For the endless hours of silly role-playing games, growing friendship, bad jokes, and ongoing inspiration. This book wouldn't exist without you and your annoying perfectionism. Thanks for Nothing.

—Ale

To my best friend, who told me not to dedicate it to her, then pulled the reverse Uno card on me. May we wander into more worlds beyond Nothing together.

—Fanny

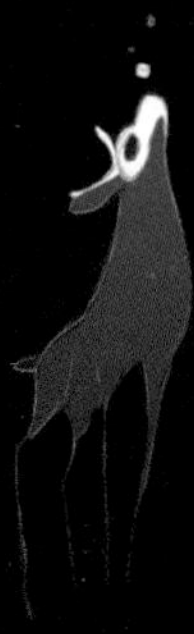

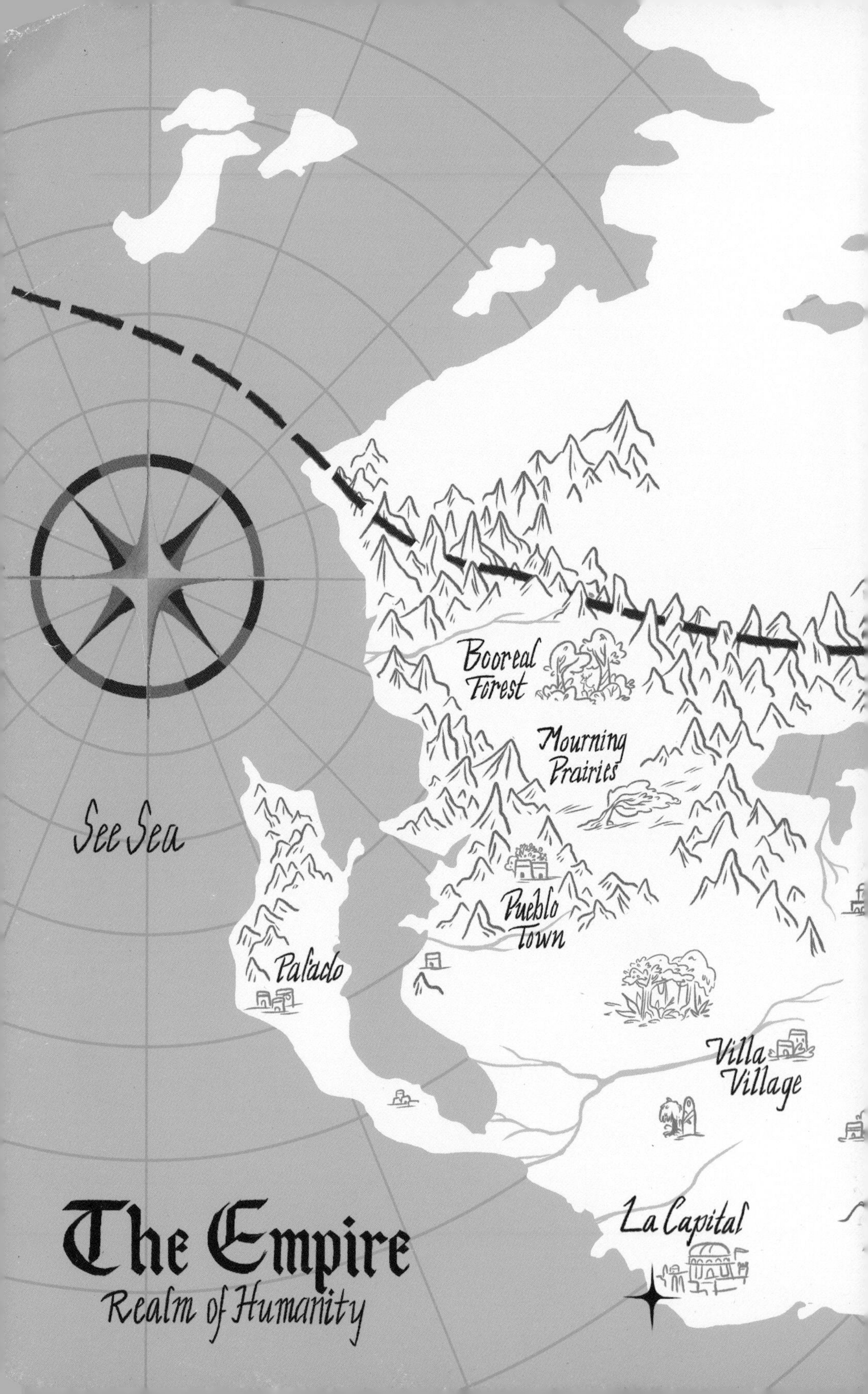
Booreal
Forest
Mourning
Prairies
See Sea
Pueblo
Town
Palado
Villa
Village
La Capital
The Empire
Realm of Humanity

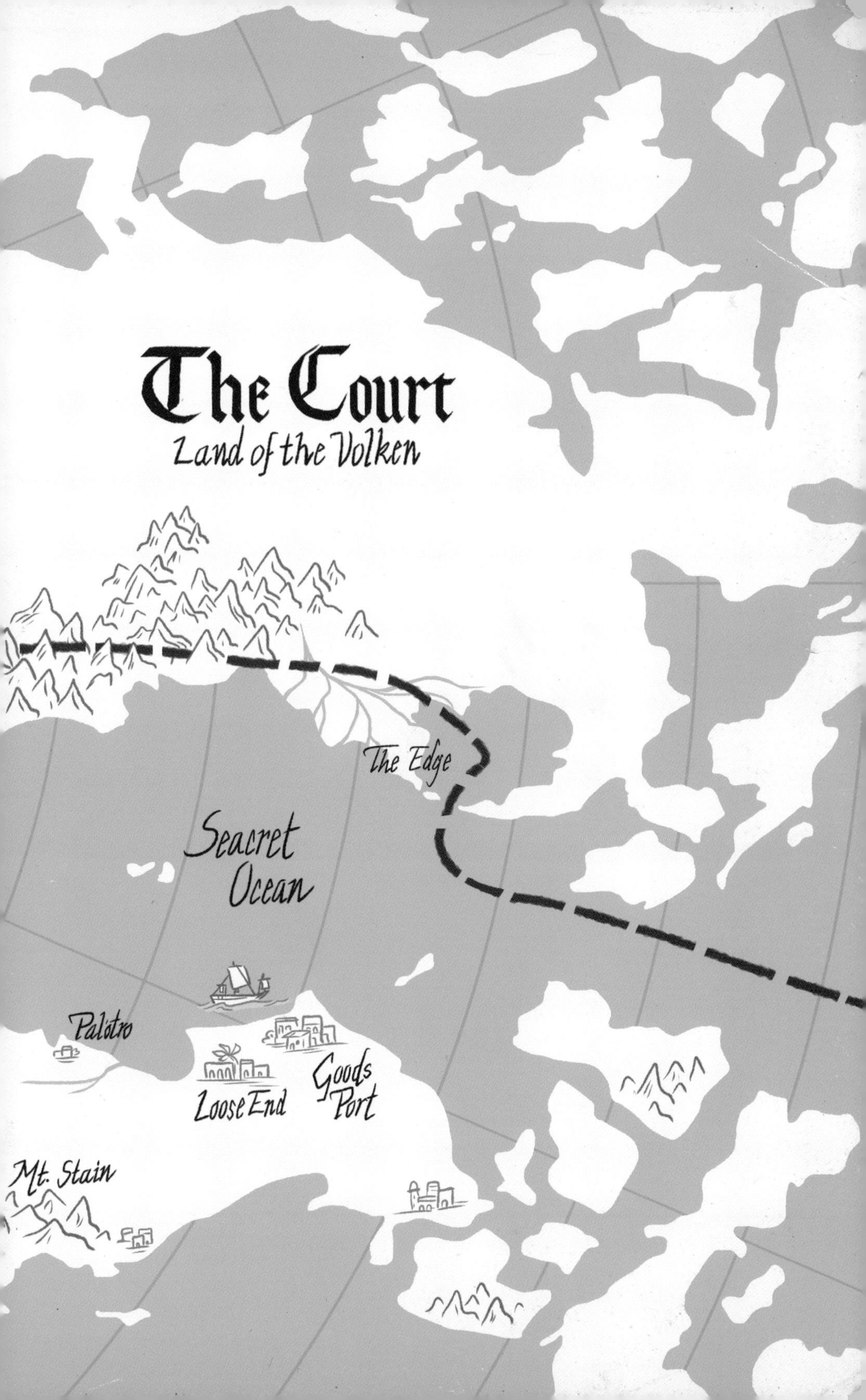
The Court
Land of the Volken
The Edge
Seacret
Ocean
Palótro
Goods
Port
Loose End
Mt. Stain

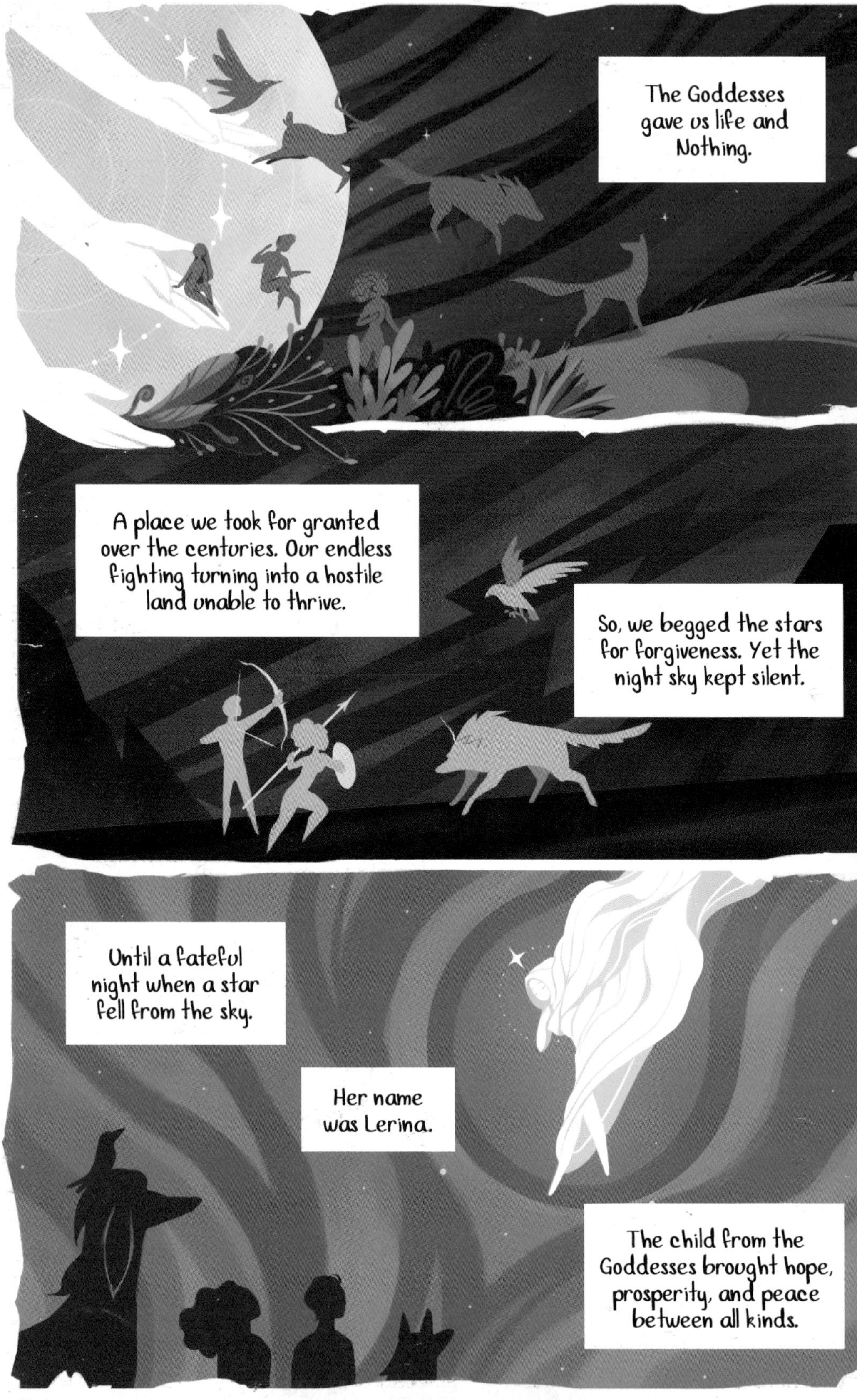
The Goddesses gave us life and Nothing.
A place we took for granted over the centuries. Our endless fighting turning into a hostile land unable to thrive.
So, we begged the stars for forgiveness. Yet the night sky kept silent.
Until a fateful night when a star fell from the sky.
Her name was Lerina.
The child from the Goddesses brought hope, prosperity, and peace between all kinds.

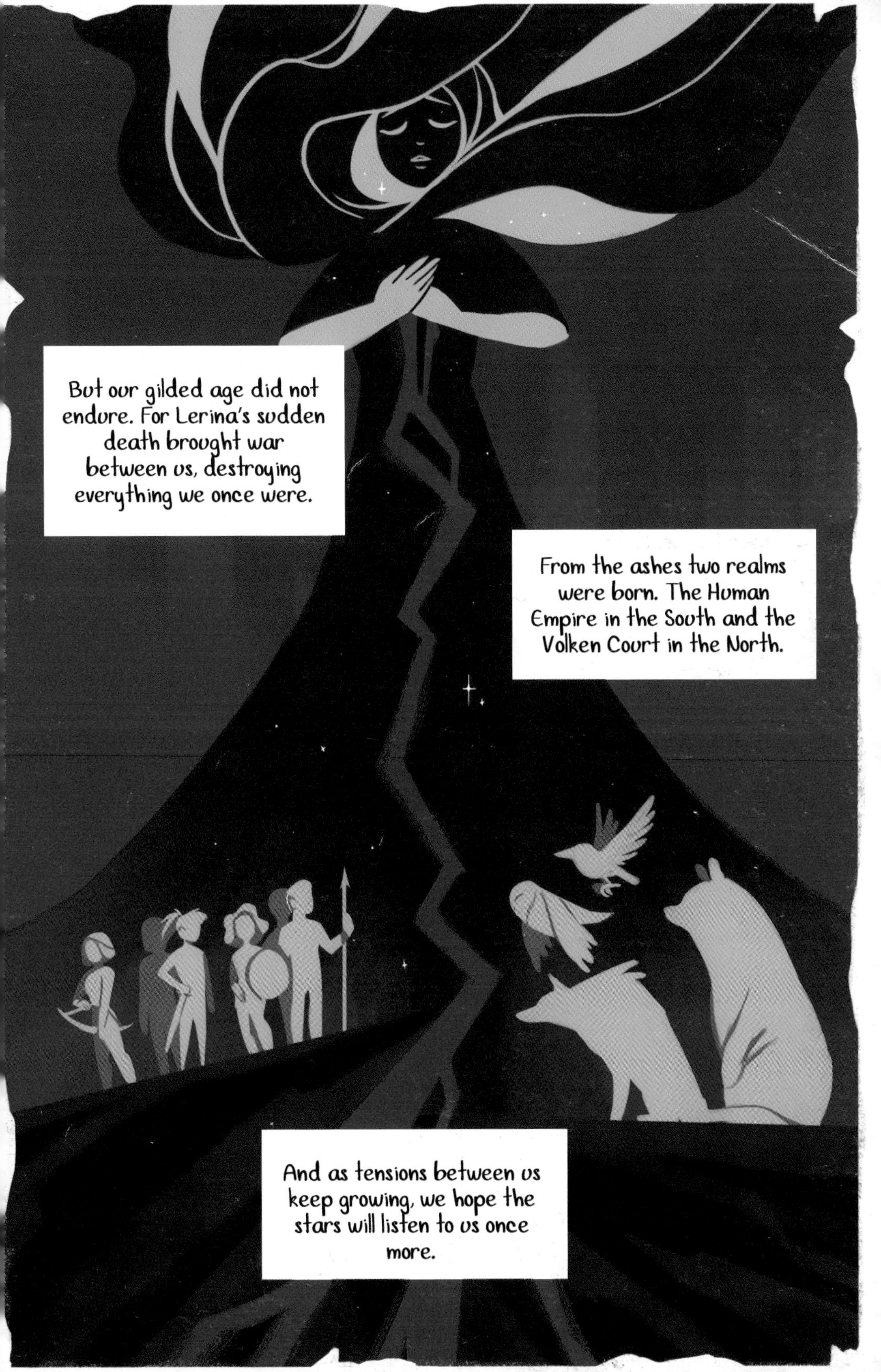
But our gilded age did not endure. For Lerina's sudden death brought war between us, destroying everything we once were.
From the ashes two realms were born. The Human Empire in the South and the Volken Court in the North.
And as tensions between us keep growing, we hope the stars will listen to us once more.

Alejandra Green & Fanny Rodriguez

Fantastic tales of Nothing

KATHERINE TEGEN BOOKS
An Imprint of HarperCollins Publishers

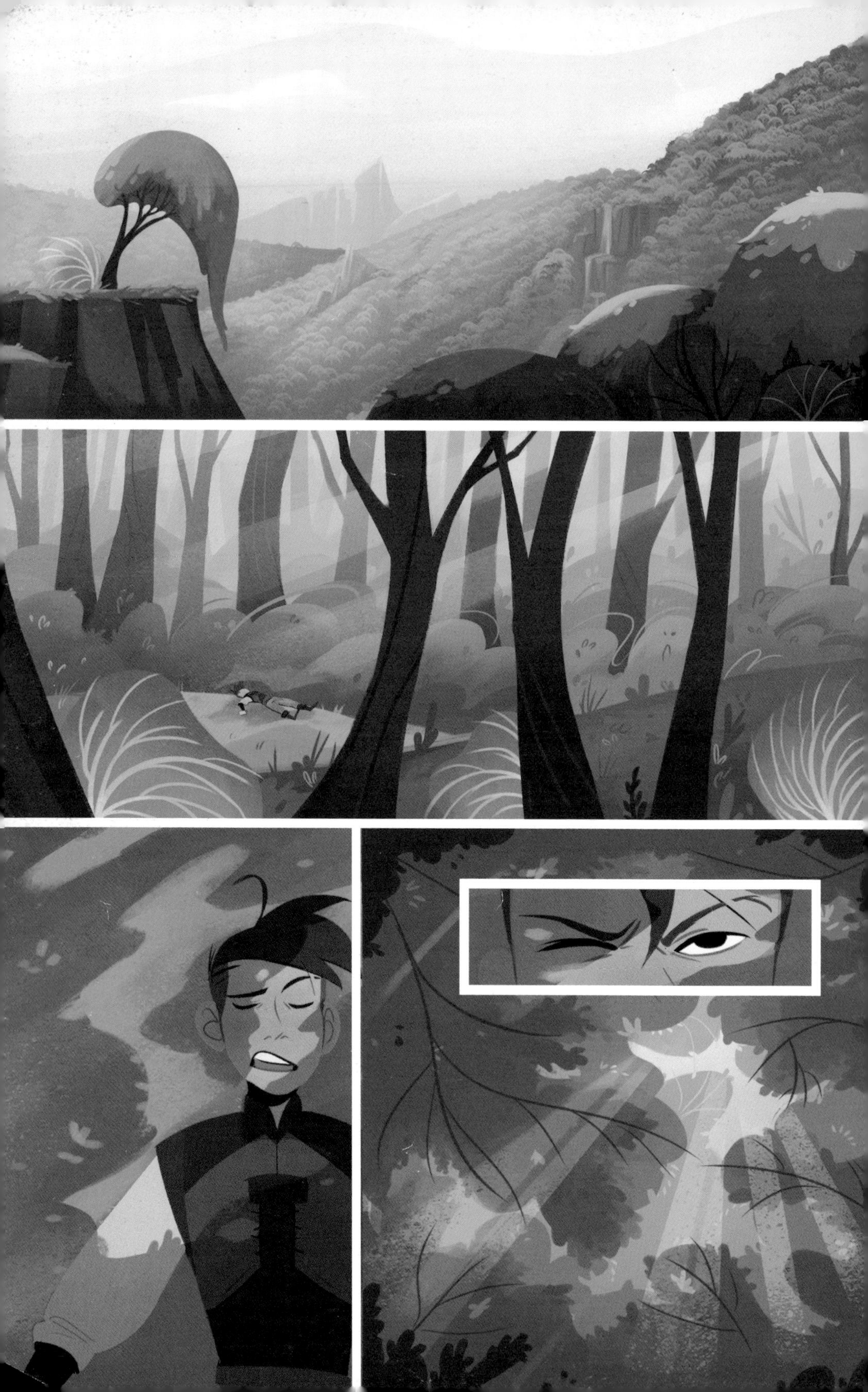

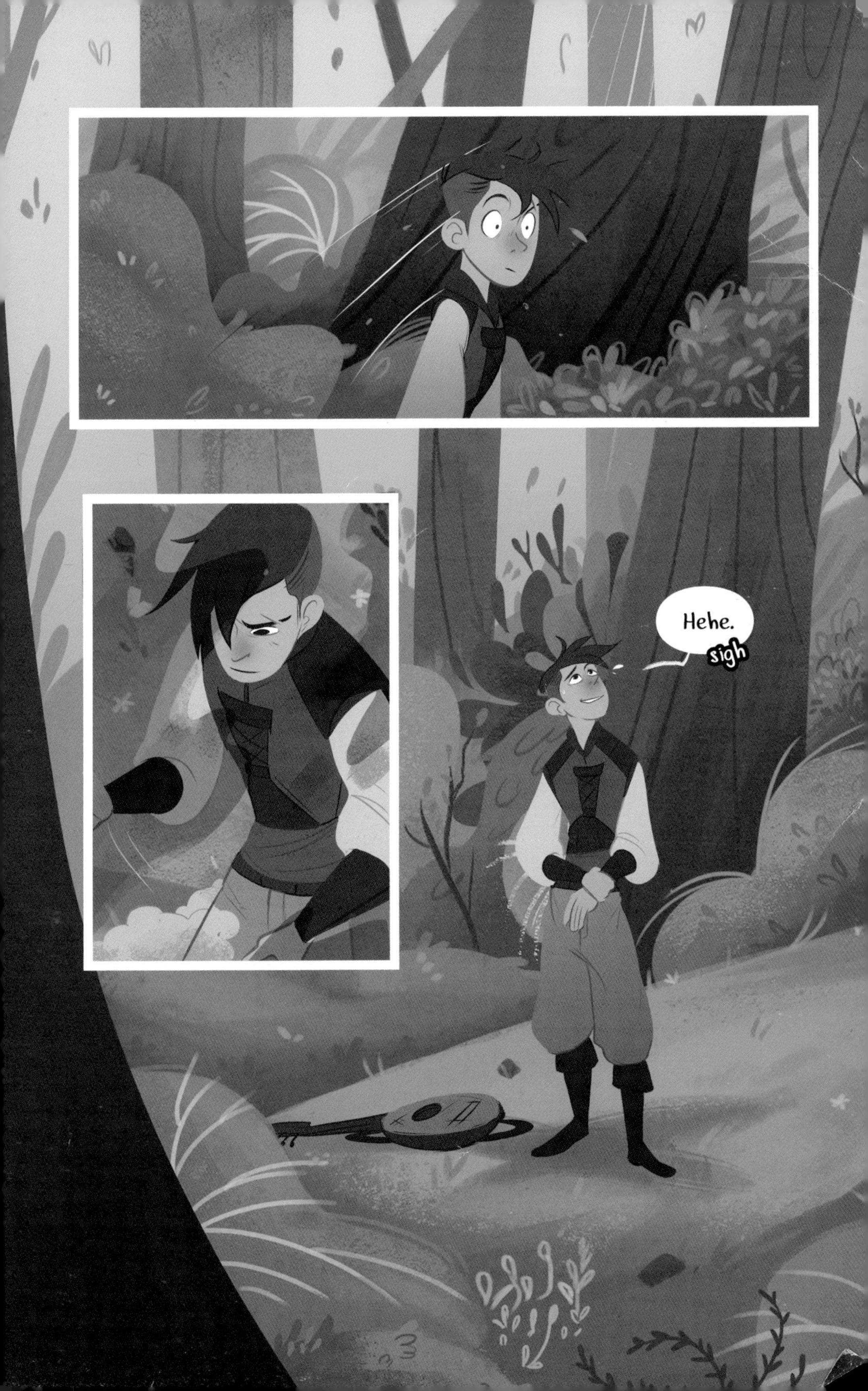
Hehe.
sigh

Chapter 1
Is This the Everafter?

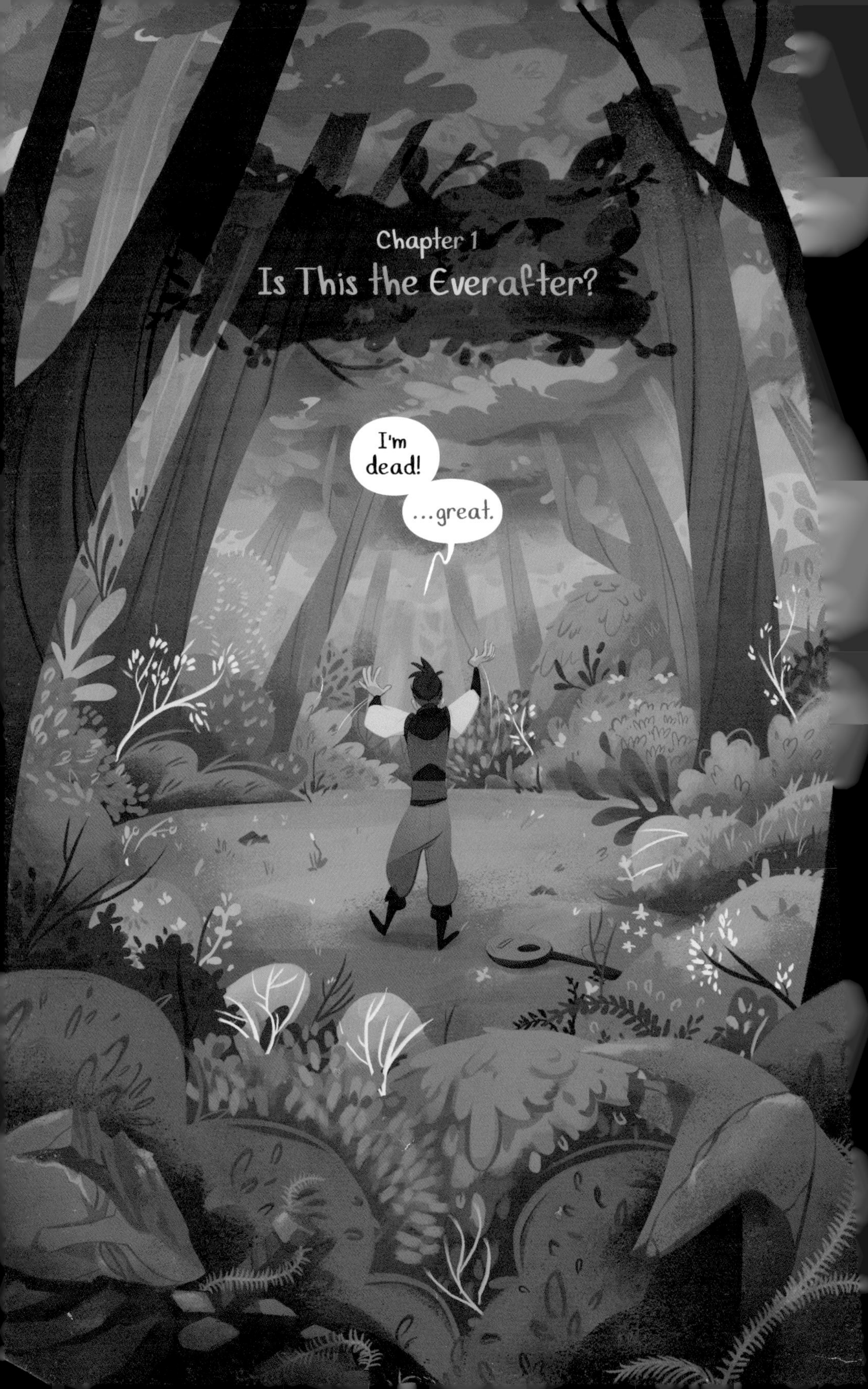
I'm dead!
...great.

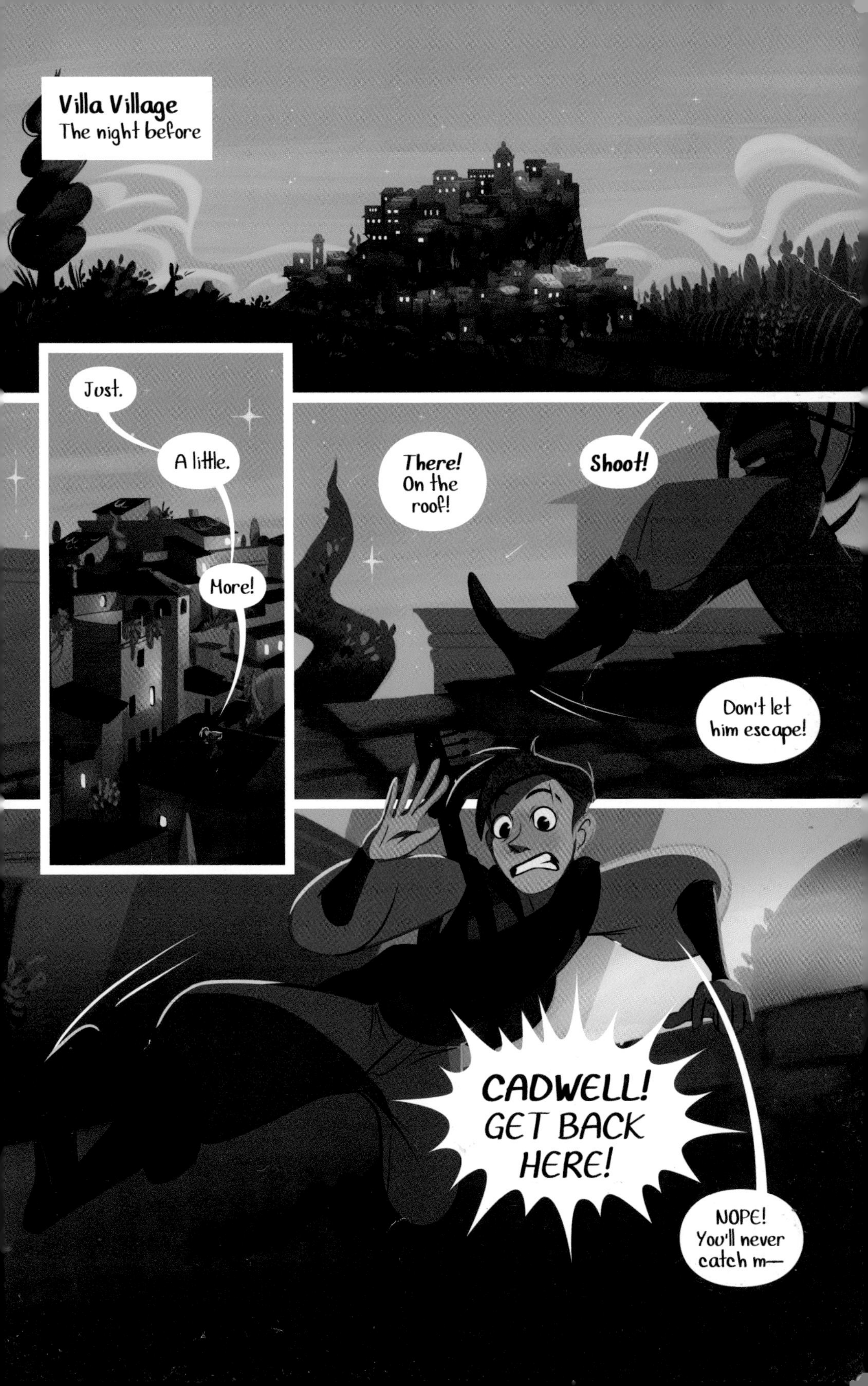
Villa Village
The night before
Just.
A little.
More!
There! On the roof!
Shoot!
Don't let him escape!
CADWELL! GET BACK HERE!
NOPE! You'll never catch m—

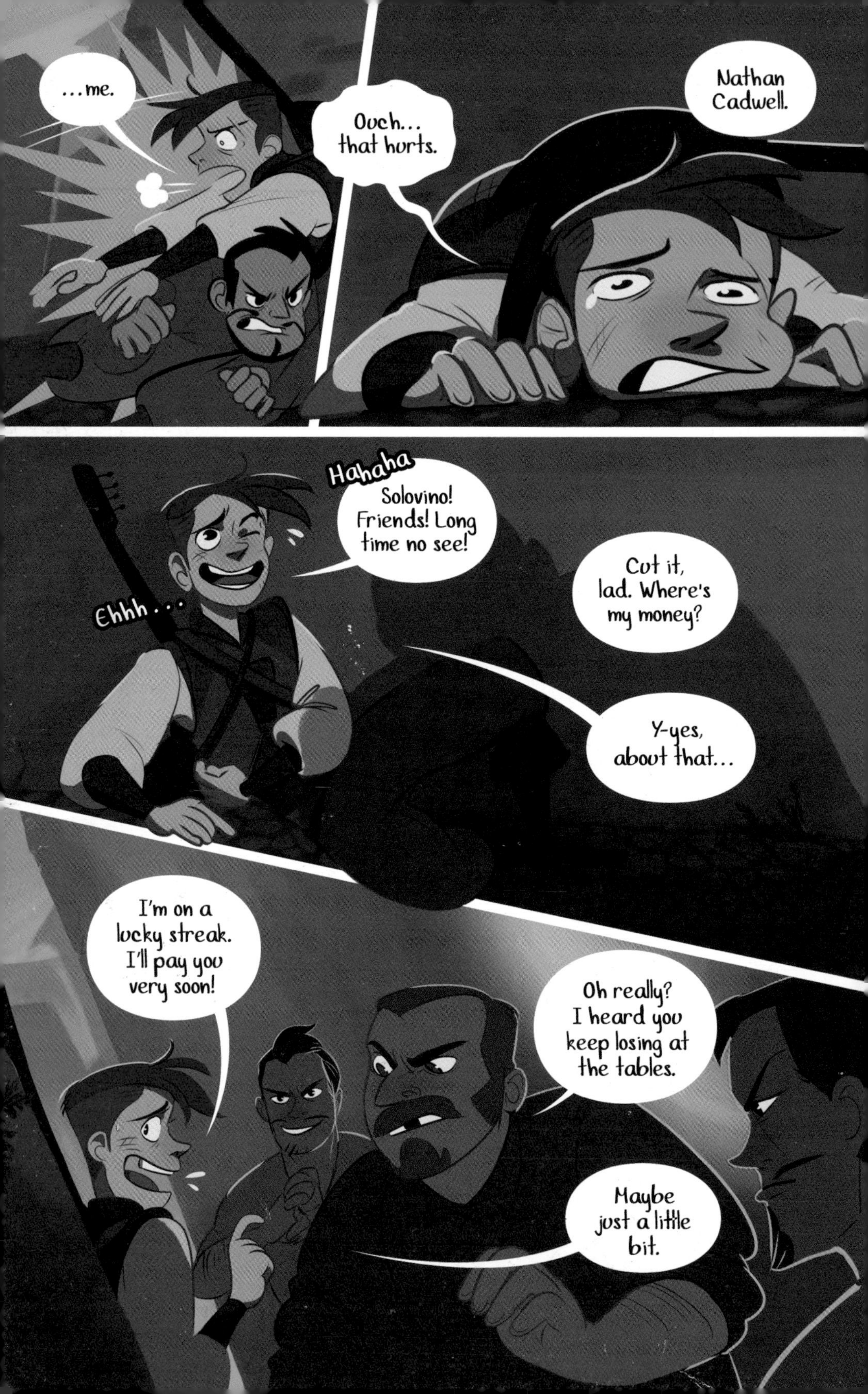
...me.
Ouch... that hurts.
Nathan Cadwell.
Hahaha
Solovino! Friends! Long time no see!
Ehhh...
Cut it, lad. Where's my money?
Y-yes, about that...
I'm on a lucky streak. I'll pay you very soon!
Oh really? I heard you keep losing at the tables.
Maybe just a little bit.

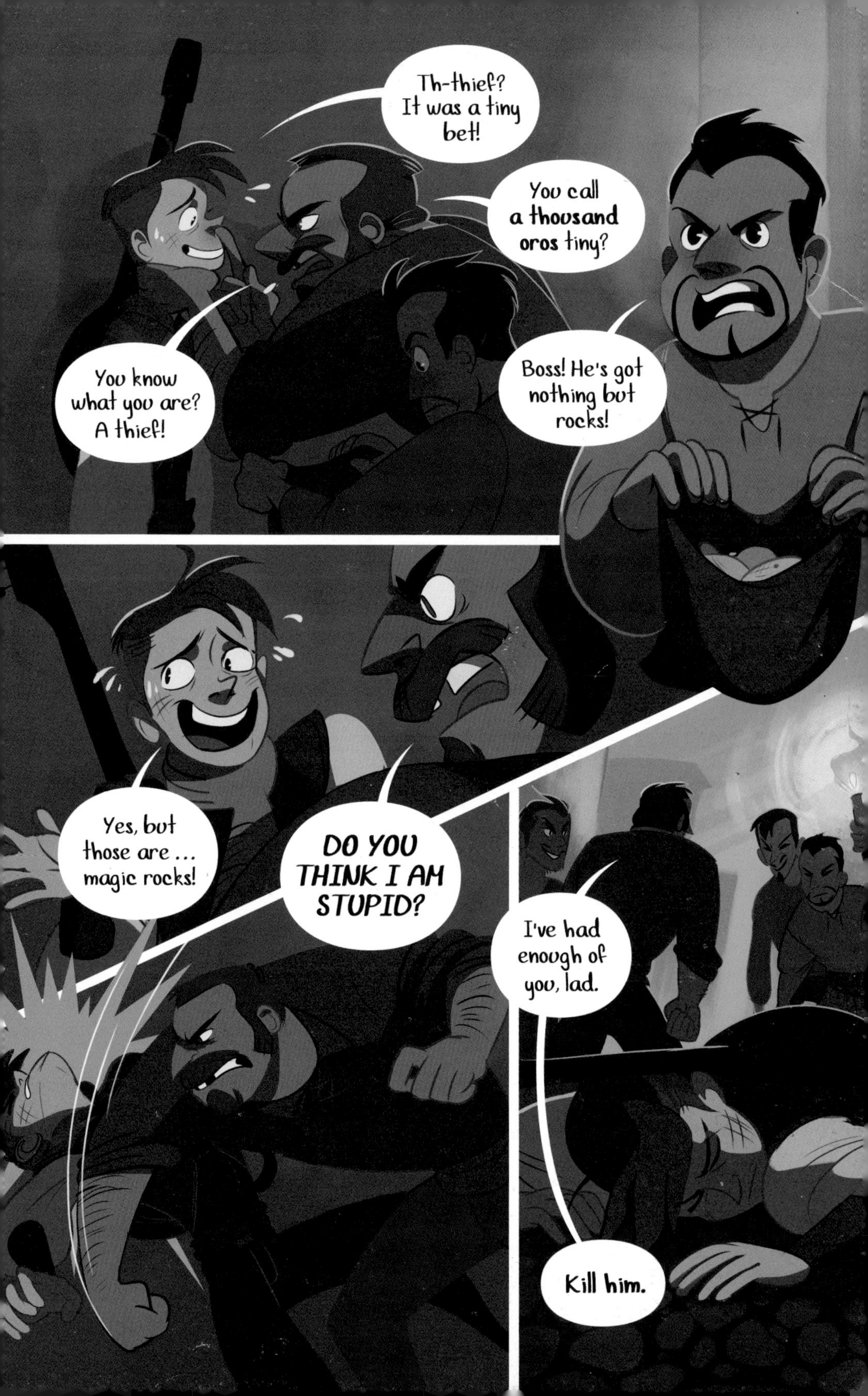
You know what you are? A thief!
Th-thief? It was a tiny bet!
You call a thousand oros tiny?
Boss! He's got nothing but rocks!
Yes, but those are ... magic rocks!
DO YOU THINK I AM STUPID?
I've had enough of you, lad.
Kill him.

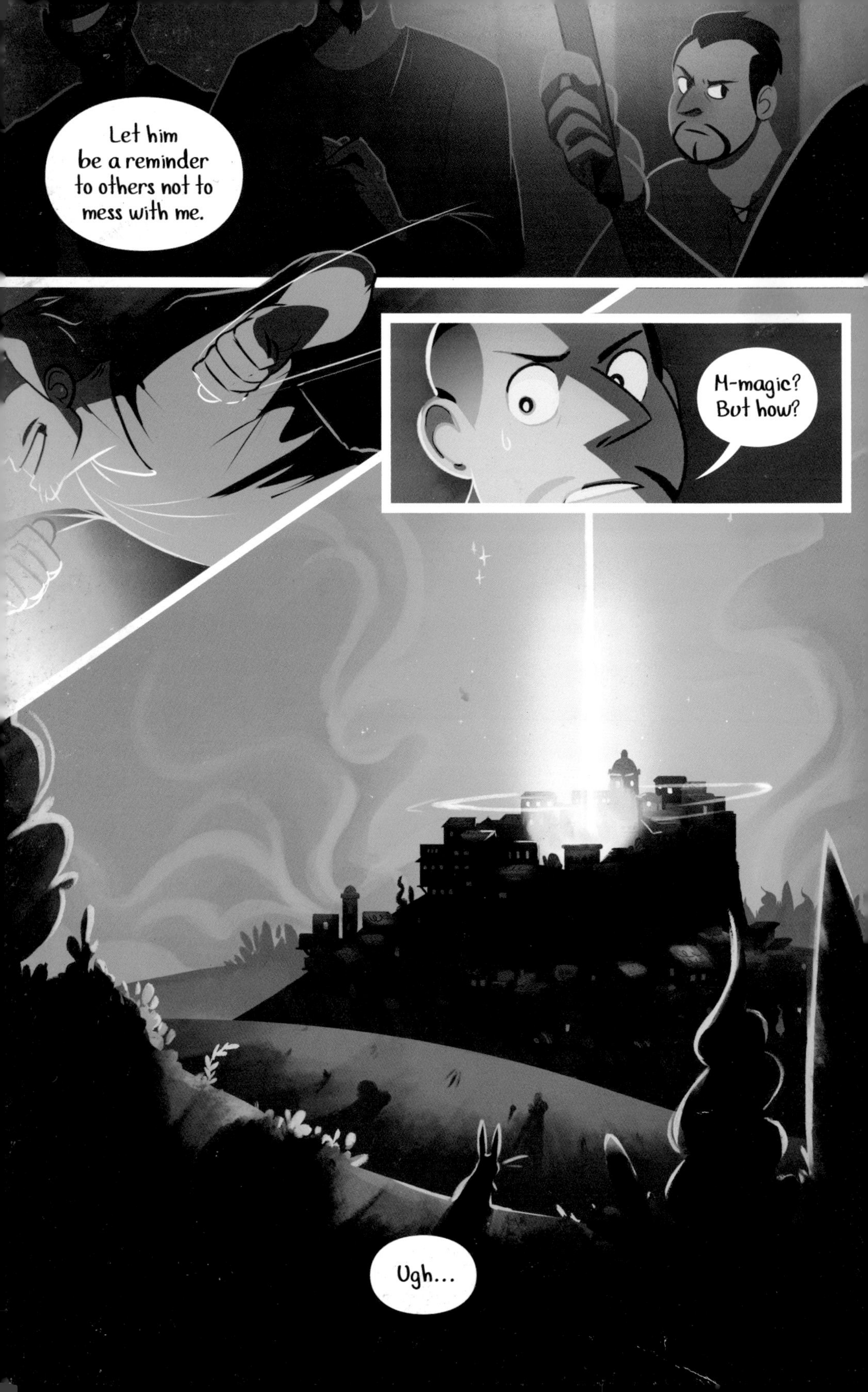
Let him be a reminder to others not to mess with me.
M-magic? But how?
Ugh...

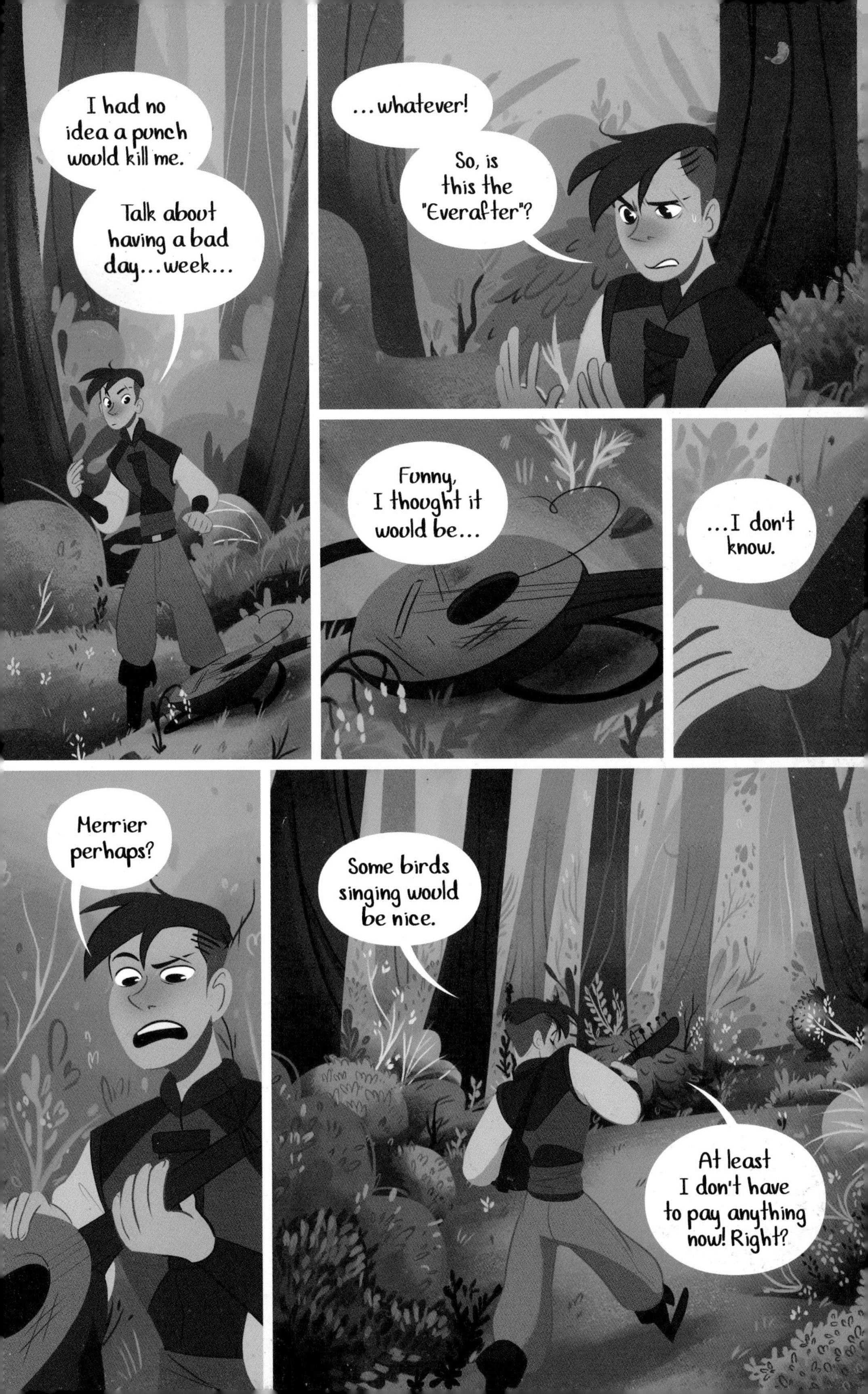
I had no idea a punch would kill me.
Talk about having a bad day...week...
...whatever!
So, is this the "Everafter"?
Funny, I thought it would be...
...I don't know.
Merrier perhaps?
Some birds singing would be nice.
At least I don't have to pay anything now! Right?

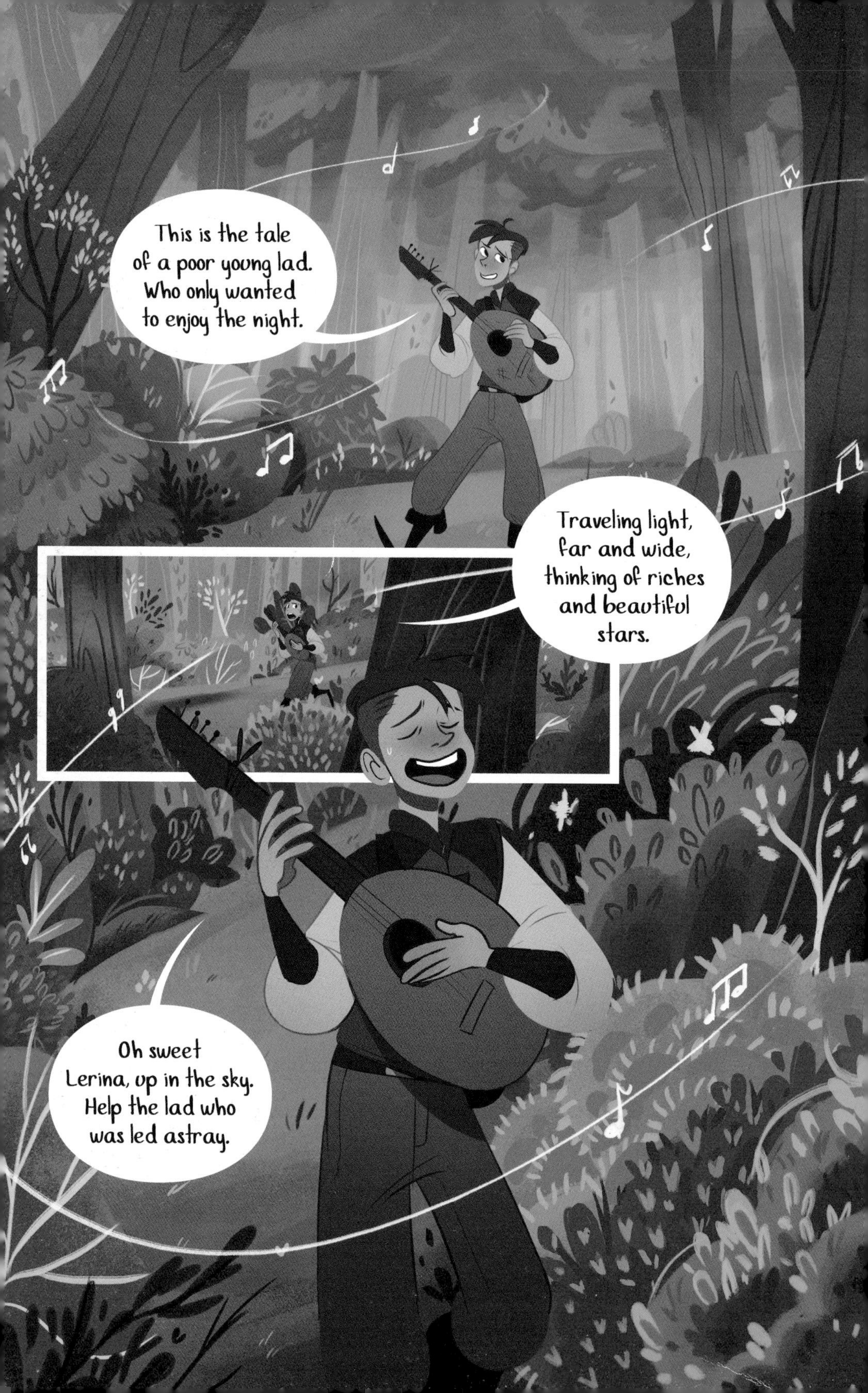
This is the tale of a poor young lad. Who only wanted to enjoy the night.
Traveling light, far and wide, thinking of riches and beautiful stars.
Oh sweet Lerina, up in the sky. Help the lad who was led astray.

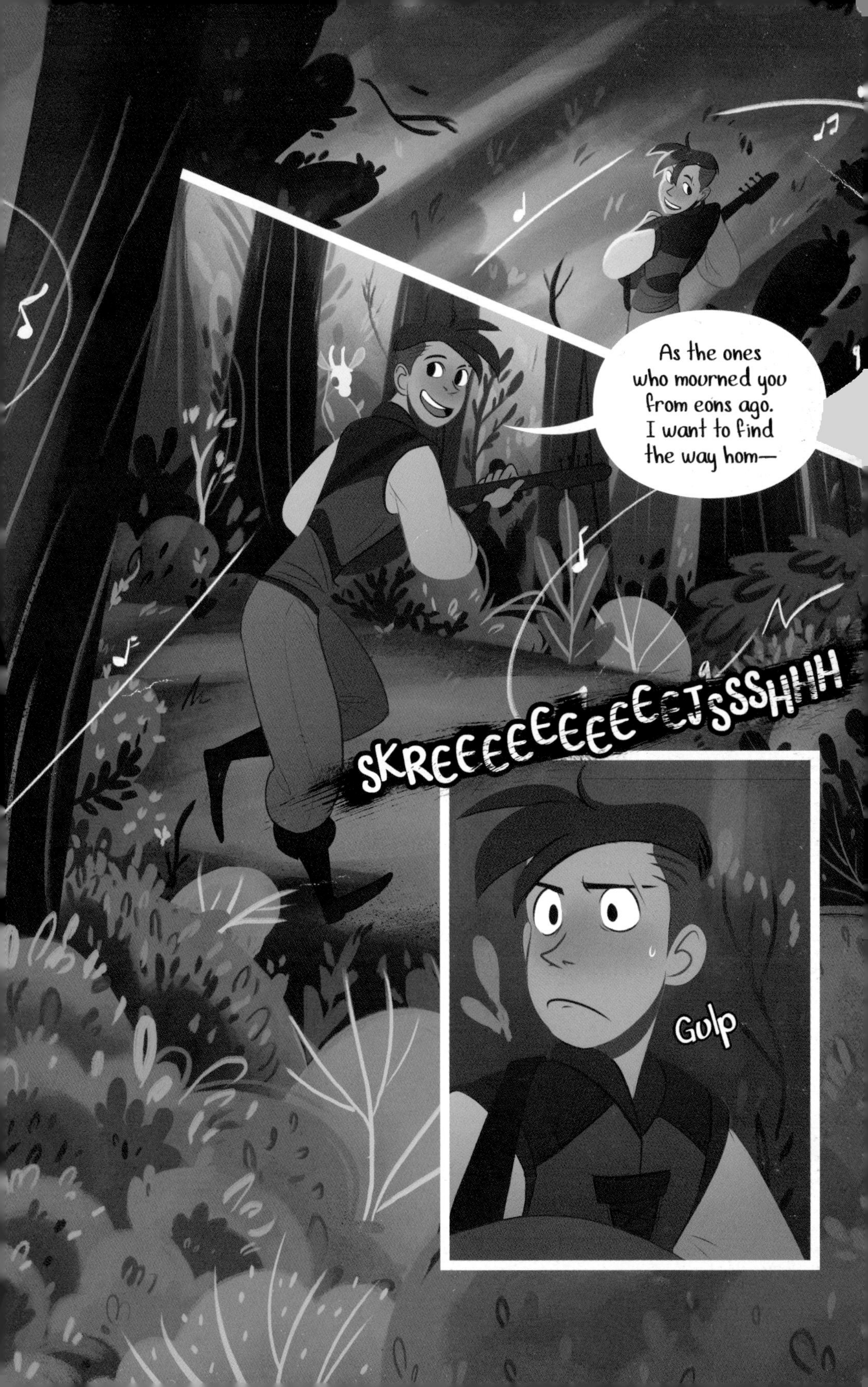
As the ones who mourned you from eons ago. I want to find the way hom—
SKREEEEEEEEEEEJSSSHHHH
Gulp

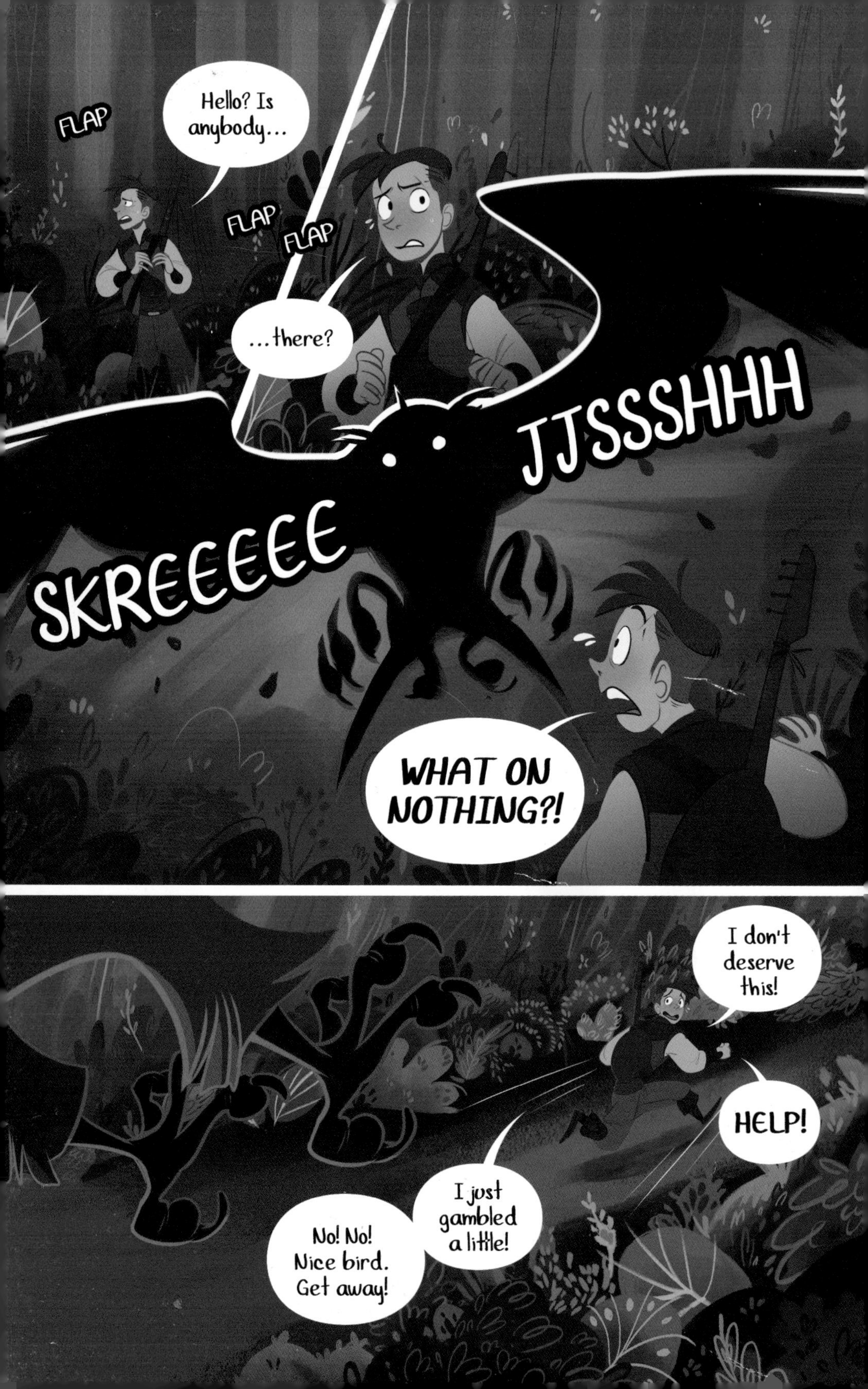
FLAP
Hello? Is anybody…
FLAP
FLAP
…there?
JJSSSHHH
SKREEEEEE
WHAT ON NOTHING?!
I don't deserve this!
HELP!
I just gambled a little!
No! No! Nice bird. Get away!

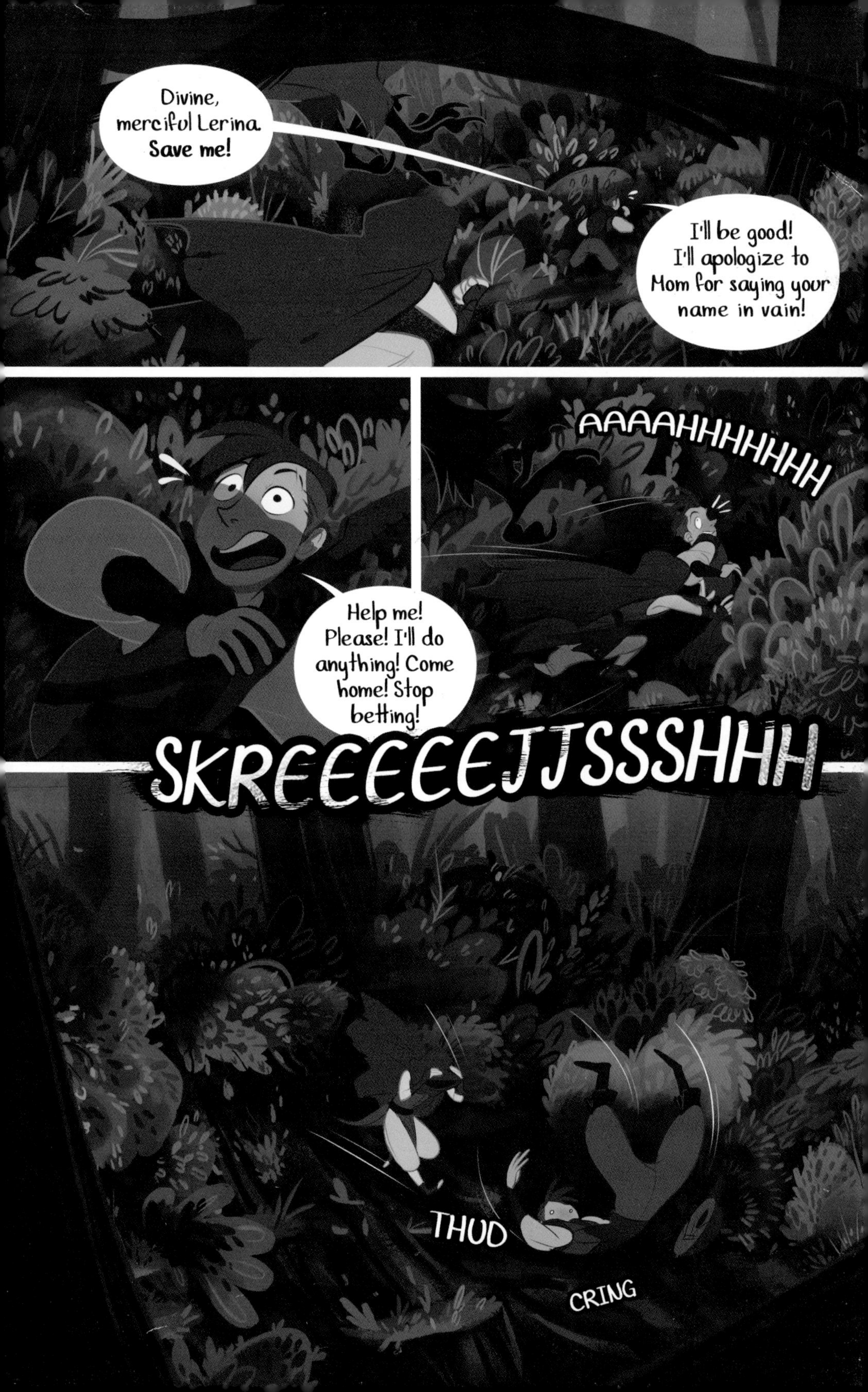
Divine, merciful Lerina. Save me!
I'll be good! I'll apologize to Mom for saying your name in vain!
Help me! Please! I'll do anything! Come home! Stop betting!
AAAAHHHHHHH
SKREEEEEEJJSSSHHH
THUD
CRING

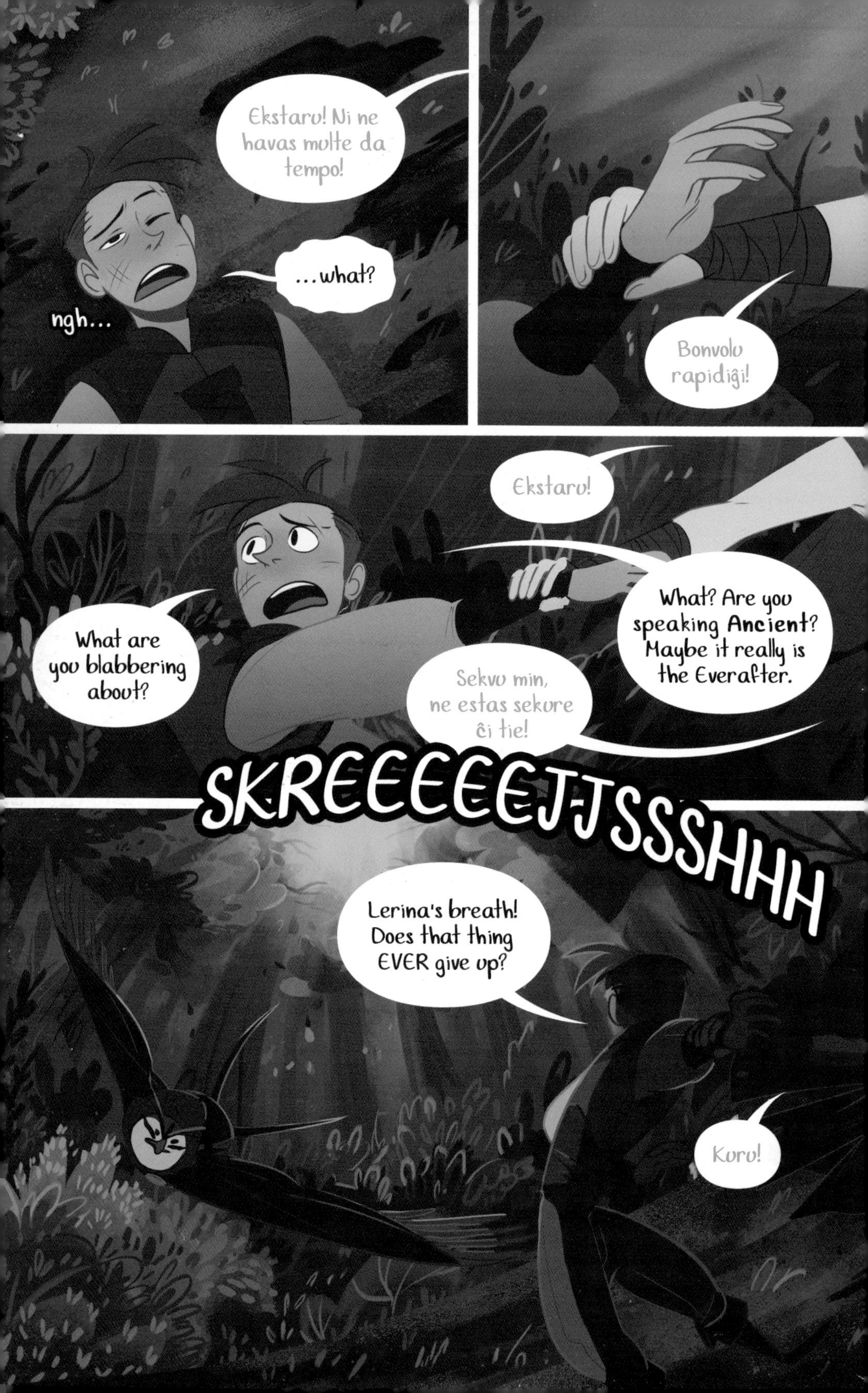
Ekstaru! Ni ne havas multe da tempo!
ngh...
...what?
Bonvolu rapidiĝi!
Ekstaru!
What are you blabbering about?
What? Are you speaking **Ancient**? Maybe it really is the Everafter.
Sekvu min, ne estas sekure ĉi tie!
SKREEEEEEJJSSSHHH
Lerina's breath! Does that thing EVER give up?
Kuru!

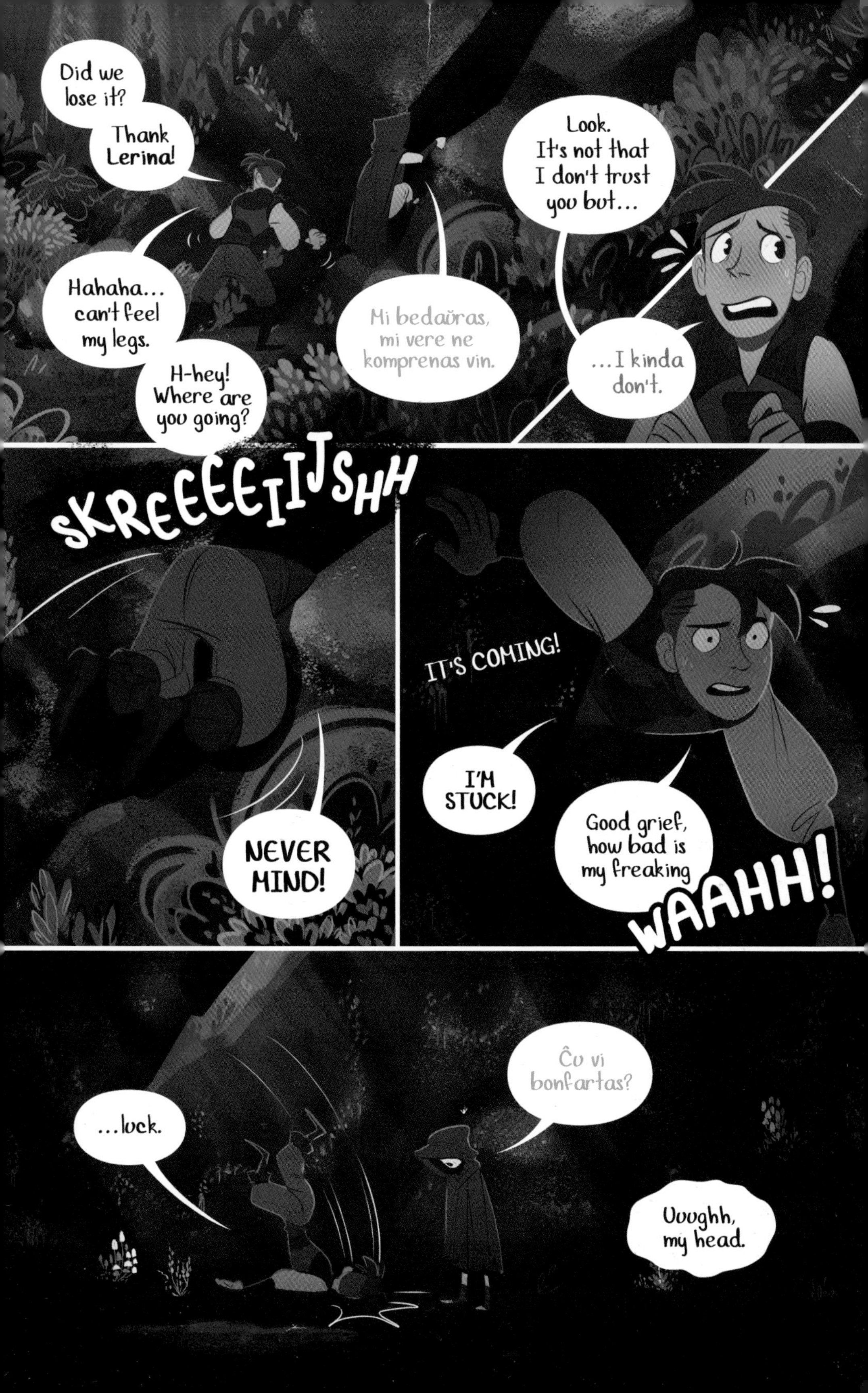
Did we lose it?
Thank Lerina!
Hahaha… can't feel my legs.
H-hey! Where are you going?
Mi bedaŭras, mi vere ne komprenas vin.
Look. It's not that I don't trust you but…
…I kinda don't.
SKREEEEIIJSHH
NEVER MIND!
IT'S COMING!
I'M STUCK!
Good grief, how bad is my freaking
WAAHH!
…luck.
Ĉu vi bonfartas?
Uuughh, my head.

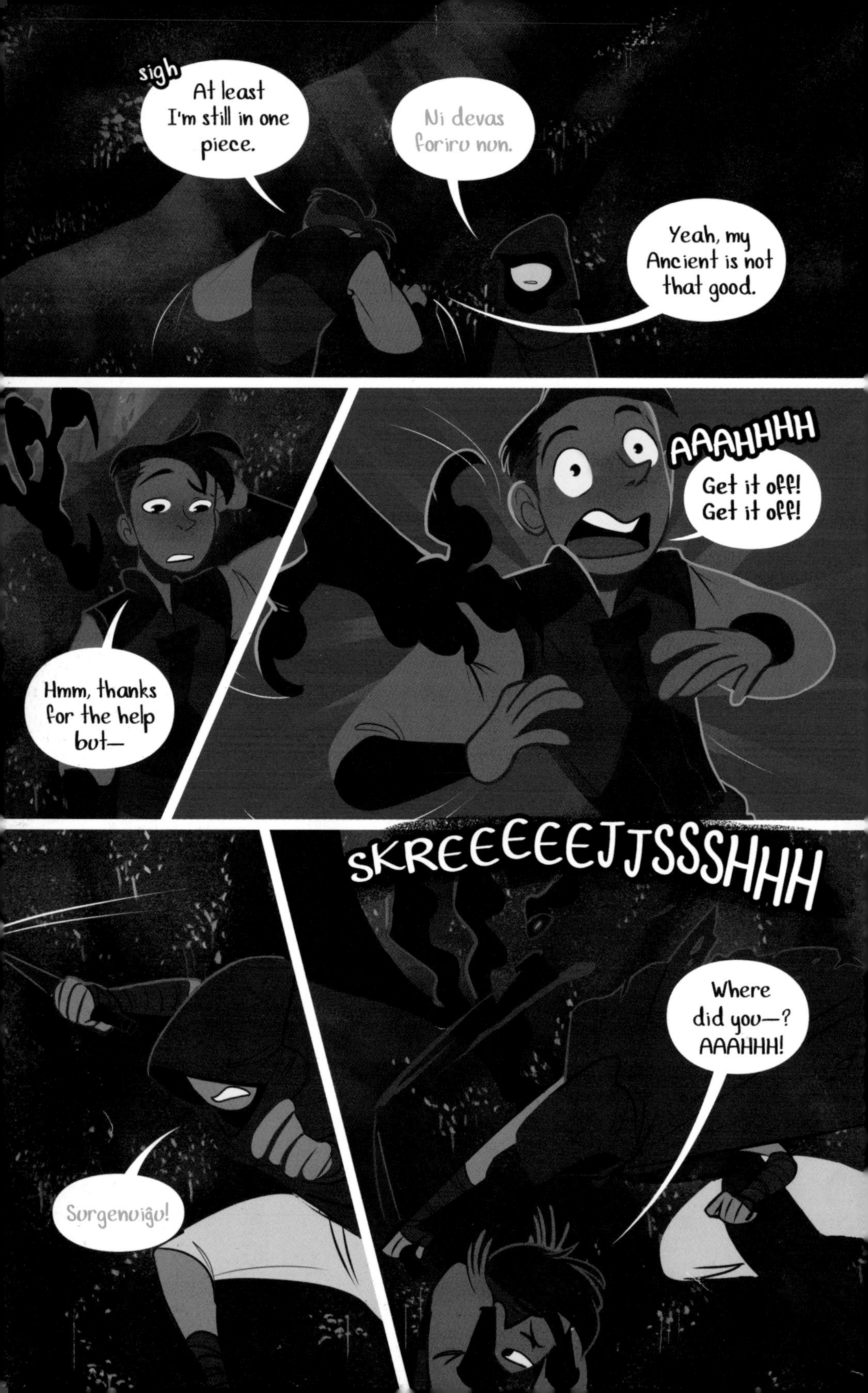
sigh
At least I'm still in one piece.
Ni devas foriru non.
Yeah, my Ancient is not that good.
Hmm, thanks for the help but—
AAAHHHH
Get it off! Get it off!
SKREEEEEEJJSSSHHH
Surgenviĝu!
Where did you—? AAAHHH!

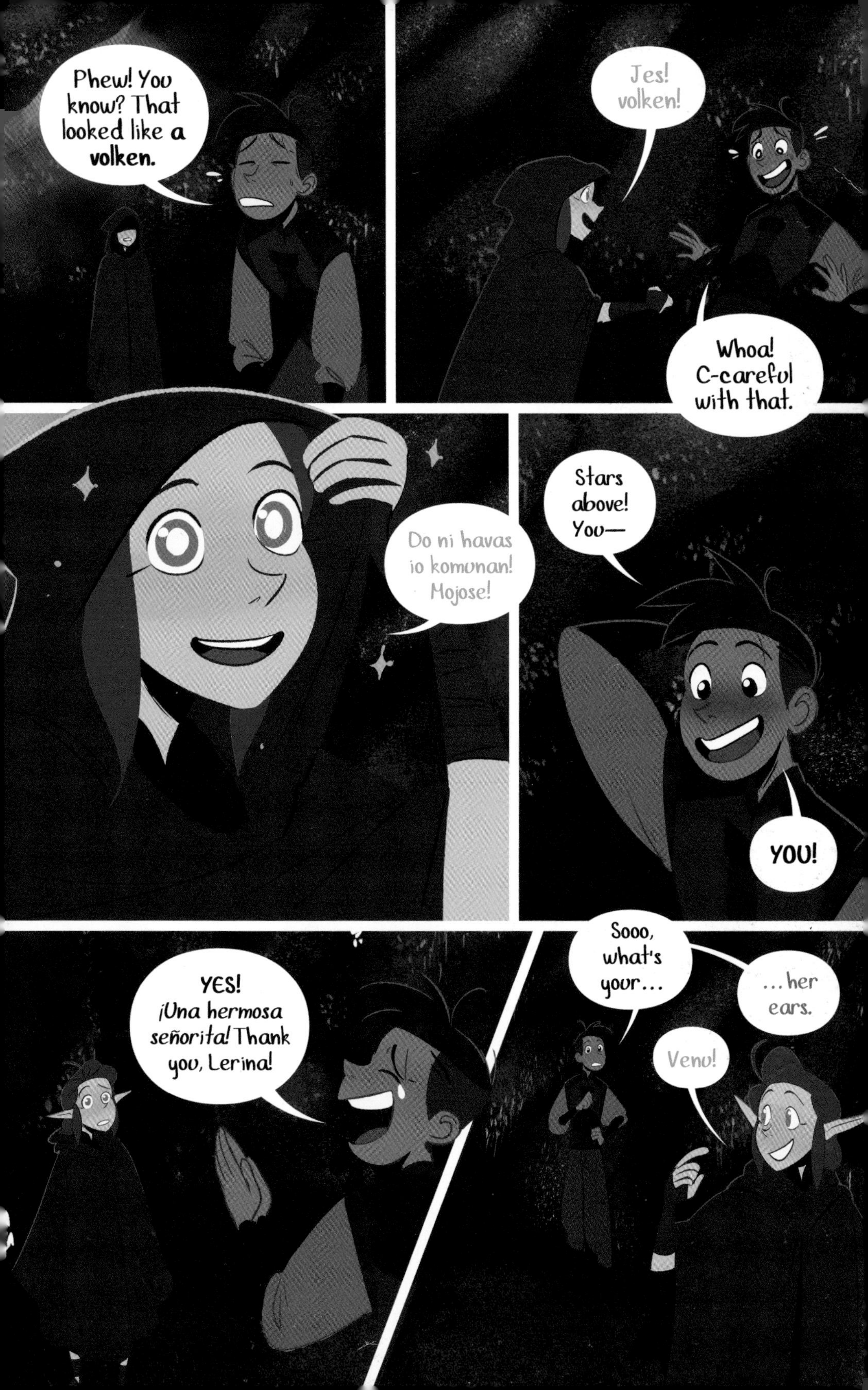
Phew! You know? That looked like a volken.
Jes! volken!
Whoa! C-careful with that.
Do ni havas io komunan! Mojose!
Stars above! You—
YOU!
YES! ¡Una hermosa señorita! Thank you, Lerina!
Sooo, what's your…
…her ears.
Venu!

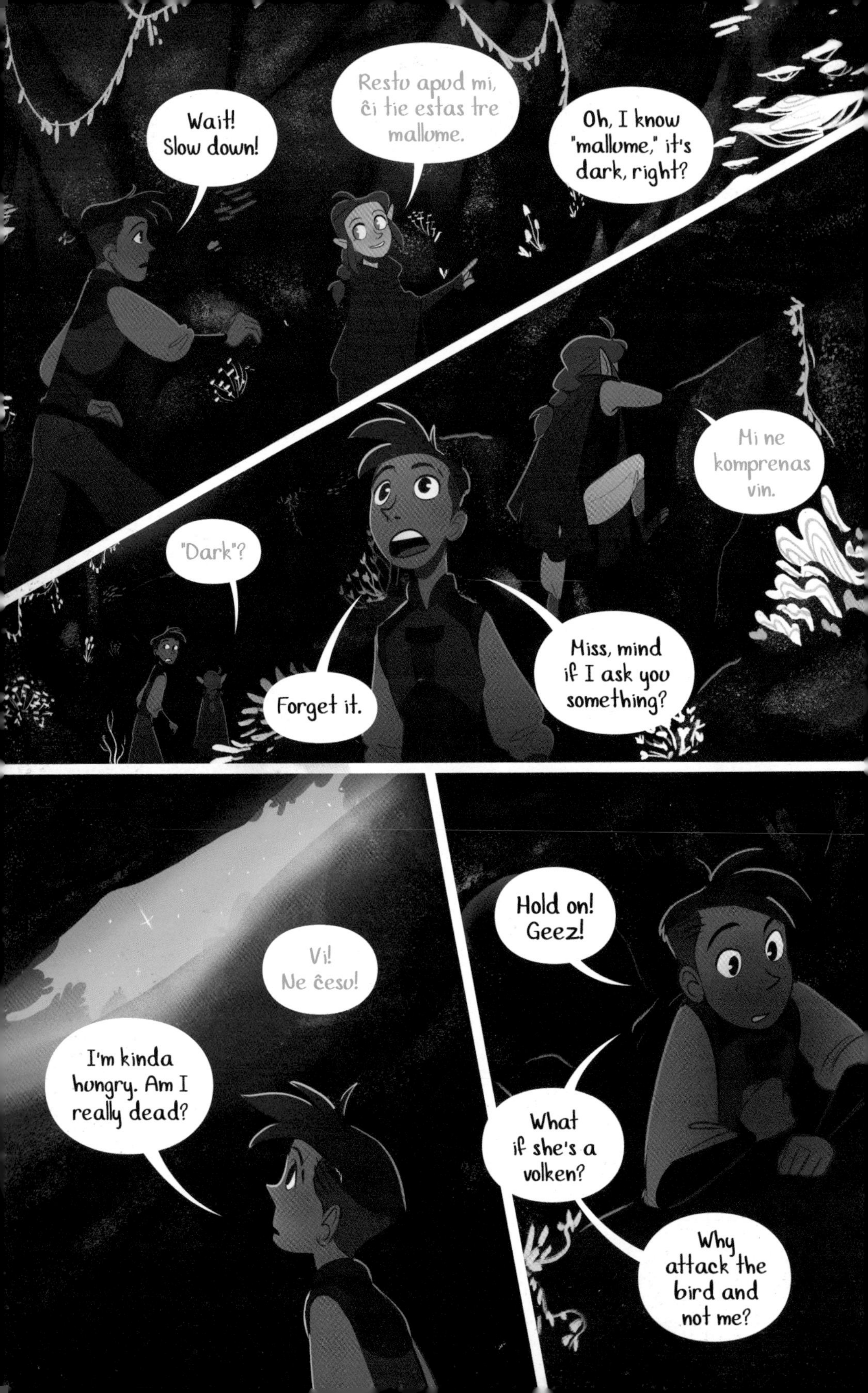
Wait! Slow down!
Restu apud mi, ĉi tie estas tre mallume.
Oh, I know "mallume," it's dark, right?
Mi ne komprenas vin.
"Dark"?
Forget it.
Miss, mind if I ask you something?
Vi! Ne ĉesu!
I'm kinda hungry. Am I really dead?
Hold on! Geez!
What if she's a volken?
Why attack the bird and not me?

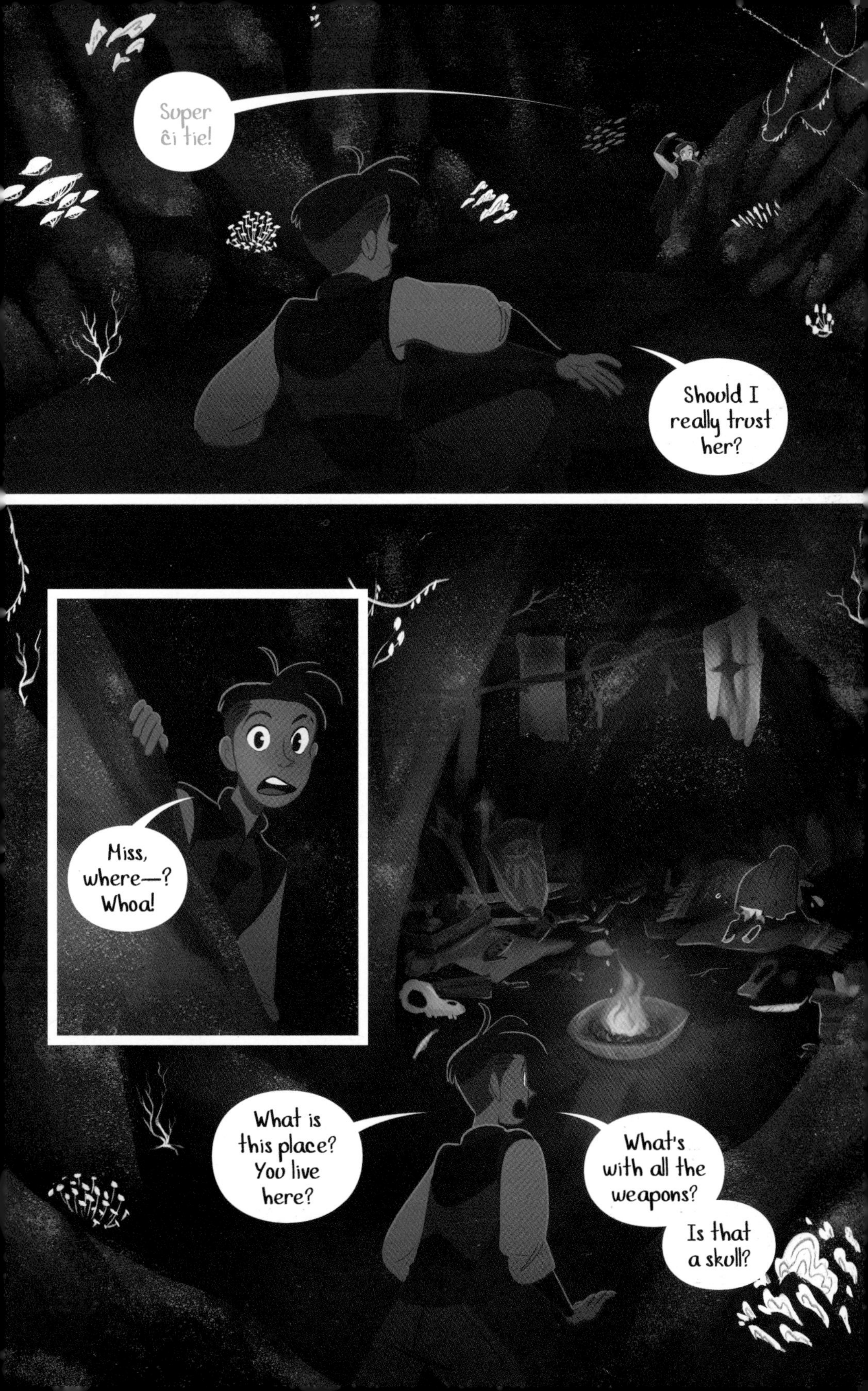
Super ĉi tie!
Should I really trust her?
Miss, where—? Whoa!
What is this place? You live here?
What's with all the weapons?
Is that a skull?

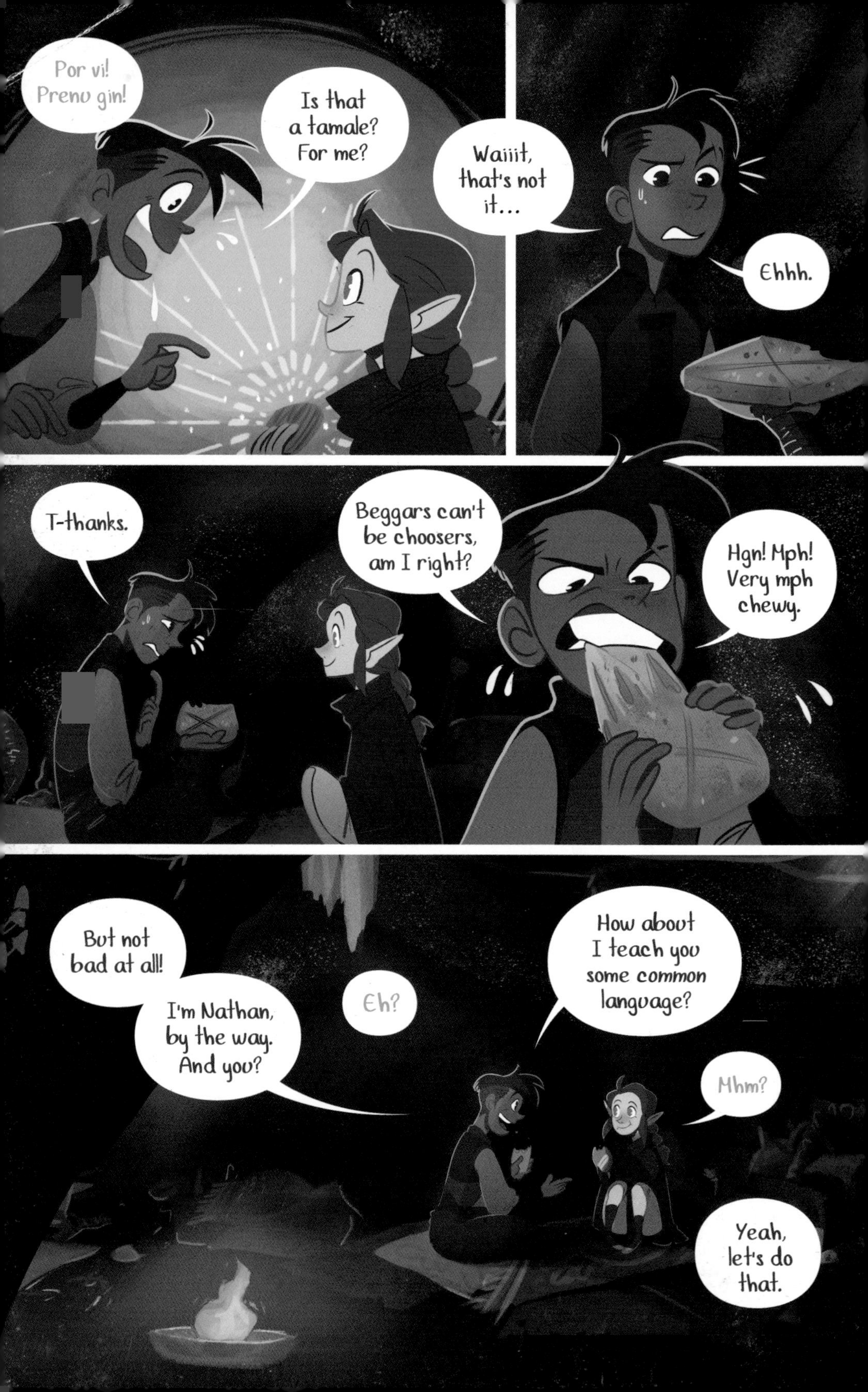
Por vi! Prenu gin!
Is that a tamale? For me?
Waiiit, that's not it...
Ehhh.
T-thanks.
Beggars can't be choosers, am I right?
Hgn! Mph! Very mph chewy.
But not bad at all!
I'm Nathan, by the way. And you?
Eh?
How about I teach you some common language?
Mhm?
Yeah, let's do that.

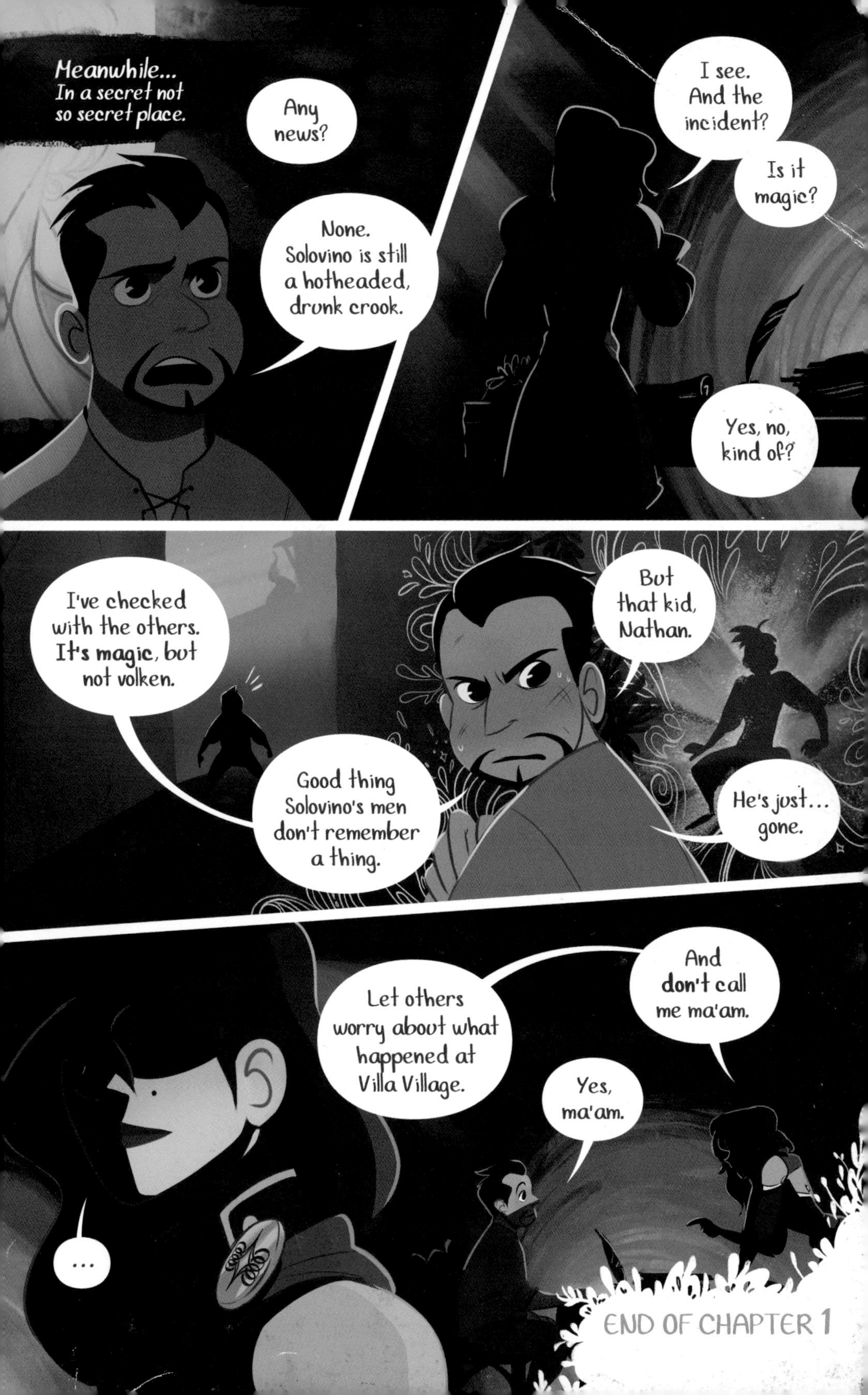
Meanwhile... In a secret not so secret place.
Any news?
None. Solovino is still a hotheaded, drunk crook.
I see. And the incident?
Is it magic?
Yes, no, kind of?
I've checked with the others. It's magic, but not volken.
Good thing Solovino's men don't remember a thing.
But that kid, Nathan.
He's just... gone.
...
Let others worry about what happened at Villa Village.
And don't call me ma'am.
Yes, ma'am.
END OF CHAPTER 1

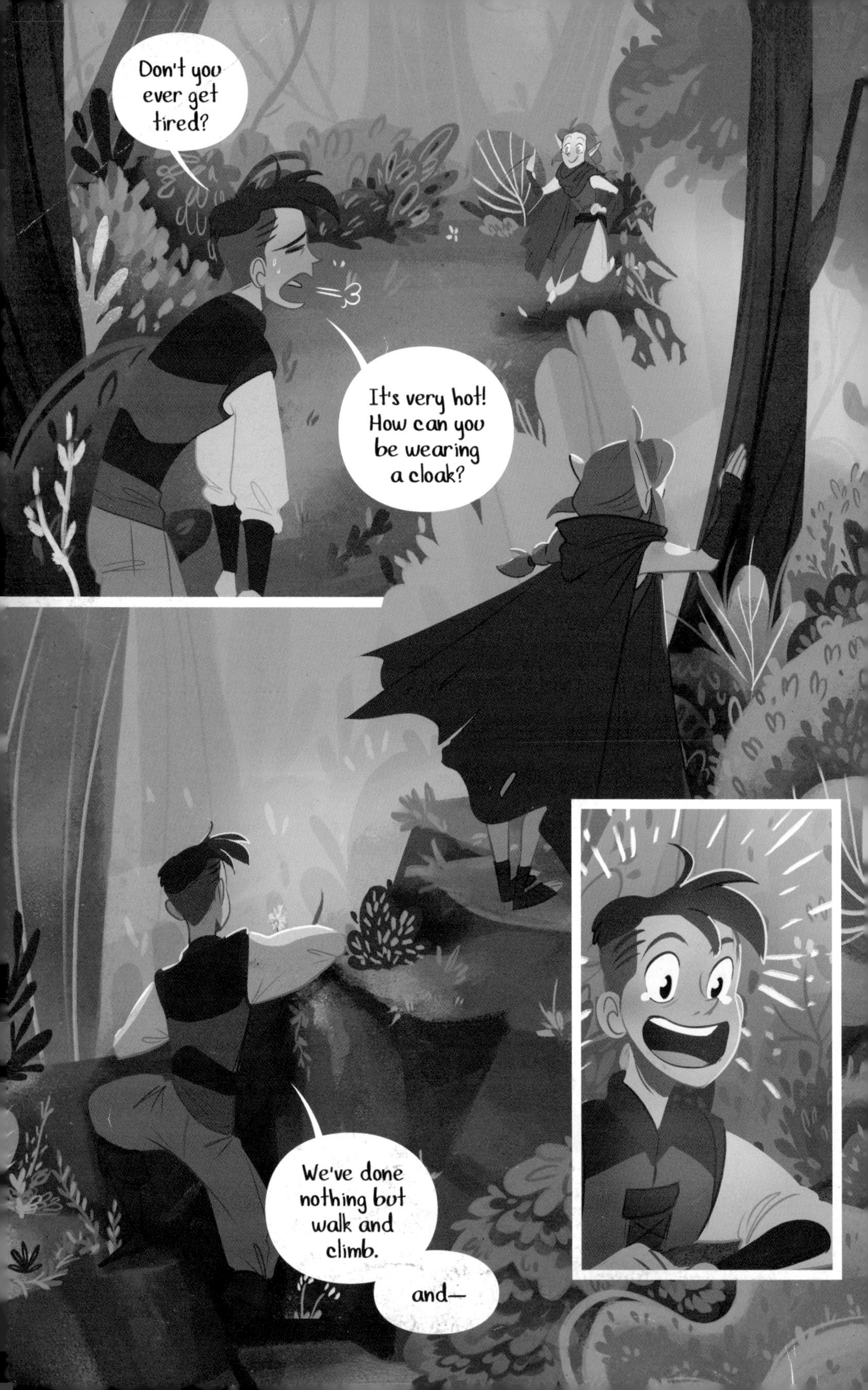
Don't you ever get tired?
It's very hot! How can you be wearing a cloak?
We've done nothing but walk and climb.
and—

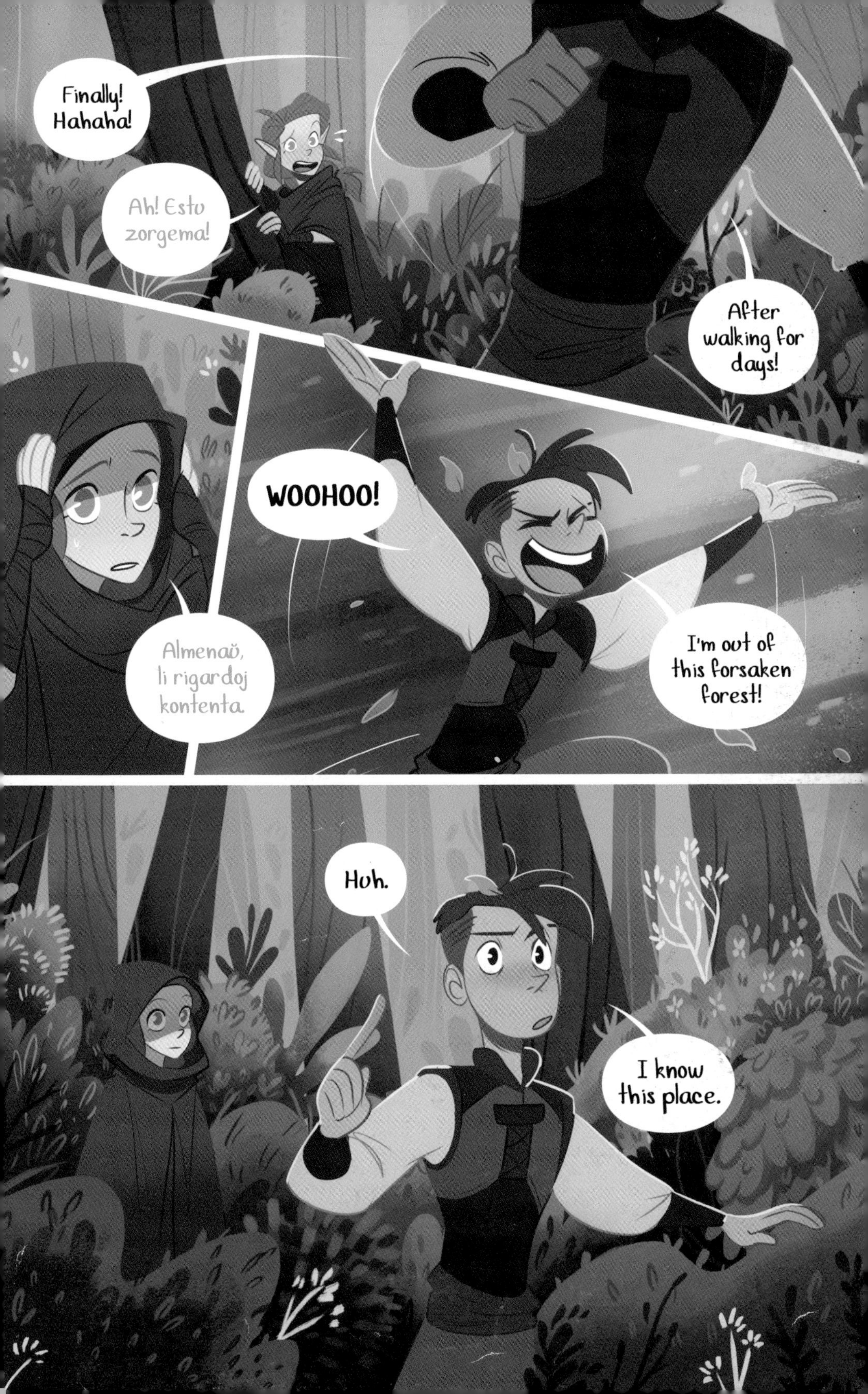
Finally! Hahaha!
Ah! Estu zorgema!
After walking for days!
Almenaŭ, li rigardoj kontenta.
WOOHOO!
I'm out of this forsaken forest!
Huh.
I know this place.

Chapter 2
Still on Nothing

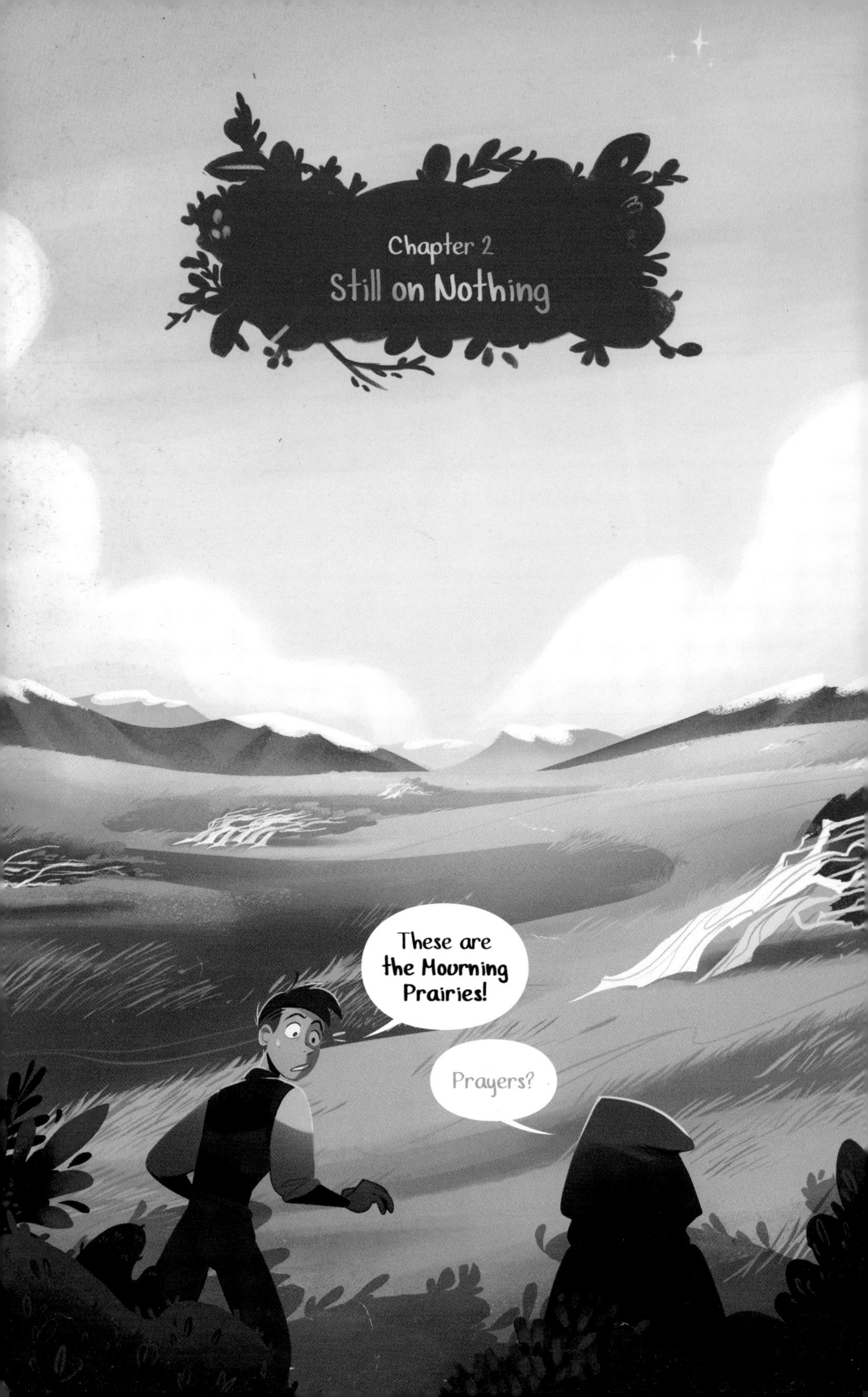
These are the Mourning Prairies!
Prayers?

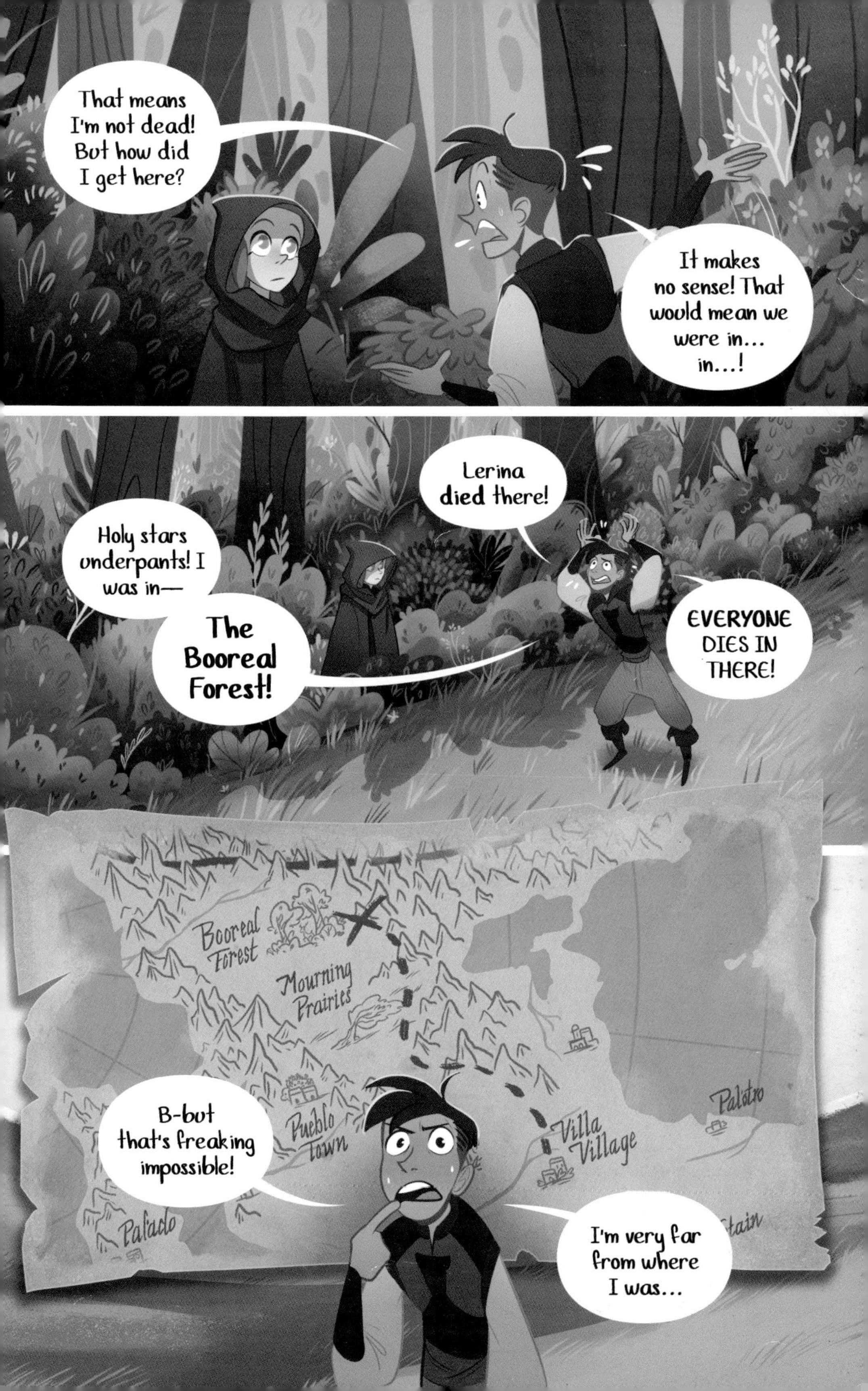
That means I'm not dead! But how did I get here?
It makes no sense! That would mean we were in... in...!
Holy stars underpants! I was in—
Lerina died there!
The Booreal Forest!
EVERYONE DIES IN THERE!
Booreal Forest
Mourning Prairies
Pueblo Town
Villa Village
Palotro
Palado
B-but that's freaking impossible!
I'm very far from where I was...

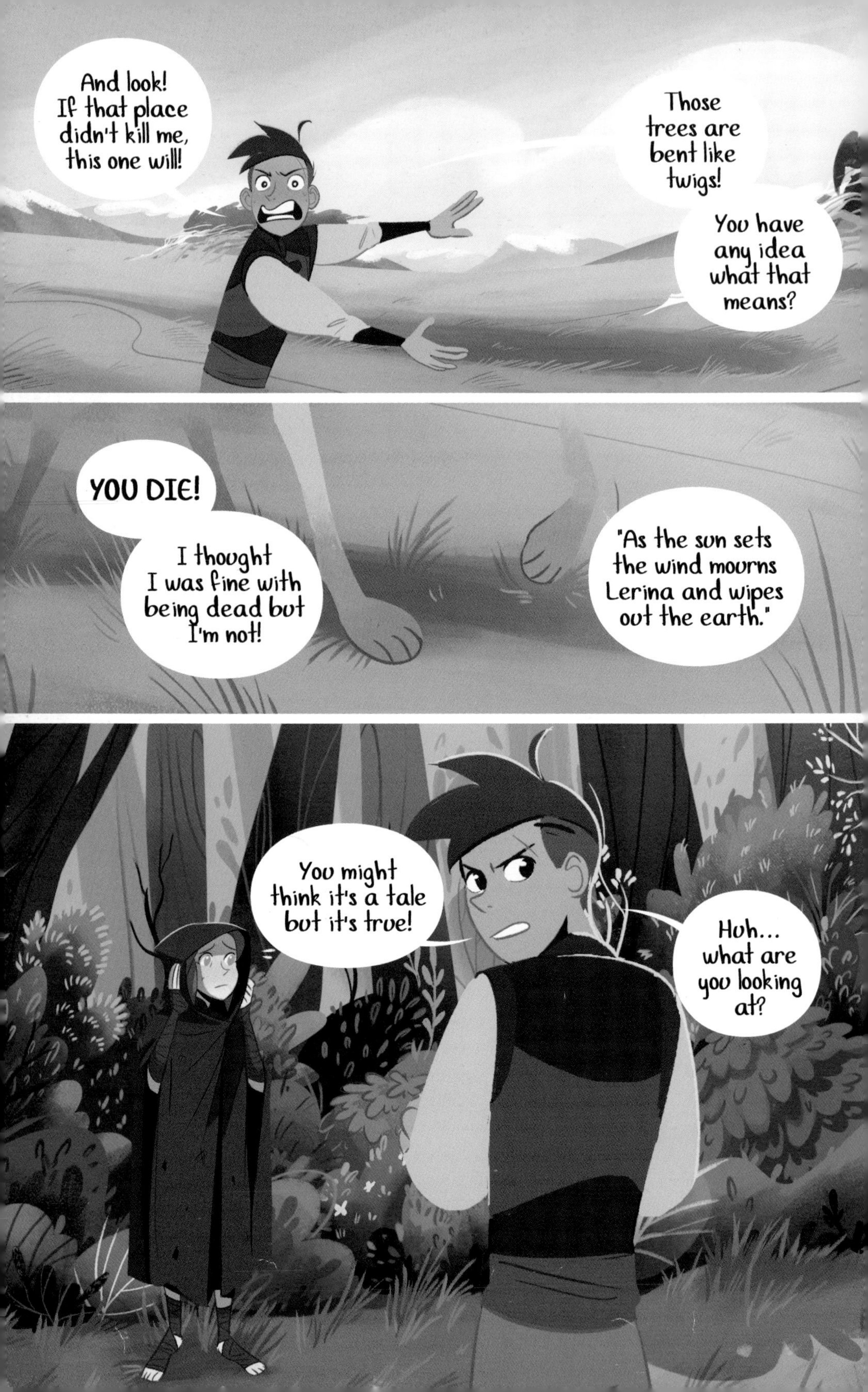
And look! If that place didn't kill me, this one will!
Those trees are bent like twigs!
You have any idea what that means?
YOU DIE!
I thought I was fine with being dead but I'm not!
"As the sun sets the wind mourns Lerina and wipes out the earth."
You might think it's a tale but it's true!
Huh... what are you looking at?

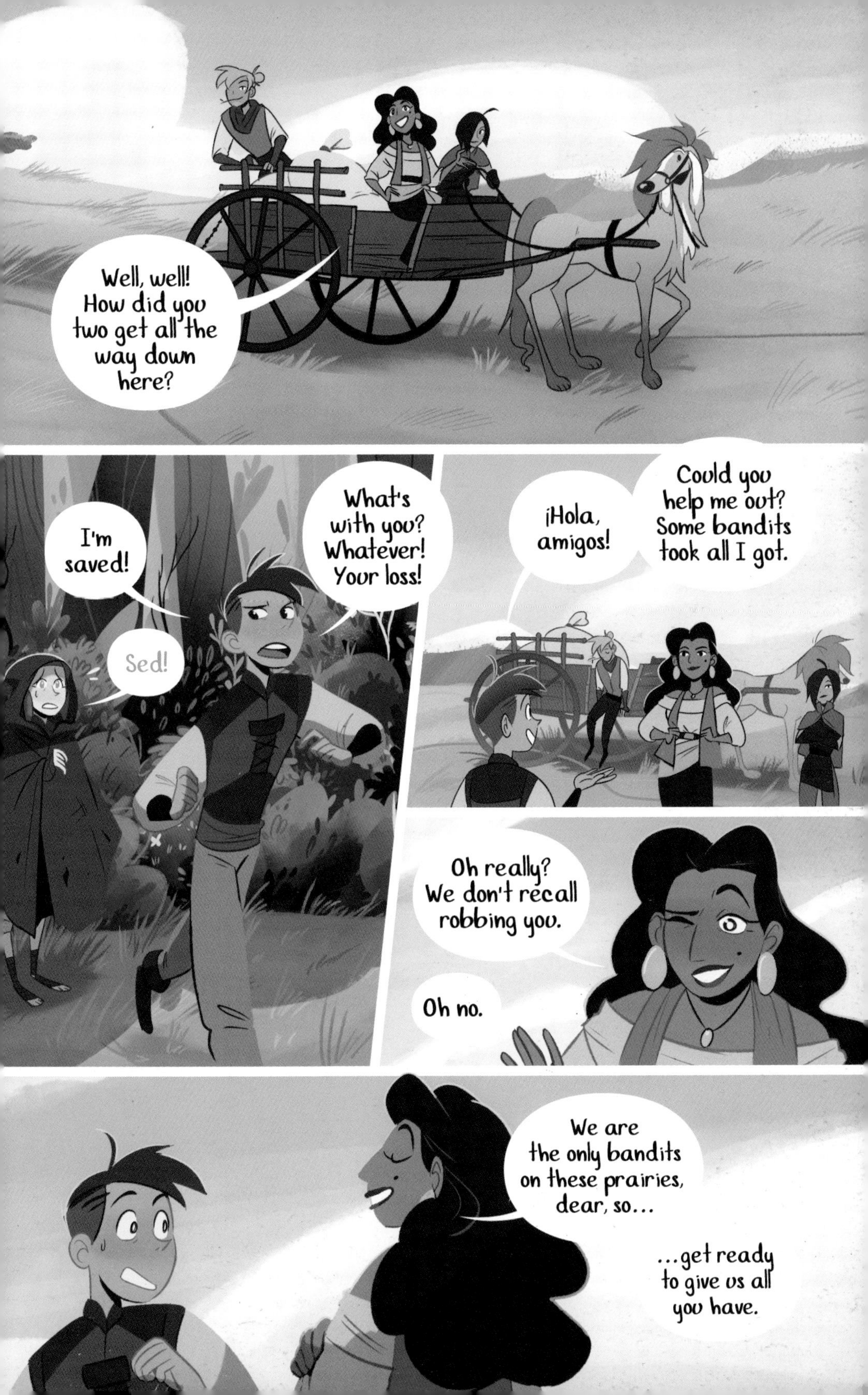

Well, well! How did you two get all the way down here?
I'm saved!
What's with you? Whatever! Your loss!
Sed!
¡Hola, amigos!
Could you help me out? Some bandits took all I got.
Oh really? We don't recall robbing you.
Oh no.
We are the only bandits on these prairies, dear, so...
...get ready to give us all you have.

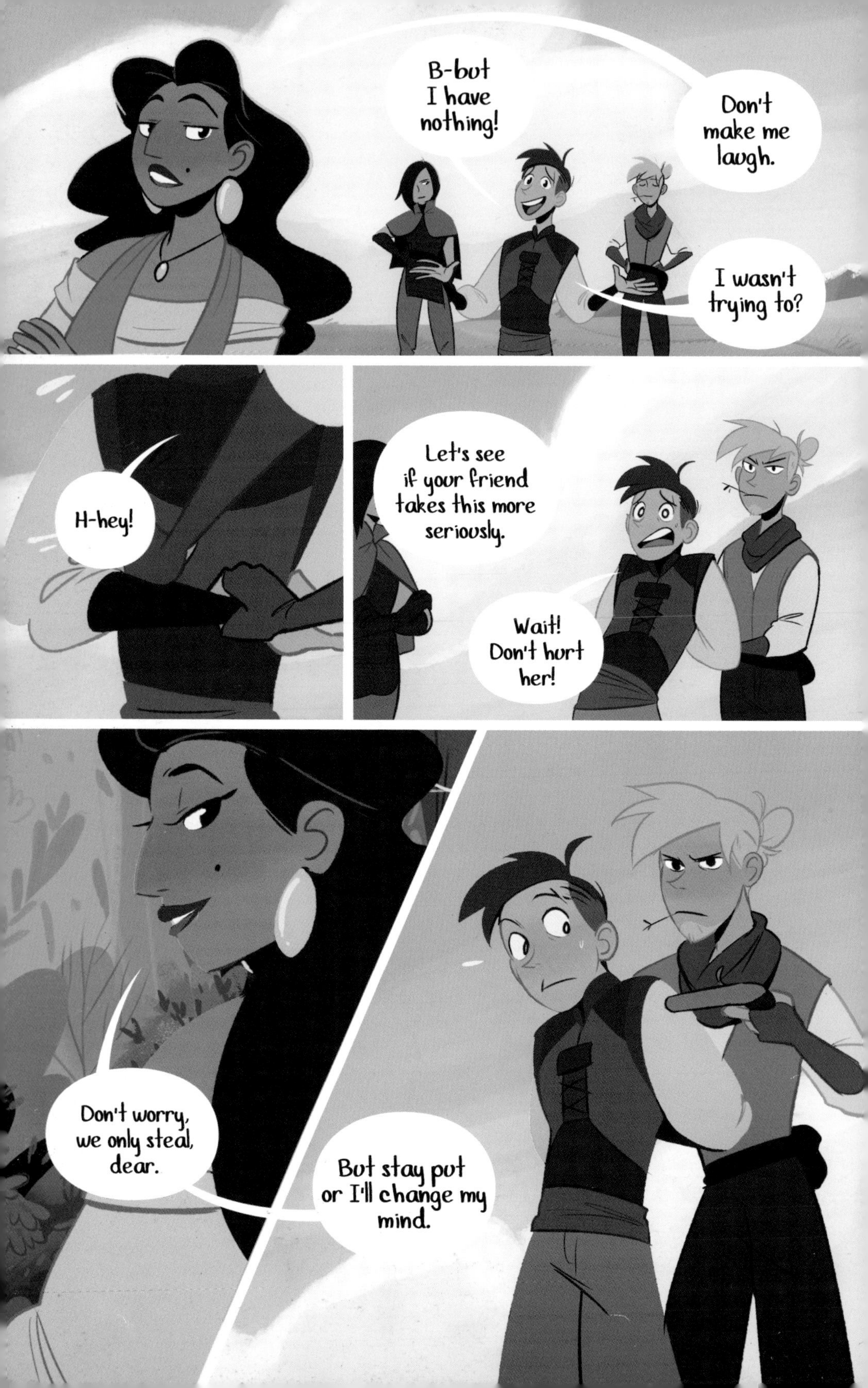
B-but I have nothing!
Don't make me laugh.
I wasn't trying to?
H-hey!
Let's see if your friend takes this more seriously.
Wait! Don't hurt her!
Don't worry, we only steal, dear.
But stay put or I'll change my mind.

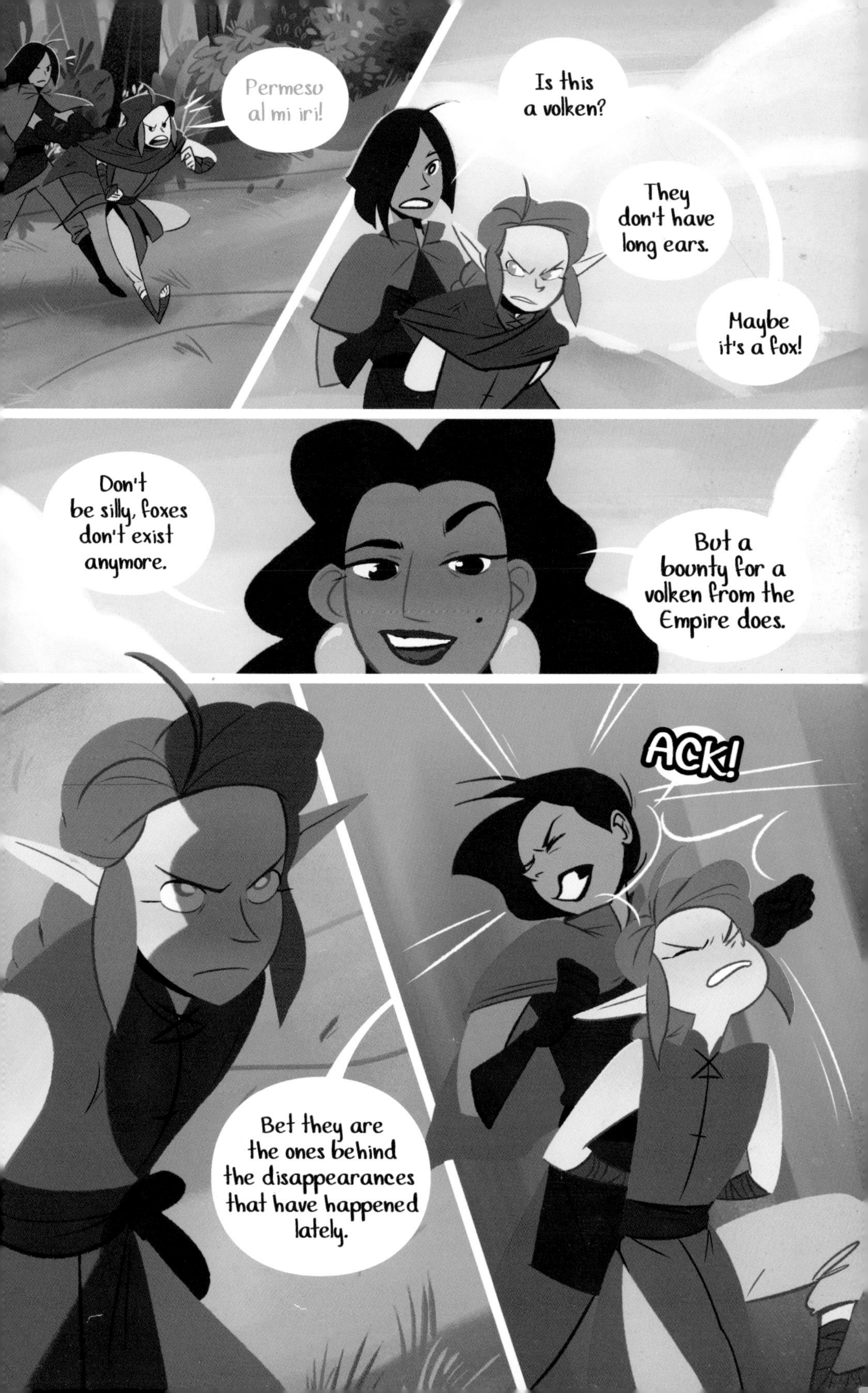
Permesu al mi iri!
Is this a volken?
They don't have long ears.
Maybe it's a fox!
Don't be silly, foxes don't exist anymore.
But a bounty for a volken from the Empire does.
ACK!
Bet they are the ones behind the disappearances that have happened lately.

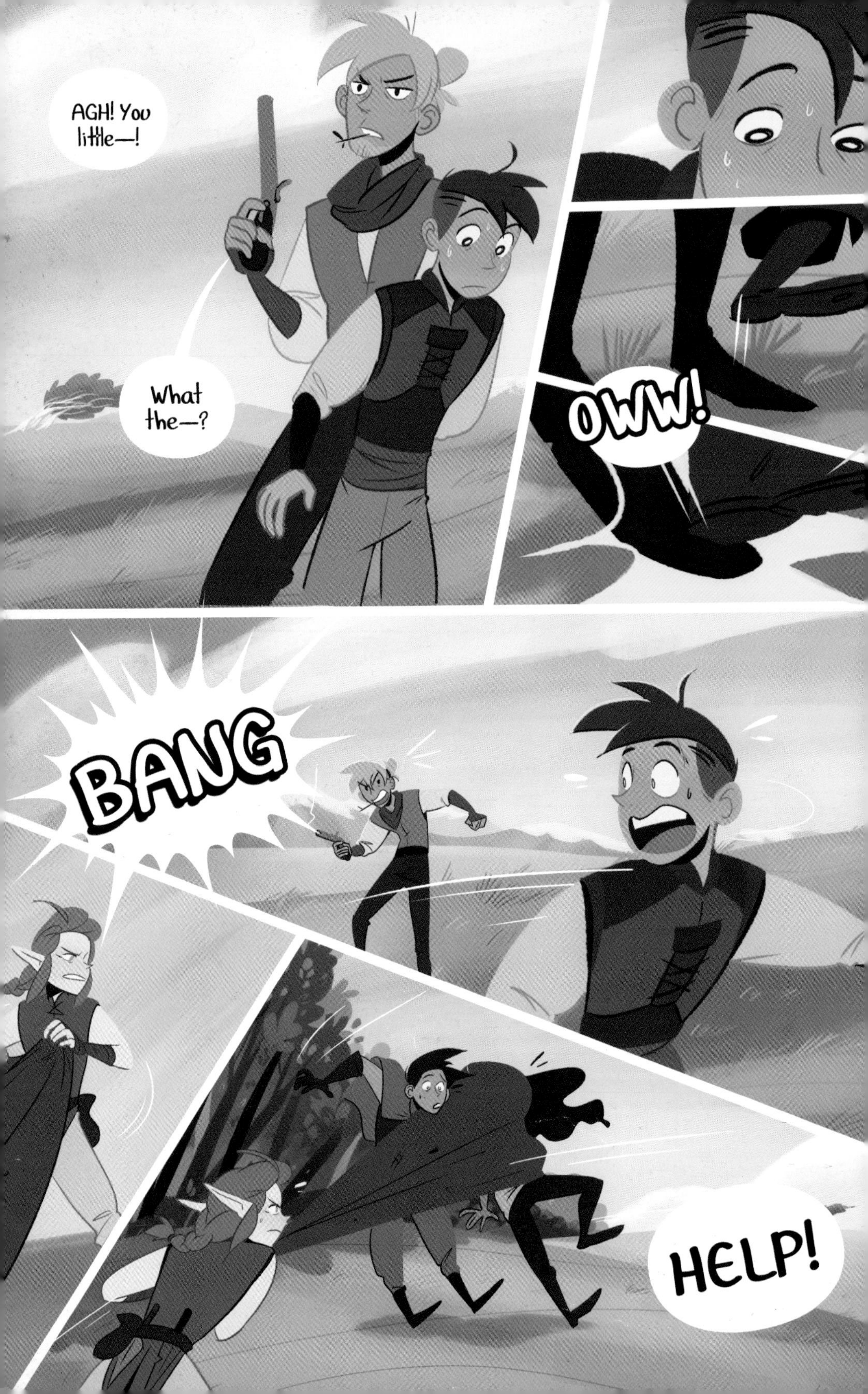
AGH! You little—!
What the—?
OWW!
BANG
HELP!

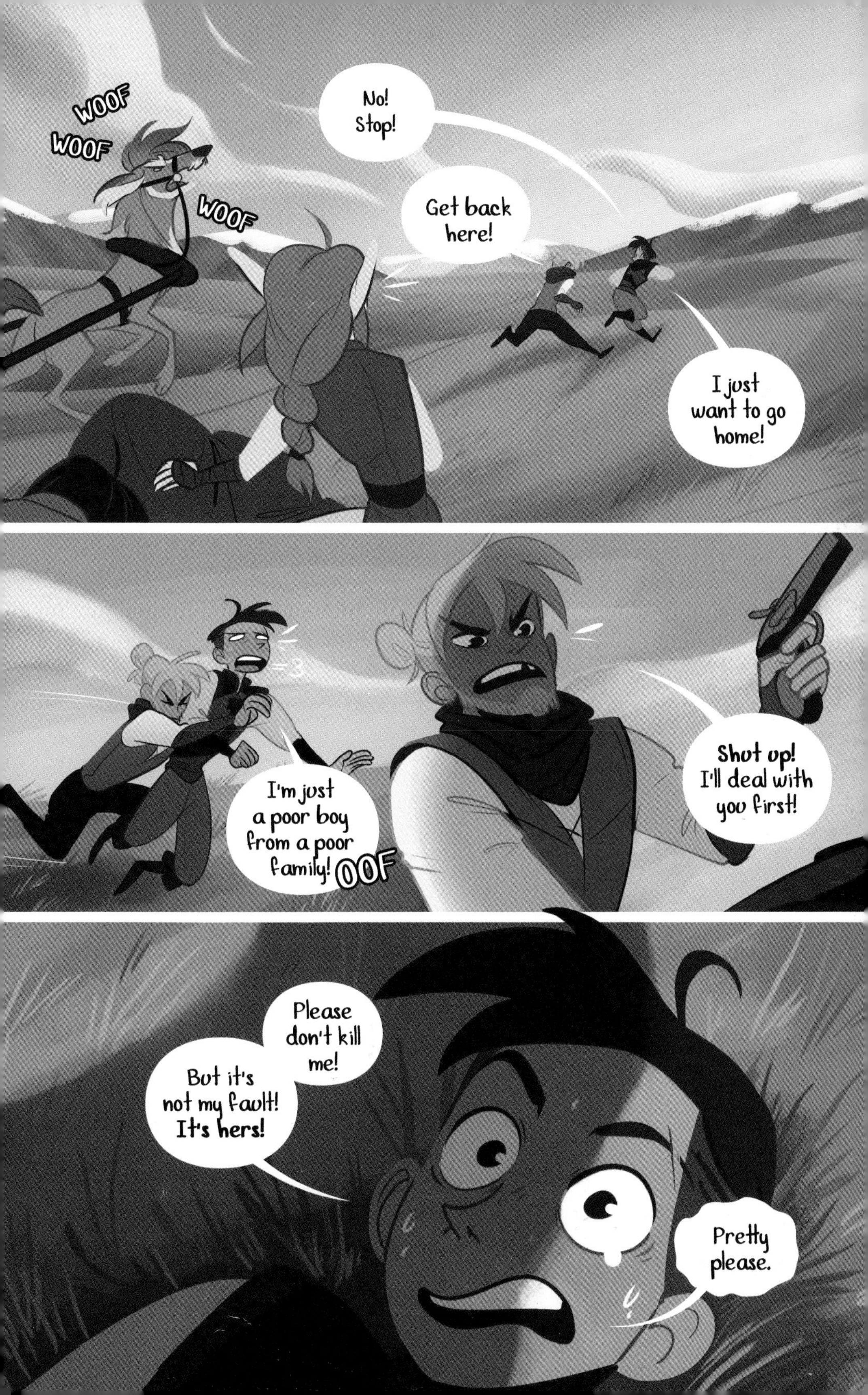
WOOF
WOOF
WOOF
No! Stop!
Get back here!
I just want to go home!
I'm just a poor boy from a poor family!
OOF
Shut up! I'll deal with you first!
Please don't kill me!
But it's not my fault! It's hers!
Pretty please.

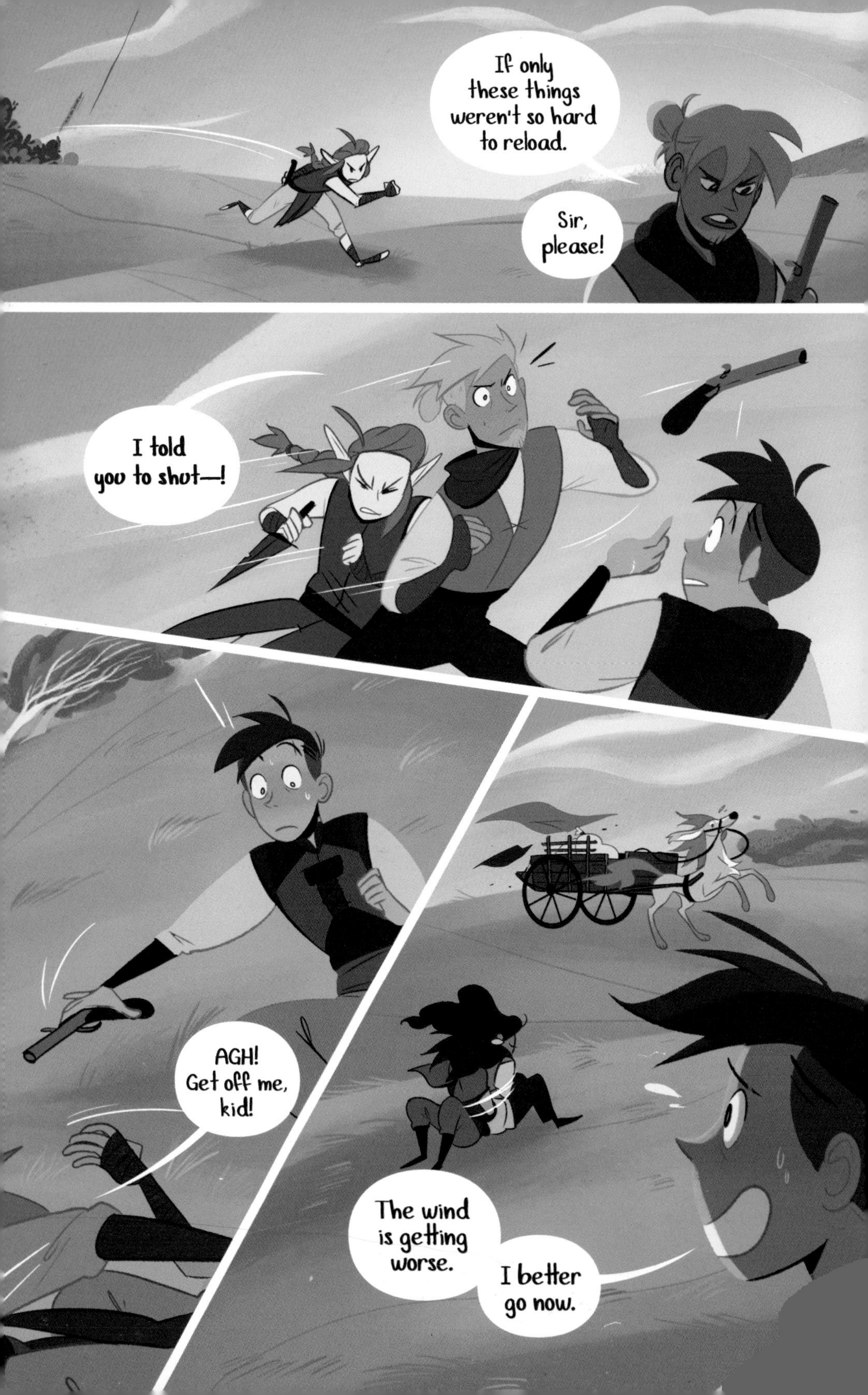
If only these things weren't so hard to reload.
Sir, please!
I told you to shut—!
AGH! Get off me, kid!
The wind is getting worse.
I better go now.

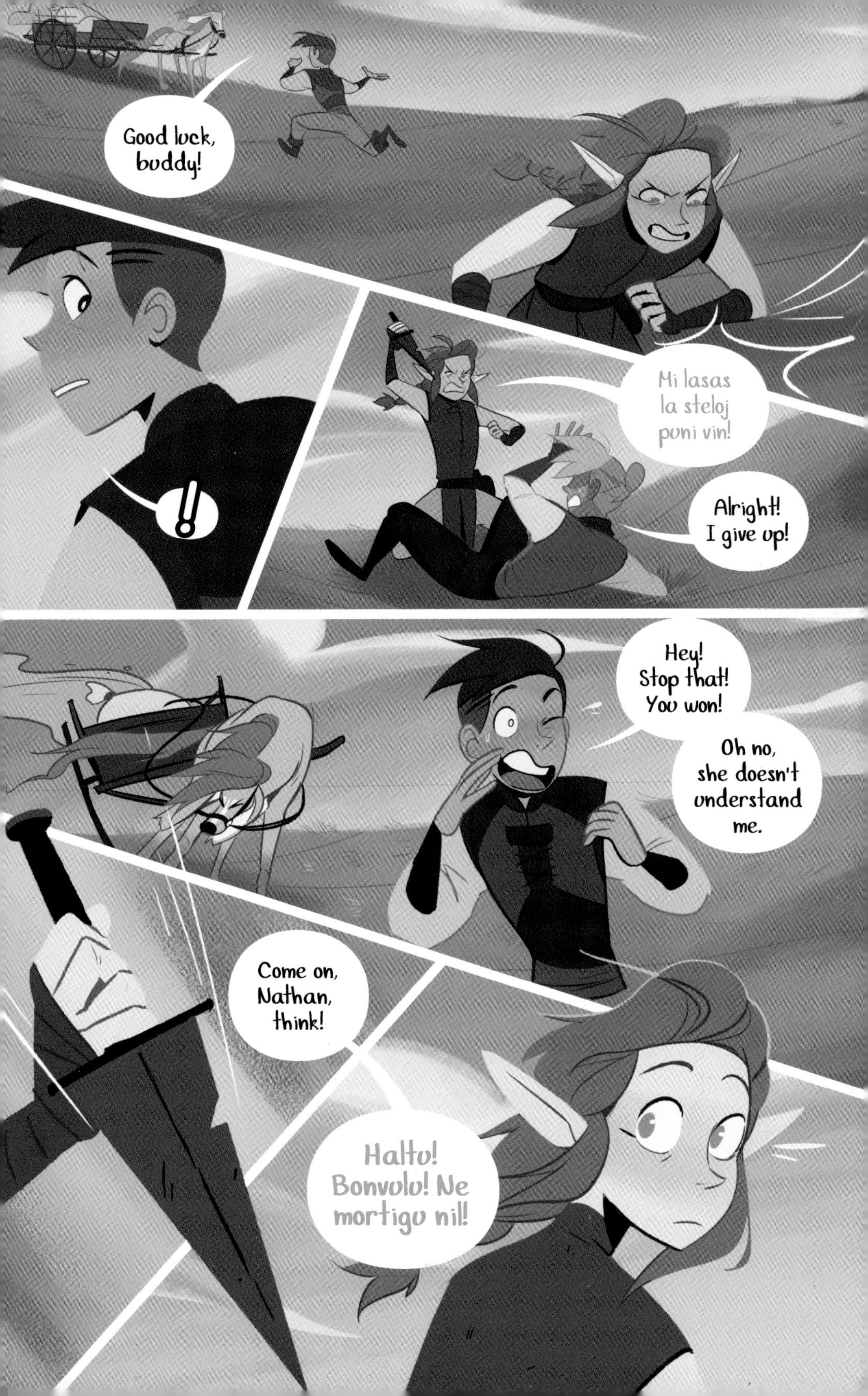
Good luck, buddy!
!
Mi lasas la steloj poni vin!
Alright! I give up!
Hey! Stop that! You won!
Oh no, she doesn't understand me.
Come on, Nathan, think!
Haltu! Bonvolu! Ne mortigu nin!

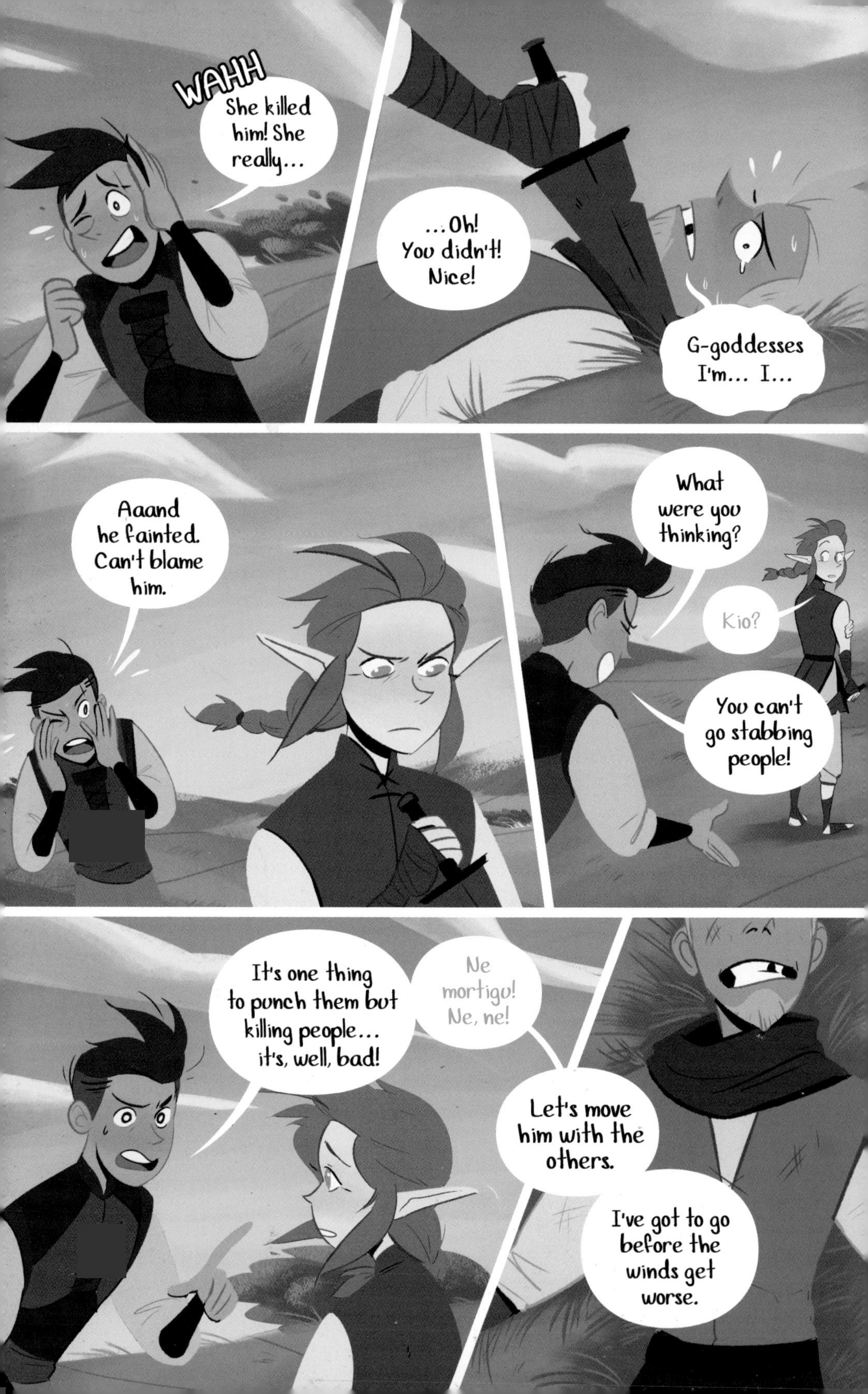

WAHH
She killed him! She really...
...Oh! You didn't! Nice!
G-goddesses I'm... I...
Aaand he fainted. Can't blame him.
What were you thinking?
Kio?
You can't go stabbing people!
It's one thing to punch them but killing people... it's, well, bad!
Ne mortigu! Ne, ne!
Let's move him with the others.
I've got to go before the winds get worse.

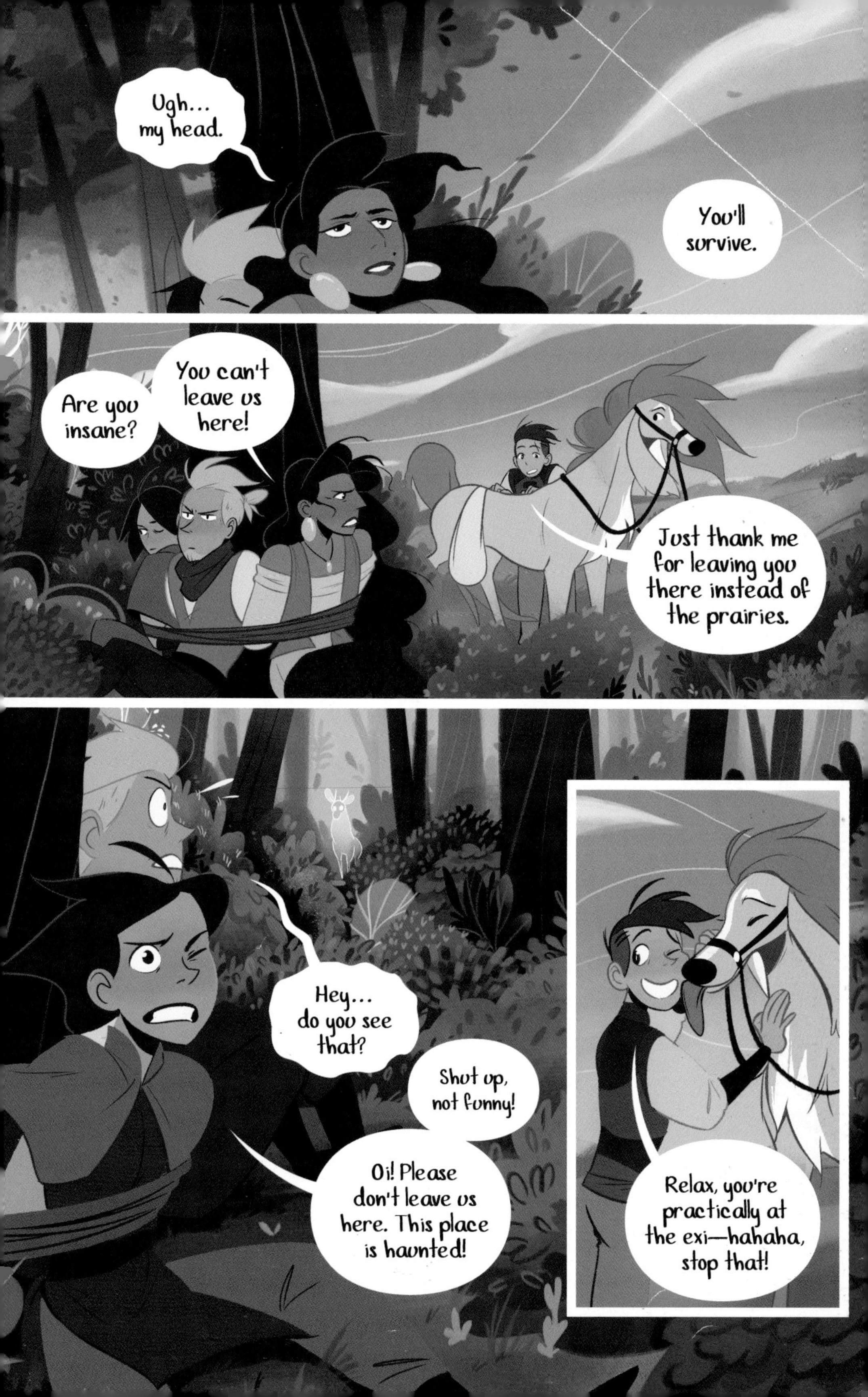
Ugh... my head.
You'll survive.
Are you insane?
You can't leave us here!
Just thank me for leaving you there instead of the prairies.
Hey... do you see that?
Shut up, not funny!
Oi! Please don't leave us here. This place is haunted!
Relax, you're practically at the exi—hahaha, stop that!

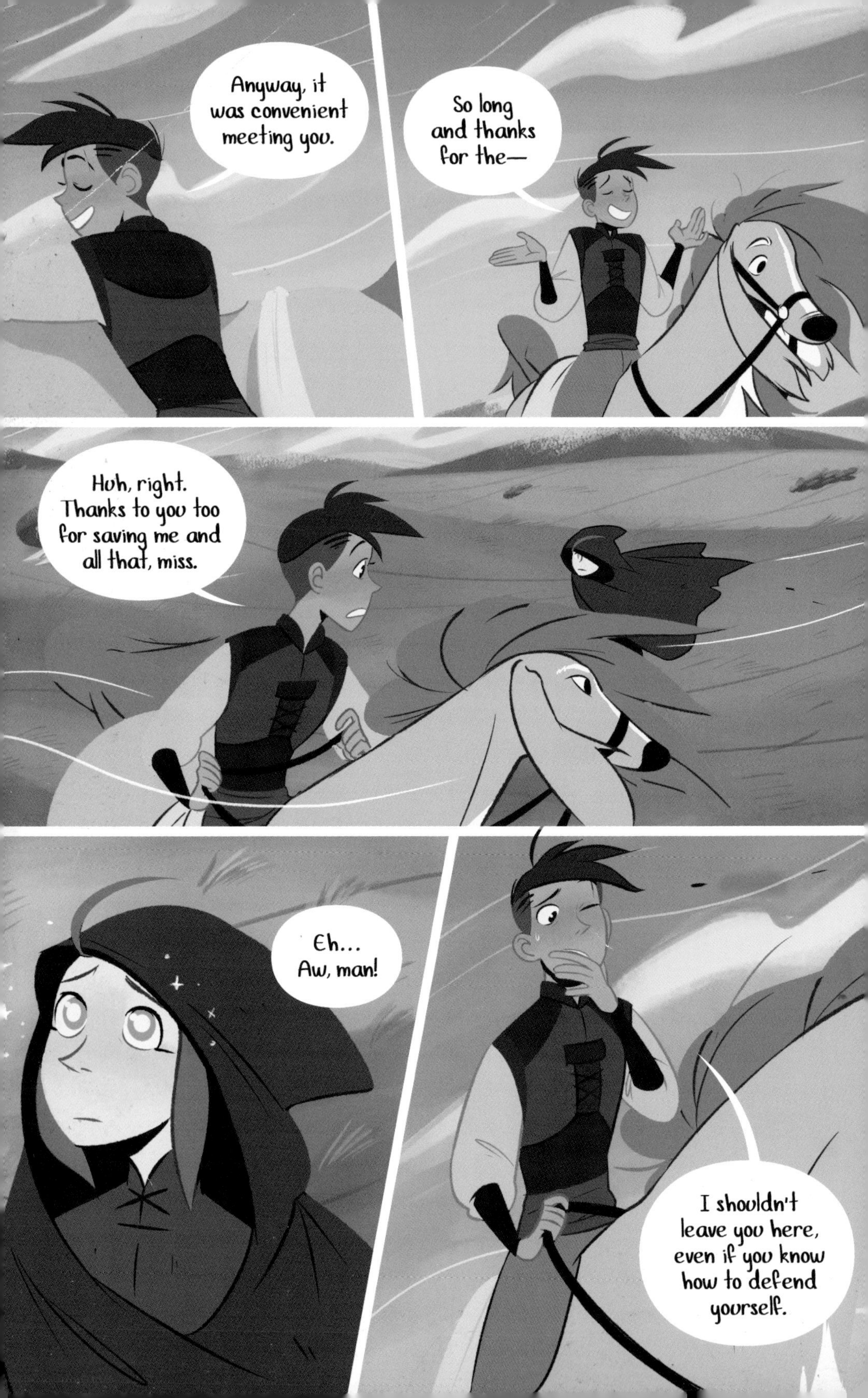
Anyway, it was convenient meeting you.
So long and thanks for the—
Huh, right. Thanks to you too for saving me and all that, miss.
Eh... Aw, man!
I shouldn't leave you here, even if you know how to defend yourself.

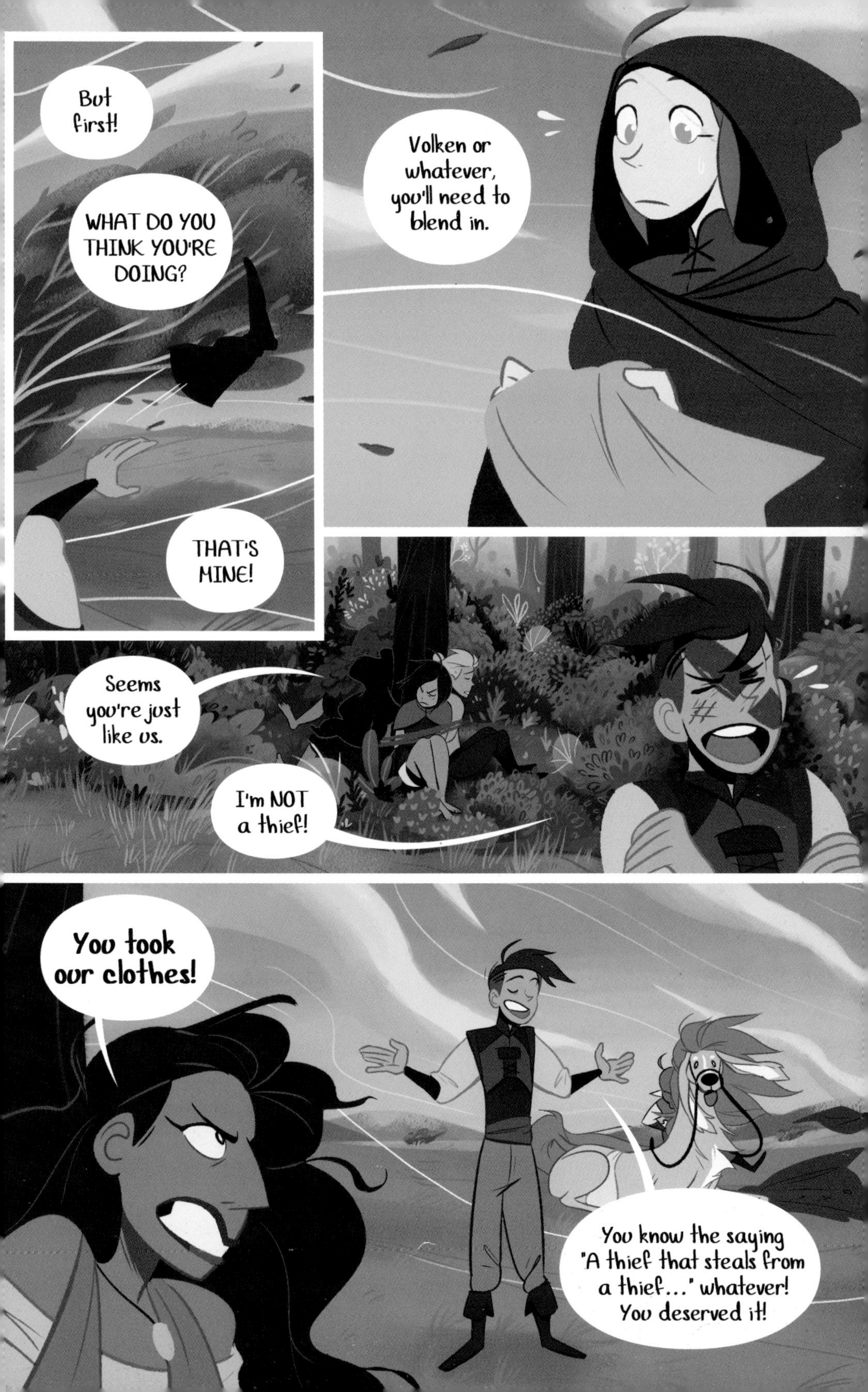
But first!
WHAT DO YOU THINK YOU'RE DOING?
THAT'S MINE!
Volken or whatever, you'll need to blend in.
Seems you're just like us.
I'm NOT a thief!
You took our clothes!
You know the saying "A thief that steals from a thief..." whatever! You deserved it!

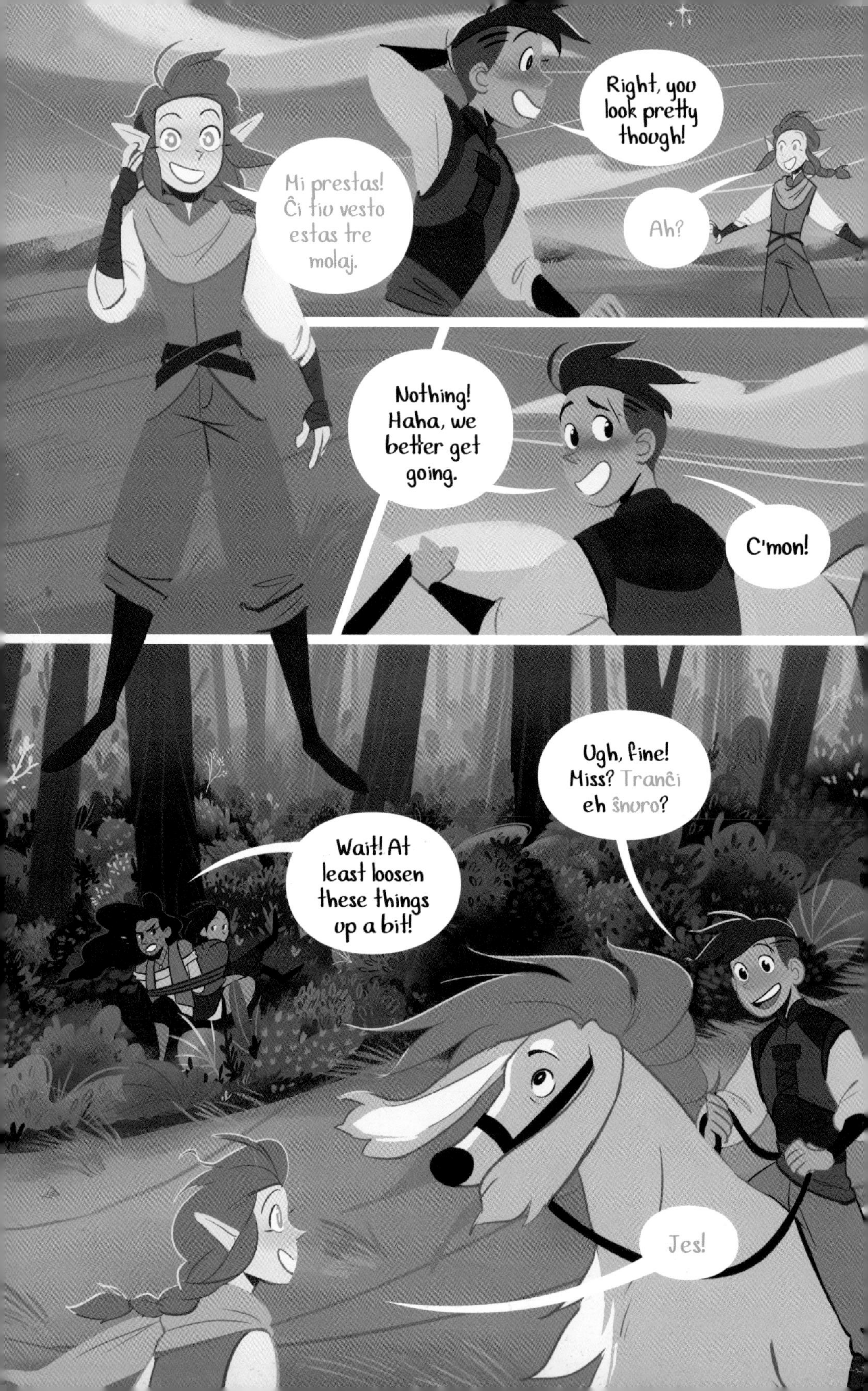
Mi prestas! Ĉi tiu vesto estas tre molaj.
Right, you look pretty though!
Ah?
Nothing! Haha, we better get going.
C'mon!
Ugh, fine! Miss? Tranĉi eh ŝnuro?
Wait! At least loosen these things up a bit!
Jes!

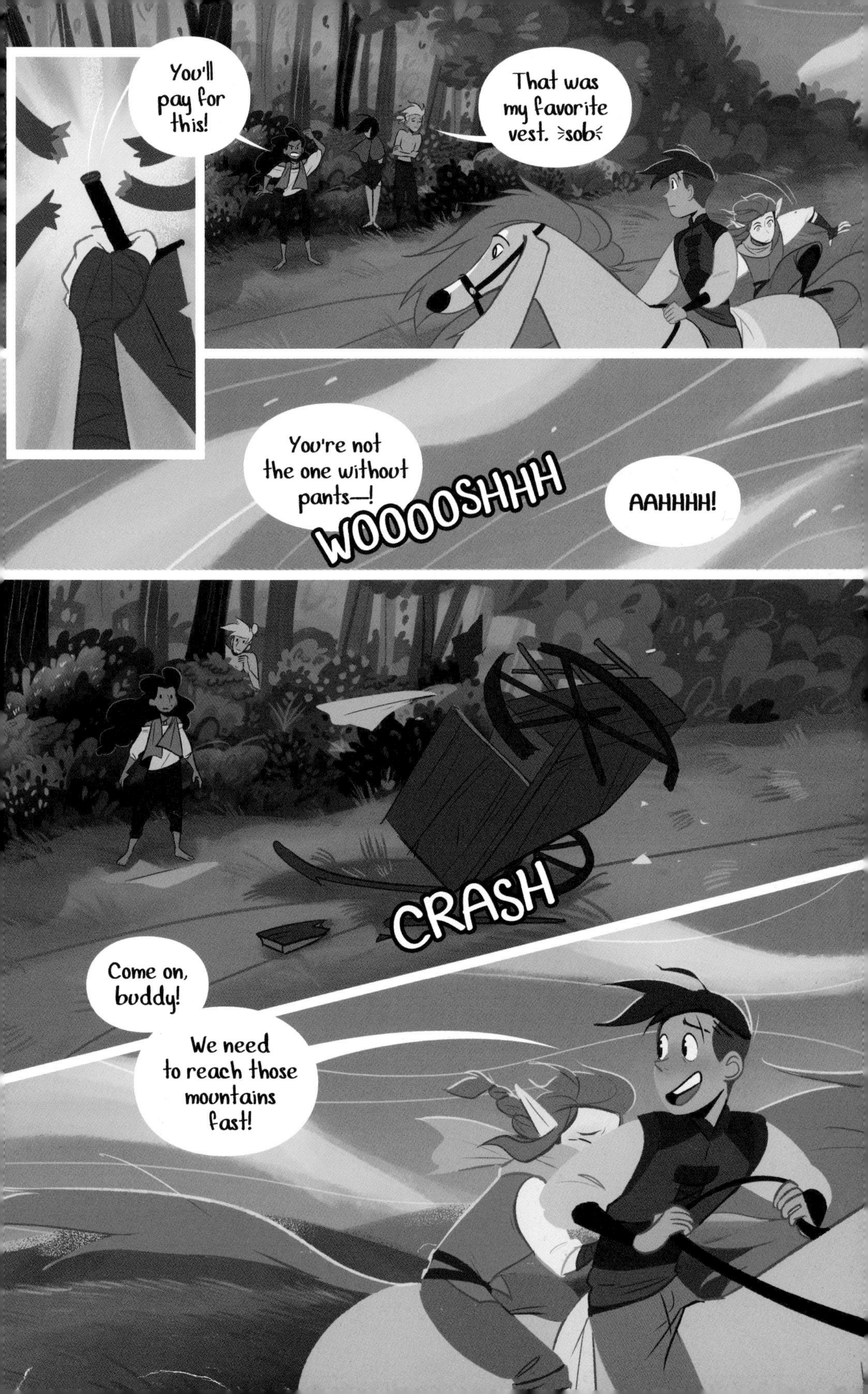
You'll pay for this!
That was my favorite vest. ⩺sob⩹
You're not the one without pants—!
WOOOOSHHH
AAHHHH!
CRASH
Come on, buddy!
We need to reach those mountains fast!

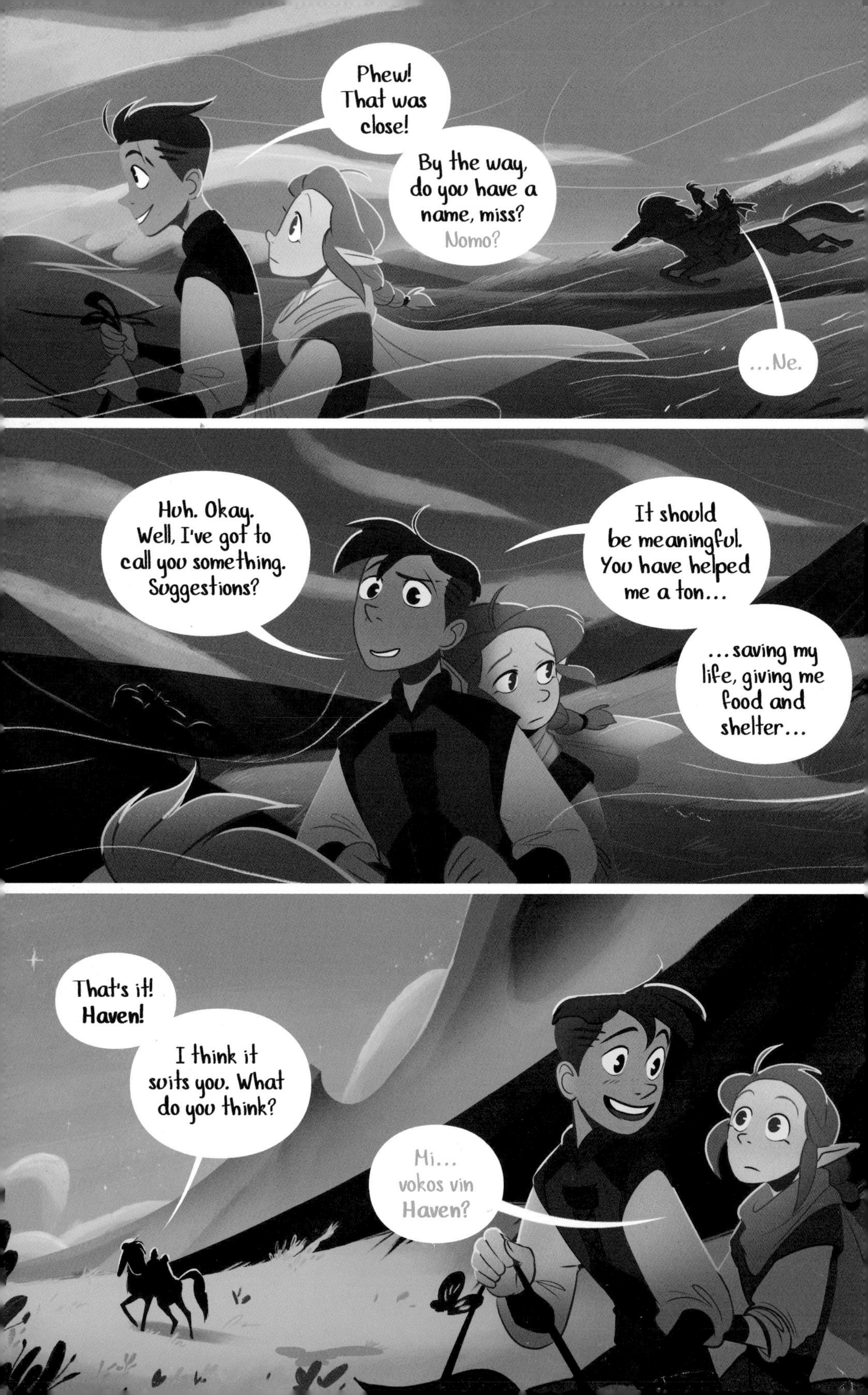
Phew! That was close!
By the way, do you have a name, miss? Nomo?
...Ne.
Huh. Okay. Well, I've got to call you something. Suggestions?
It should be meaningful. You have helped me a ton...
...saving my life, giving me food and shelter...
That's it! Haven!
I think it suits you. What do you think?
Mi... vokos vin Haven?

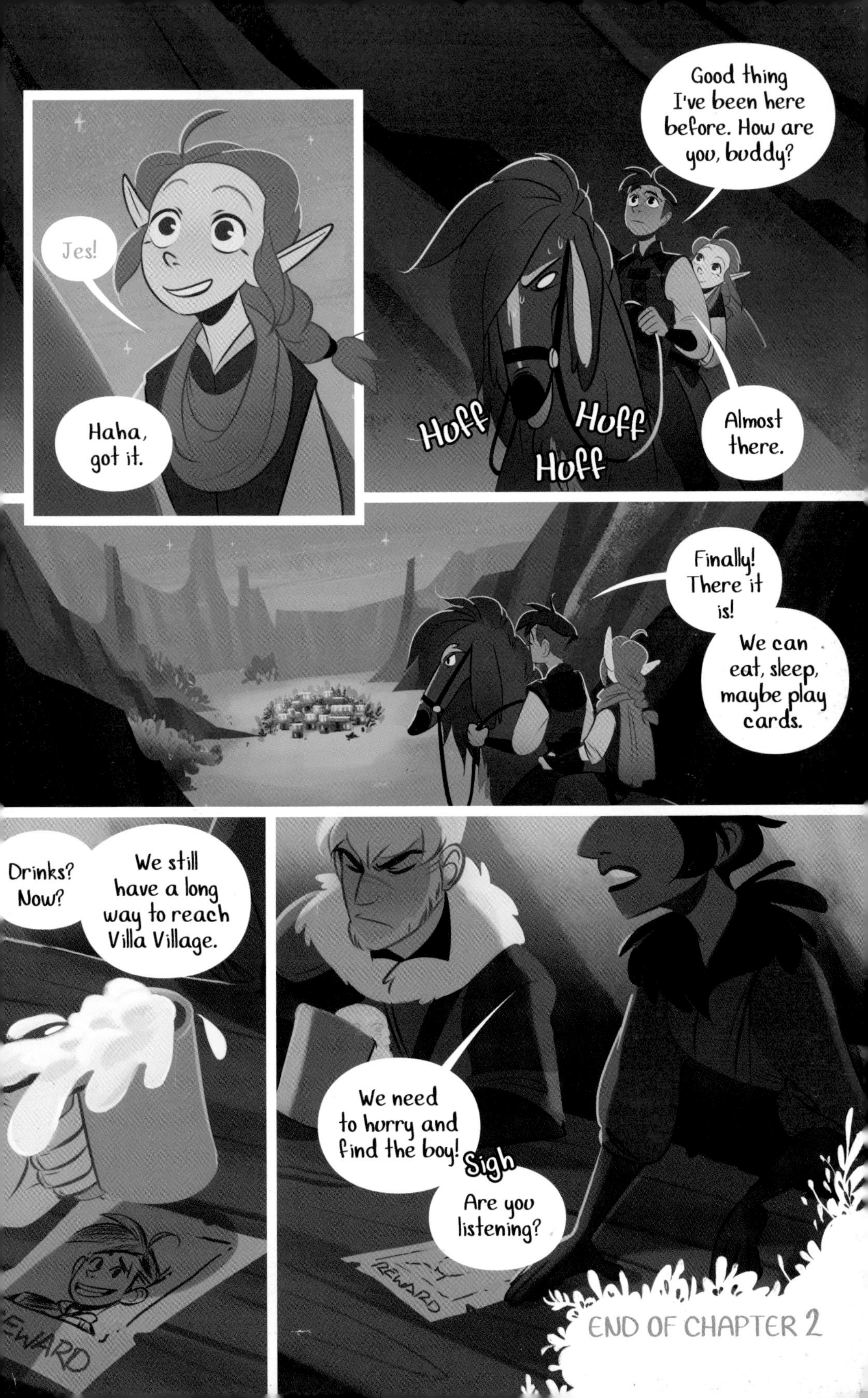
Jes!
Haha, got it.
Good thing I've been here before. How are you, buddy?
Huff
Huff
Huff
Almost there.
Finally! There it is!
We can eat, sleep, maybe play cards.
Drinks? Now?
We still have a long way to reach Villa Village.
REWARD
We need to hurry and find the boy!
Sigh
Are you listening?
REWARD
END OF CHAPTER 2

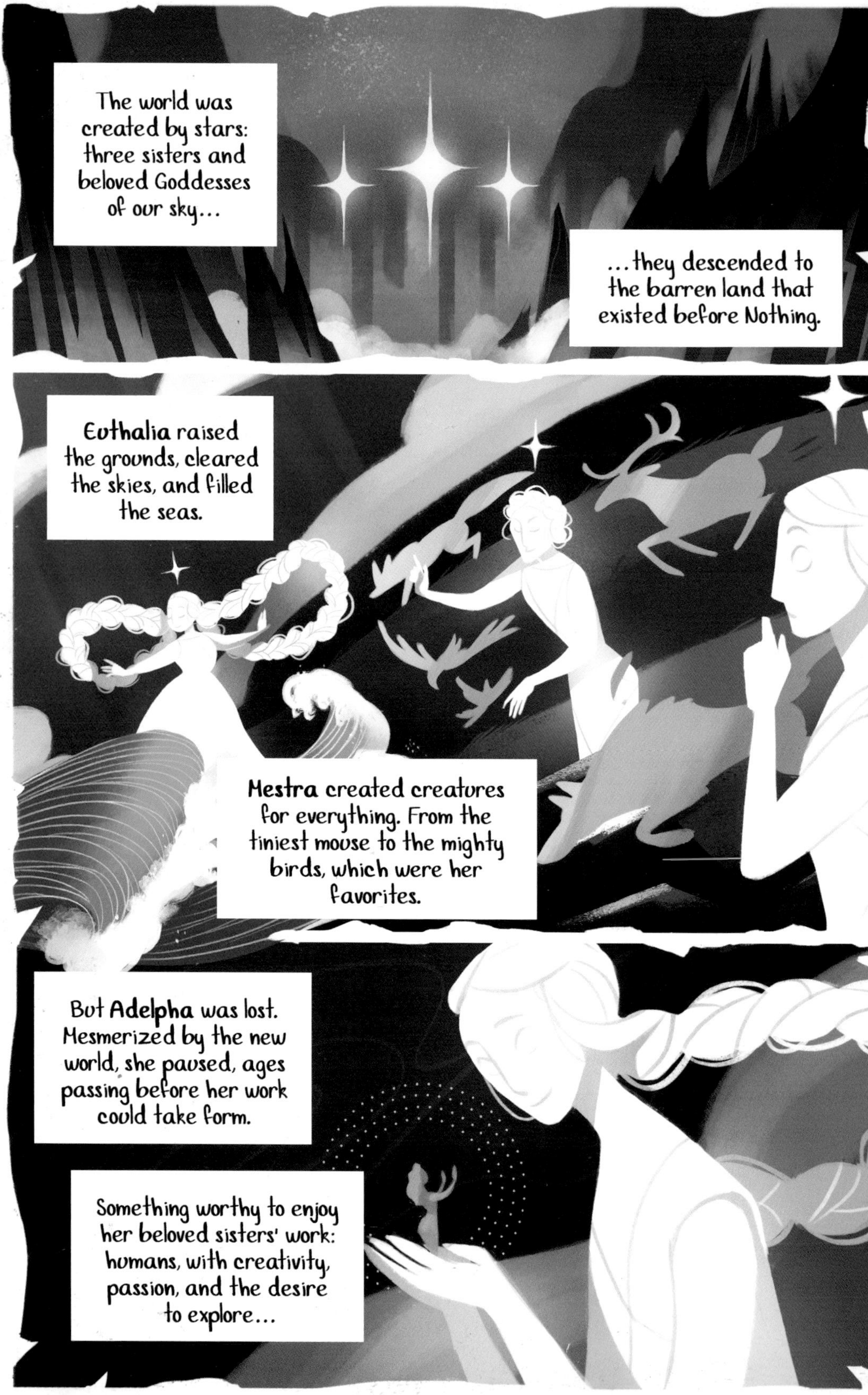
The world was created by stars: three sisters and beloved Goddesses of our sky...
...they descended to the barren land that existed before Nothing.
Euthalia raised the grounds, cleared the skies, and filled the seas.
Mestra created creatures for everything. From the tiniest mouse to the mighty birds, which were her favorites.
But **Adelpha** was lost. Mesmerized by the new world, she paused, ages passing before her work could take form.
Something worthy to enjoy her beloved sisters' work: humans, with creativity, passion, and the desire to explore...

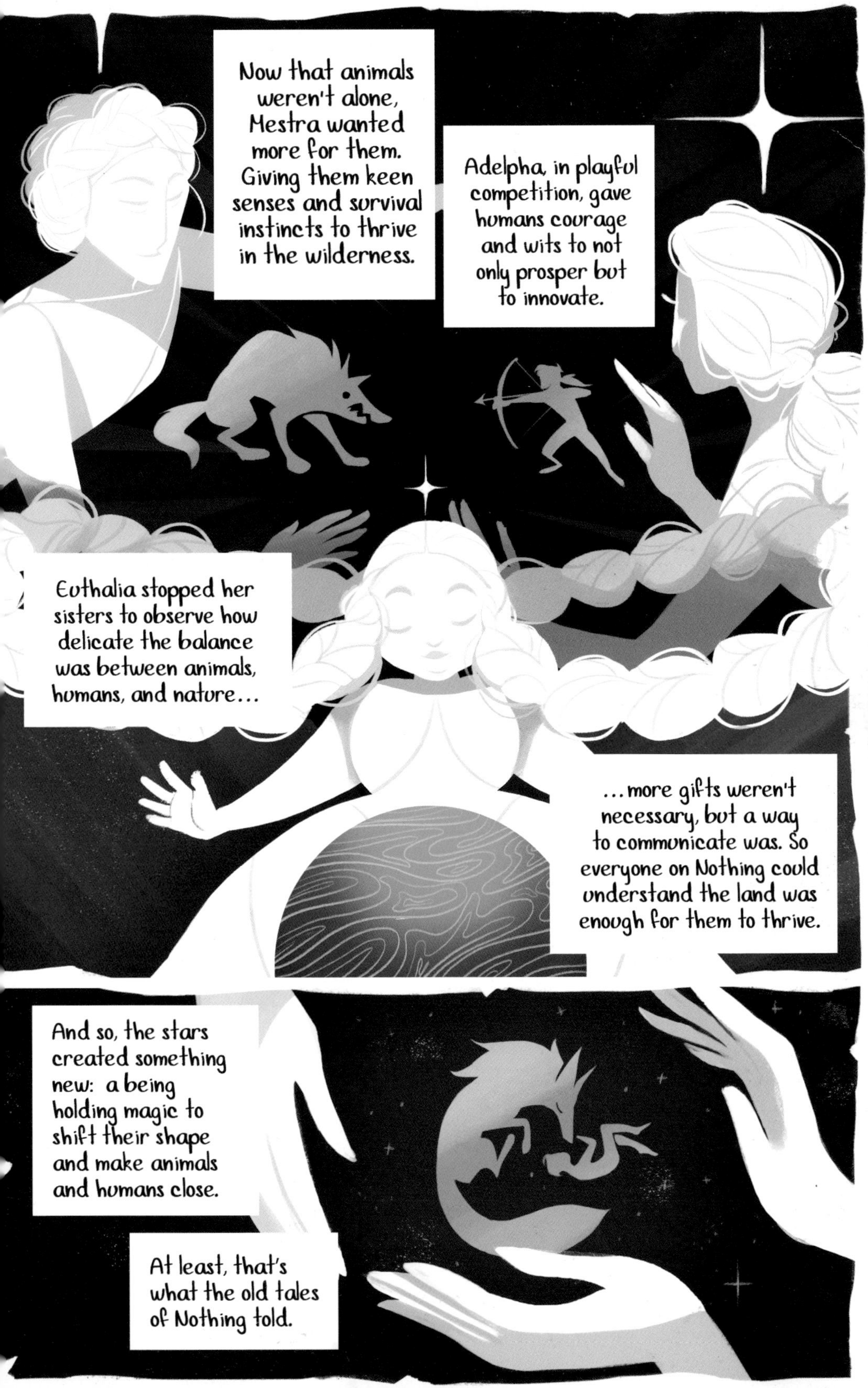
Now that animals weren't alone, Mestra wanted more for them. Giving them keen senses and survival instincts to thrive in the wilderness.
Adelpha, in playful competition, gave humans courage and wits to not only prosper but to innovate.
Euthalia stopped her sisters to observe how delicate the balance was between animals, humans, and nature…
…more gifts weren't necessary, but a way to communicate was. So everyone on Nothing could understand the land was enough for them to thrive.
And so, the stars created something new: a being holding magic to shift their shape and make animals and humans close.
At least, that's what the old tales of Nothing told.

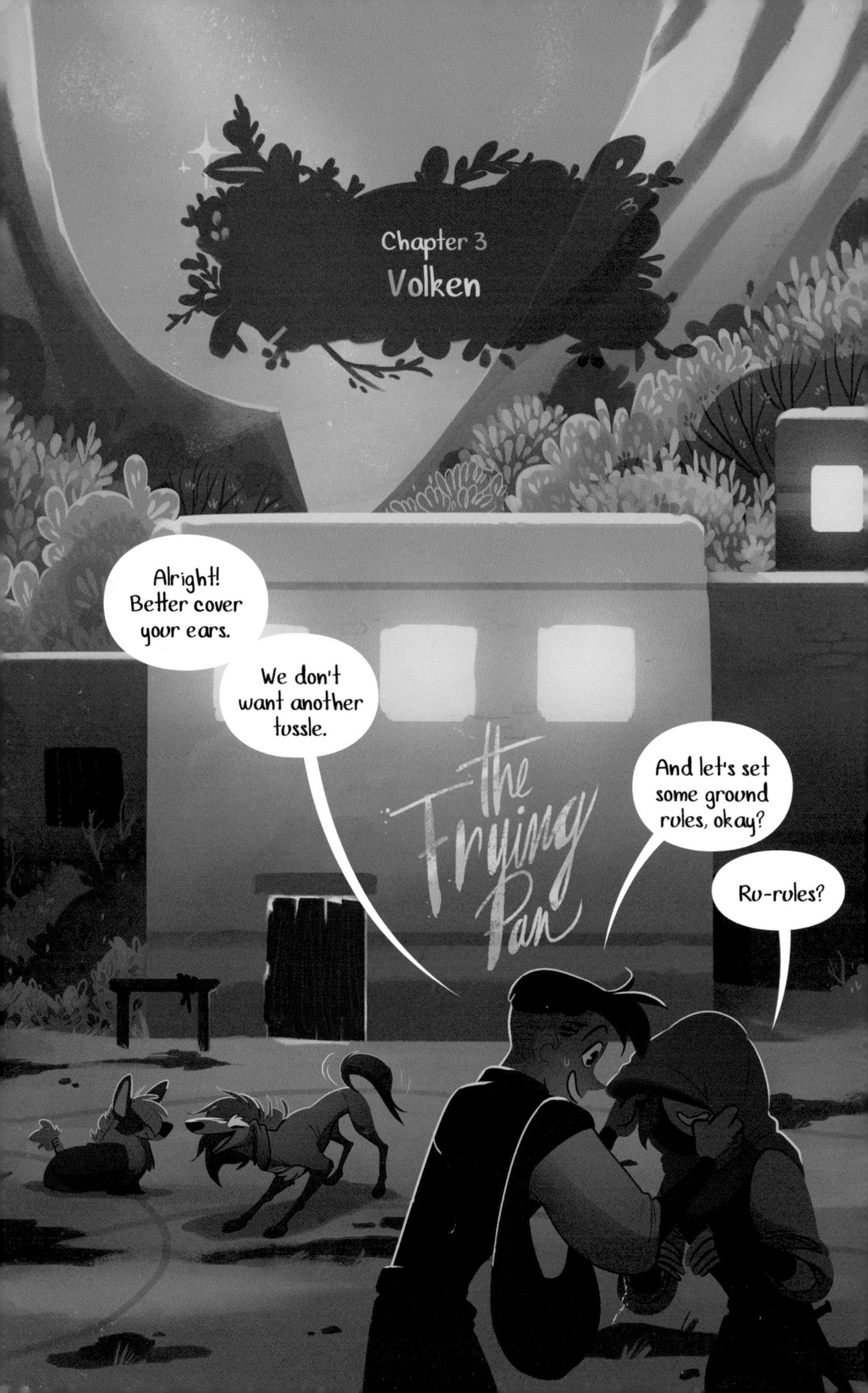
Chapter 3
Volken
Alright! Better cover your ears.
We don't want another tussle.
The Frying Pan
And let's set some ground rules, okay?
Ru-rules?

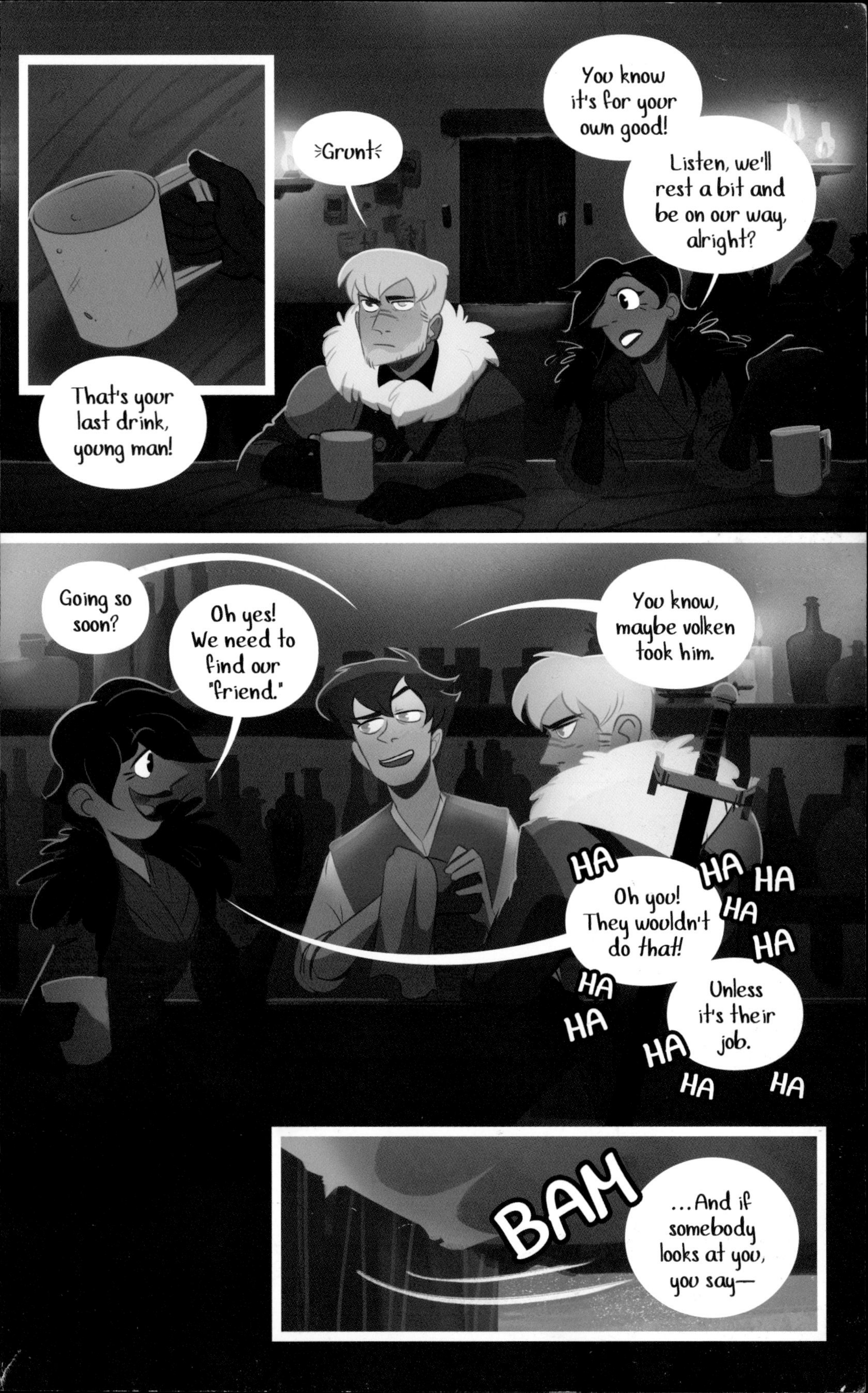
That's your last drink, young man!
≶Grunt≶
You know it's for your own good!
Listen, we'll rest a bit and be on our way, alright?
Going so soon?
Oh yes! We need to find our "friend."
You know, maybe volken took him.
Oh you! They wouldn't do that!
Unless it's their job.
HA HA HA HA HA HA HA HA HA HA
BAM
...And if somebody looks at you, you say—

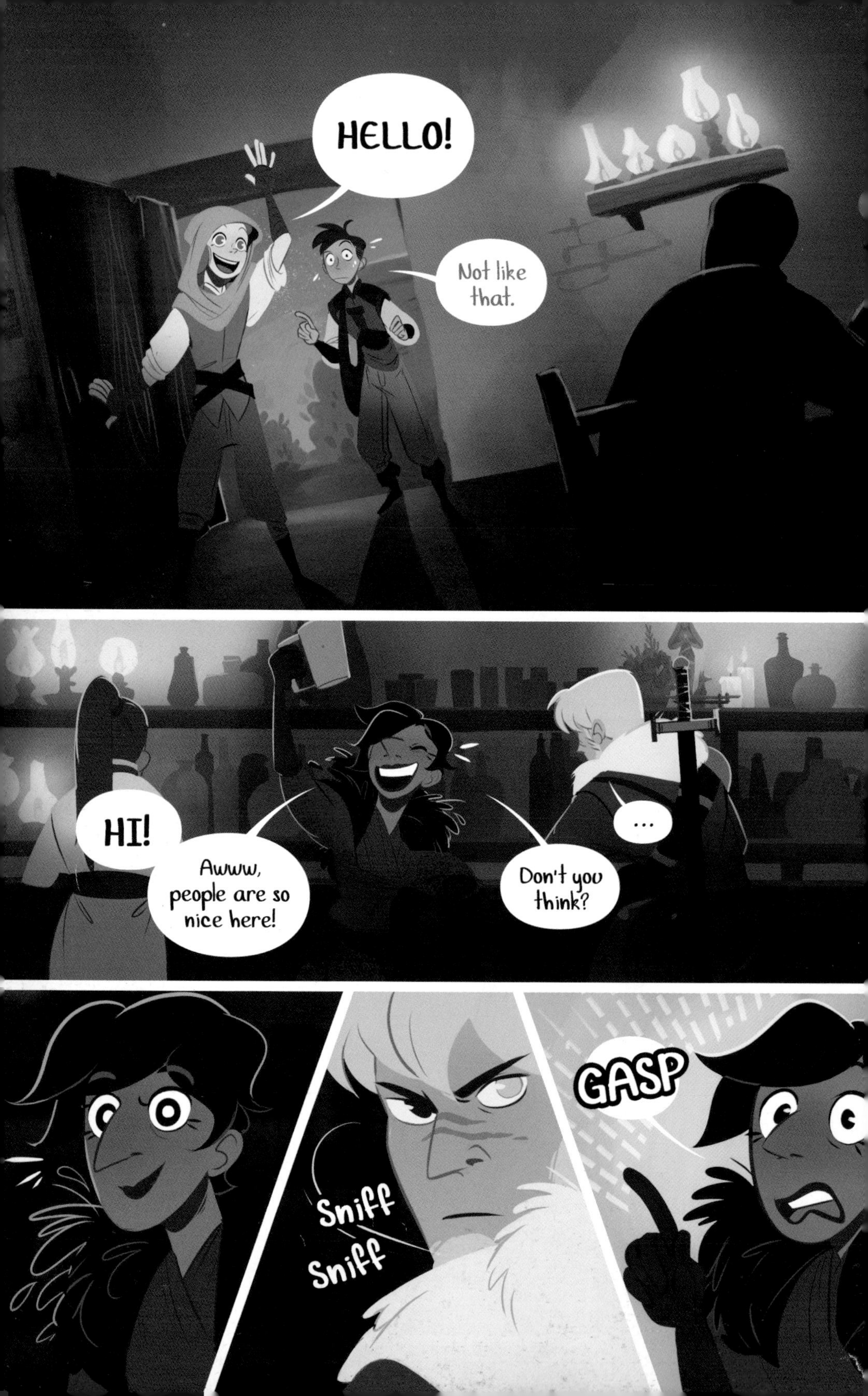
HELLO!
Not like that.
HI!
Awww, people are so nice here!
Don't you think?
...
Sniff
Sniff
GASP

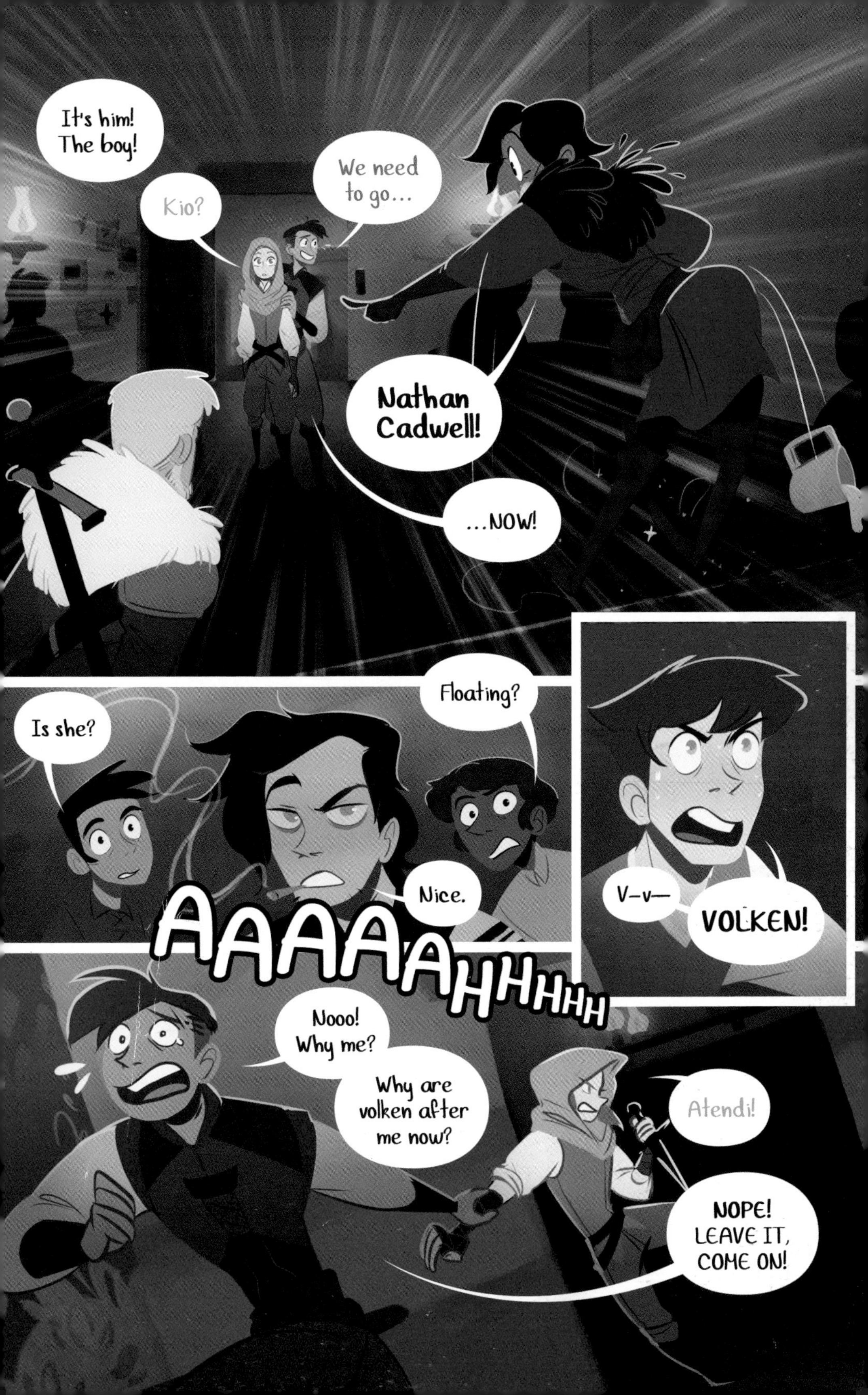
It's him! The boy!
Kio?
We need to go...
Nathan Cadwell!
...NOW!
Is she?
Floating?
Nice.
V—v—
VOLKEN!
AAAAAAHHHHH
Nooo! Why me?
Why are volken after me now?
Atendi!
NOPE! LEAVE IT, COME ON!

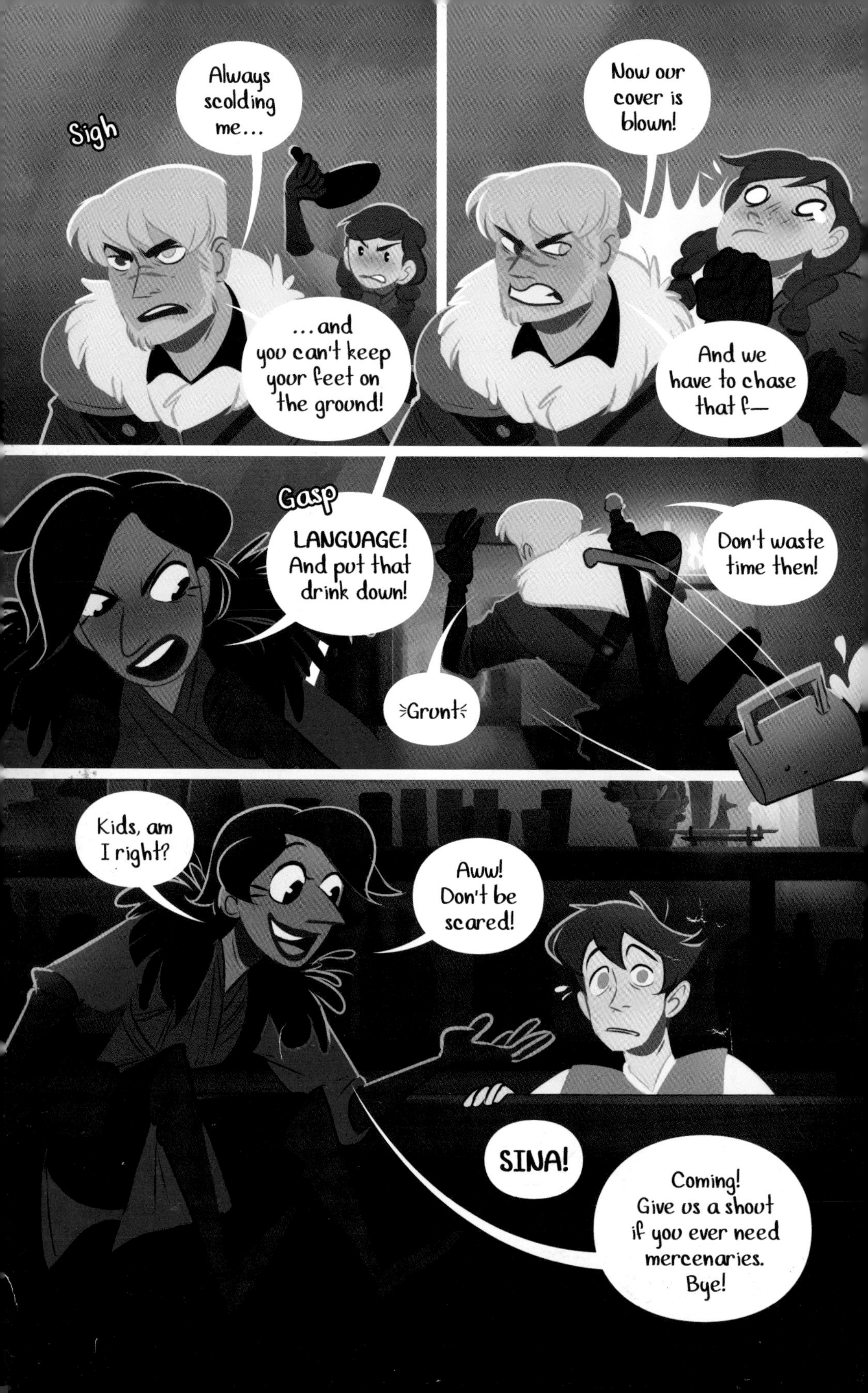
Sigh
Always scolding me...
...and you can't keep your feet on the ground!
Now our cover is blown!
And we have to chase that f—
Gasp
LANGUAGE! And put that drink down!
Grunt
Don't waste time then!
Kids, am I right?
Aww! Don't be scared!
SINA!
Coming! Give us a shout if you ever need mercenaries. Bye!

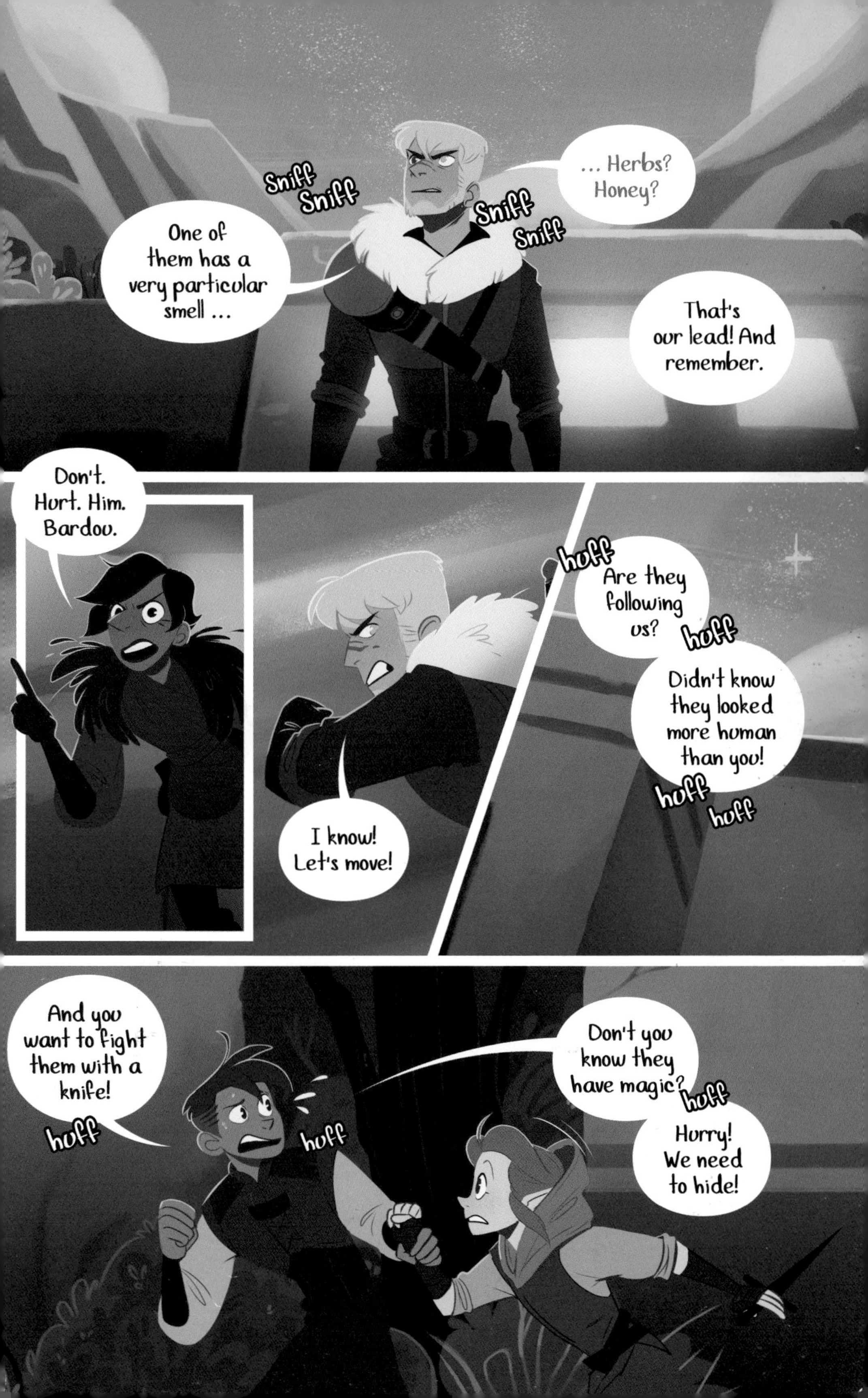
Sniff
Sniff
... Herbs? Honey?
Sniff
Sniff
One of them has a very particular smell ...
That's our lead! And remember.
Don't. Hurt. Him. Bardou.
I know! Let's move!
hoff
Are they following us?
hoff
Didn't know they looked more human than you!
hoff
hoff
And you want to fight them with a knife!
hoff
hoff
Don't you know they have magic?
hoff
Hurry! We need to hide!

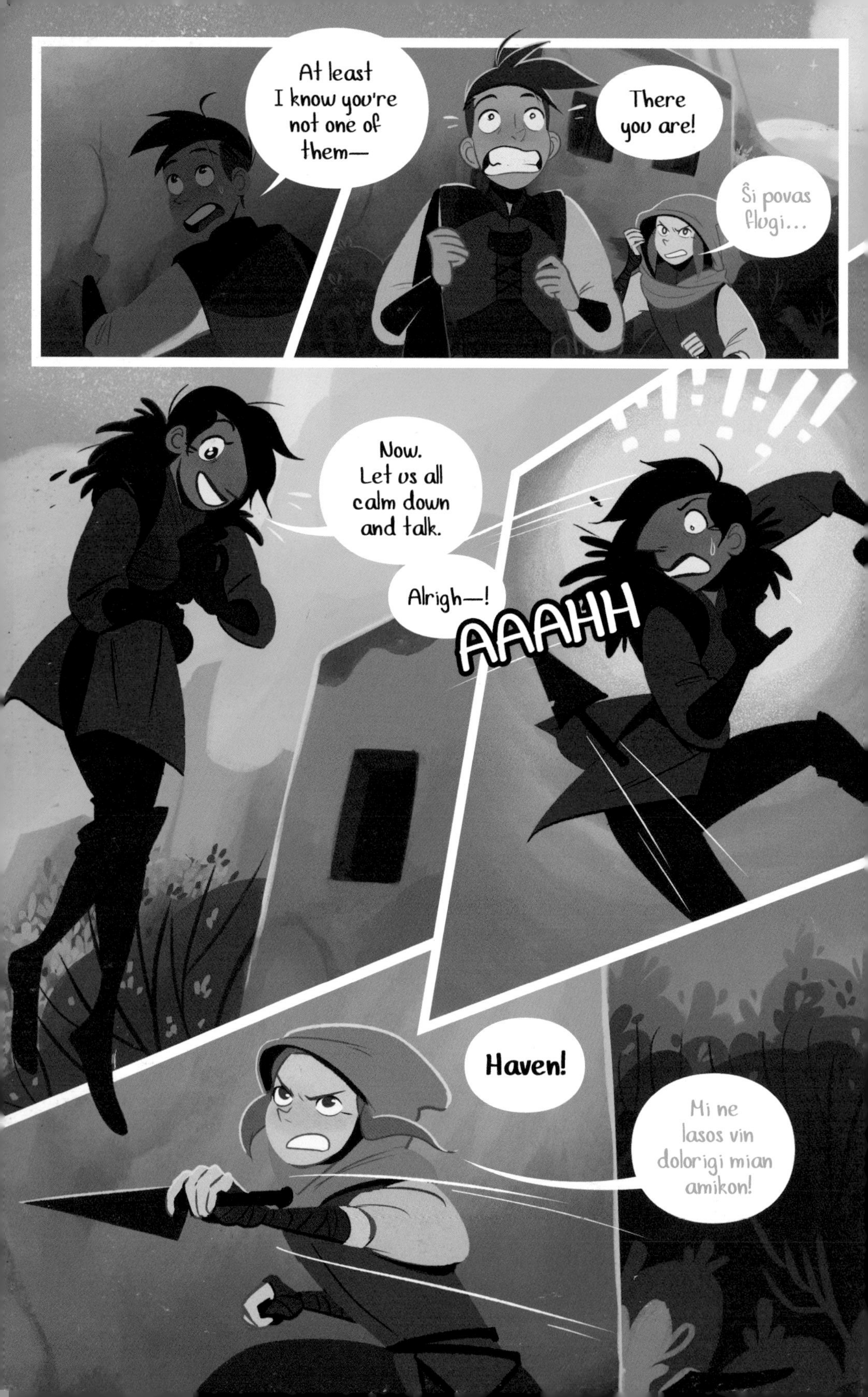
At least I know you're not one of them—
There you are!
Ŝi povas flugi…
Now. Let us all calm down and talk.
Alrigh—!
AAAHH
Haven!
Mi ne lasos vin dolorigi mian amikon!

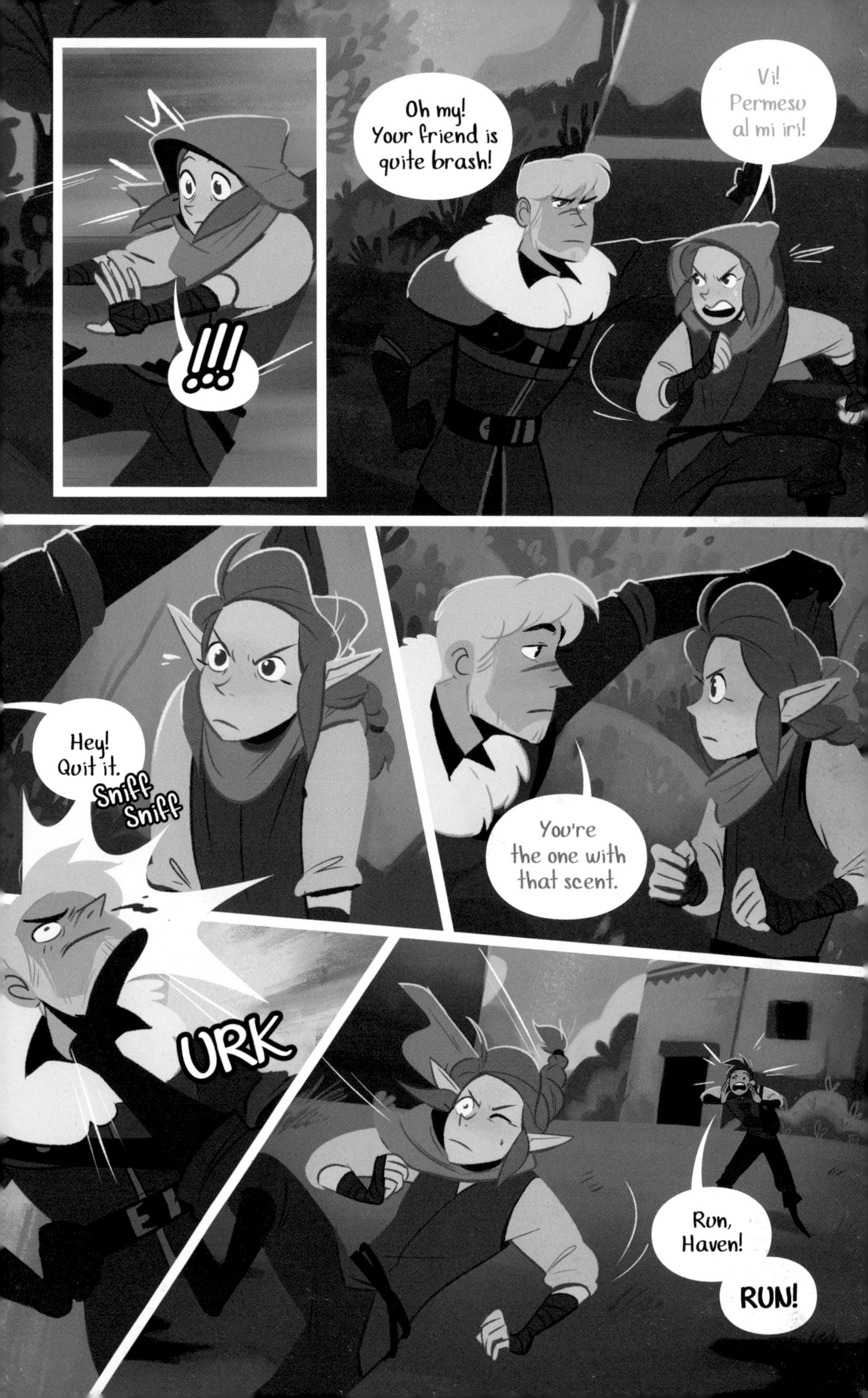
!!!
Oh my! Your friend is quite brash!
Vi! Permeso al mi iri!
Hey! Quit it.
Sniff Sniff
You're the one with that scent.
URK
Run, Haven!
RUN!

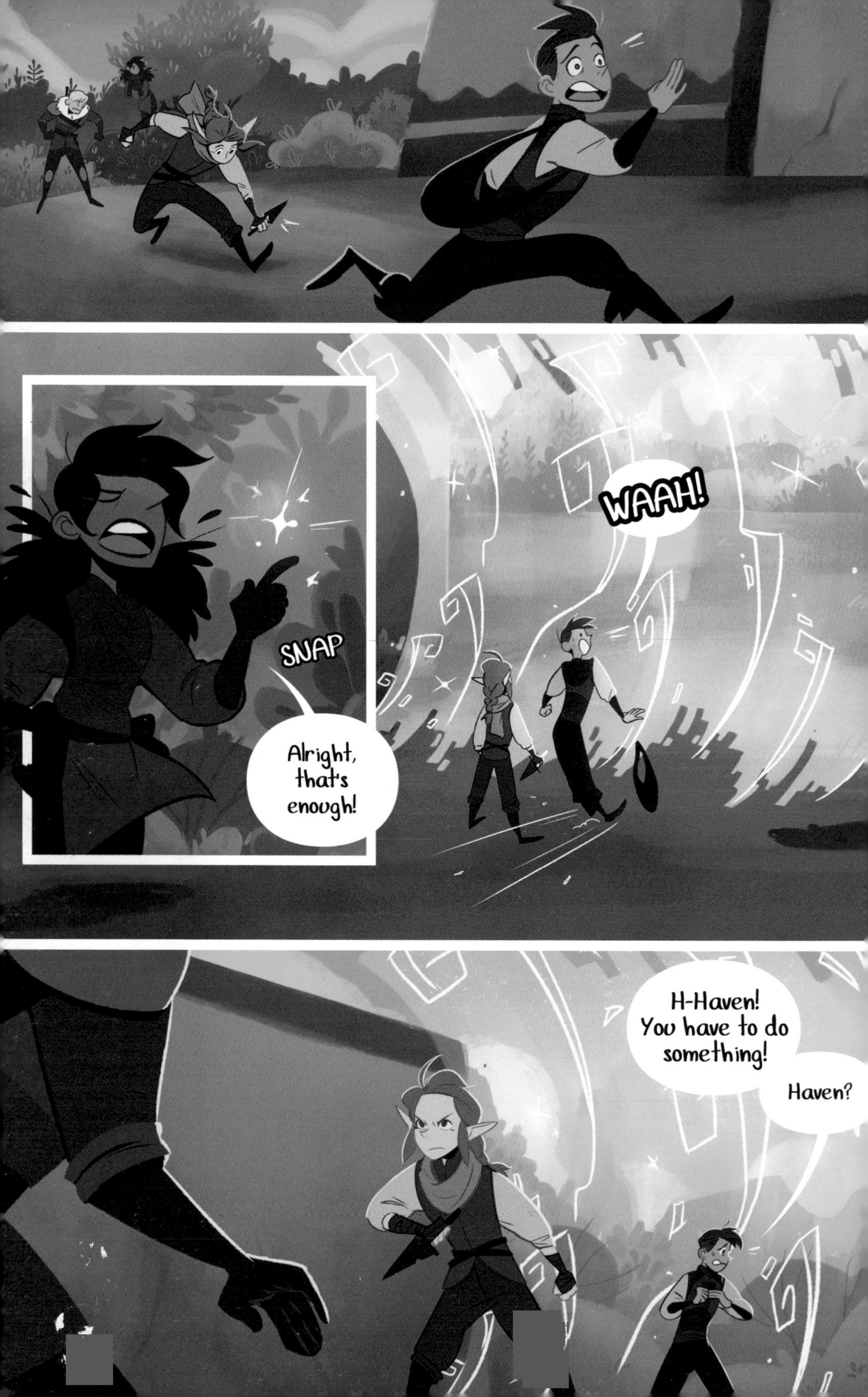
SNAP
Alright, that's enough!
WAAH!
H-Haven! You have to do something!
Haven?

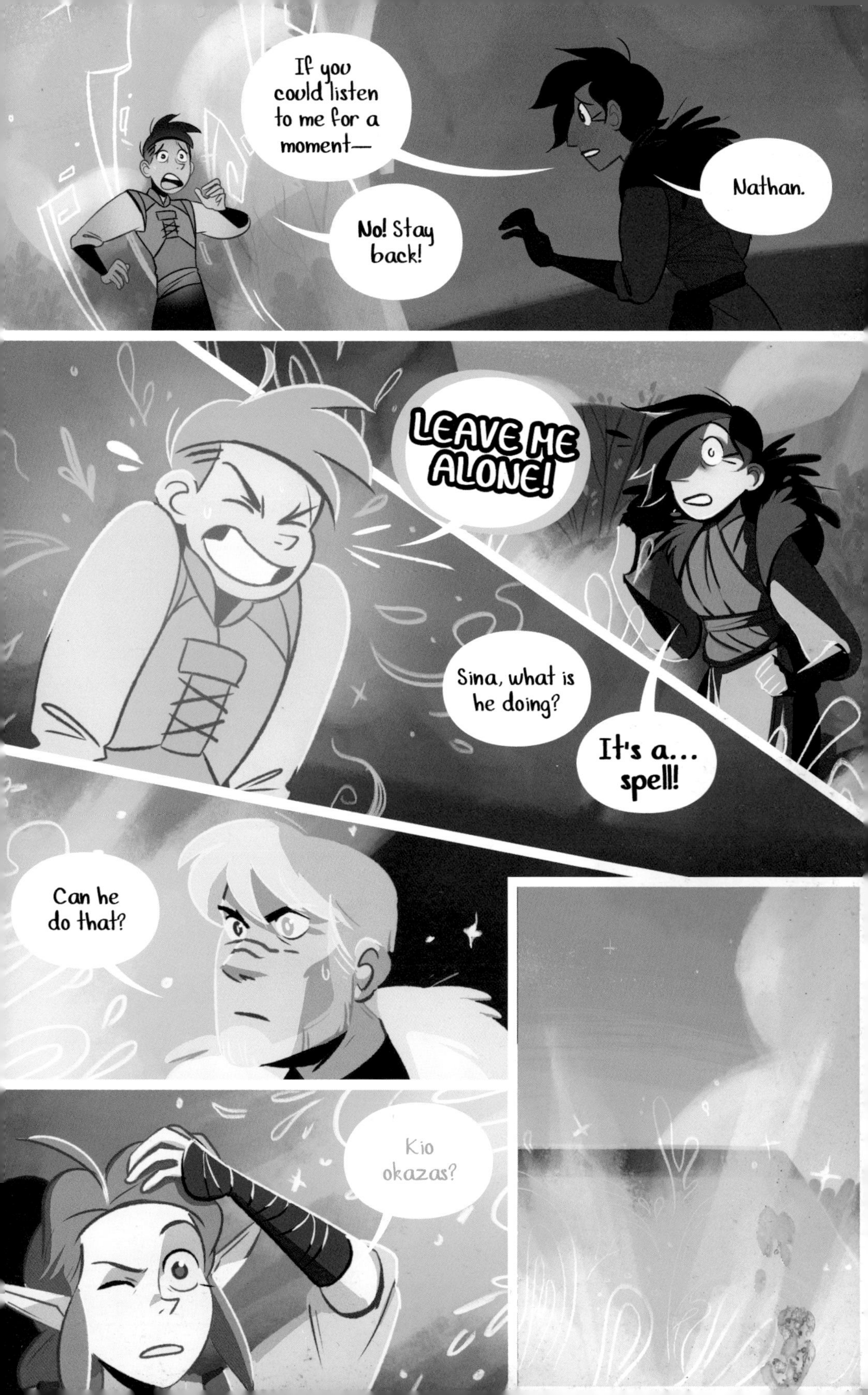
If you could listen to me for a moment—
Nathan.
No! Stay back!
LEAVE ME ALONE!
Sina, what is he doing?
It's a... spell!
Can he do that?
Kio okazas?

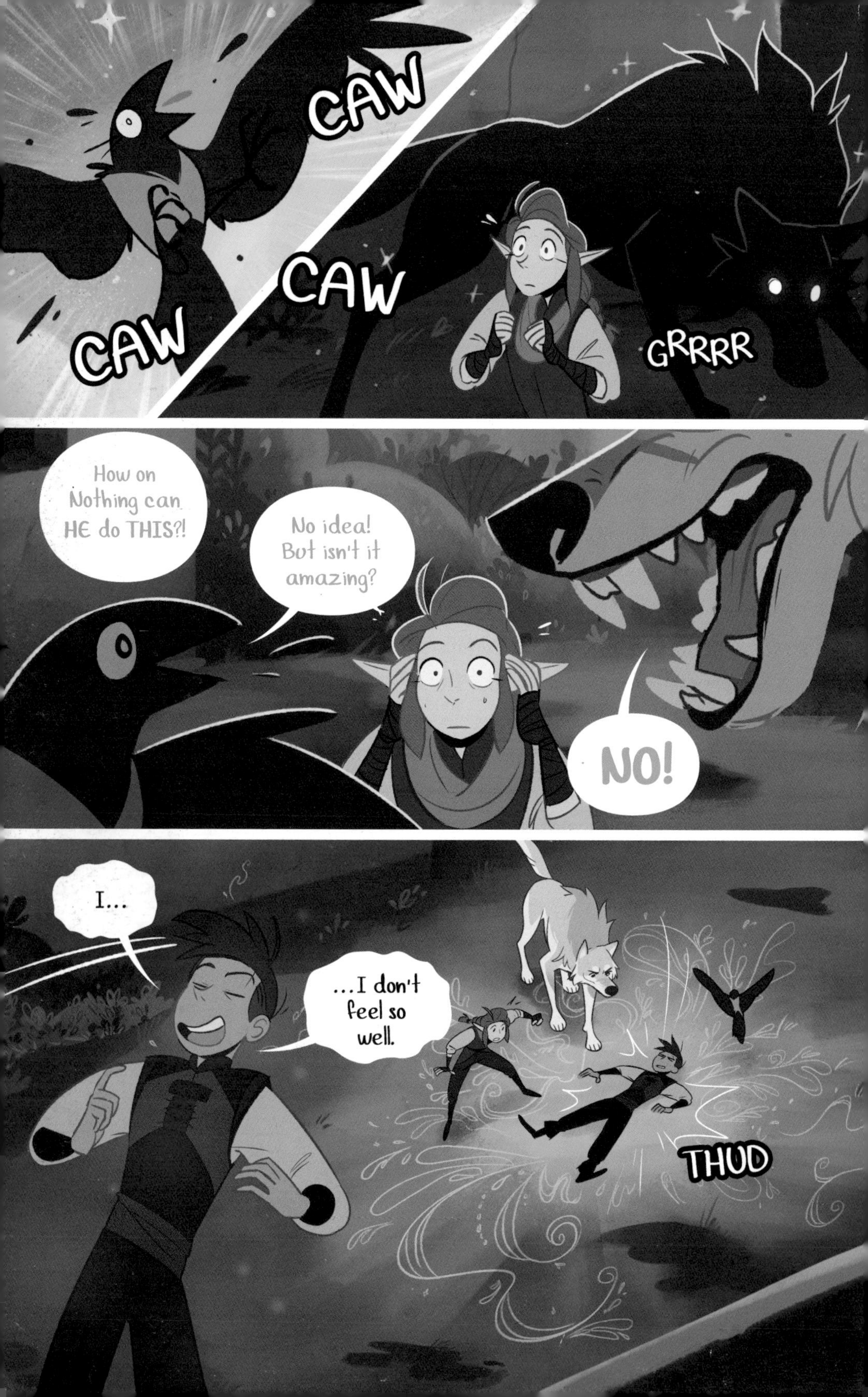

CAW
CAW
CAW
GRRRR
How on Nothing can HE do THIS?!
No idea! But isn't it amazing?
NO!
I...
...I don't feel so well.
THUD

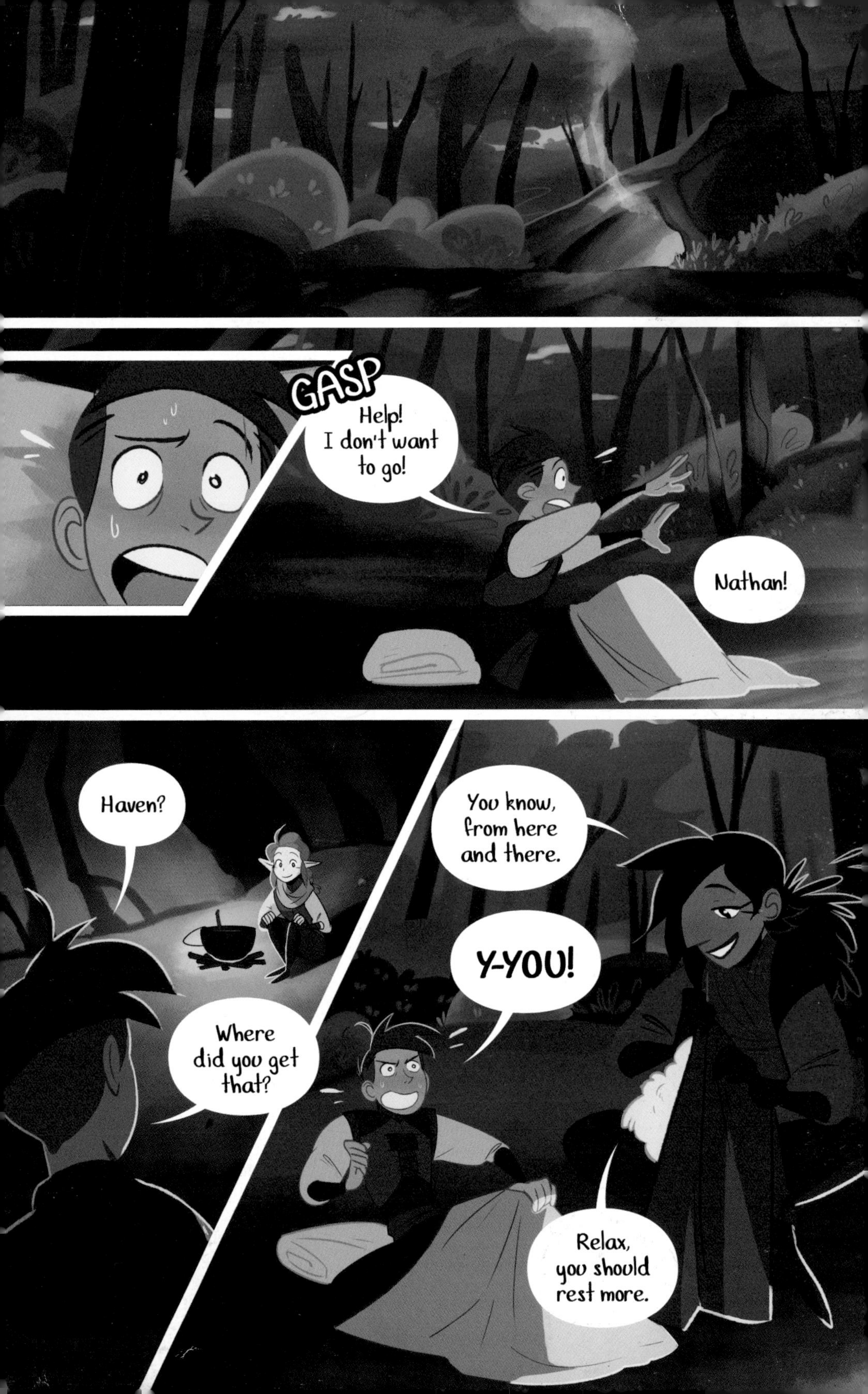
GASP
Help! I don't want to go!
Nathan!
Haven?
Where did you get that?
You know, from here and there.
Y-YOU!
Relax, you should rest more.

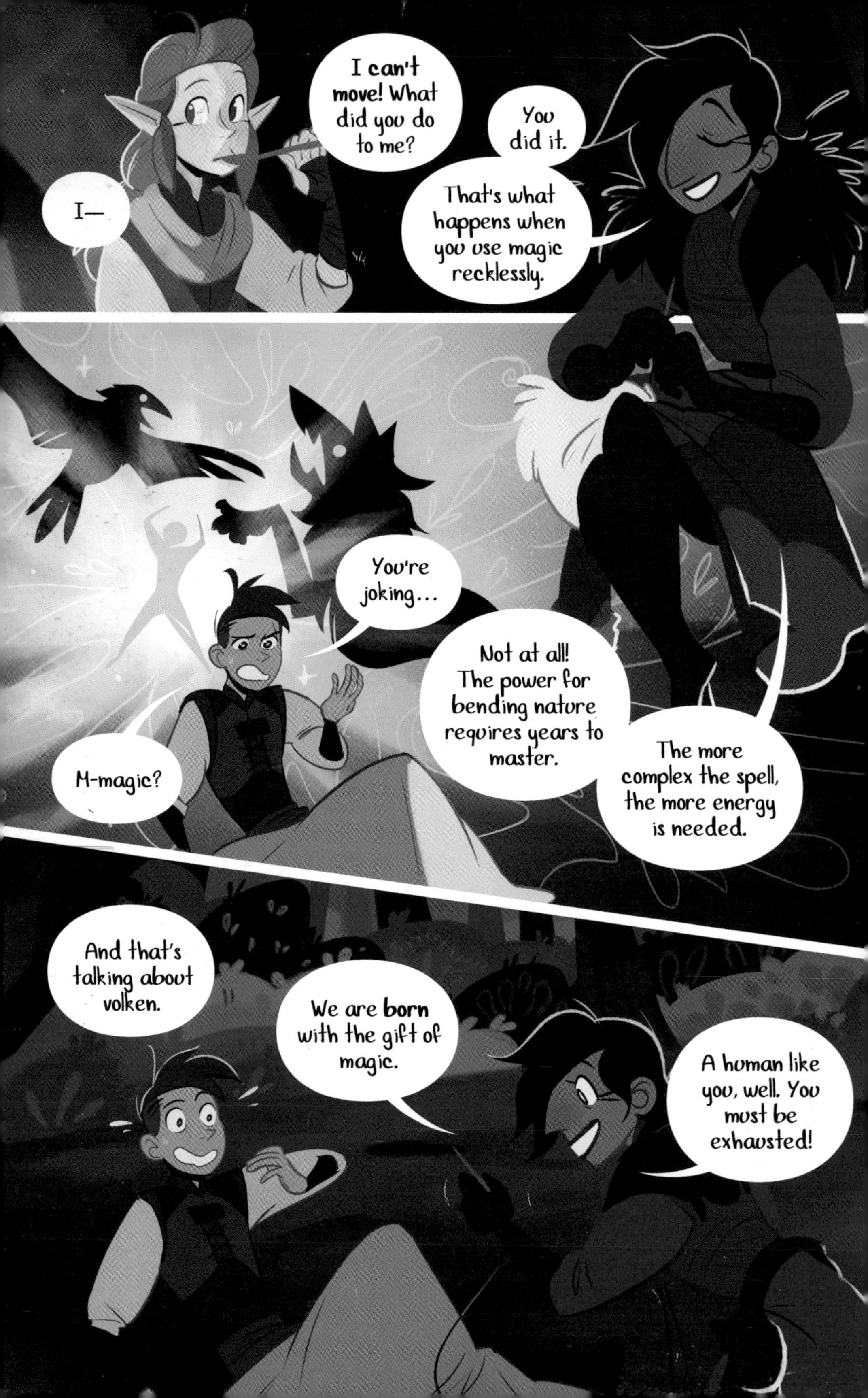
I can't move! What did you do to me?
I—
You did it.
That's what happens when you use magic recklessly.
You're joking...
M-magic?
Not at all! The power for bending nature requires years to master.
The more complex the spell, the more energy is needed.
And that's talking about volken.
We are born with the gift of magic.
A human like you, well. You must be exhausted!

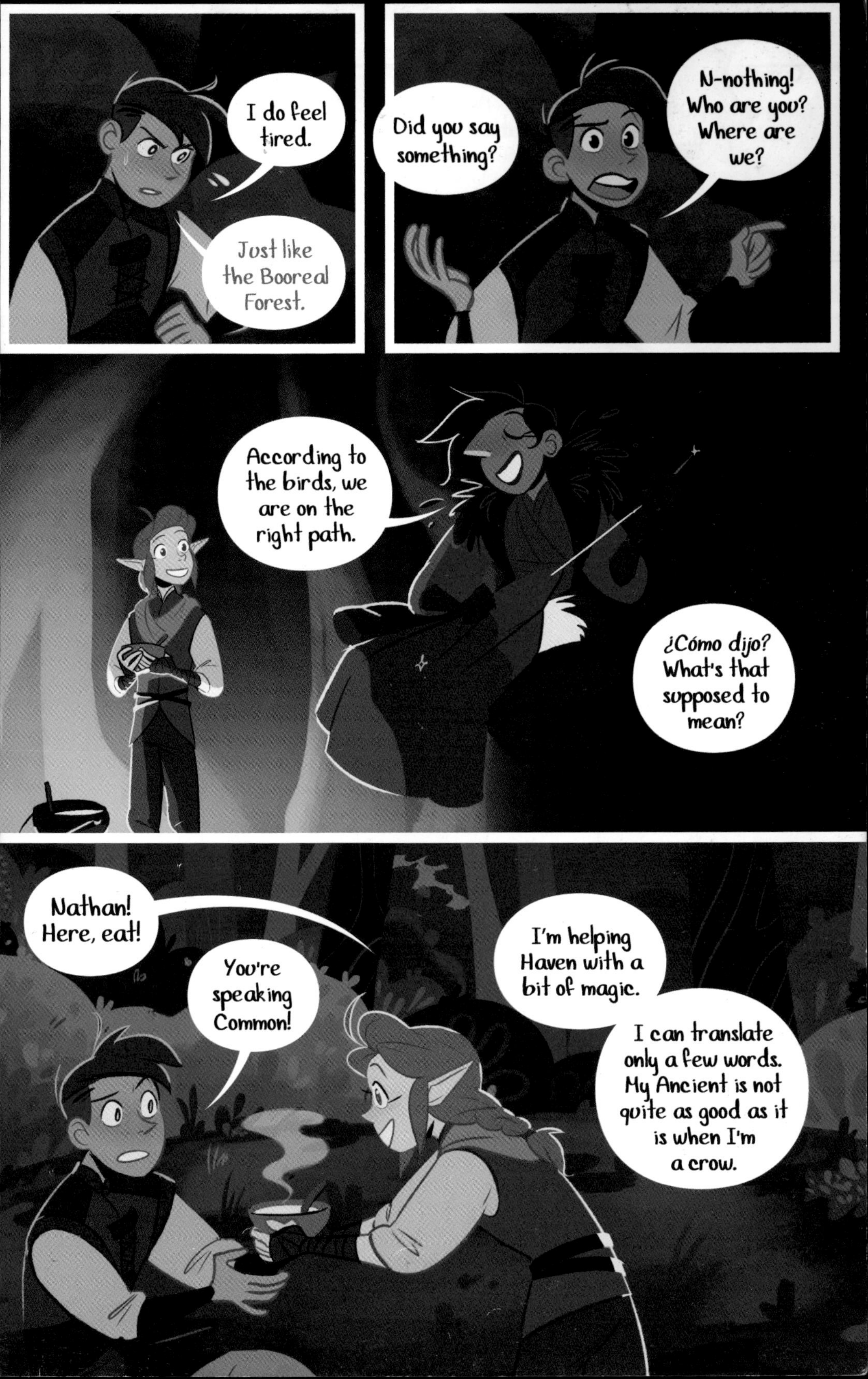
I do feel tired.
Just like the Booreal Forest.
Did you say something?
N-nothing! Who are you? Where are we?
According to the birds, we are on the right path.
¿Cómo dijo? What's that supposed to mean?
Nathan! Here, eat!
You're speaking Common!
I'm helping Haven with a bit of magic.
I can translate only a few words. My Ancient is not quite as good as it is when I'm a crow.

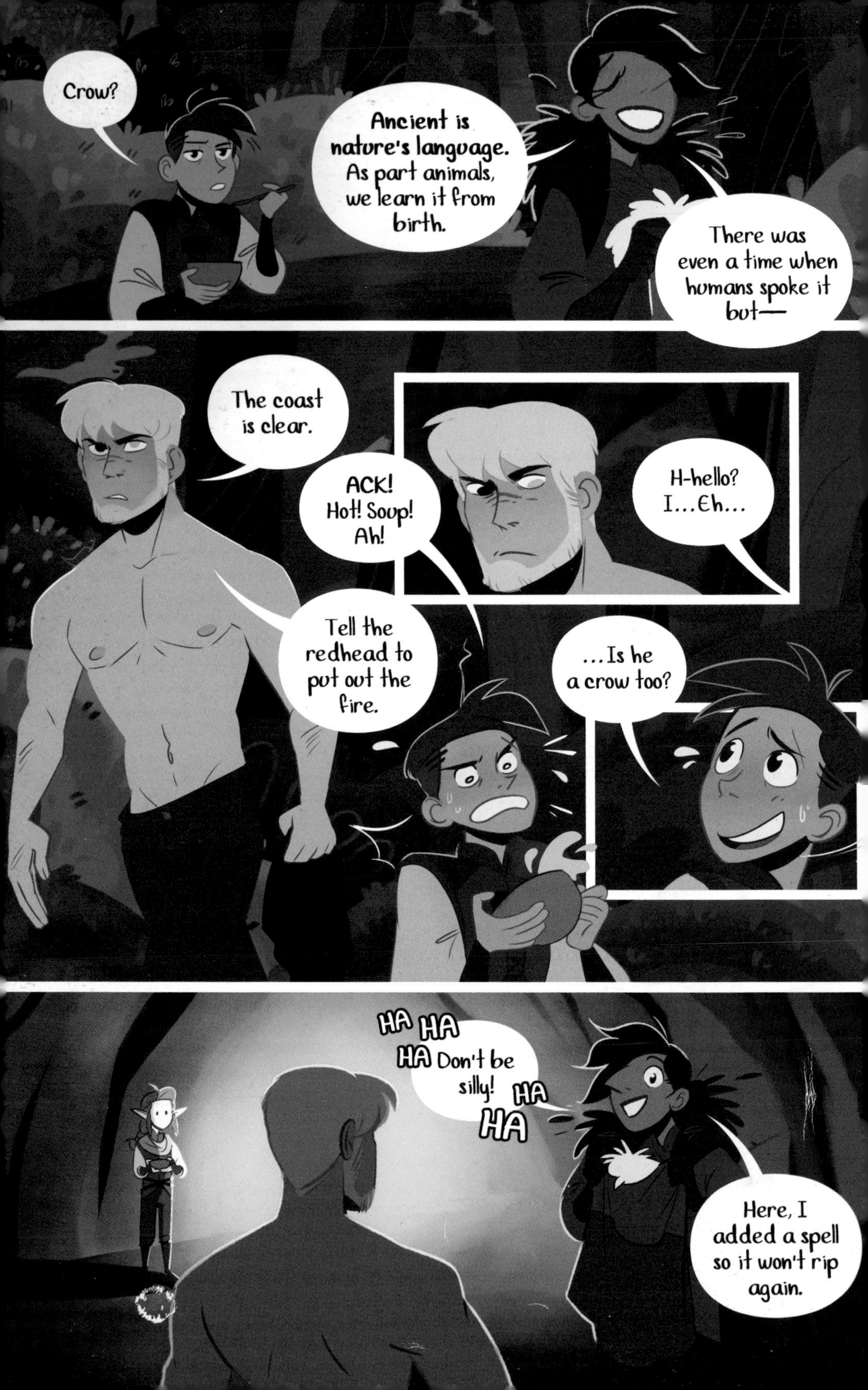
Crow?
Ancient is nature's language. As part animals, we learn it from birth.
There was even a time when humans spoke it but—
The coast is clear.
ACK! Hot! Soup! Ah!
H-hello? I...Eh...
Tell the redhead to put out the fire.
...Is he a crow too?
HA HA HA Don't be silly! HA HA
Here, I added a spell so it won't rip again.

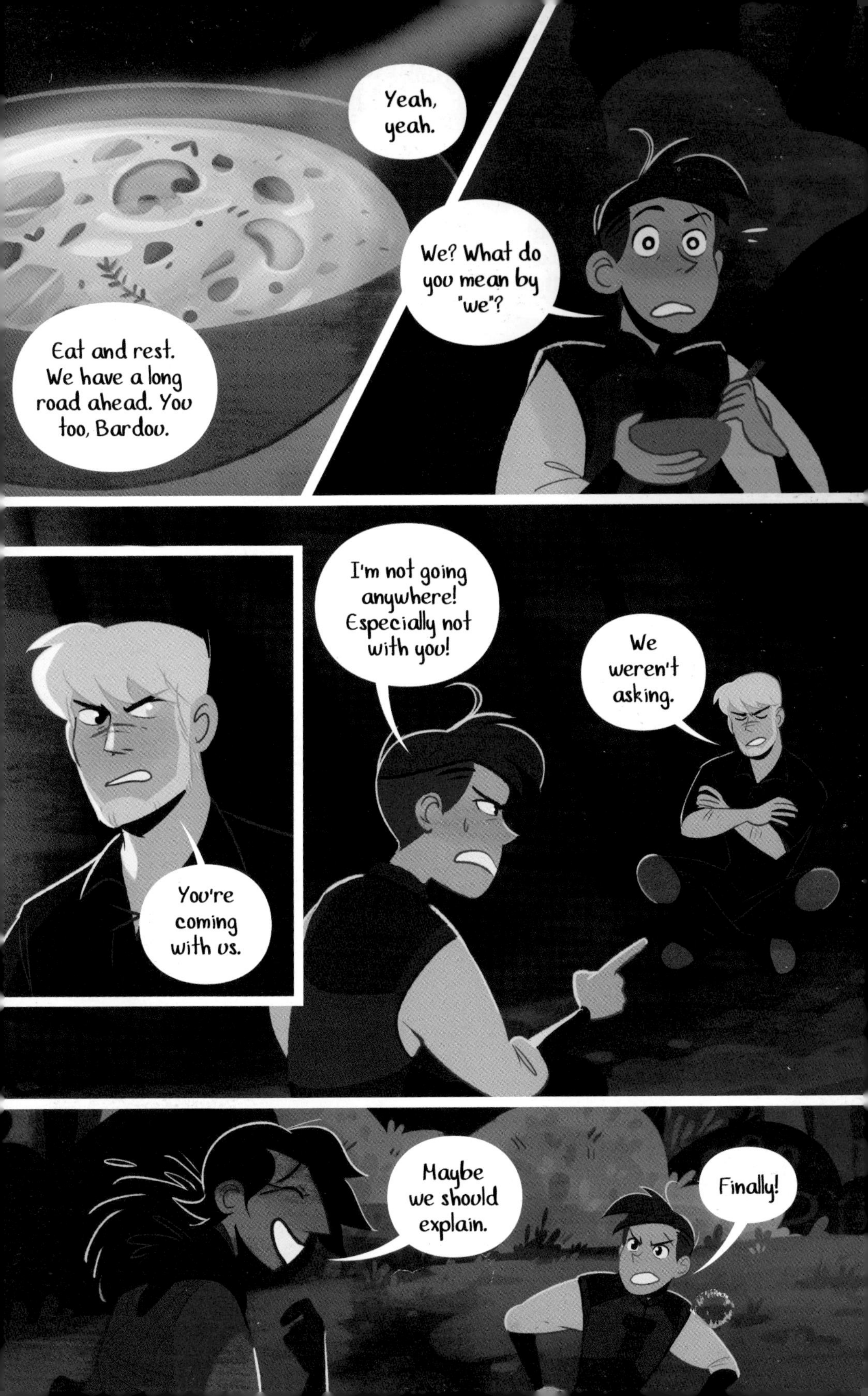
Yeah, yeah.
Eat and rest. We have a long road ahead. You too, Bardou.
We? What do you mean by "we"?
You're coming with us.
I'm not going anywhere! Especially not with you!
We weren't asking.
Maybe we should explain.
Finally!

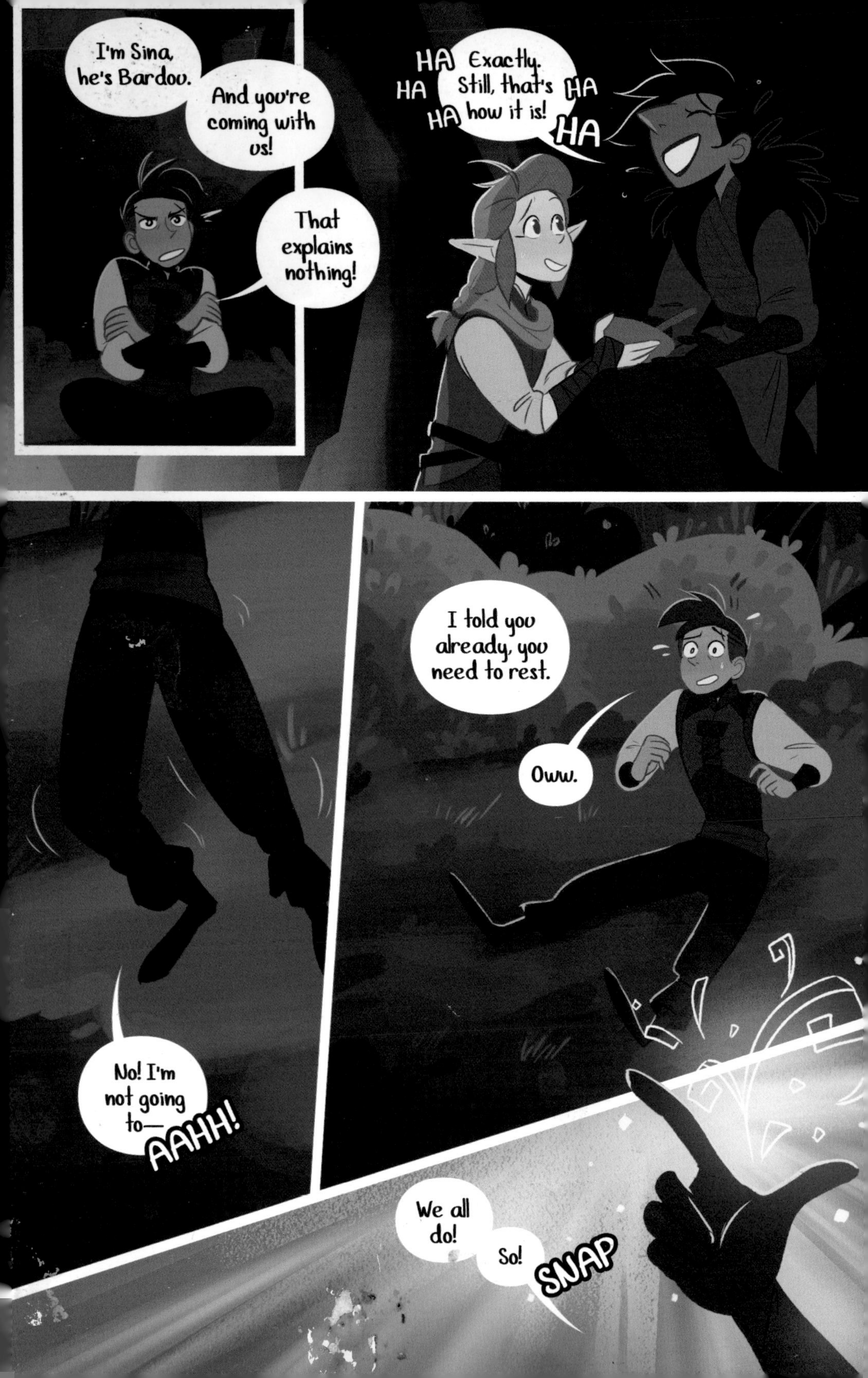
I'm Sina, he's Bardou.
And you're coming with us!
That explains nothing!
HA HA HA
Exactly. Still, that's how it is!
HA HA
No! I'm not going to—
AAHH!
I told you already, you need to rest.
Oww.
We all do!
So!
SNAP

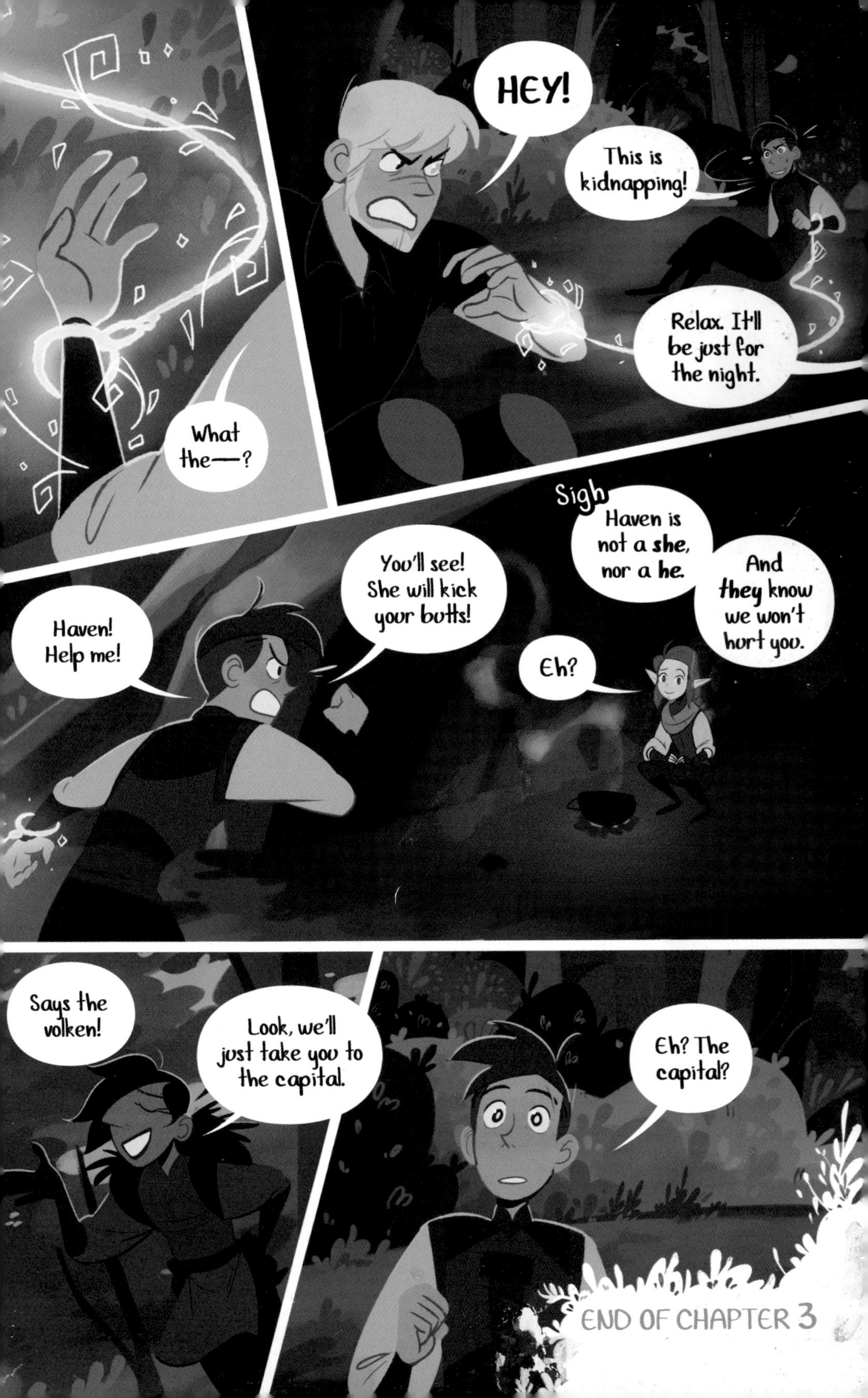

HEY!
This is kidnapping!
What the—?
Relax. It'll be just for the night.
Haven! Help me!
You'll see! She will kick your butts!
Sigh
Haven is not a she, nor a he.
And they know we won't hurt you.
Eh?
Says the volken!
Look, we'll just take you to the capital.
Eh? The capital?
END OF CHAPTER 3

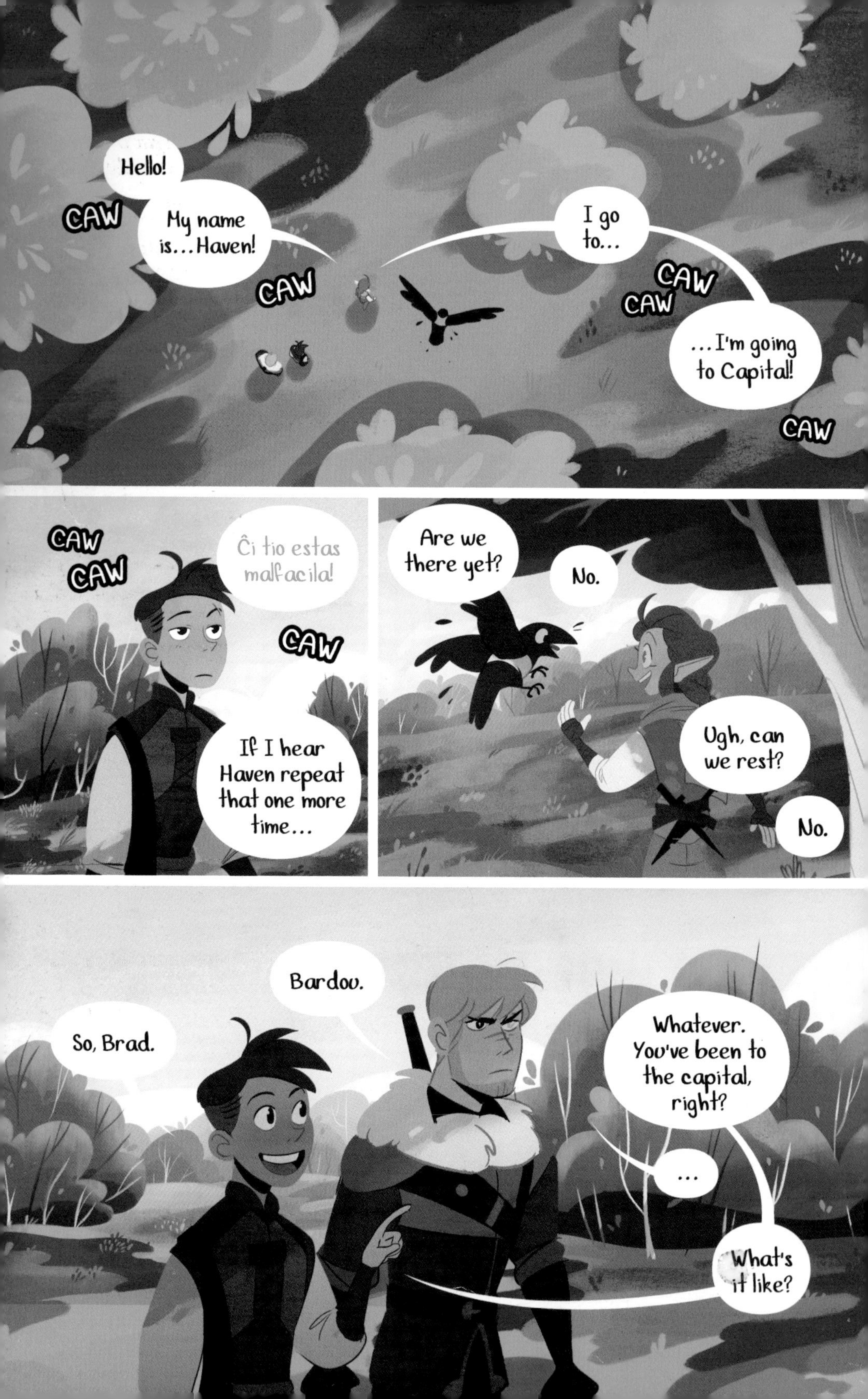
Hello!
CAW
My name is...Haven!
CAW
I go to...
CAW
CAW
...I'm going to Capital!
CAW
CAW
CAW
Ĉi tio estas malfacila!
CAW
If I hear Haven repeat that one more time...
Are we there yet?
No.
Ugh, can we rest?
No.
So, Brad.
Bardou.
Whatever. You've been to the capital, right?
...
What's it like?

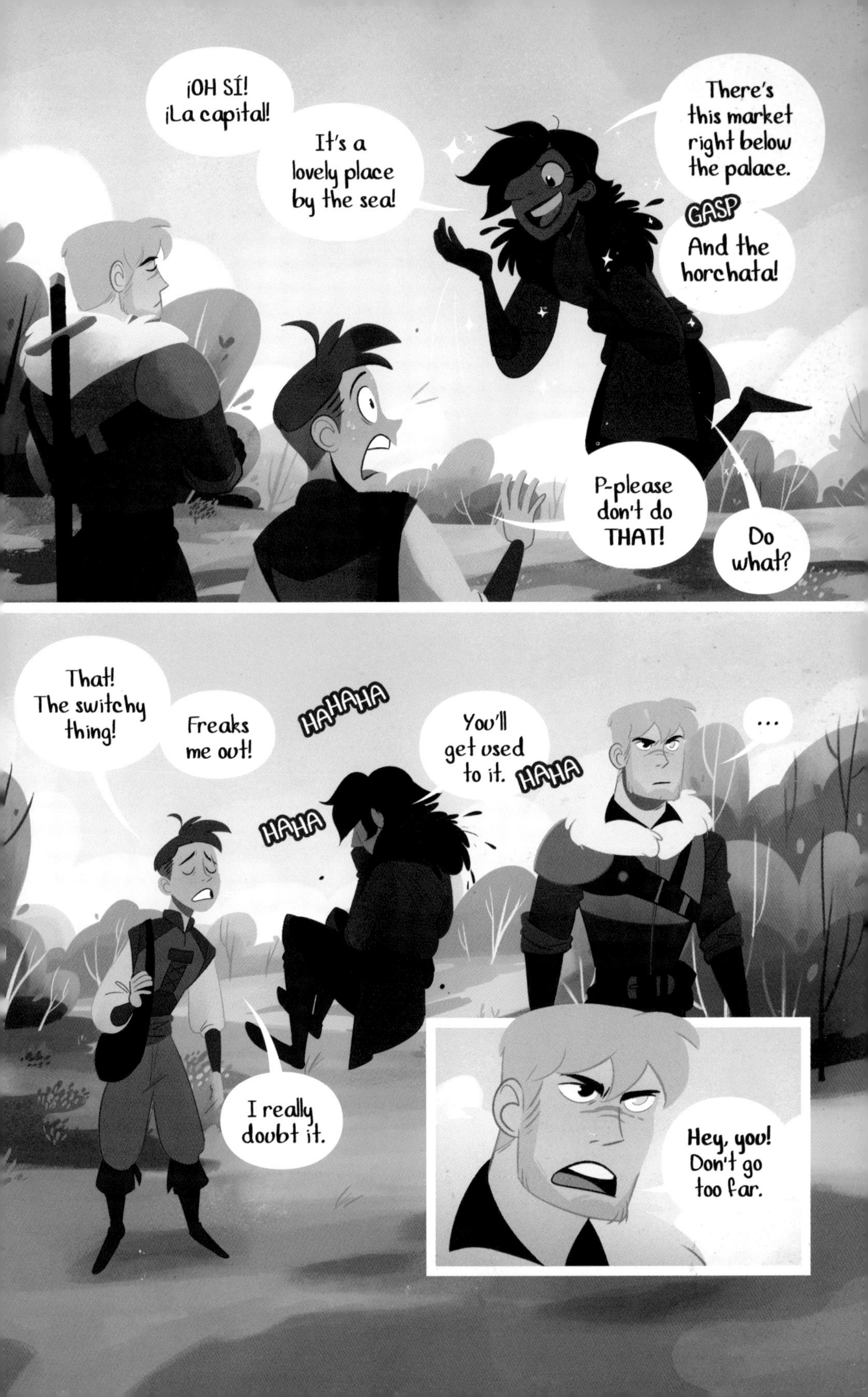
¡OH SÍ!
¡La capital!
It's a lovely place by the sea!
There's this market right below the palace.
GASP
And the horchata!
P-please don't do THAT!
Do what?
That! The switchy thing!
Freaks me out!
HAHAHA
You'll get used to it.
HAHA
HAHA
...
I really doubt it.
Hey, you! Don't go too far.

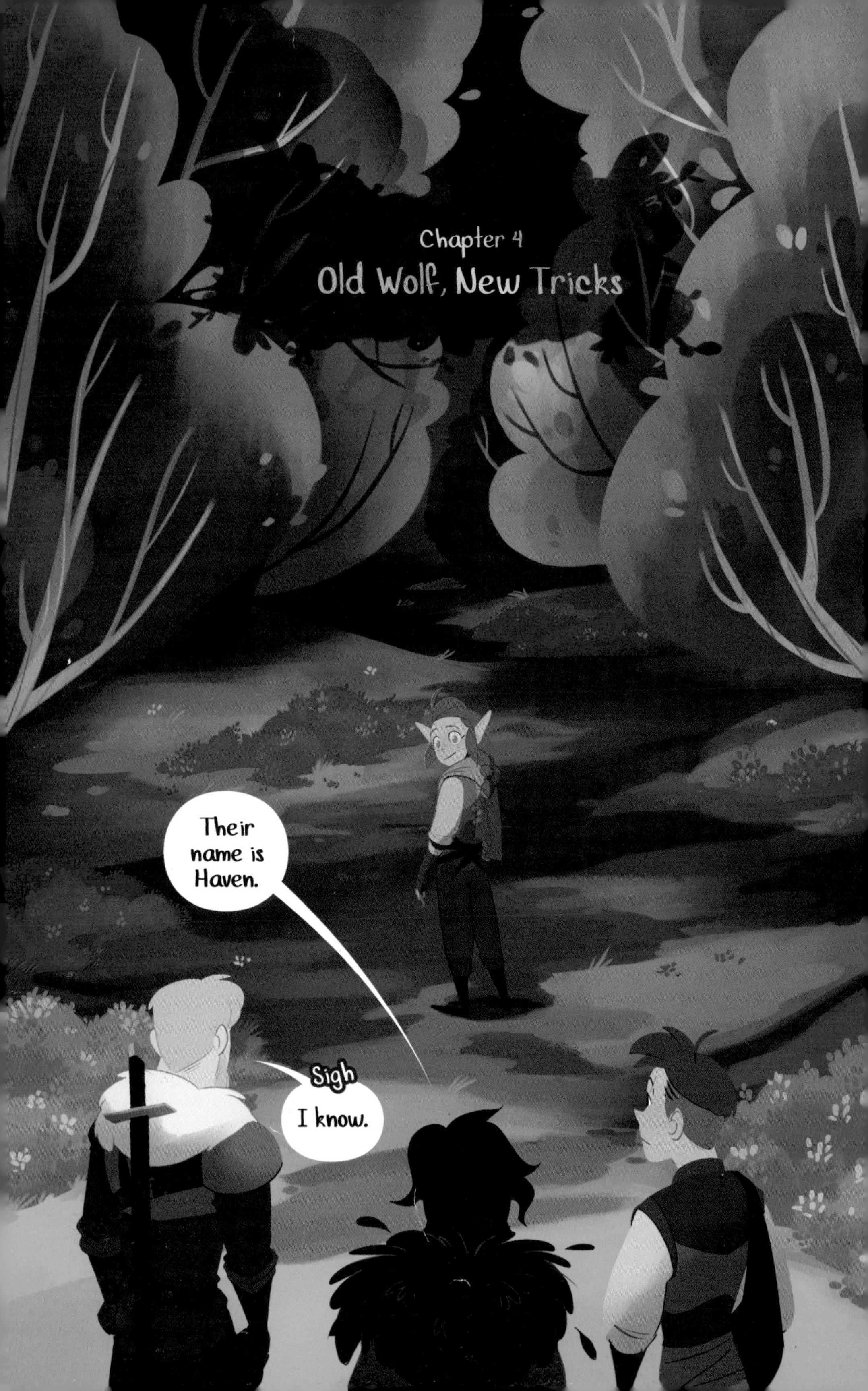
Chapter 4
Old Wolf, New Tricks
Their name is Haven.
Sigh
I know.

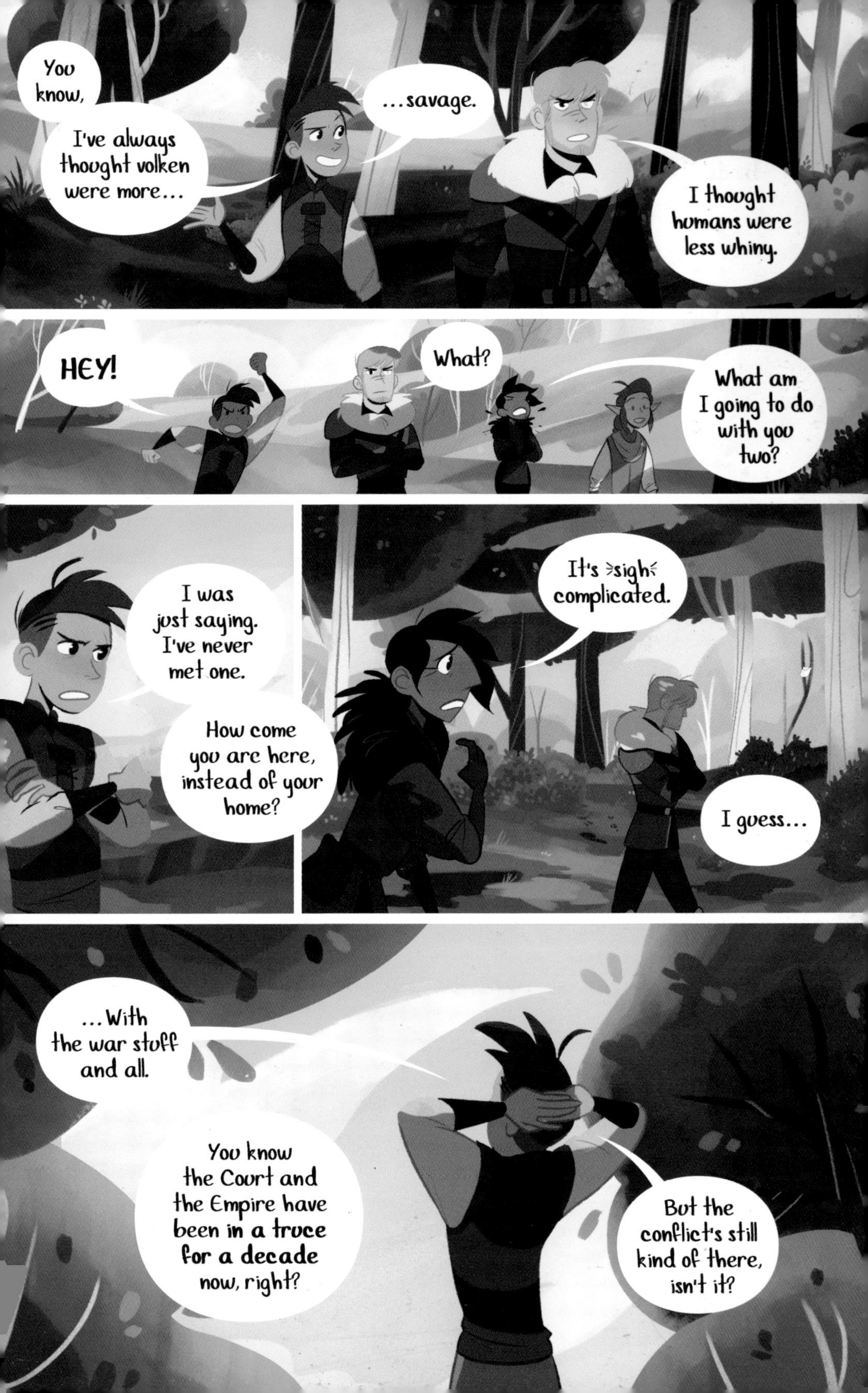
You know,
I've always thought volken were more...
...savage.
I thought humans were less whiny.
HEY!
What?
What am I going to do with you two?
I was just saying. I've never met one.
How come you are here, instead of your home?
It's >sigh< complicated.
I guess...
...With the war stuff and all.
You know the Court and the Empire have been in a truce for a decade now, right?
But the conflict's still kind of there, isn't it?

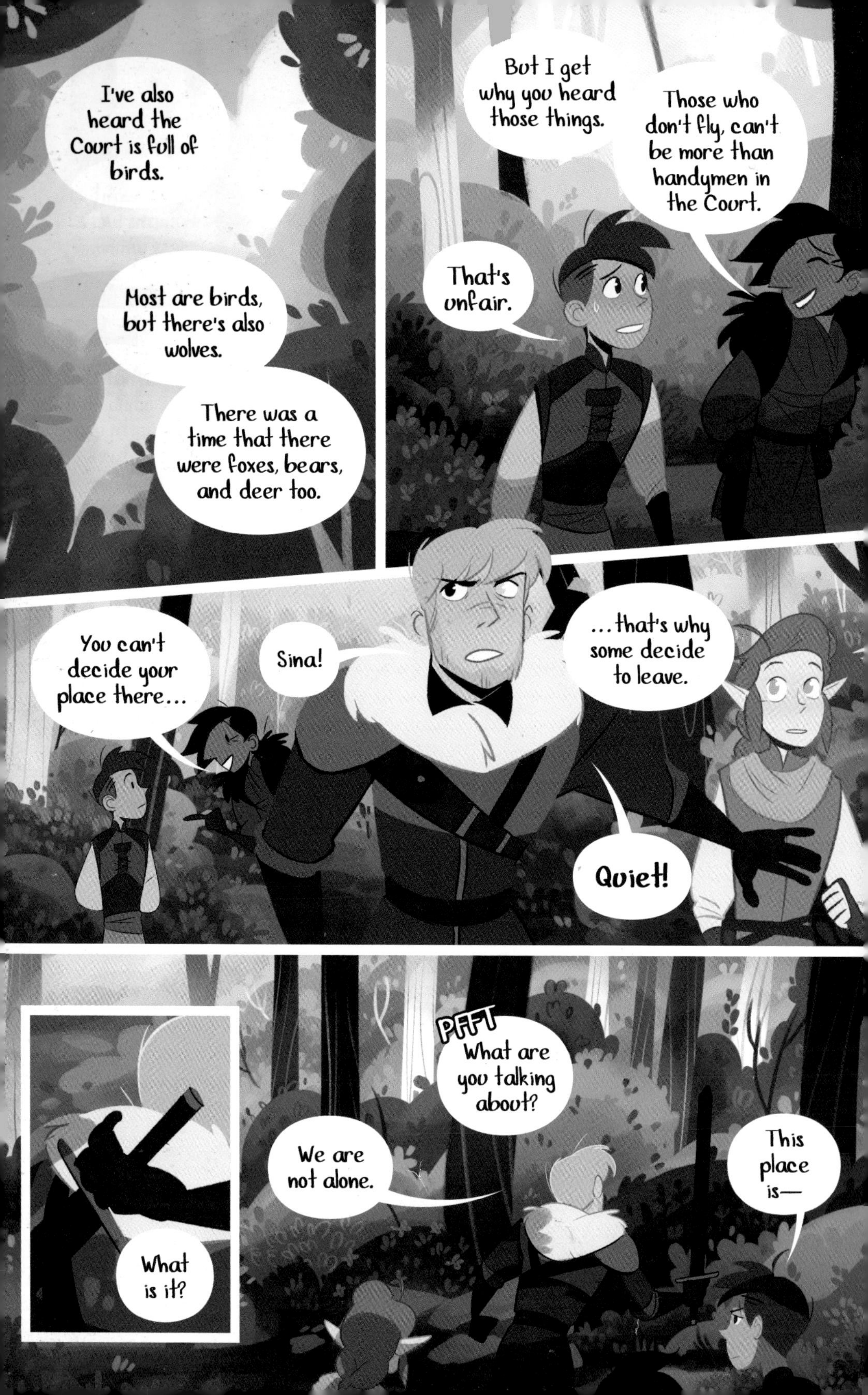
I've also heard the Court is full of birds.
Most are birds, but there's also wolves.
There was a time that there were foxes, bears, and deer too.
But I get why you heard those things.
Those who don't fly, can't be more than handymen in the Court.
That's unfair.
You can't decide your place there...
Sina!
...that's why some decide to leave.
Quiet!
What is it?
PFFT
What are you talking about?
We are not alone.
This place is—

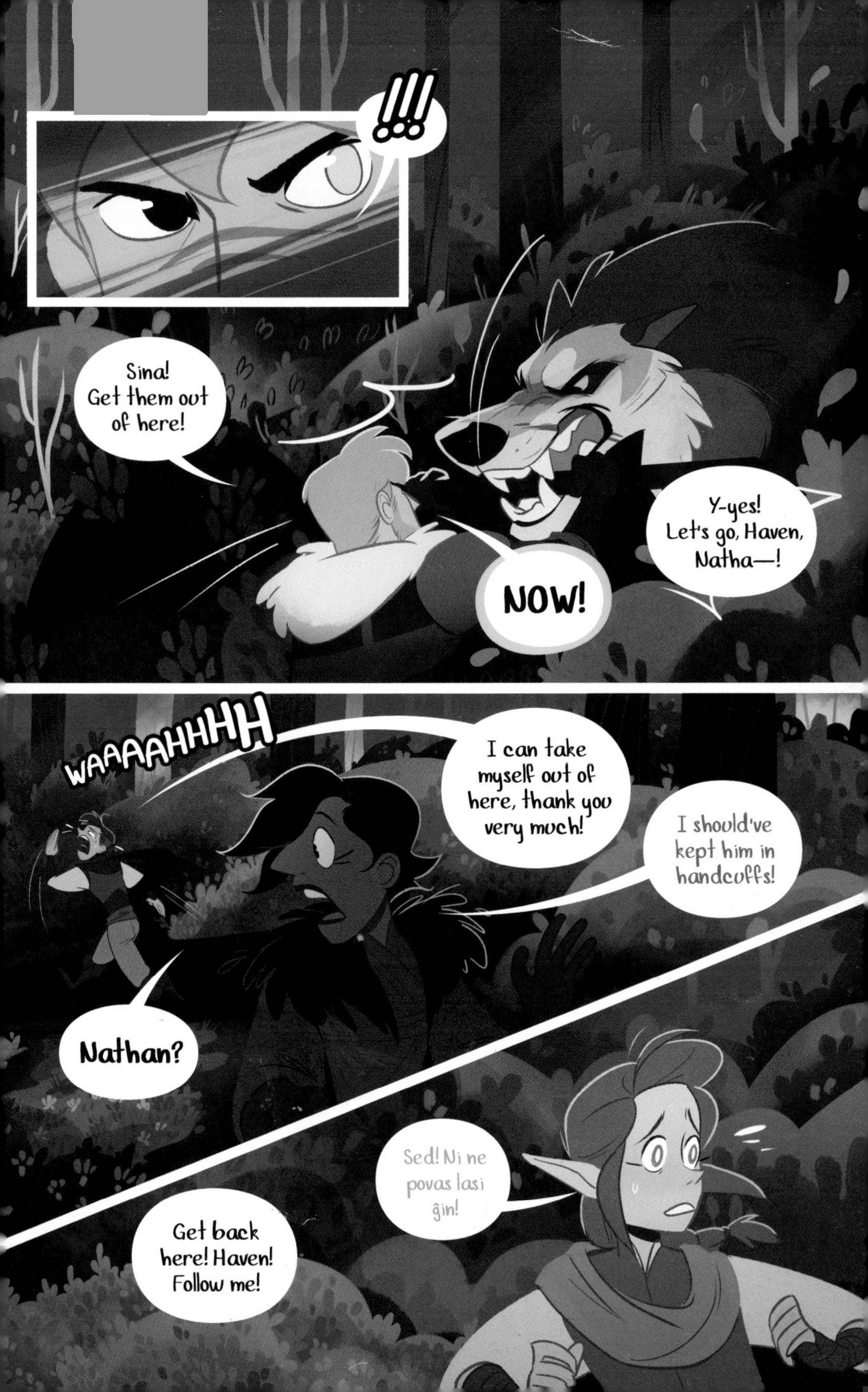
!!!
Sina! Get them out of here!
NOW!
Y-yes! Let's go, Haven, Natha—!
WAAAAHHHH
I can take myself out of here, thank you very much!
I should've kept him in handcuffs!
Nathan?
Sed! Ni ne povas lasi ĝin!
Get back here! Haven! Follow me!

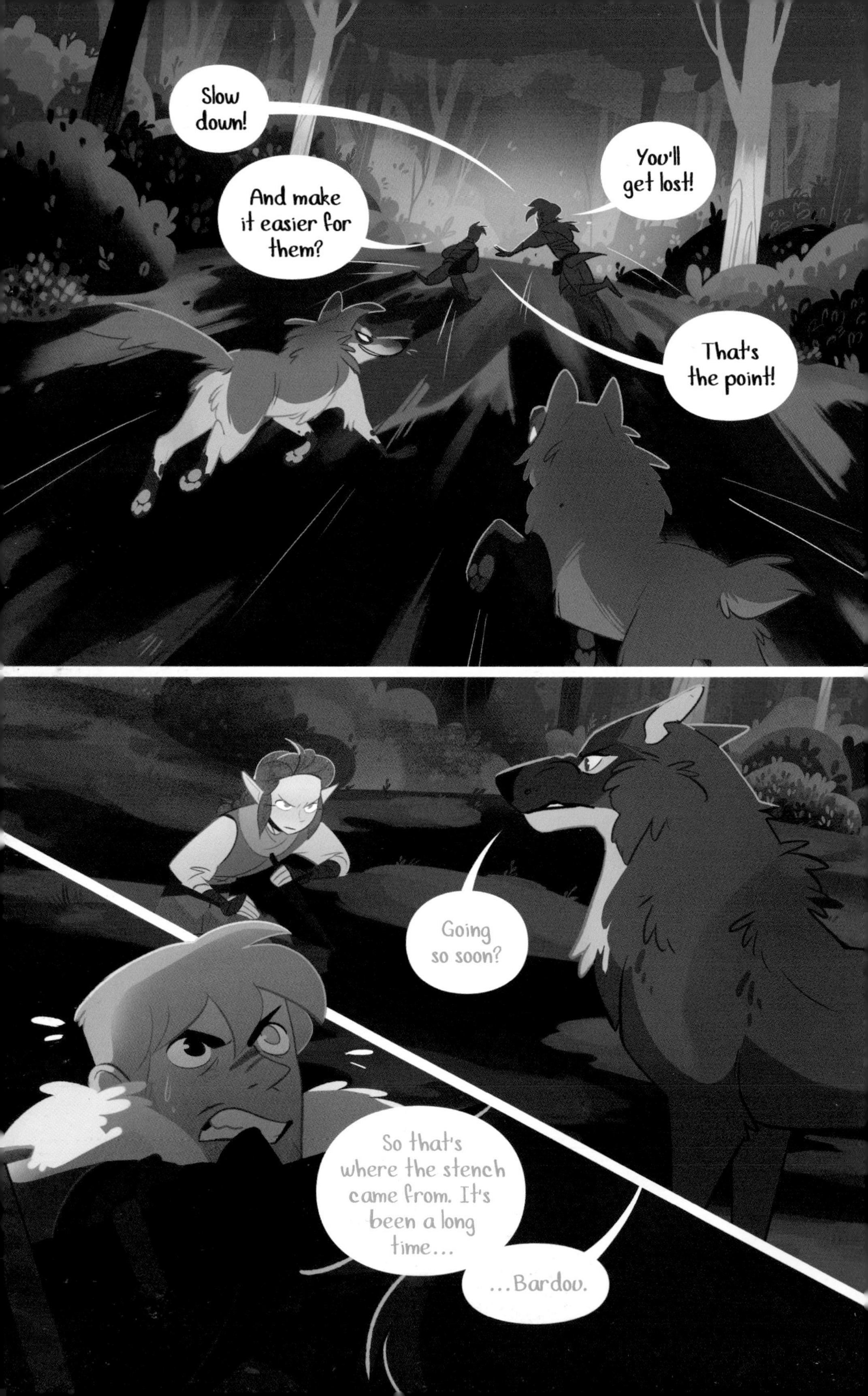
Slow down!
You'll get lost!
And make it easier for them?
That's the point!
Going so soon?
So that's where the stench came from. It's been a long time...
...Bardou.

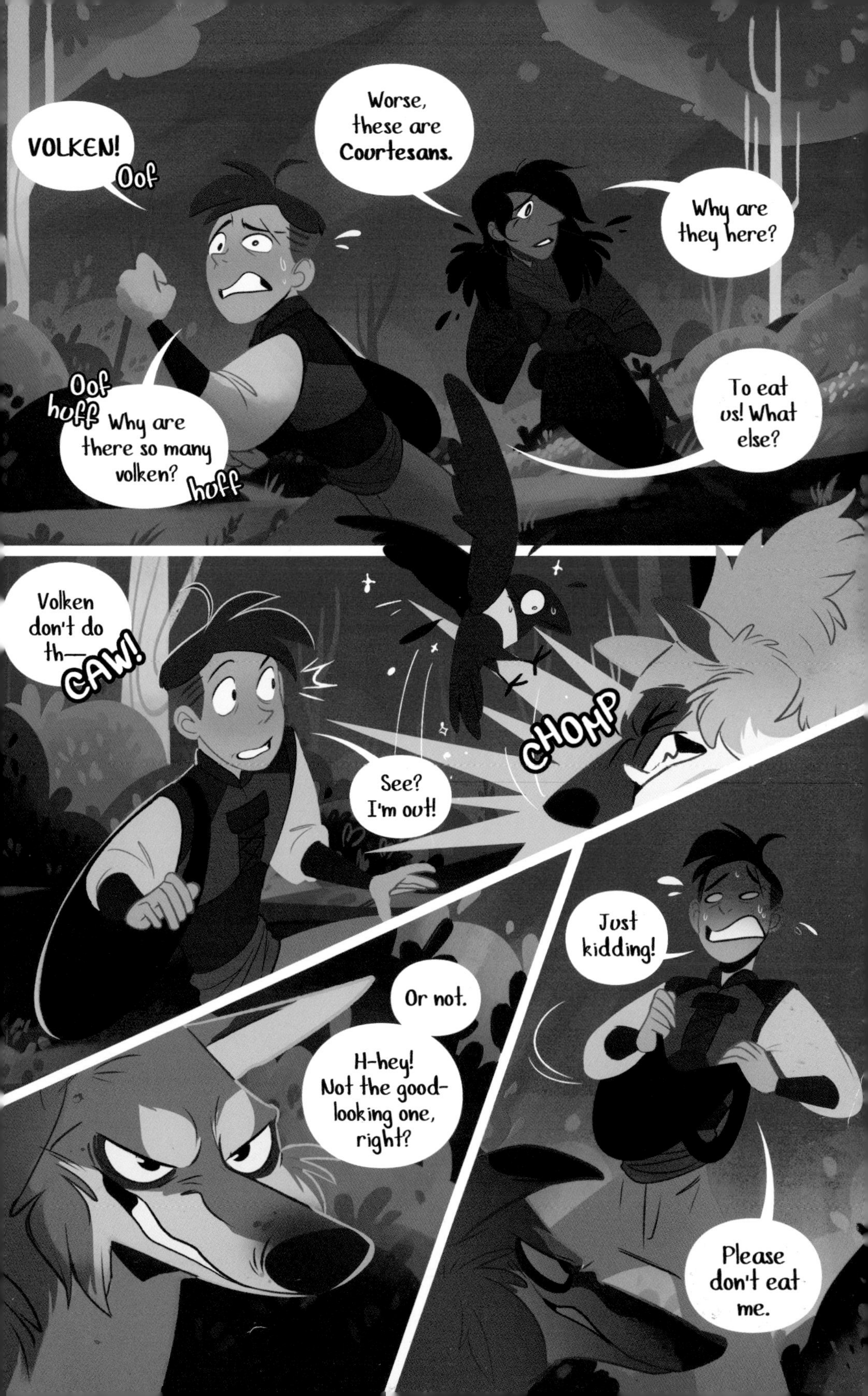
VOLKEN! Oof
Worse, these are Courtesans.
Why are they here?
Oof huff Why are there so many volken? huff
To eat us! What else?
Volken don't do th— CAW!
CHOMP
See? I'm out!
Just kidding!
Or not.
H-hey! Not the good-looking one, right?
Please don't eat me.

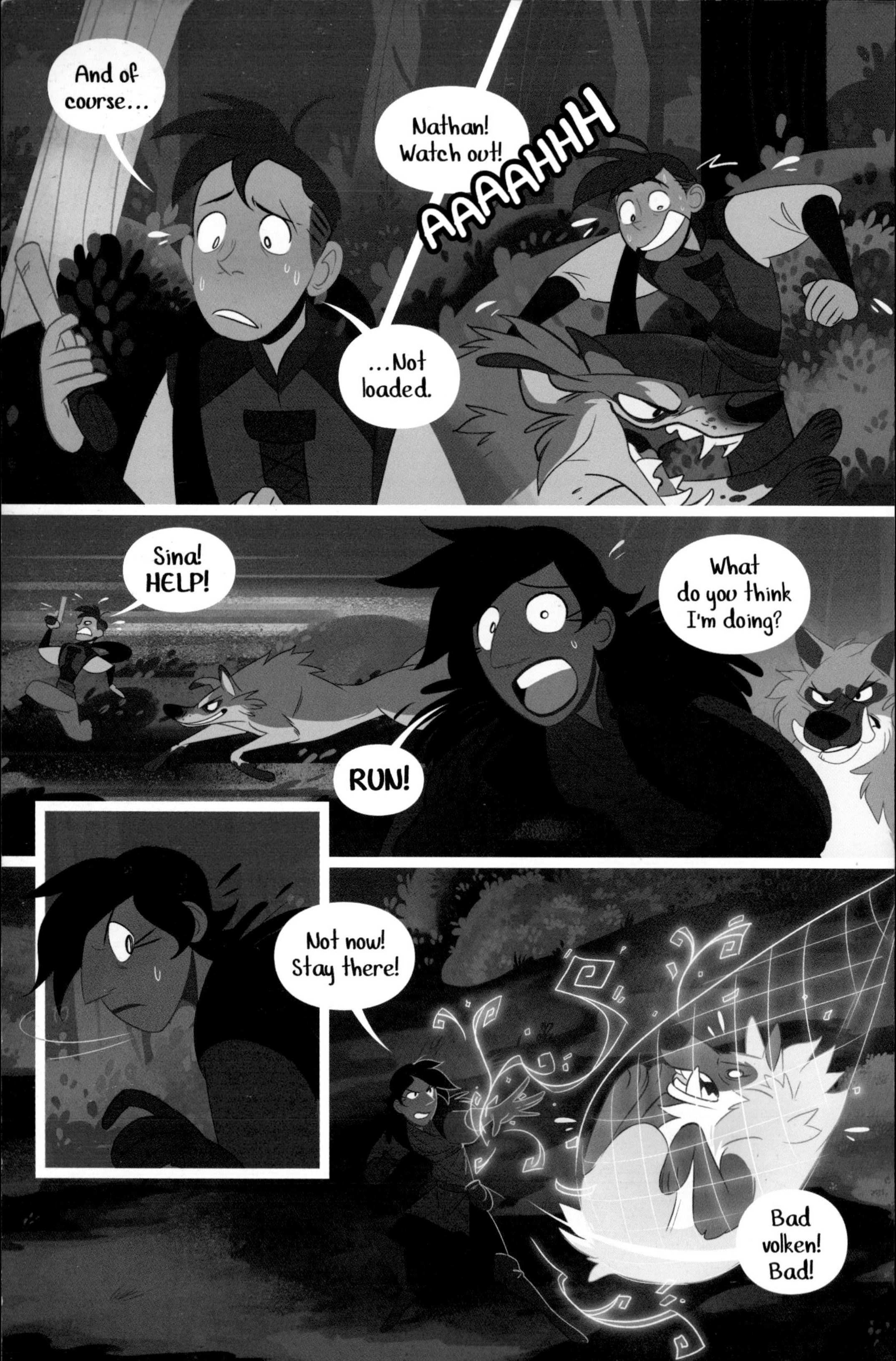
And of course...
...Not loaded.
Nathan! Watch out!
AAAAHHH
Sina! HELP!
What do you think I'm doing?
RUN!
Not now! Stay there!
Bad volken! Bad!

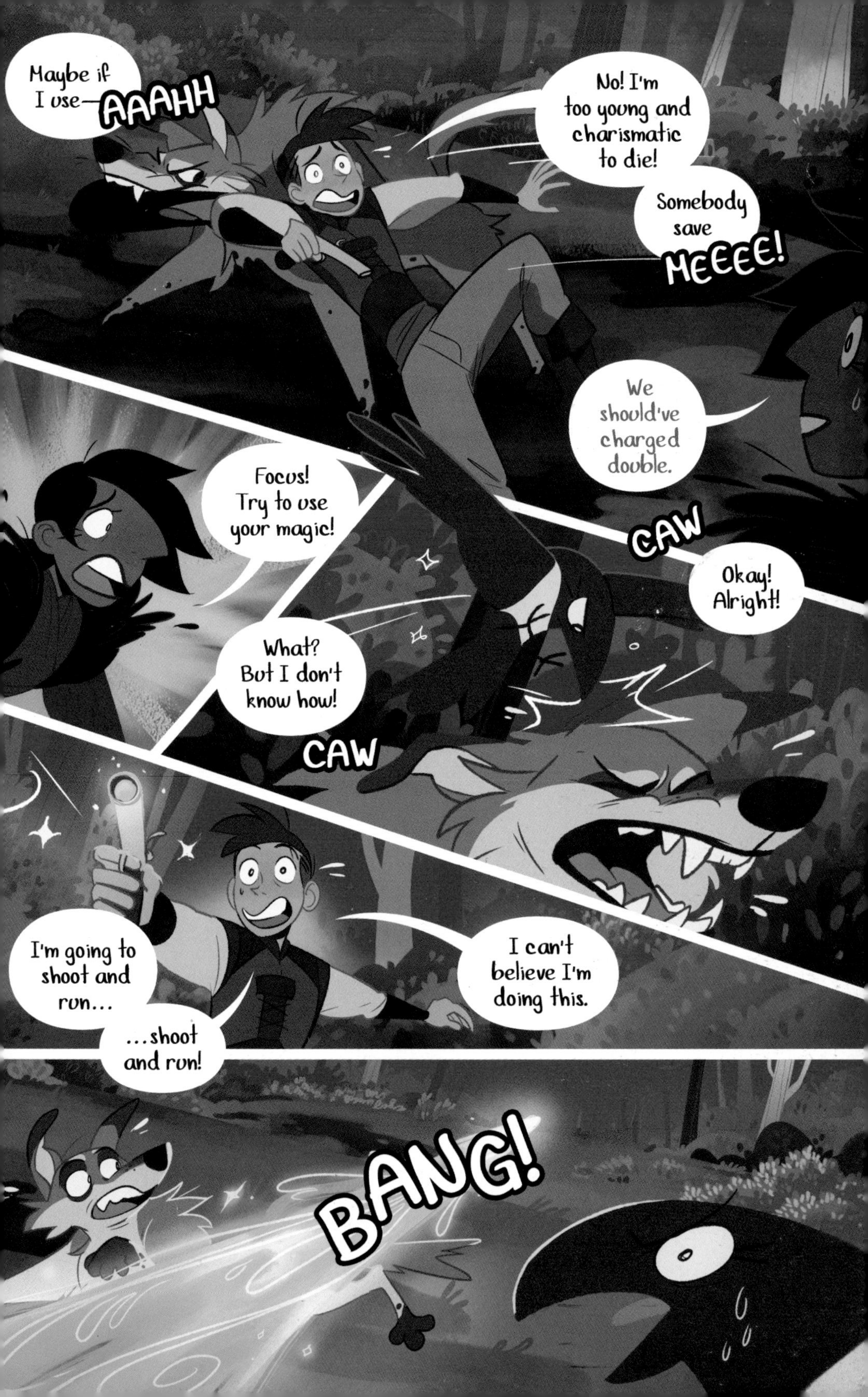
Maybe if I use—AAAHH
No! I'm too young and charismatic to die!
Somebody save MEEEE!
We should've charged double.
Focus! Try to use your magic!
CAW
Okay! Alright!
What? But I don't know how!
CAW
I can't believe I'm doing this.
I'm going to shoot and run...
...shoot and run!
BANG!

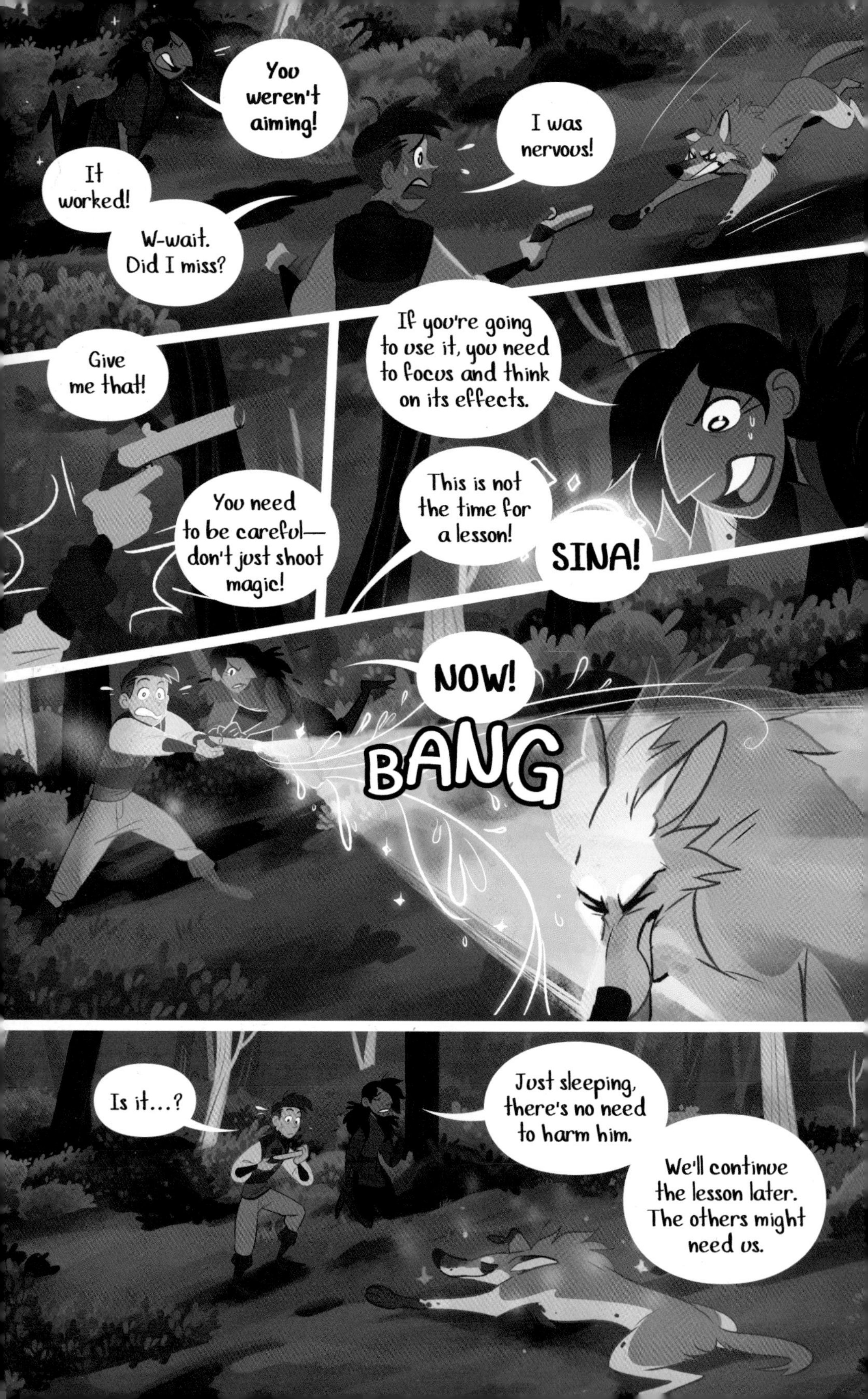

You weren't aiming!
I was nervous!
It worked!
W-wait. Did I miss?
Give me that!
If you're going to use it, you need to focus and think on its effects.
You need to be careful—don't just shoot magic!
This is not the time for a lesson!
SINA!
NOW!
BANG
Is it...?
Just sleeping, there's no need to harm him.
We'll continue the lesson later. The others might need us.

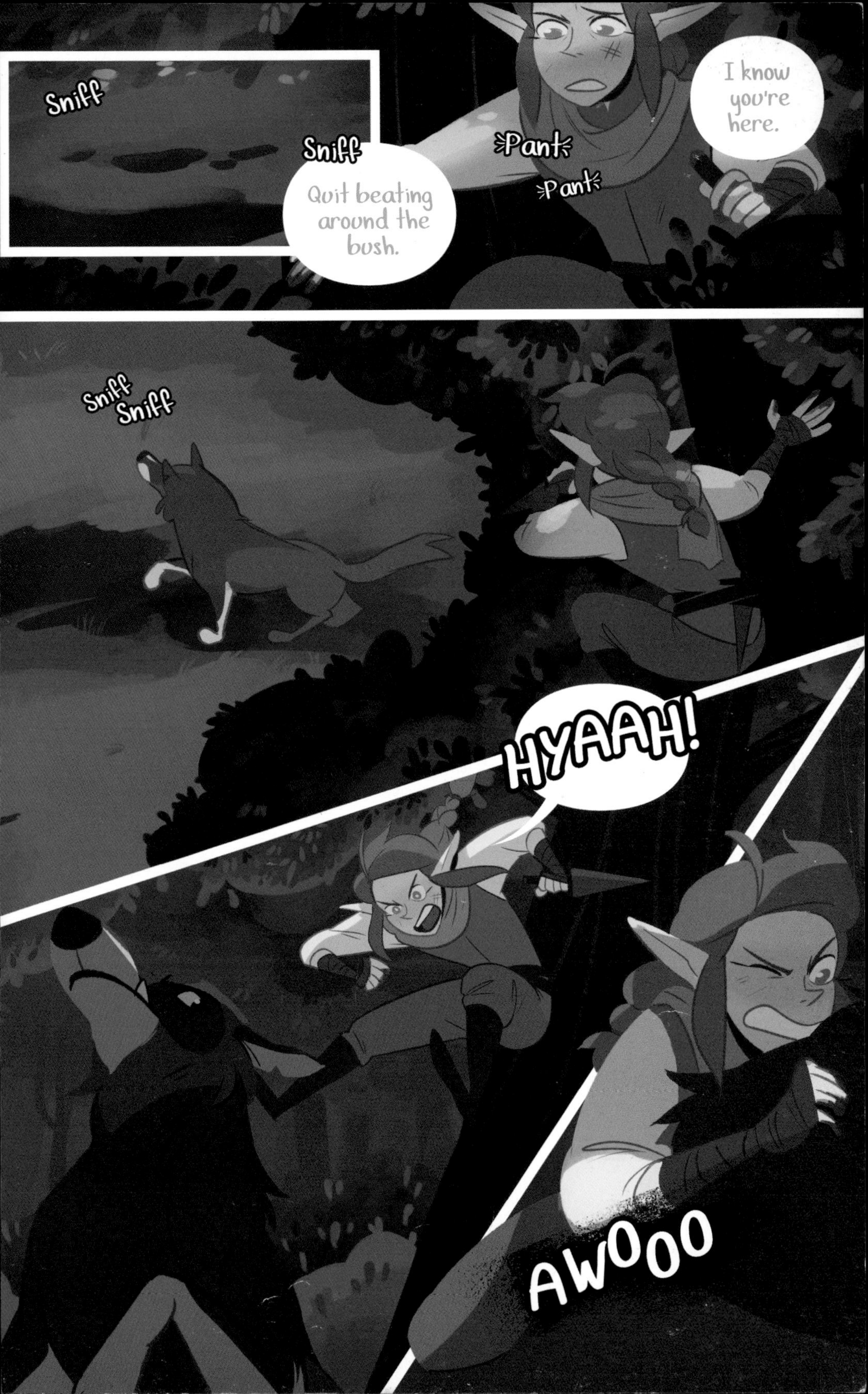
Sniff
Sniff
Quit beating around the bush.
Pant
Pant
I know you're here.
Sniff Sniff
HYAAH!
AWOOO

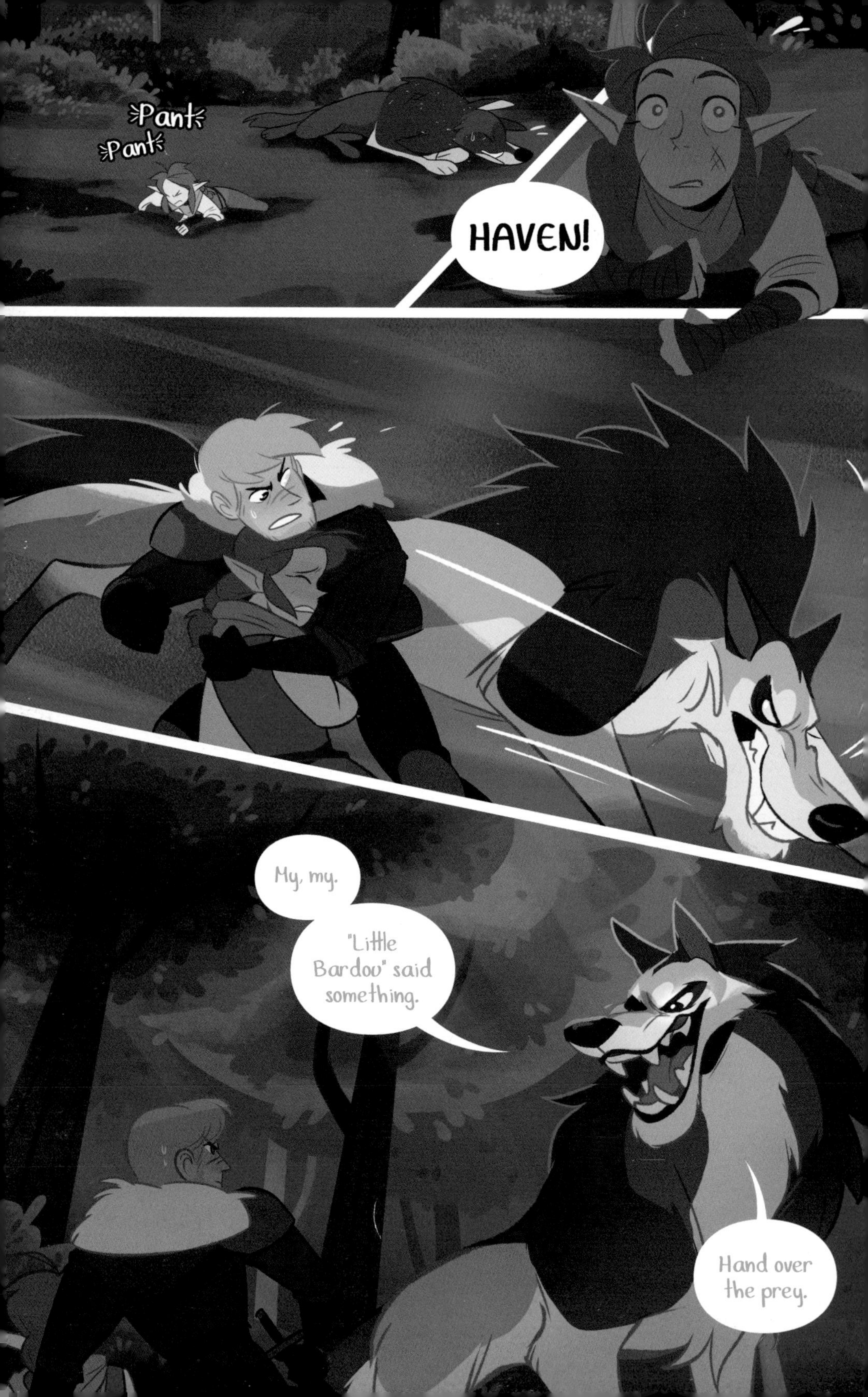
Pant
Pant
HAVEN!
My, my.
"Little Bardou" said something.
Hand over the prey.

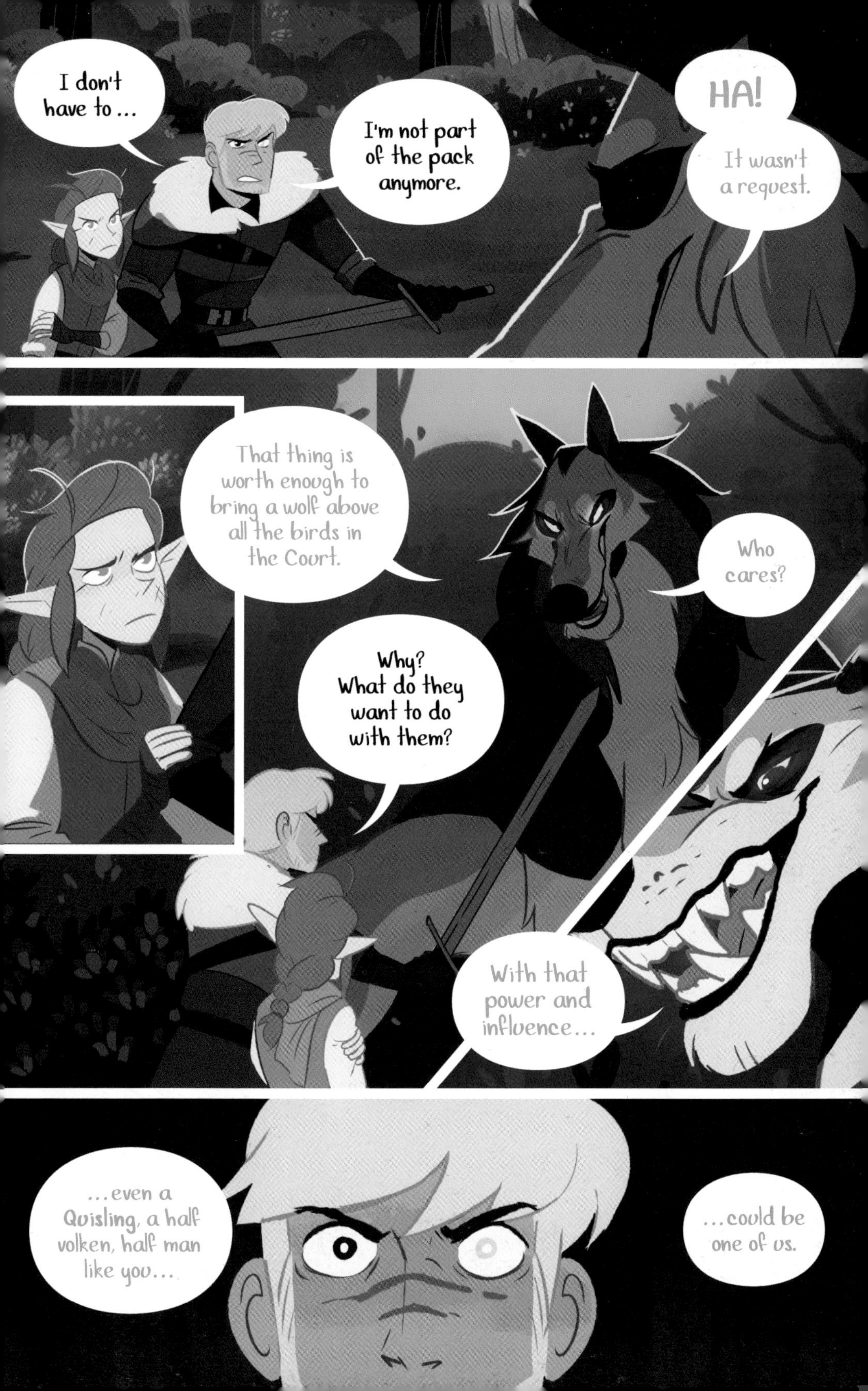
I don't have to ...
I'm not part of the pack anymore.
HA!
It wasn't a request.
That thing is worth enough to bring a wolf above all the birds in the Court.
Who cares?
Why? What do they want to do with them?
With that power and influence...
...even a Quisling, a half volken, half man like you...
...could be one of us.

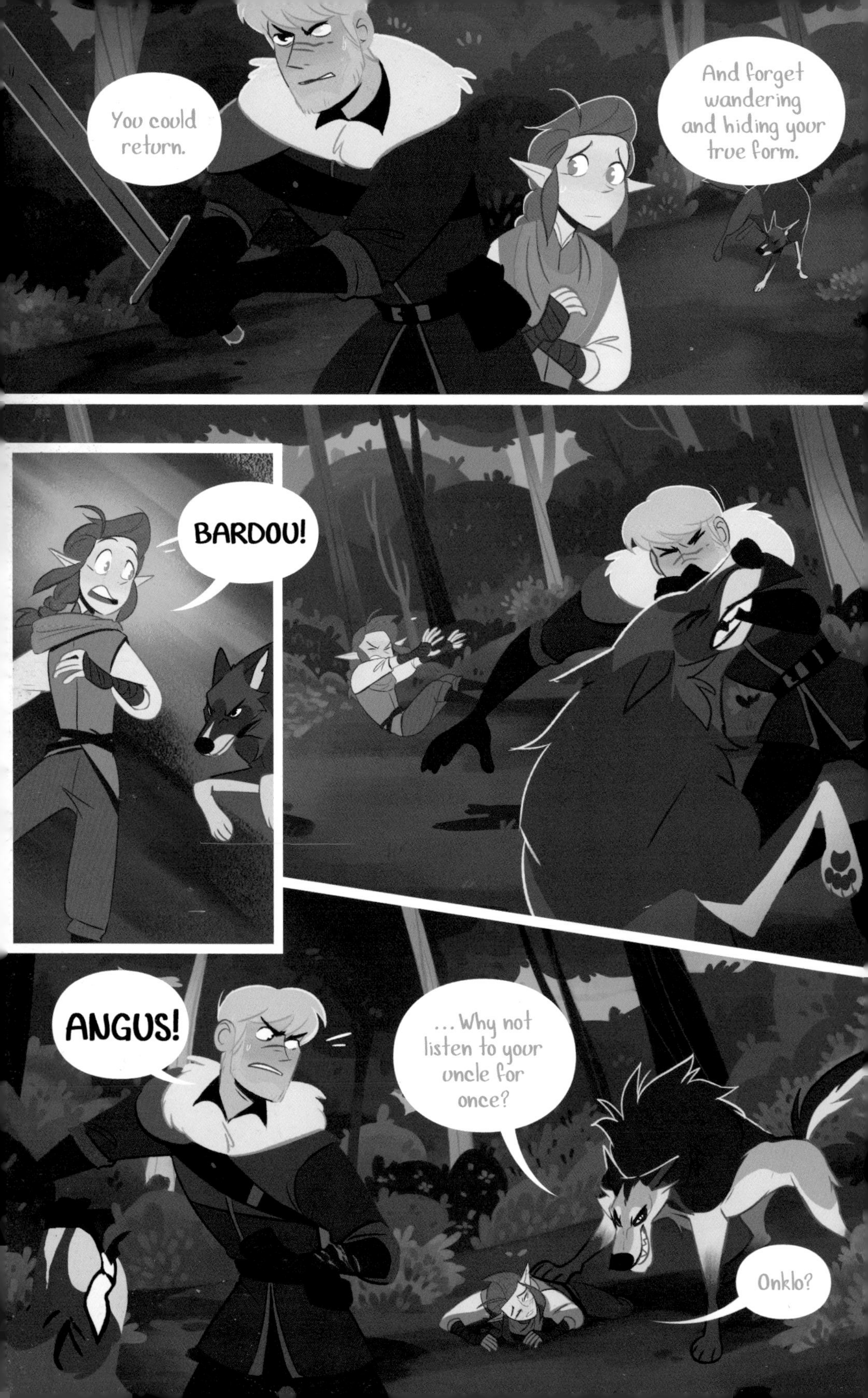
You could return.
And forget wandering and hiding your true form.
BARDOU!
ANGUS!
...Why not listen to your uncle for once?
Onklo?

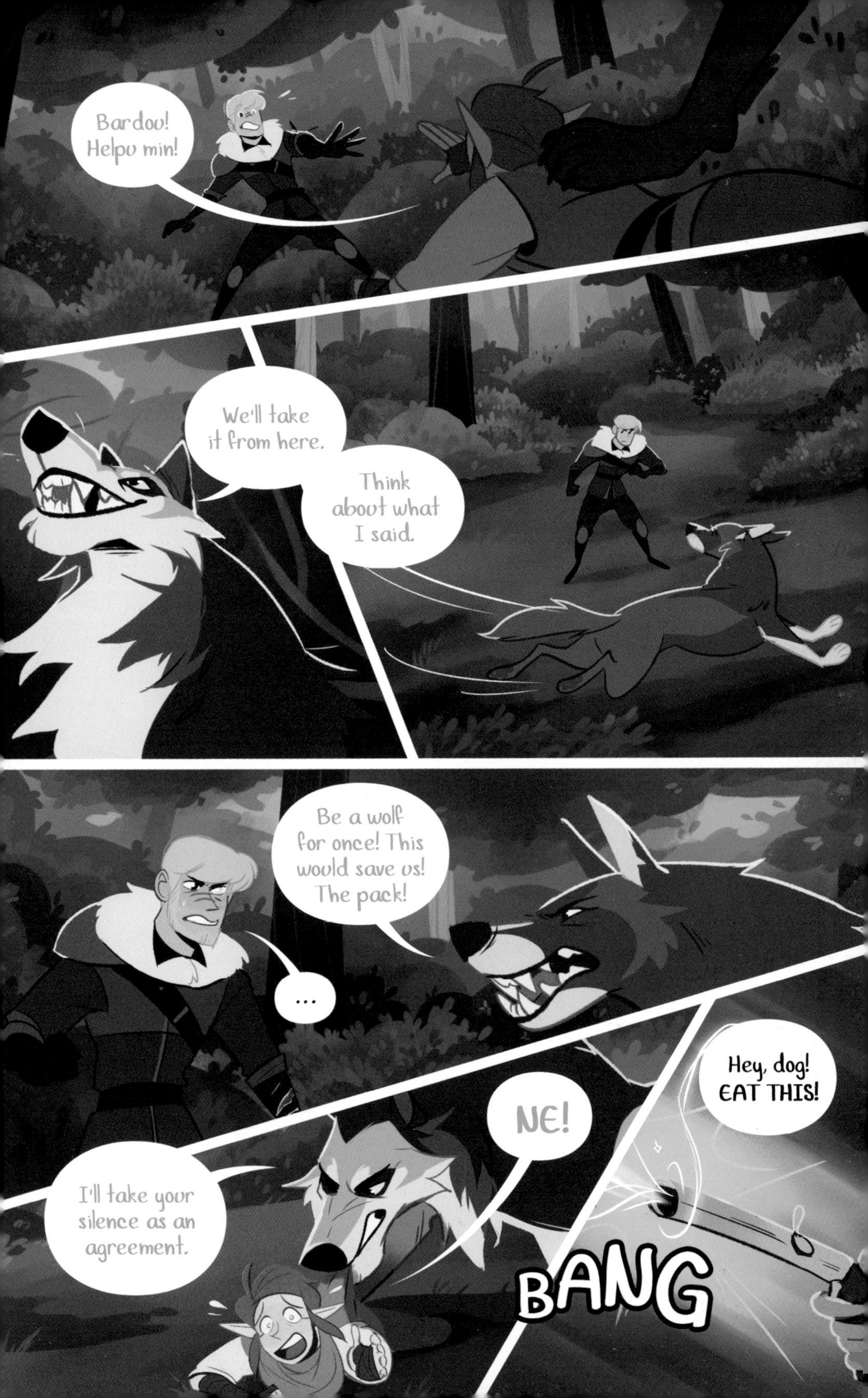
Bardou!
Helpu min!
We'll take it from here.
Think about what I said.
Be a wolf for once! This would save us! The pack!
...
Hey, dog! EAT THIS!
NE!
I'll take your silence as an agreement.
BANG

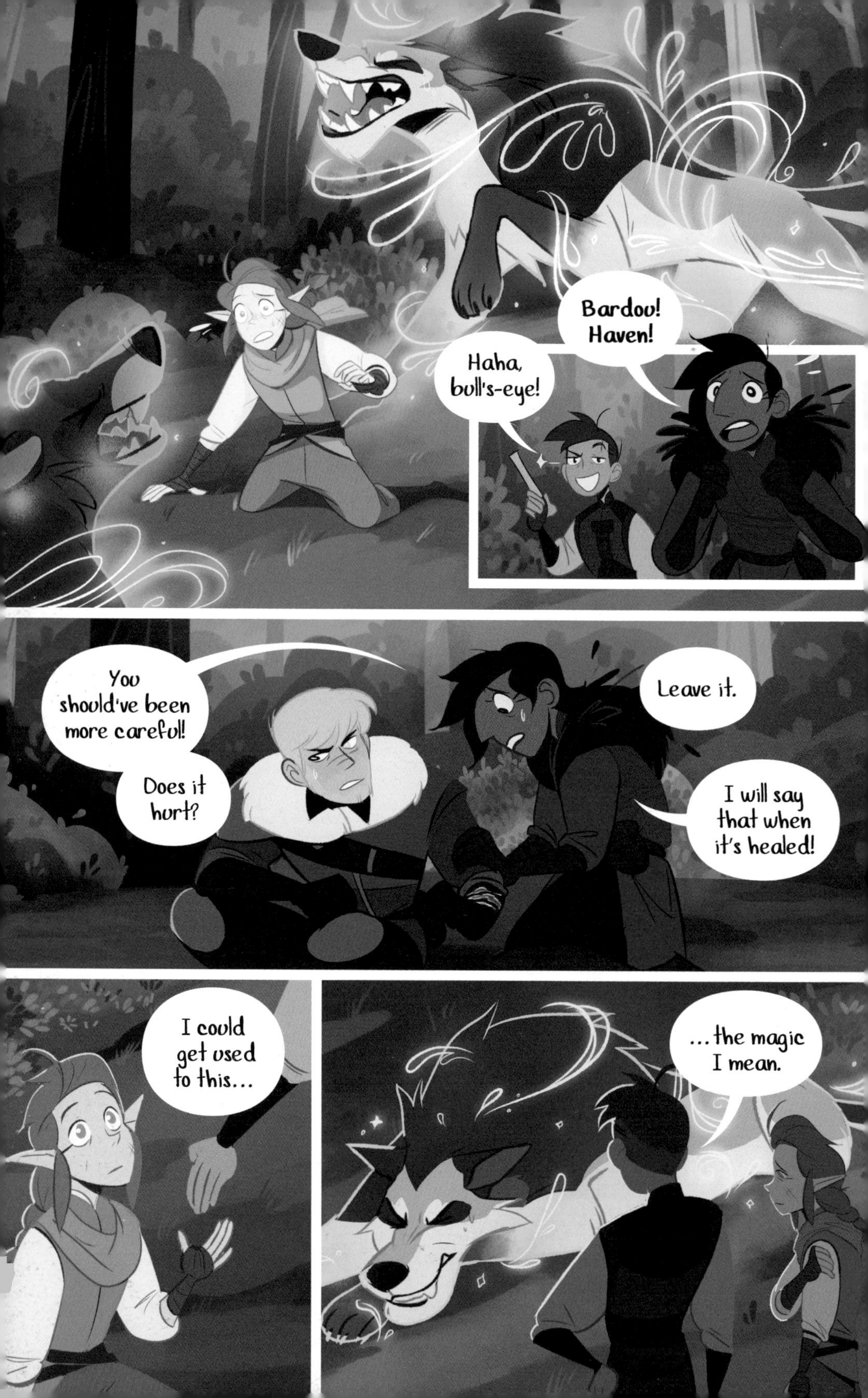

Bardou!
Haven!
Haha, bull's-eye!
You should've been more careful!
Does it hurt?
Leave it.
I will say that when it's healed!
I could get used to this...
...the magic I mean.

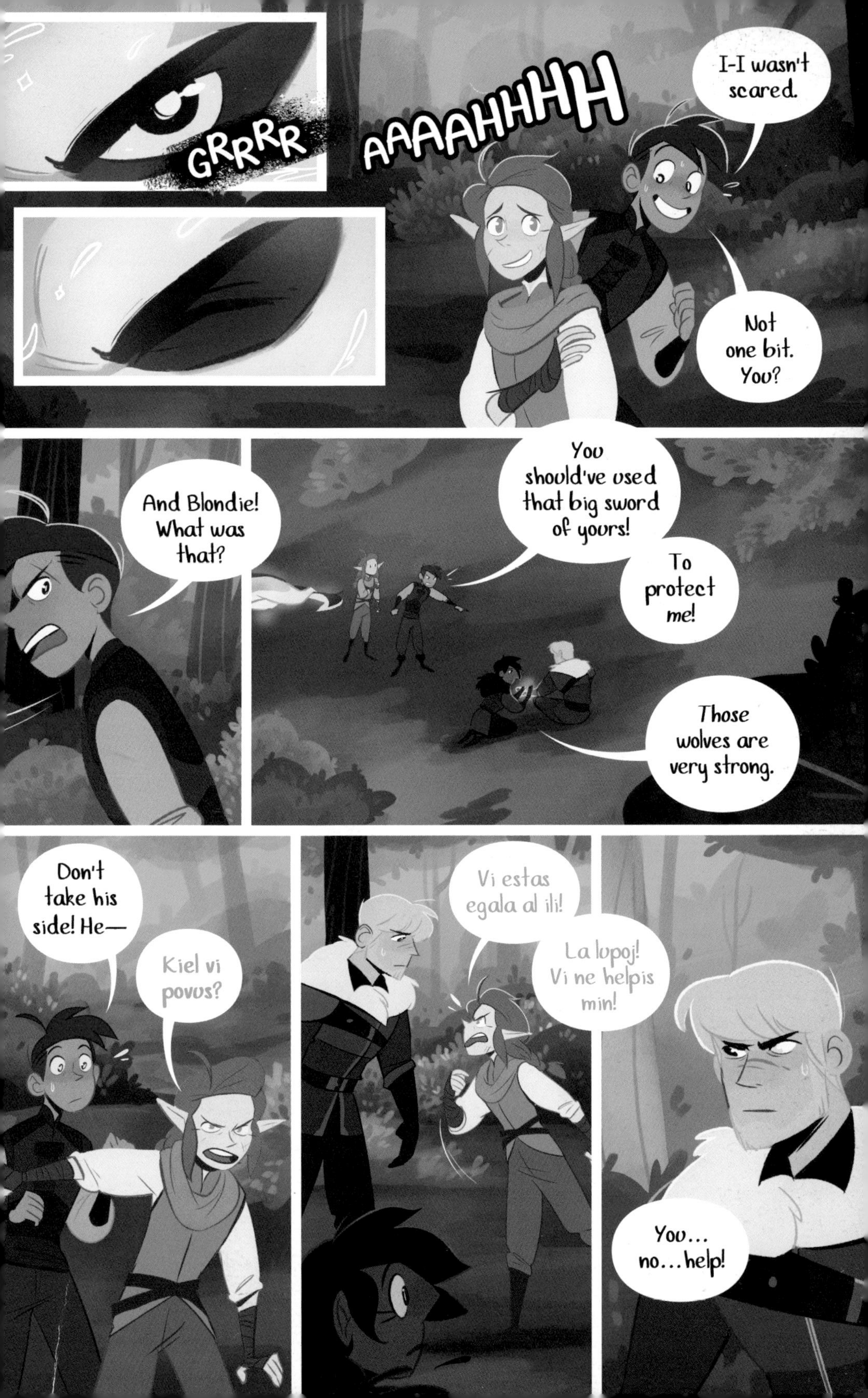
GRRRR
AAAAHHHHH
I-I wasn't scared.
Not one bit. You?
And Blondie! What was that?
You should've used that big sword of yours!
To protect me!
Those wolves are very strong.
Don't take his side! He—
Kiel vi povus?
Vi estas egala al ili!
La lupoj! Vi ne helpis min!
You... no... help!

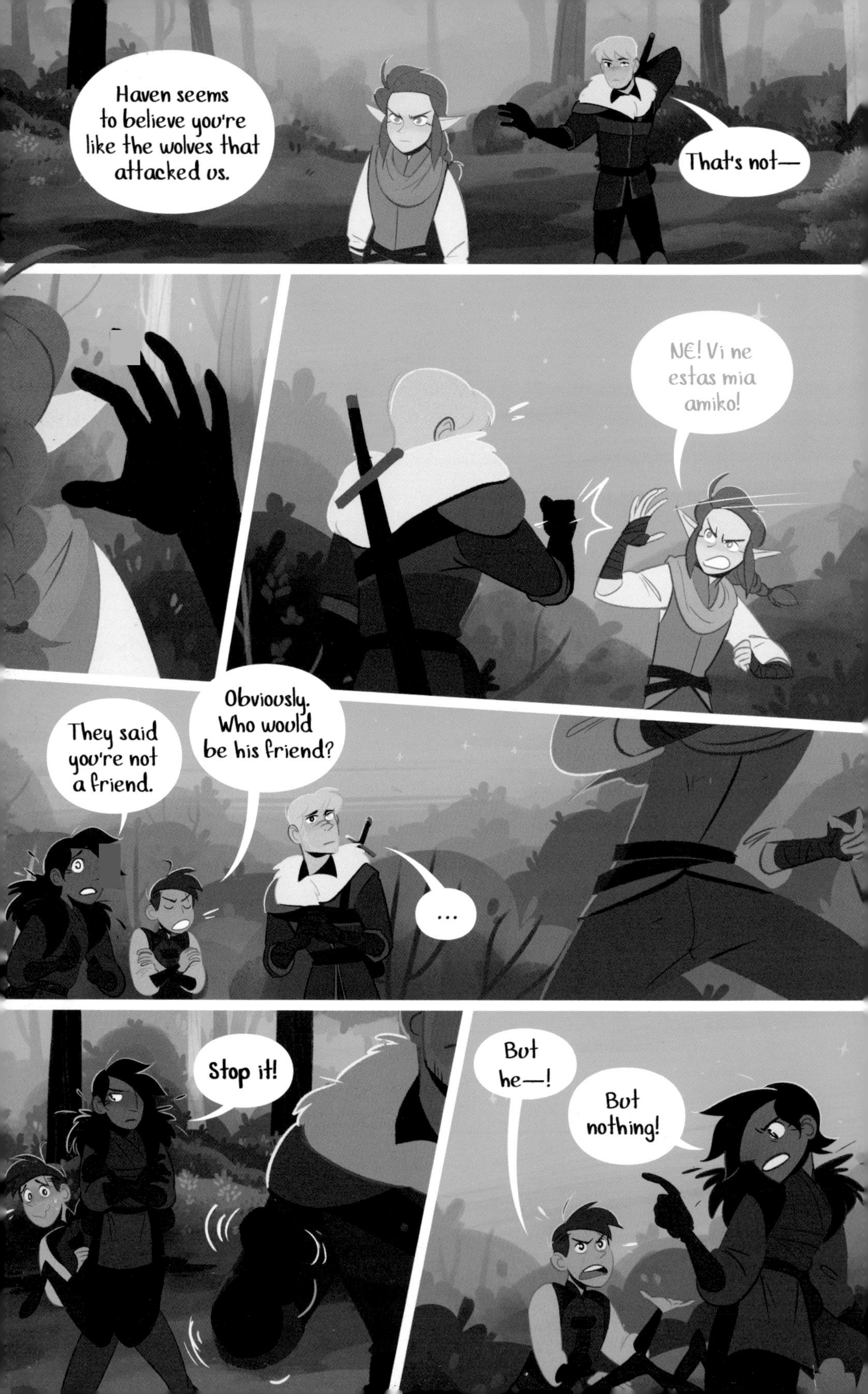
Haven seems to believe you're like the wolves that attacked us.
That's not—
NE! Vi ne estas mia amiko!
They said you're not a friend.
Obviously. Who would be his friend?
...
Stop it!
But he—!
But nothing!

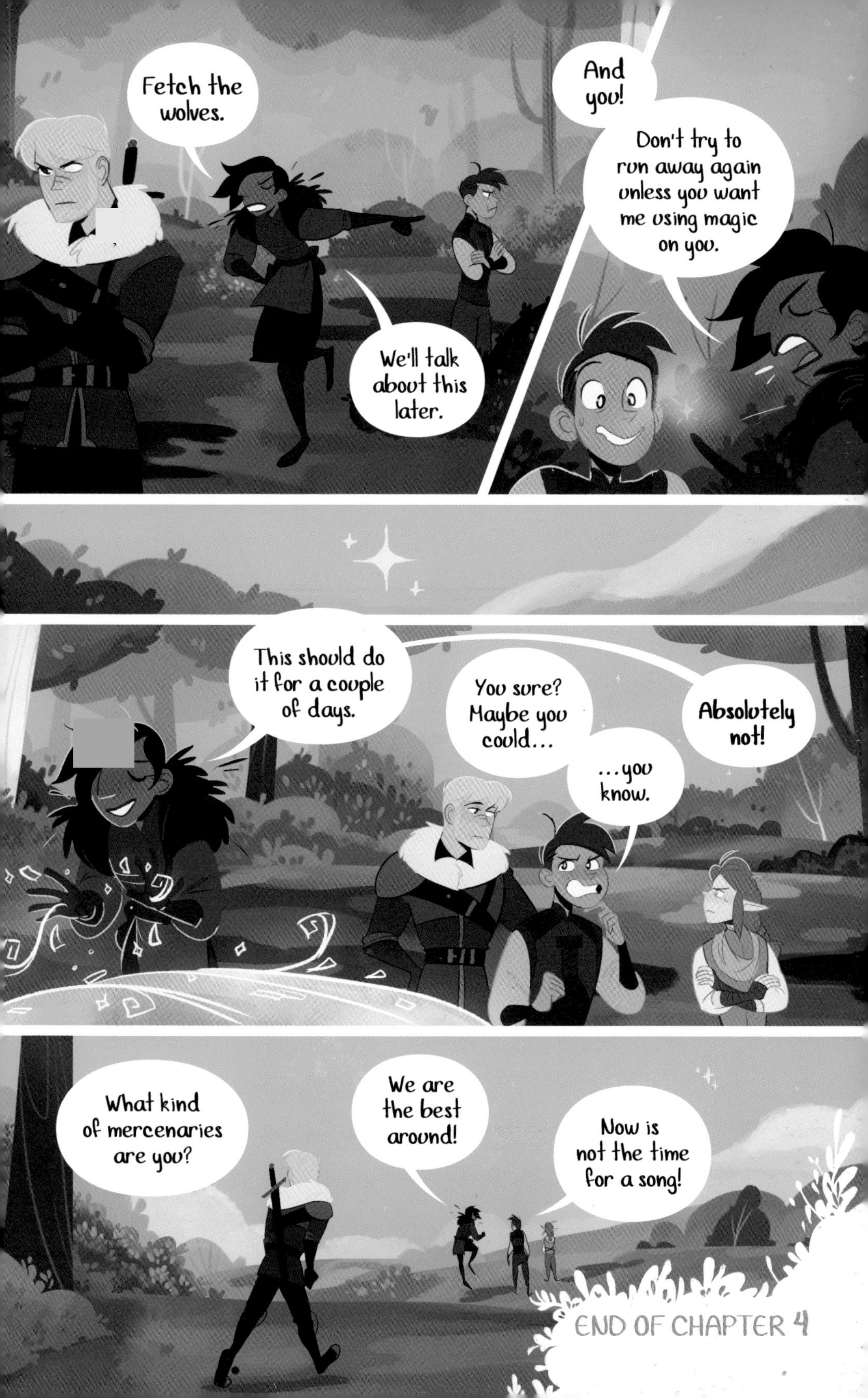
Fetch the wolves.
We'll talk about this later.
And you!
Don't try to run away again unless you want me using magic on you.
This should do it for a couple of days.
You sure? Maybe you could...
...you know.
Absolutely not!
What kind of mercenaries are you?
We are the best around!
Now is not the time for a song!
END OF CHAPTER 4

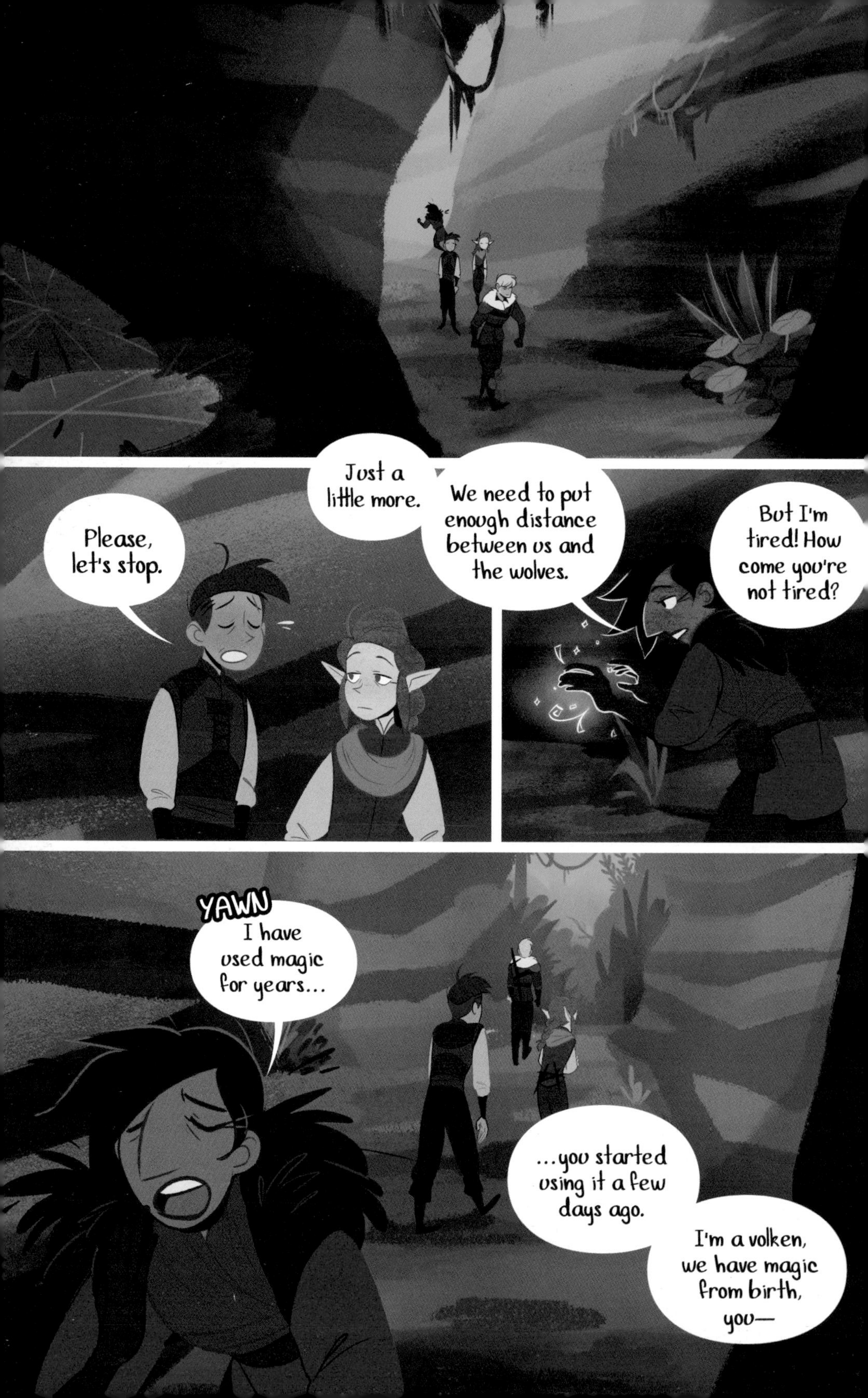
Please, let's stop.
Just a little more.
We need to put enough distance between us and the wolves.
But I'm tired! How come you're not tired?
YAWN
I have used magic for years...
...you started using it a few days ago.
I'm a volken, we have magic from birth, you—

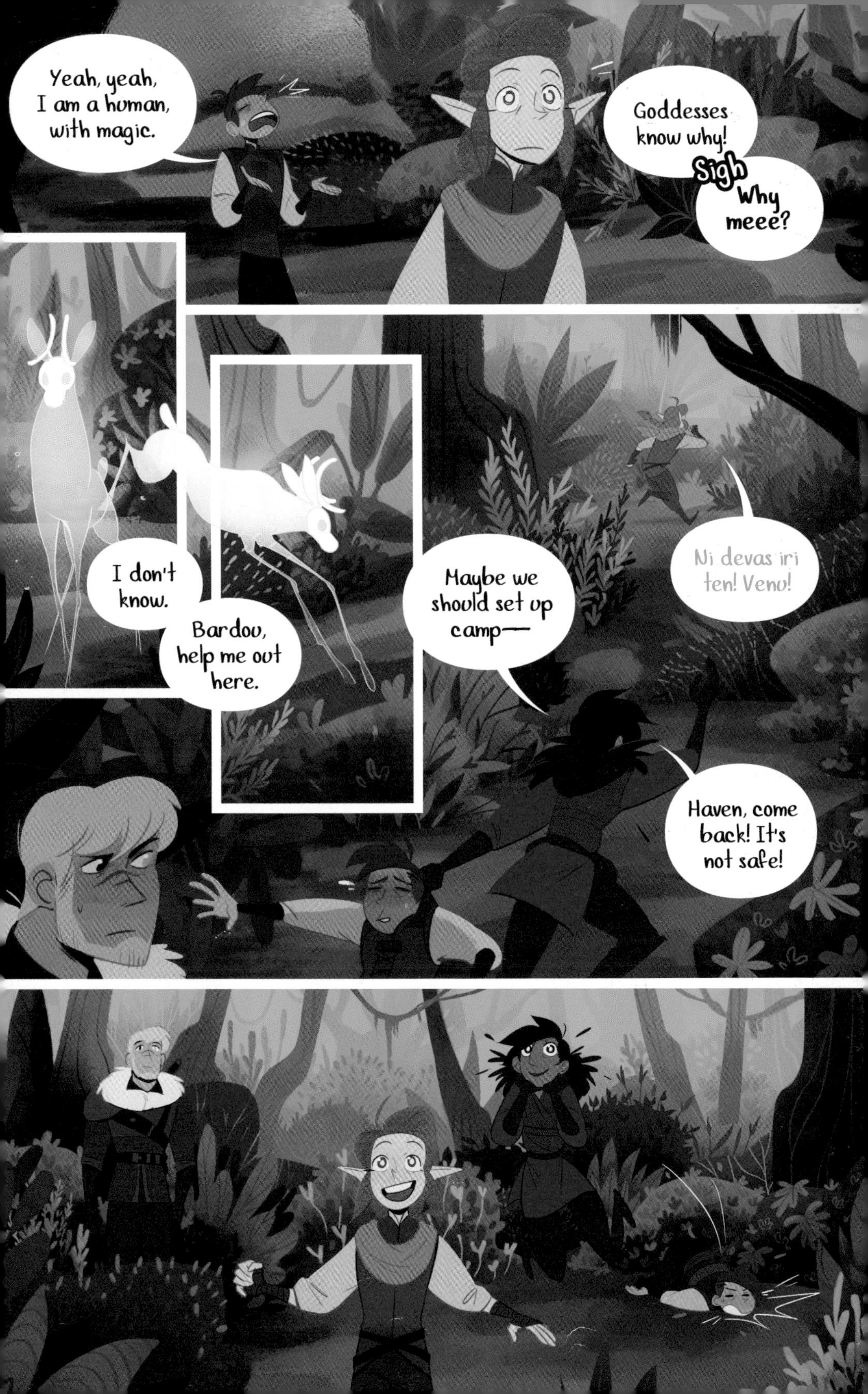

Yeah, yeah, I am a human, with magic.
Goddesses know why!
Sigh
Why meee?
I don't know.
Bardou, help me out here.
Maybe we should set up camp—
Ni devas iri ten! Veno!
Haven, come back! It's not safe!

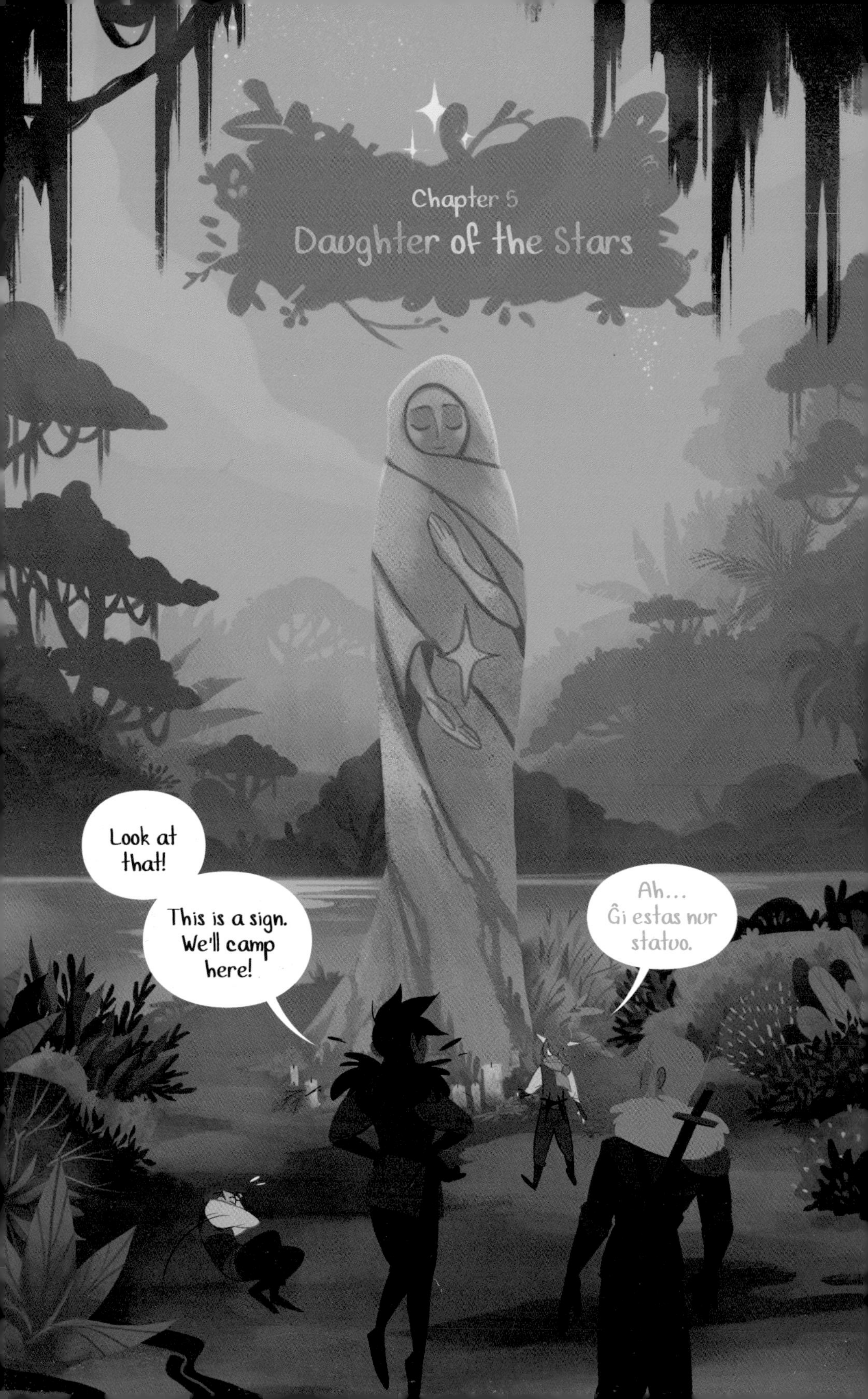
Chapter 5
Daughter of the Stars
Look at that!
This is a sign. We'll camp here!
Ah... Ĝi estas nur statuo.

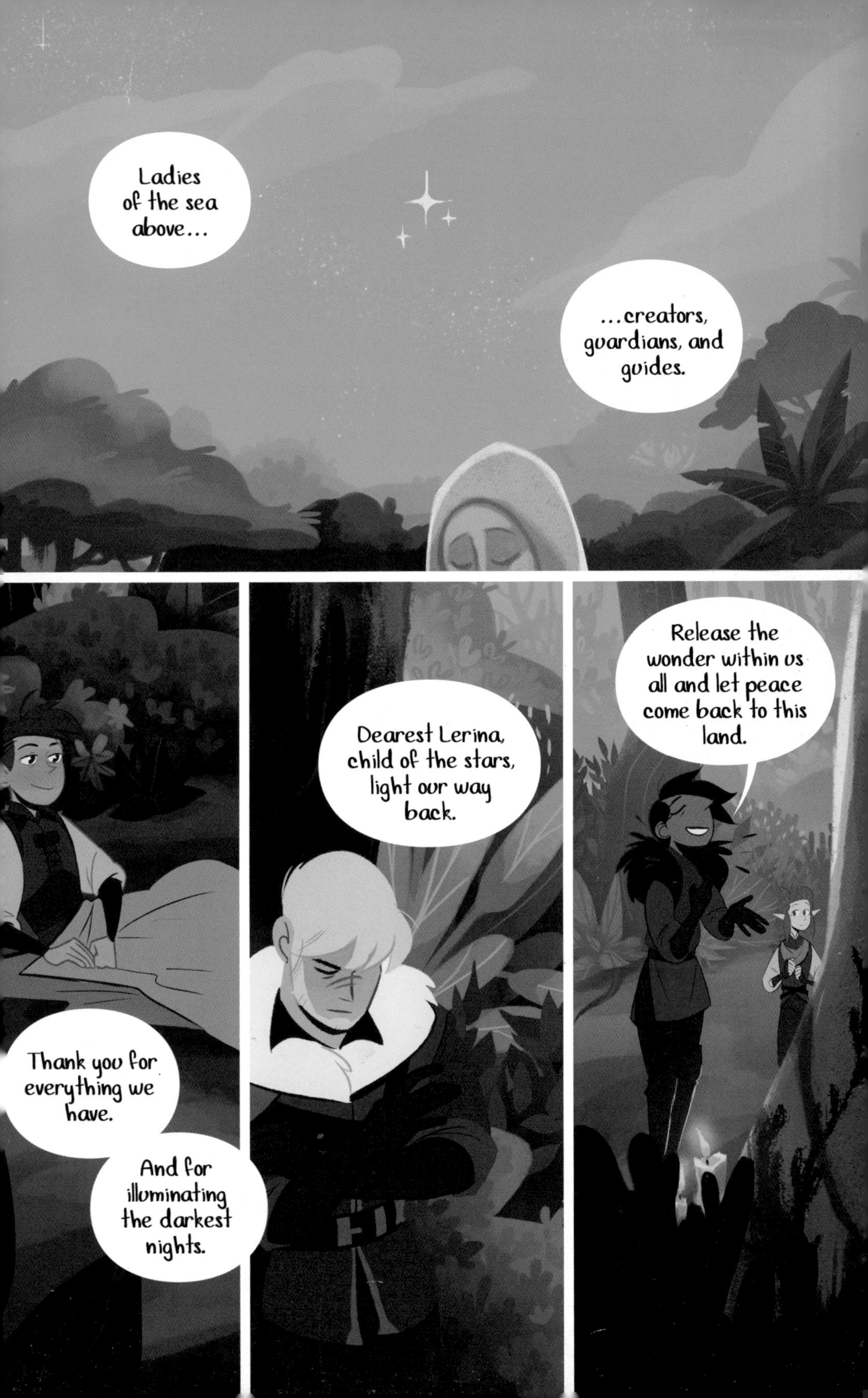

Ladies of the sea above...
...creators, guardians, and guides.
Thank you for everything we have.
And for illuminating the darkest nights.
Dearest Lerina, child of the stars, light our way back.
Release the wonder within us all and let peace come back to this land.

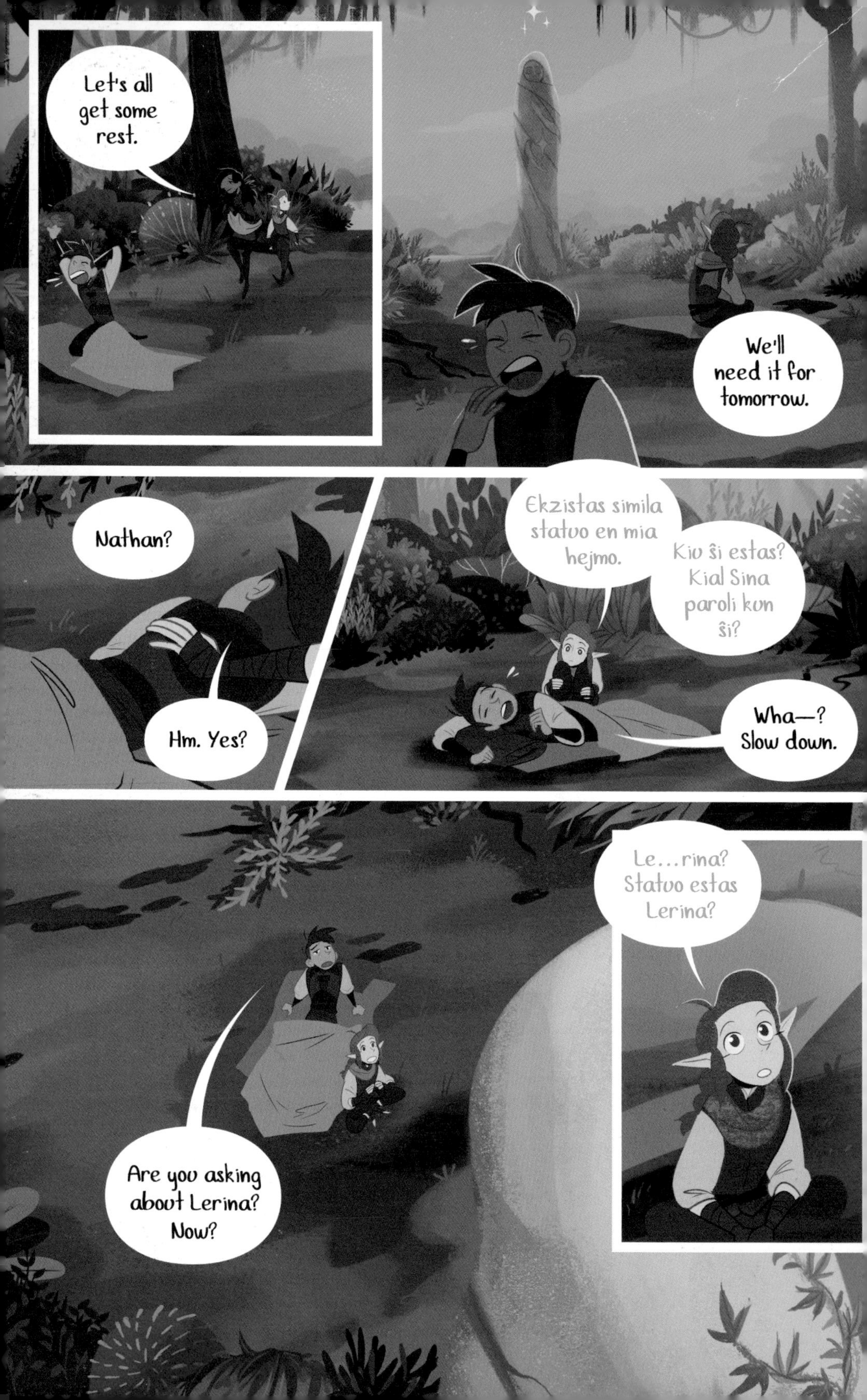
Let's all get some rest.
We'll need it for tomorrow.
Nathan?
Hm. Yes?
Ekzistas simila statuo en mia hejmo.
Kiu ŝi estas? Kial Sina paroli kun ŝi?
Wha—? Slow down.
Are you asking about Lerina? Now?
Le...rina? Statuo estas Lerina?

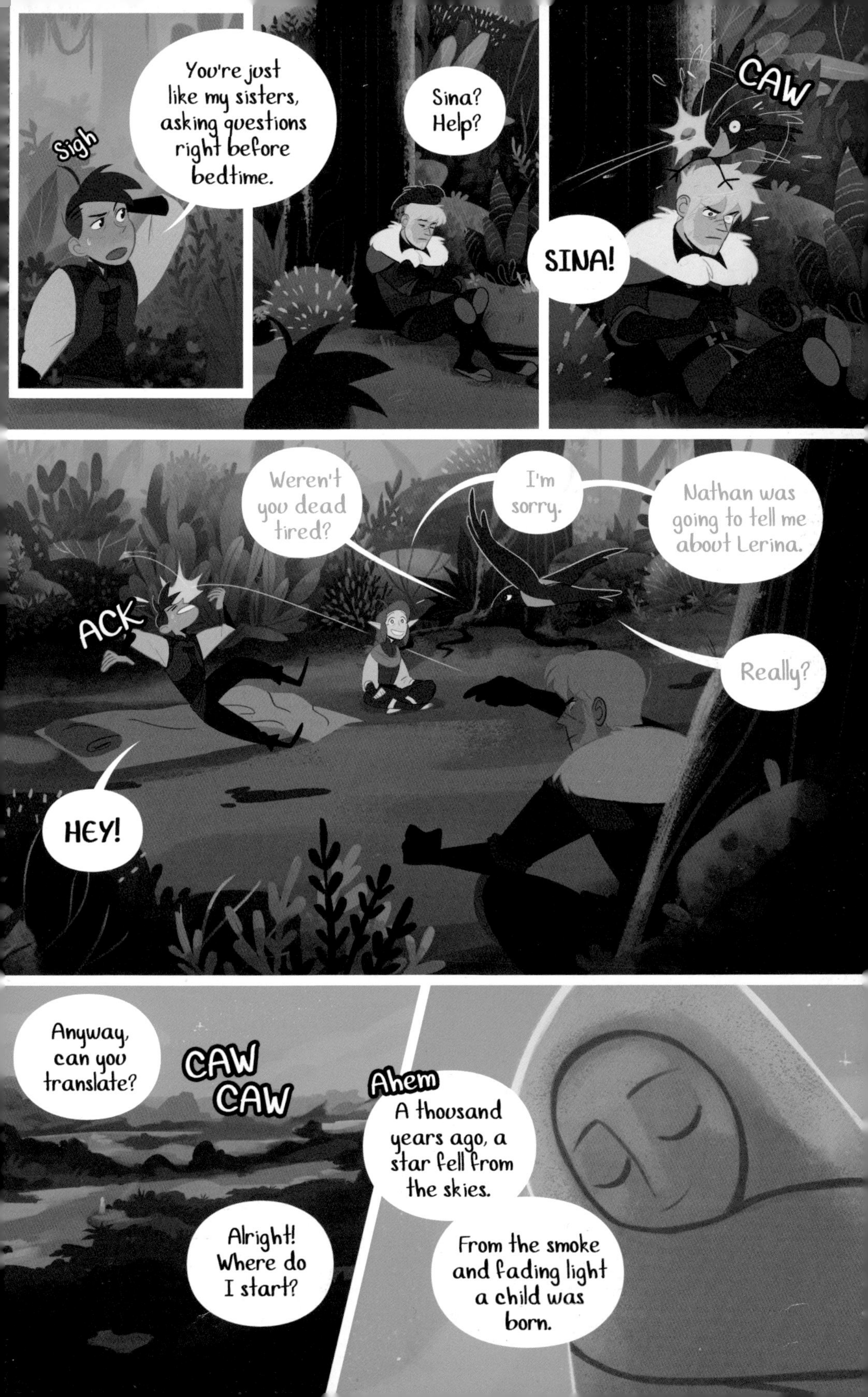
Sigh
You're just like my sisters, asking questions right before bedtime.
Sina? Help?
CAW
SINA!
ACK
Weren't you dead tired?
I'm sorry.
Nathan was going to tell me about Lerina.
Really?
HEY!
Anyway, can you translate?
CAW CAW
Alright! Where do I start?
Ahem
A thousand years ago, a star fell from the skies.
From the smoke and fading light a child was born.

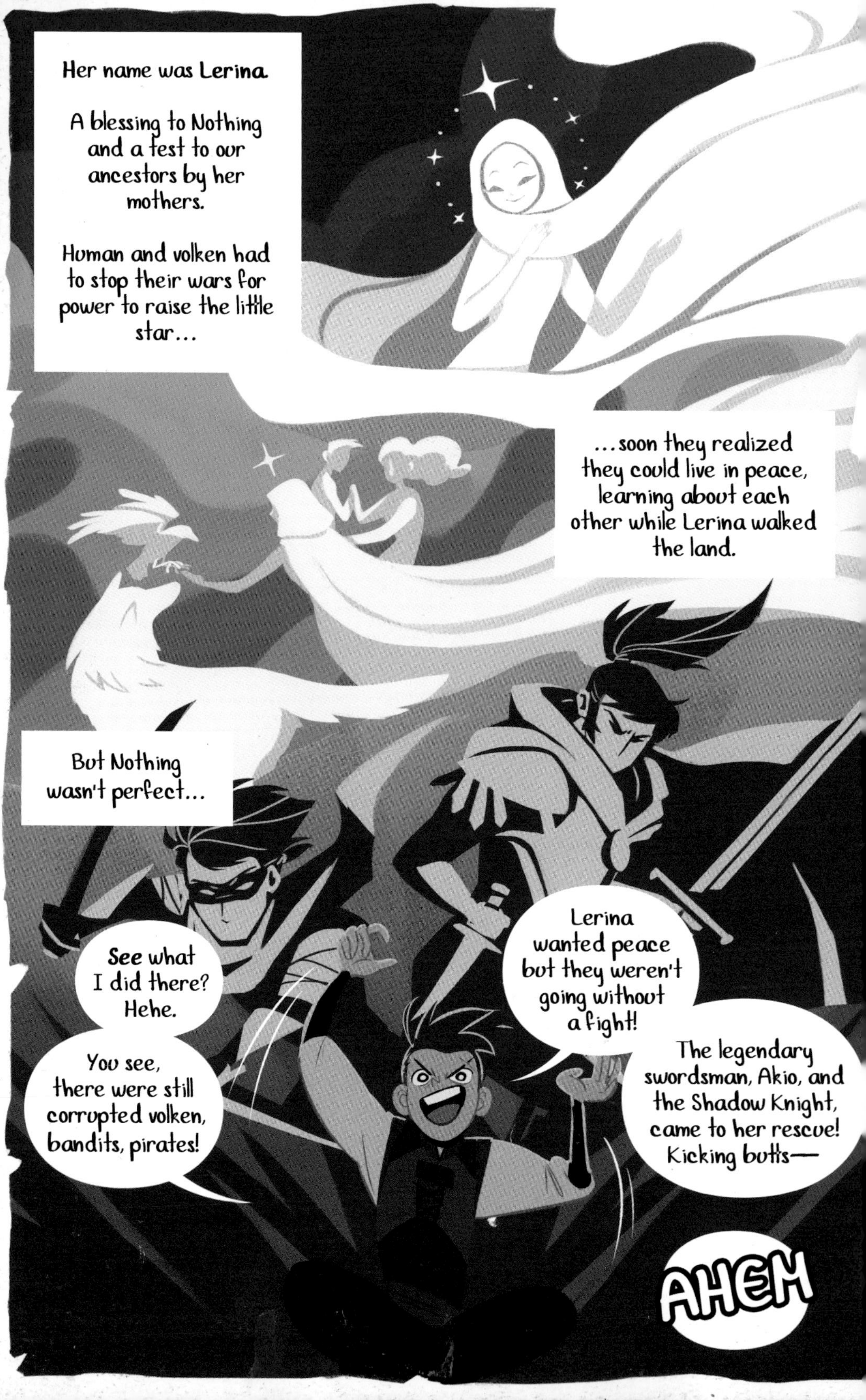
Her name was Lerina
A blessing to Nothing and a test to our ancestors by her mothers.
Human and volken had to stop their wars for power to raise the little star...
...soon they realized they could live in peace, learning about each other while Lerina walked the land.
But Nothing wasn't perfect...
See what I did there? Hehe.
Lerina wanted peace but they weren't going without a fight!
You see, there were still corrupted volken, bandits, pirates!
The legendary swordsman, Akio, and the Shadow Knight, came to her rescue! Kicking butts—
AHEM

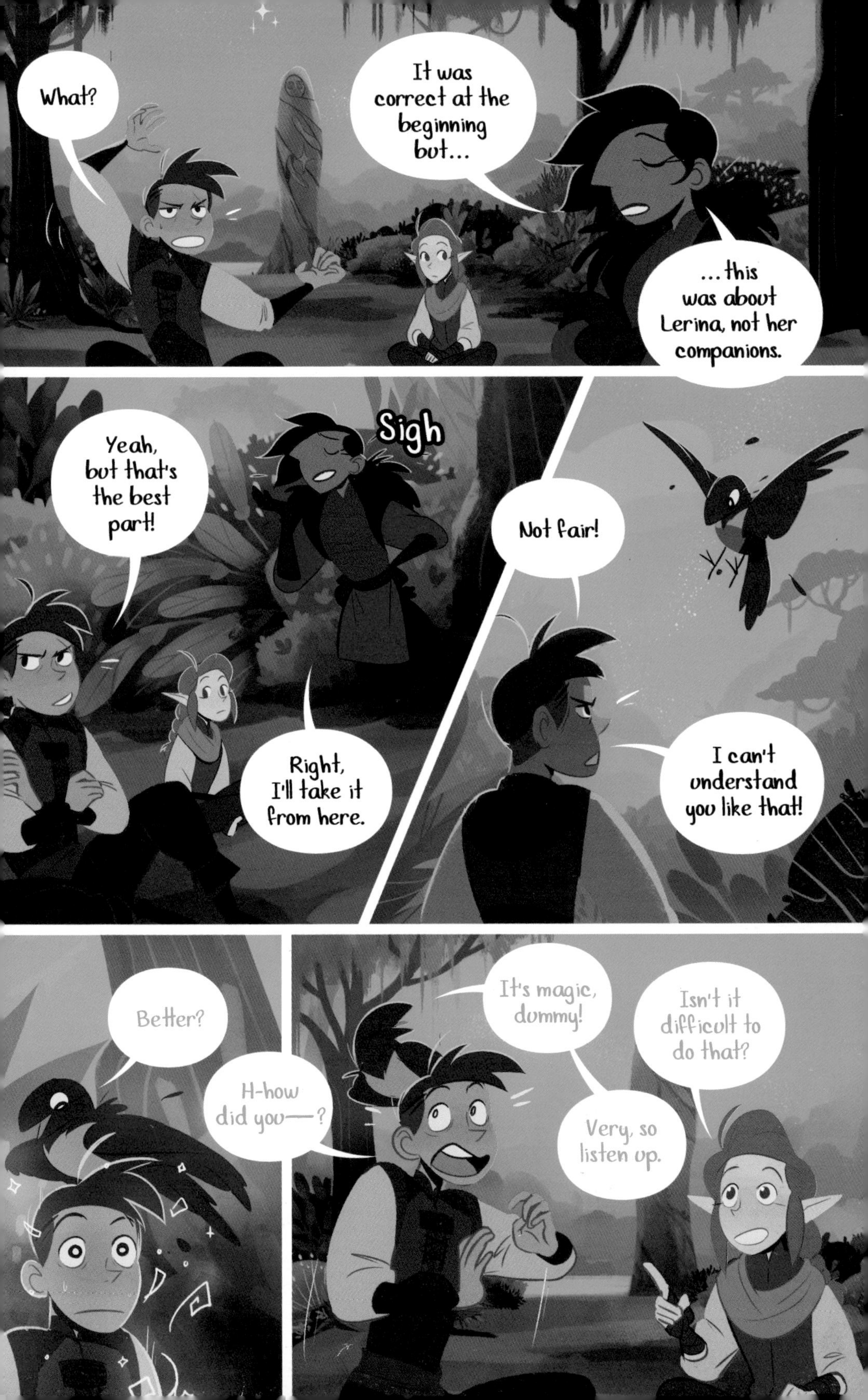
What?
It was correct at the beginning but...
...this was about Lerina, not her companions.
Sigh
Yeah, but that's the best part!
Right, I'll take it from here.
Not fair!
I can't understand you like that!
Better?
H-how did you—?
It's magic, dummy!
Very, so listen up.
Isn't it difficult to do that?

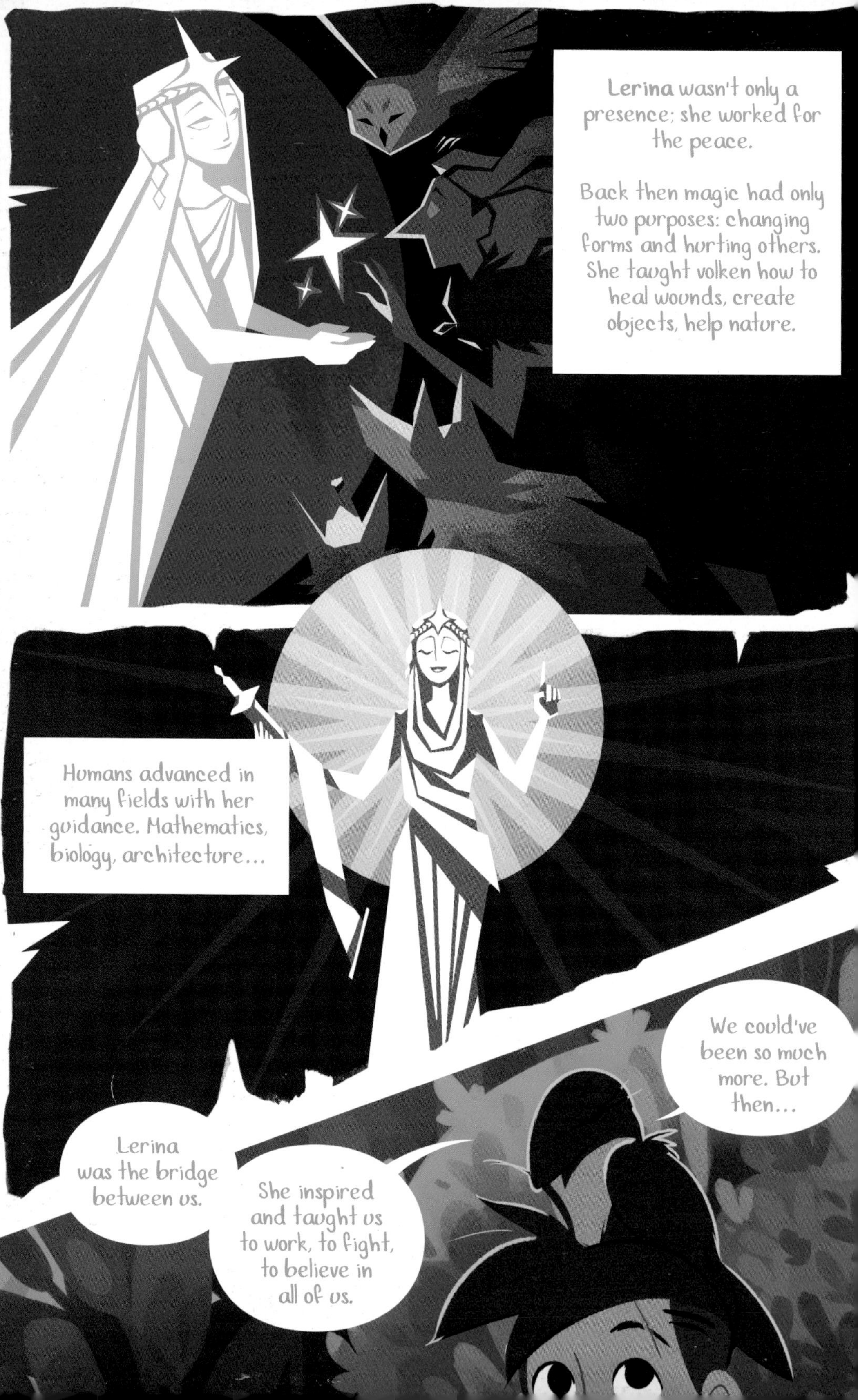
Lerina wasn't only a presence; she worked for the peace.
Back then magic had only two purposes: changing forms and hurting others. She taught volken how to heal wounds, create objects, help nature.
Humans advanced in many fields with her guidance. Mathematics, biology, architecture...
Lerina was the bridge between us.
She inspired and taught us to work, to fight, to believe in all of us.
We could've been so much more. But then...

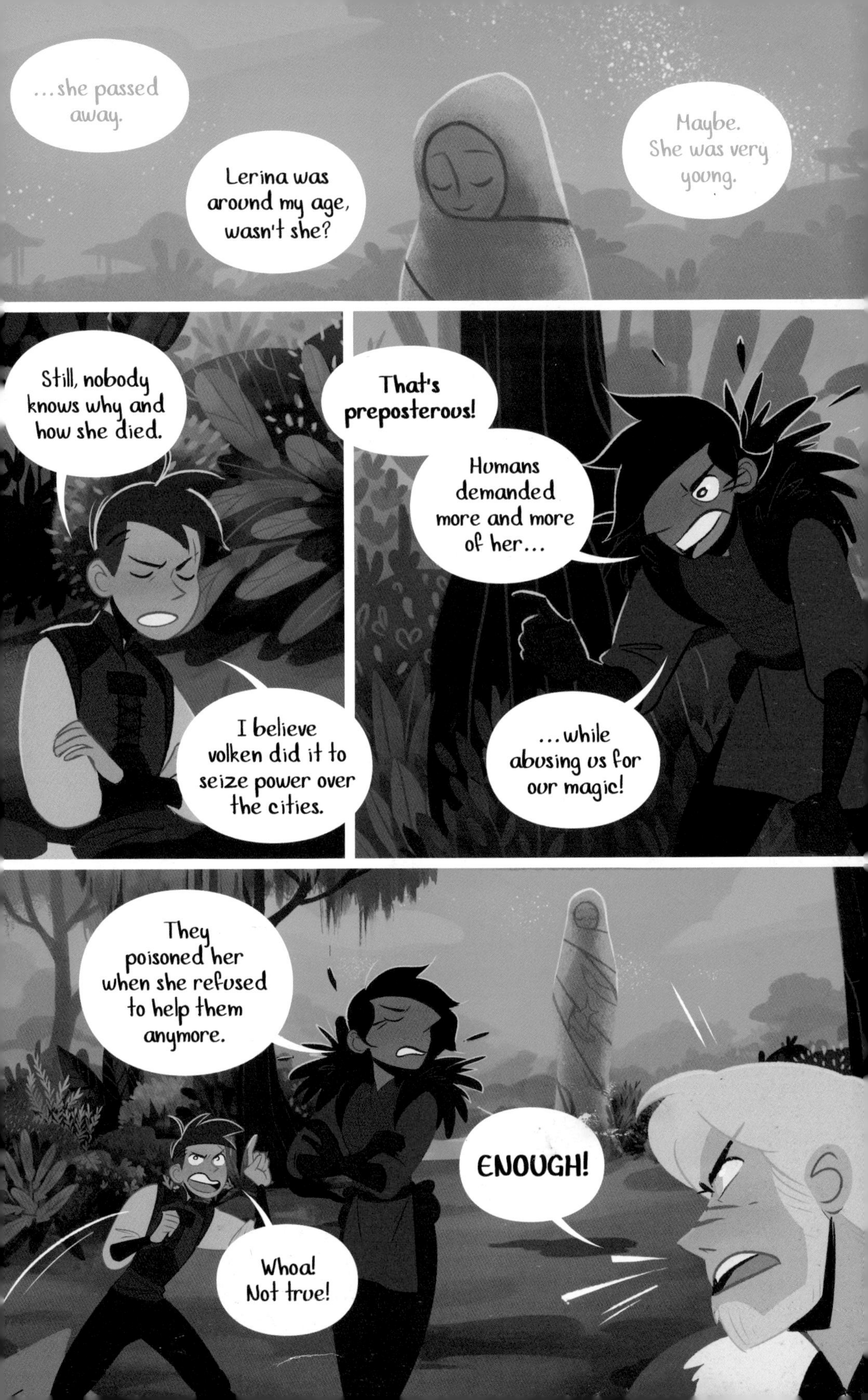
...she passed away.
Lerina was around my age, wasn't she?
Maybe. She was very young.
Still, nobody knows why and how she died.
I believe volken did it to seize power over the cities.
That's preposterous!
Humans demanded more and more of her...
...while abusing us for our magic!
They poisoned her when she refused to help them anymore.
Whoa! Not true!
ENOUGH!

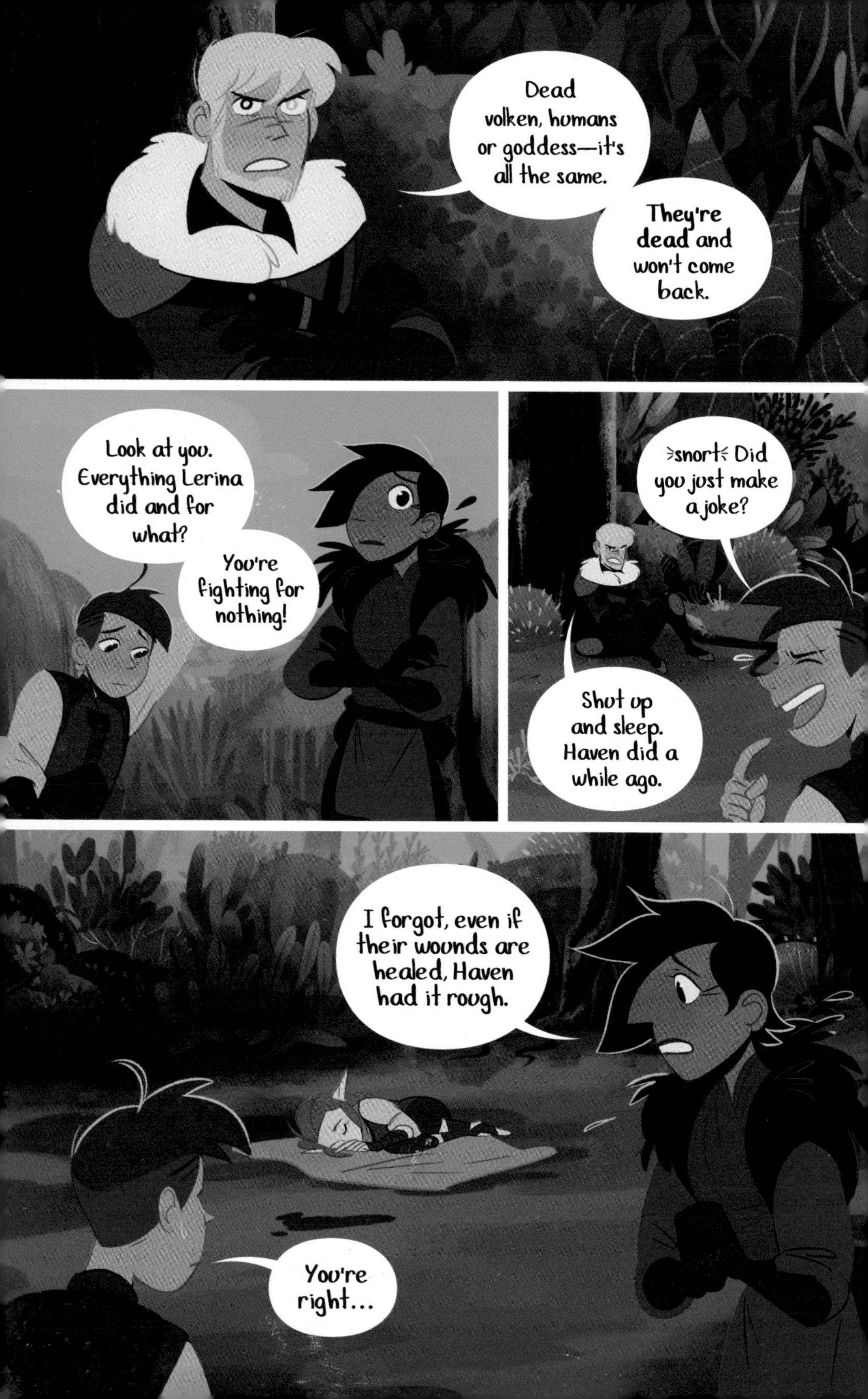

Dead volken, humans or goddess—it's all the same.
They're dead and won't come back.
Look at you. Everything Lerina did and for what?
You're fighting for nothing!
⪢snort⪡ Did you just make a joke?
Shut up and sleep. Haven did a while ago.
I forgot, even if their wounds are healed, Haven had it rough.
You're right...

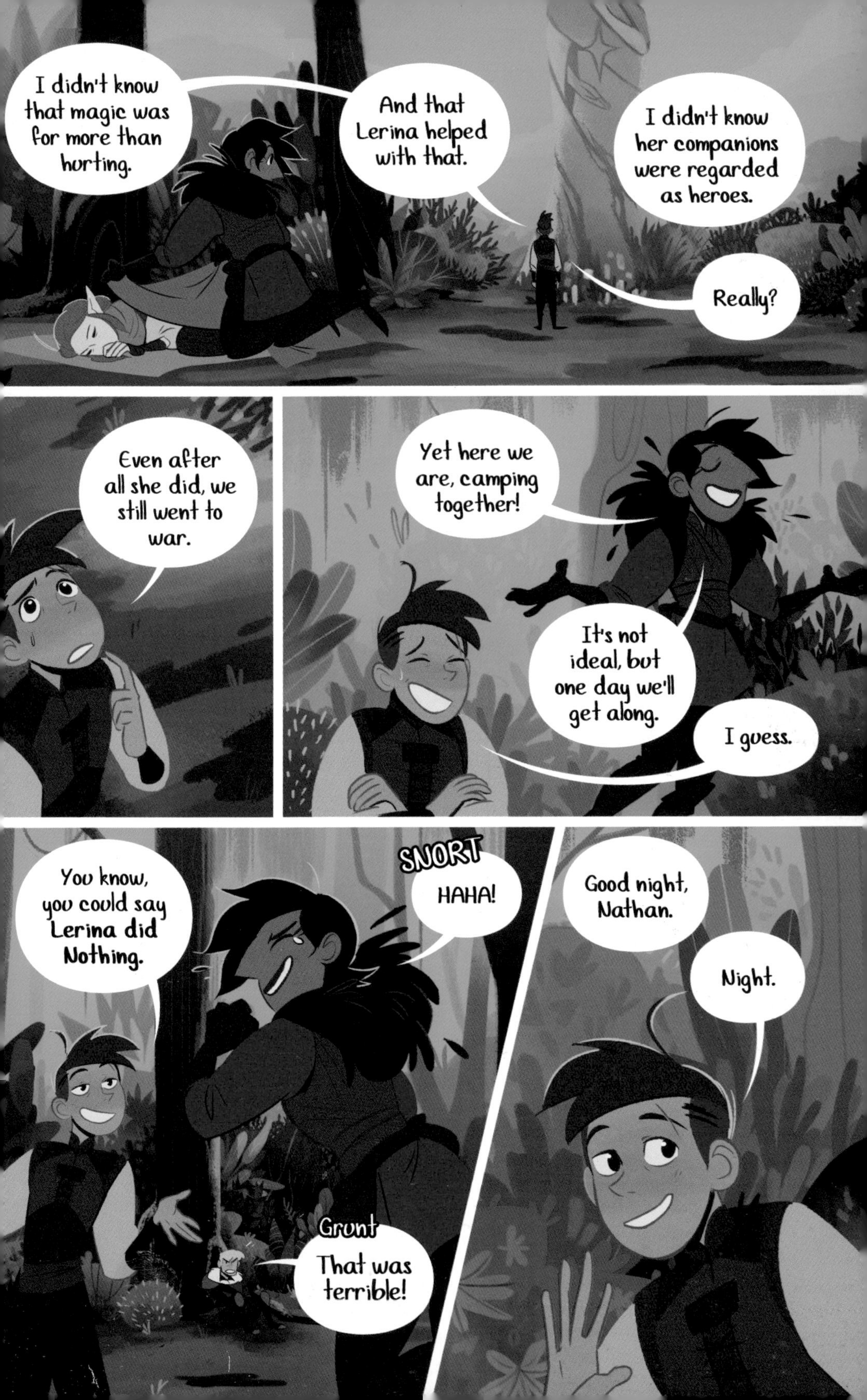
I didn't know that magic was for more than hurting.
And that Lerina helped with that.
I didn't know her companions were regarded as heroes.
Really?
Even after all she did, we still went to war.
Yet here we are, camping together!
It's not ideal, but one day we'll get along.
I guess.
You know, you could say Lerina did Nothing.
SNORT
HAHA!
Grunt
That was terrible!
Good night, Nathan.
Night.

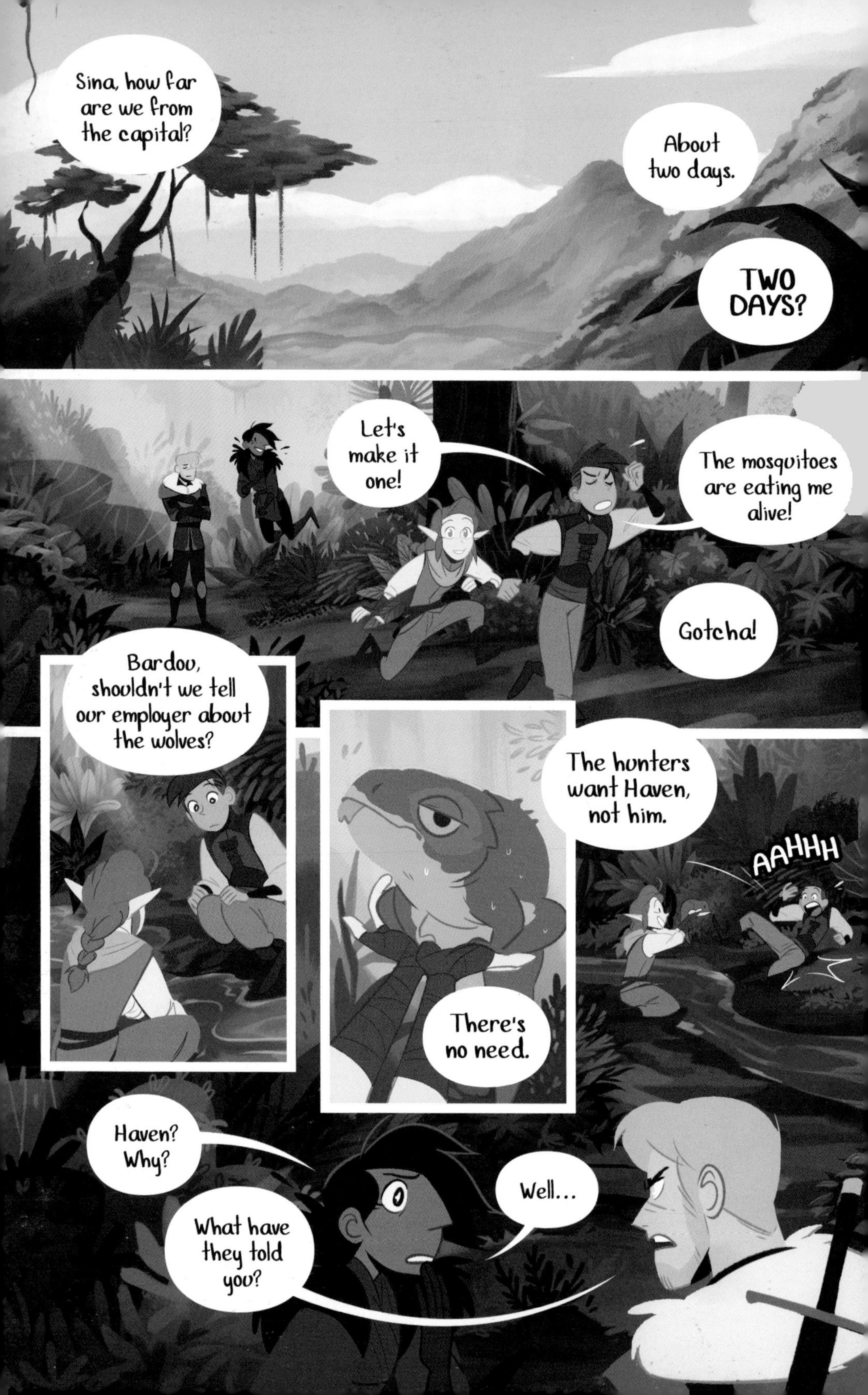
Sina, how far are we from the capital?
About two days.
TWO DAYS?
Let's make it one!
The mosquitoes are eating me alive!
Gotcha!
Bardou, shouldn't we tell our employer about the wolves?
There's no need.
The hunters want Haven, not him.
AAHHH
Haven? Why?
What have they told you?
Well...

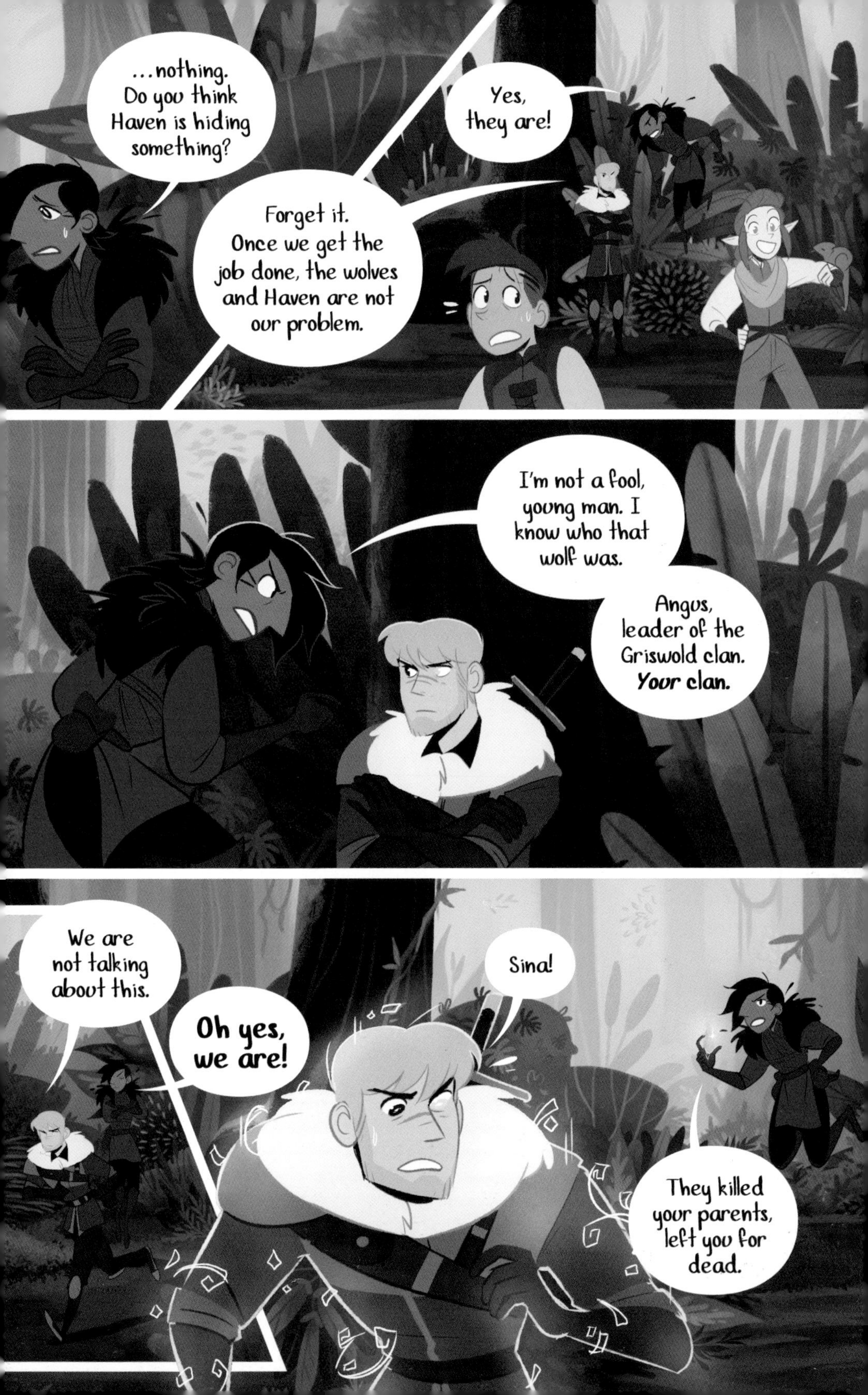
...nothing. Do you think Haven is hiding something?
Yes, they are!
Forget it. Once we get the job done, the wolves and Haven are not our problem.
I'm not a fool, young man. I know who that wolf was.
Angus, leader of the Griswold clan. **Your clan.**
We are not talking about this.
Oh yes, we are!
Sina!
They killed your parents, left you for dead.

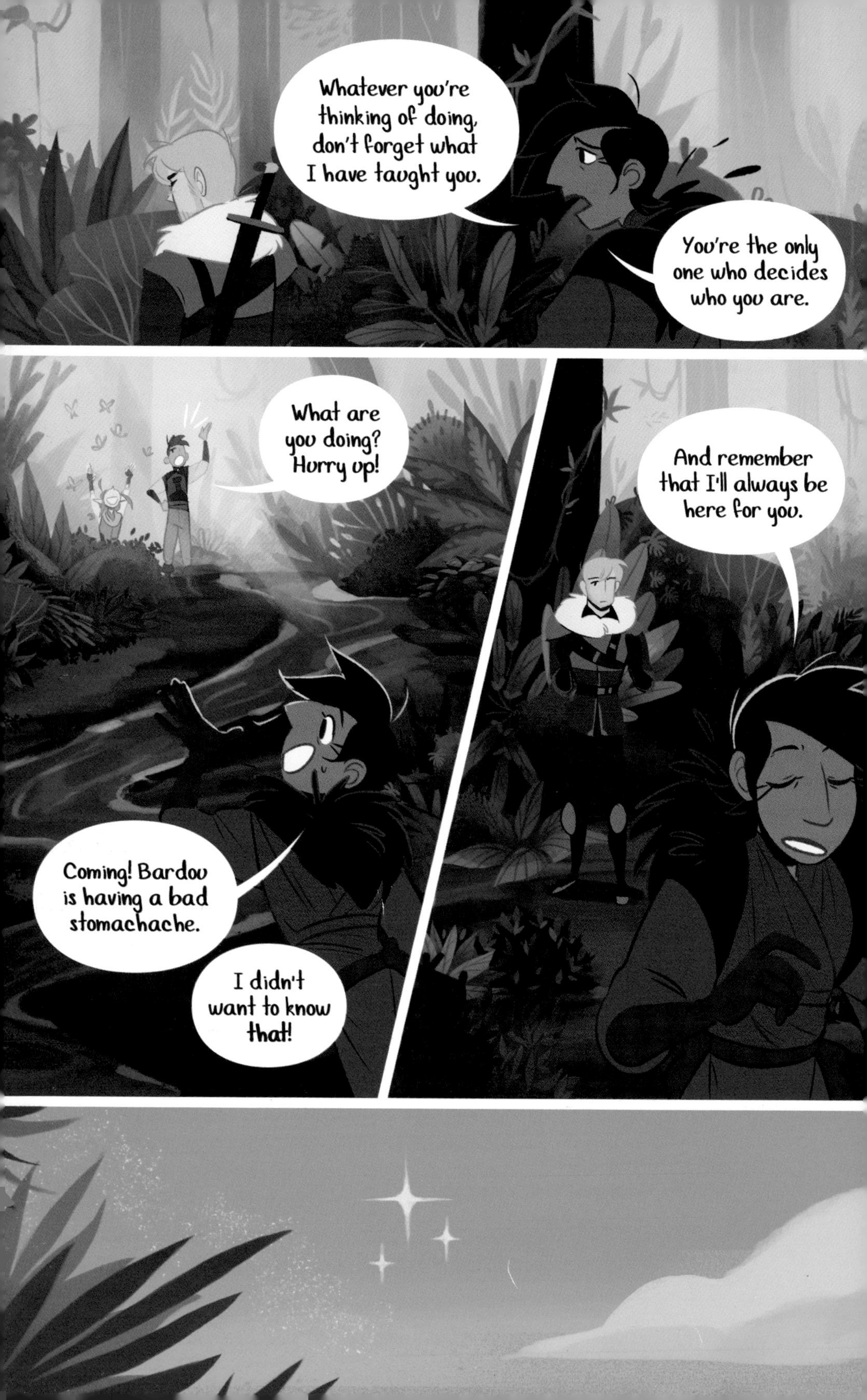
Whatever you're thinking of doing, don't forget what I have taught you.
You're the only one who decides who you are.
What are you doing? Hurry up!
Coming! Bardou is having a bad stomachache.
I didn't want to know that!
And remember that I'll always be here for you.

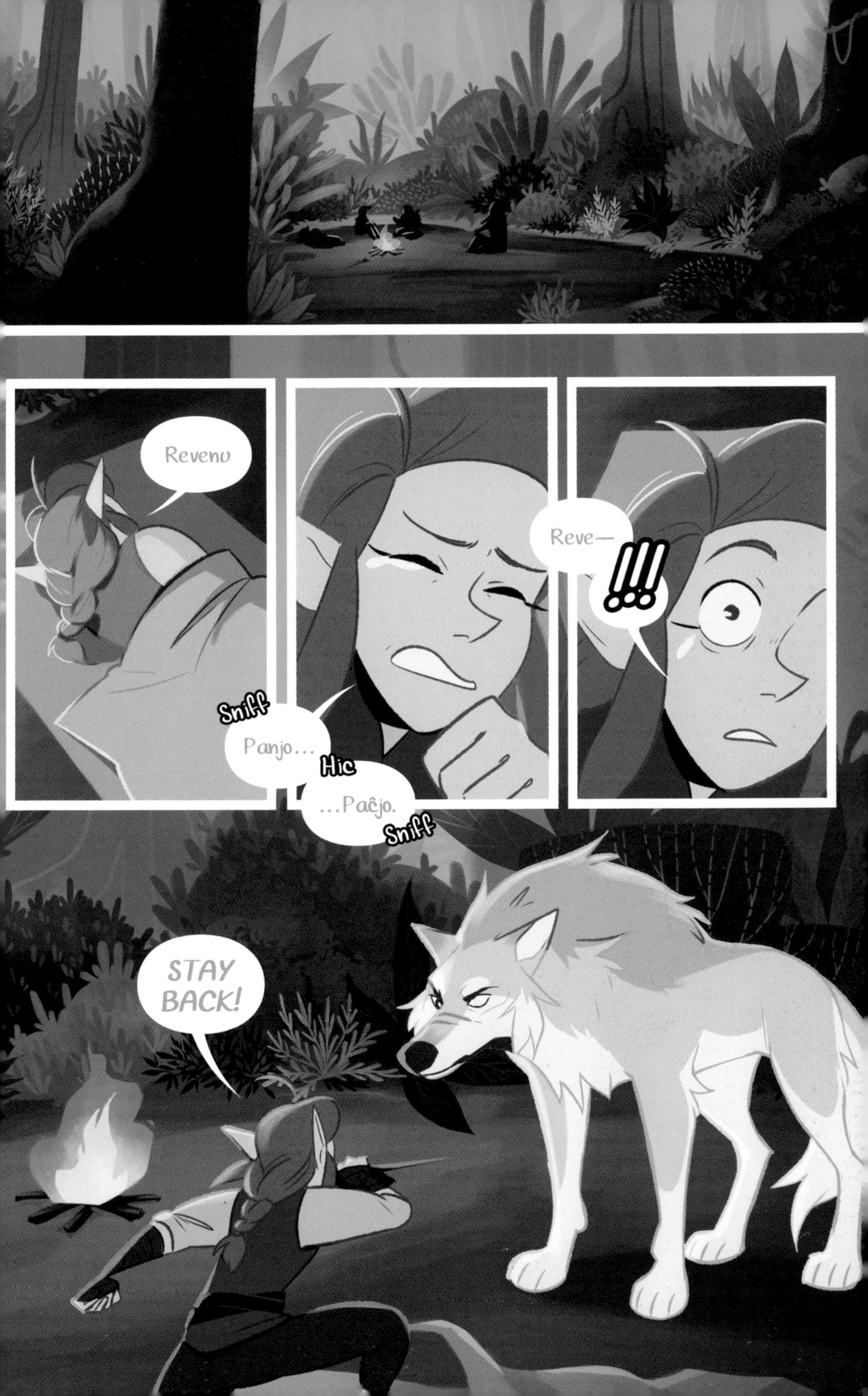
Reveno
Sniff
Panjo...
Hic
...Paĉjo.
Sniff
Reve—
!!!
STAY BACK!

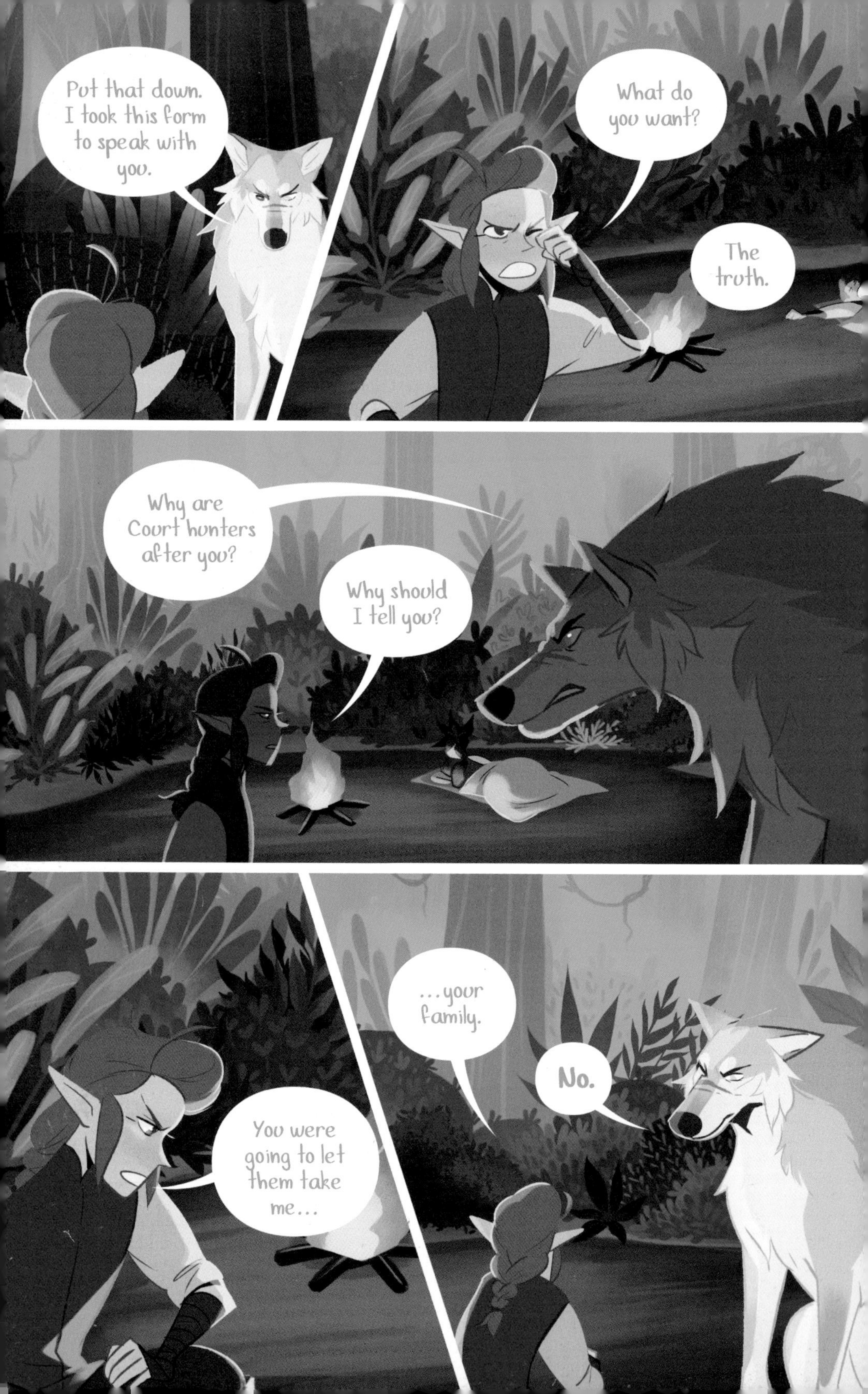
Put that down. I took this form to speak with you.
What do you want?
The truth.
Why are Court hunters after you?
Why should I tell you?
You were going to let them take me...
...your family.
No.

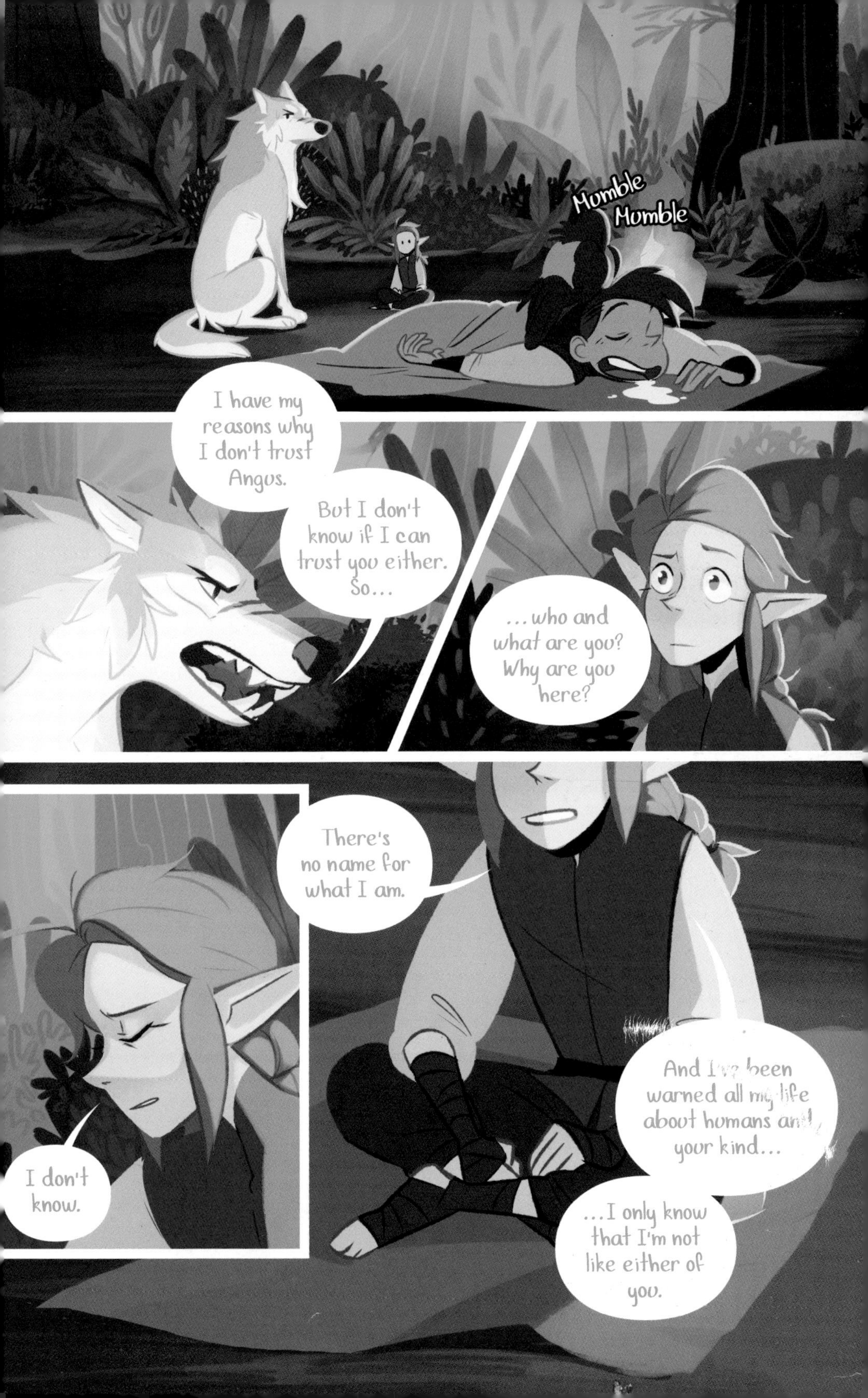
Mumble
Mumble
I have my reasons why I don't trust Angus.
But I don't know if I can trust you either. So...
...who and what are you? Why are you here?
There's no name for what I am.
I don't know.
And I've been warned all my life about humans and your kind...
...I only know that I'm not like either of you.

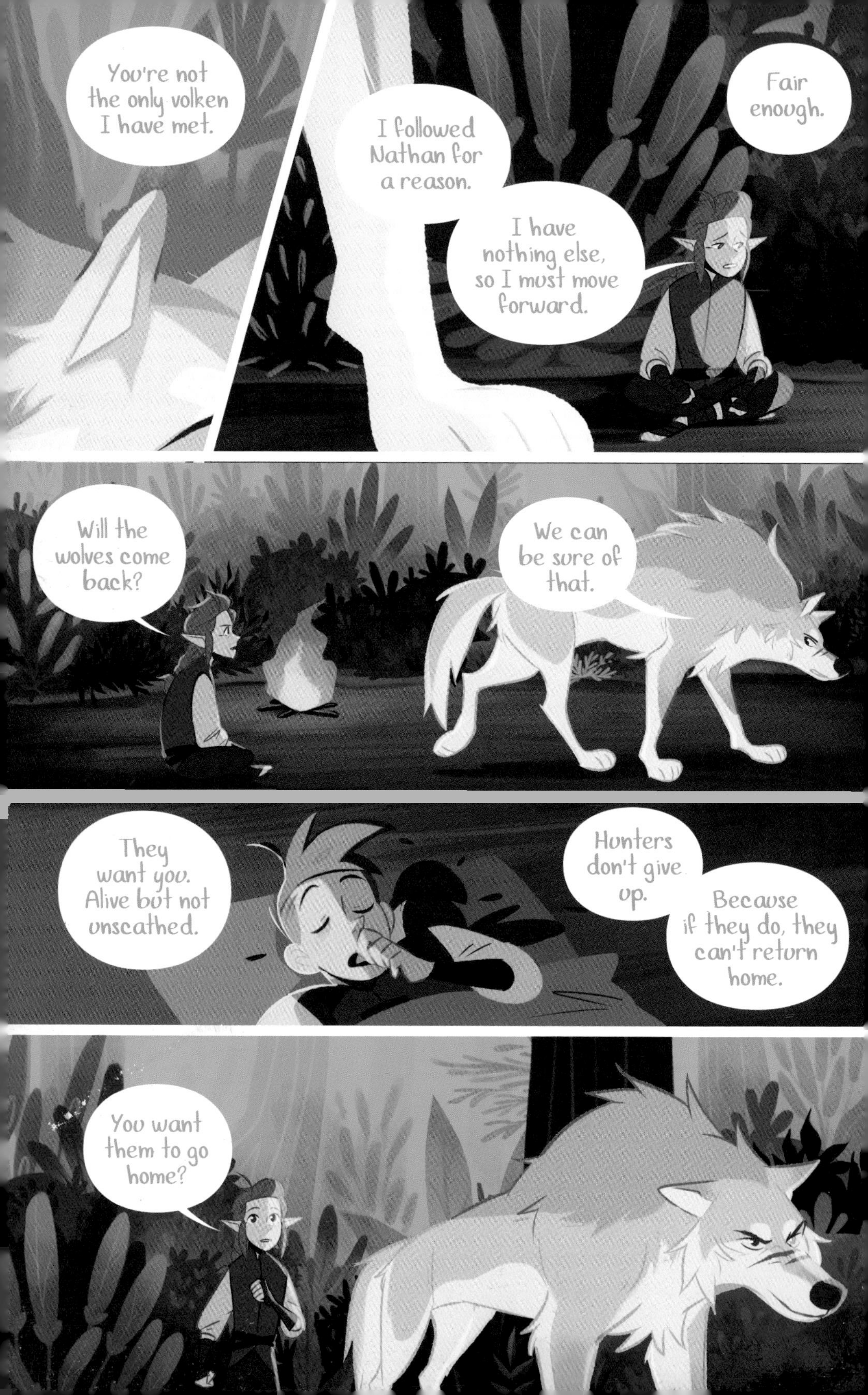
You're not the only volken I have met.
I followed Nathan for a reason.
I have nothing else, so I must move forward.
Fair enough.
Will the wolves come back?
We can be sure of that.
They want you. Alive but not unscathed.
Hunters don't give up.
Because if they do, they can't return home.
You want them to go home?

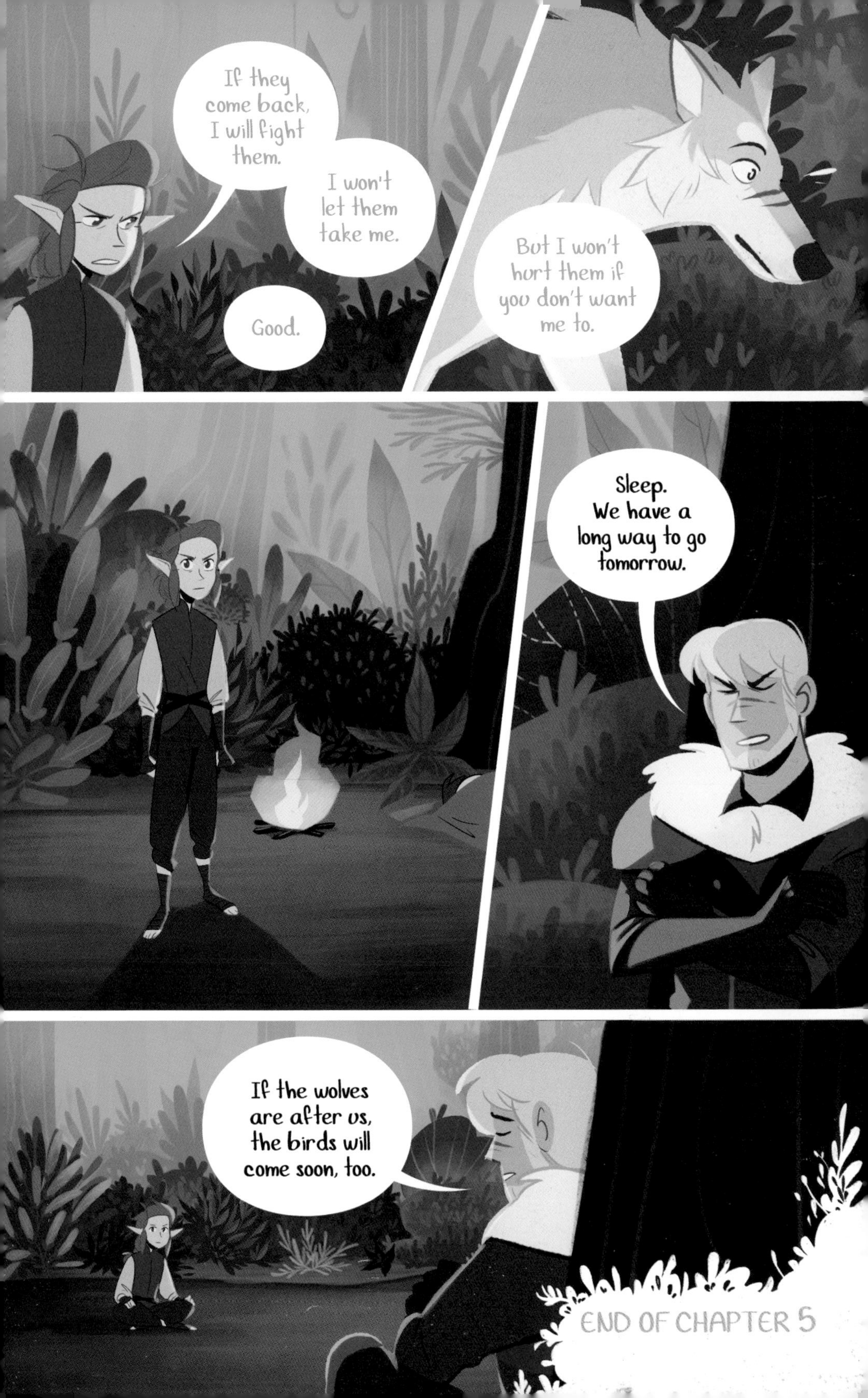

If they come back, I will fight them.
I won't let them take me.
Good.
But I won't hurt them if you don't want me to.
Sleep. We have a long way to go tomorrow.
If the wolves are after us, the birds will come soon, too.
END OF CHAPTER 5

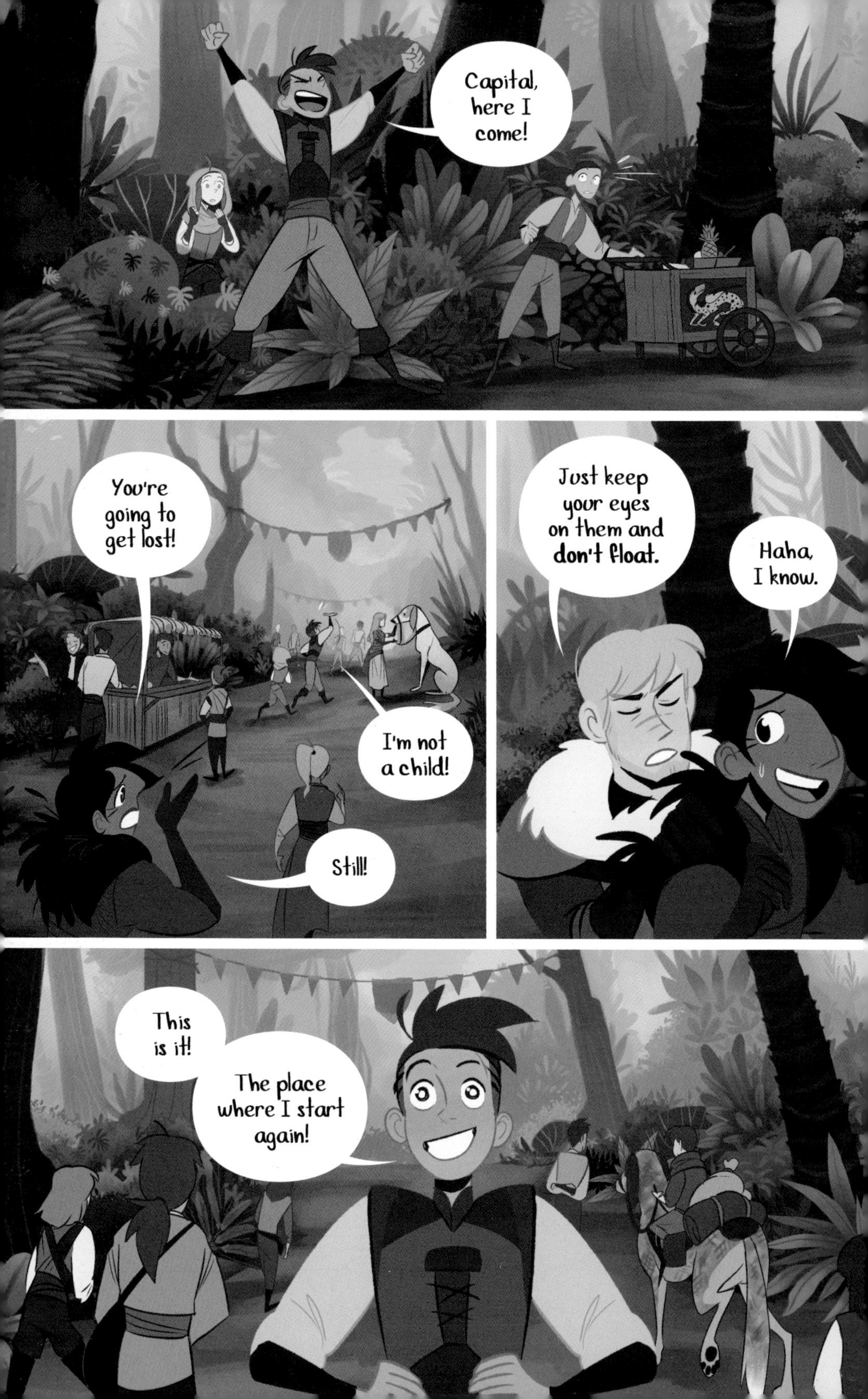
Capital, here I come!
You're going to get lost!
I'm not a child!
Still!
Just keep your eyes on them and **don't float.**
Haha, I know.
This is it!
The place where I start again!

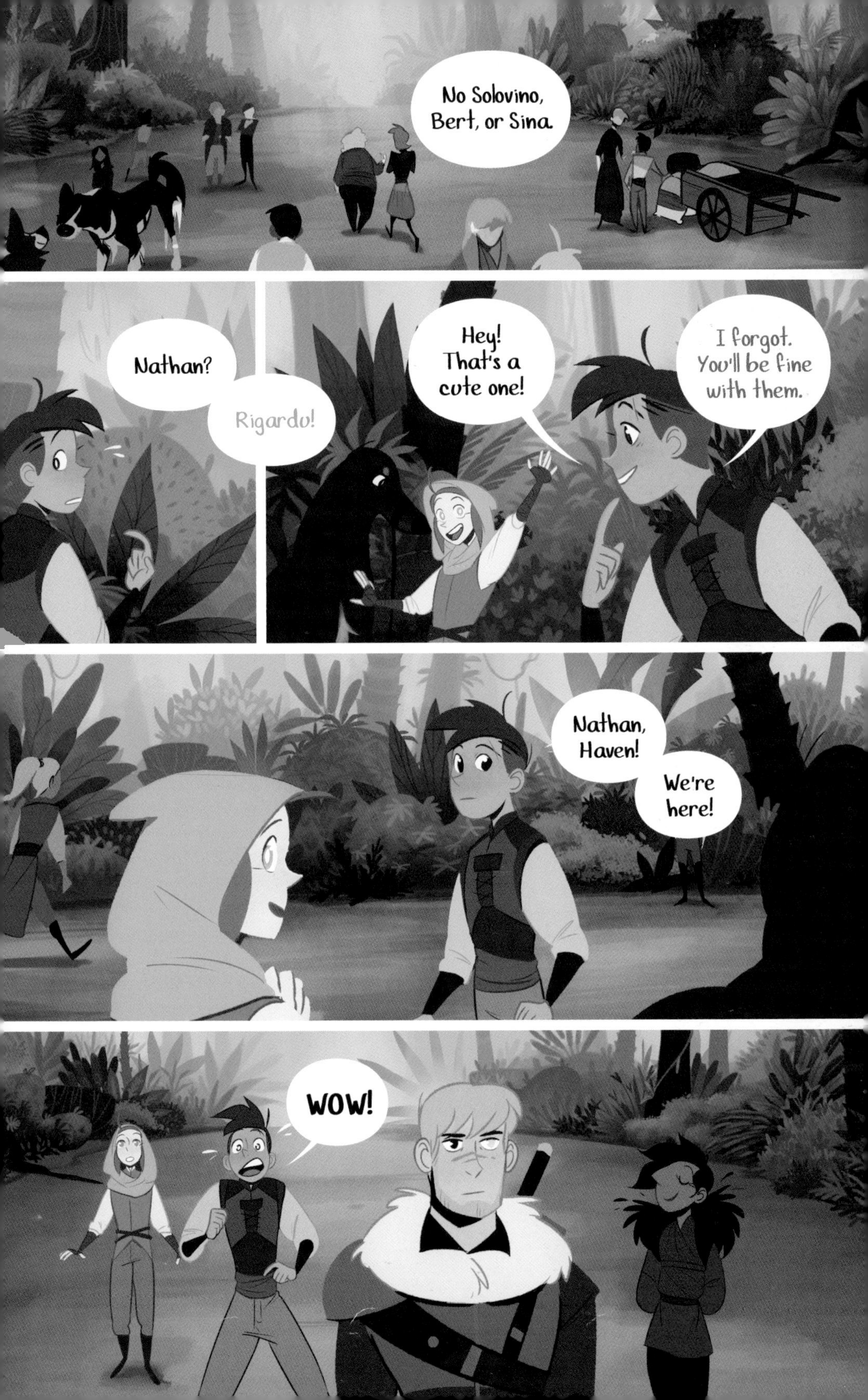
No Solovino, Bert, or Sina.
Nathan?
Rigardo!
Hey! That's a cute one!
I forgot. You'll be fine with them.
Nathan, Haven!
We're here!
WOW!

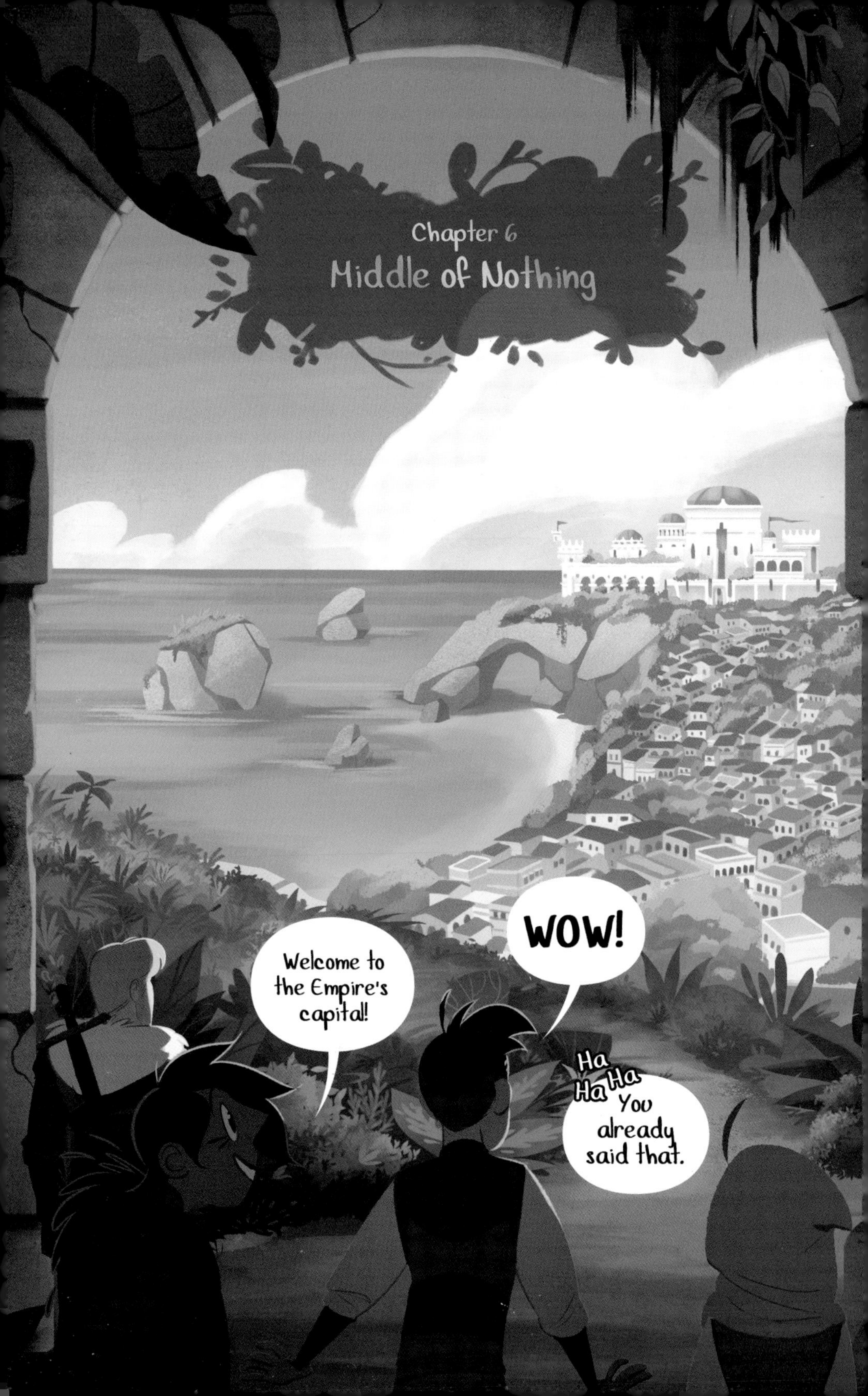
Chapter 6
Middle of Nothing
Welcome to the Empire's capital!
WOW!
Ha Ha Ha
You already said that.

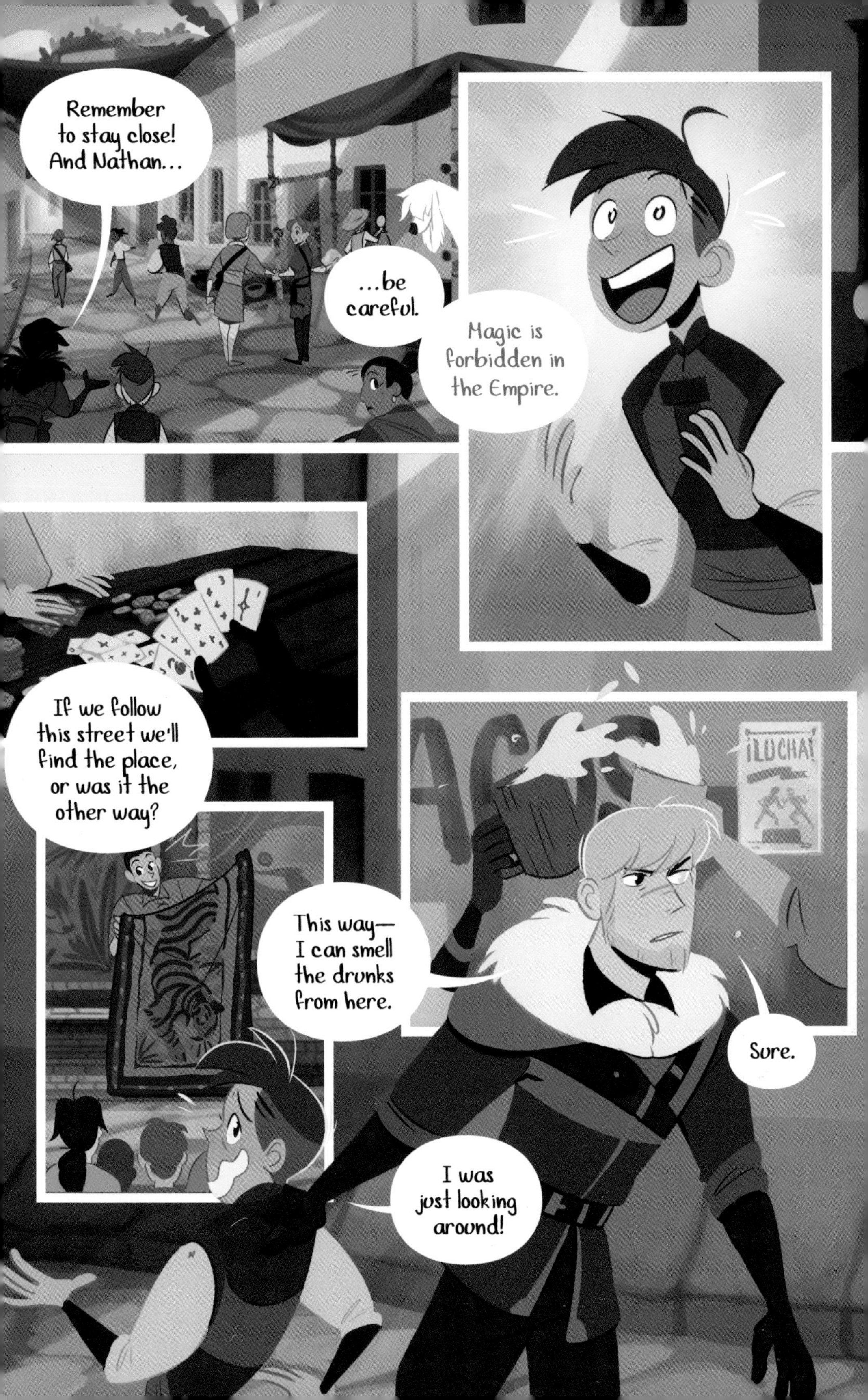
Remember to stay close! And Nathan...
...be careful.
Magic is forbidden in the Empire.
¡LUCHA!
If we follow this street we'll find the place, or was it the other way?
This way— I can smell the drunks from here.
Sure.
I was just looking around!

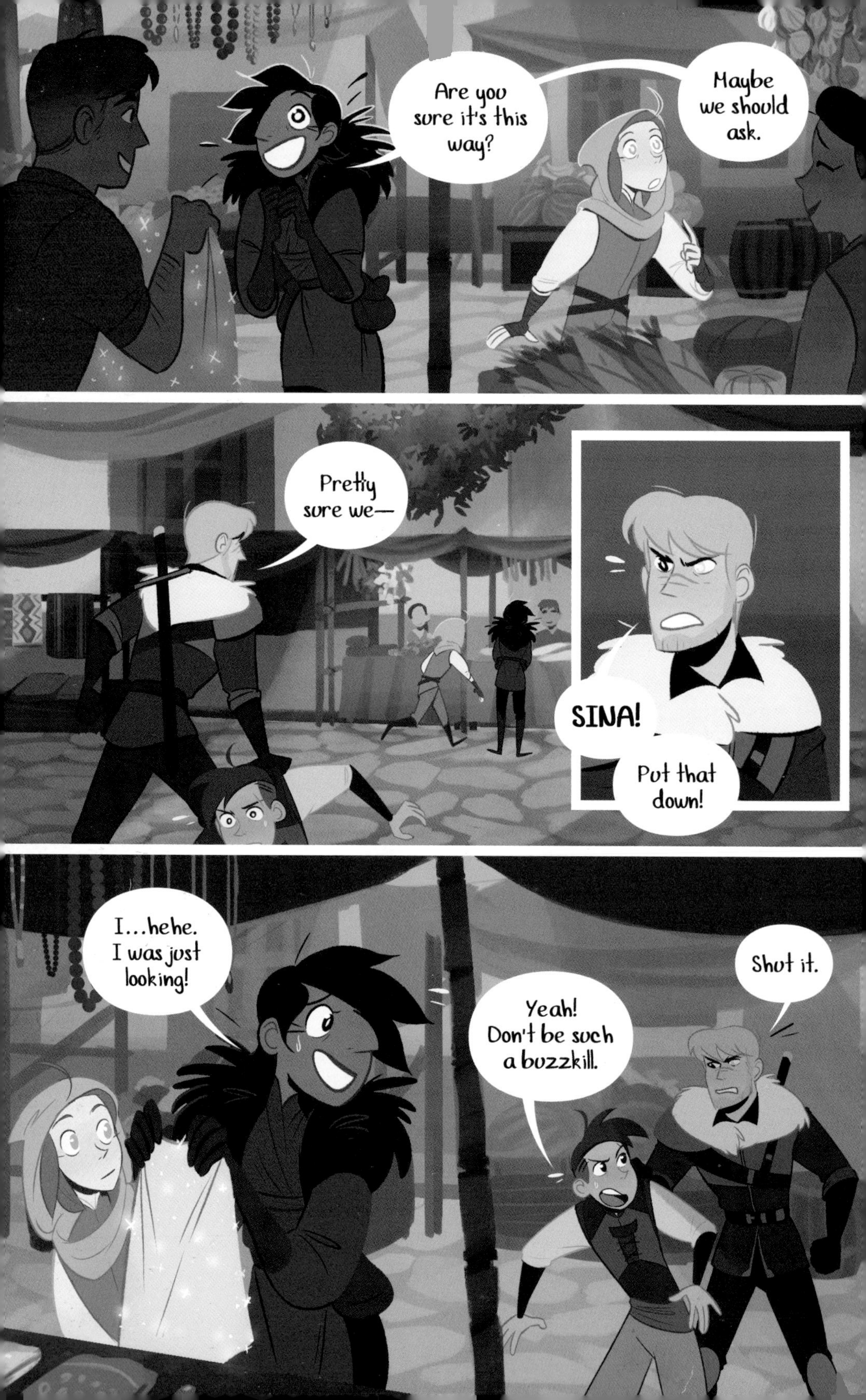
Are you sure it's this way?
Maybe we should ask.
Pretty sure we—
SINA!
Put that down!
I...hehe. I was just looking!
Yeah! Don't be such a buzzkill.
Shut it.

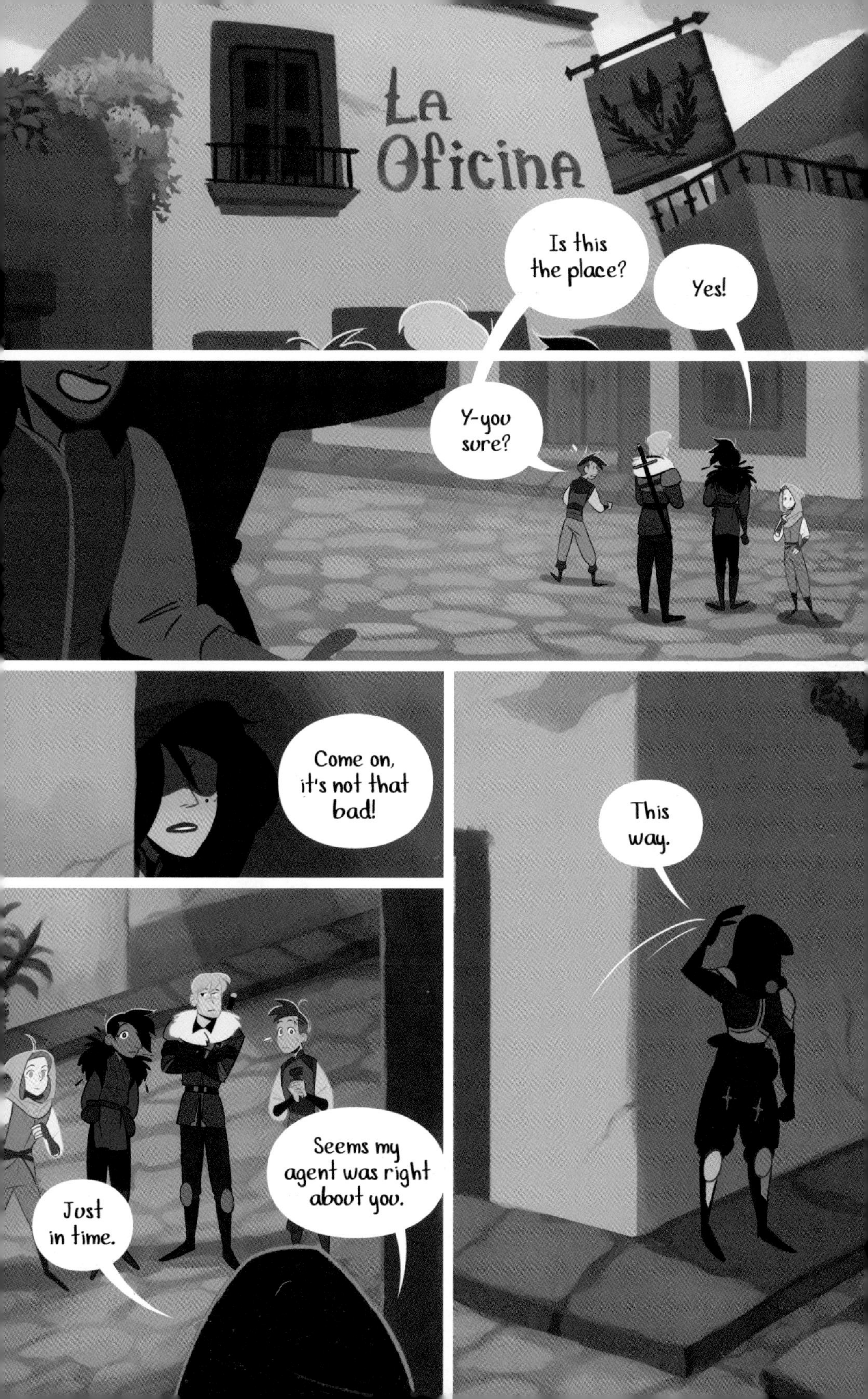
La Oficina
Is this the place?
Yes!
Y-you sure?
Come on, it's not that bad!
This way.
Seems my agent was right about you.
Just in time.

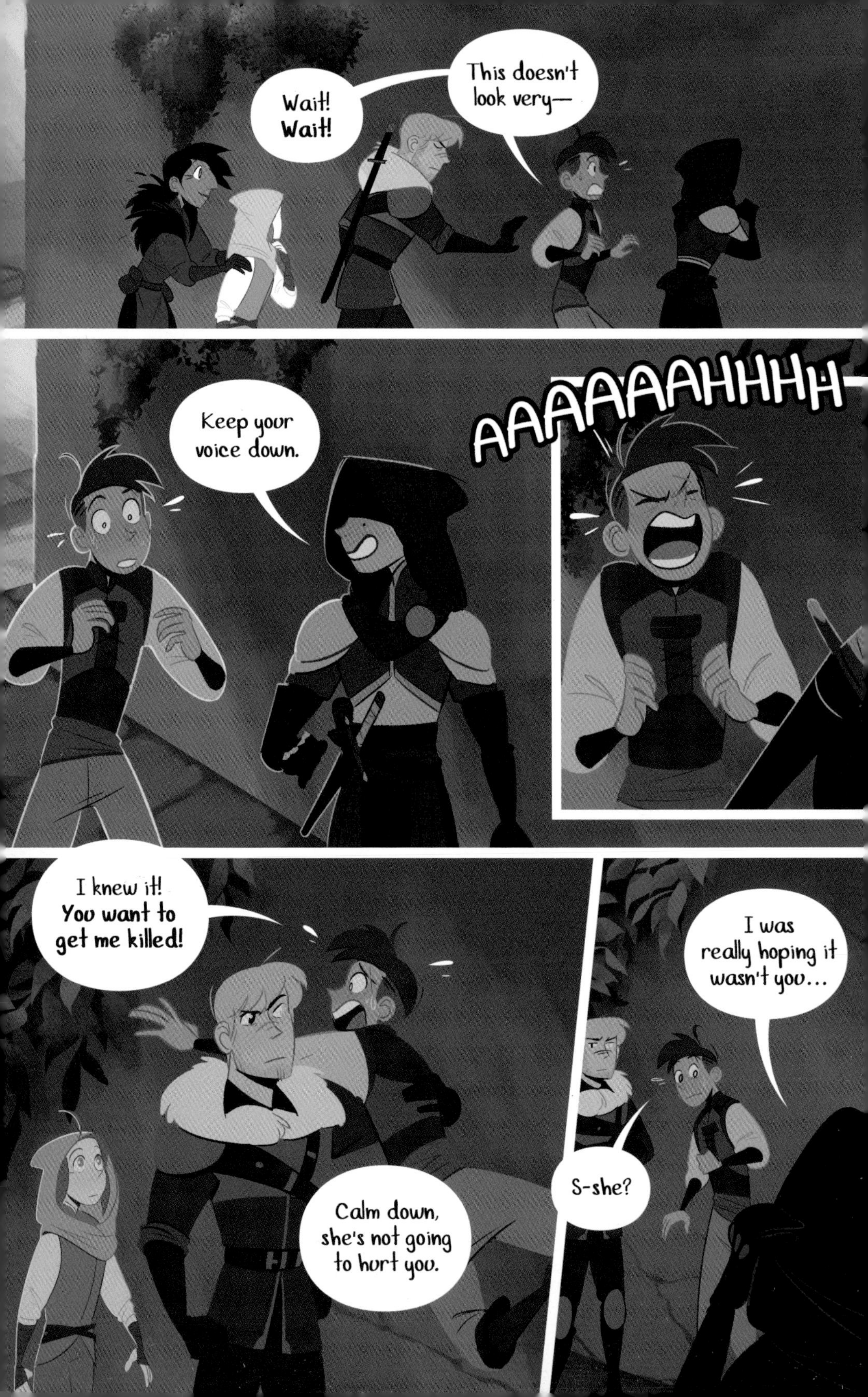
Wait! Wait!
This doesn't look very—
Keep your voice down.
AAAAAAAHHHH
I knew it! You want to get me killed!
Calm down, she's not going to hurt you.
I was really hoping it wasn't you...
S-she?

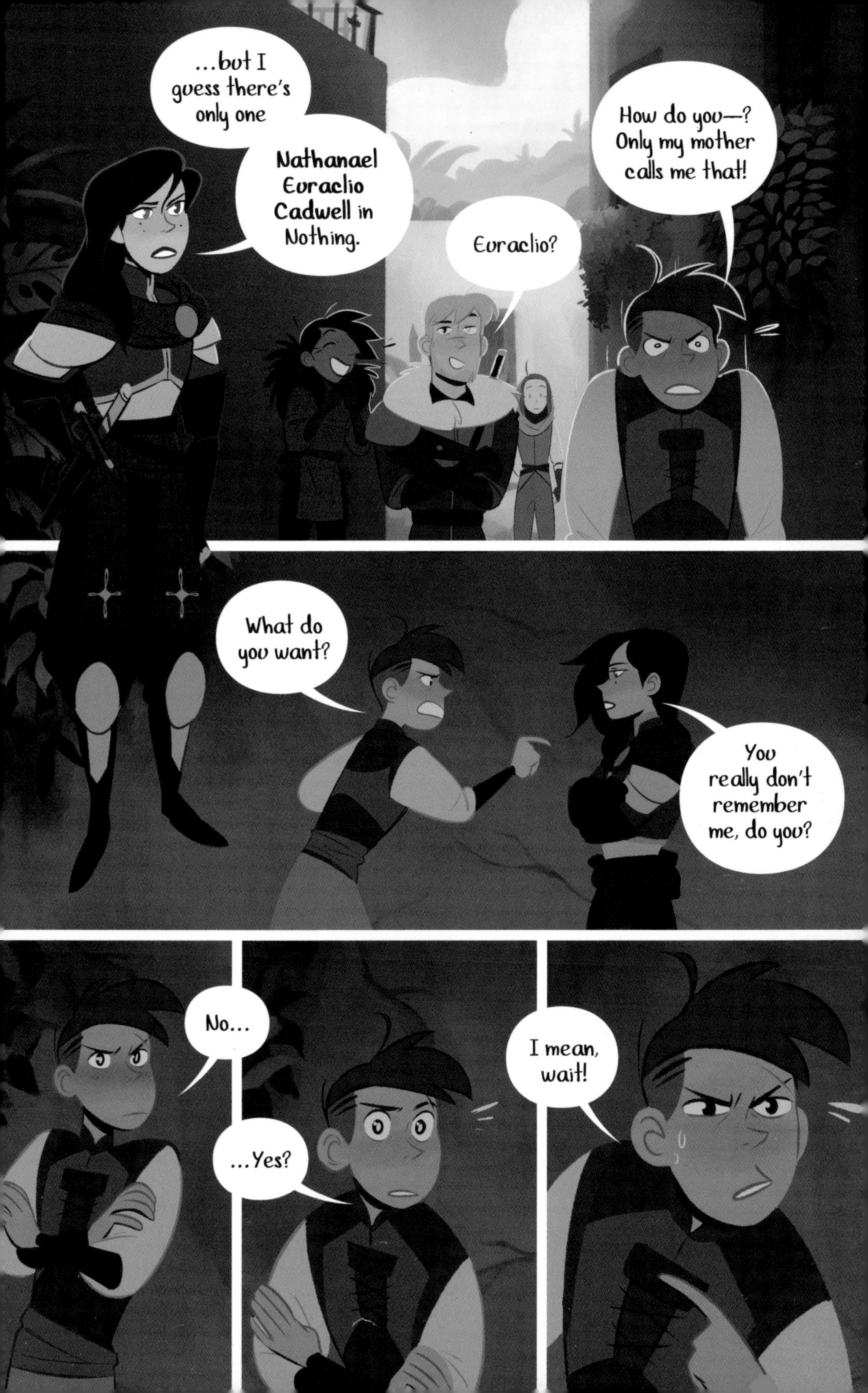
...but I guess there's only one
Nathanael Euraclio Cadwell in Nothing.
Euraclio?
How do you—? Only my mother calls me that!
What do you want?
You really don't remember me, do you?
No...
...Yes?
I mean, wait!

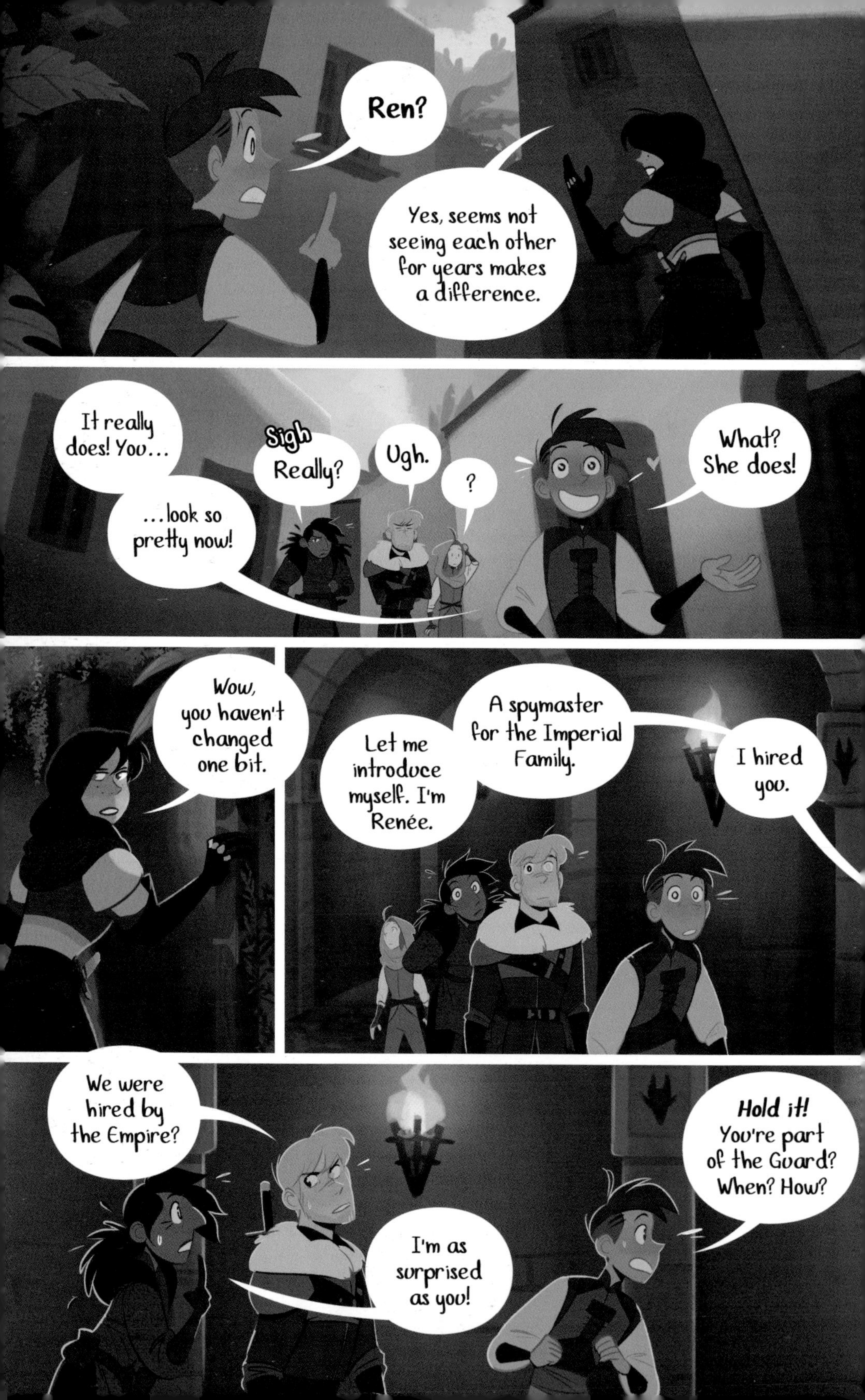
Ren?
Yes, seems not seeing each other for years makes a difference.
It really does! You...
...look so pretty now!
Sigh
Really?
Ugh.
?
What? She does!
Wow, you haven't changed one bit.
Let me introduce myself. I'm Renée.
A spymaster for the Imperial Family.
I hired you.
We were hired by the Empire?
I'm as surprised as you!
Hold it! You're part of the Guard? When? How?

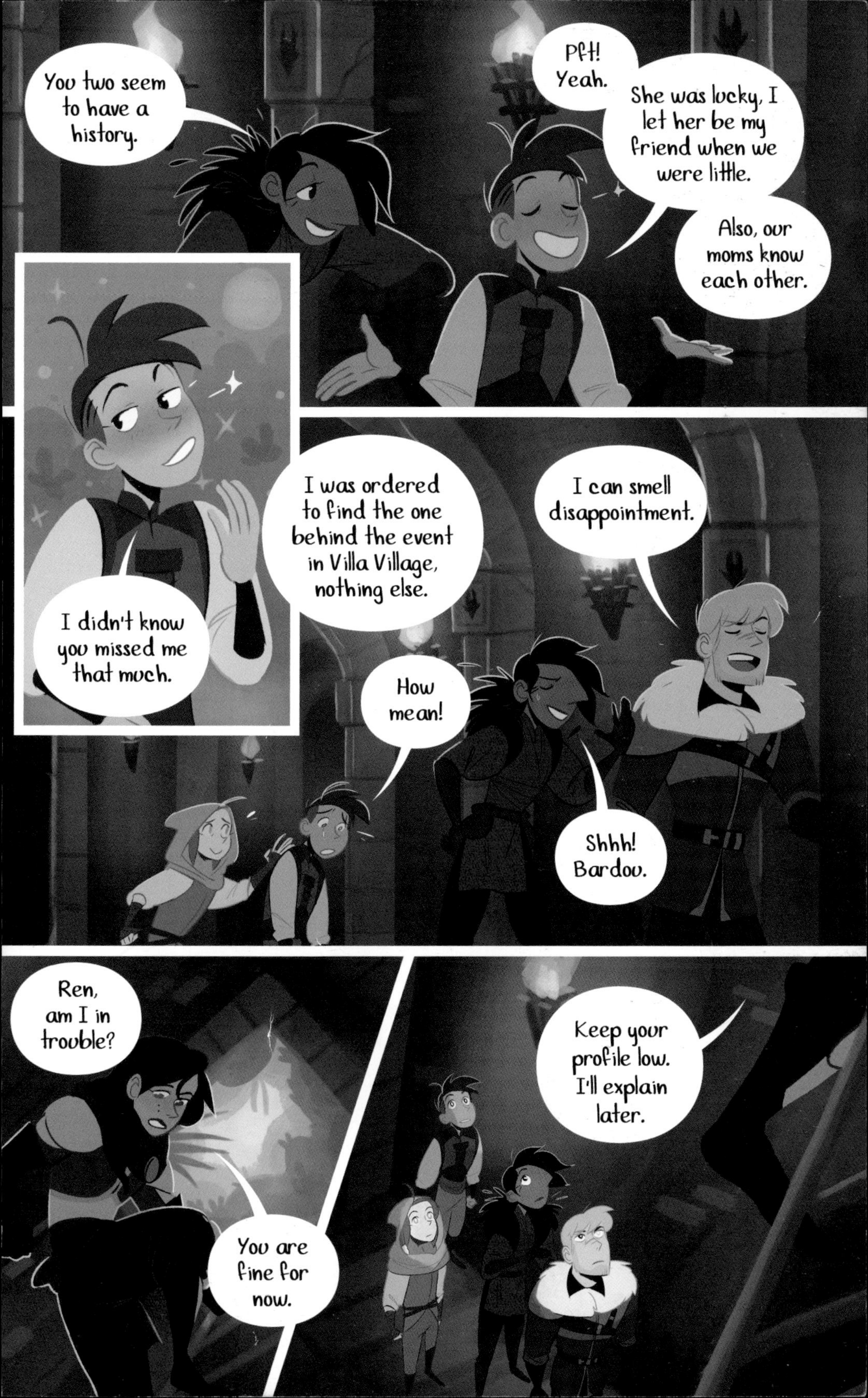
You two seem to have a history.
Pft! Yeah.
She was lucky, I let her be my friend when we were little.
Also, our moms know each other.
I didn't know you missed me that much.
I was ordered to find the one behind the event in Villa Village, nothing else.
I can smell disappointment.
How mean!
Shhh! Bardou.
Ren, am I in trouble?
You are fine for now.
Keep your profile low. I'll explain later.

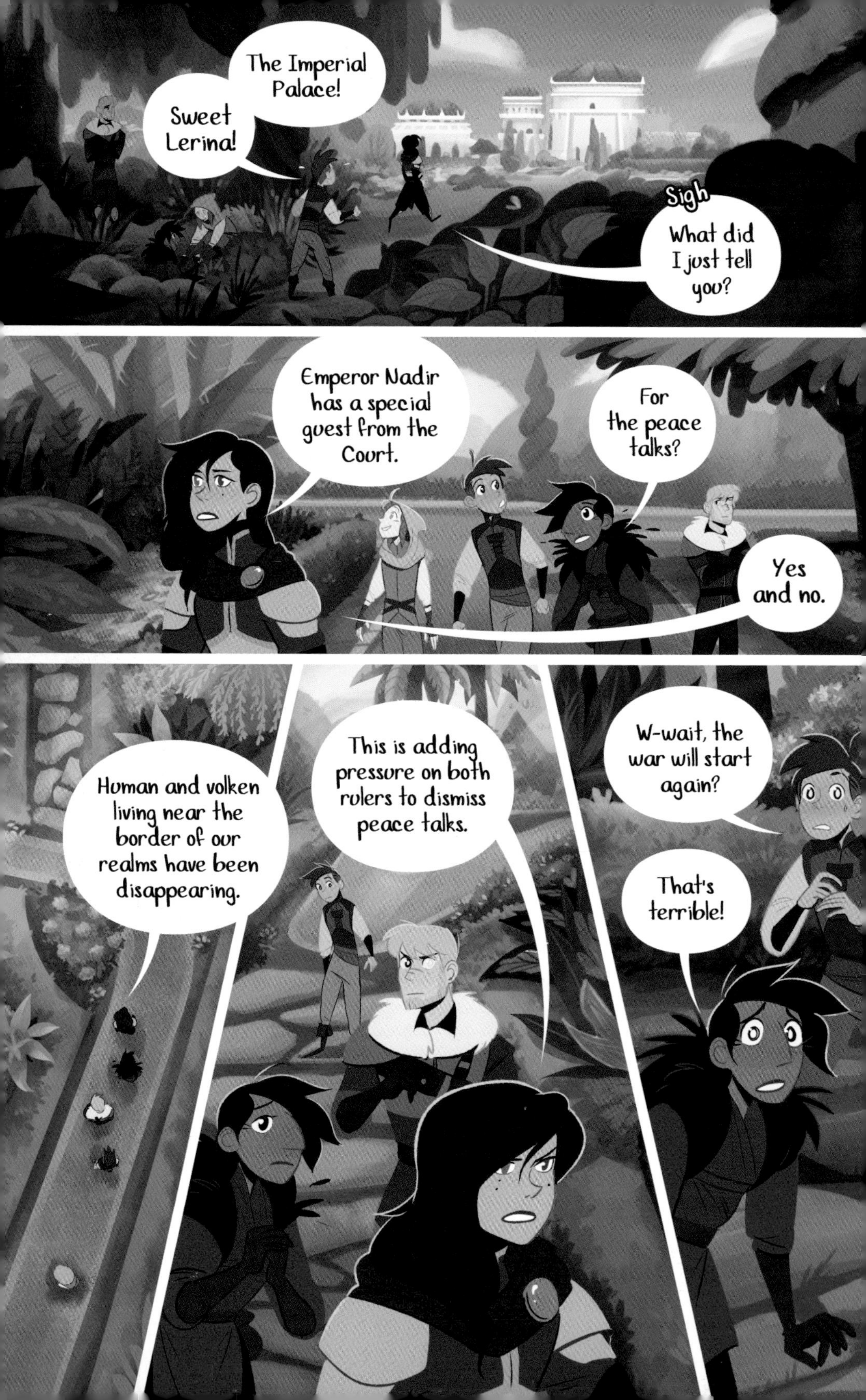
Sweet Lerina!
The Imperial Palace!
Sigh
What did I just tell you?
Emperor Nadir has a special guest from the Court.
For the peace talks?
Yes and no.
Human and volken living near the border of our realms have been disappearing.
This is adding pressure on both rulers to dismiss peace talks.
W-wait, the war will start again?
That's terrible!

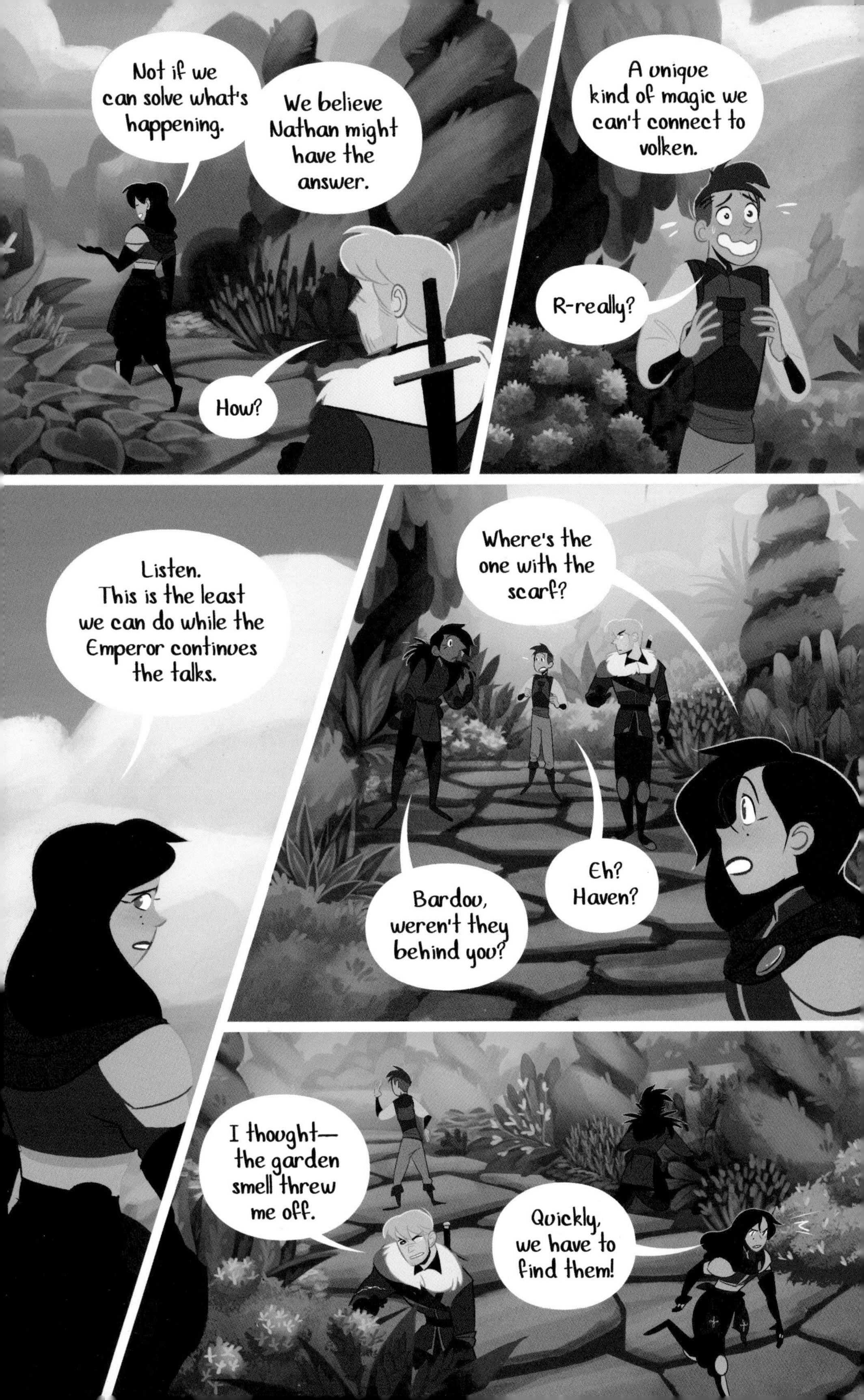
Not if we can solve what's happening.
We believe Nathan might have the answer.
How?
A unique kind of magic we can't connect to volken.
R-really?
Listen. This is the least we can do while the Emperor continues the talks.
Where's the one with the scarf?
Bardou, weren't they behind you?
Eh? Haven?
I thought— the garden smell threw me off.
Quickly, we have to find them!

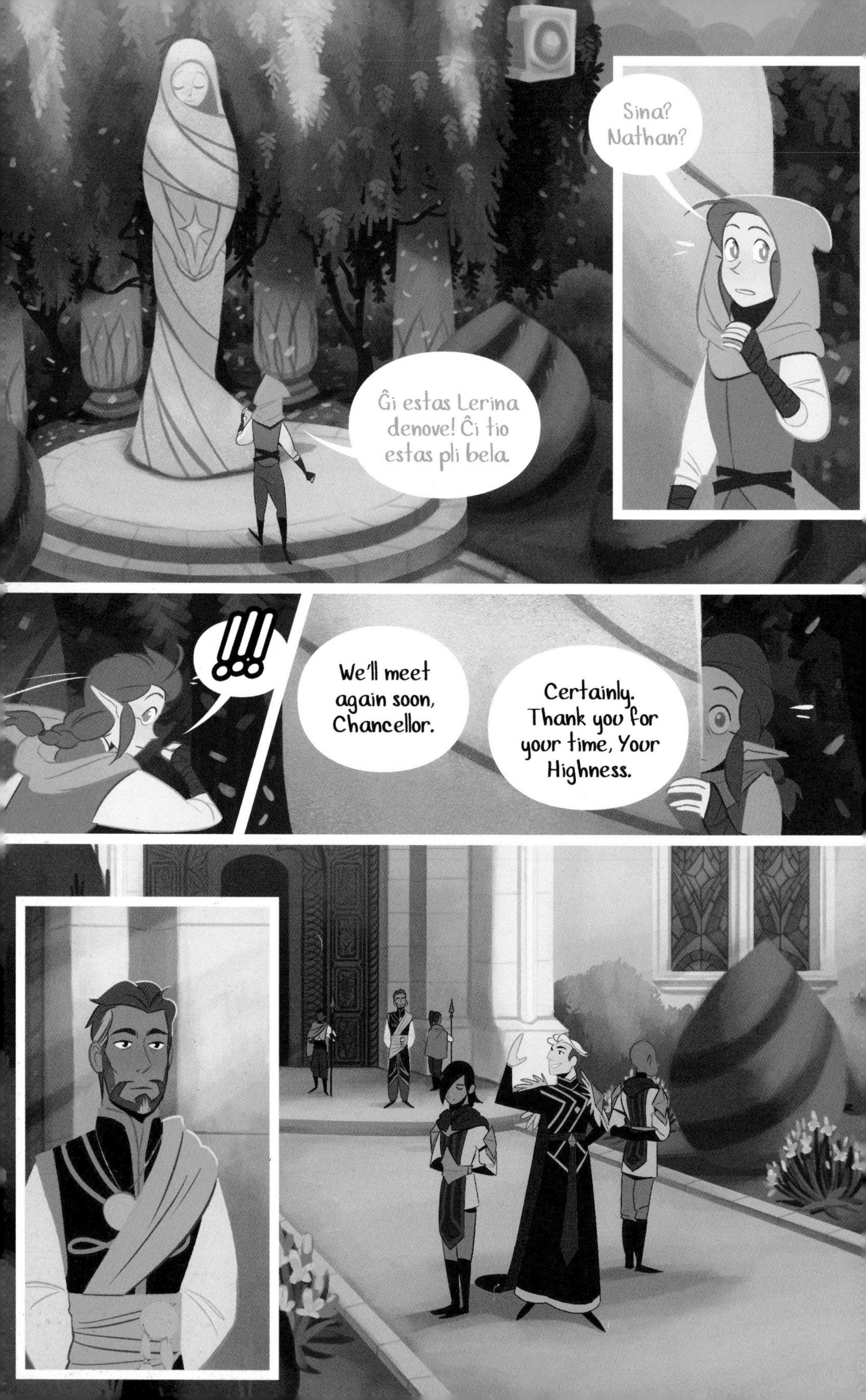
Ĝi estas Lerina denove! Ĉi tio estas pli bela
Sina? Nathan?
!!!
We'll meet again soon, Chancellor.
Certainly. Thank you for your time, Your Highness.

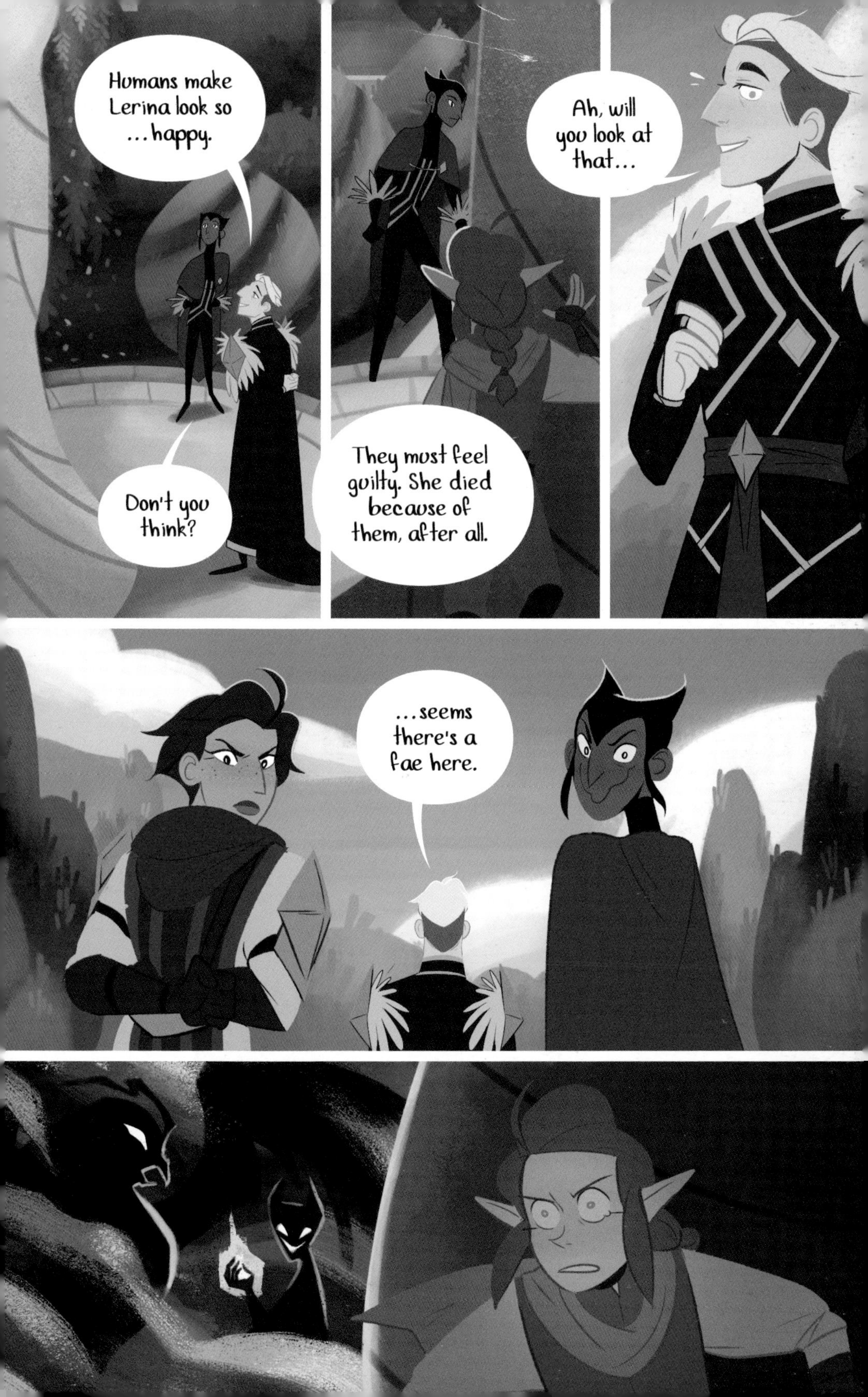
Humans make Lerina look so ...happy.
Don't you think?
They must feel guilty. She died because of them, after all.
Ah, will you look at that...
...seems there's a fae here.

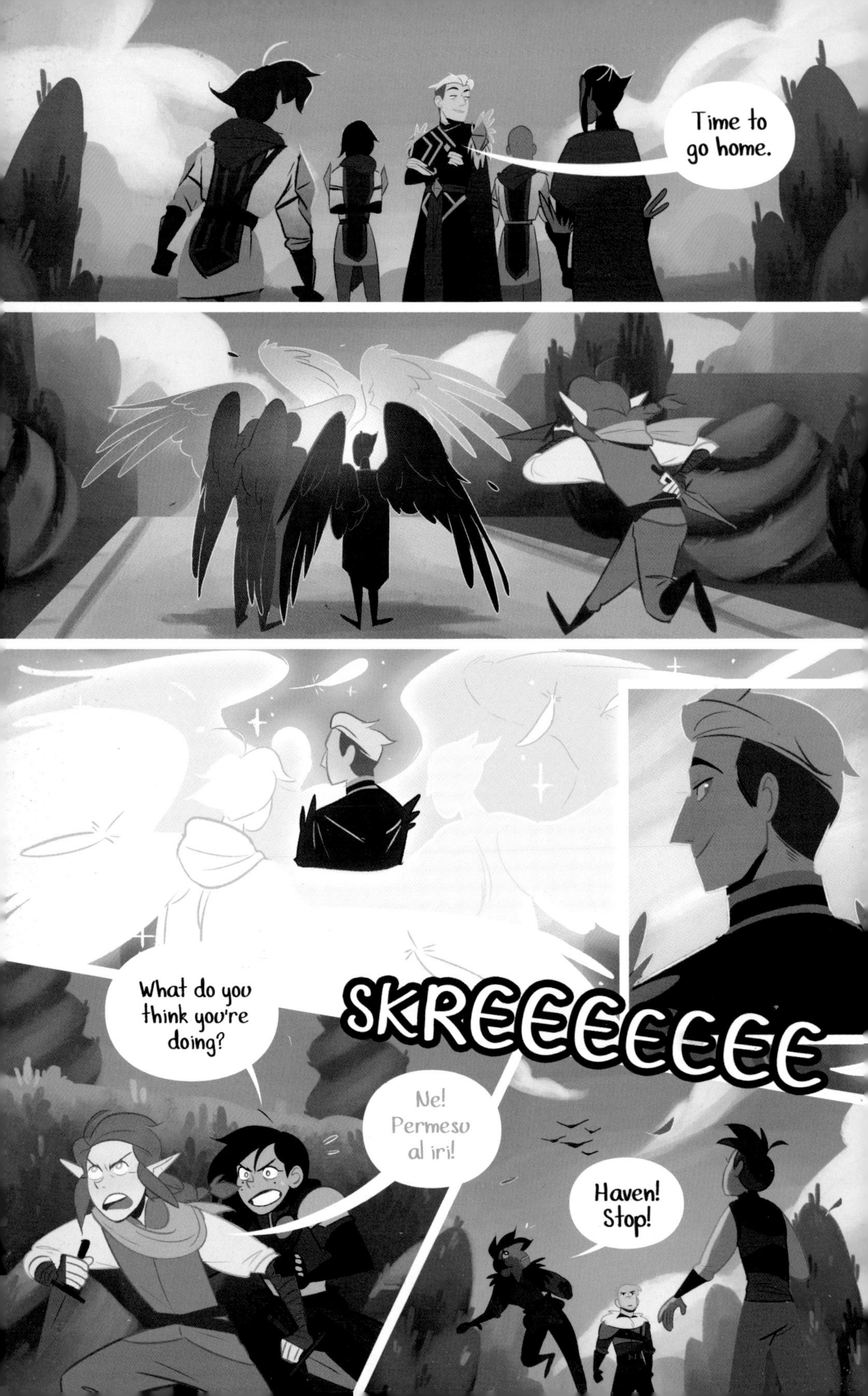
Time to go home.
What do you think you're doing?
SKREEEEEEEE
Ne! Permeso al iri!
Haven! Stop!

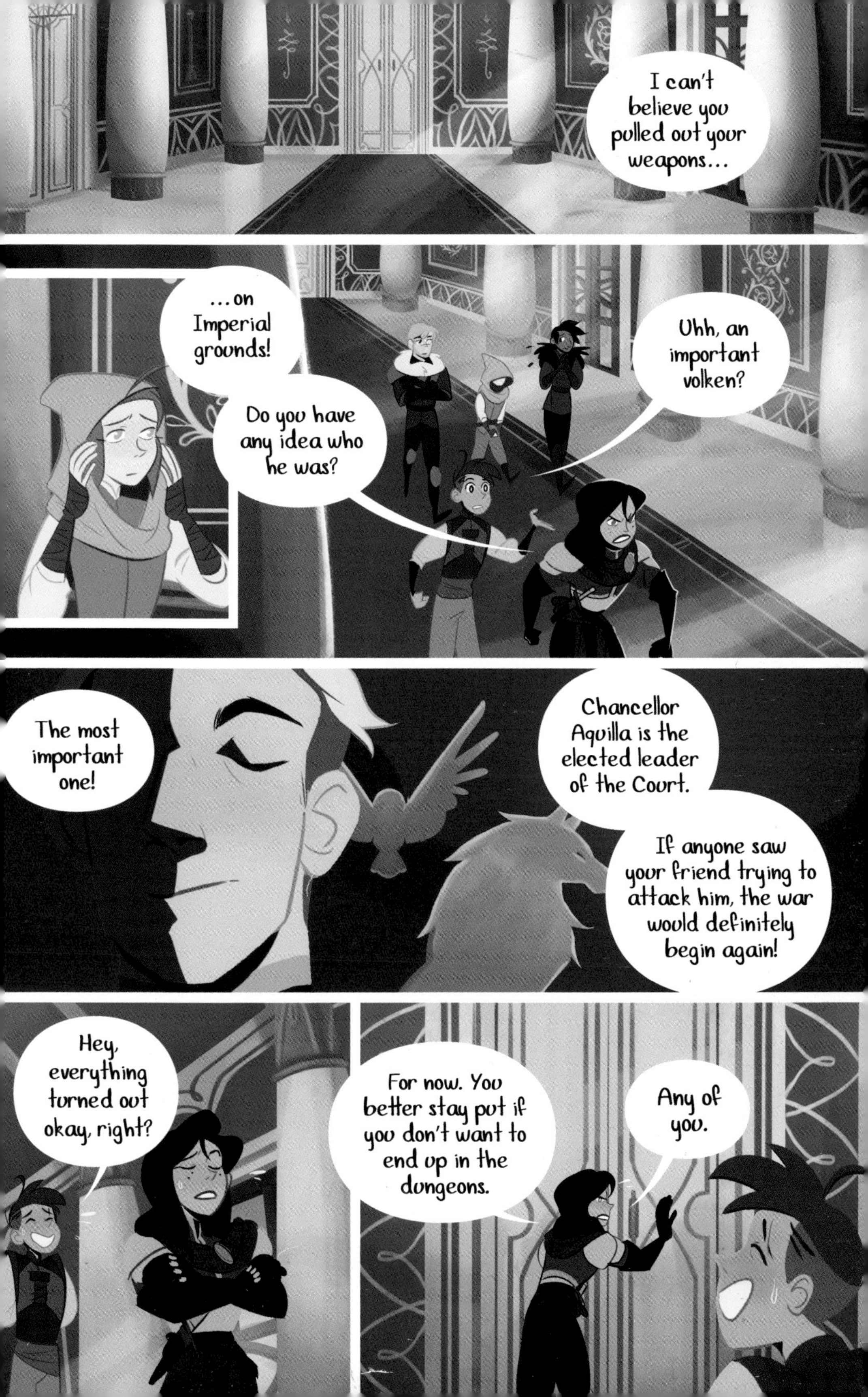
I can't believe you pulled out your weapons...
...on Imperial grounds!
Do you have any idea who he was?
Uhh, an important volken?
The most important one!
Chancellor Aquilla is the elected leader of the Court.
If anyone saw your friend trying to attack him, the war would definitely begin again!
Hey, everything turned out okay, right?
For now. You better stay put if you don't want to end up in the dungeons.
Any of you.

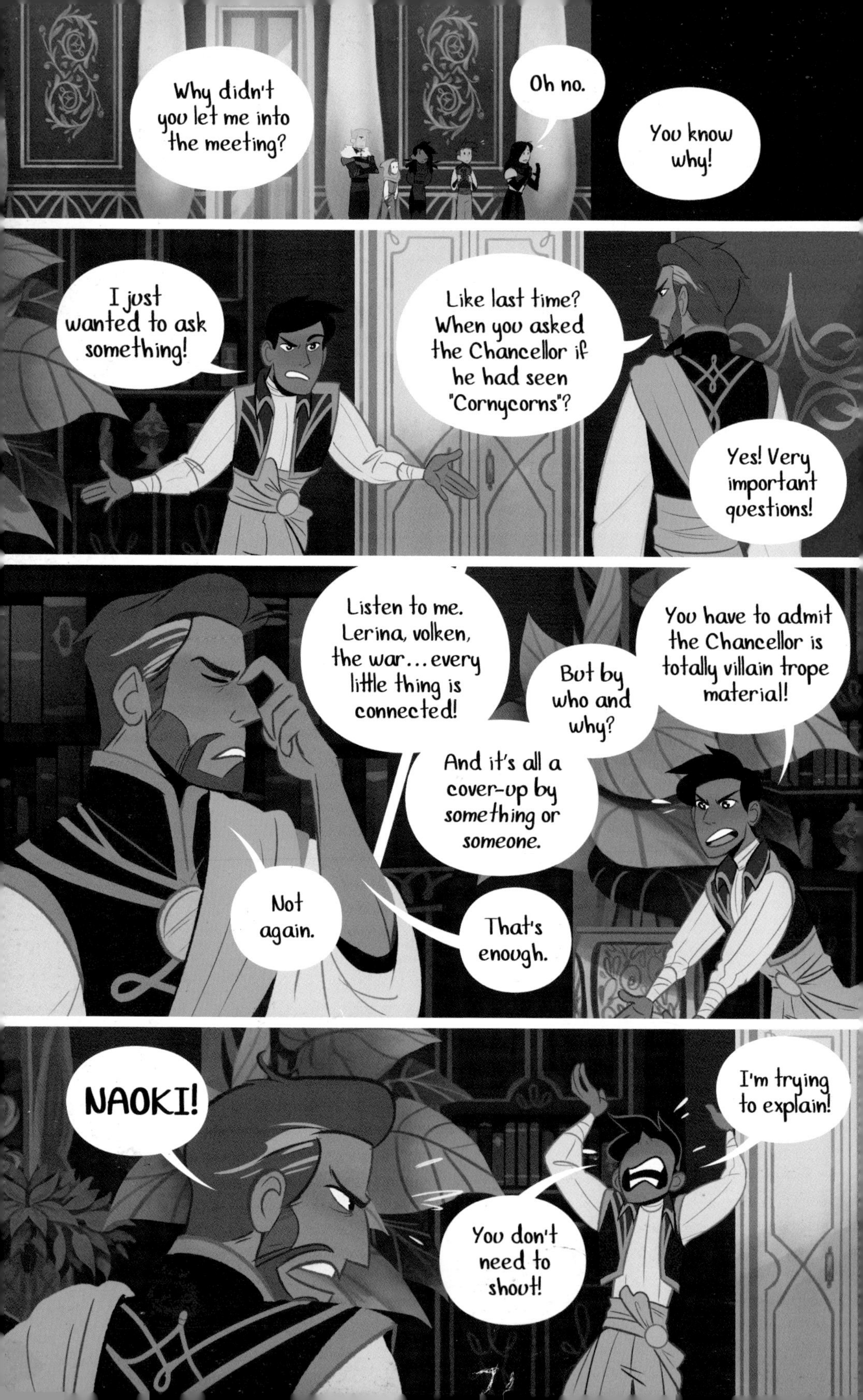

Why didn't you let me into the meeting?
Oh no.
You know why!
I just wanted to ask something!
Like last time? When you asked the Chancellor if he had seen "Cornycorns"?
Yes! Very important questions!
Listen to me. Lerina, volken, the war... every little thing is connected!
But by who and why?
You have to admit the Chancellor is totally villain trope material!
And it's all a cover-up by something or someone.
Not again.
That's enough.
NAOKI!
I'm trying to explain!
You don't need to shout!

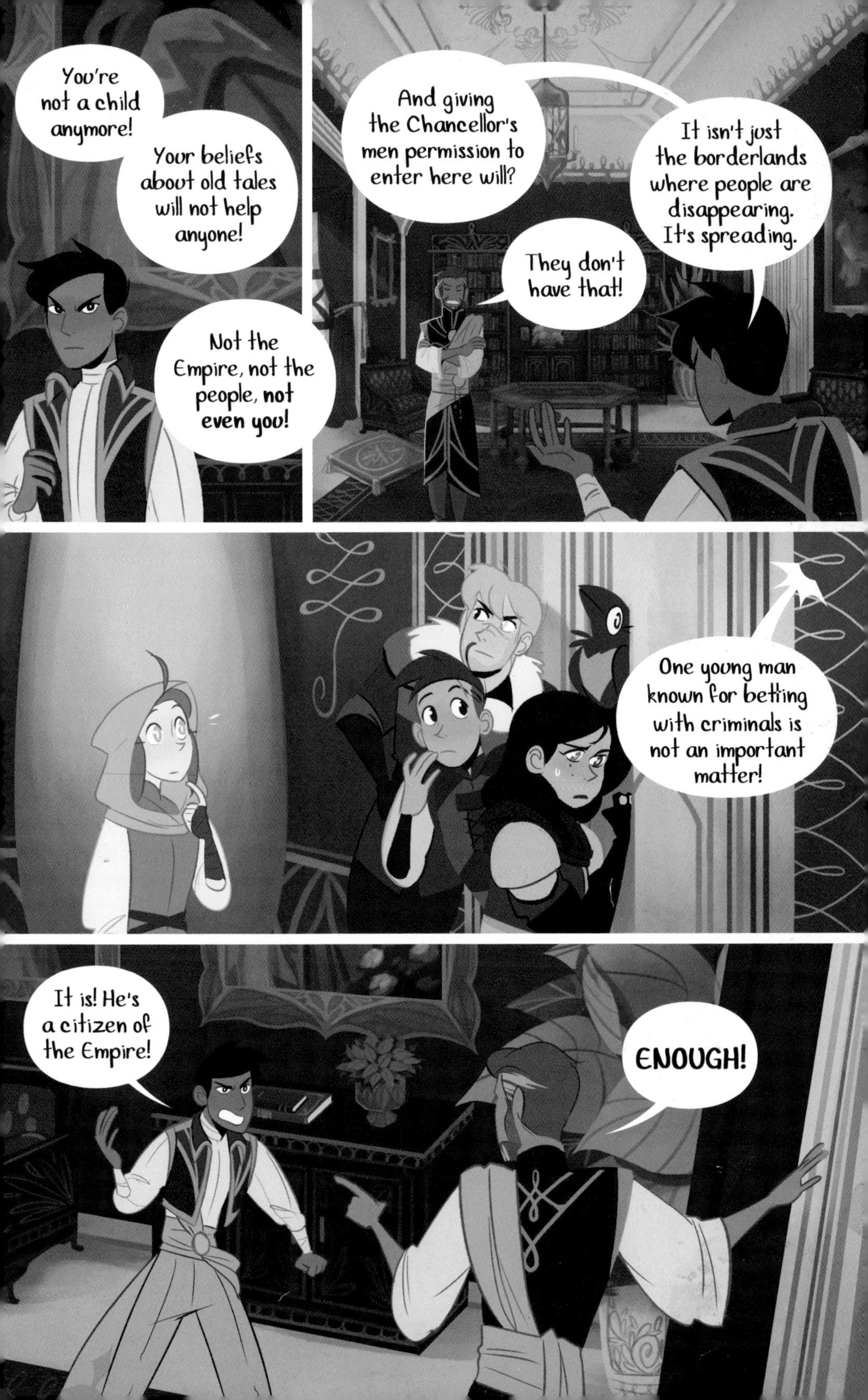
You're not a child anymore!
Your beliefs about old tales will not help anyone!
Not the Empire, not the people, not even you!
And giving the Chancellor's men permission to enter here will?
They don't have that!
It isn't just the borderlands where people are disappearing. It's spreading.
One young man known for betting with criminals is not an important matter!
It is! He's a citizen of the Empire!
ENOUGH!

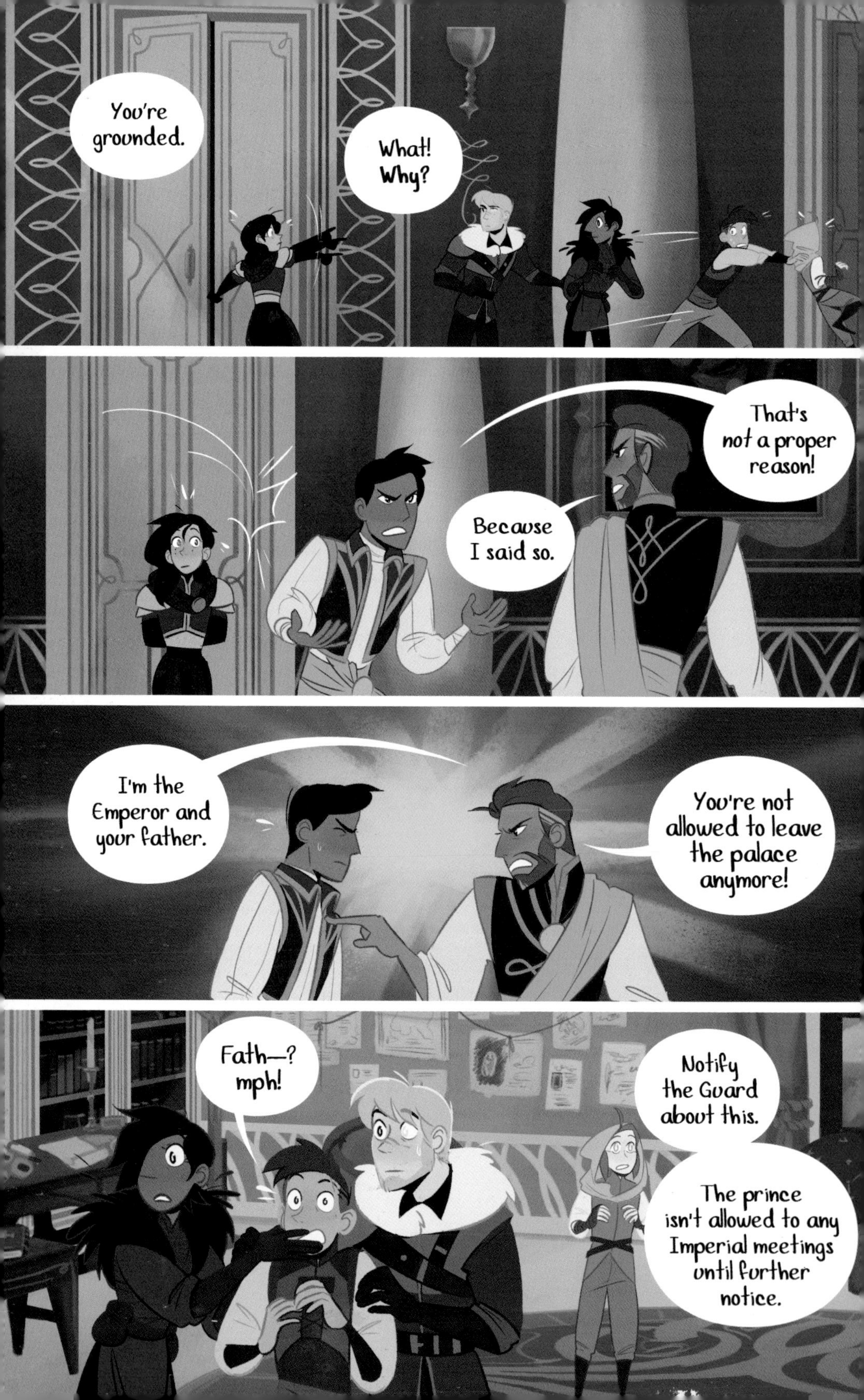
You're grounded.
What! Why?
That's not a proper reason!
Because I said so.
I'm the Emperor and your father.
You're not allowed to leave the palace anymore!
Fath—? mph!
Notify the Guard about this.
The prince isn't allowed to any Imperial meetings until further notice.

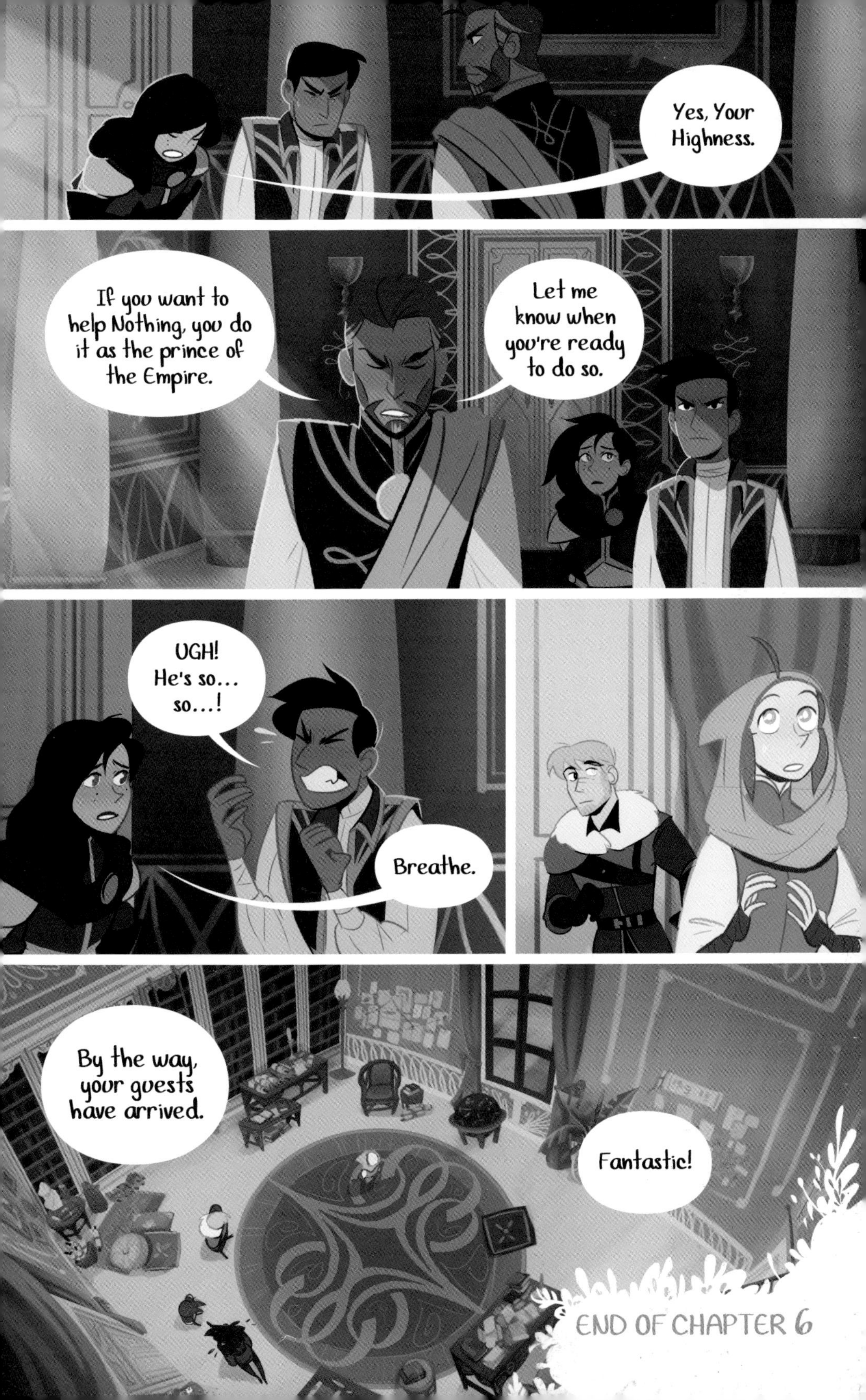
Yes, Your Highness.
If you want to help Nothing, you do it as the prince of the Empire.
Let me know when you're ready to do so.
UGH! He's so... so...!
Breathe.
By the way, your guests have arrived.
Fantastic!
END OF CHAPTER 6

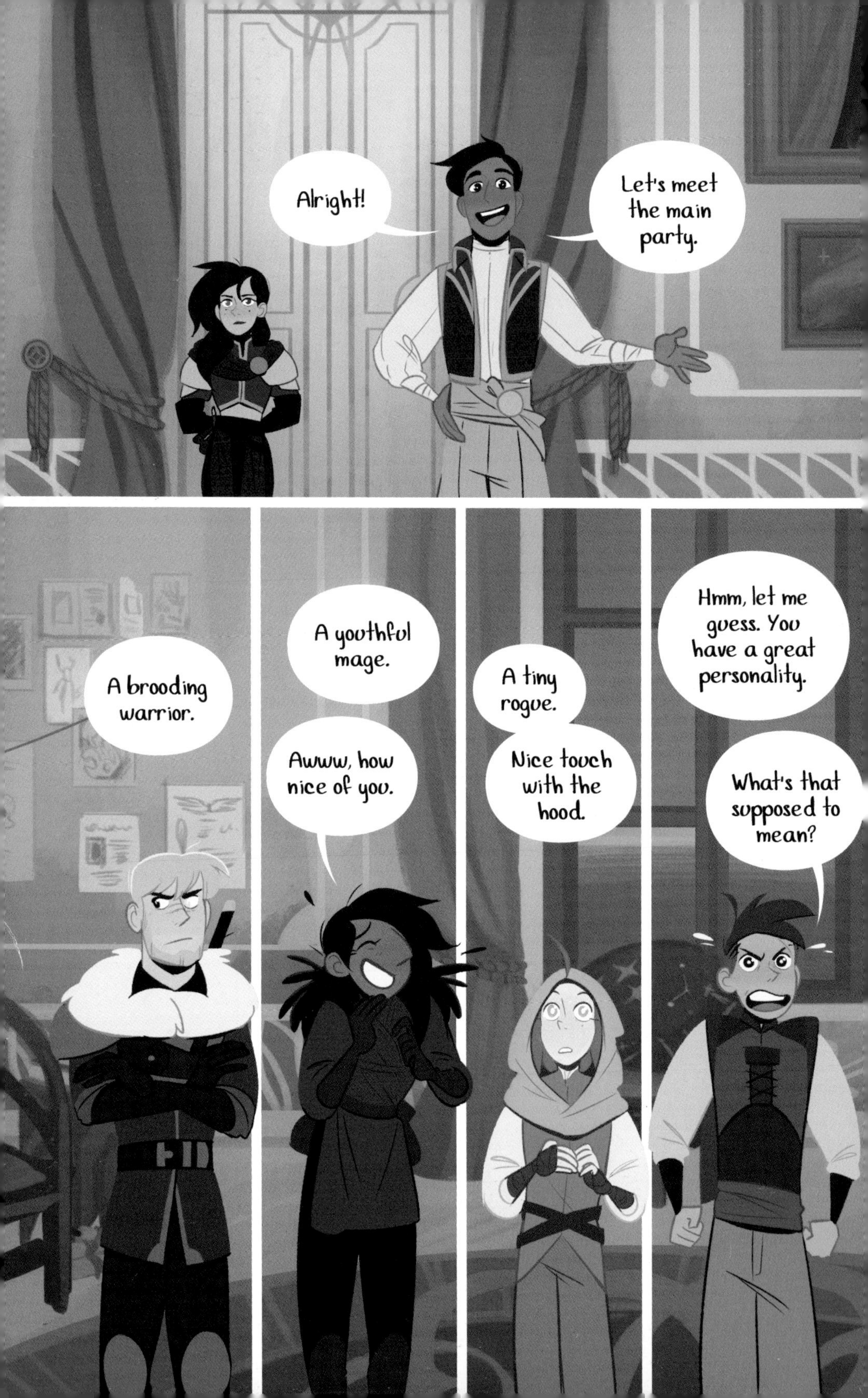
Alright!
Let's meet the main party.
A brooding warrior.
A youthful mage.
Awww, how nice of you.
A tiny rogue.
Nice touch with the hood.
Hmm, let me guess. You have a great personality.
What's that supposed to mean?

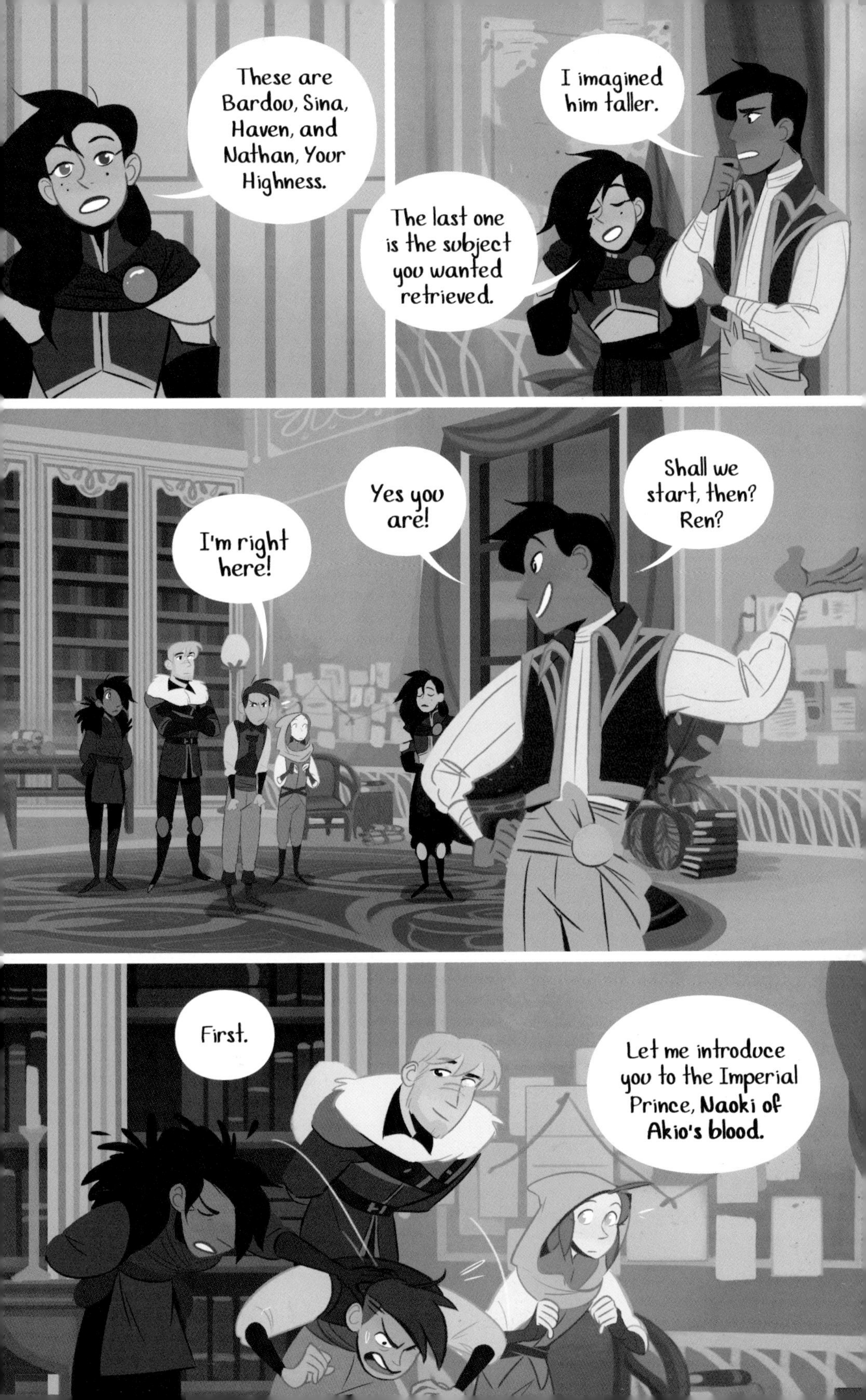
These are Bardou, Sina, Haven, and Nathan, Your Highness.
I imagined him taller.
The last one is the subject you wanted retrieved.
I'm right here!
Yes you are!
Shall we start, then? Ren?
First.
Let me introduce you to the Imperial Prince, **Naoki of Akio's blood.**

Chapter 7
Lerina's Light

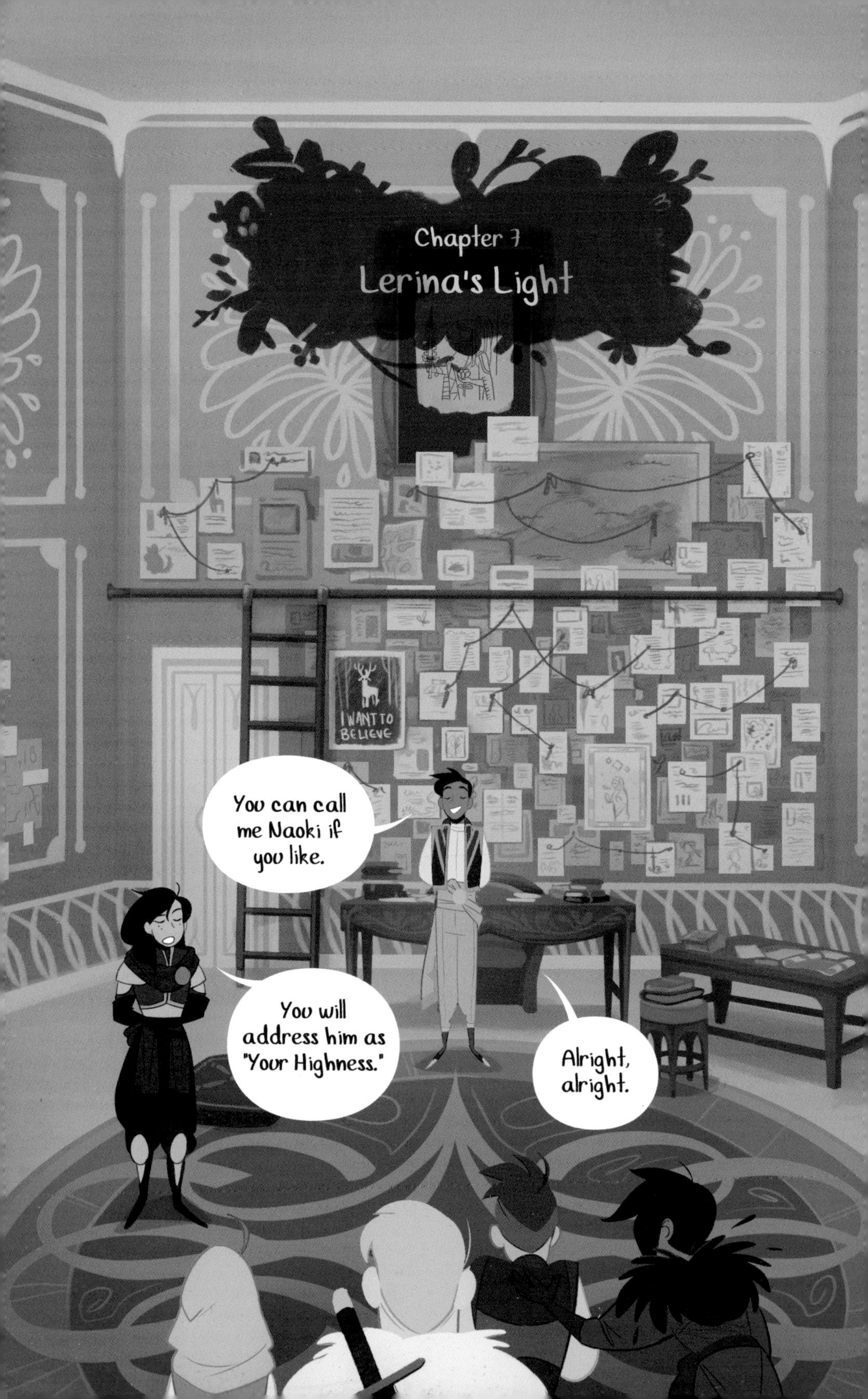
I WANT TO BELIEVE
You can call me Naoki if you like.
You will address him as "Your Highness."
Alright, alright.

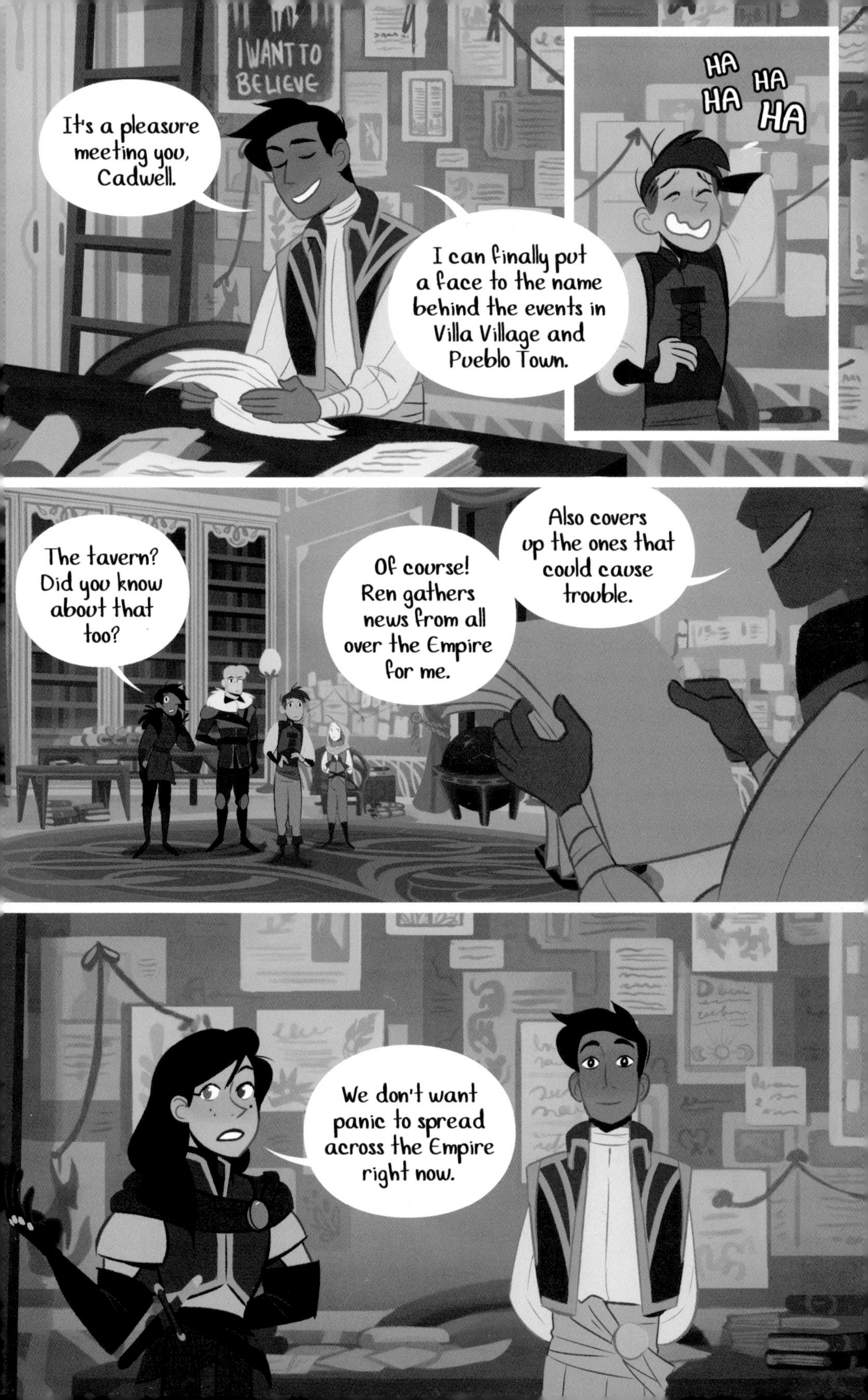
I WANT TO BELIEVE
It's a pleasure meeting you, Cadwell.
I can finally put a face to the name behind the events in Villa Village and Pueblo Town.
HA HA HA HA
The tavern? Did you know about that too?
Of course! Ren gathers news from all over the Empire for me.
Also covers up the ones that could cause trouble.
We don't want panic to spread across the Empire right now.

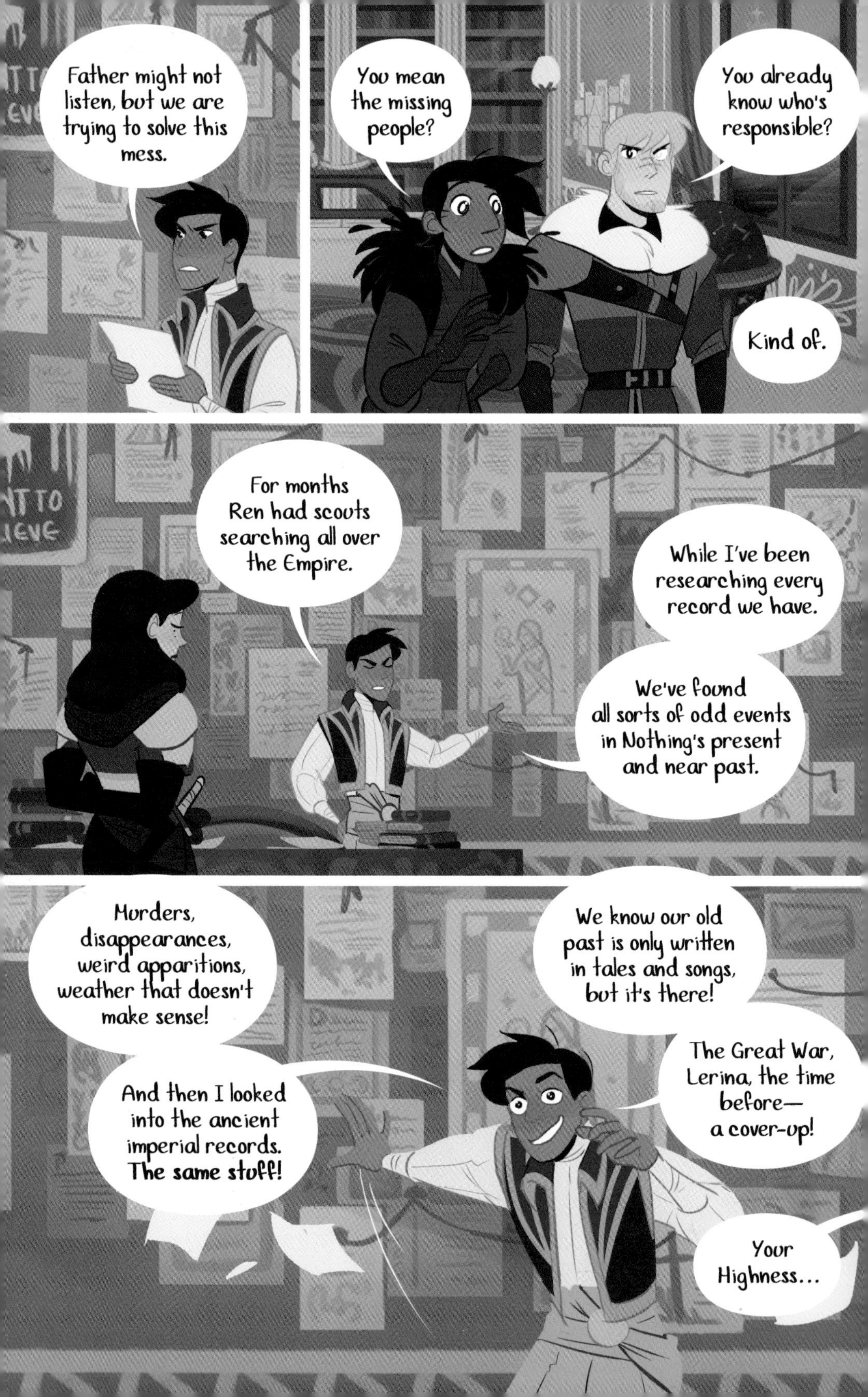

Father might not listen, but we are trying to solve this mess.
You mean the missing people?
You already know who's responsible?
Kind of.
For months Ren had scouts searching all over the Empire.
While I've been researching every record we have.
We've found all sorts of odd events in Nothing's present and near past.
Murders, disappearances, weird apparitions, weather that doesn't make sense!
And then I looked into the ancient imperial records. **The same stuff!**
We know our old past is only written in tales and songs, but it's there!
The Great War, Lerina, the time before— a cover-up!
Your Highness...

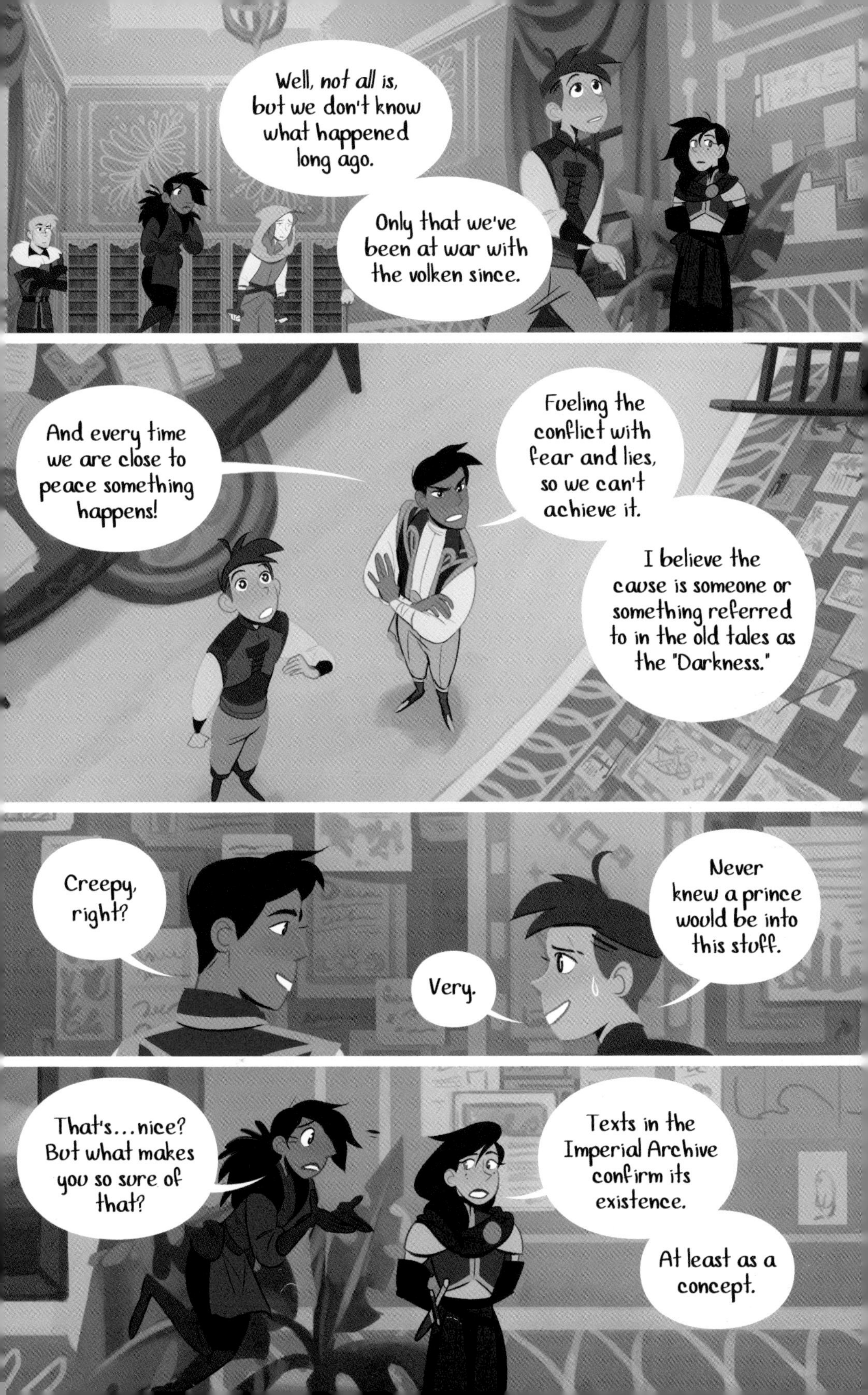
Well, not all is, but we don't know what happened long ago.
Only that we've been at war with the volken since.
And every time we are close to peace something happens!
Fueling the conflict with fear and lies, so we can't achieve it.
I believe the cause is someone or something referred to in the old tales as the "Darkness."
Creepy, right?
Very.
Never knew a prince would be into this stuff.
That's...nice? But what makes you so sure of that?
Texts in the Imperial Archive confirm its existence.
At least as a concept.

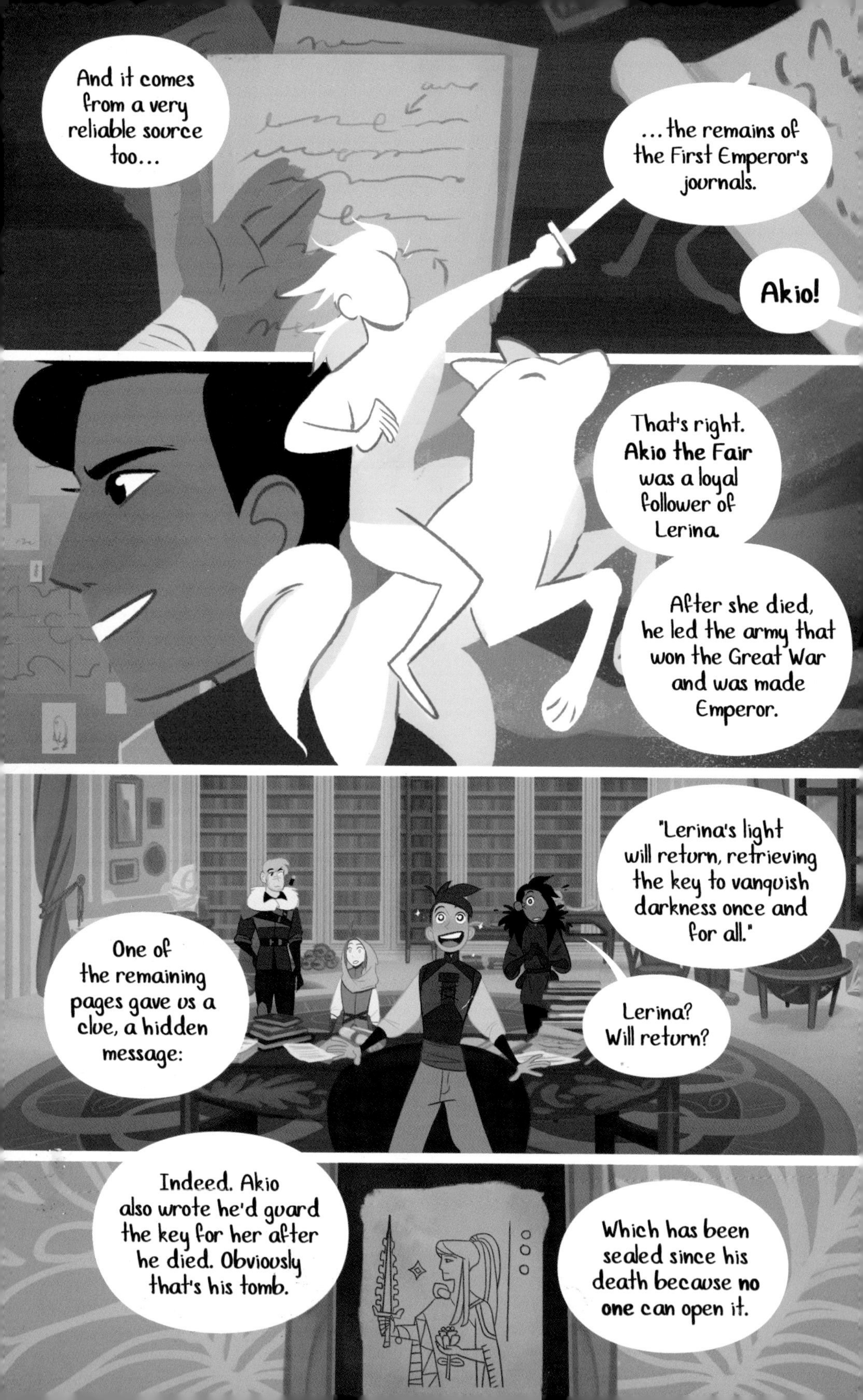
And it comes from a very reliable source too...
...the remains of the First Emperor's journals.
Akio!
That's right. Akio the Fair was a loyal follower of Lerina.
After she died, he led the army that won the Great War and was made Emperor.
One of the remaining pages gave us a clue, a hidden message:
"Lerina's light will return, retrieving the key to vanquish darkness once and for all."
Lerina? Will return?
Indeed. Akio also wrote he'd guard the key for her after he died. Obviously that's his tomb.
Which has been sealed since his death because no one can open it.

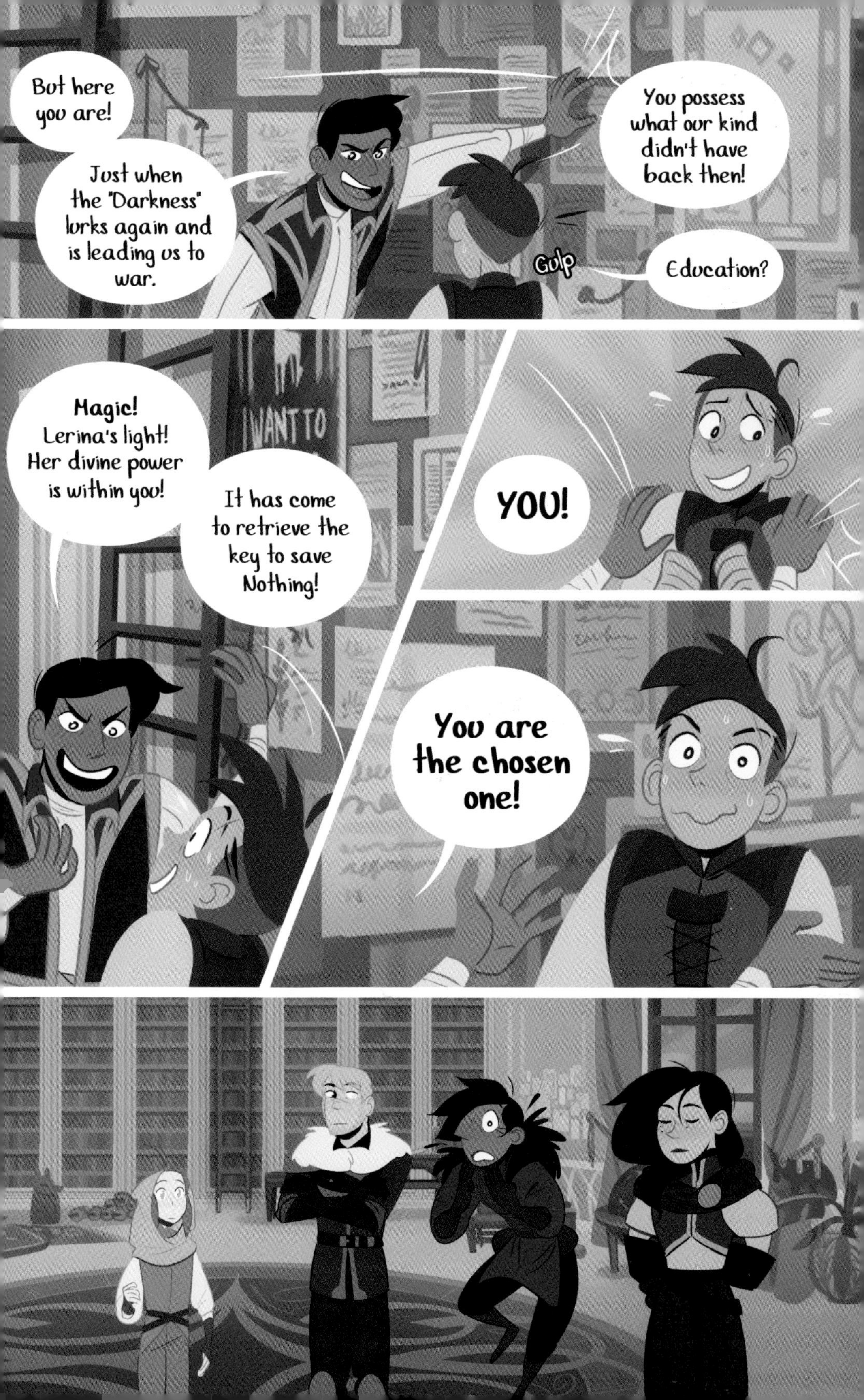
But here you are!
Just when the "Darkness" lurks again and is leading us to war.
You possess what our kind didn't have back then!
Gulp
Education?
Magic! Lerina's light! Her divine power is within you!
It has come to retrieve the key to save Nothing!
I WANT TO
YOU!
You are the chosen one!

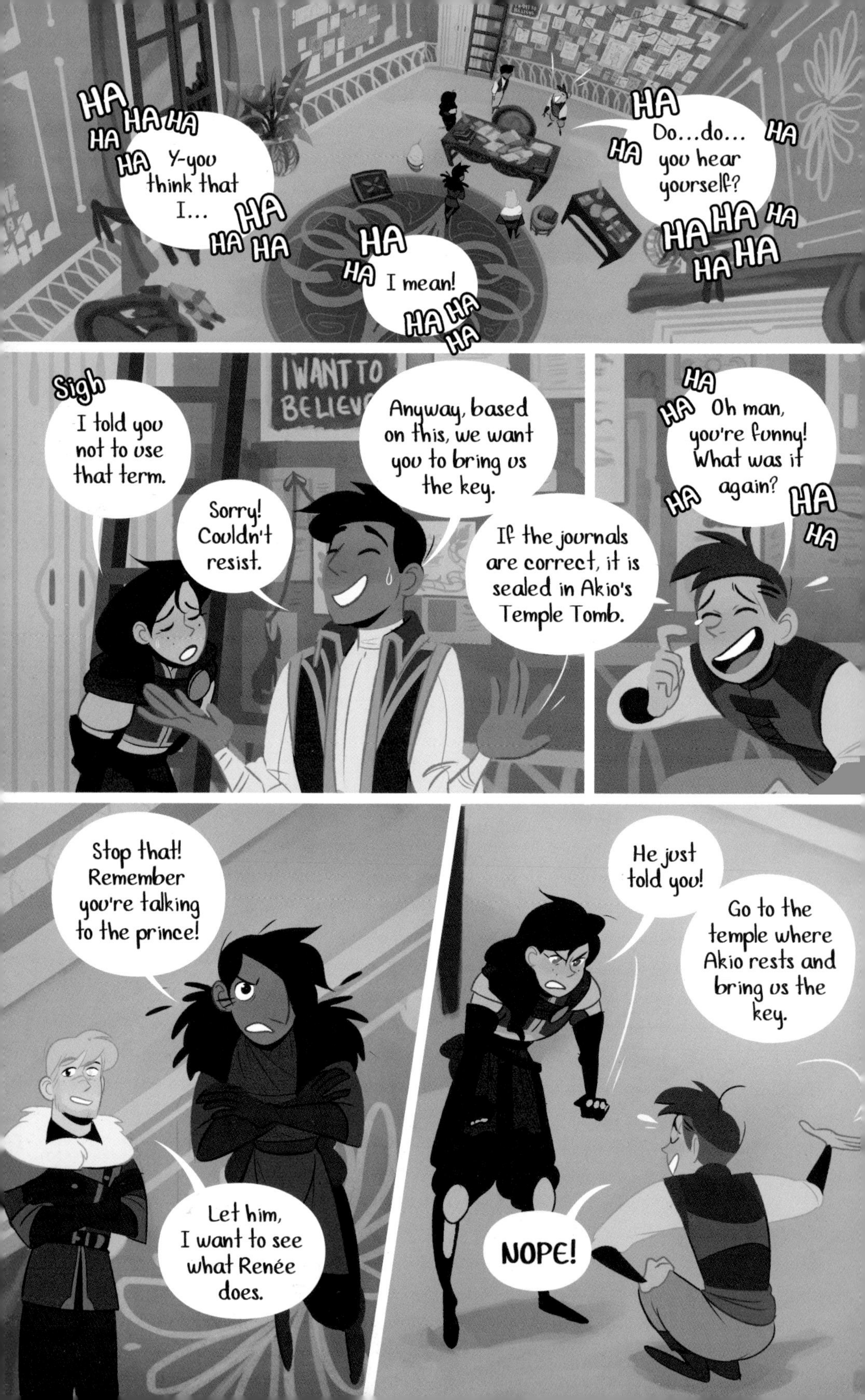
HA HA HA HA HA HA
Y-you think that I...
HA HA HA
HA HA
Do...do... you hear yourself?
HA HA HA HA HA HA HA HA
HA HA
I mean!
HA HA HA
Sigh
I told you not to use that term.
I WANT TO BELIEVE
Sorry! Couldn't resist.
Anyway, based on this, we want you to bring us the key.
If the journals are correct, it is sealed in Akio's Temple Tomb.
HA HA
Oh man, you're funny! What was it again?
HA HA HA
Stop that! Remember you're talking to the prince!
Let him, I want to see what Renée does.
He just told you!
Go to the temple where Akio rests and bring us the key.
NOPE!

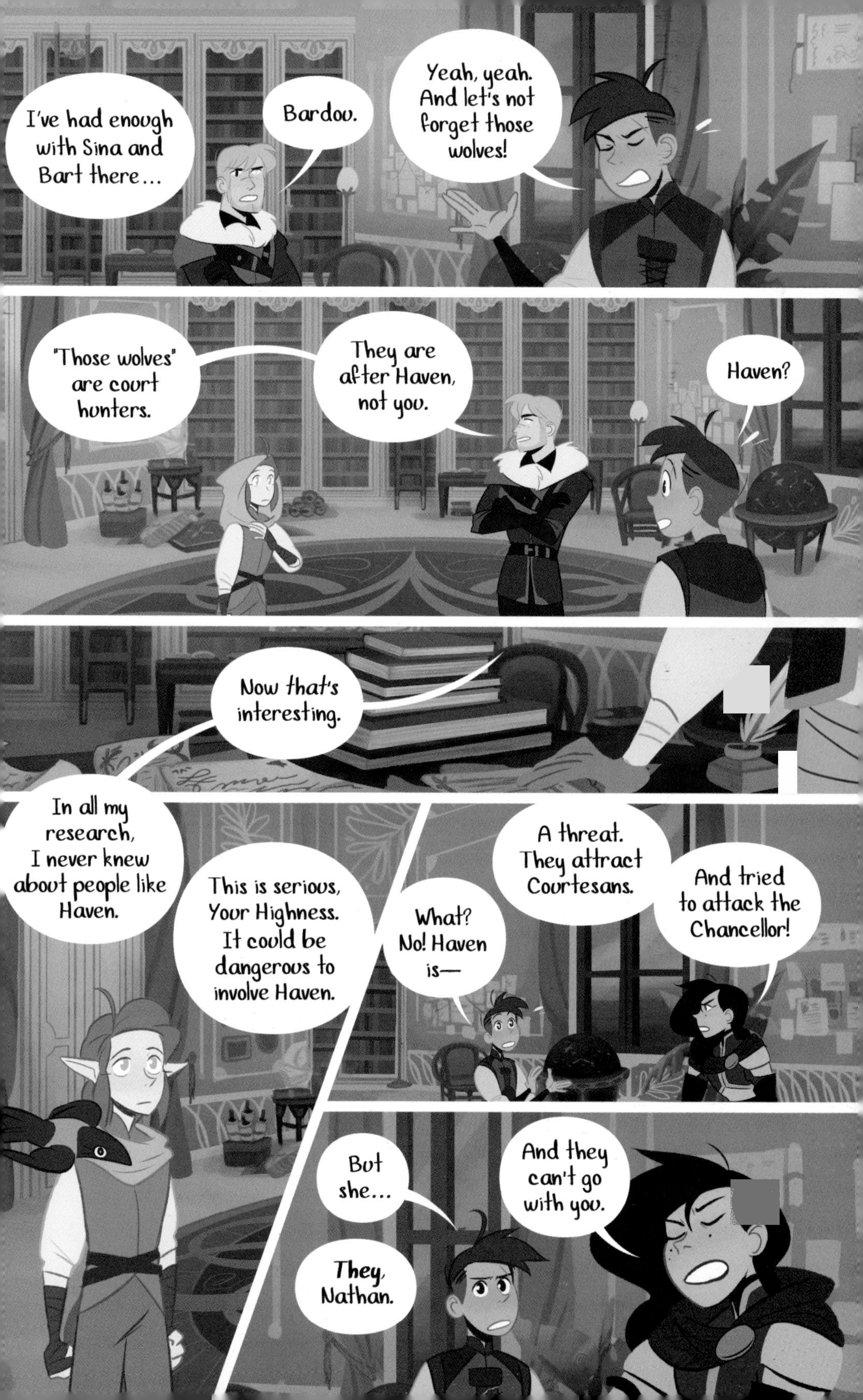
I've had enough with Sina and Bart there...
Bardou.
Yeah, yeah. And let's not forget those wolves!
"Those wolves" are court hunters.
They are after Haven, not you.
Haven?
Now that's interesting.
In all my research, I never knew about people like Haven.
This is serious, Your Highness. It could be dangerous to involve Haven.
What? No! Haven is—
A threat. They attract Courtesans.
And tried to attack the Chancellor!
But she...
They, Nathan.
And they can't go with you.

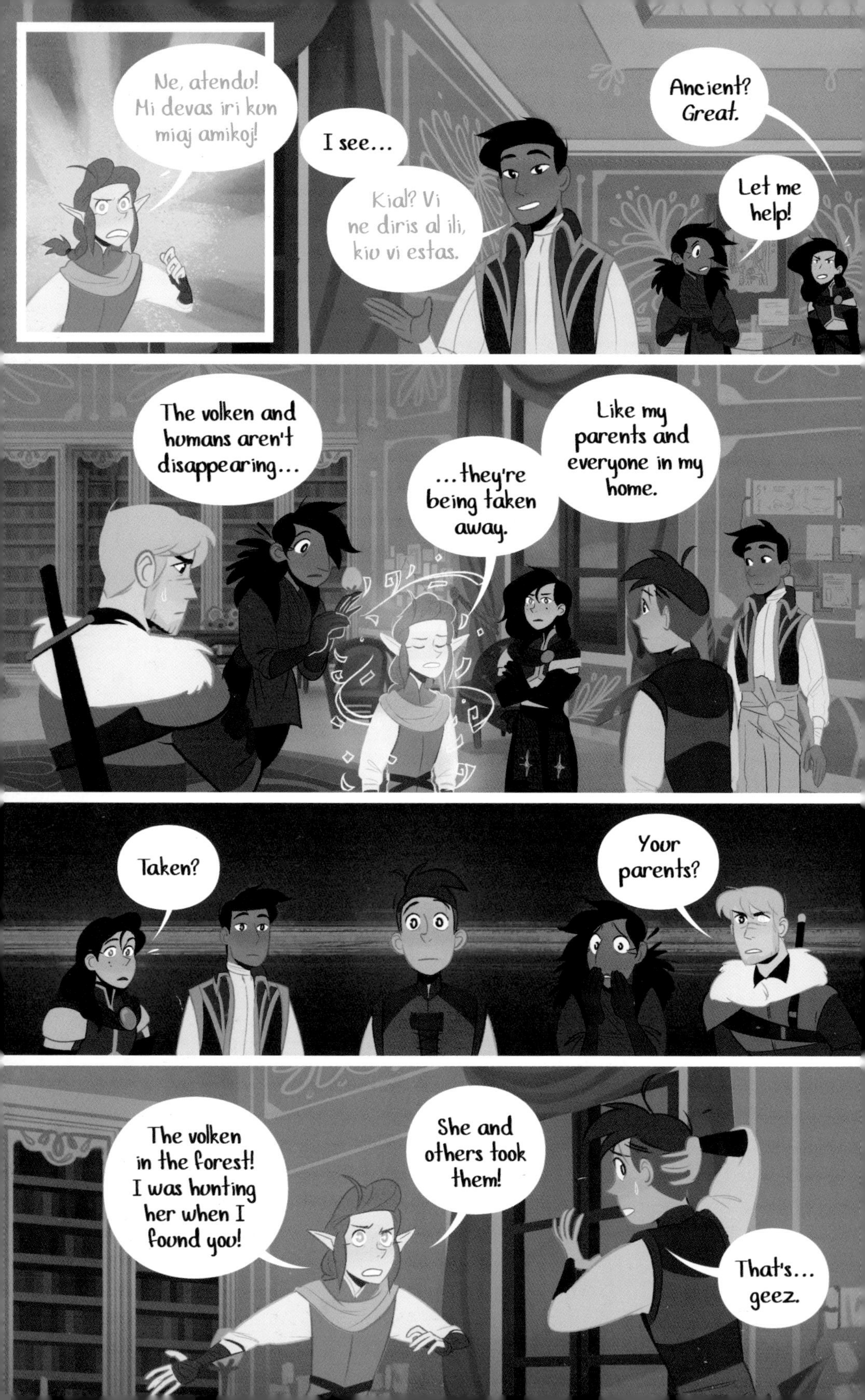
Ne, atendu! Mi devas iri kun miaj amikoj!
I see...
Kial? Vi ne diris al ili, kiu vi estas.
Ancient? Great.
Let me help!
The volken and humans aren't disappearing...
...they're being taken away.
Like my parents and everyone in my home.
Taken?
Your parents?
The volken in the forest! I was hunting her when I found you!
She and others took them!
That's... geez.

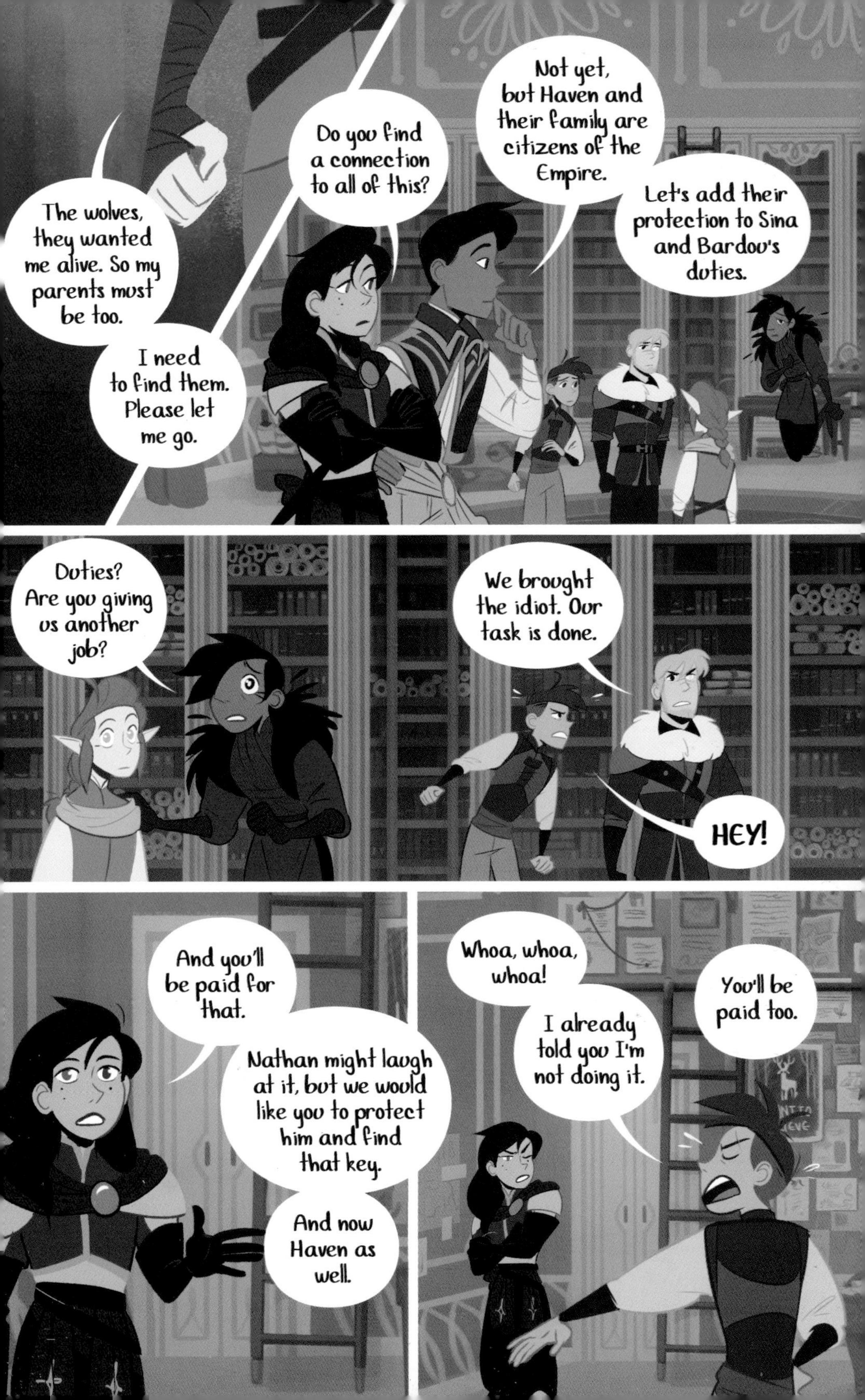

The wolves, they wanted me alive. So my parents must be too.
I need to find them. Please let me go.
Do you find a connection to all of this?
Not yet, but Haven and their family are citizens of the Empire.
Let's add their protection to Sina and Bardou's duties.
Duties? Are you giving us another job?
We brought the idiot. Our task is done.
HEY!
And you'll be paid for that.
Nathan might laugh at it, but we would like you to protect him and find that key.
And now Haven as well.
Whoa, whoa, whoa!
I already told you I'm not doing it.
You'll be paid too.

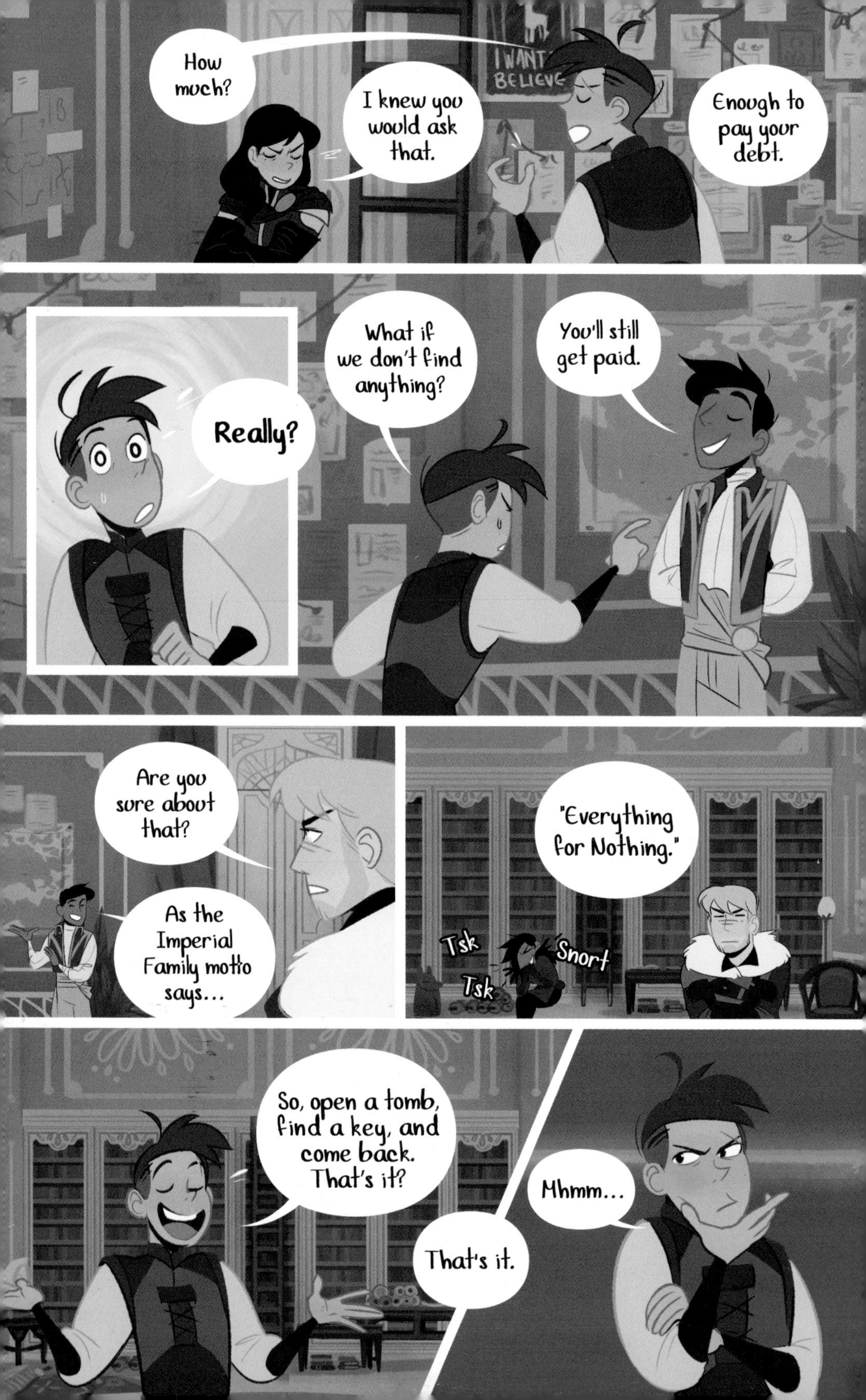
How much?
I knew you would ask that.
Enough to pay your debt.
What if we don't find anything?
You'll still get paid.
Really?
Are you sure about that?
As the Imperial Family motto says...
"Everything for Nothing."
Tsk
Tsk
Snort
So, open a tomb, find a key, and come back. That's it?
That's it.
Mhmm...

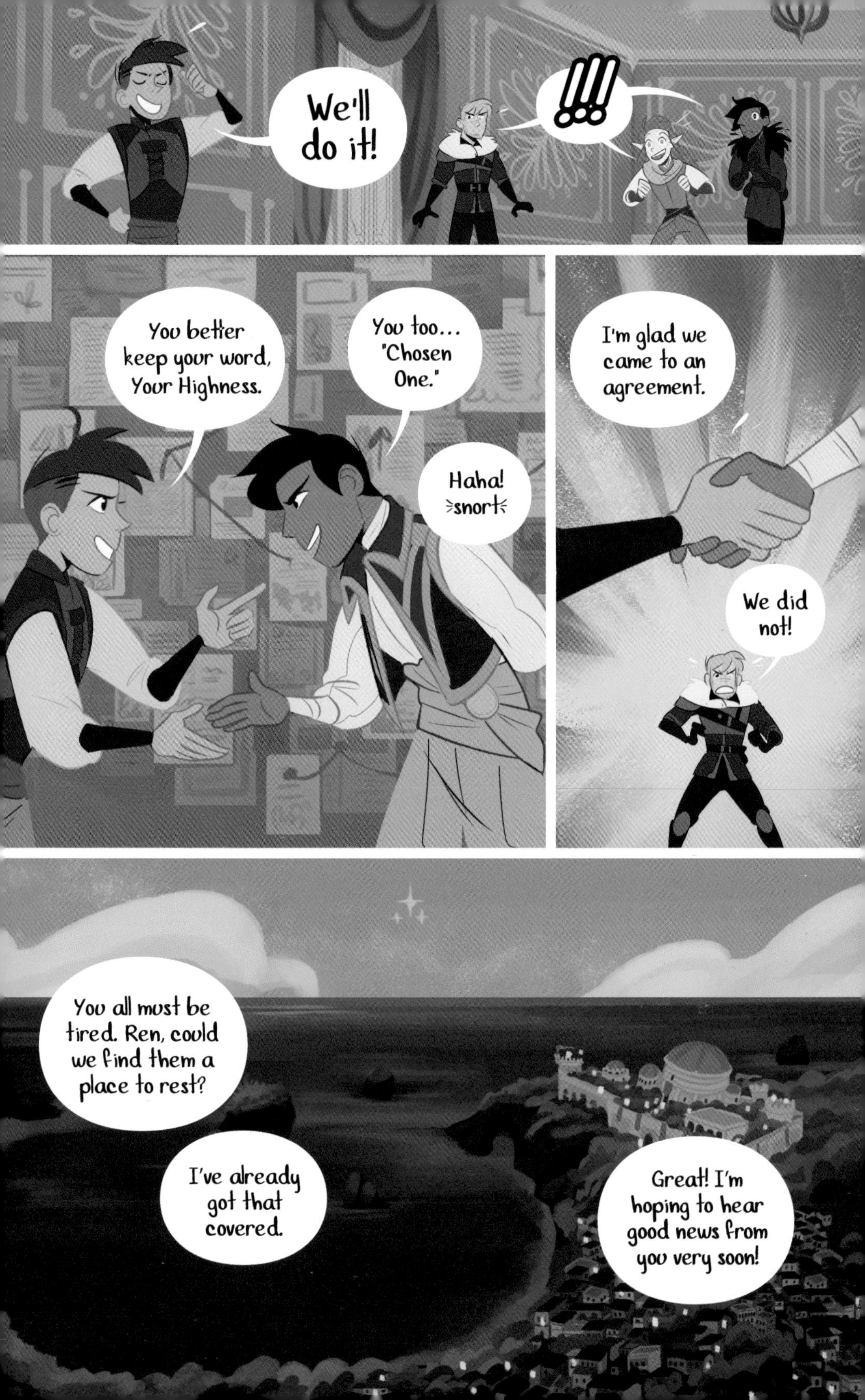

We'll do it!
!!!
You better keep your word, Your Highness.
You too... "Chosen One."
Haha! ≥snort≤
I'm glad we came to an agreement.
We did not!
You all must be tired. Ren, could we find them a place to rest?
I've already got that covered.
Great! I'm hoping to hear good news from you very soon!

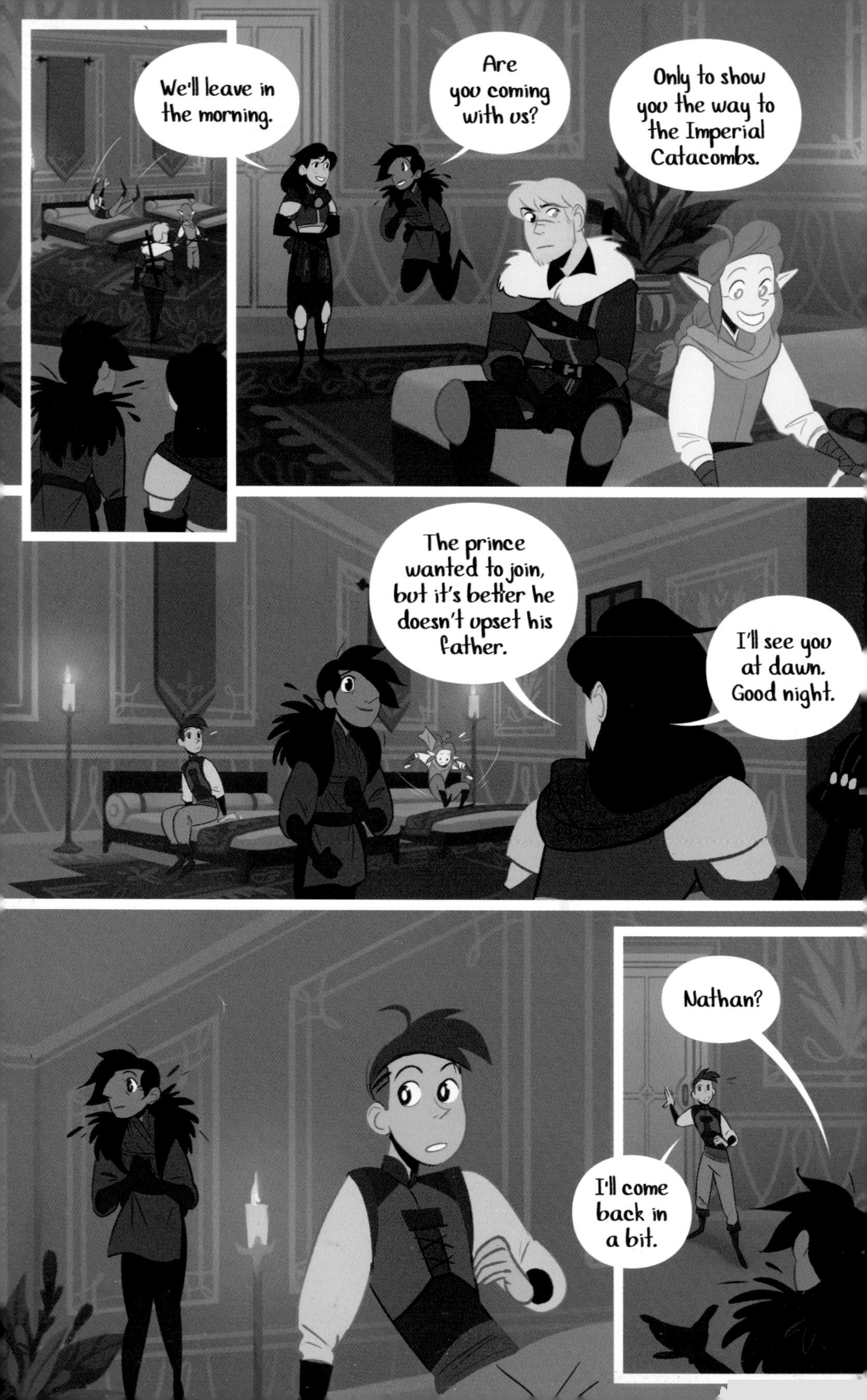
We'll leave in the morning.
Are you coming with us?
Only to show you the way to the Imperial Catacombs.
The prince wanted to join, but it's better he doesn't upset his father.
I'll see you at dawn. Good night.
Nathan?
I'll come back in a bit.

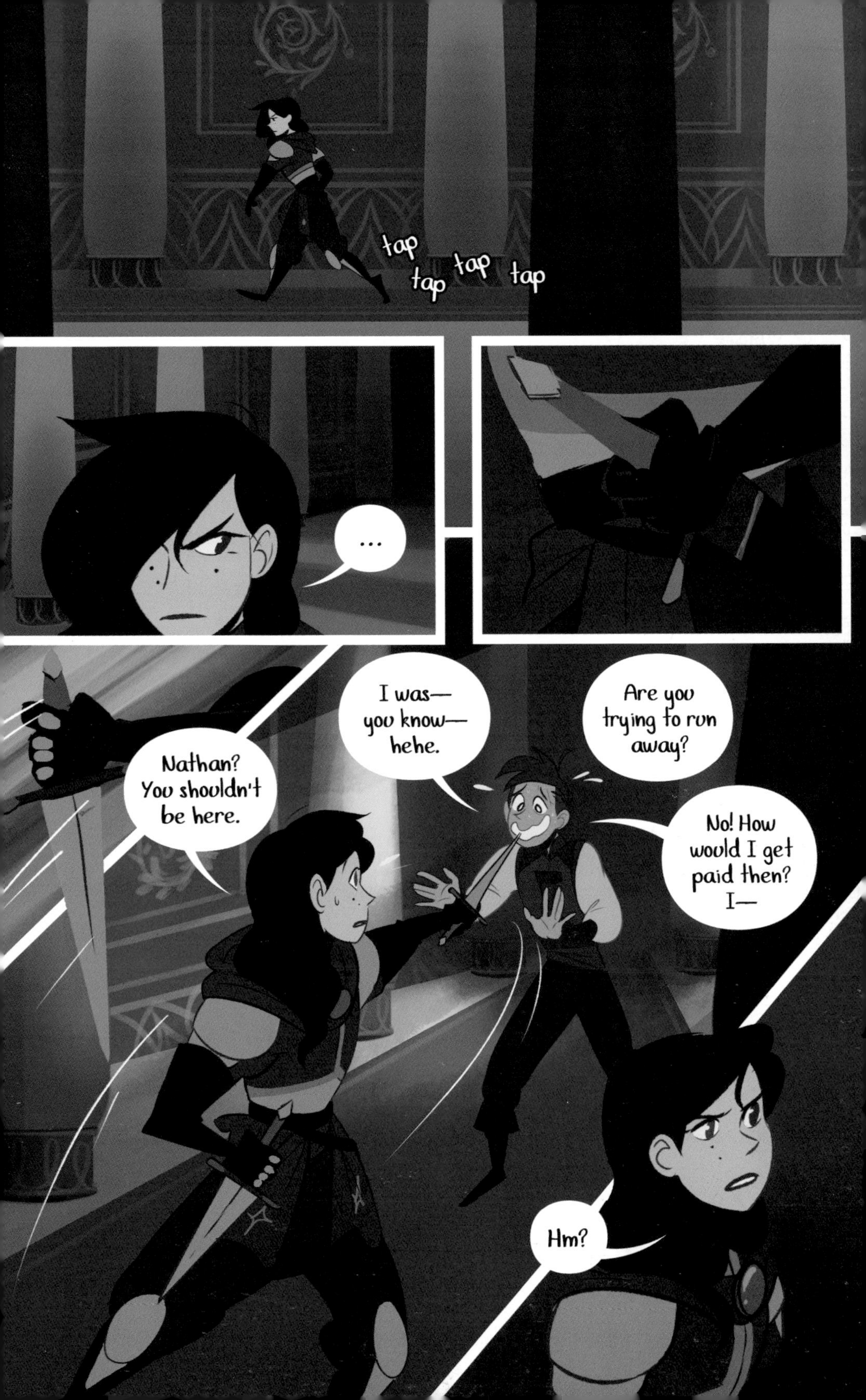
tap
tap
tap
tap
...
Nathan? You shouldn't be here.
I was— you know— hehe.
Are you trying to run away?
No! How would I get paid then? I—
Hm?

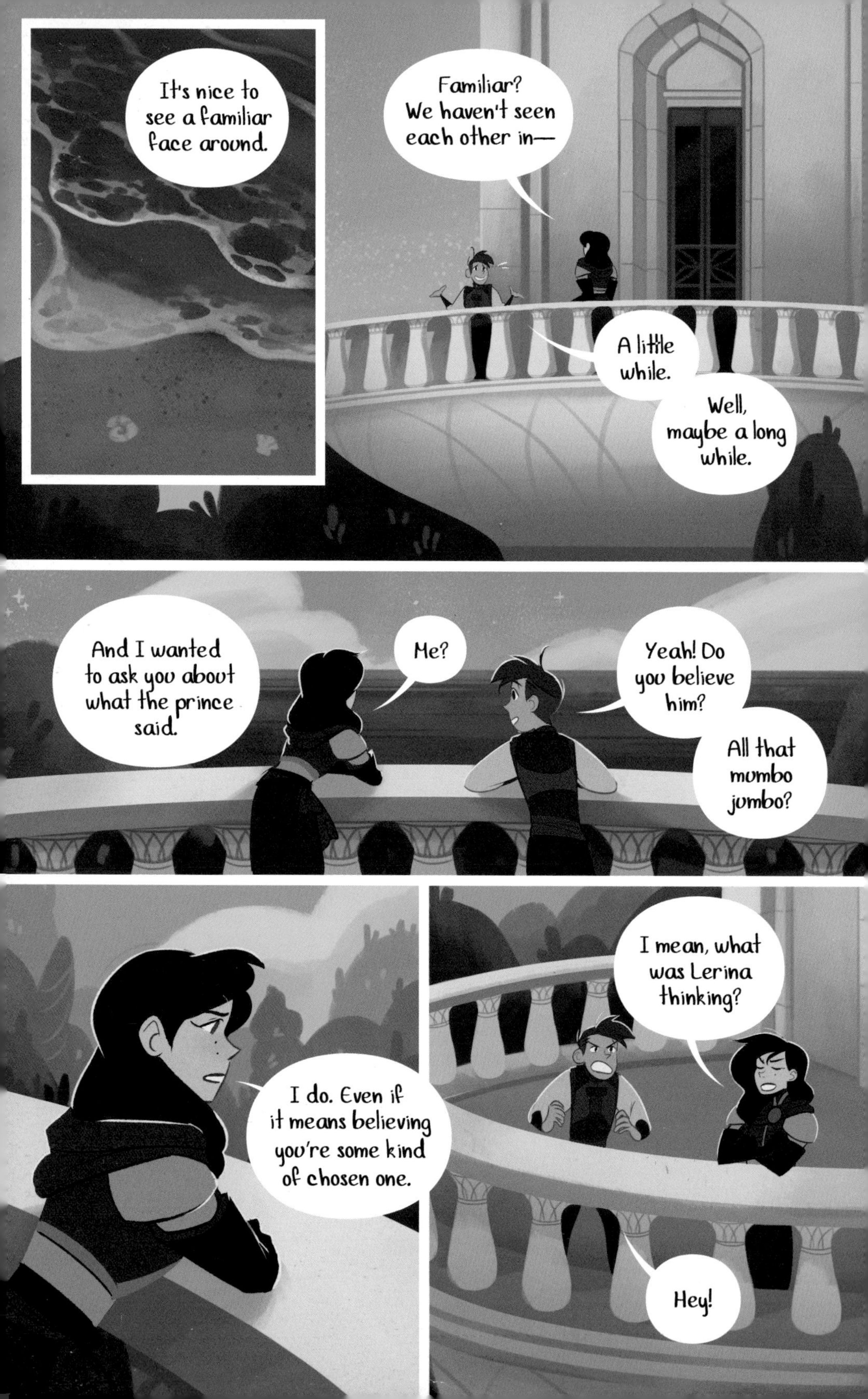
It's nice to see a familiar face around.
Familiar? We haven't seen each other in—
A little while.
Well, maybe a long while.
And I wanted to ask you about what the prince said.
Me?
Yeah! Do you believe him?
All that mumbo jumbo?
I do. Even if it means believing you're some kind of chosen one.
I mean, what was Lerina thinking?
Hey!

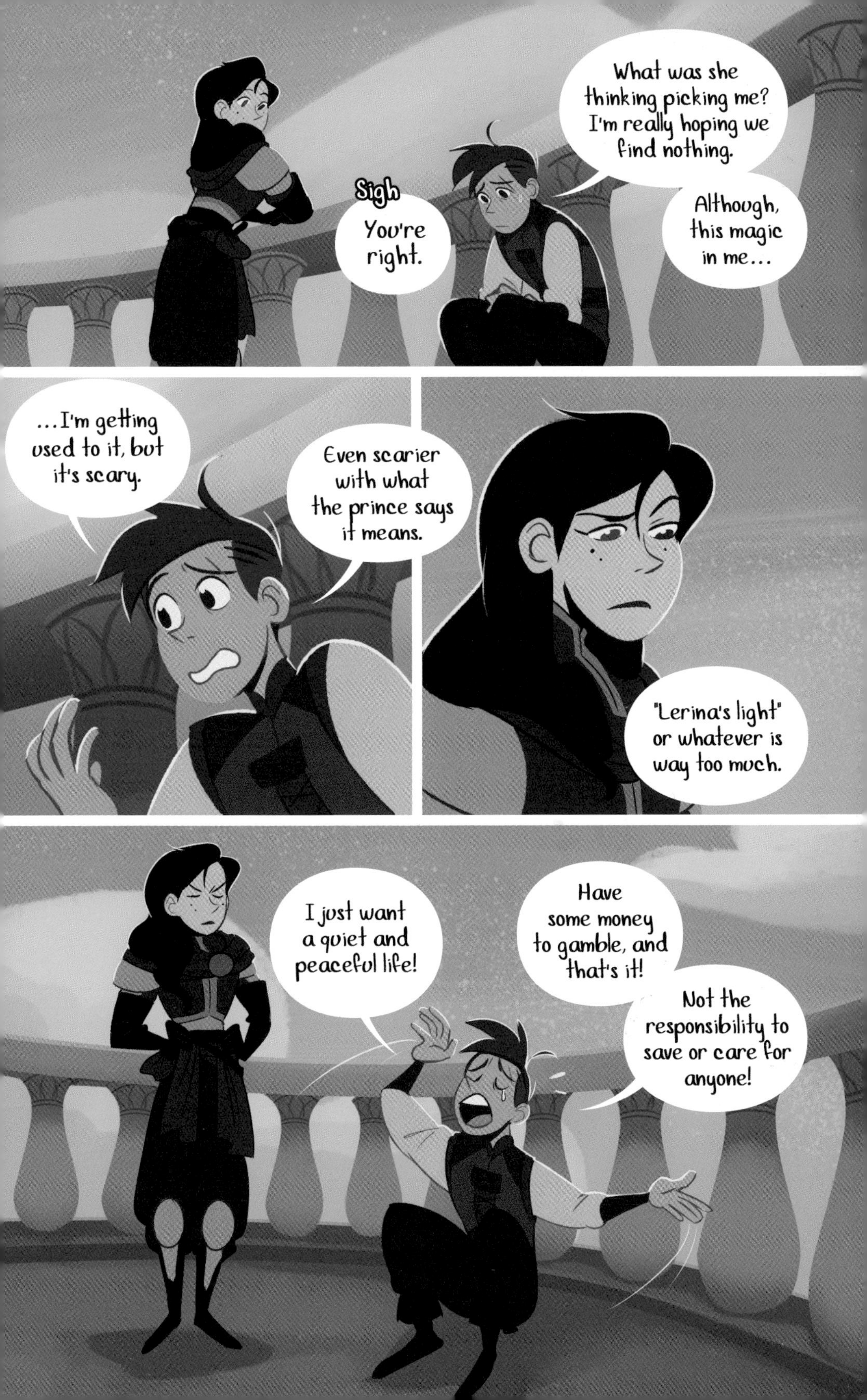
What was she thinking picking me? I'm really hoping we find nothing.
Sigh
You're right.
Although, this magic in me...
...I'm getting used to it, but it's scary.
Even scarier with what the prince says it means.
"Lerina's light" or whatever is way too much.
I just want a quiet and peaceful life!
Have some money to gamble, and that's it!
Not the responsibility to save or care for anyone!

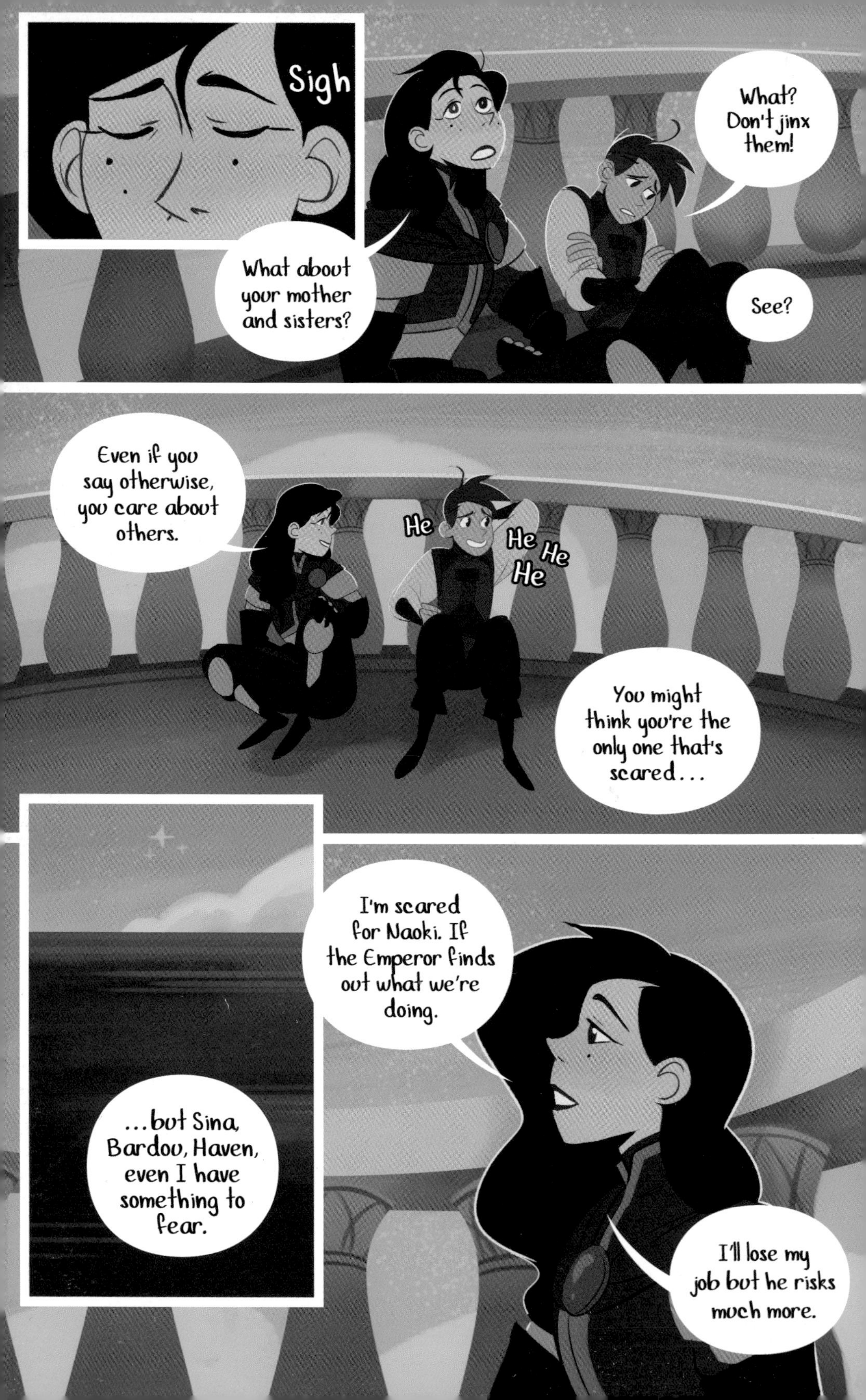

Sigh
What about your mother and sisters?
What? Don't jinx them!
See?
Even if you say otherwise, you care about others.
He
He He He
You might think you're the only one that's scared...
I'm scared for Naoki. If the Emperor finds out what we're doing.
...but Sina, Bardou, Haven, even I have something to fear.
I'll lose my job but he risks much more.

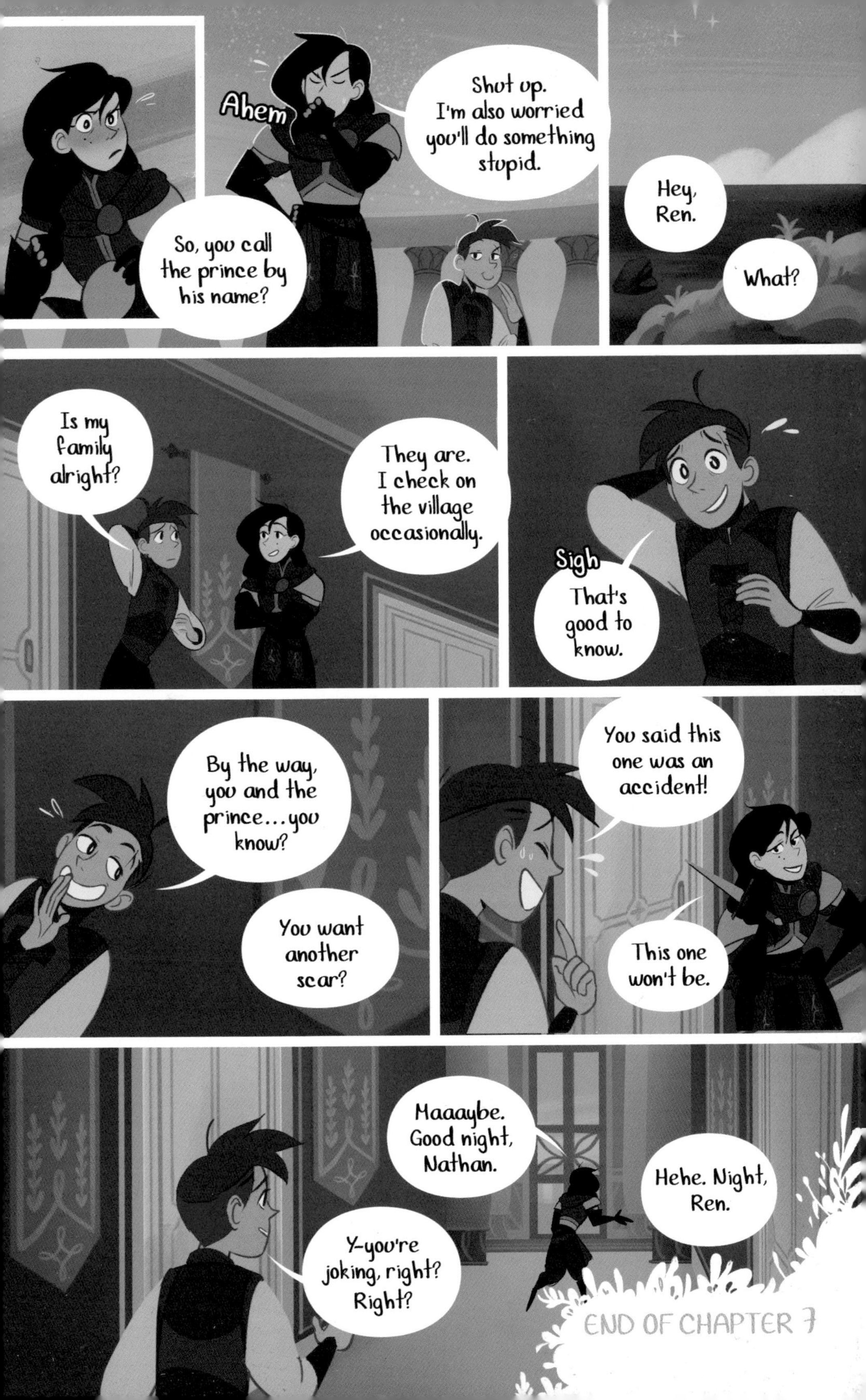
Ahem
Shut up.
I'm also worried you'll do something stupid.
So, you call the prince by his name?
Hey, Ren.
What?
Is my family alright?
They are.
I check on the village occasionally.
Sigh
That's good to know.
By the way, you and the prince... you know?
You want another scar?
You said this one was an accident!
This one won't be.
Maaaybe. Good night, Nathan.
Y-you're joking, right? Right?
Hehe. Night, Ren.
END OF CHAPTER 7

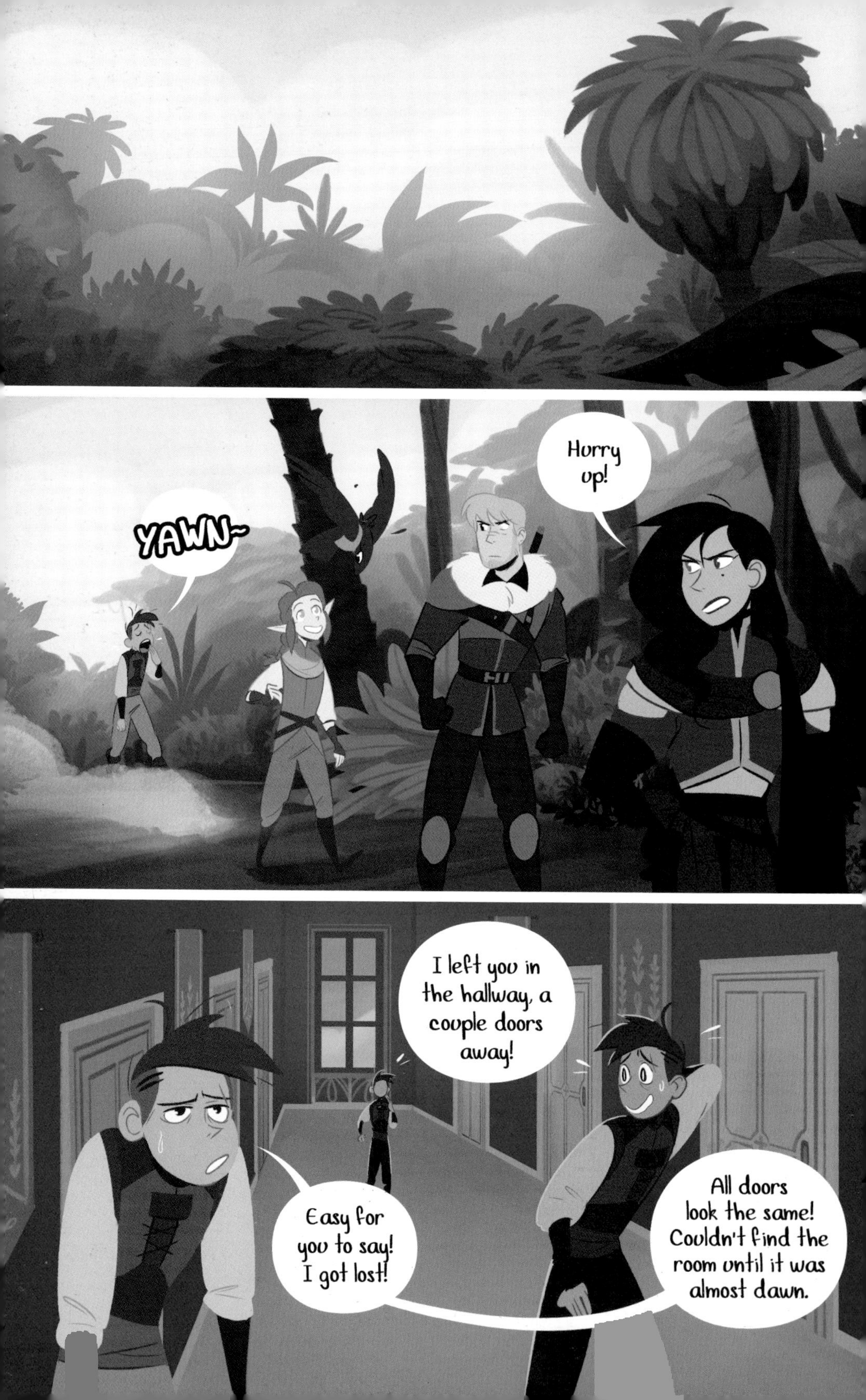
YAWN~
Hurry up!
I left you in the hallway, a couple doors away!
Easy for you to say! I got lost!
All doors look the same! Couldn't find the room until it was almost dawn.

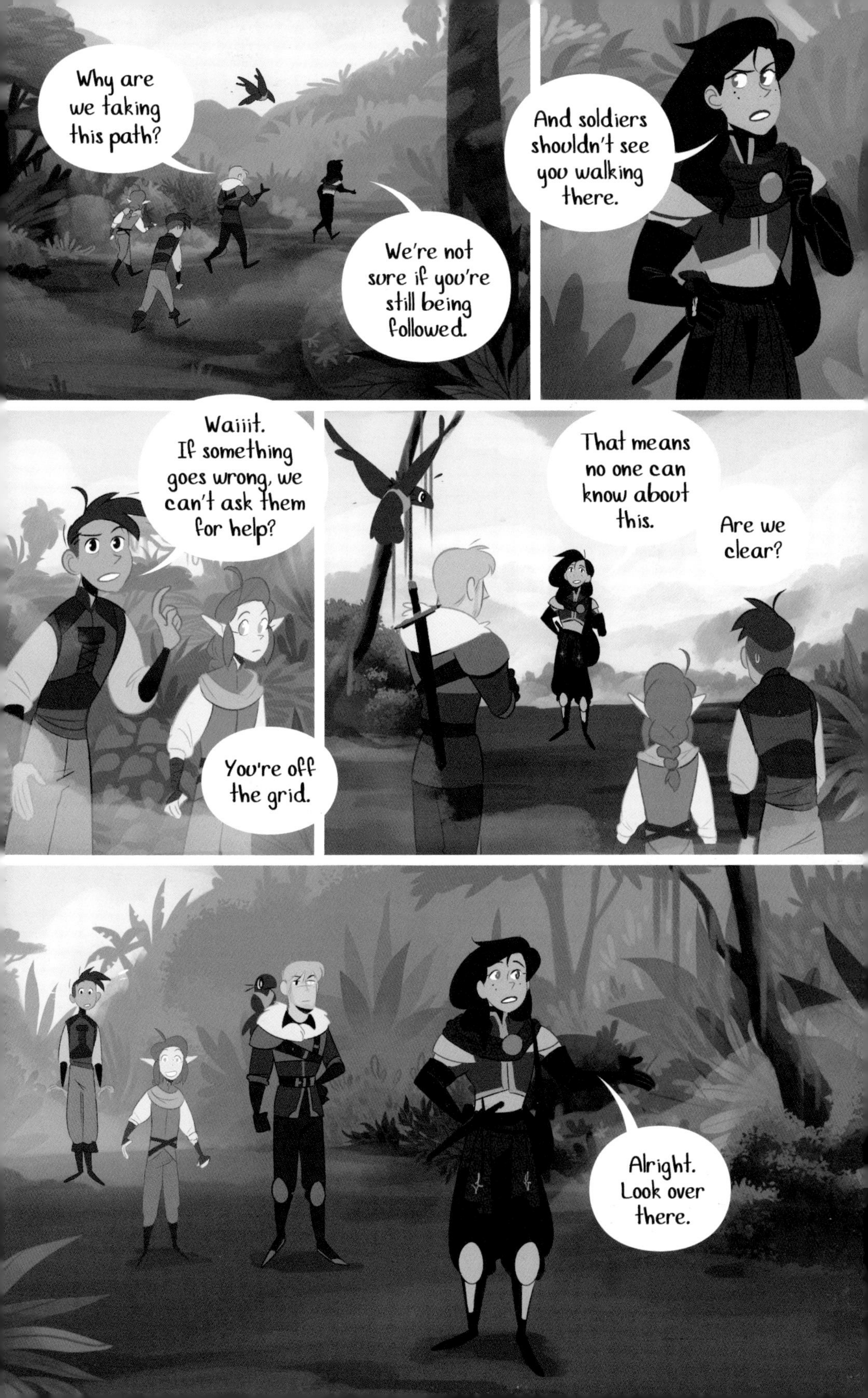
Why are we taking this path?
We're not sure if you're still being followed.
And soldiers shouldn't see you walking there.
Waiiit. If something goes wrong, we can't ask them for help?
You're off the grid.
That means no one can know about this.
Are we clear?
Alright. Look over there.

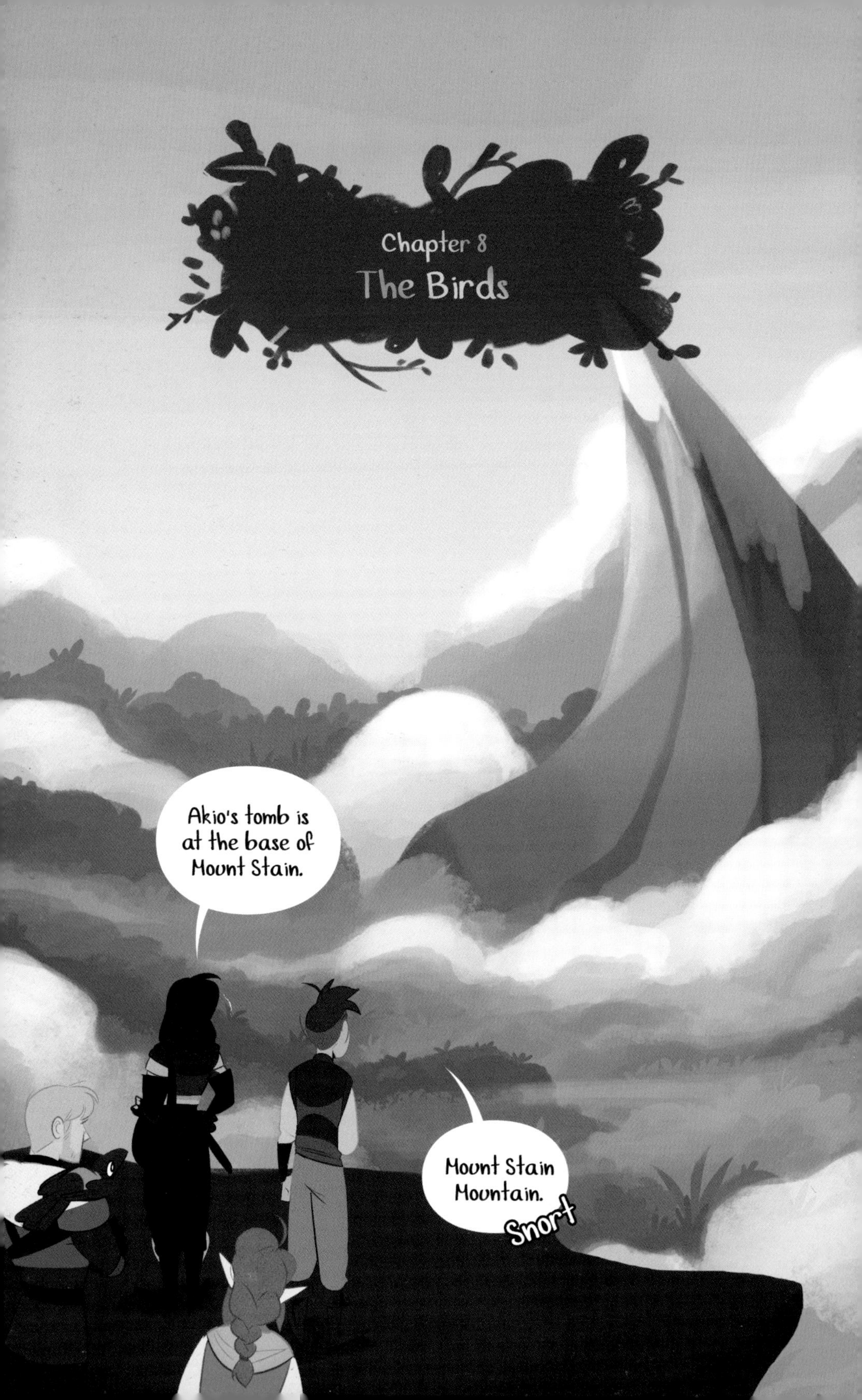
Chapter 8
The Birds
Akio's tomb is at the base of Mount Stain.
Mount Stain Mountain.
Snort

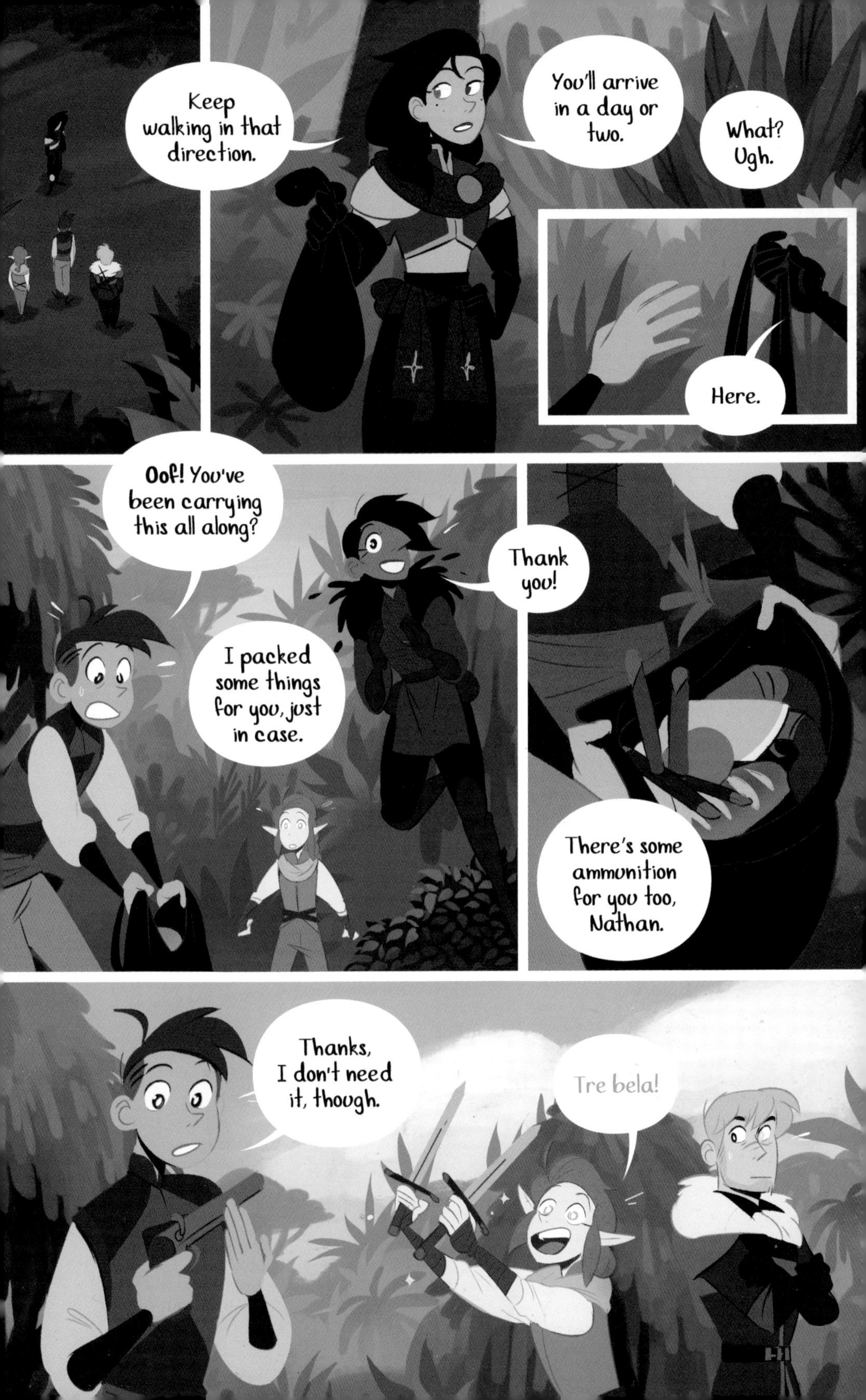
Keep walking in that direction.
You'll arrive in a day or two.
What? Ugh.
Here.
Oof! You've been carrying this all along?
Thank you!
I packed some things for you, just in case.
There's some ammunition for you too, Nathan.
Thanks, I don't need it, though.
Tre bela!

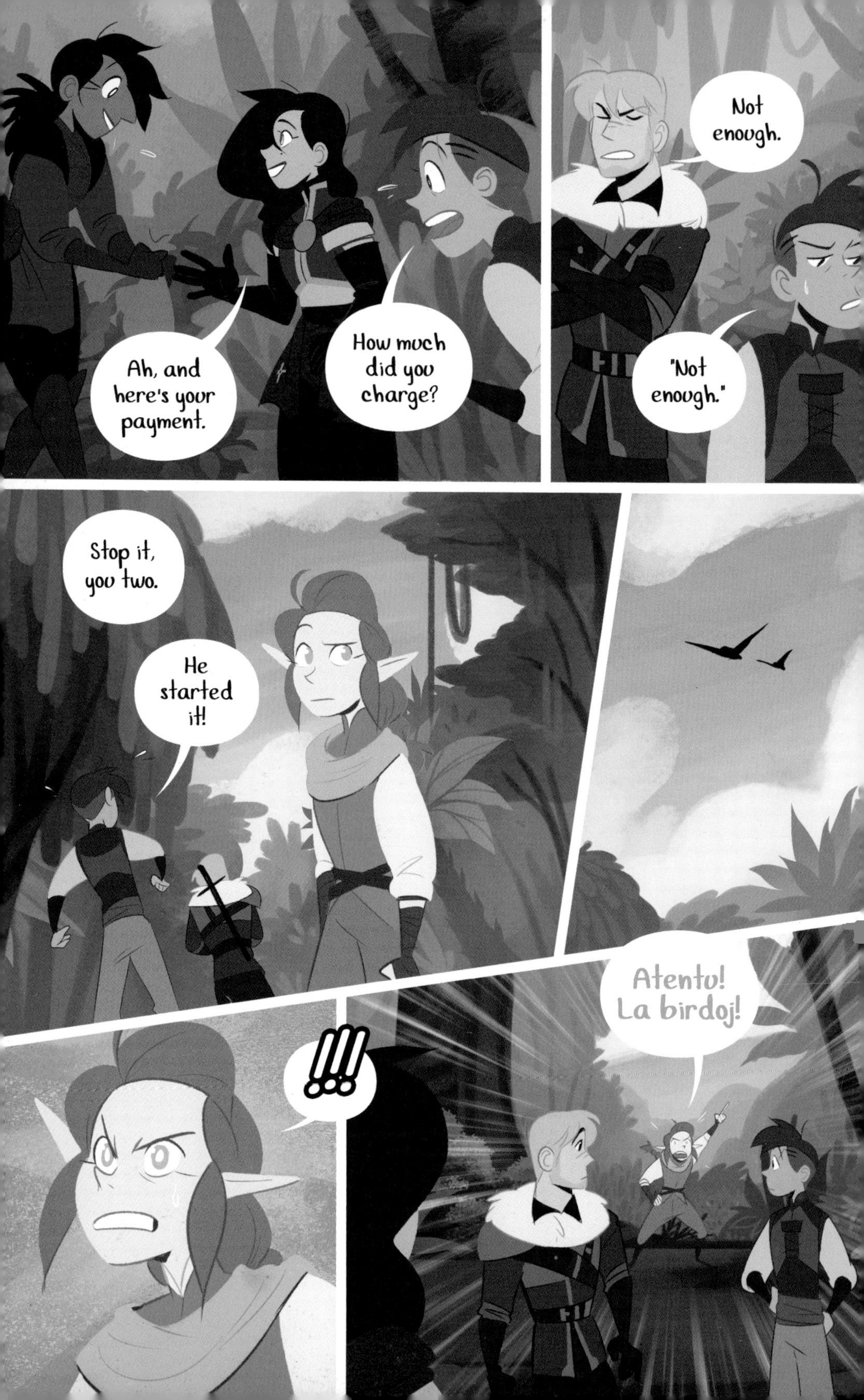
Ah, and here's your payment.
How much did you charge?
Not enough.
"Not enough."
Stop it, you two.
He started it!
!!!
Atentu! La birdoj!

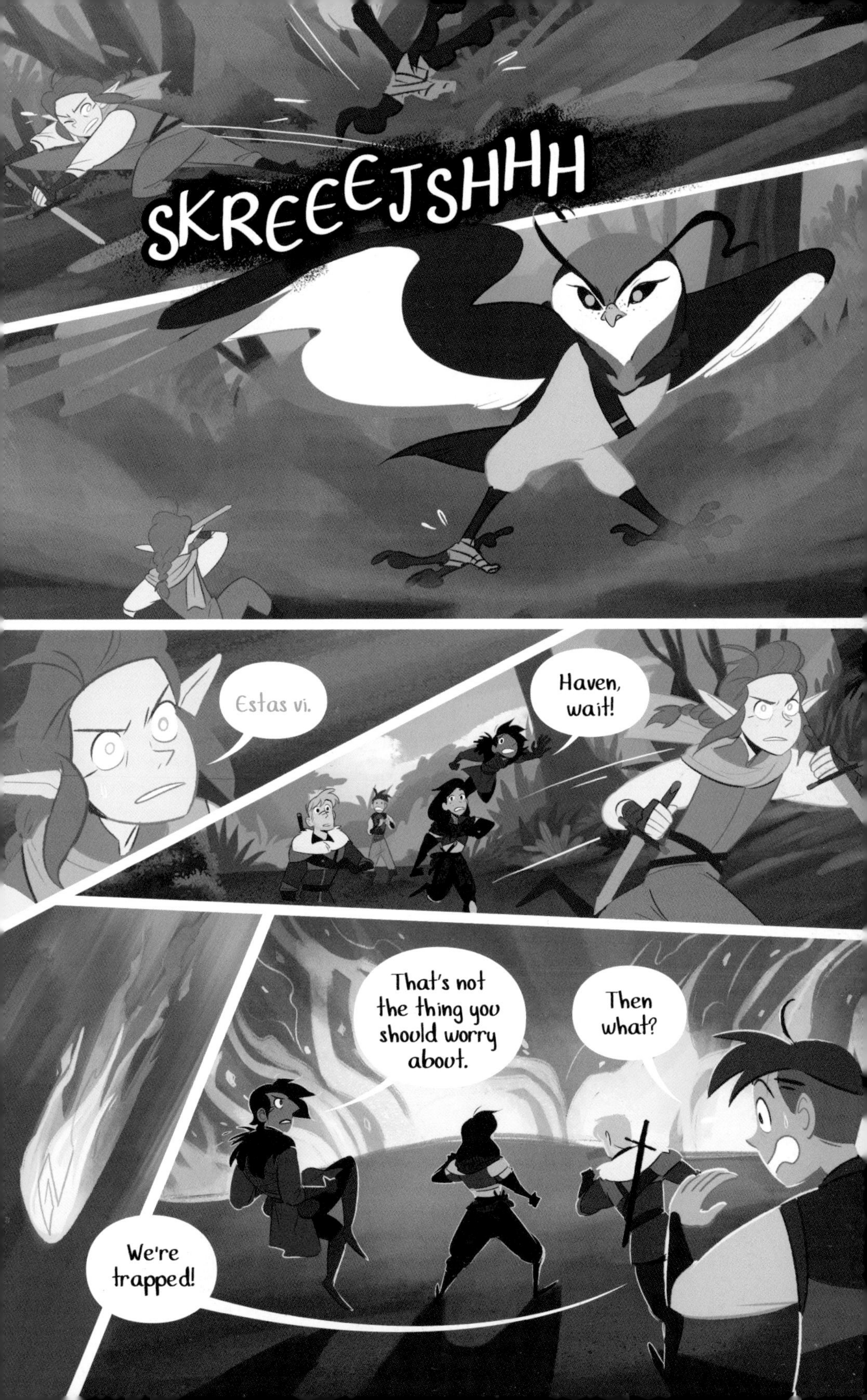
SKREEEJSHHH
Estas vi.
Haven, wait!
That's not the thing you should worry about.
Then what?
We're trapped!

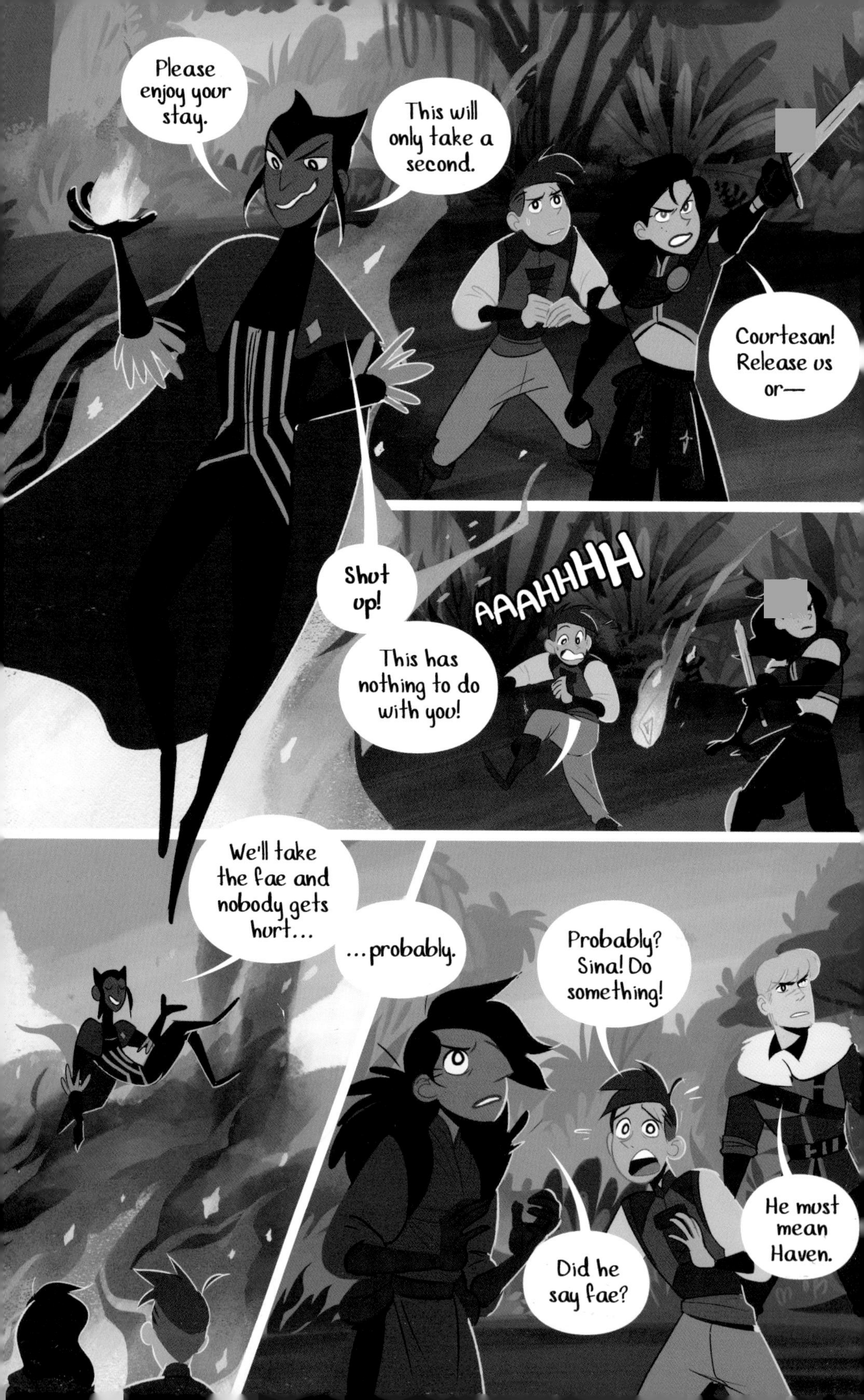
Please enjoy your stay.
This will only take a second.
Courtesan! Release us or—
Shut up!
This has nothing to do with you!
AAAHHHH
We'll take the fae and nobody gets hurt...
...probably.
Probably? Sina! Do something!
Did he say fae?
He must mean Haven.

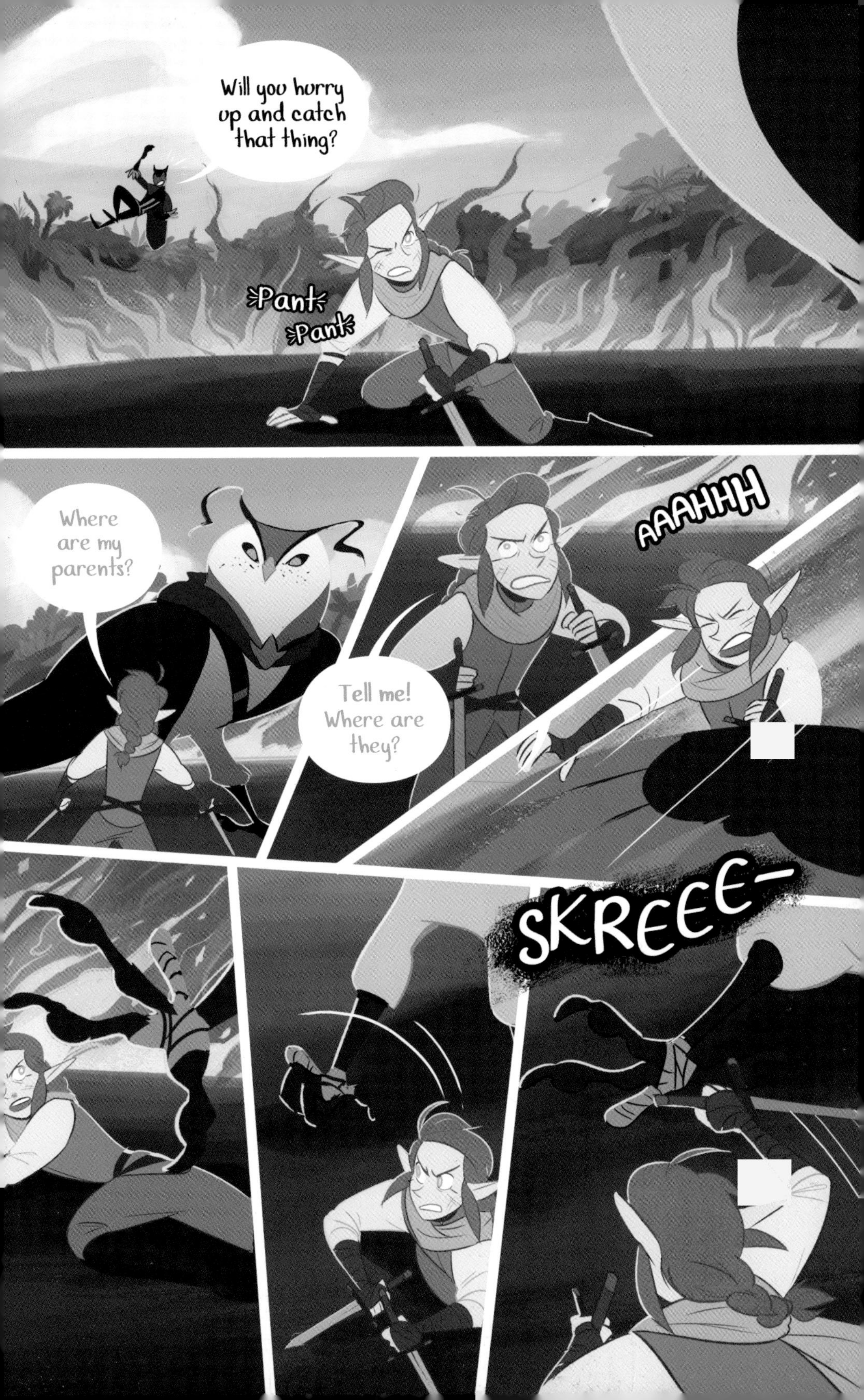
Will you hurry up and catch that thing?
Pant
Pant
Where are my parents?
Tell me! Where are they?
AAAHHH
SKREEE-

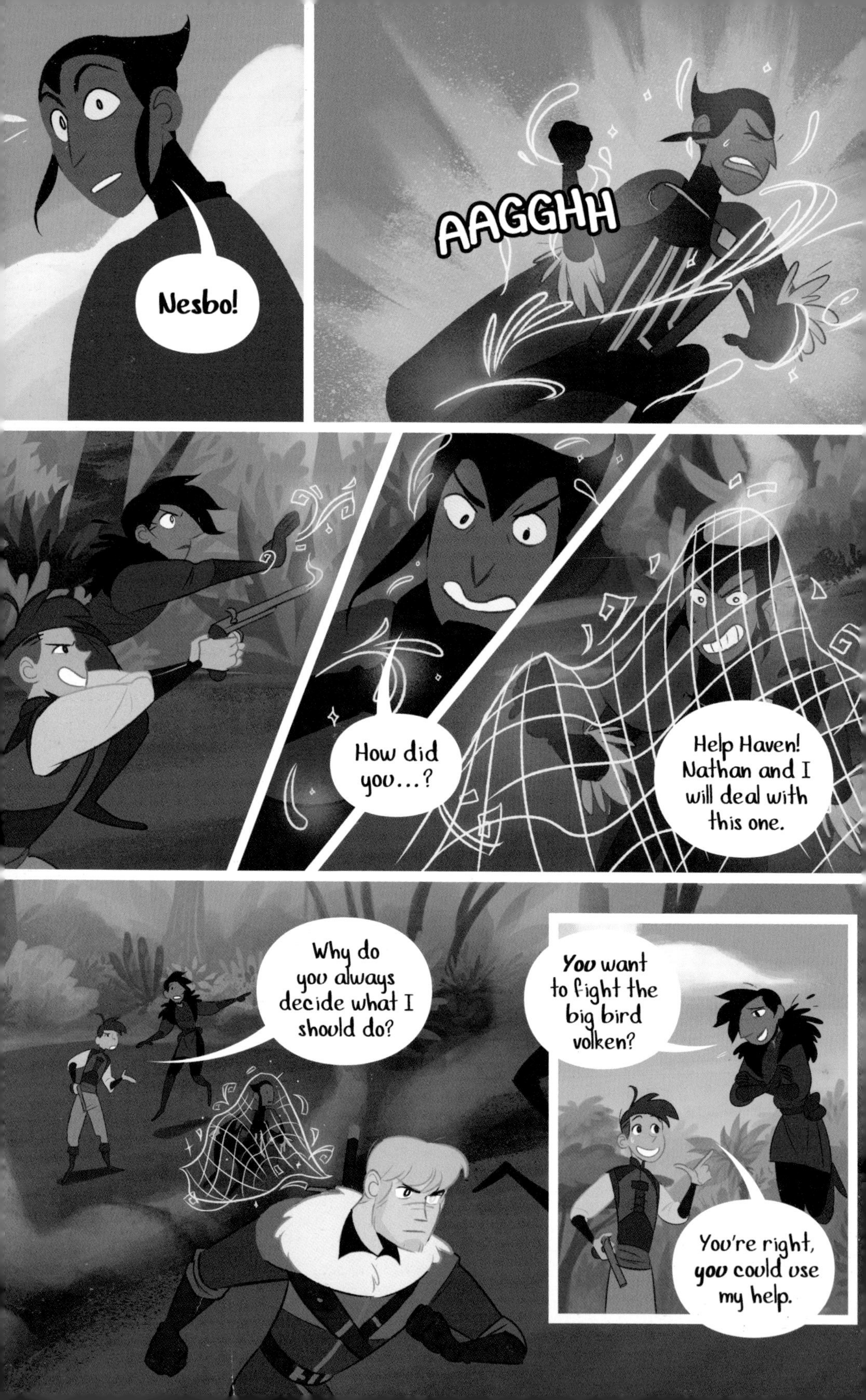
Nesbo!
AAGGHH
How did you...?
Help Haven! Nathan and I will deal with this one.
Why do you always decide what I should do?
You want to fight the big bird volken?
You're right, *you* could use my help.

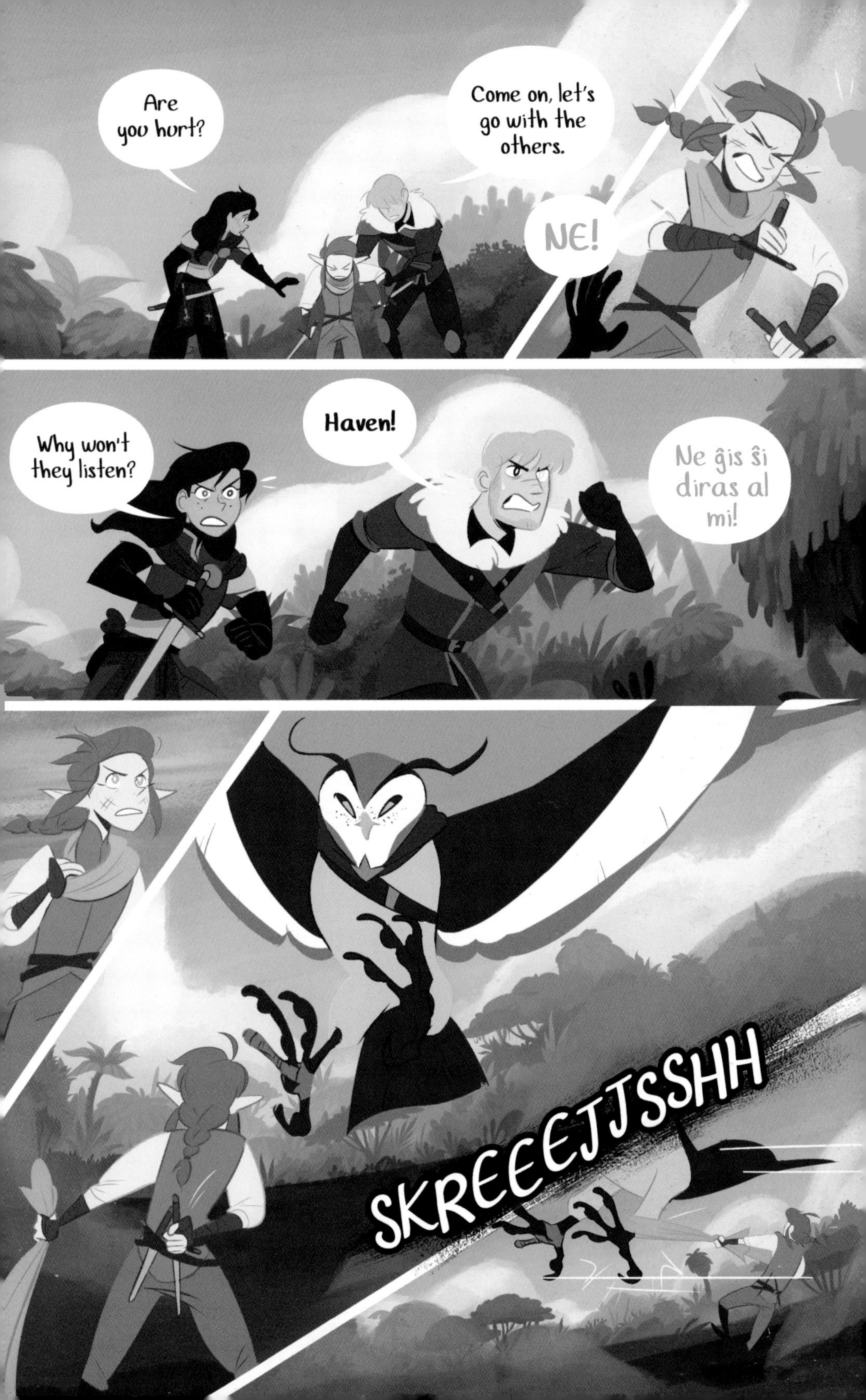
Are you hurt?
Come on, let's go with the others.
NE!
Why won't they listen?
Haven!
Ne ĝis ŝi diras al mi!
SKREEEJJSSHH

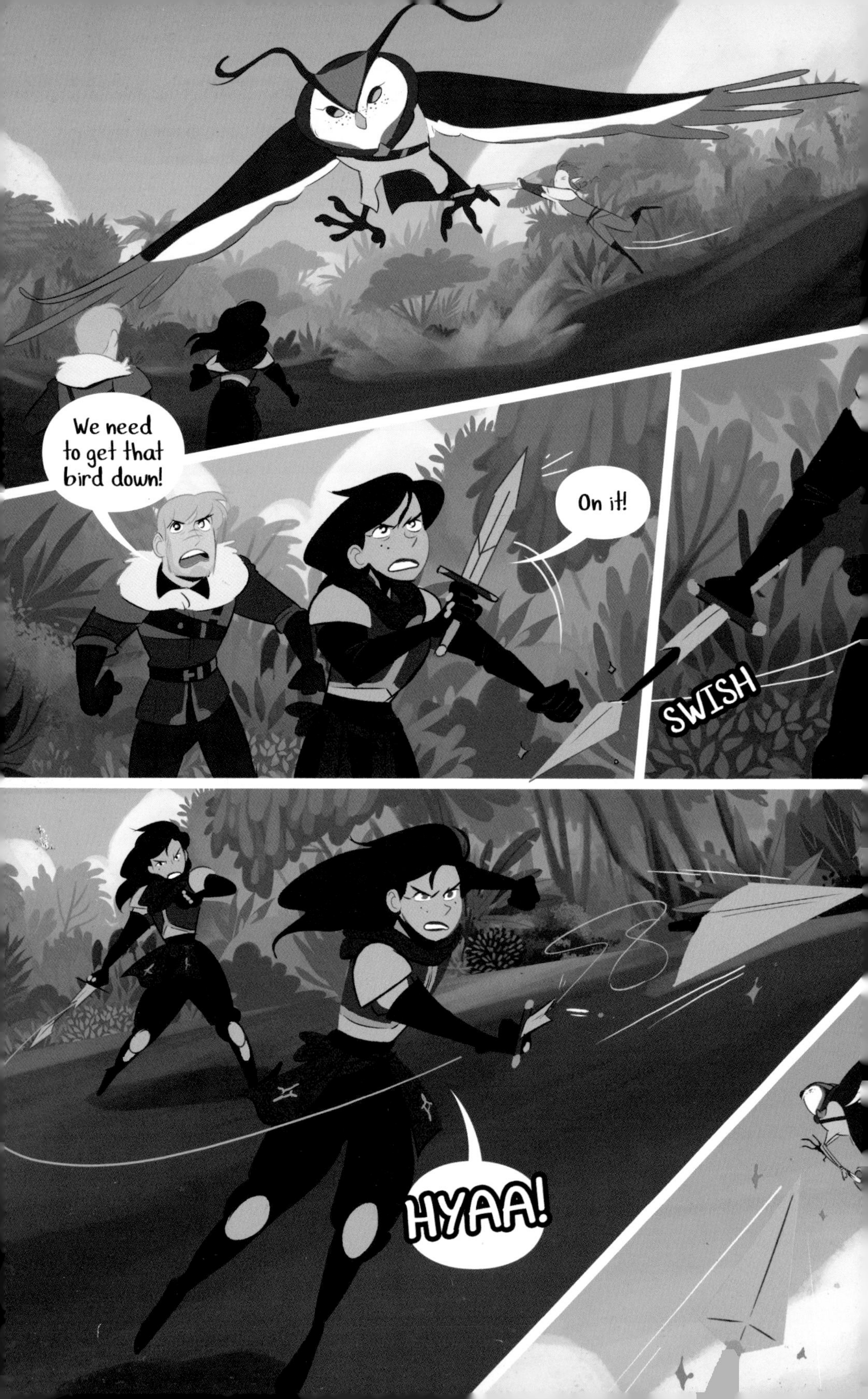
We need to get that bird down!
On it!
SWISH
HYAA!

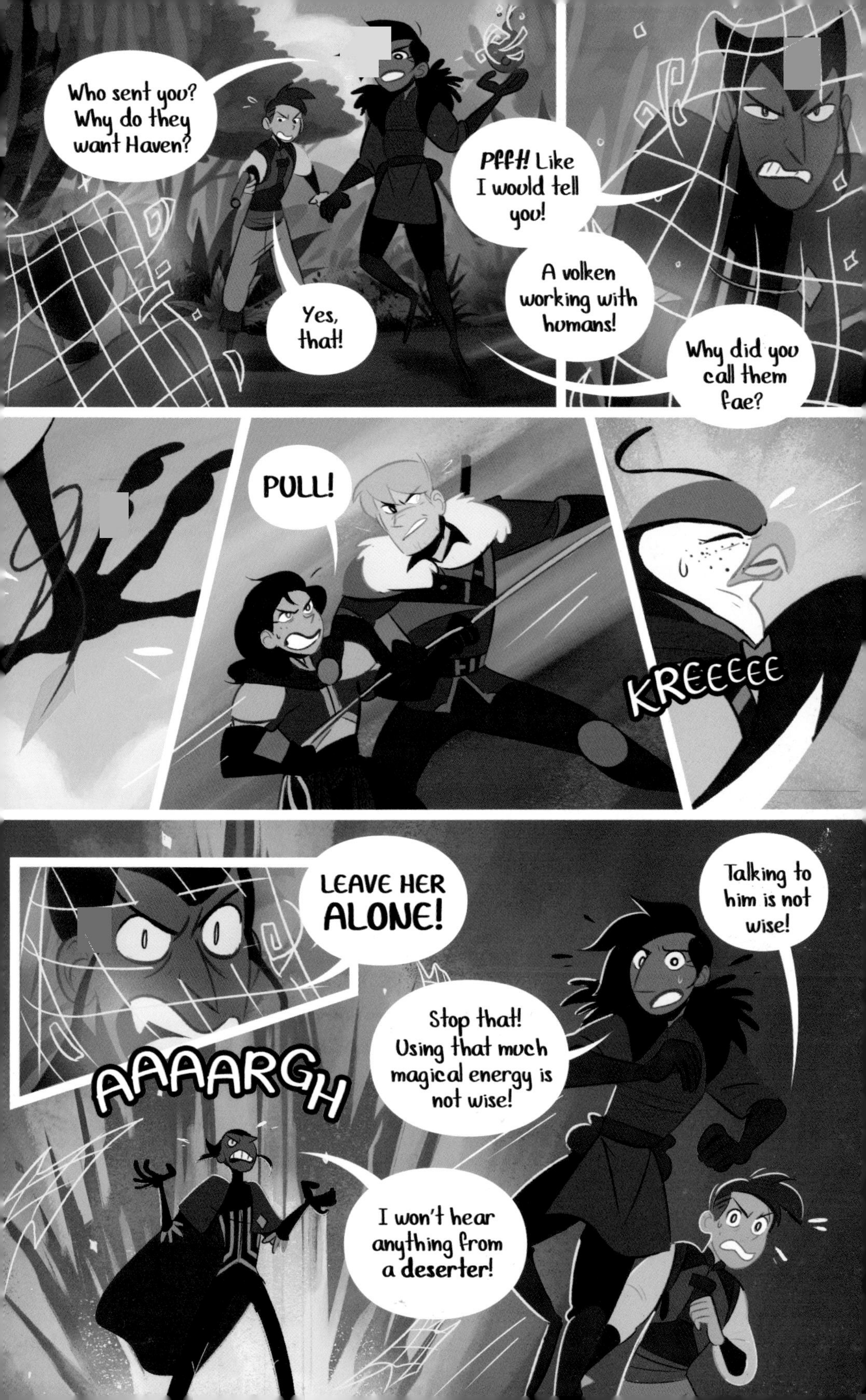

Who sent you? Why do they want Haven?
Yes, that!
Pfft! Like I would tell you!
A volken working with humans!
Why did you call them fae?
PULL!
KREEEEE
LEAVE HER ALONE!
AAAARGH
Talking to him is not wise!
Stop that! Using that much magical energy is not wise!
I won't hear anything from a deserter!

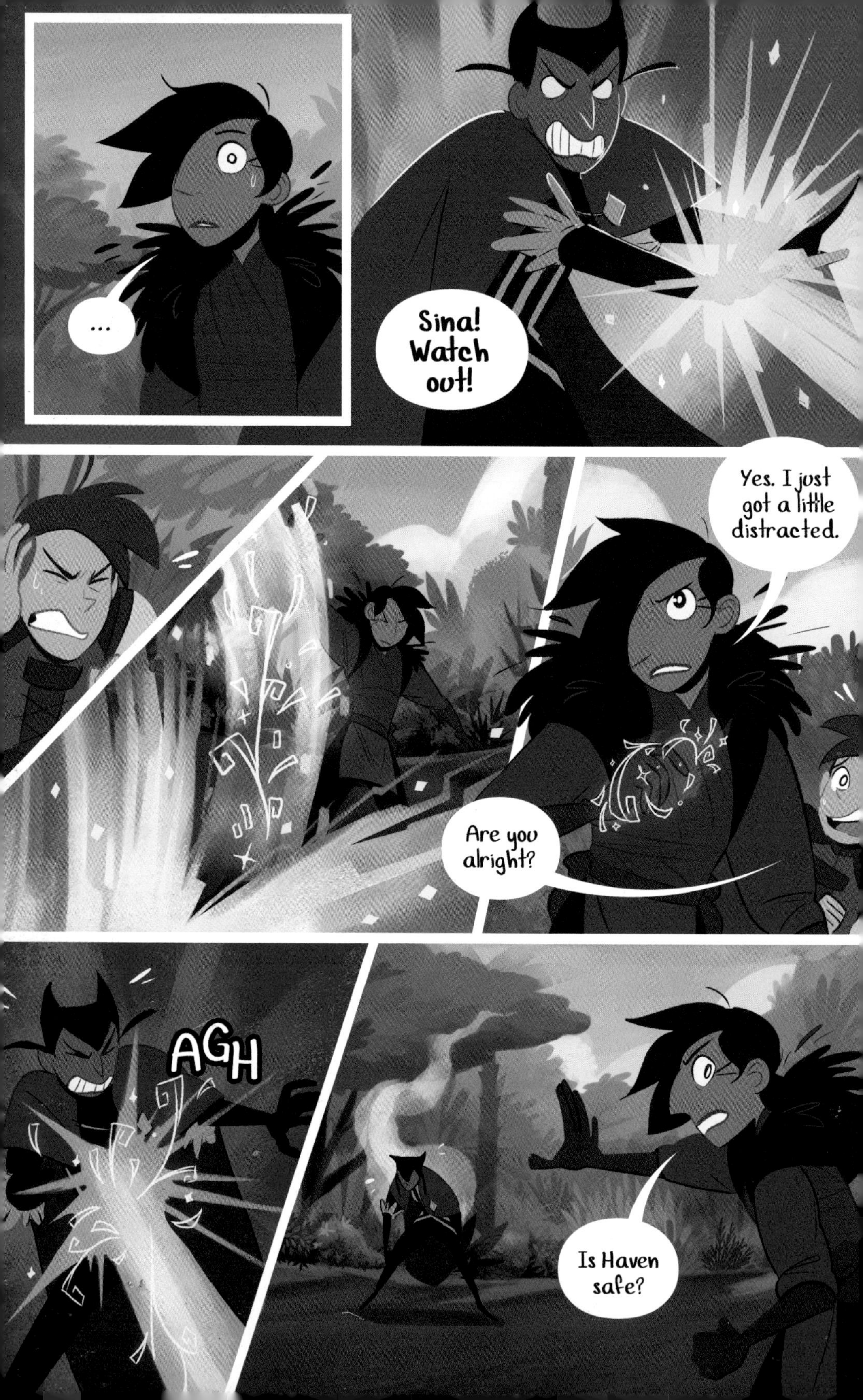
...
Sina! Watch out!
Are you alright?
Yes. I just got a little distracted.
AGH
Is Haven safe?

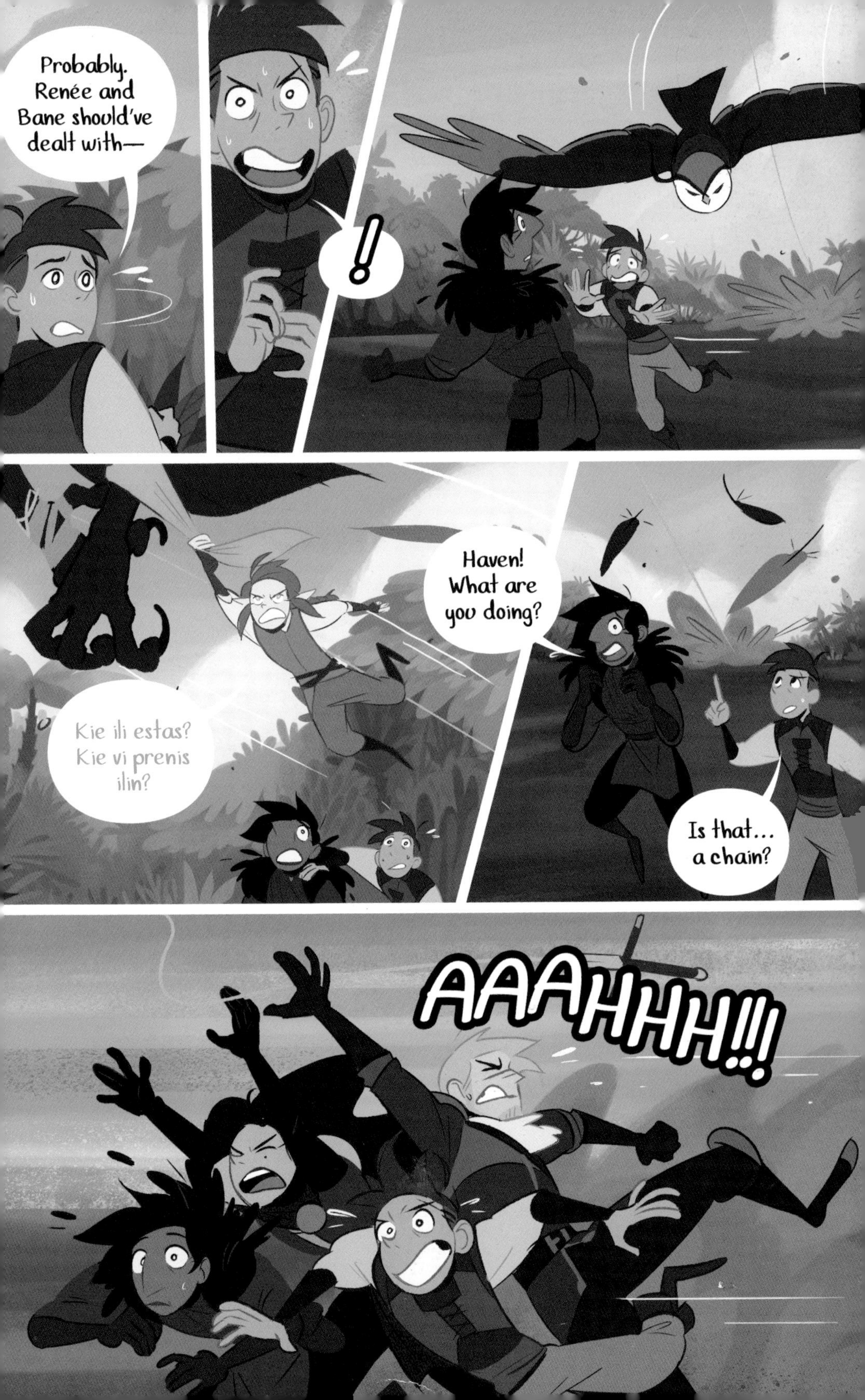
Probably. Renée and Bane should've dealt with—
!
Haven! What are you doing?
Kie ili estas? Kie vi prenis ilin?
Is that... a chain?
AAAHHHH!!!

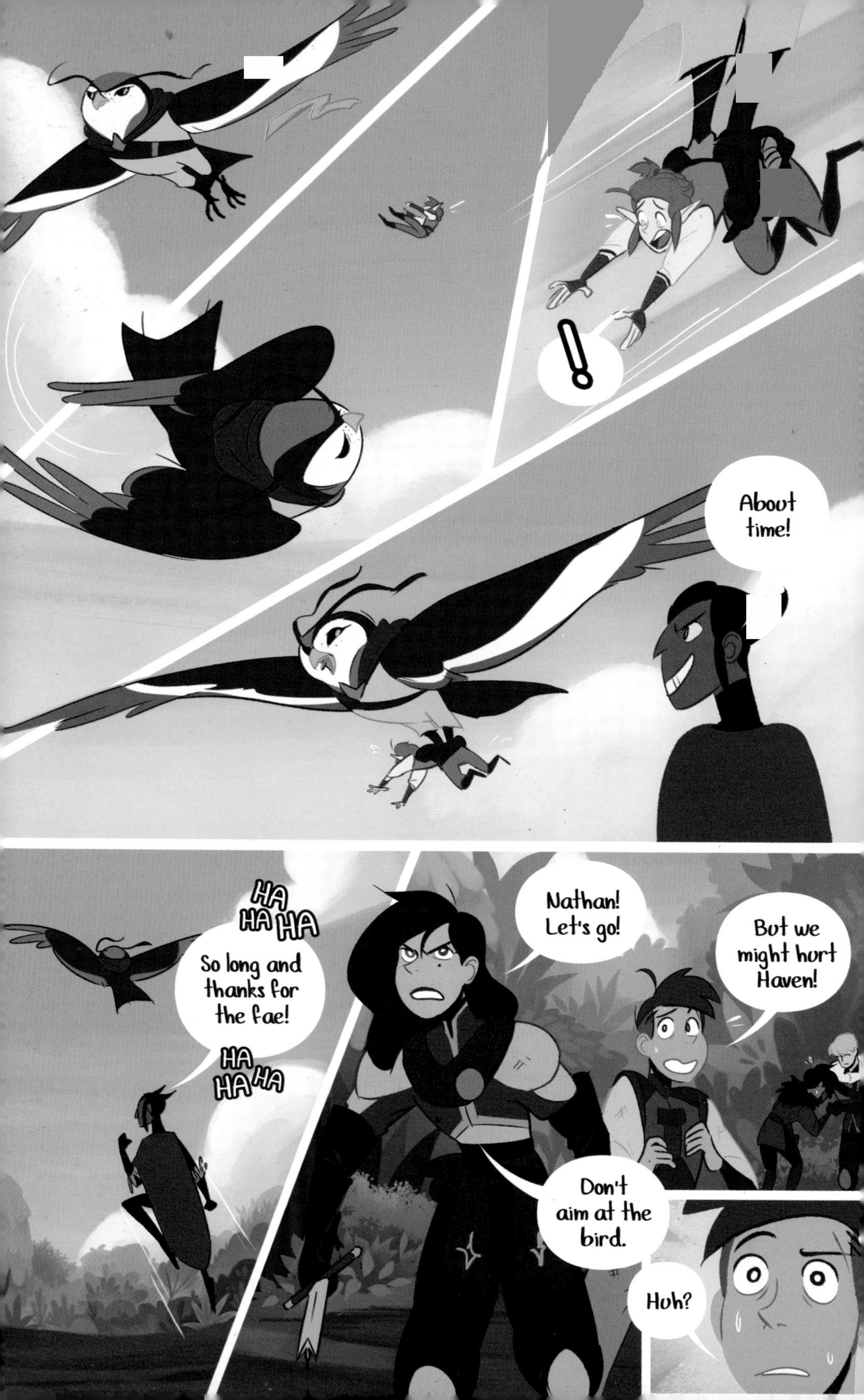
!
About time!
HA HA HA
So long and thanks for the fae!
HA HA HA
Nathan! Let's go!
But we might hurt Haven!
Don't aim at the bird.
Huh?

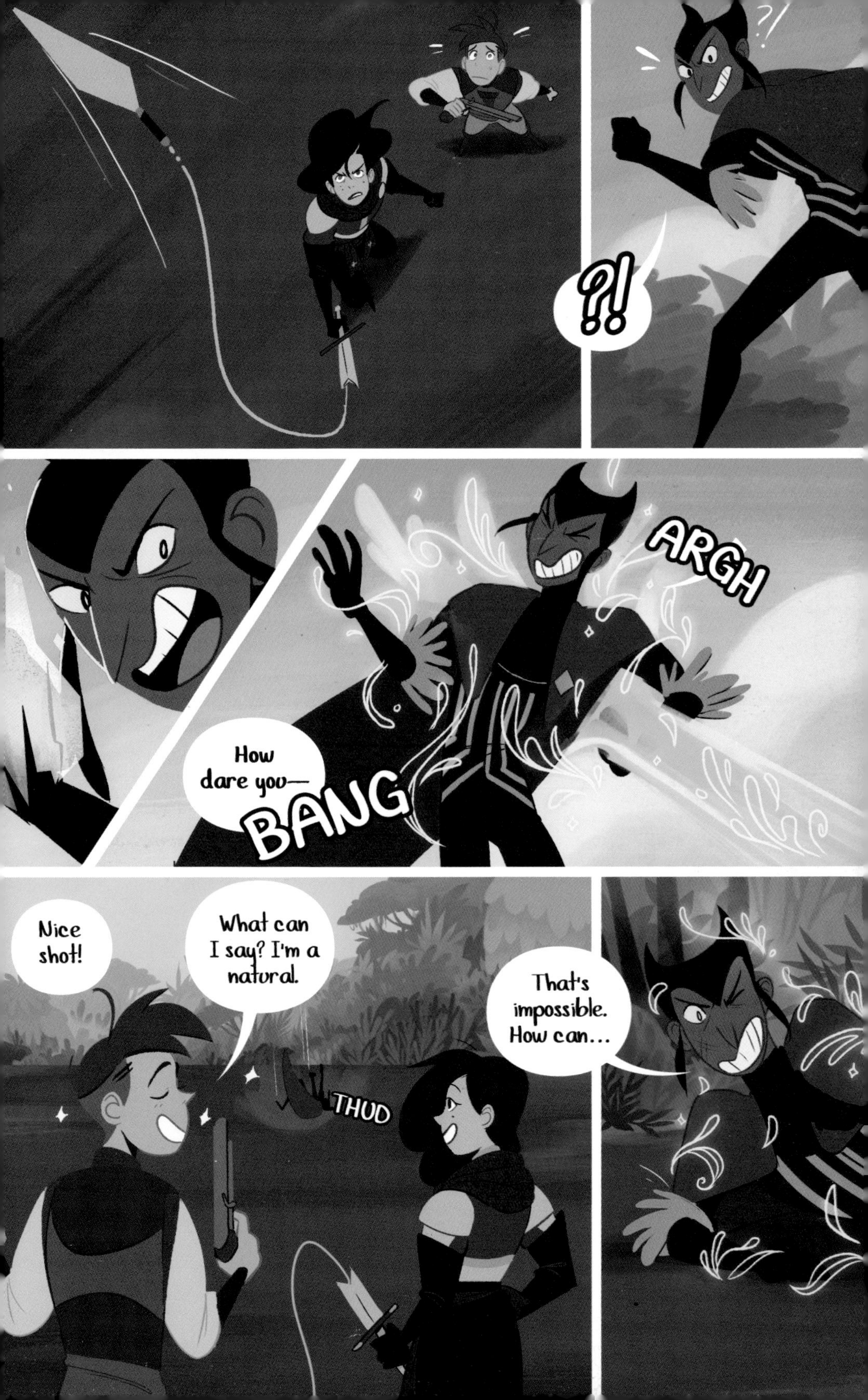
?!
?!
ARGH
How dare you—
BANG
Nice shot!
What can I say? I'm a natural.
THUD
That's impossible. How can...

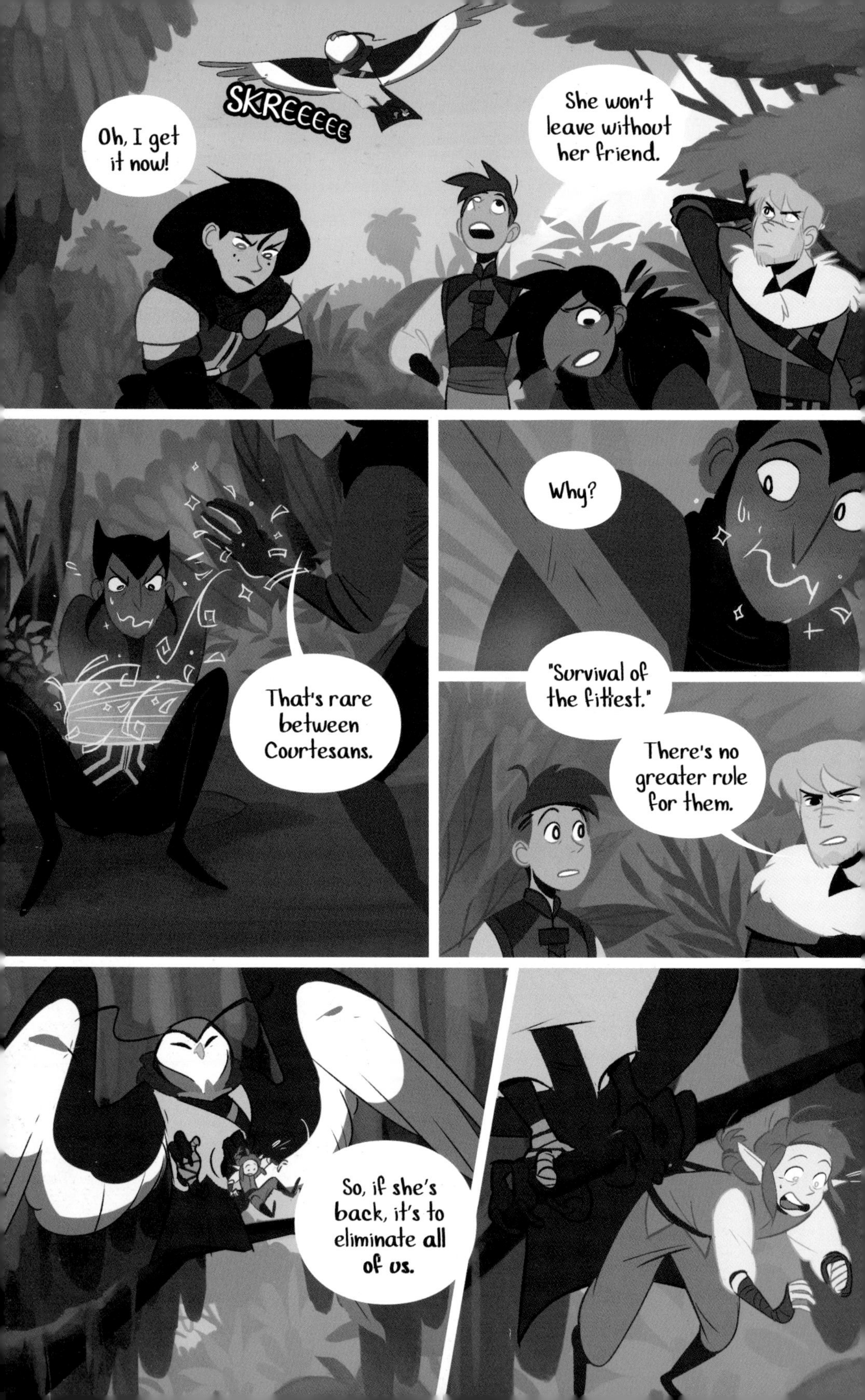
SKREEEEEE
Oh, I get it now!
She won't leave without her friend.
That's rare between Courtesans.
Why?
"Survival of the fittest."
There's no greater rule for them.
So, if she's back, it's to eliminate all of us.

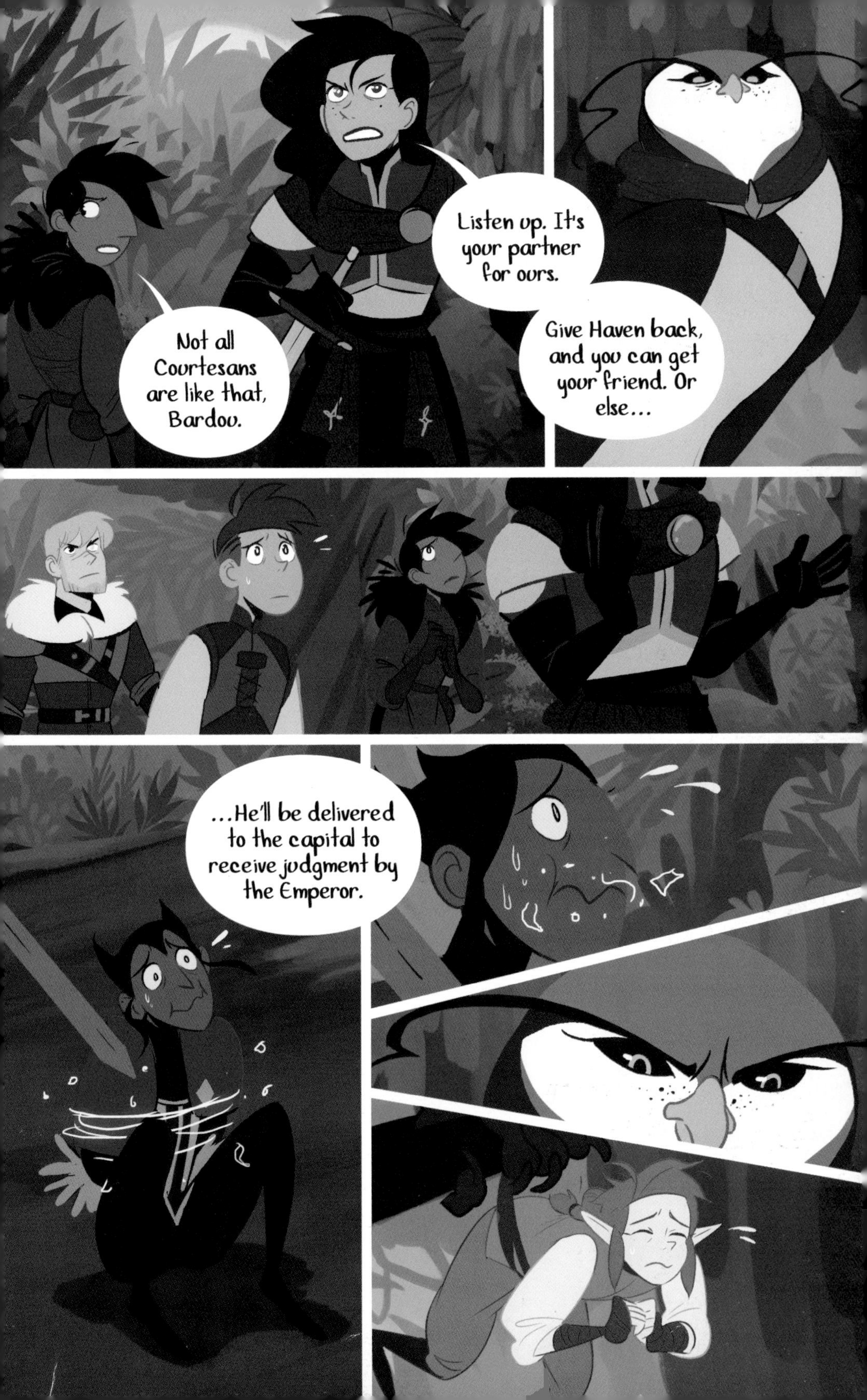
Not all Courtesans are like that, Bardou.
Listen up. It's your partner for ours.
Give Haven back, and you can get your friend. Or else...
...He'll be delivered to the capital to receive judgment by the Emperor.

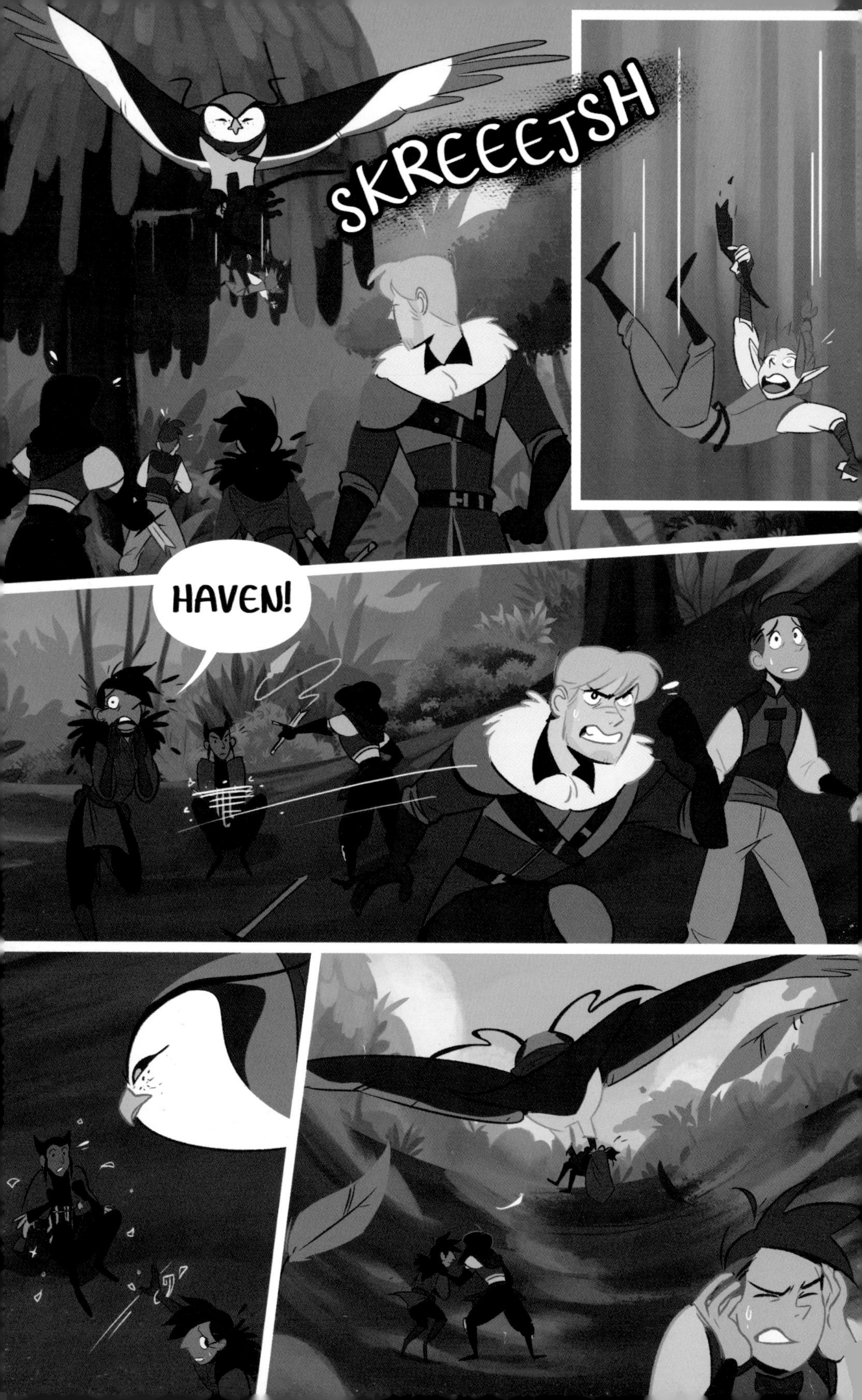
SKREEEJSH
HAVEN!

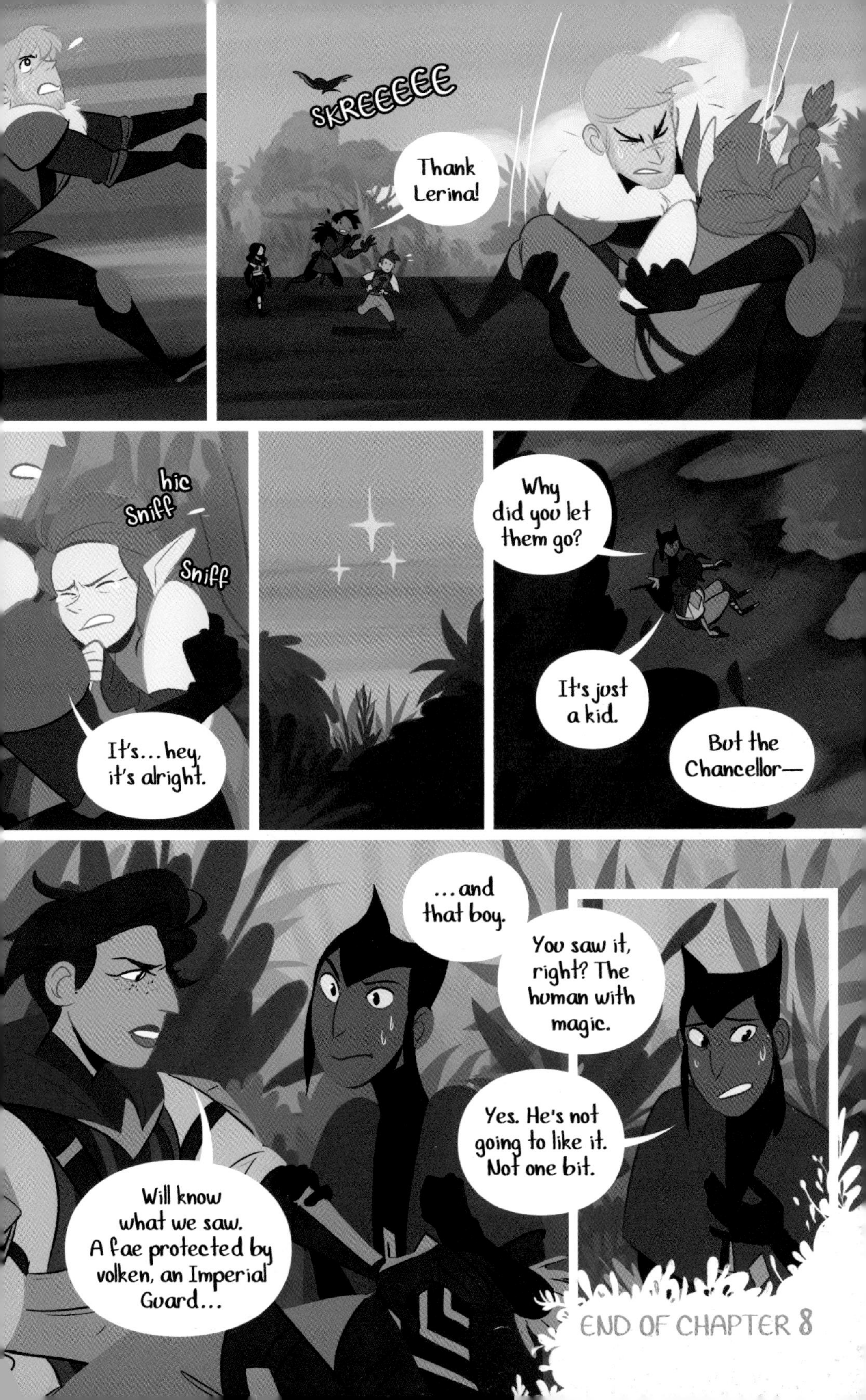
SKREEEEEE
Thank Lerina!
hic
Sniff
Sniff
It's... hey, it's alright.
Why did you let them go?
It's just a kid.
But the Chancellor—
...and that boy.
You saw it, right? The human with magic.
Yes. He's not going to like it. Not one bit.
Will know what we saw. A fae protected by volken, an Imperial Guard...
END OF CHAPTER 8

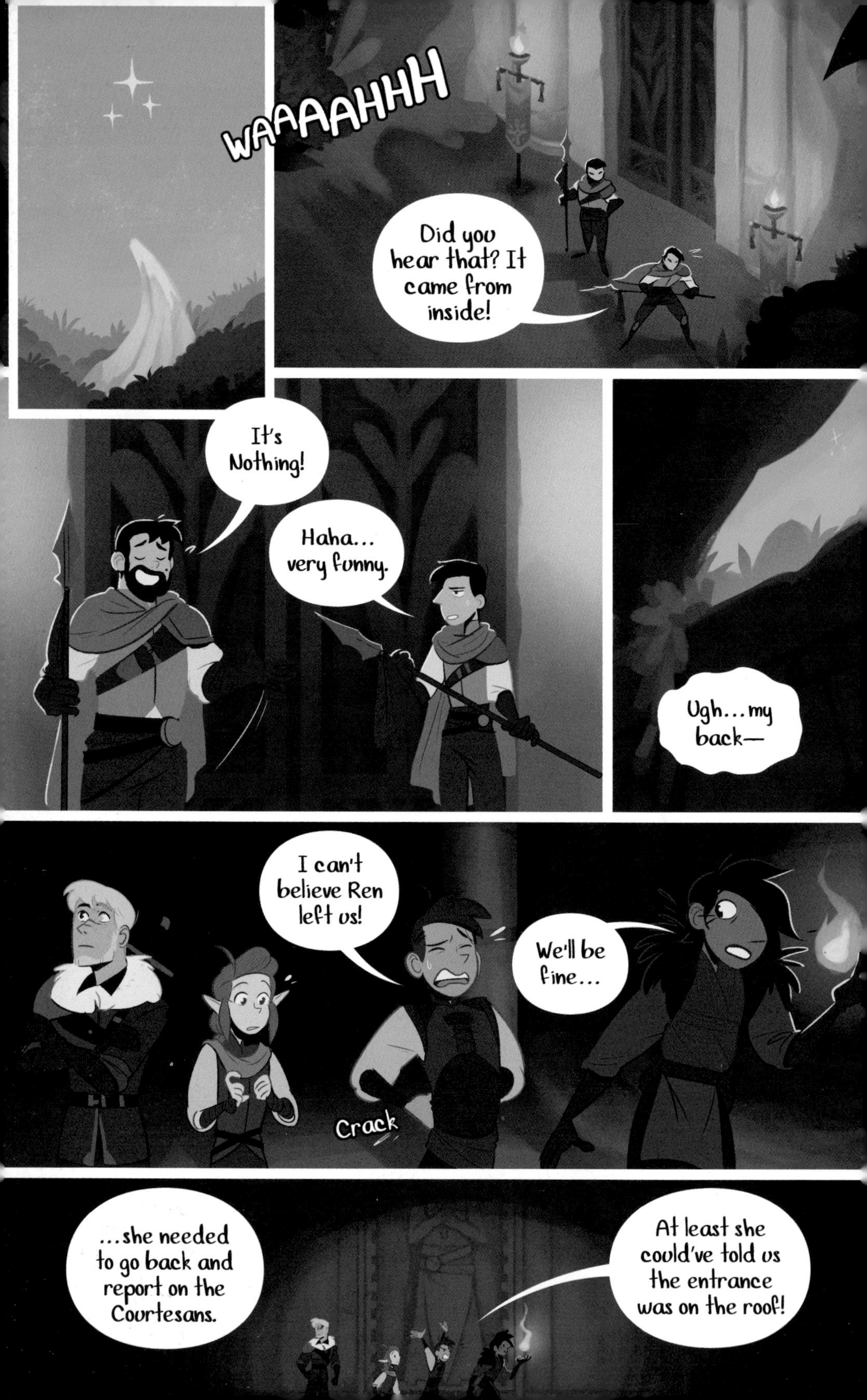
WAAAAHHH
Did you hear that? It came from inside!
It's Nothing!
Haha... very funny.
Ugh...my back—
I can't believe Ren left us!
We'll be fine...
Crack
...she needed to go back and report on the Courtesans.
At least she could've told us the entrance was on the roof!

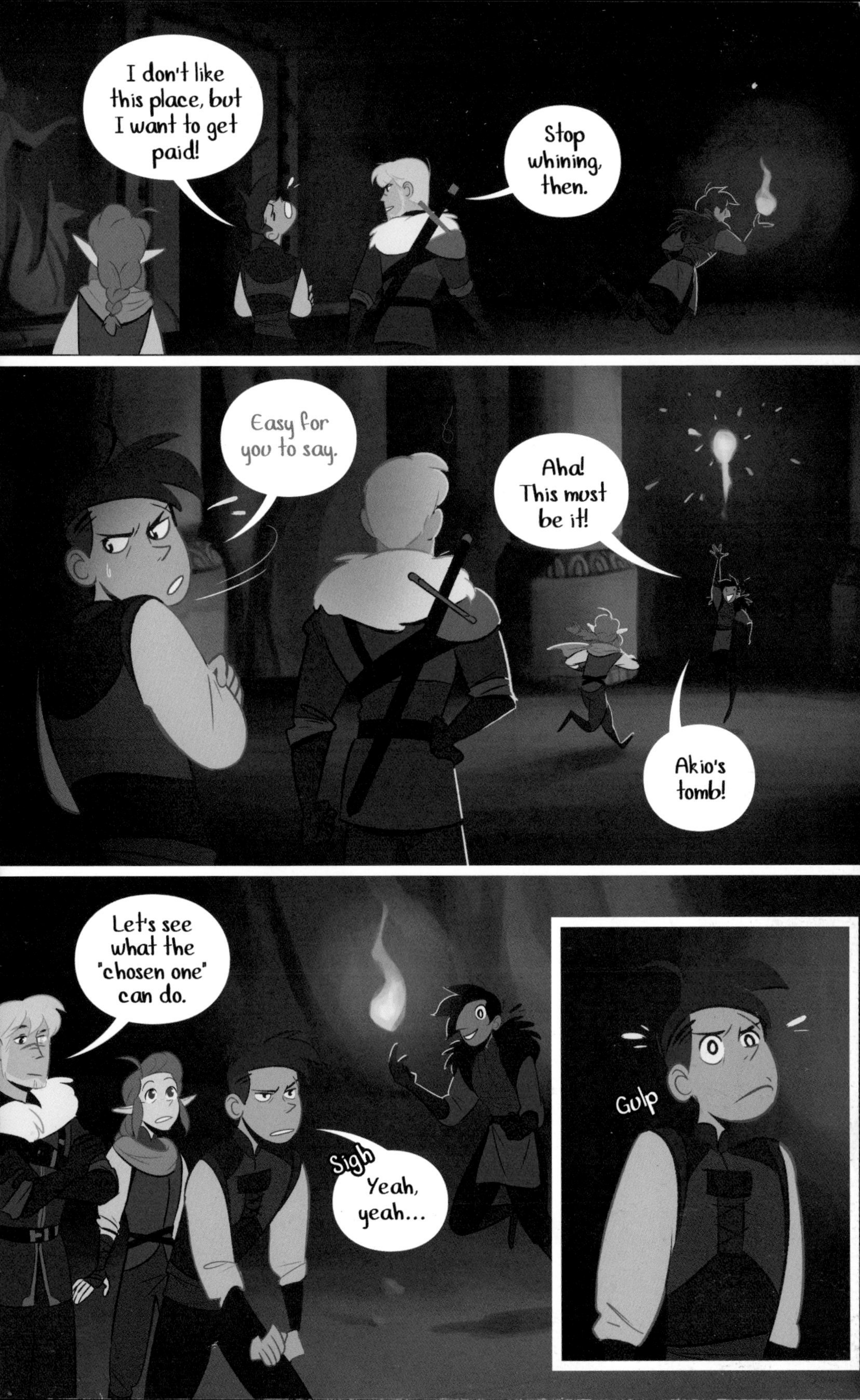
I don't like this place, but I want to get paid!
Stop whining, then.
Easy for you to say.
Aha! This must be it!
Akio's tomb!
Let's see what the "chosen one" can do.
Sigh
Yeah, yeah...
Gulp

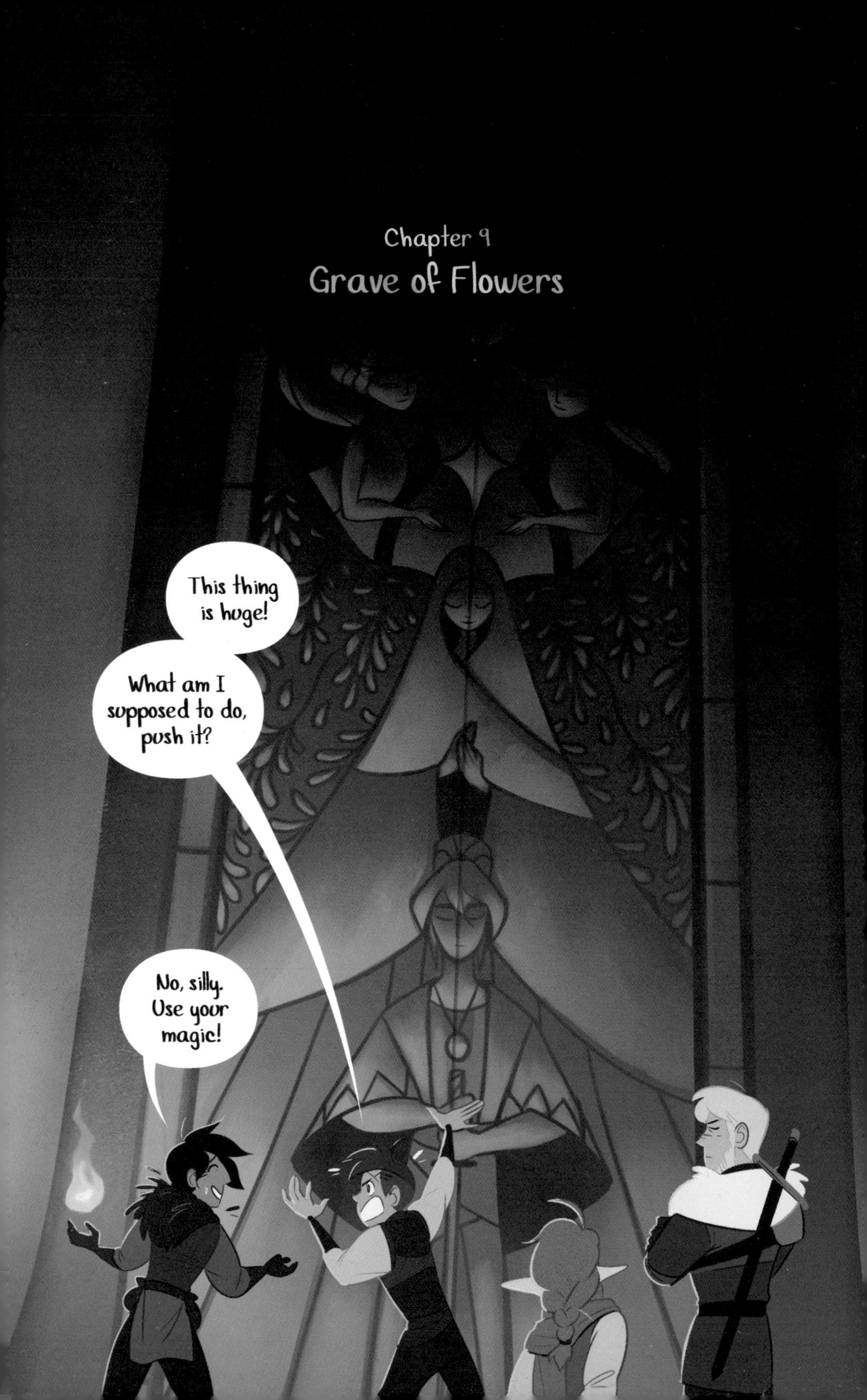
Chapter 9
Grave of Flowers
This thing is huge!
What am I supposed to do, push it?
No, silly. Use your magic!

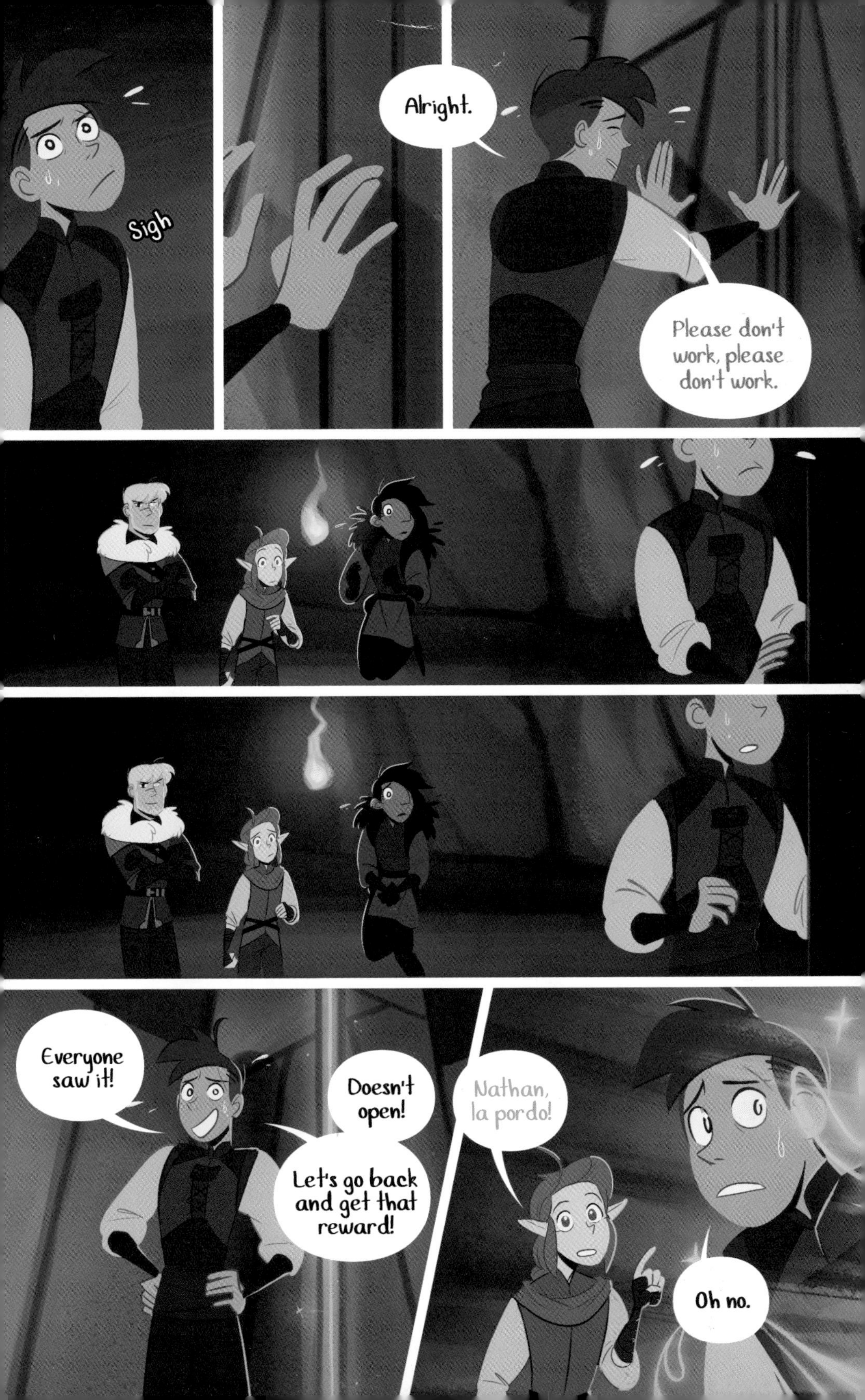
Sigh
Alright.
Please don't work, please don't work.
Everyone saw it!
Doesn't open!
Let's go back and get that reward!
Nathan, la pordo!
Oh no.

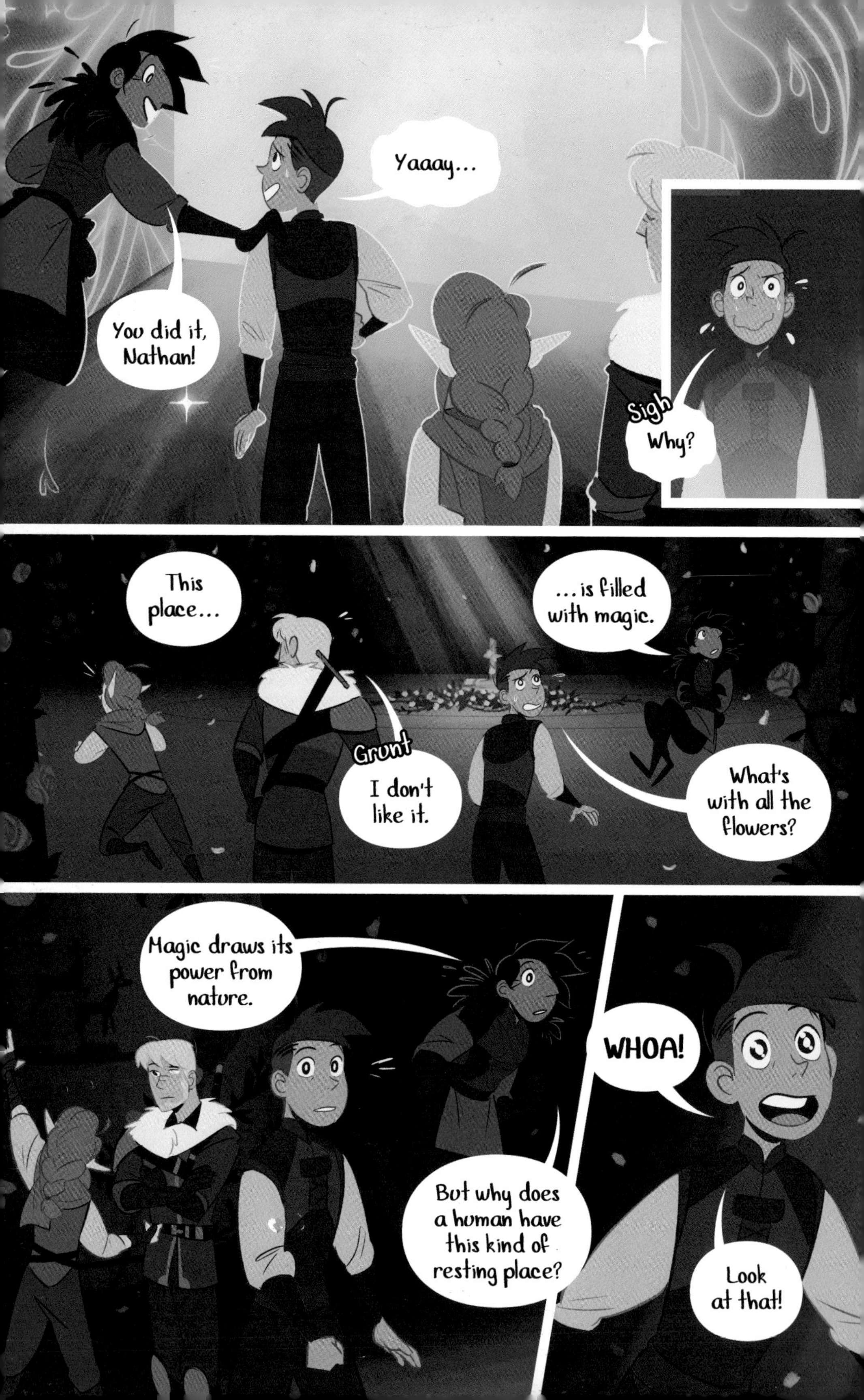
Yaaay...
You did it, Nathan!
Sigh
Why?
This place...
...is filled with magic.
Grunt
I don't like it.
What's with all the flowers?
Magic draws its power from nature.
But why does a human have this kind of resting place?
WHOA!
Look at that!

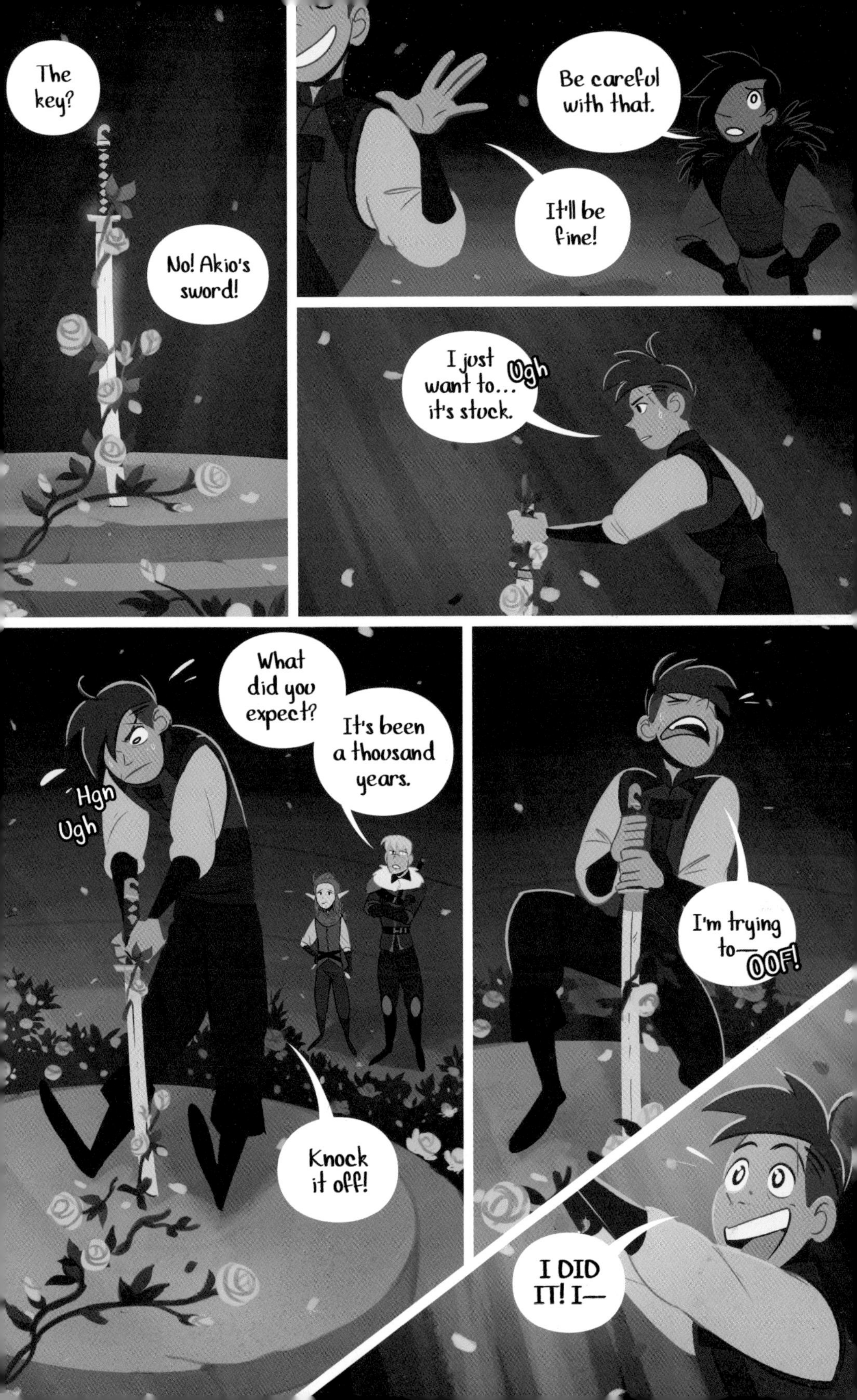
The key?
No! Akio's sword!
Be careful with that.
It'll be fine!
I just want to… Ugh it's stuck.
What did you expect?
It's been a thousand years.
Hgn
Ugh
Knock it off!
I'm trying to— OOF!
I DID IT! I—

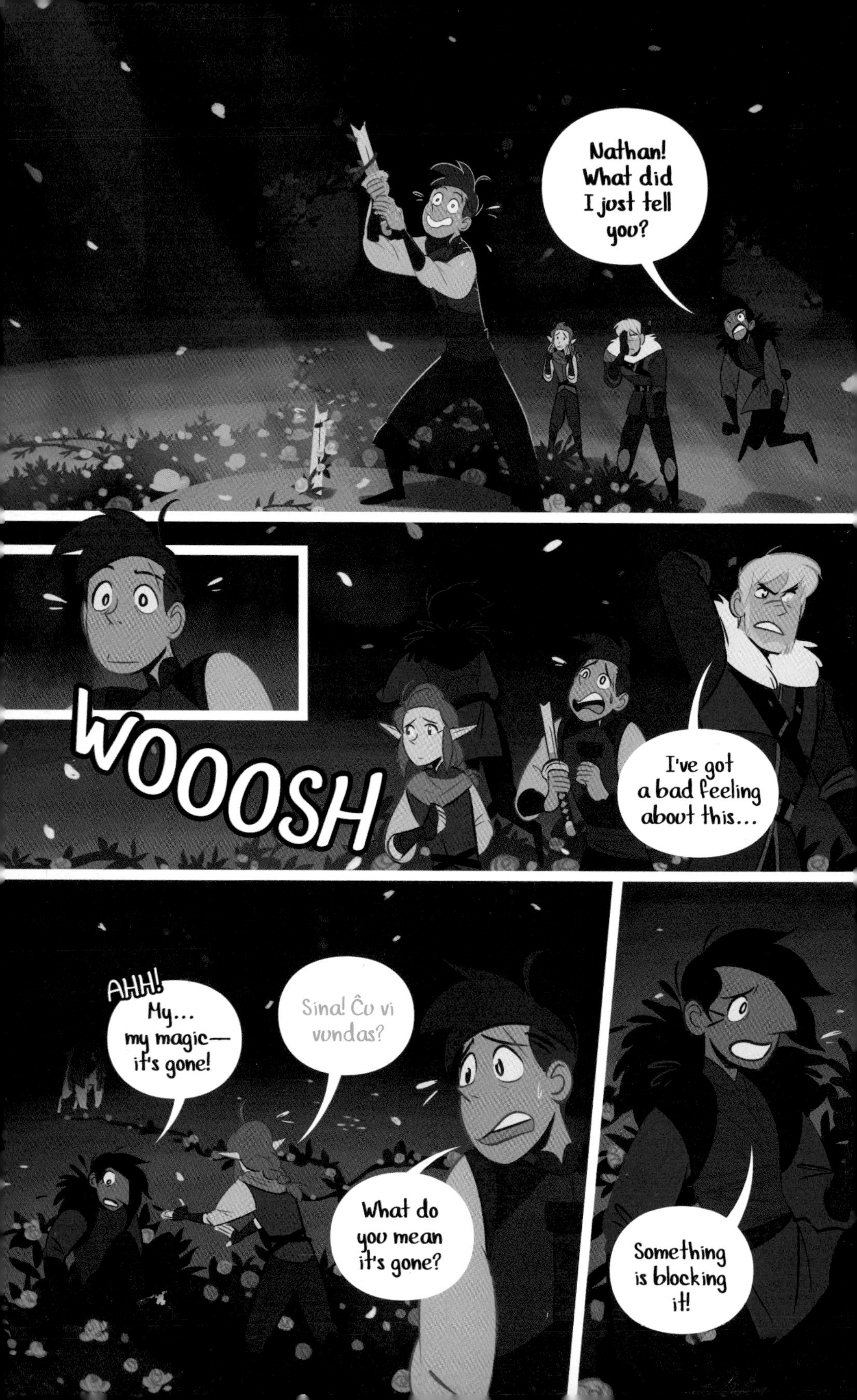
Nathan! What did I just tell you?
WOOOSH
I've got a bad feeling about this...
AHH! My... my magic— it's gone!
Sina! Ĉu vi vundas?
What do you mean it's gone?
Something is blocking it!

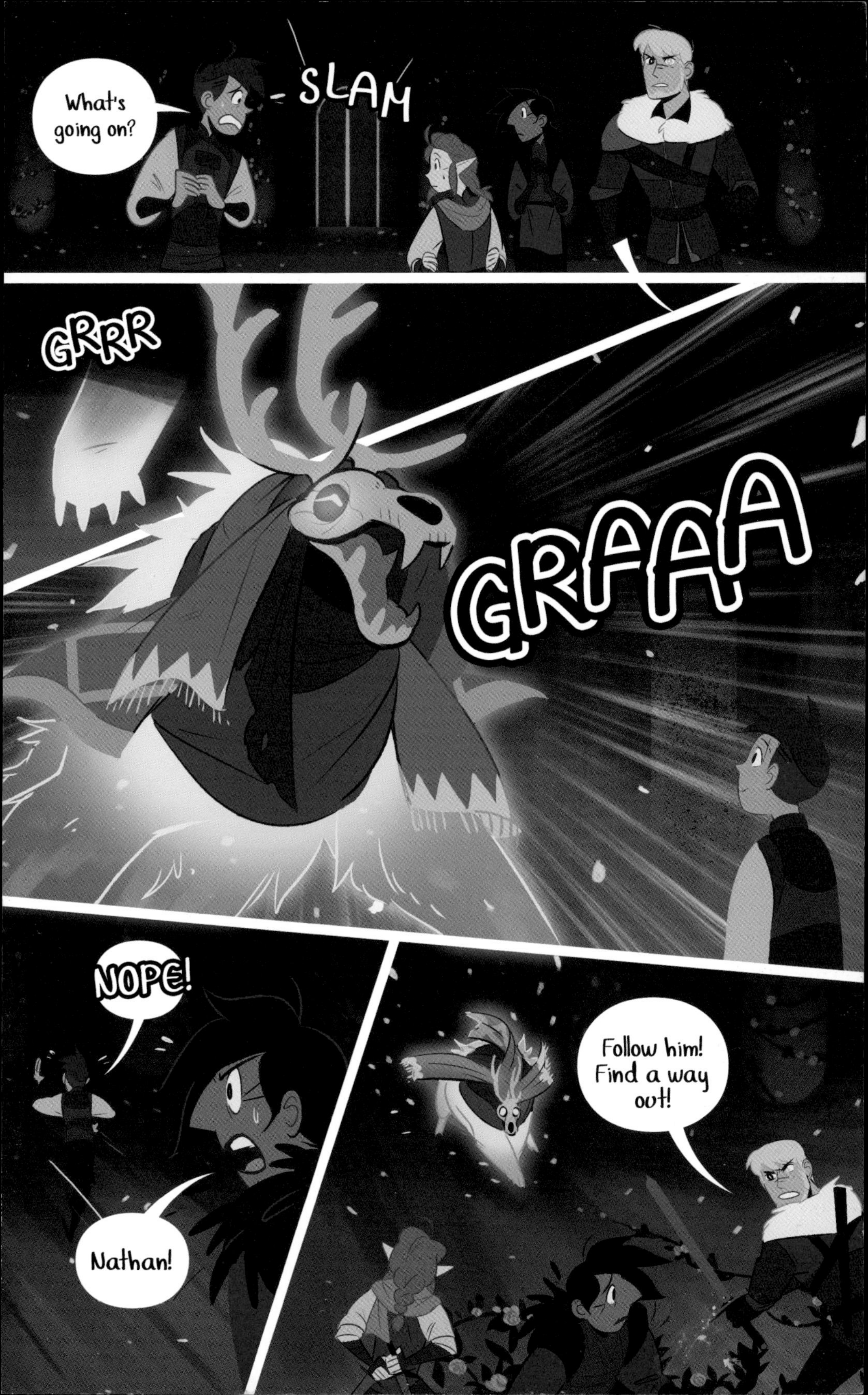
What's going on?
SLAM
GRRR
GRAAA
NOPE!
Nathan!
Follow him! Find a way out!

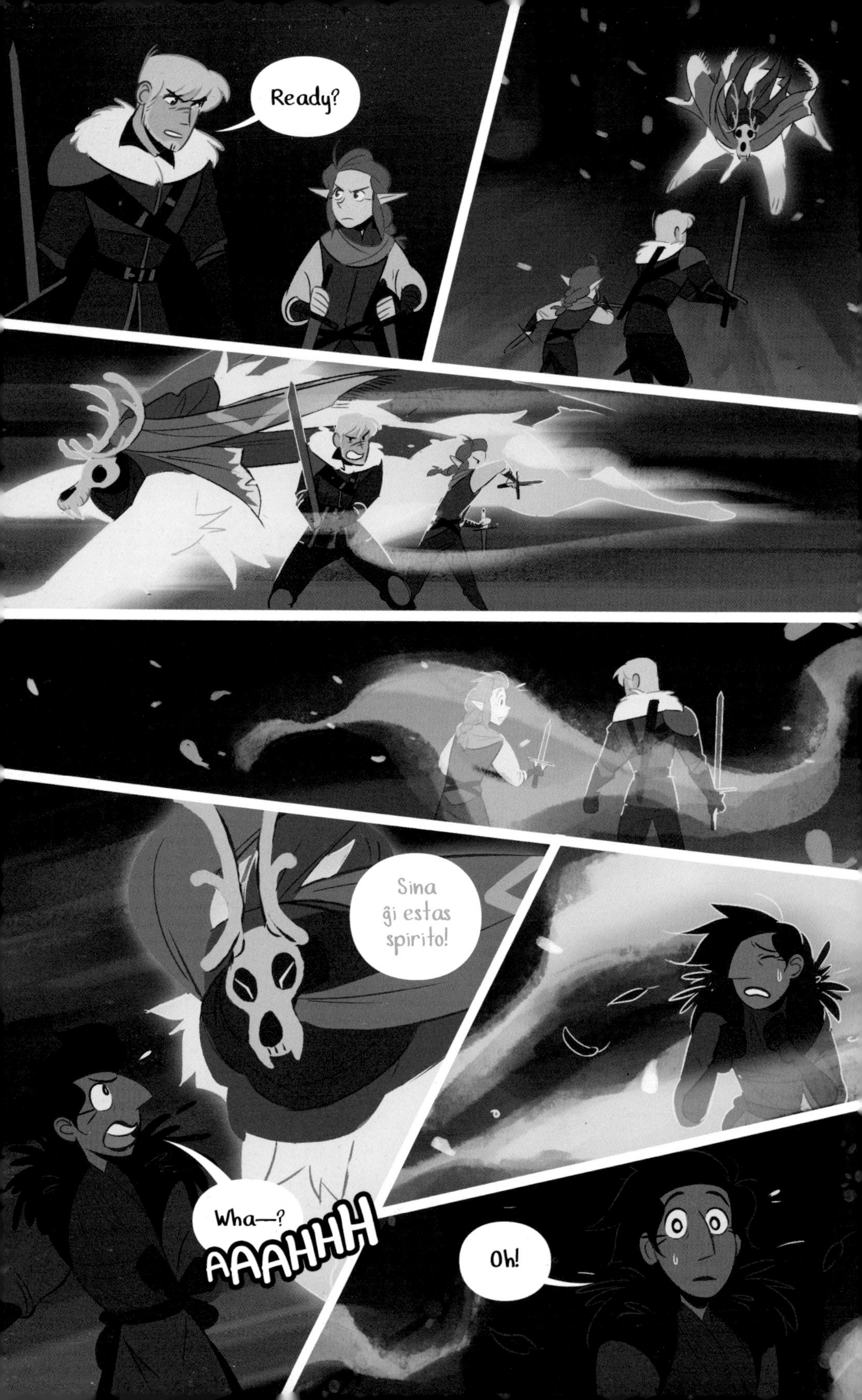

Ready?
Sina ĝi estas spirito!
Wha—?
AAAHHH
Oh!

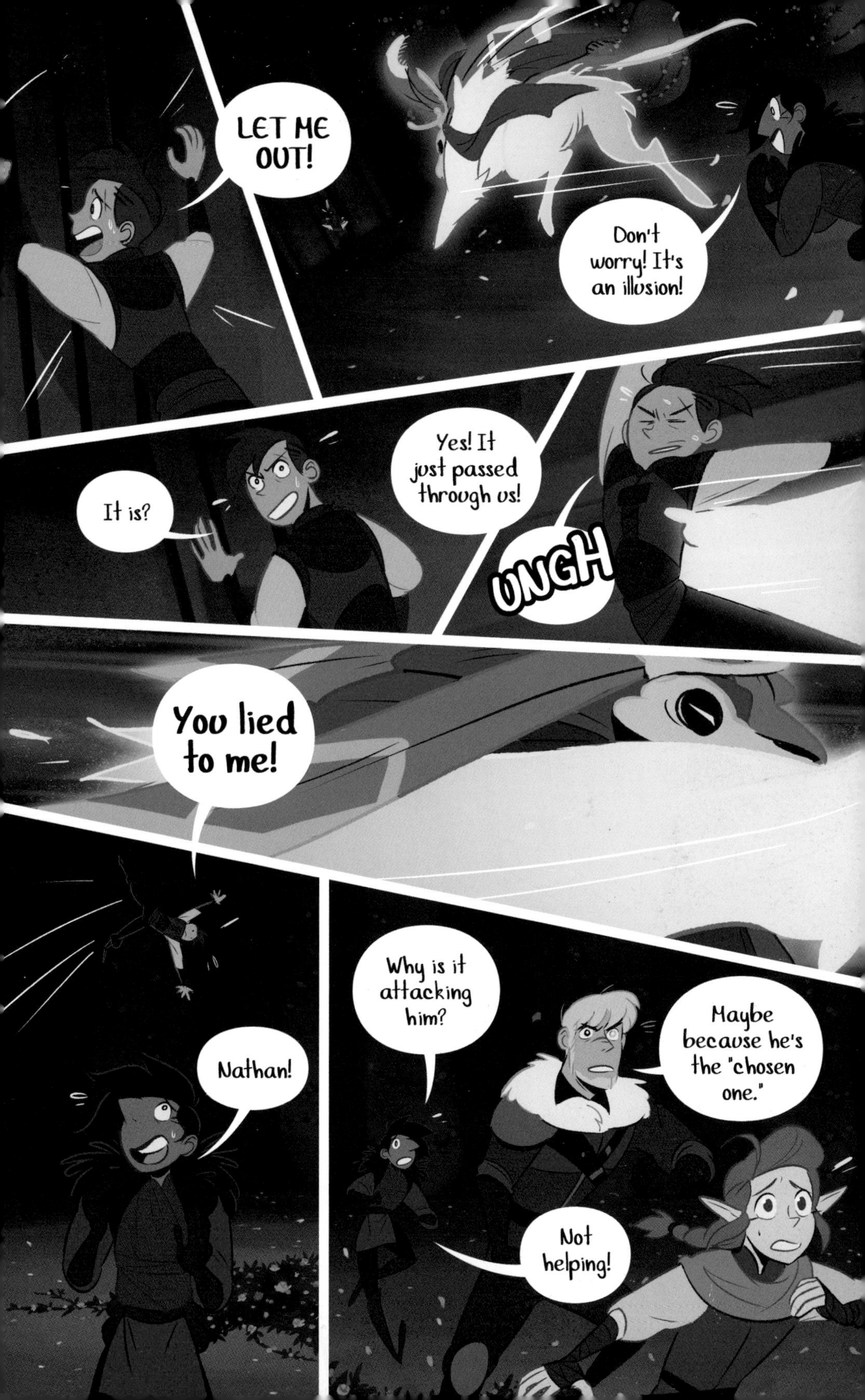
LET ME OUT!
Don't worry! It's an illusion!
It is?
Yes! It just passed through us!
UNGH
You lied to me!
Nathan!
Why is it attacking him?
Maybe because he's the "chosen one."
Not helping!

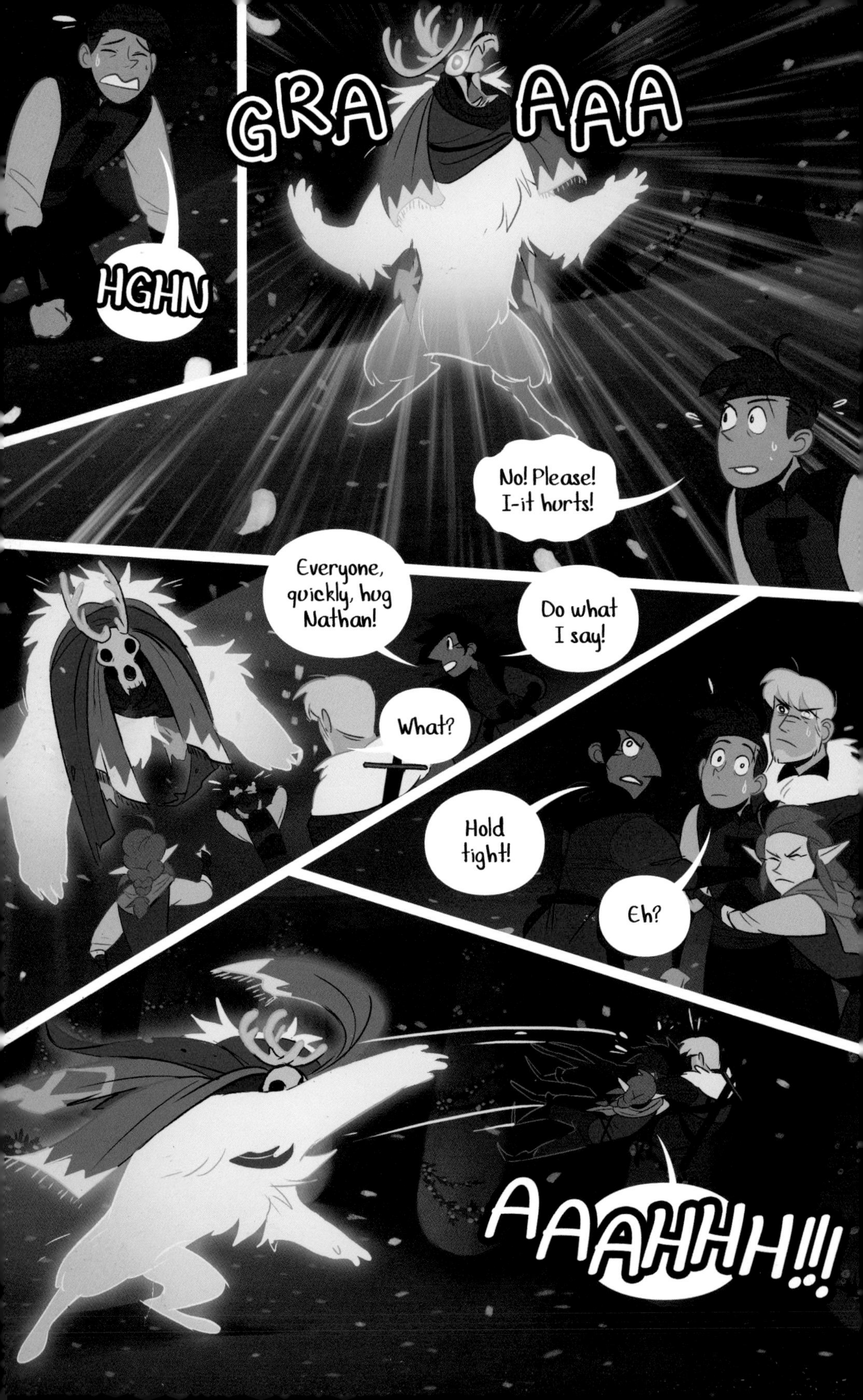
GRAAAA
HGHN
No! Please! I-it hurts!
Everyone, quickly, hug Nathan!
Do what I say!
What?
Hold tight!
Eh?
AAAHHHH!!!

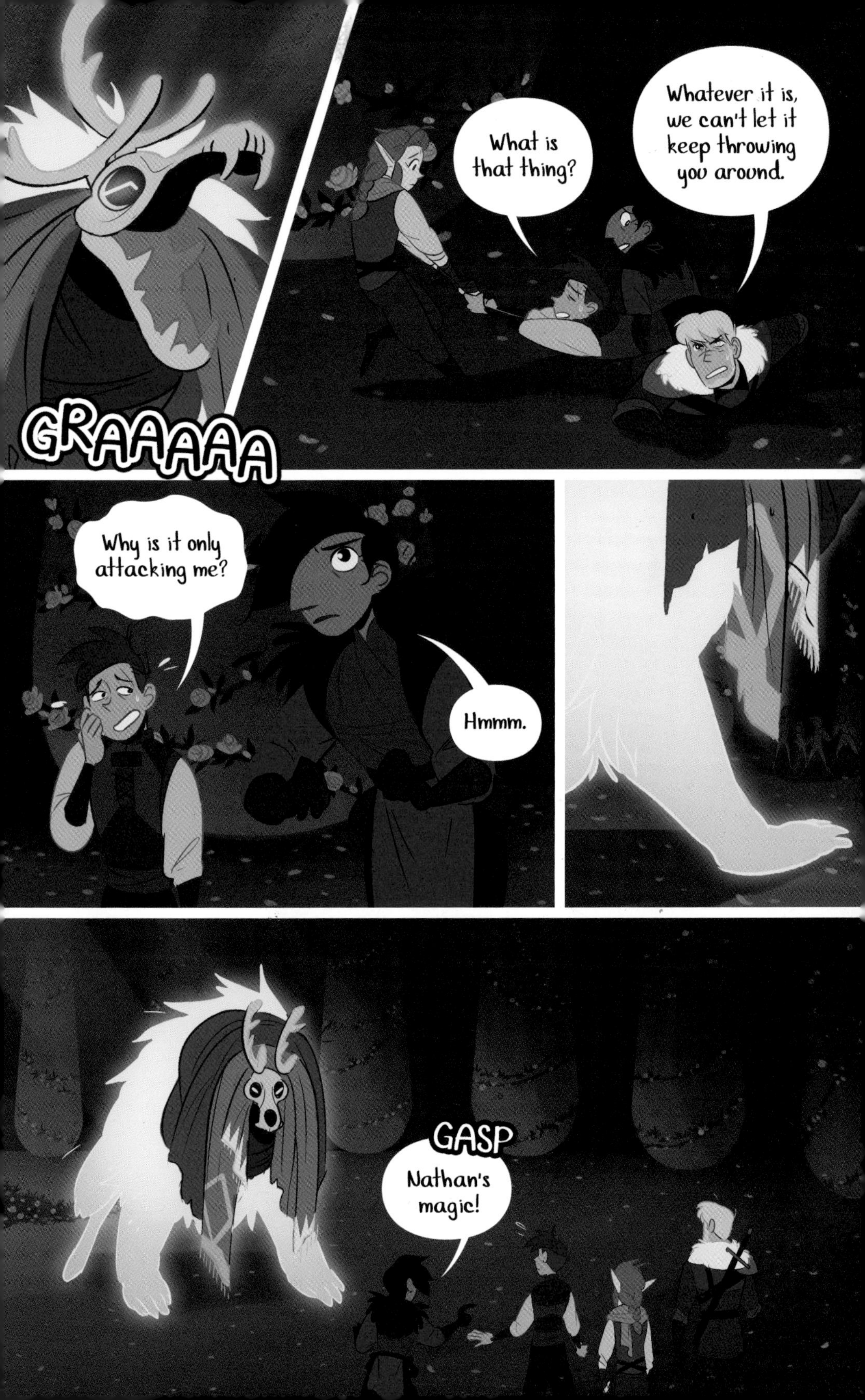
GRAAAAA
What is that thing?
Whatever it is, we can't let it keep throwing you around.
Why is it only attacking me?
Hmmm.
GASP
Nathan's magic!

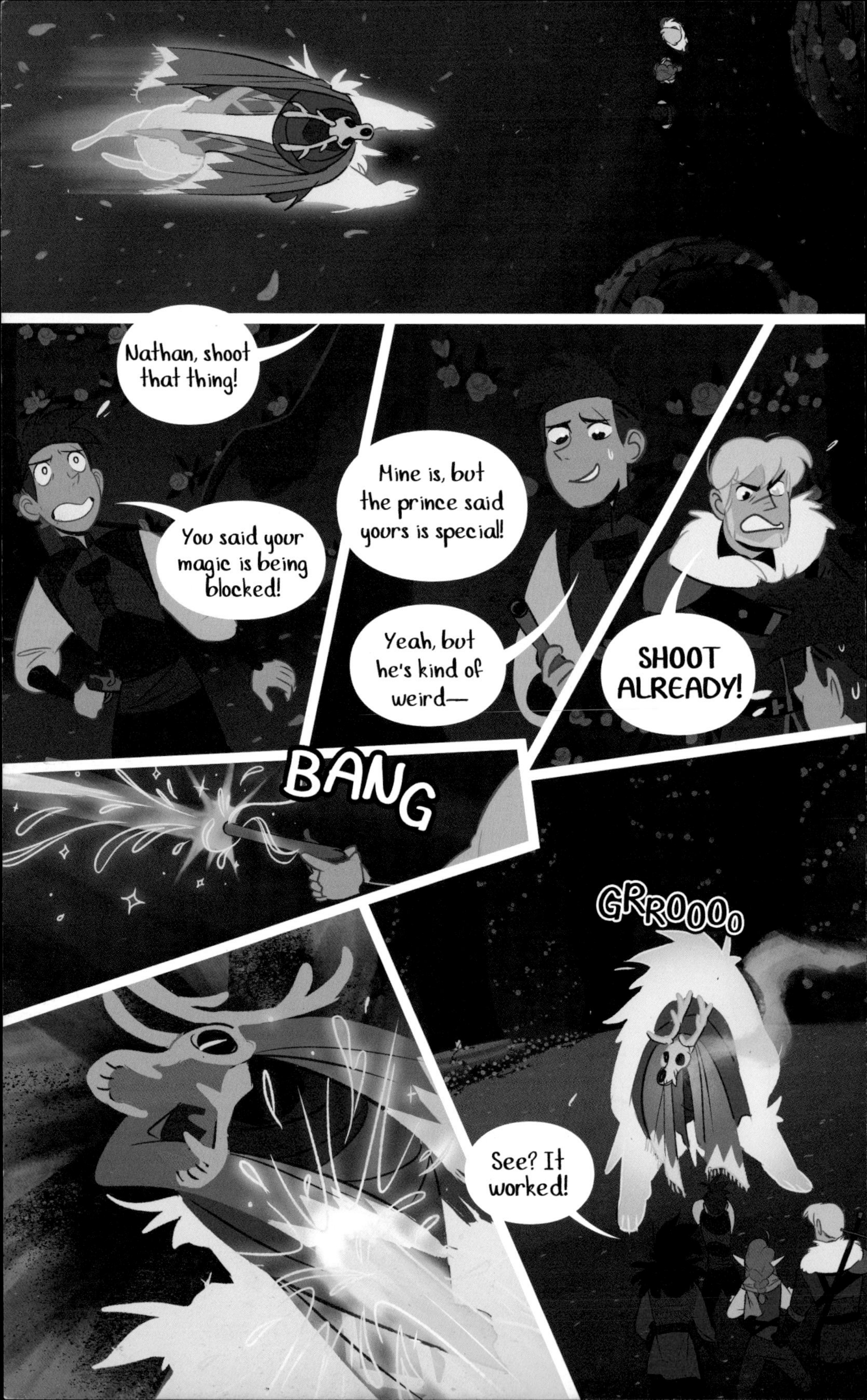
Nathan, shoot that thing!
You said your magic is being blocked!
Mine is, but the prince said yours is special!
Yeah, but he's kind of weird—
SHOOT ALREADY!
BANG
GRROOOO
See? It worked!

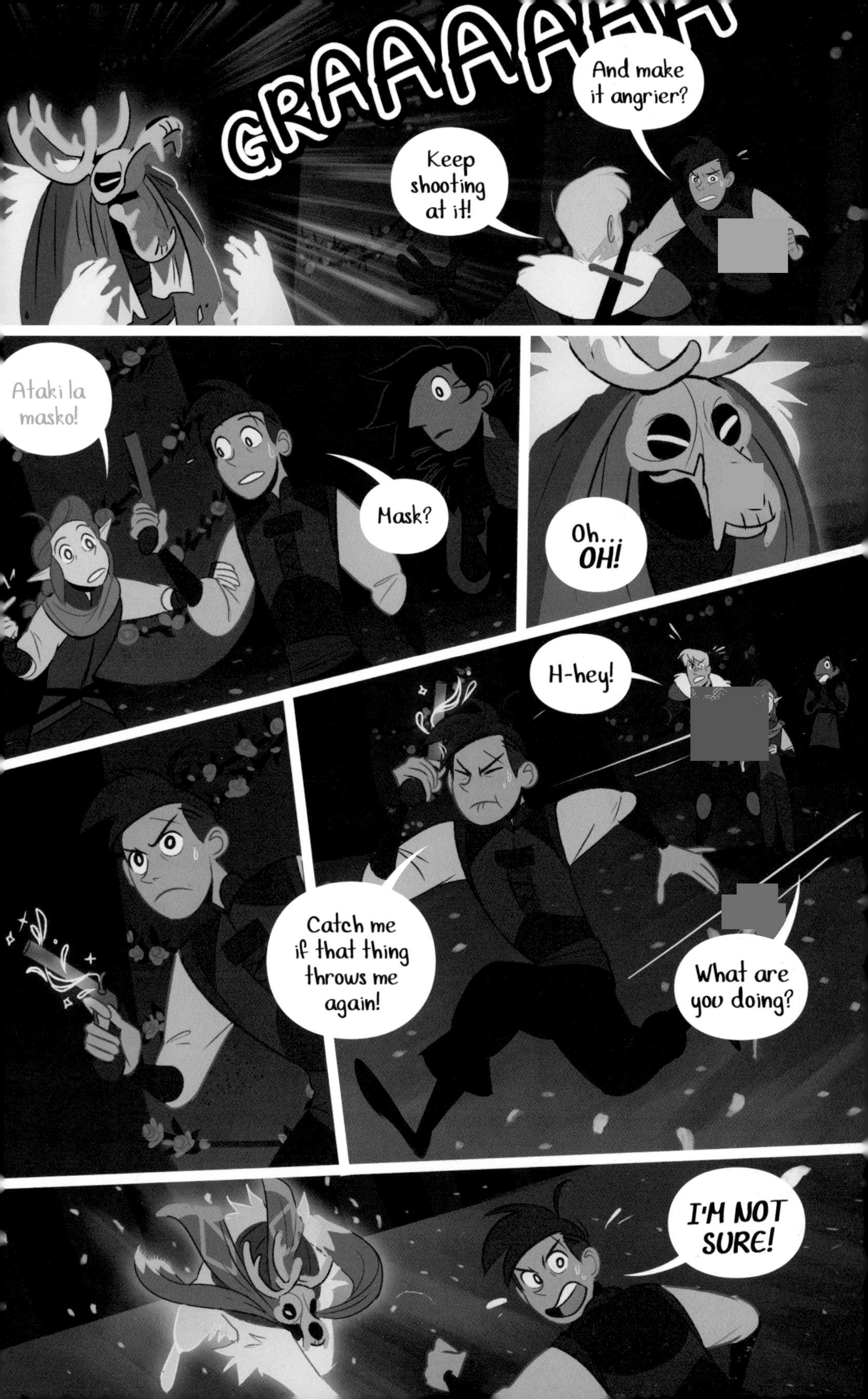
GRAAAAAH
Keep shooting at it!
And make it angrier?
Ataki la masko!
Mask?
Oh... OH!
H-hey!
Catch me if that thing throws me again!
What are you doing?
I'M NOT SURE!

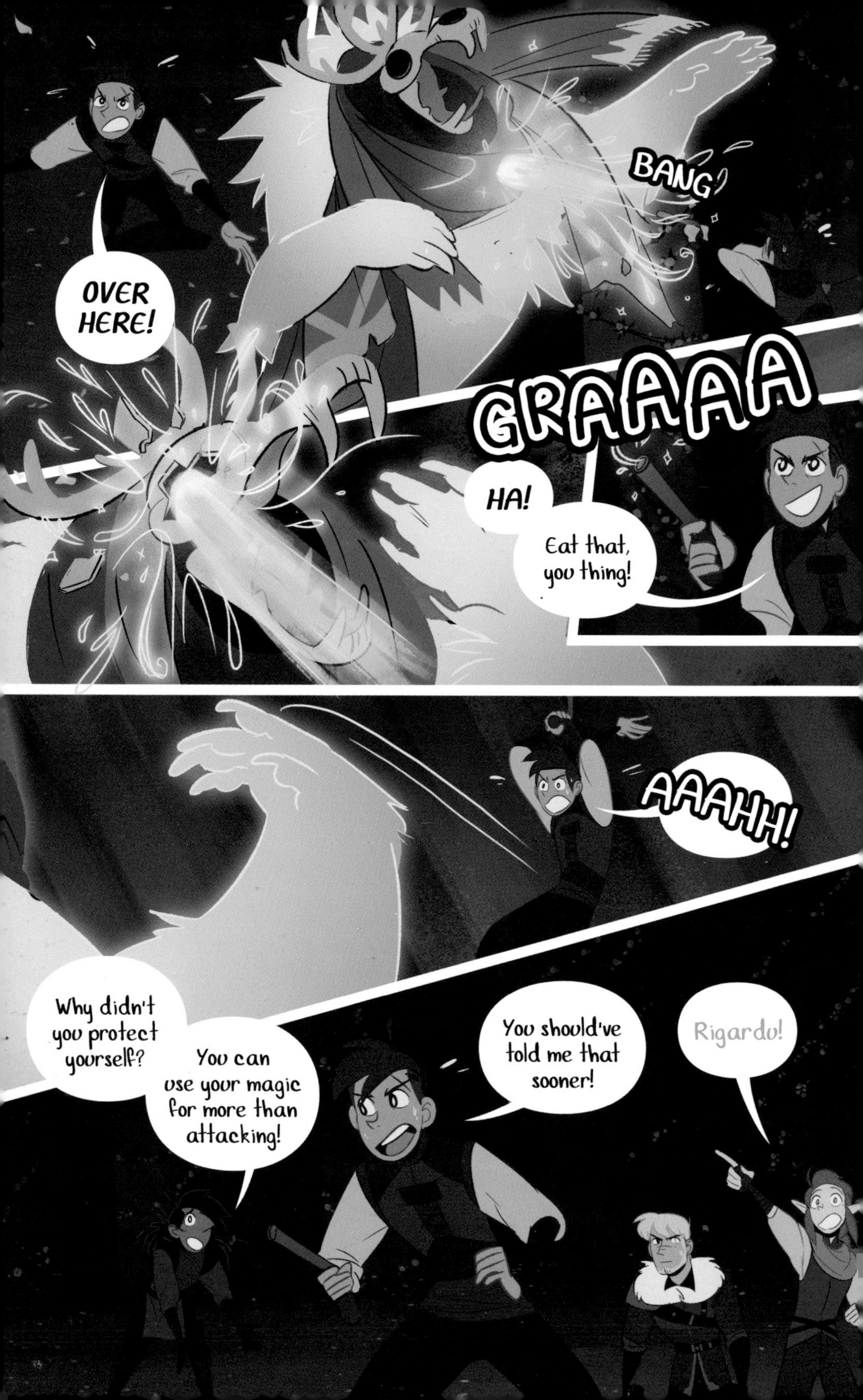
OVER HERE!
BANG
GRAAAA
HA!
Eat that, you thing!
AAAHH!
Why didn't you protect yourself?
You can use your magic for more than attacking!
You should've told me that sooner!
Rigardo!

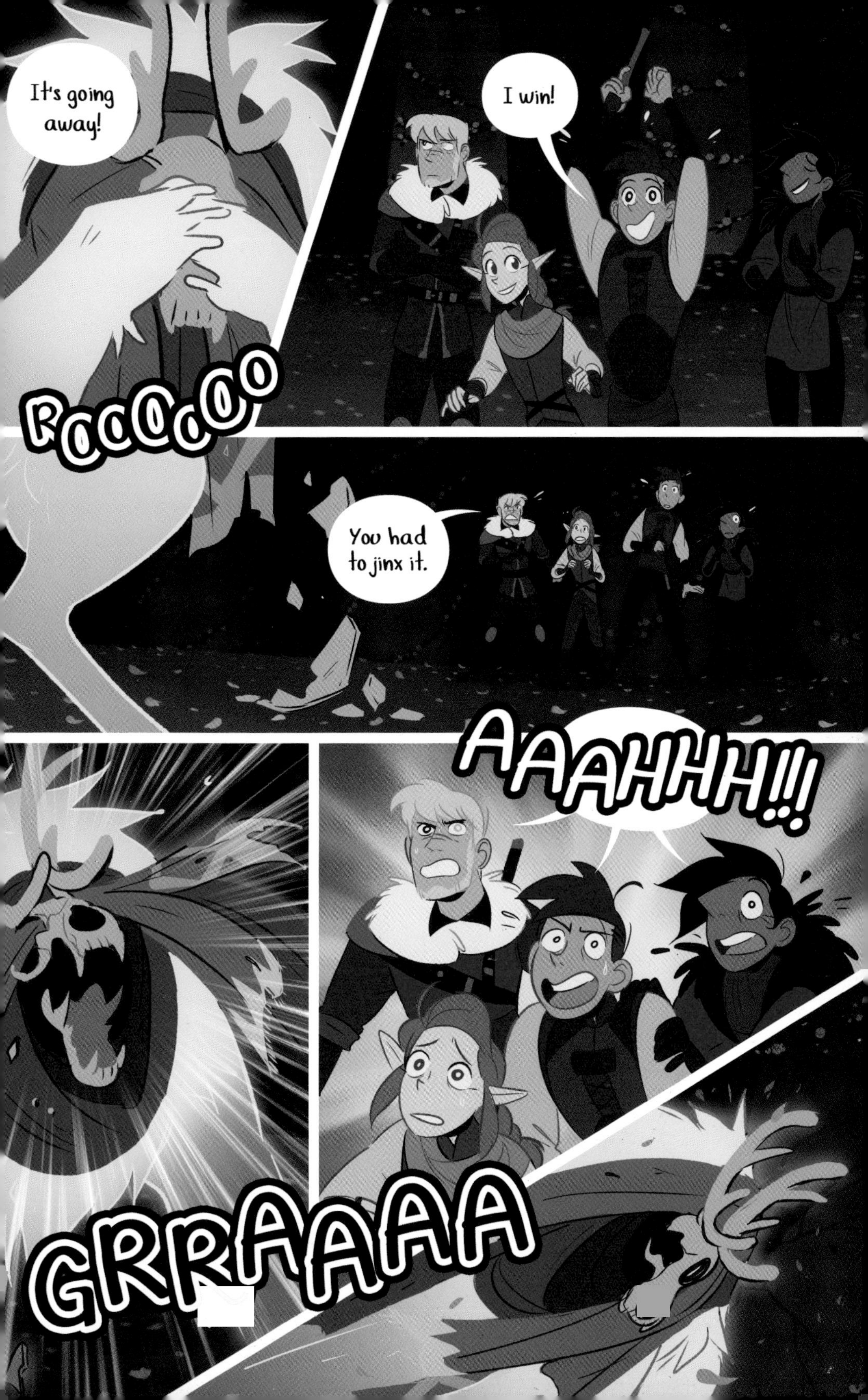
It's going away!
I win!
ROOOoOO
You had to jinx it.
AAAHHH!!!
GRRAAAAA

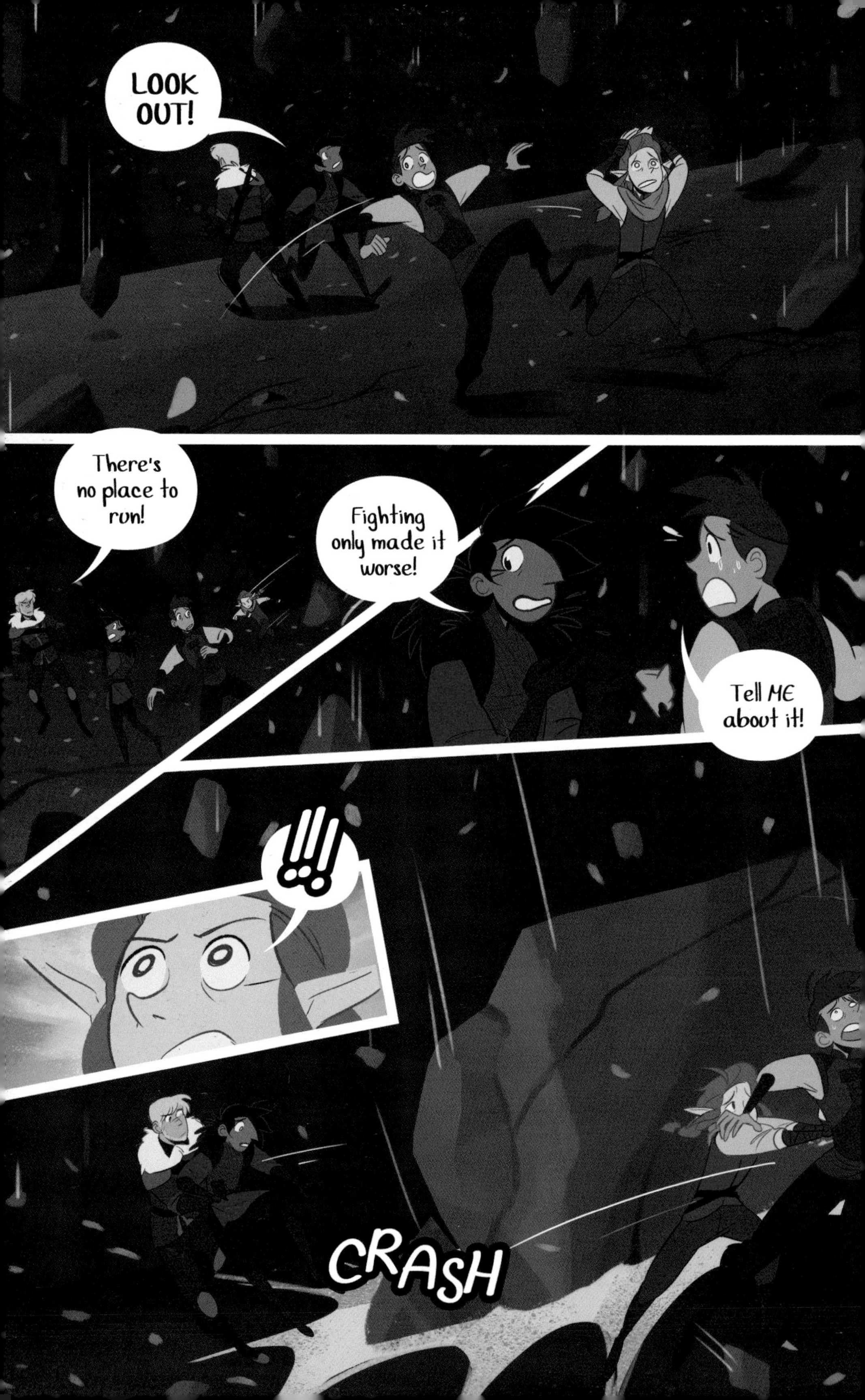
LOOK OUT!
There's no place to run!
Fighting only made it worse!
Tell ME about it!
!!!
CRASH

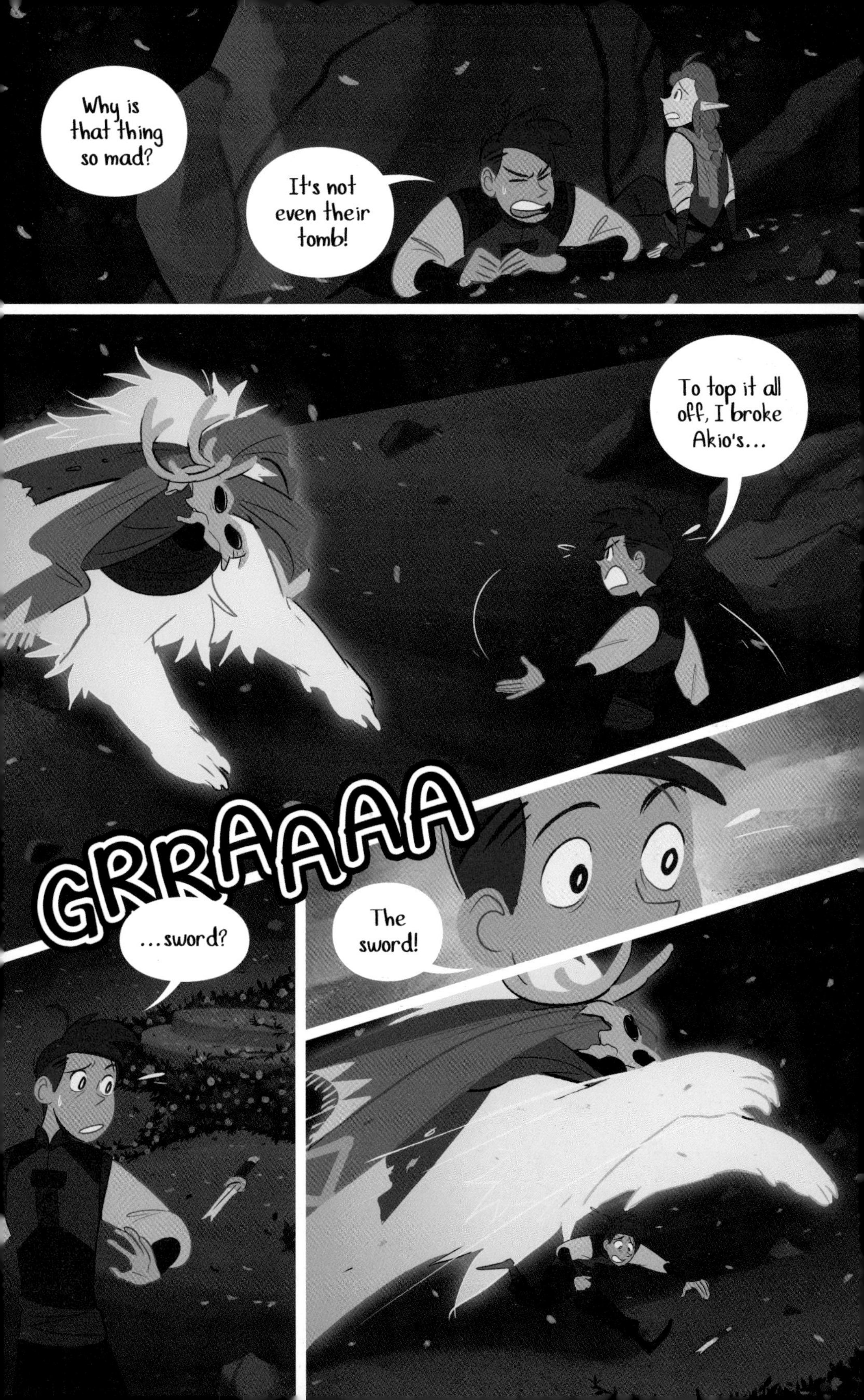
Why is that thing so mad?
It's not even their tomb!
To top it all off, I broke Akio's...
GRRAAAA
...sword?
The sword!

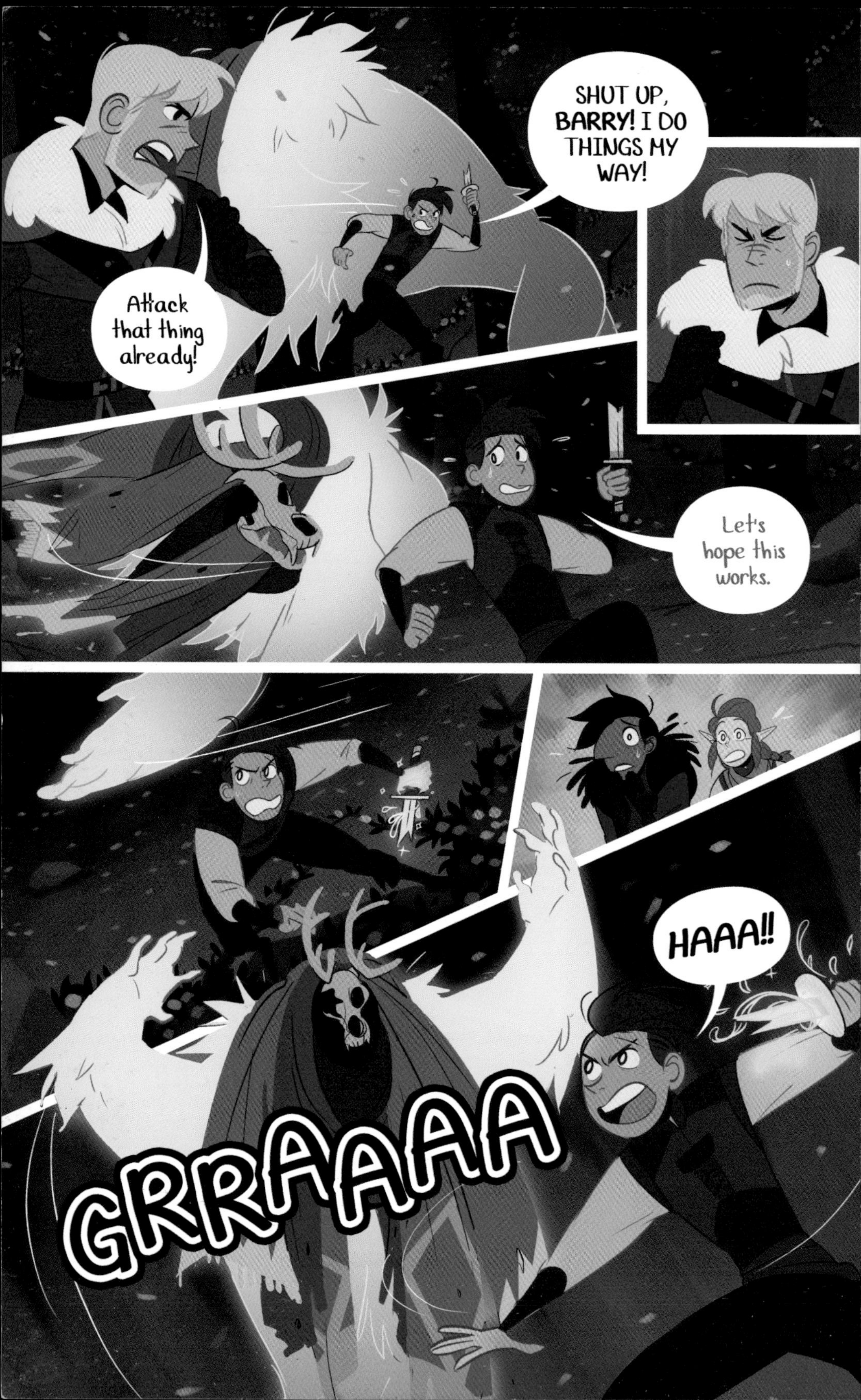

SHUT UP, BARRY! I DO THINGS MY WAY!
Attack that thing already!
Let's hope this works.
HAAA!!
GRRAAAAA

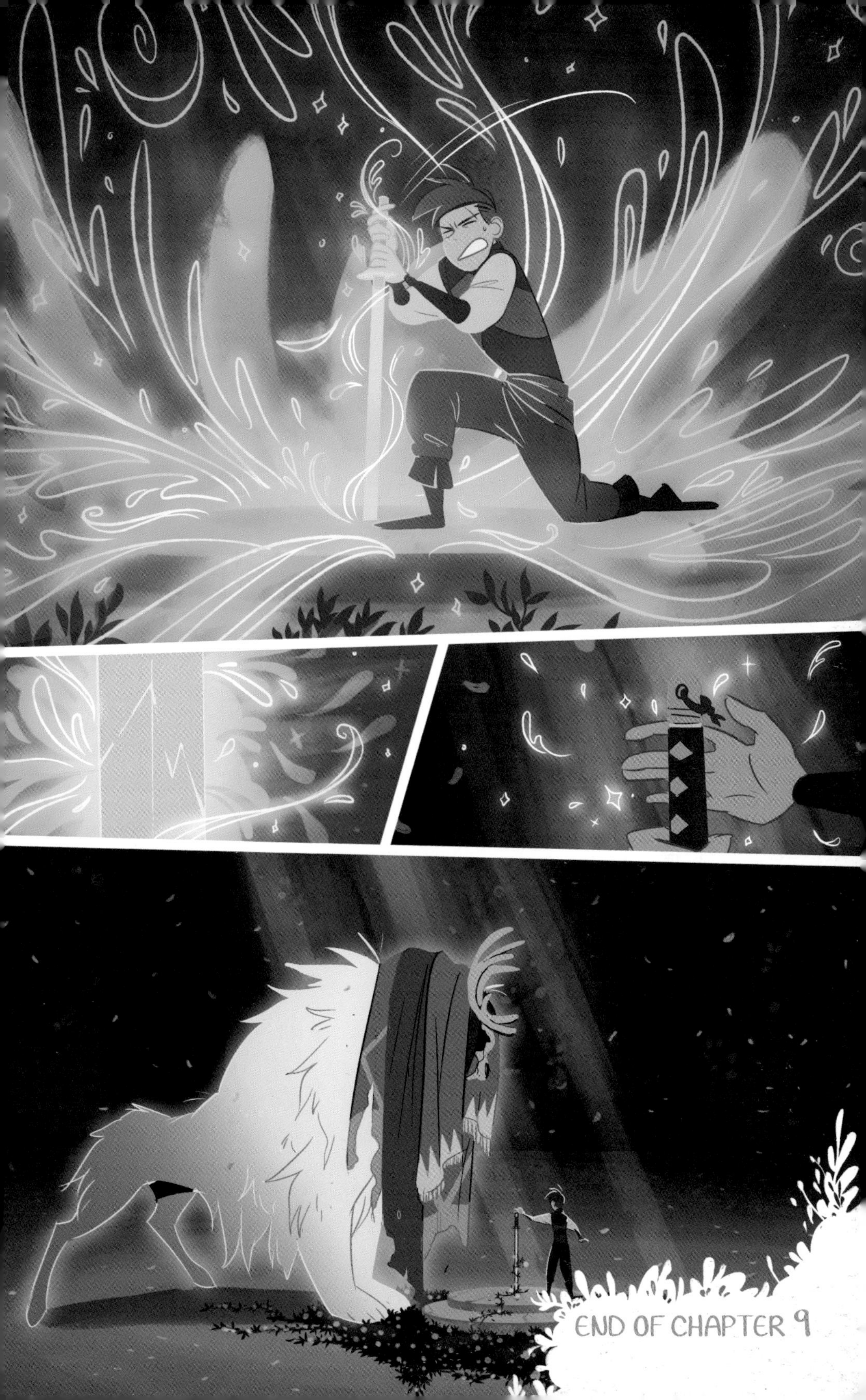
END OF CHAPTER 9

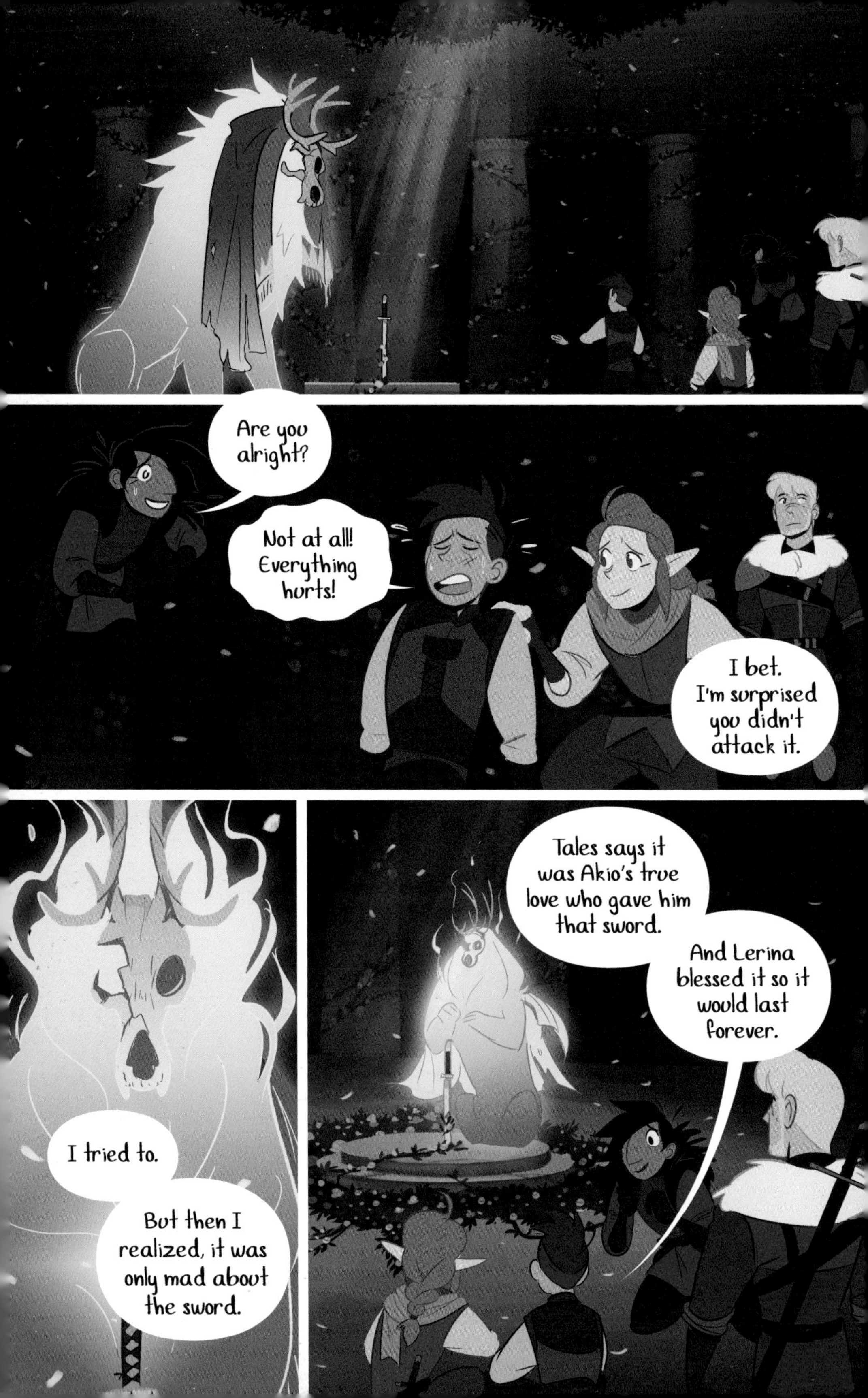
Are you alright?
Not at all! Everything hurts!
I bet. I'm surprised you didn't attack it.
I tried to.
But then I realized, it was only mad about the sword.
Tales says it was Akio's true love who gave him that sword.
And Lerina blessed it so it would last forever.

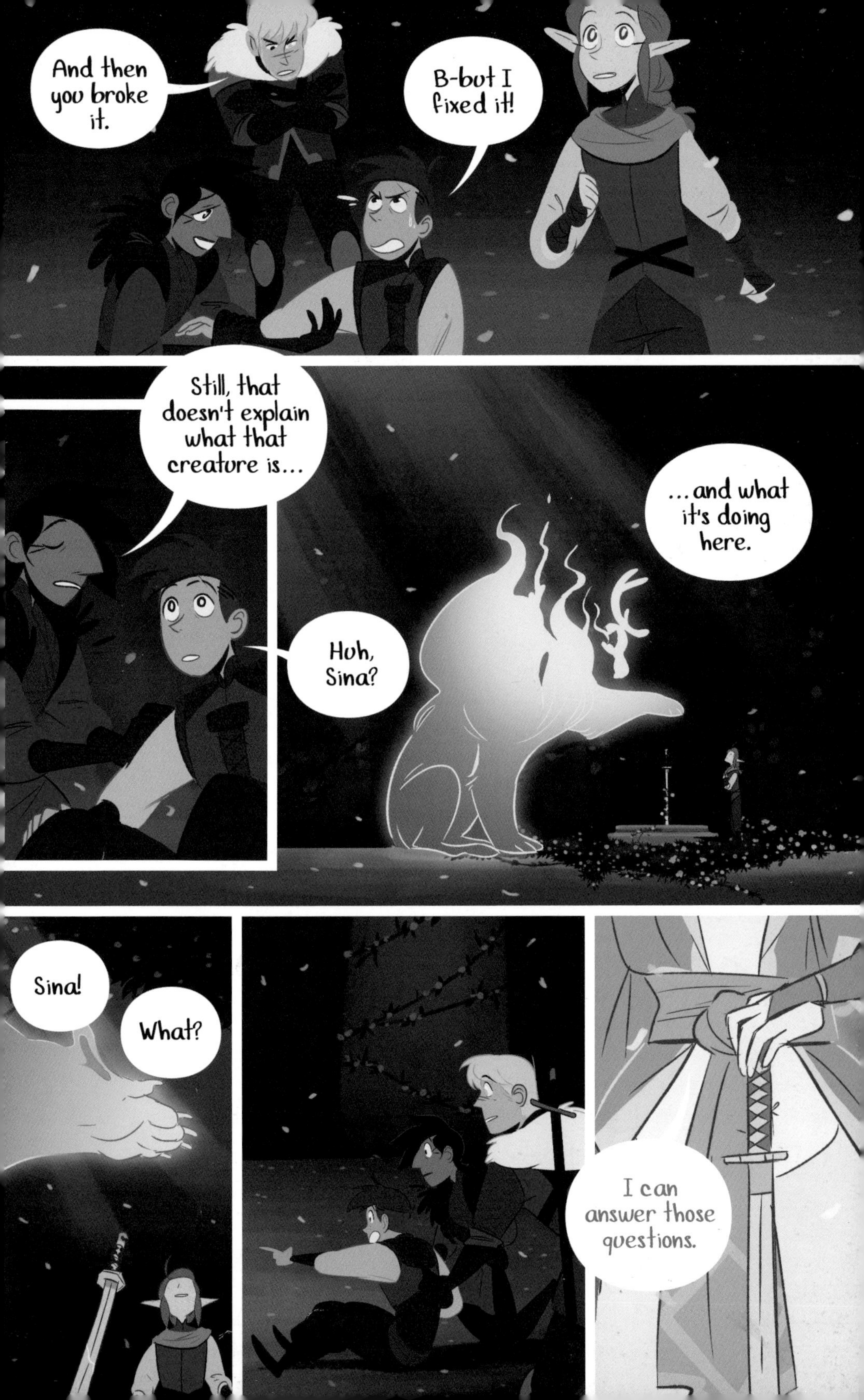
And then you broke it.
B-but I fixed it!
Still, that doesn't explain what that creature is...
...and what it's doing here.
Huh, Sina?
Sina!
What?
I can answer those questions.

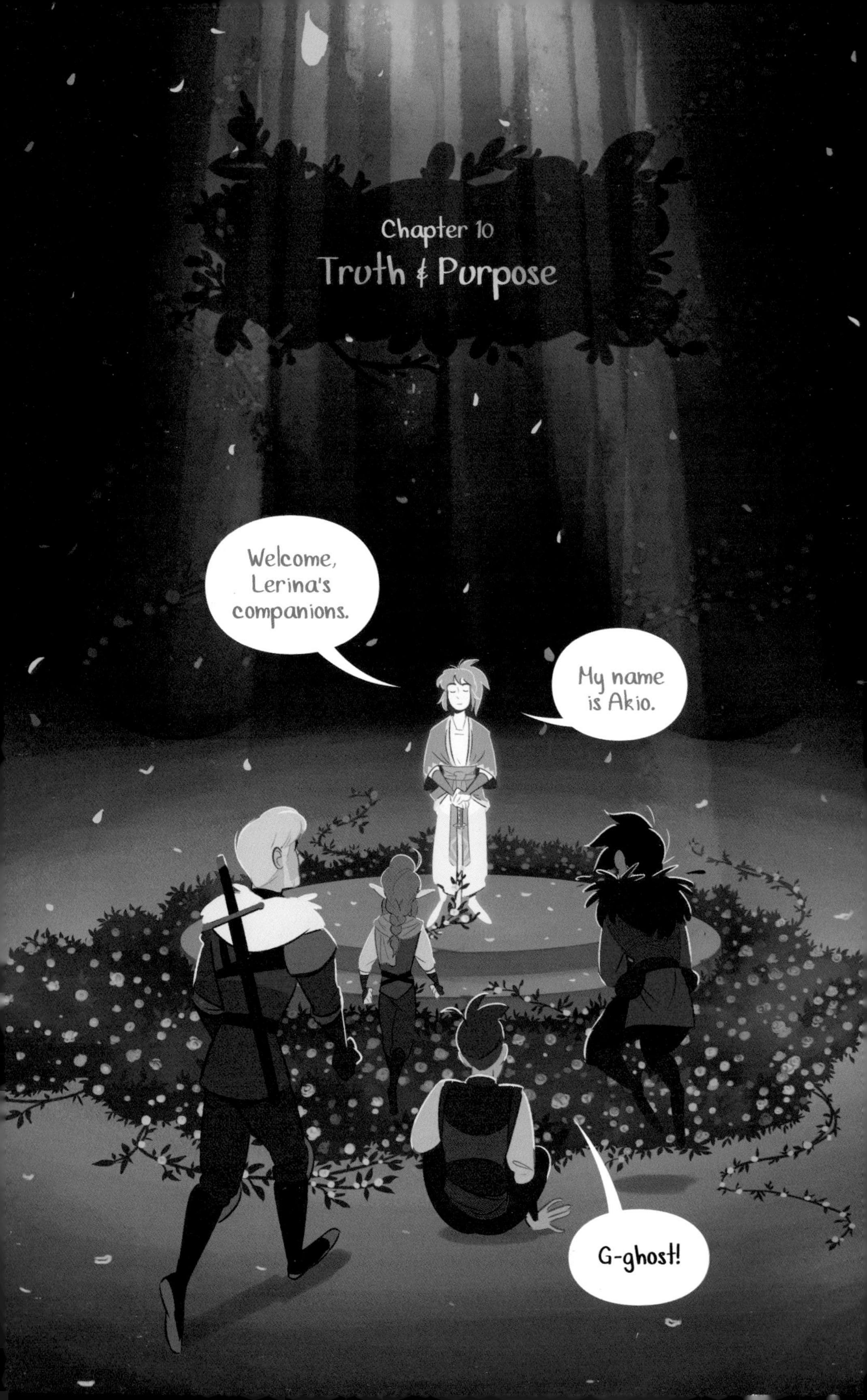
Chapter 10
Truth & Purpose
Welcome, Lerina's companions.
My name is Akio.
G-ghost!

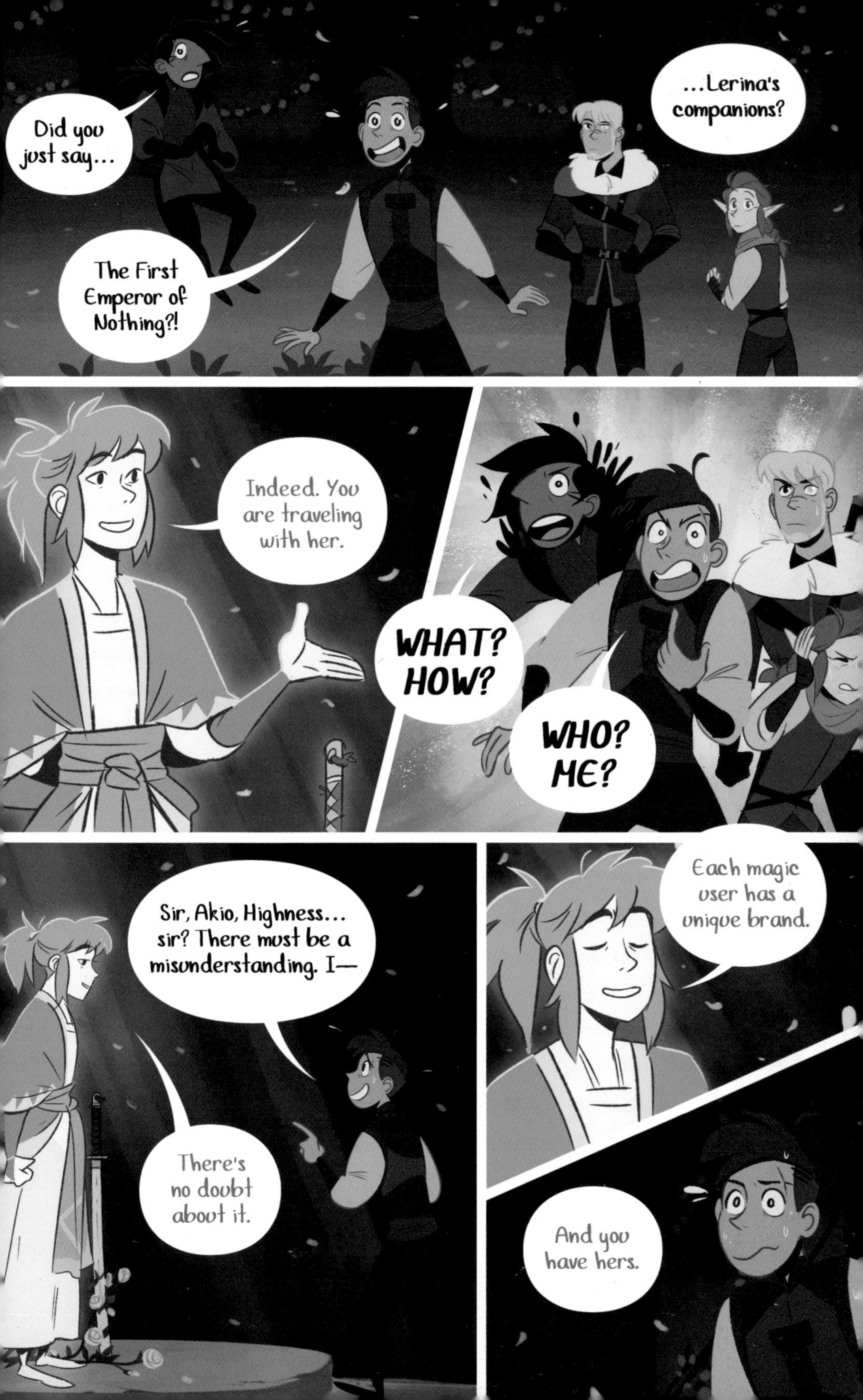
Did you just say...
The First Emperor of Nothing?!
...Lerina's companions?
Indeed. You are traveling with her.
WHAT? HOW?
WHO? ME?
Sir, Akio, Highness... sir? There must be a misunderstanding. I—
There's no doubt about it.
Each magic user has a unique brand.
And you have hers.

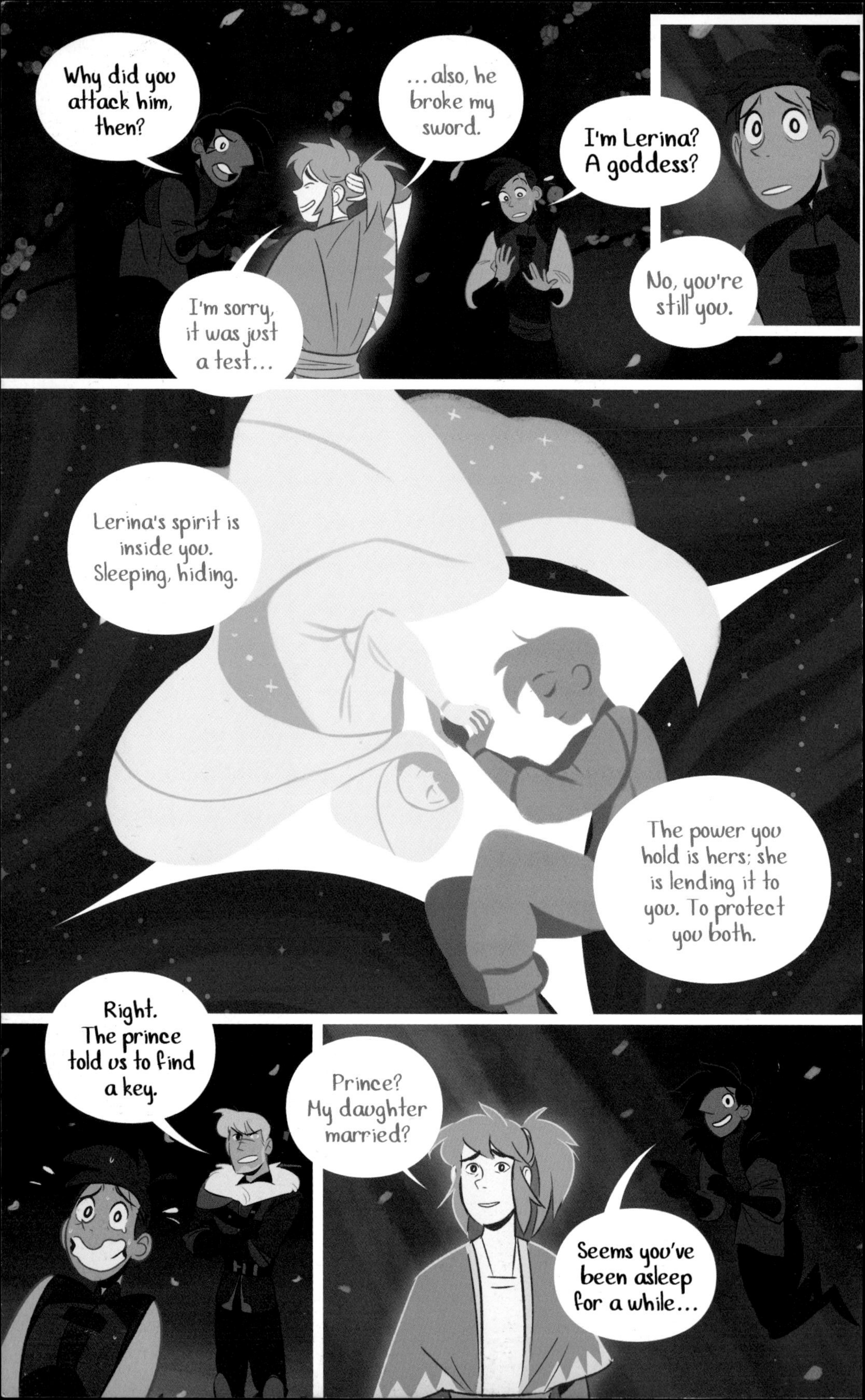
Why did you attack him, then?
...also, he broke my sword.
I'm sorry, it was just a test...
I'm Lerina? A goddess?
No, you're still you.
Lerina's spirit is inside you. Sleeping, hiding.
The power you hold is hers; she is lending it to you. To protect you both.
Right. The prince told us to find a key.
Prince? My daughter married?
Seems you've been asleep for a while...

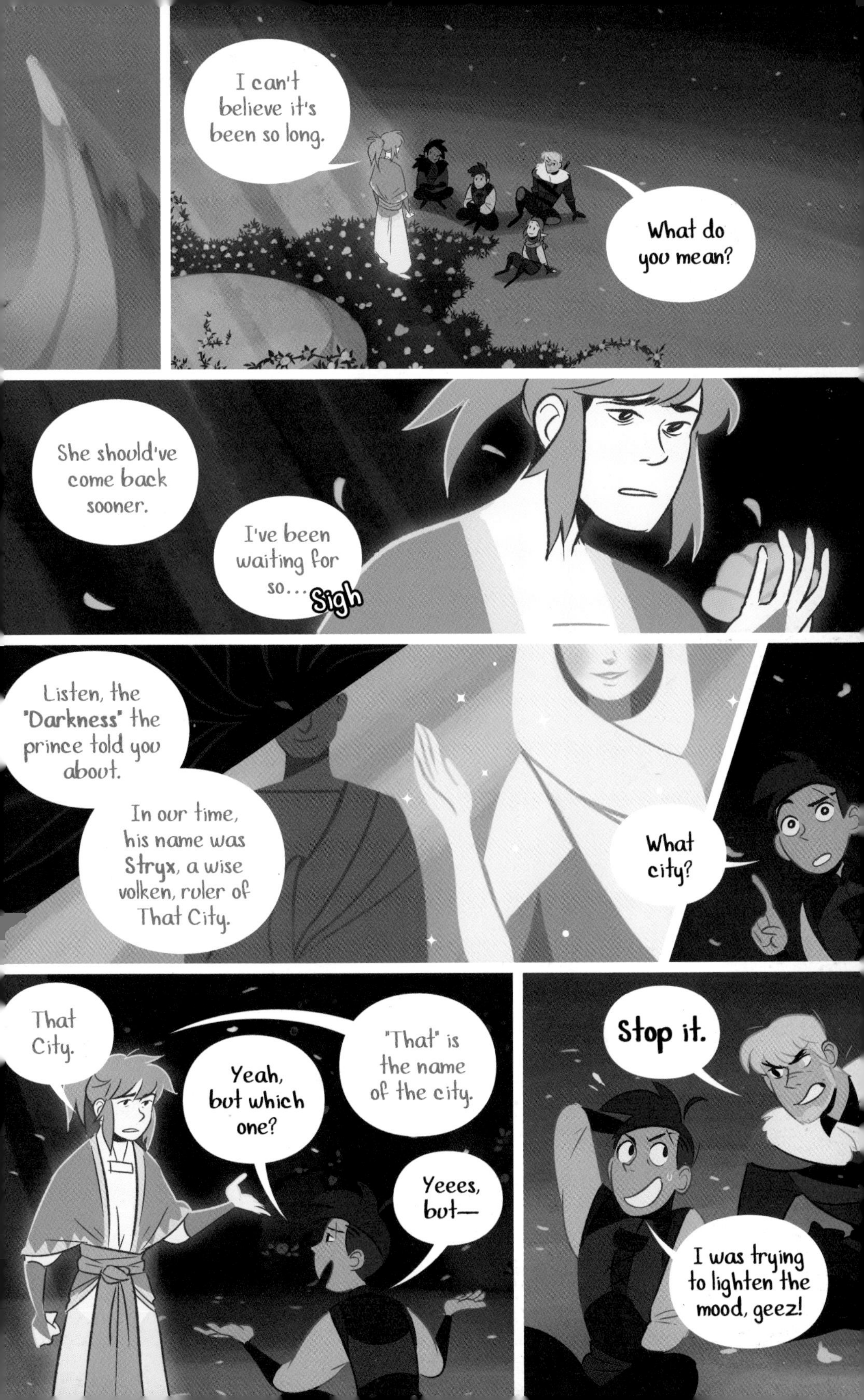
I can't believe it's been so long.
What do you mean?
She should've come back sooner.
I've been waiting for so...
Sigh
Listen, the "Darkness" the prince told you about.
In our time, his name was Stryx, a wise volken, ruler of That City.
What city?
That City.
"That" is the name of the city.
Yeah, but which one?
Yeees, but—
Stop it.
I was trying to lighten the mood, geez!

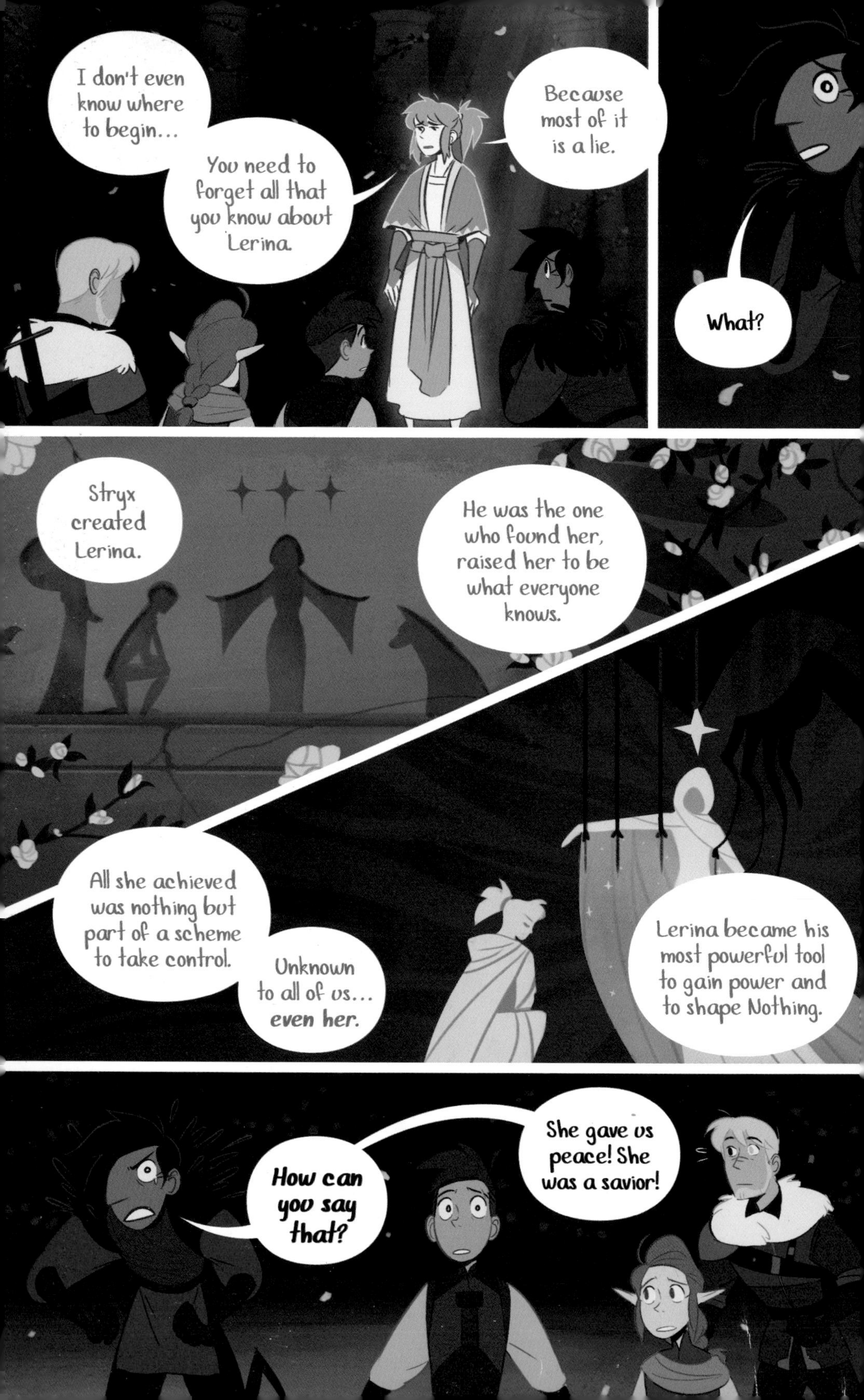
I don't even know where to begin...
You need to forget all that you know about Lerina.
Because most of it is a lie.
What?
Stryx created Lerina.
He was the one who found her, raised her to be what everyone knows.
All she achieved was nothing but part of a scheme to take control.
Unknown to all of us... even her.
Lerina became his most powerful tool to gain power and to shape Nothing.
How can you say that?
She gave us peace! She was a savior!

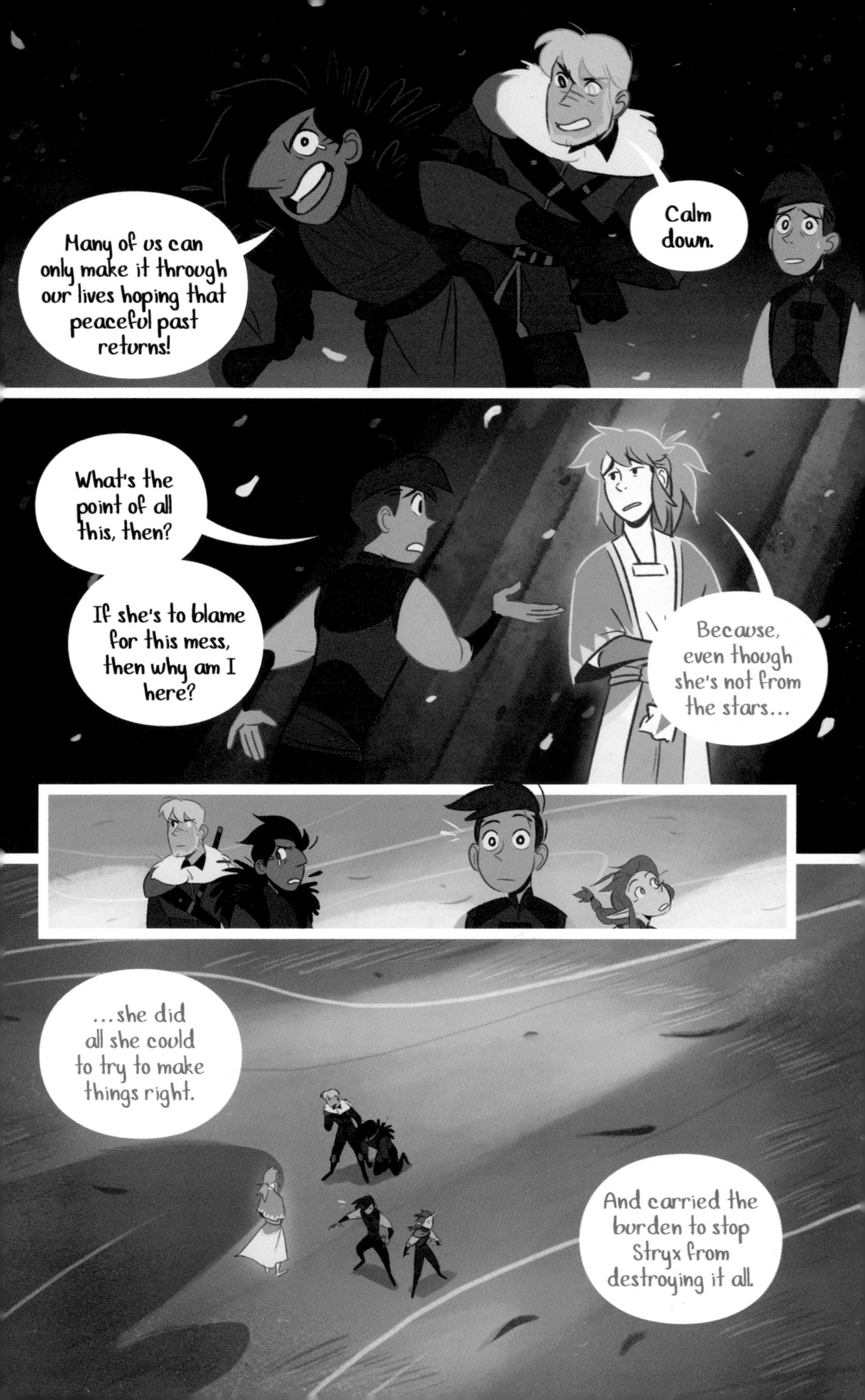
Many of us can only make it through our lives hoping that peaceful past returns!
Calm down.
What's the point of all this, then?
If she's to blame for this mess, then why am I here?
Because, even though she's not from the stars...
...she did all she could to try to make things right.
And carried the burden to stop Stryx from destroying it all.

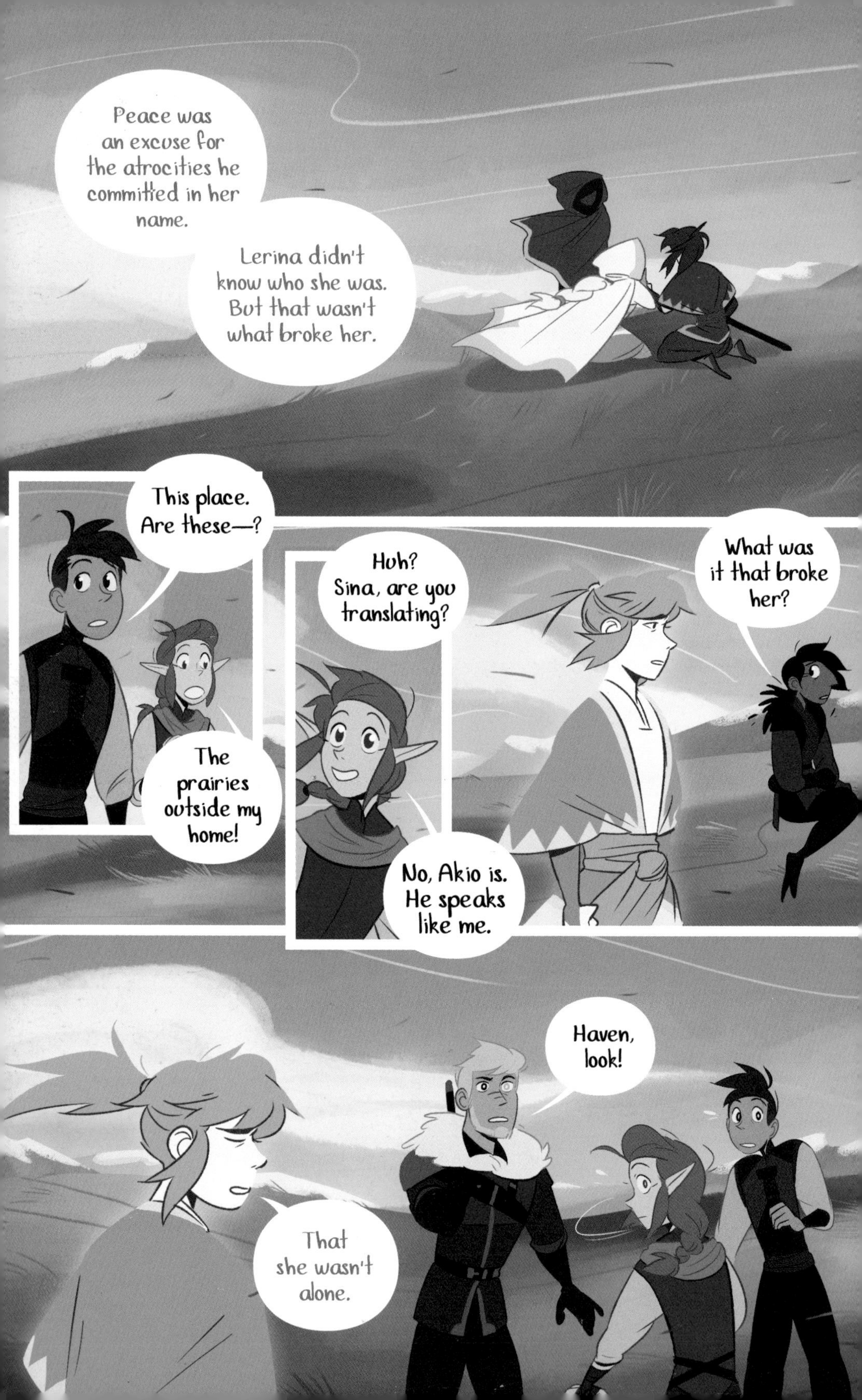
Peace was an excuse for the atrocities he committed in her name.
Lerina didn't know who she was. But that wasn't what broke her.
This place. Are these—?
The prairies outside my home!
Huh? Sina, are you translating?
No, Akio is. He speaks like me.
What was it that broke her?
That she wasn't alone.
Haven, look!

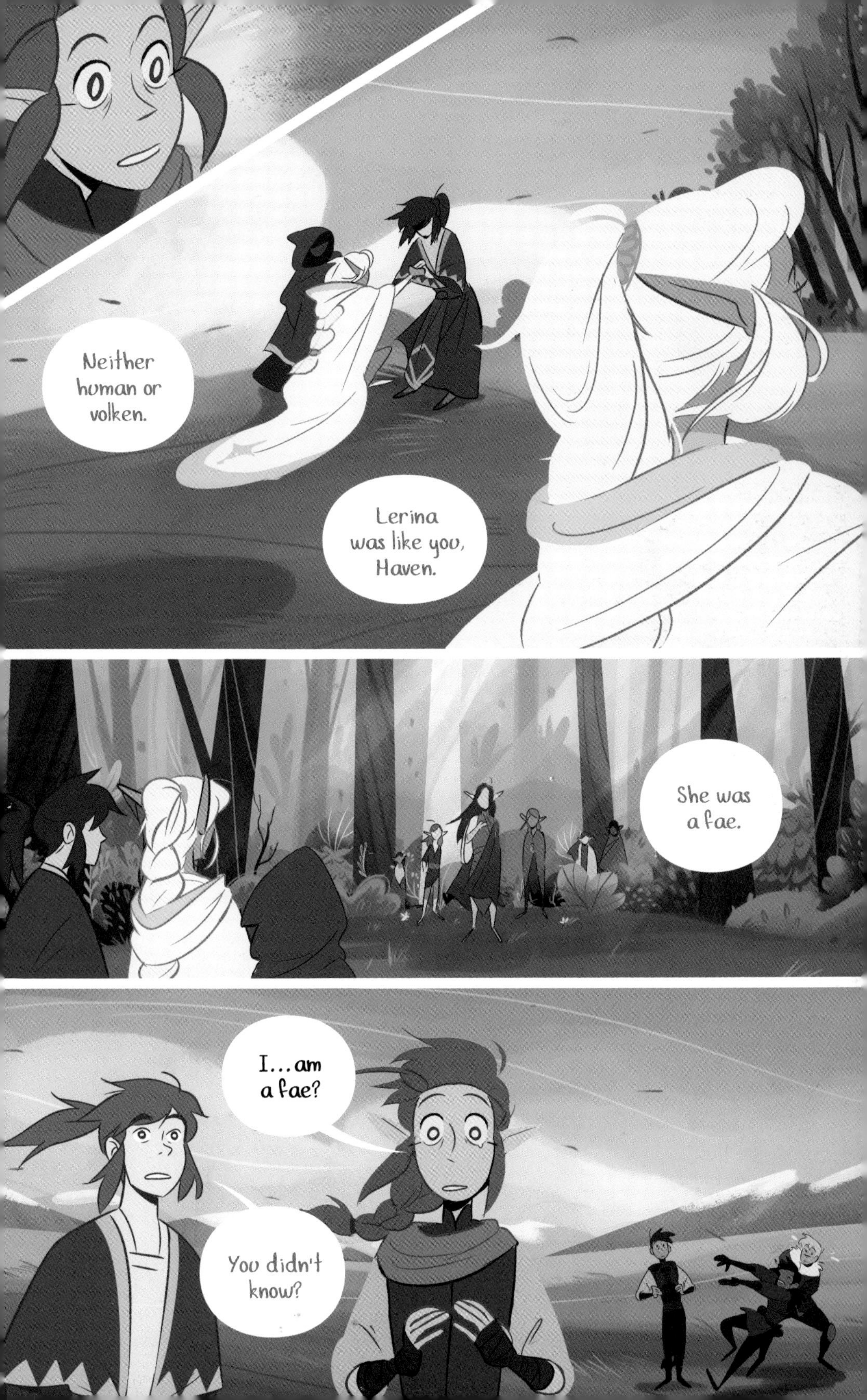
Neither human or volken.
Lerina was like you, Haven.
She was a fae.
I...am a fae?
You didn't know?

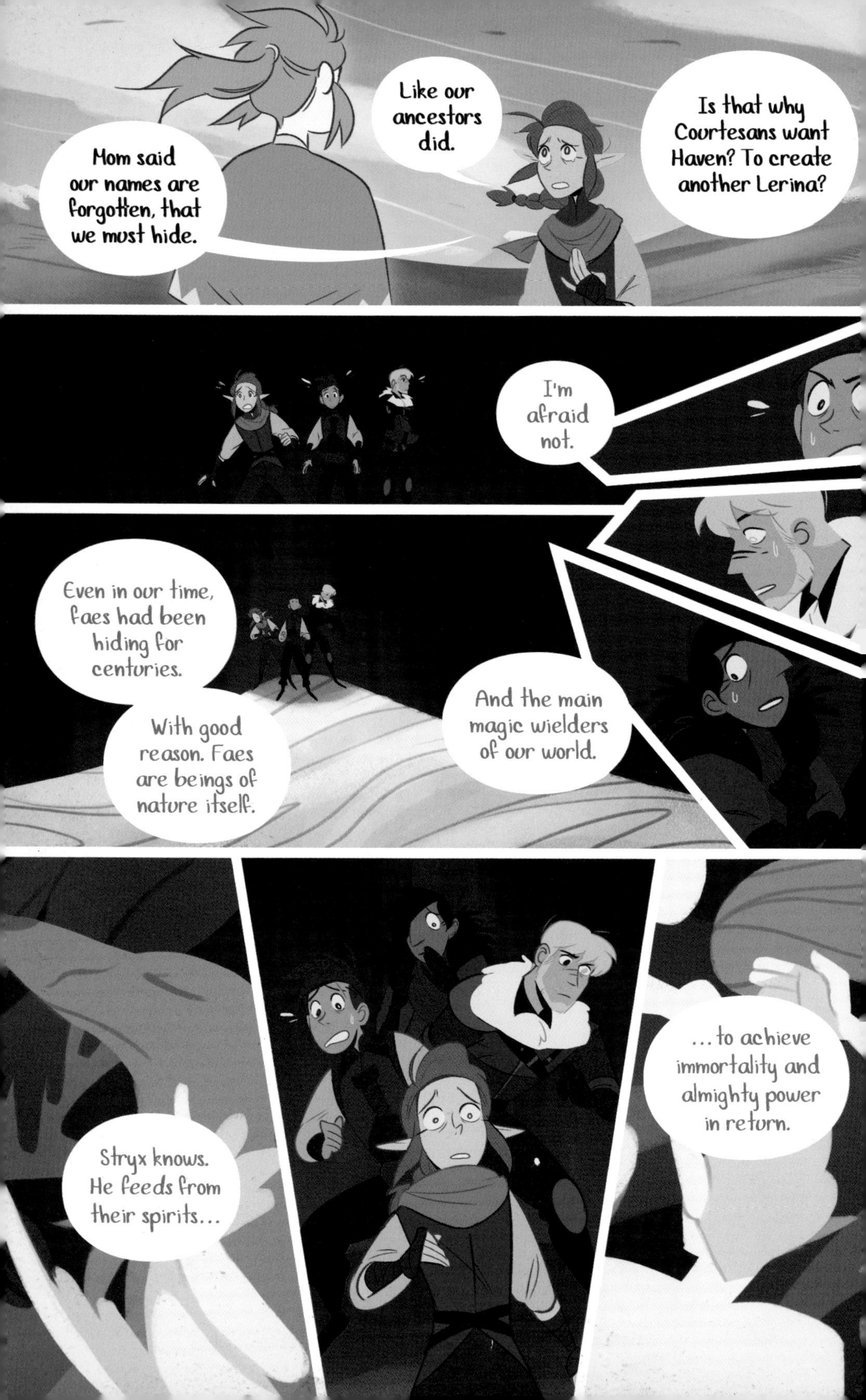
Mom said our names are forgotten, that we must hide.
Like our ancestors did.
Is that why Courtesans want Haven? To create another Lerina?
I'm afraid not.
Even in our time, faes had been hiding for centuries.
With good reason. Faes are beings of nature itself.
And the main magic wielders of our world.
Stryx knows. He feeds from their spirits...
...to achieve immortality and almighty power in return.

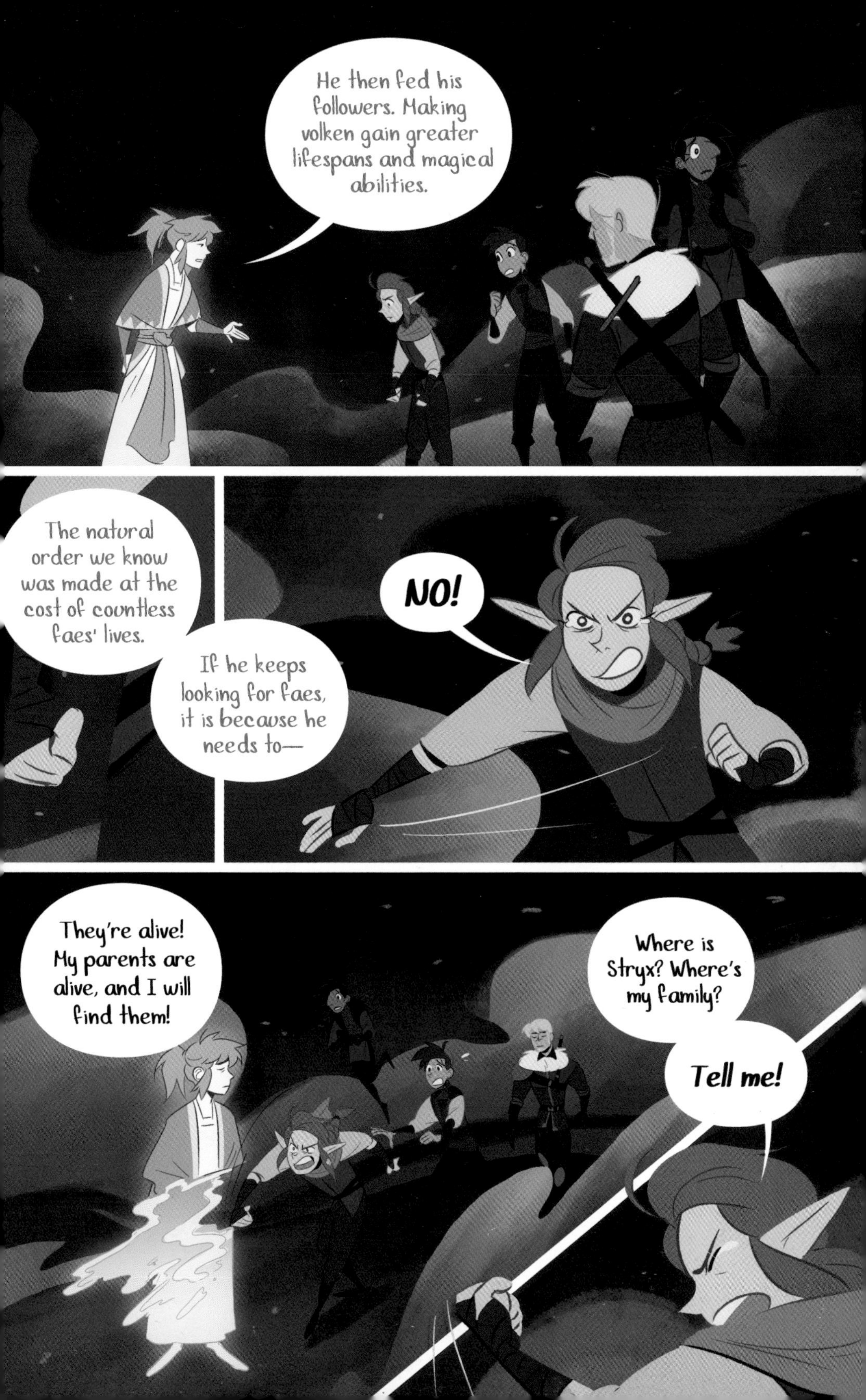
He then fed his followers. Making volken gain greater lifespans and magical abilities.
The natural order we know was made at the cost of countless faes' lives.
If he keeps looking for faes, it is because he needs to—
NO!
They're alive! My parents are alive, and I will find them!
Where is Stryx? Where's my family?
Tell me!

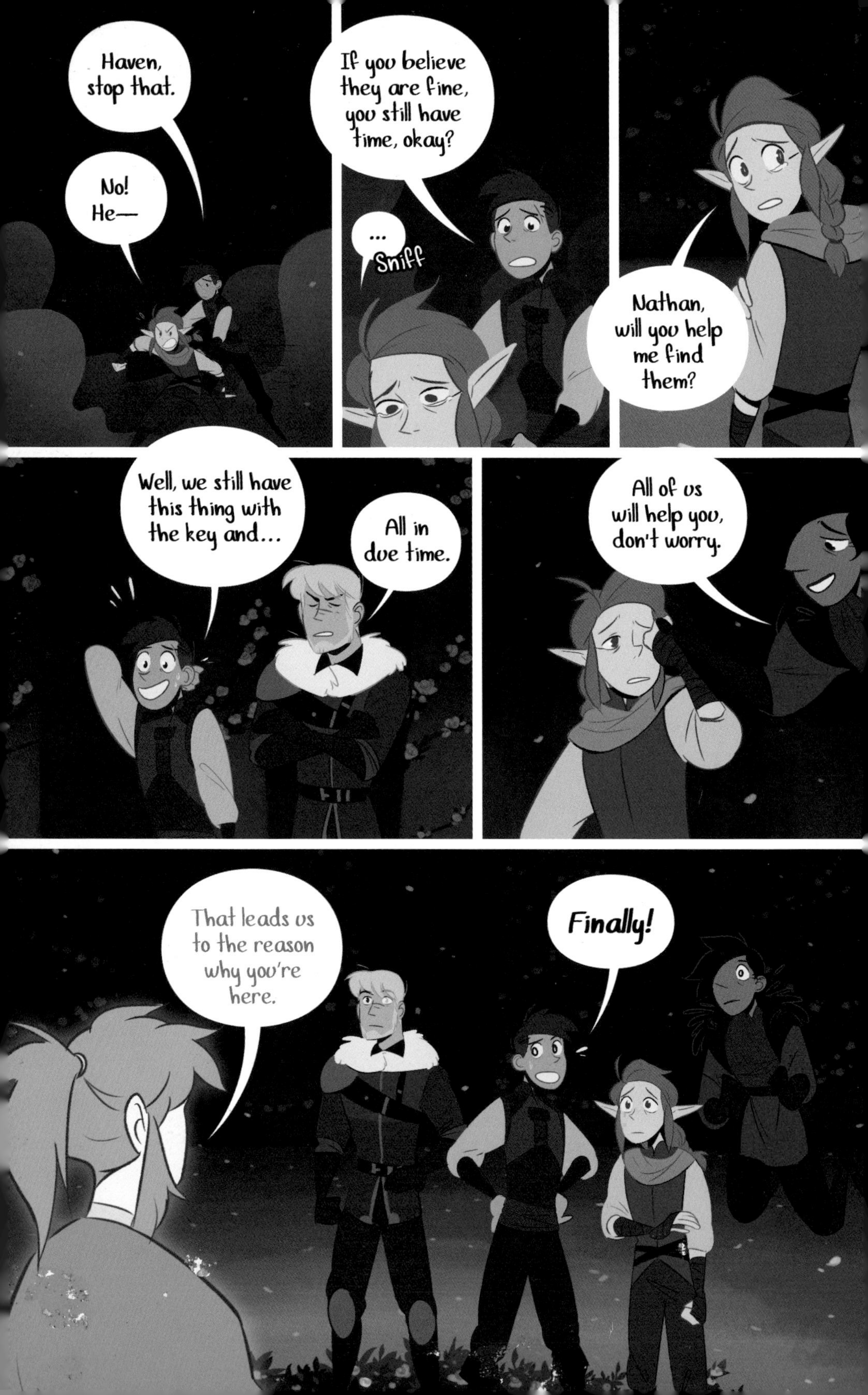
Haven, stop that.
No! He—
If you believe they are fine, you still have time, okay?
... Sniff
Nathan, will you help me find them?
Well, we still have this thing with the key and...
All in due time.
All of us will help you, don't worry.
That leads us to the reason why you're here.
Finally!

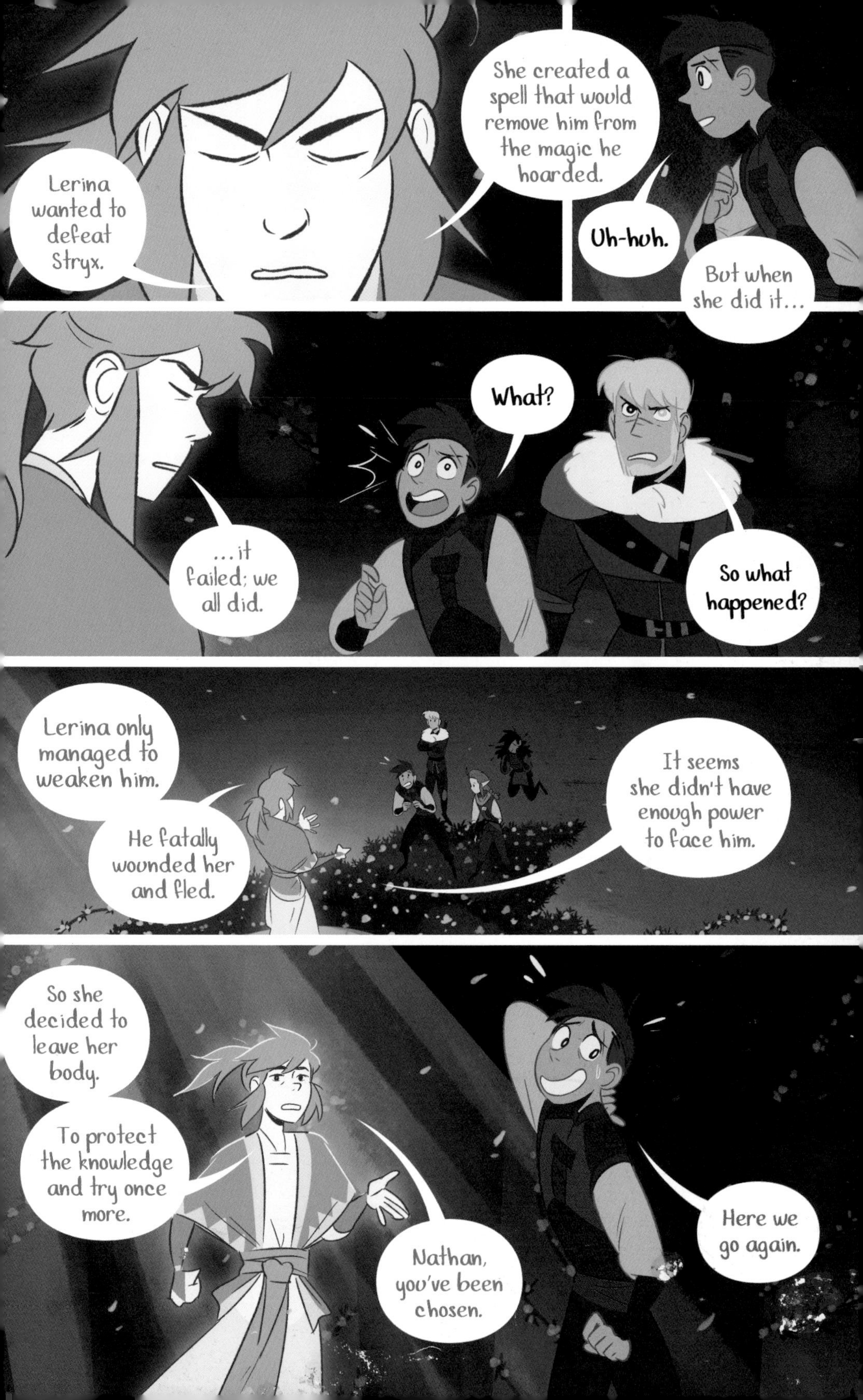
Lerina wanted to defeat Stryx.
She created a spell that would remove him from the magic he hoarded.
Uh-huh.
But when she did it...
What?
...it failed; we all did.
So what happened?
Lerina only managed to weaken him.
He fatally wounded her and fled.
It seems she didn't have enough power to face him.
So she decided to leave her body.
To protect the knowledge and try once more.
Nathan, you've been chosen.
Here we go again.

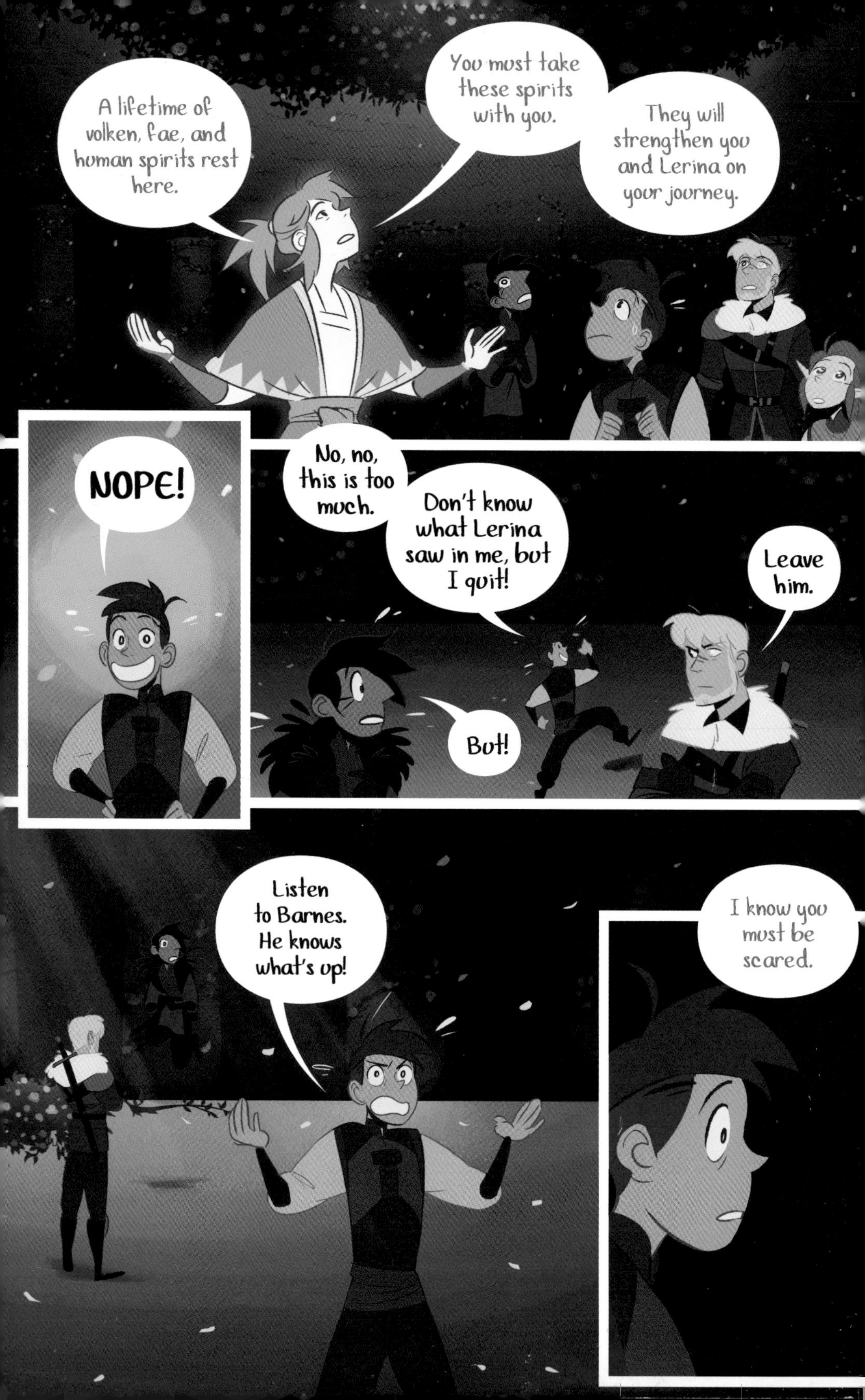
A lifetime of volken, fae, and human spirits rest here.
You must take these spirits with you.
They will strengthen you and Lerina on your journey.
NOPE!
No, no, this is too much.
Don't know what Lerina saw in me, but I quit!
Leave him.
But!
Listen to Barnes. He knows what's up!
I know you must be scared.

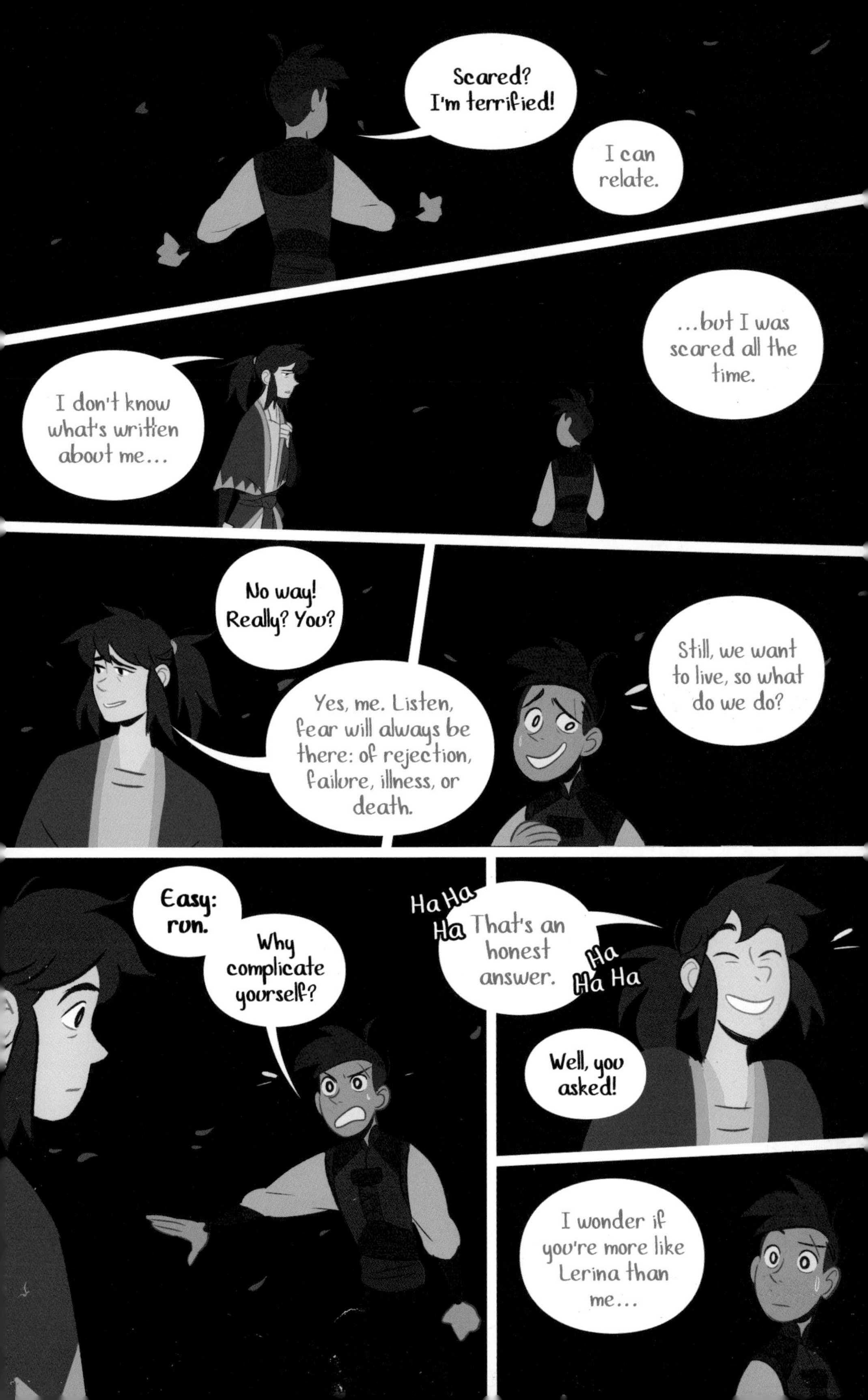
Scared? I'm terrified!
I can relate.
I don't know what's written about me...
...but I was scared all the time.
No way! Really? You?
Yes, me. Listen, fear will always be there: of rejection, failure, illness, or death.
Still, we want to live, so what do we do?
Easy: run.
Why complicate yourself?
Ha Ha Ha
That's an honest answer.
Ha Ha Ha
Well, you asked!
I wonder if you're more like Lerina than me...

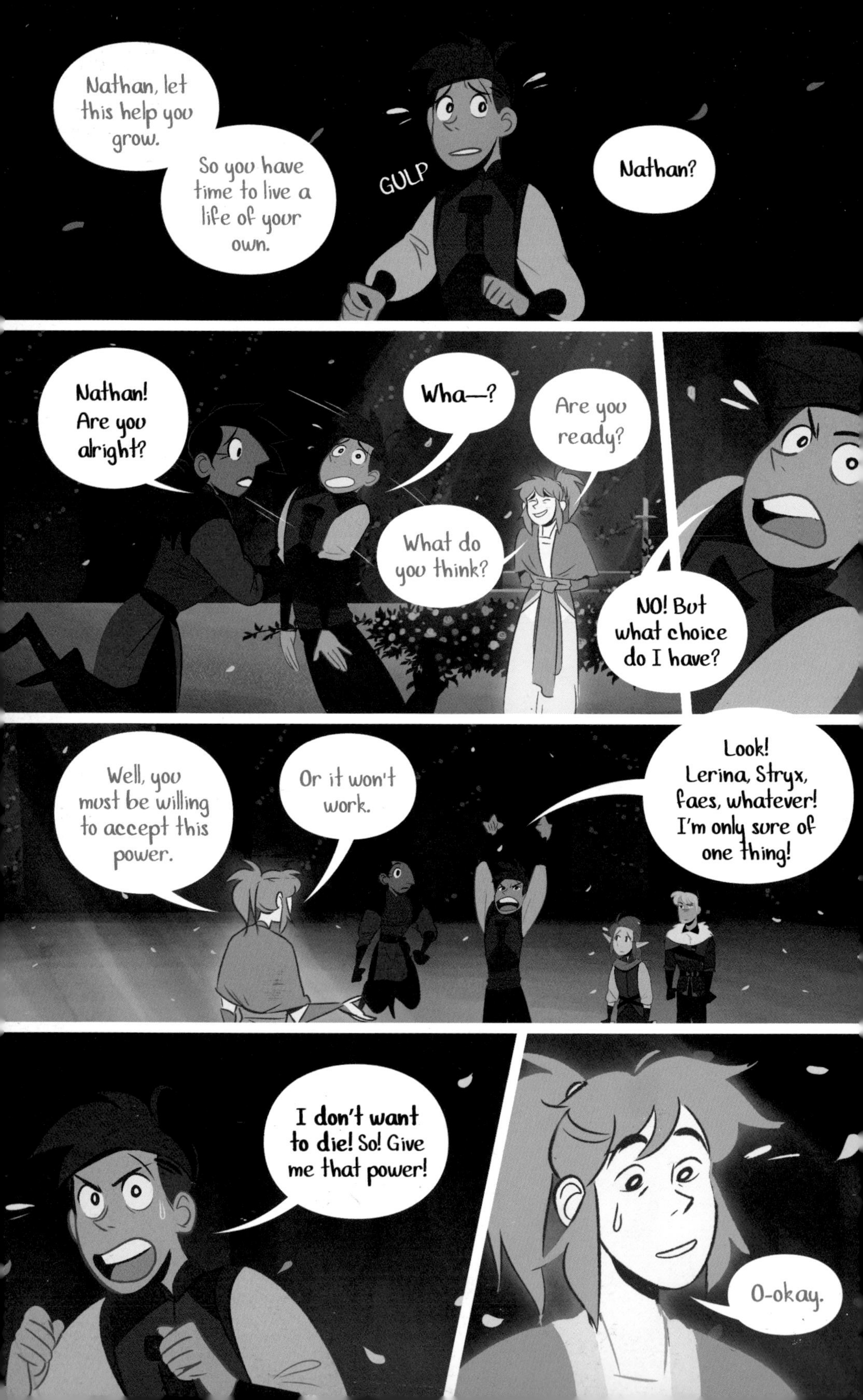
Nathan, let this help you grow.
So you have time to live a life of your own.
GULP
Nathan?
Nathan! Are you alright?
Wha—?
Are you ready?
What do you think?
NO! But what choice do I have?
Well, you must be willing to accept this power.
Or it won't work.
Look! Lerina, Stryx, faes, whatever! I'm only sure of one thing!
I don't want to die! So! Give me that power!
O-okay.

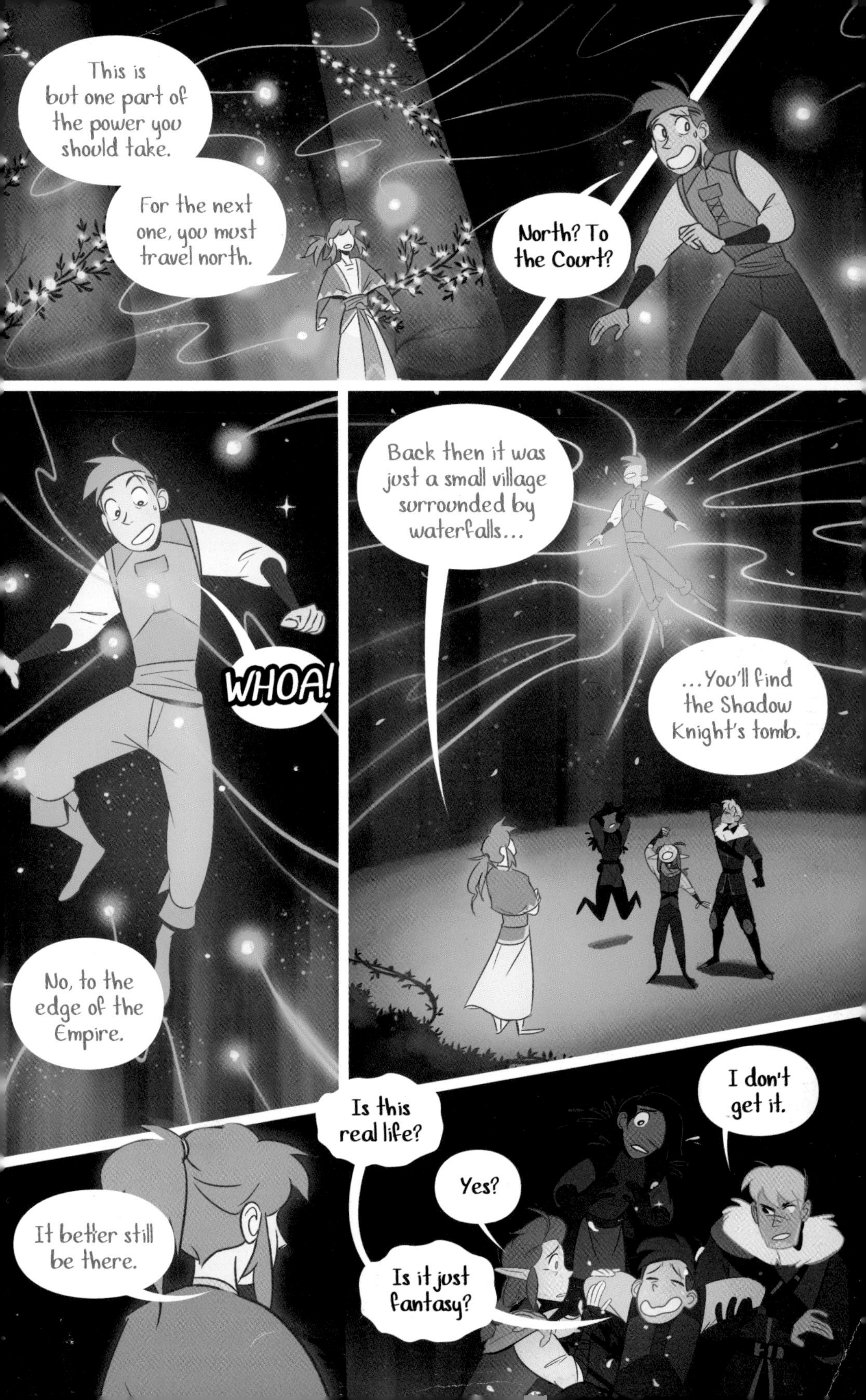
This is but one part of the power you should take.
For the next one, you must travel north.
North? To the Court?
WHOA!
No, to the edge of the Empire.
Back then it was just a small village surrounded by waterfalls...
...You'll find the Shadow Knight's tomb.
It better still be there.
Is this real life?
Yes?
Is it just fantasy?
I don't get it.

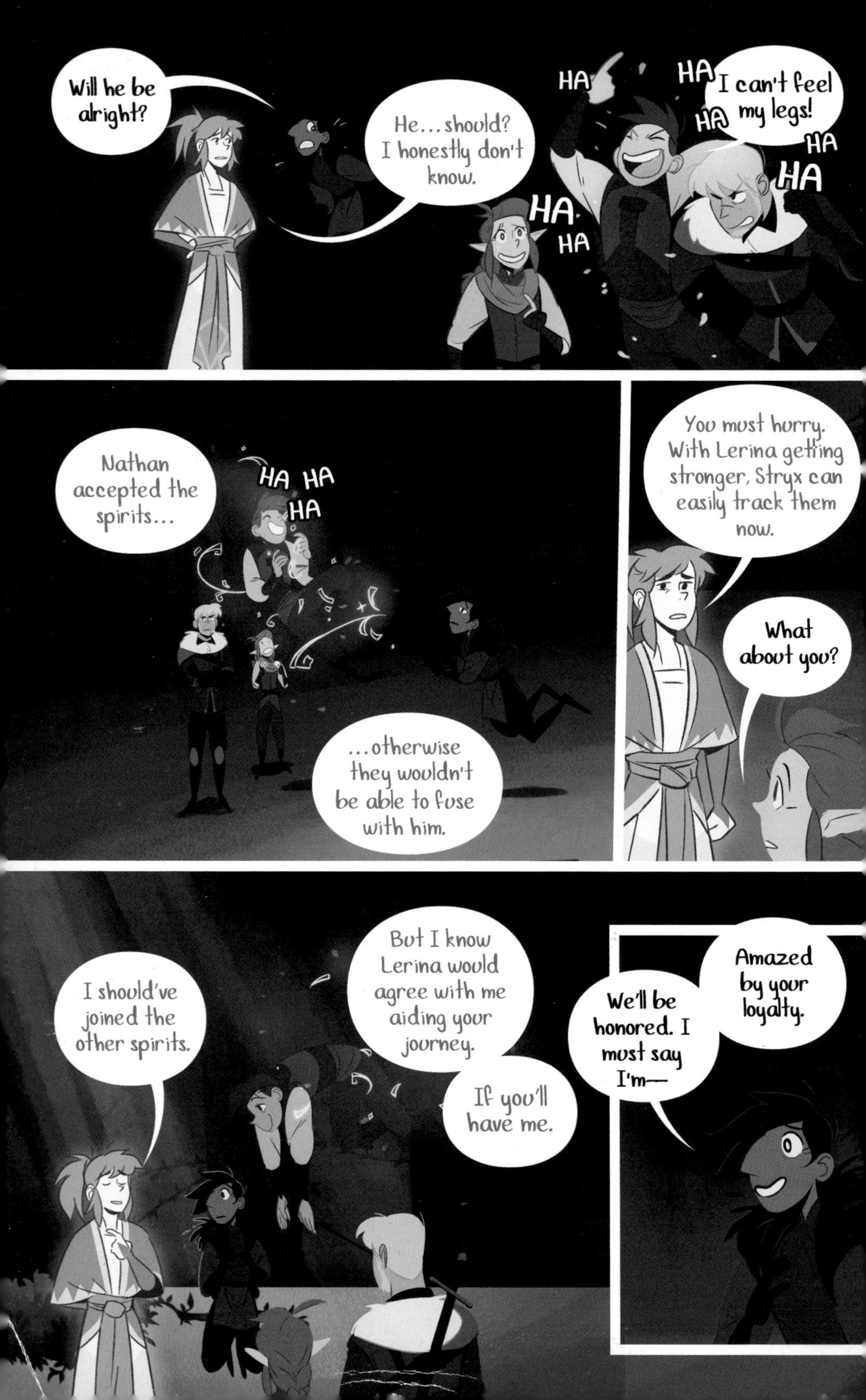

Will he be alright?
He...should? I honestly don't know.
HA HA HA HA HA HA HA HA
I can't feel my legs!
Nathan accepted the spirits...
HA HA HA
...otherwise they wouldn't be able to fuse with him.
You must hurry. With Lerina getting stronger, Stryx can easily track them now.
What about you?
I should've joined the other spirits.
But I know Lerina would agree with me aiding your journey.
If you'll have me.
We'll be honored. I must say I'm—
Amazed by your loyalty.

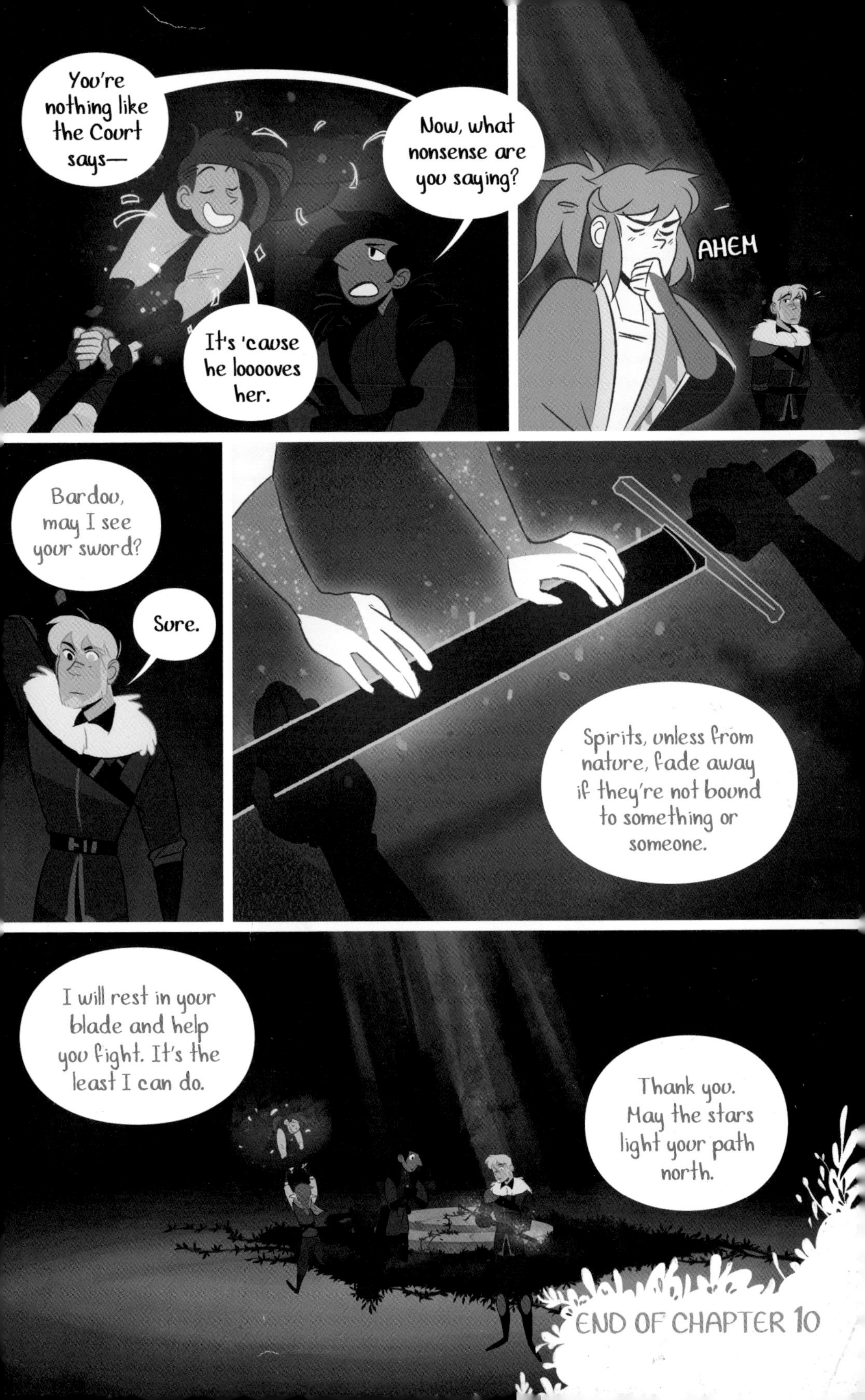
You're nothing like the Court says—
Now, what nonsense are you saying?
It's 'cause he looooves her.
AHEM
Bardou, may I see your sword?
Sure.
Spirits, unless from nature, fade away if they're not bound to something or someone.
I will rest in your blade and help you fight. It's the least I can do.
Thank you. May the stars light your path north.
END OF CHAPTER 10

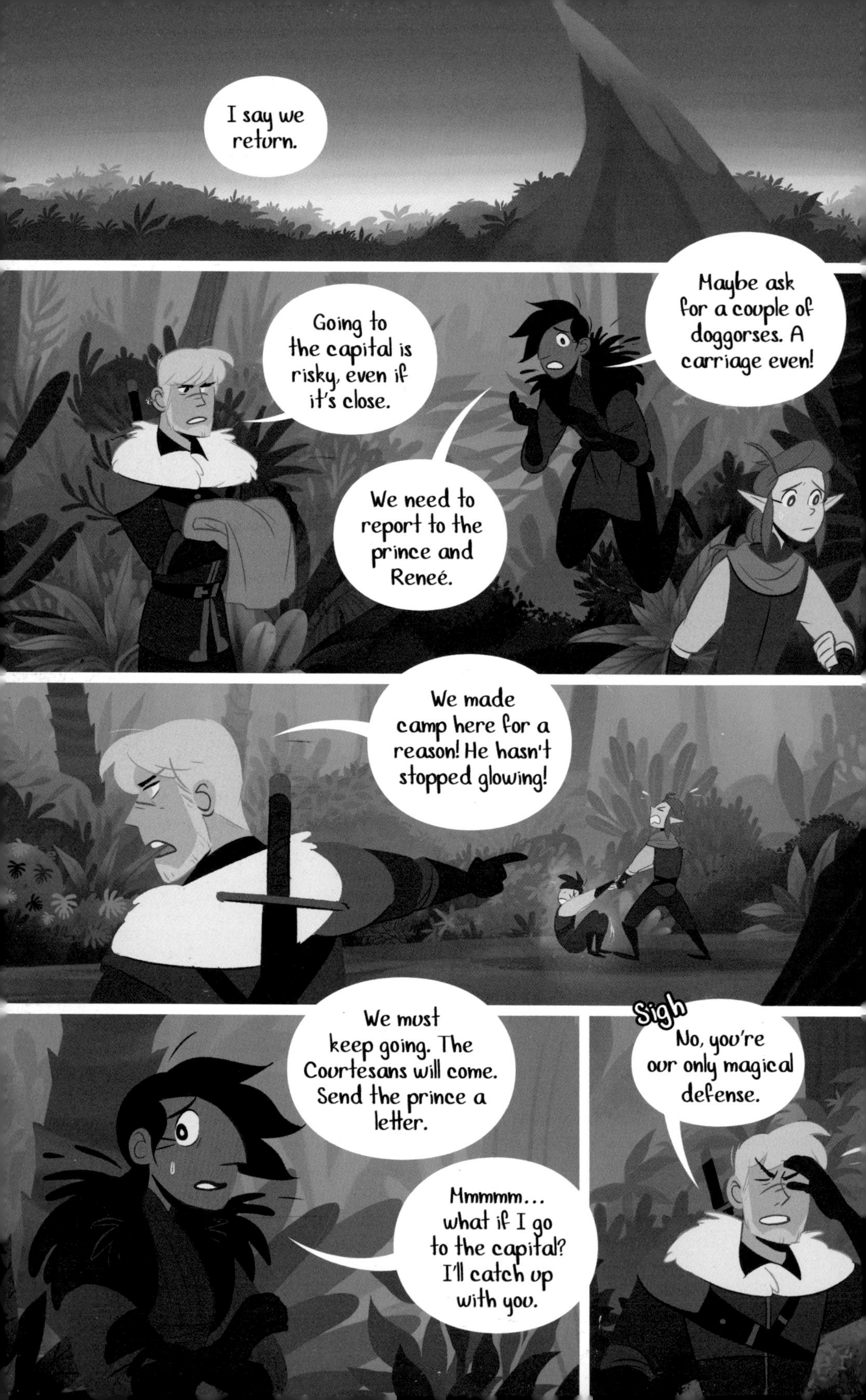
I say we return.
Going to the capital is risky, even if it's close.
We need to report to the prince and Reneé.
Maybe ask for a couple of doggorses. A carriage even!
We made camp here for a reason! He hasn't stopped glowing!
We must keep going. The Courtesans will come. Send the prince a letter.
Mmmmm... what if I go to the capital? I'll catch up with you.
Sigh
No, you're our only magical defense.

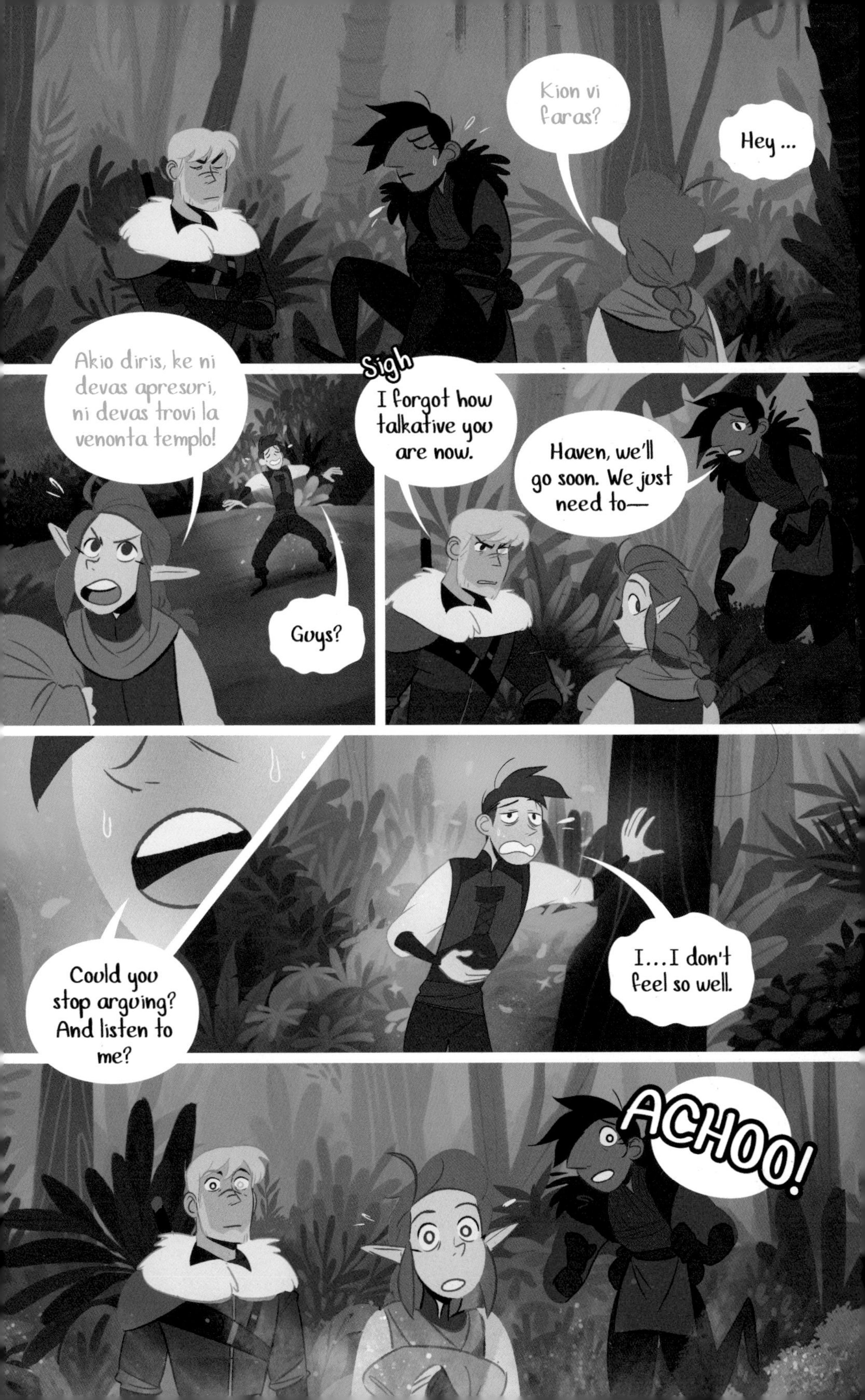
Kion vi faras?
Hey ...
Akio diris, ke ni devas apresori, ni devas trovi la venonta templo!
Guys?
Sigh
I forgot how talkative you are now.
Haven, we'll go soon. We just need to—
Could you stop arguing? And listen to me?
I...I don't feel so well.
ACHOO!

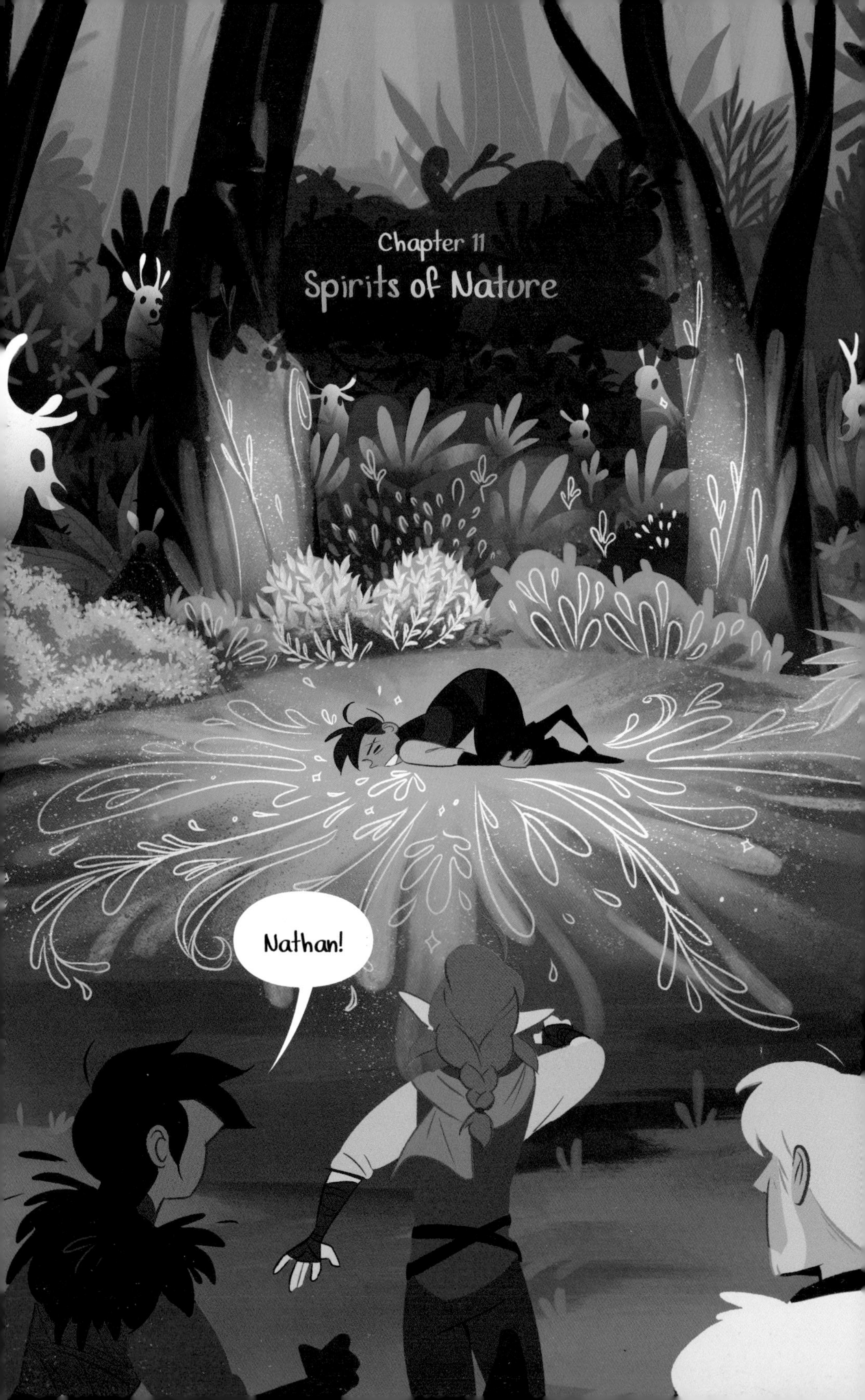
Chapter 11
Spirits of Nature
Nathan!

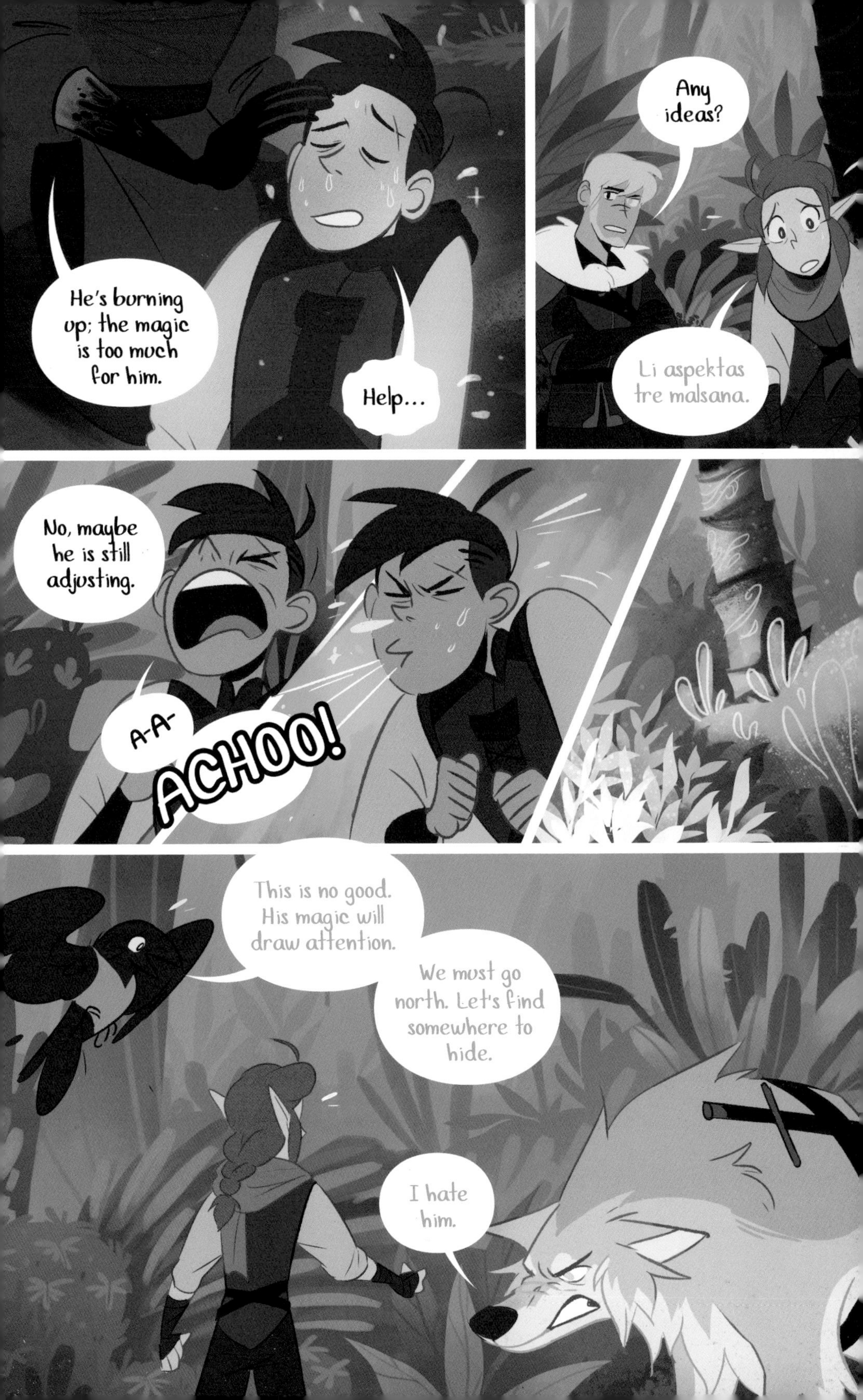
He's burning up; the magic is too much for him.
Help...
Any ideas?
Li aspektas tre malsana.
No, maybe he is still adjusting.
A-A-
ACHOO!
This is no good. His magic will draw attention.
We must go north. Let's find somewhere to hide.
I hate him.

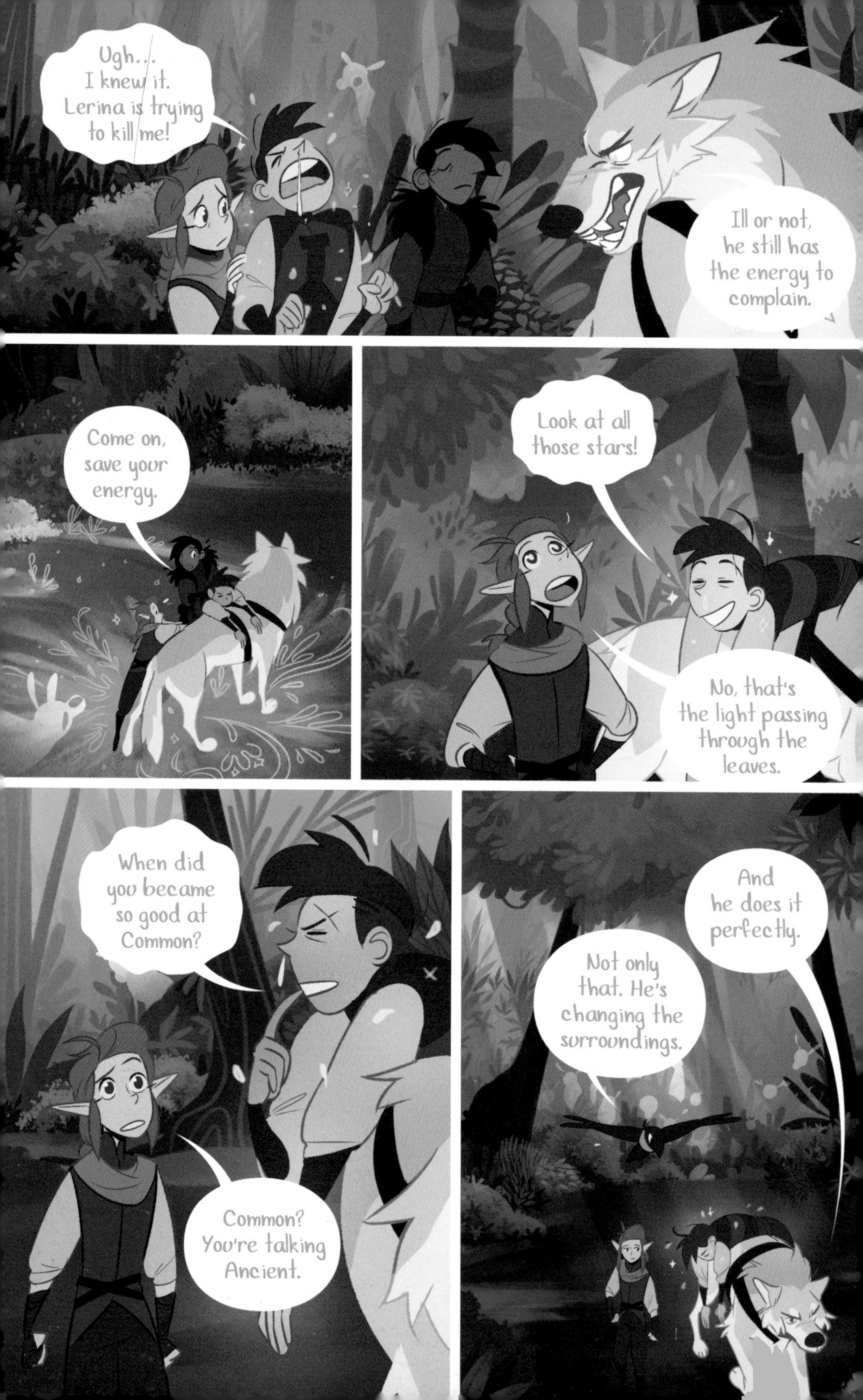
Ugh... I knew it. Lerina is trying to kill me!
Ill or not, he still has the energy to complain.
Come on, save your energy.
Look at all those stars!
No, that's the light passing through the leaves.
When did you became so good at Common?
Common? You're talking Ancient.
Not only that. He's changing the surroundings.
And he does it perfectly.

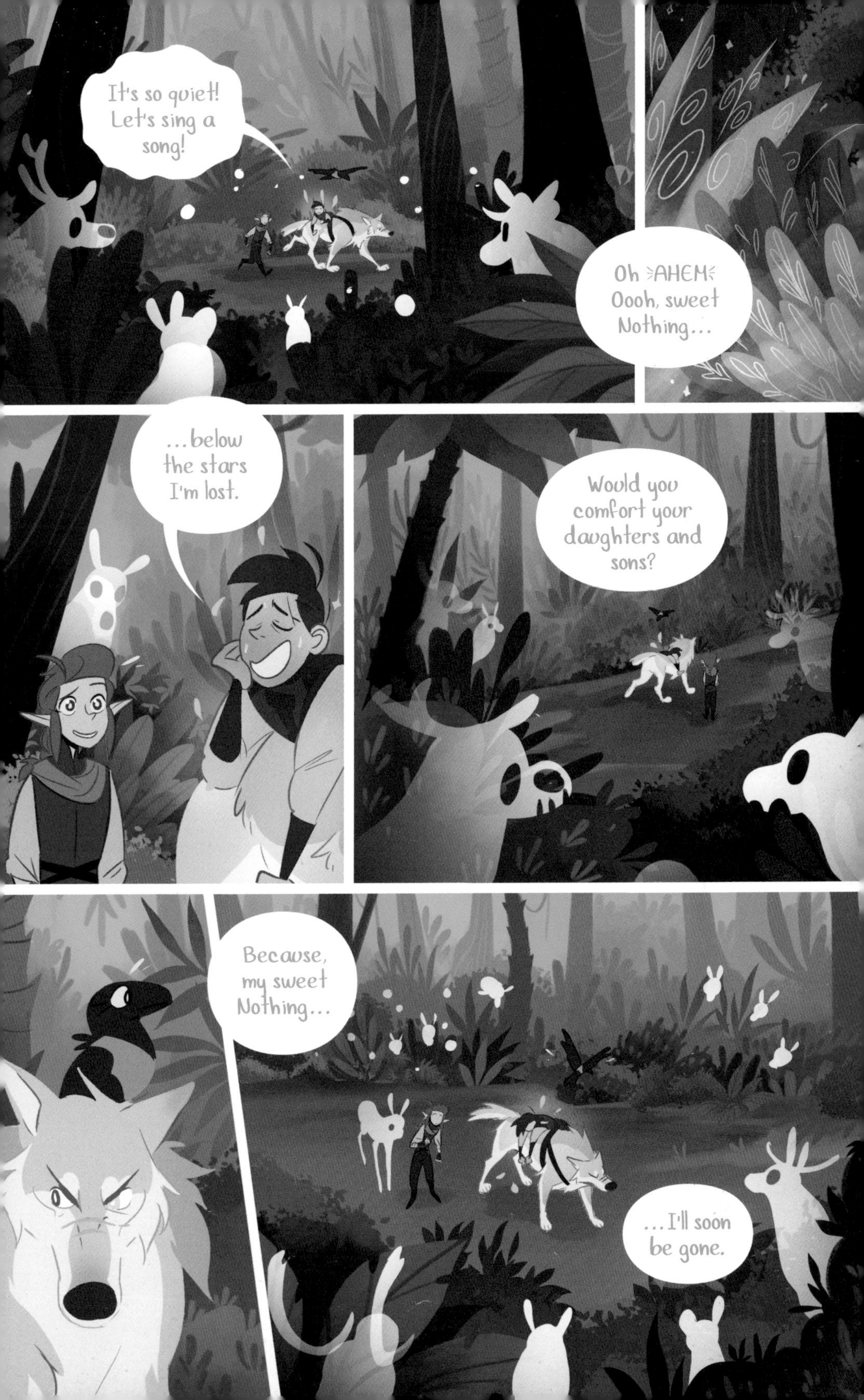
It's so quiet! Let's sing a song!
Oh ⸗AHEM⸗ Oooh, sweet Nothing...
...below the stars I'm lost.
Would you comfort your daughters and sons?
Because, my sweet Nothing...
...I'll soon be gone.

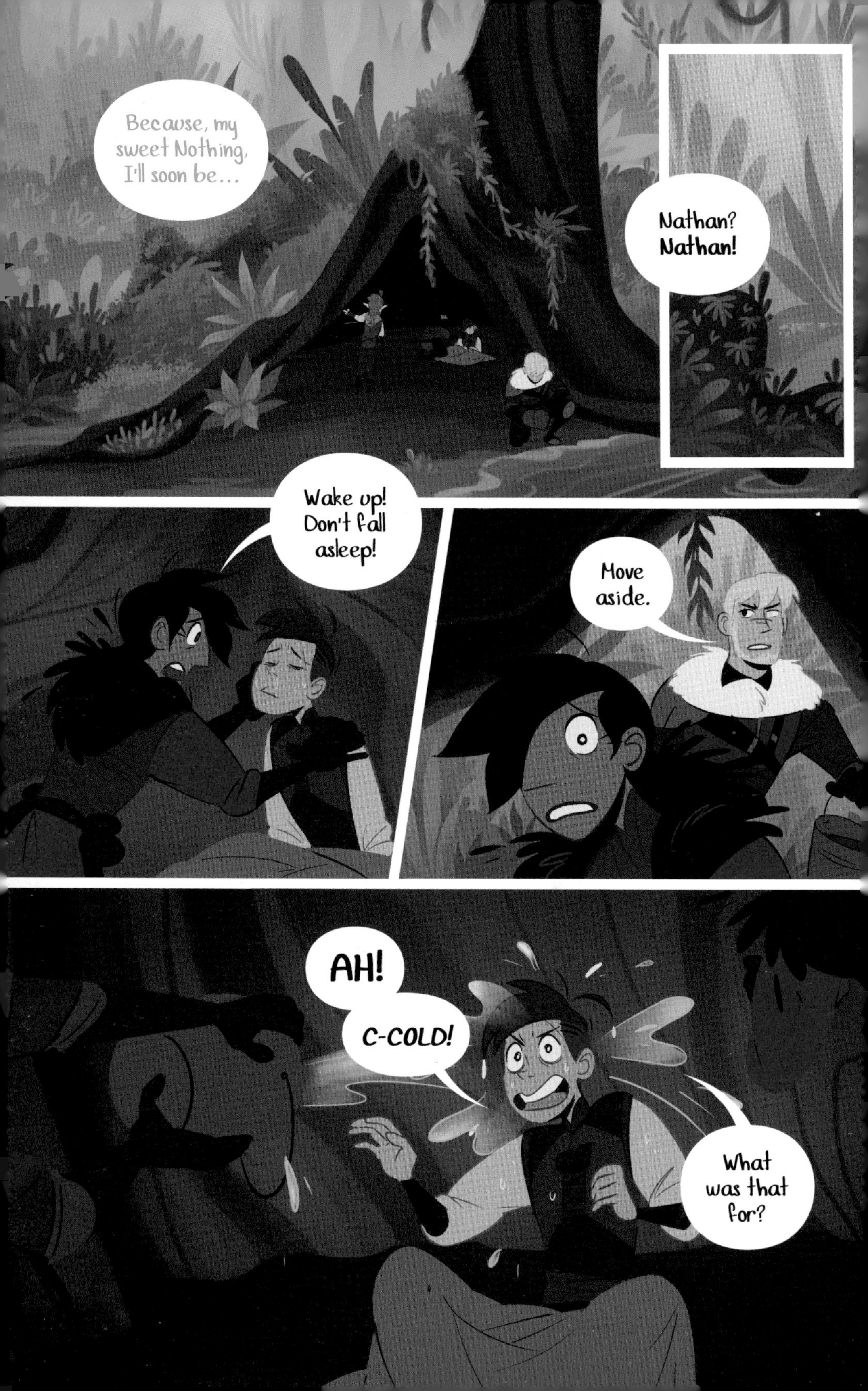
Because, my sweet Nothing, I'll soon be...
Nathan? Nathan!
Wake up! Don't fall asleep!
Move aside.
AH!
C-COLD!
What was that for?

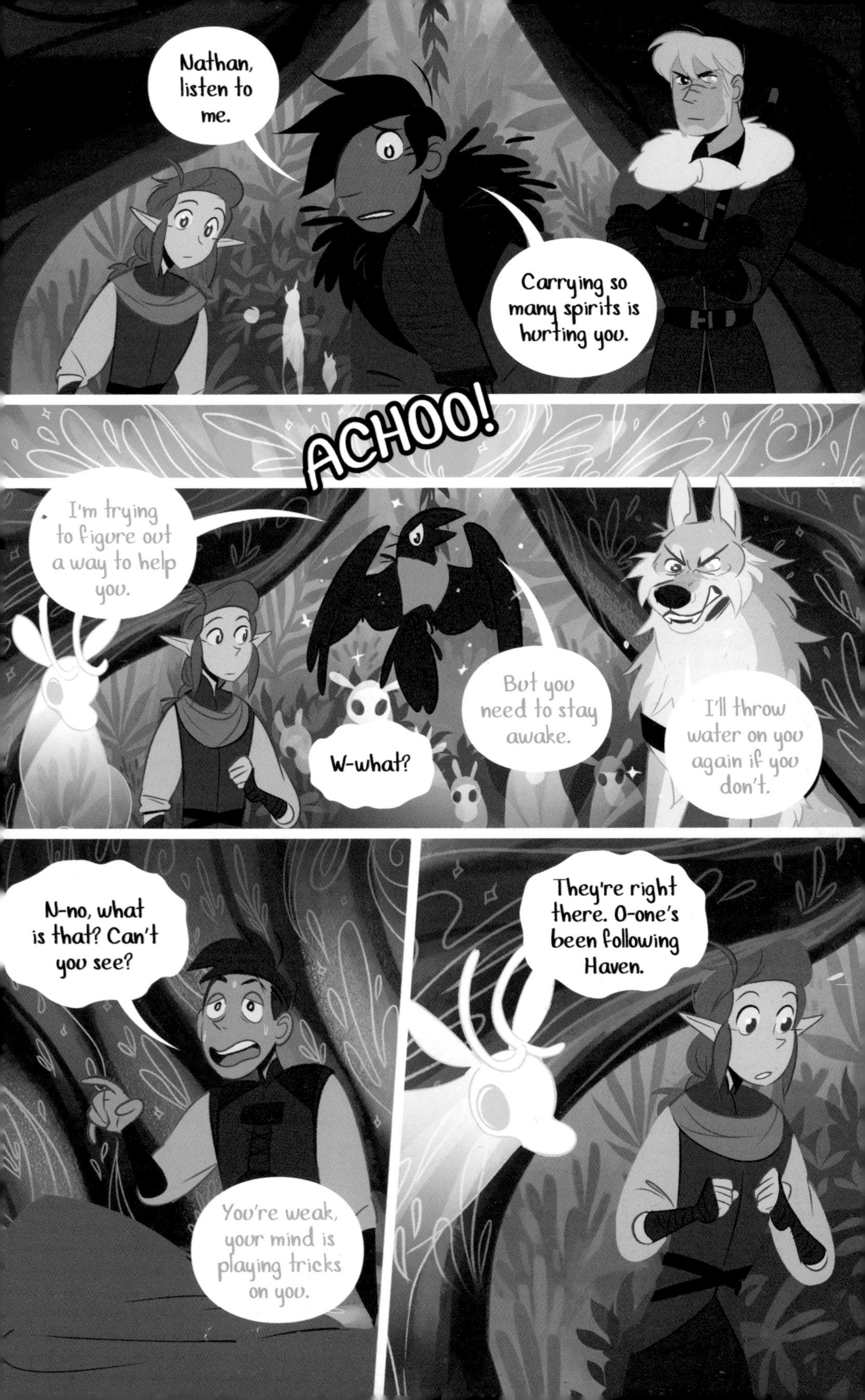
Nathan, listen to me.
Carrying so many spirits is hurting you.
ACHOO!
I'm trying to figure out a way to help you.
W-what?
But you need to stay awake.
I'll throw water on you again if you don't.
N-no, what is that? Can't you see?
You're weak, your mind is playing tricks on you.
They're right there. O-one's been following Haven.

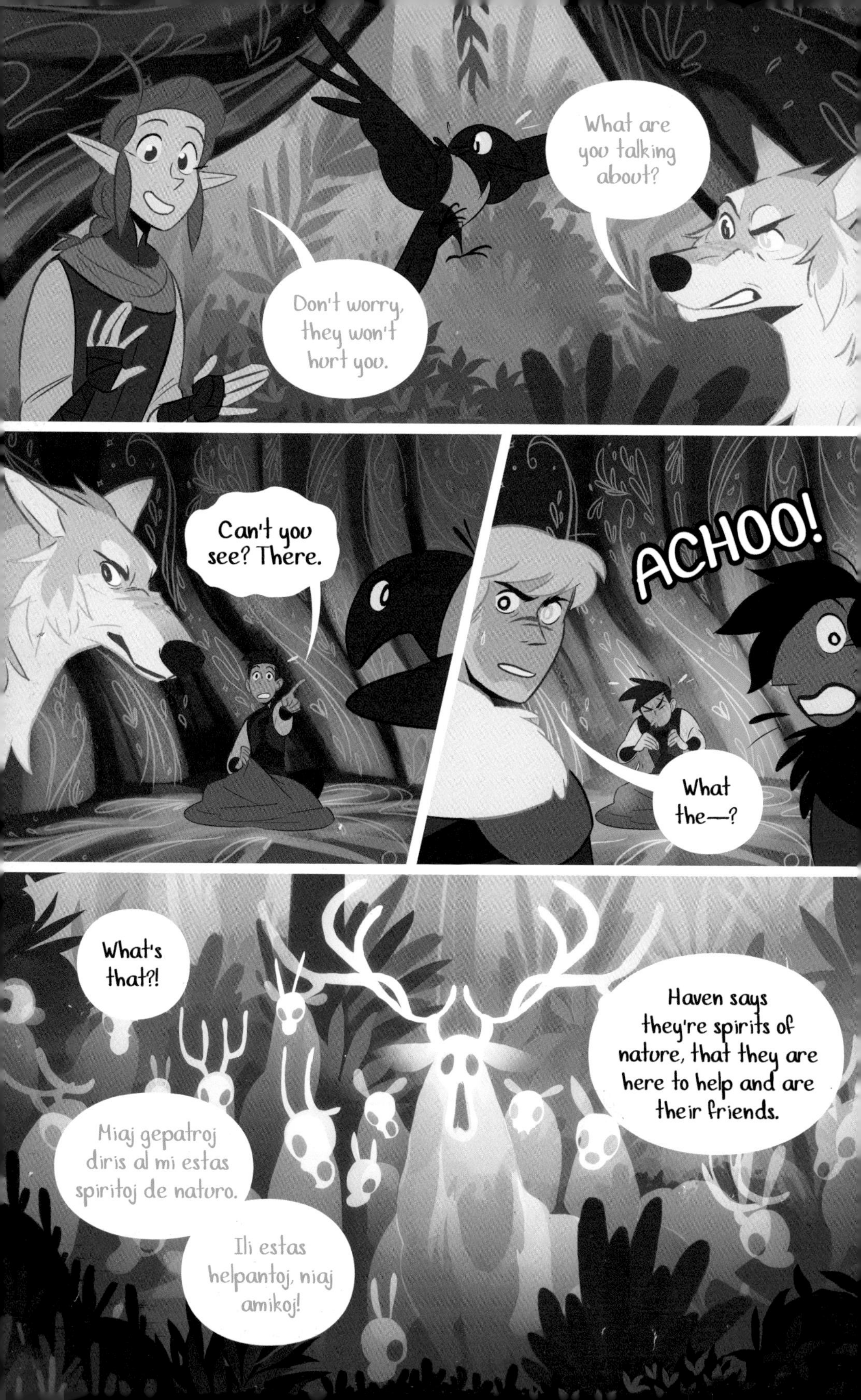

What are you talking about?
Don't worry, they won't hurt you.
Can't you see? There.
ACHOO!
What the—?
What's that?!
Haven says they're spirits of nature, that they are here to help and are their friends.
Miaj gepatroj diris al mi estas spiritoj de naturo.
Ili estas helpantoj, niaj amikoj!

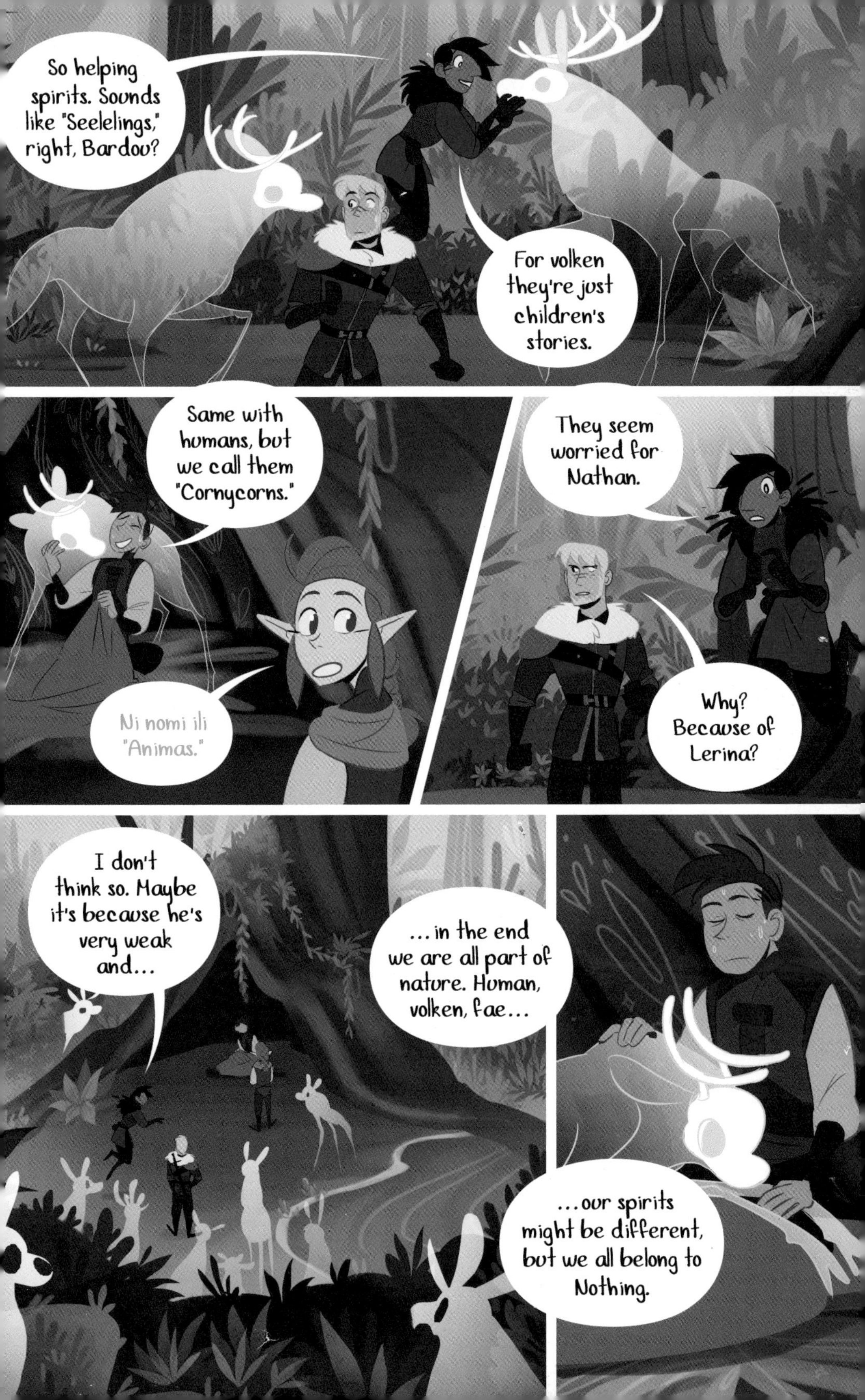
So helping spirits. Sounds like "Seelelings," right, Bardou?
For volken they're just children's stories.
Same with humans, but we call them "Cornycorns."
Ni nomi ili "Animas."
They seem worried for Nathan.
Why? Because of Lerina?
I don't think so. Maybe it's because he's very weak and...
...in the end we are all part of nature. Human, volken, fae...
...our spirits might be different, but we all belong to Nothing.

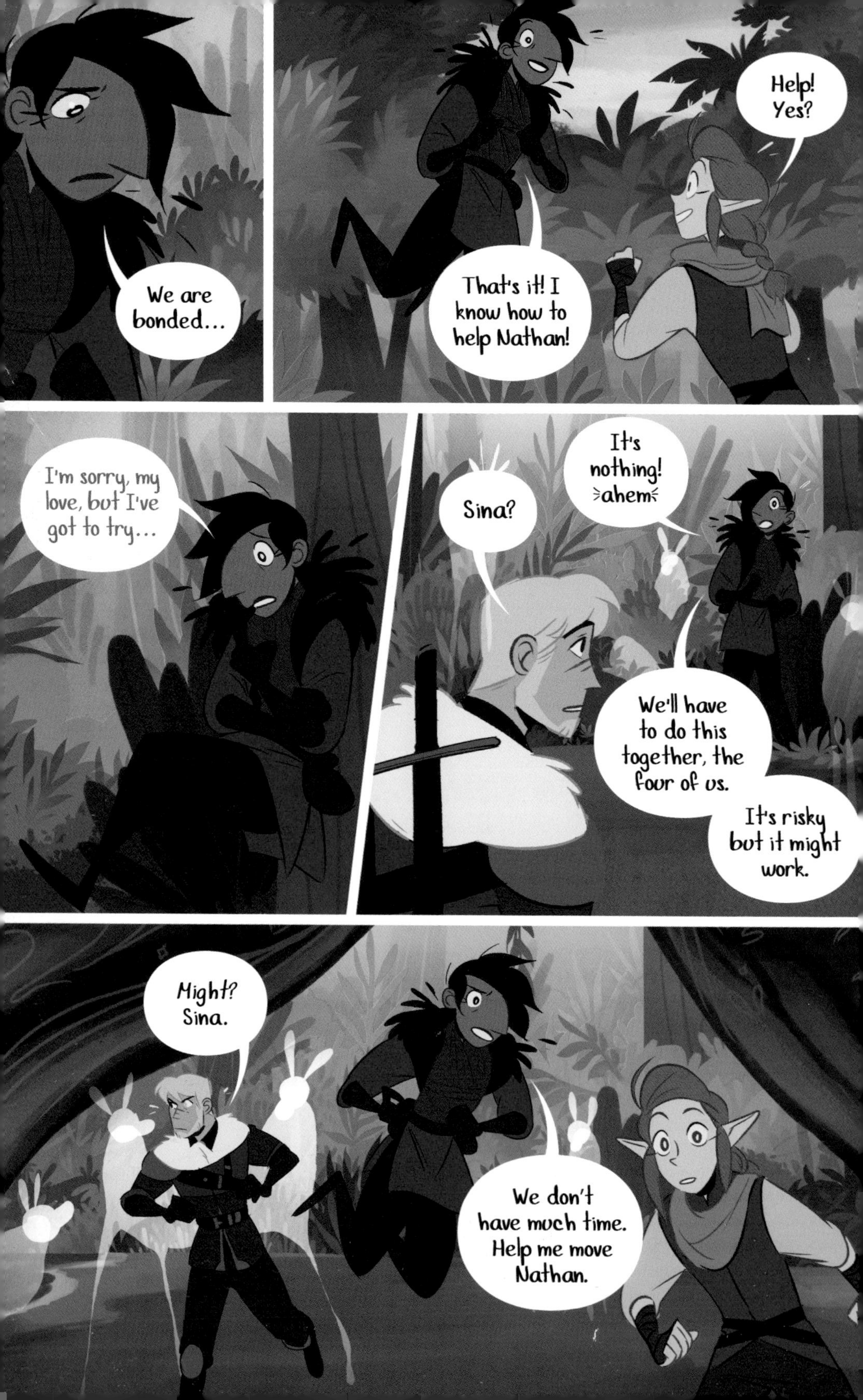
We are bonded...
That's it! I know how to help Nathan!
Help! Yes?
I'm sorry, my love, but I've got to try...
Sina?
It's nothing! ahem
We'll have to do this together, the four of us.
It's risky but it might work.
Might? Sina.
We don't have much time. Help me move Nathan.

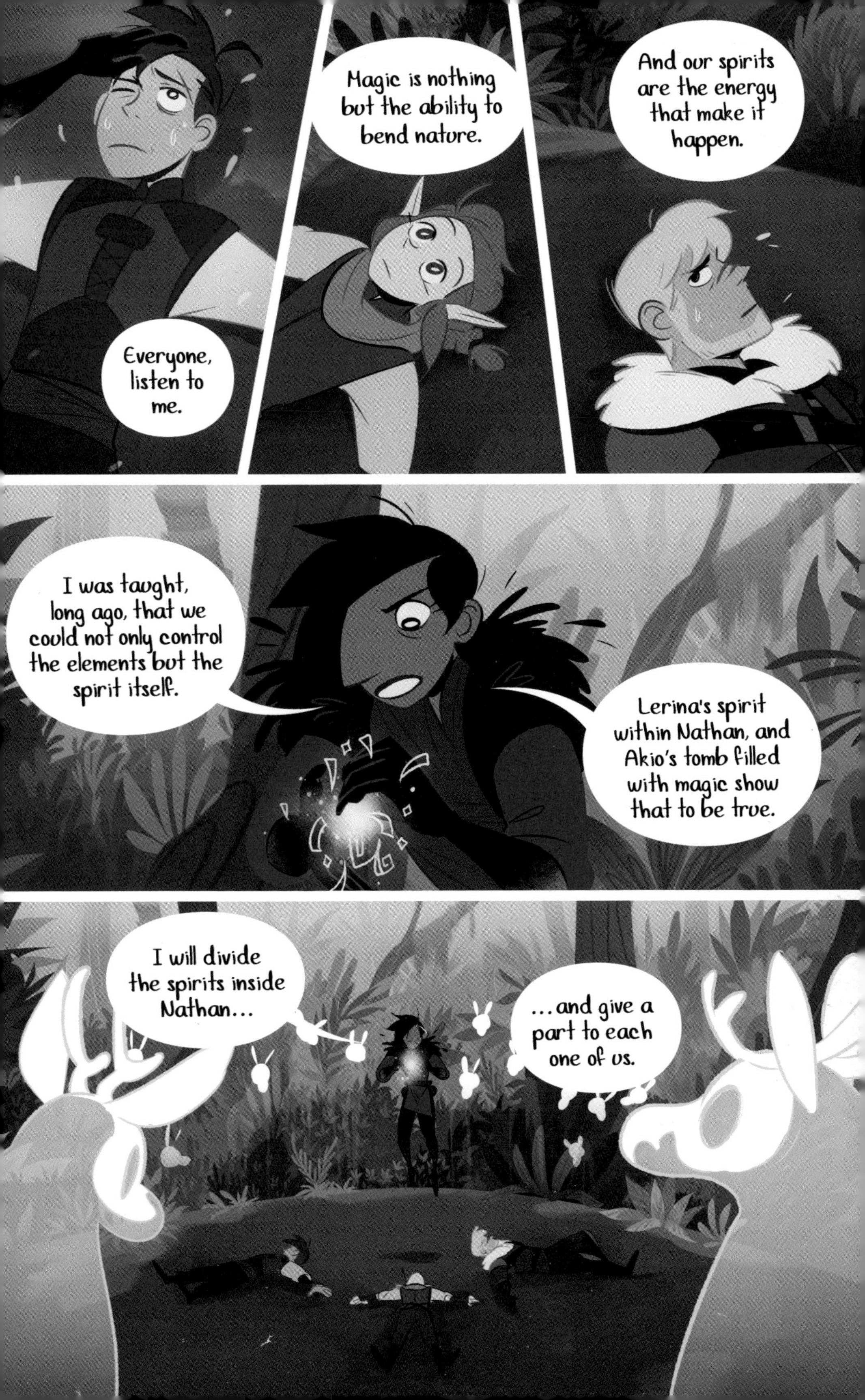
Everyone, listen to me.
Magic is nothing but the ability to bend nature.
And our spirits are the energy that make it happen.
I was taught, long ago, that we could not only control the elements but the spirit itself.
Lerina's spirit within Nathan, and Akio's tomb filled with magic show that to be true.
I will divide the spirits inside Nathan...
...and give a part to each one of us.

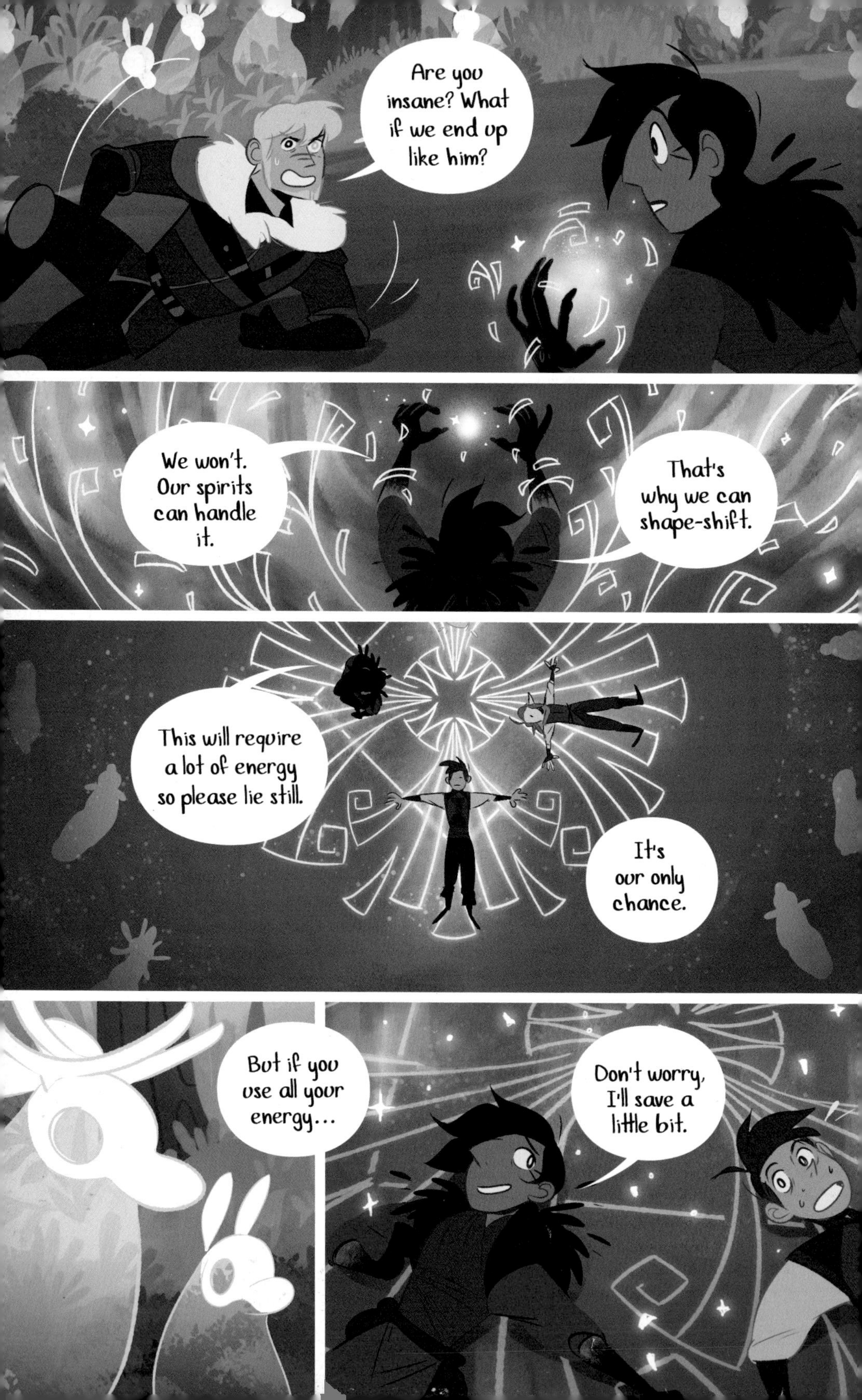
Are you insane? What if we end up like him?
We won't. Our spirits can handle it.
That's why we can shape-shift.
This will require a lot of energy so please lie still.
It's our only chance.
But if you use all your energy...
Don't worry, I'll save a little bit.

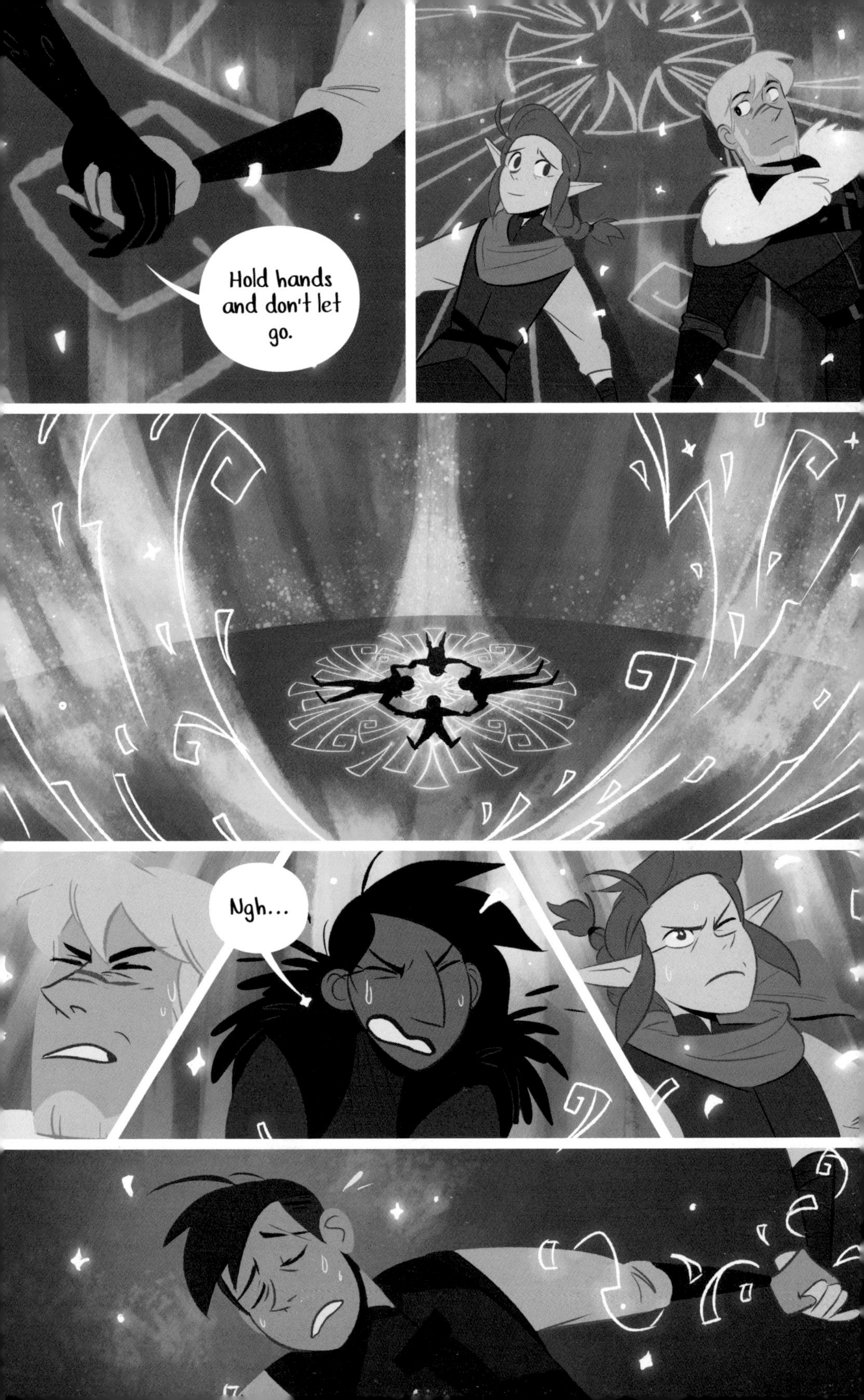
Hold hands and don't let go.
Ngh...

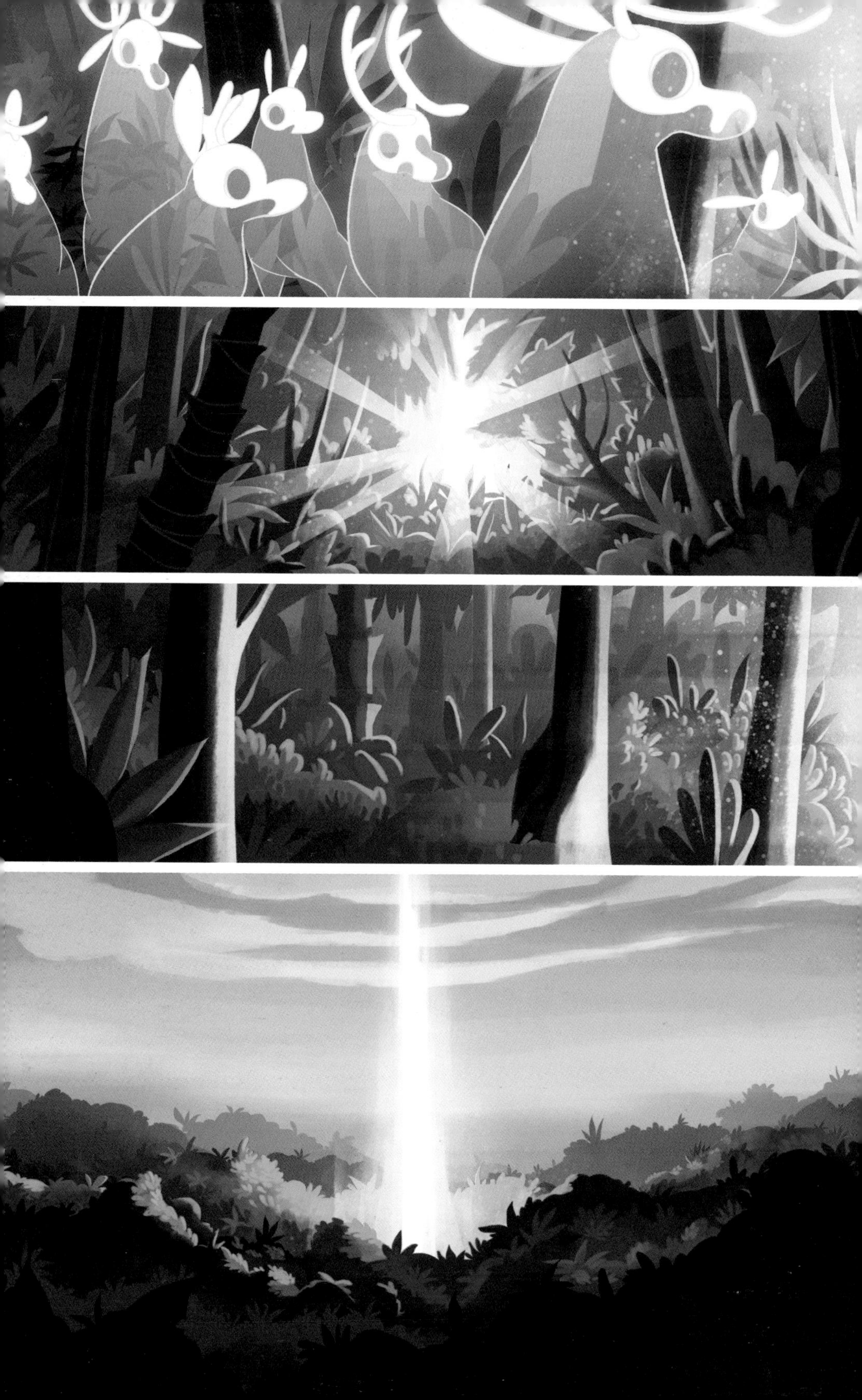

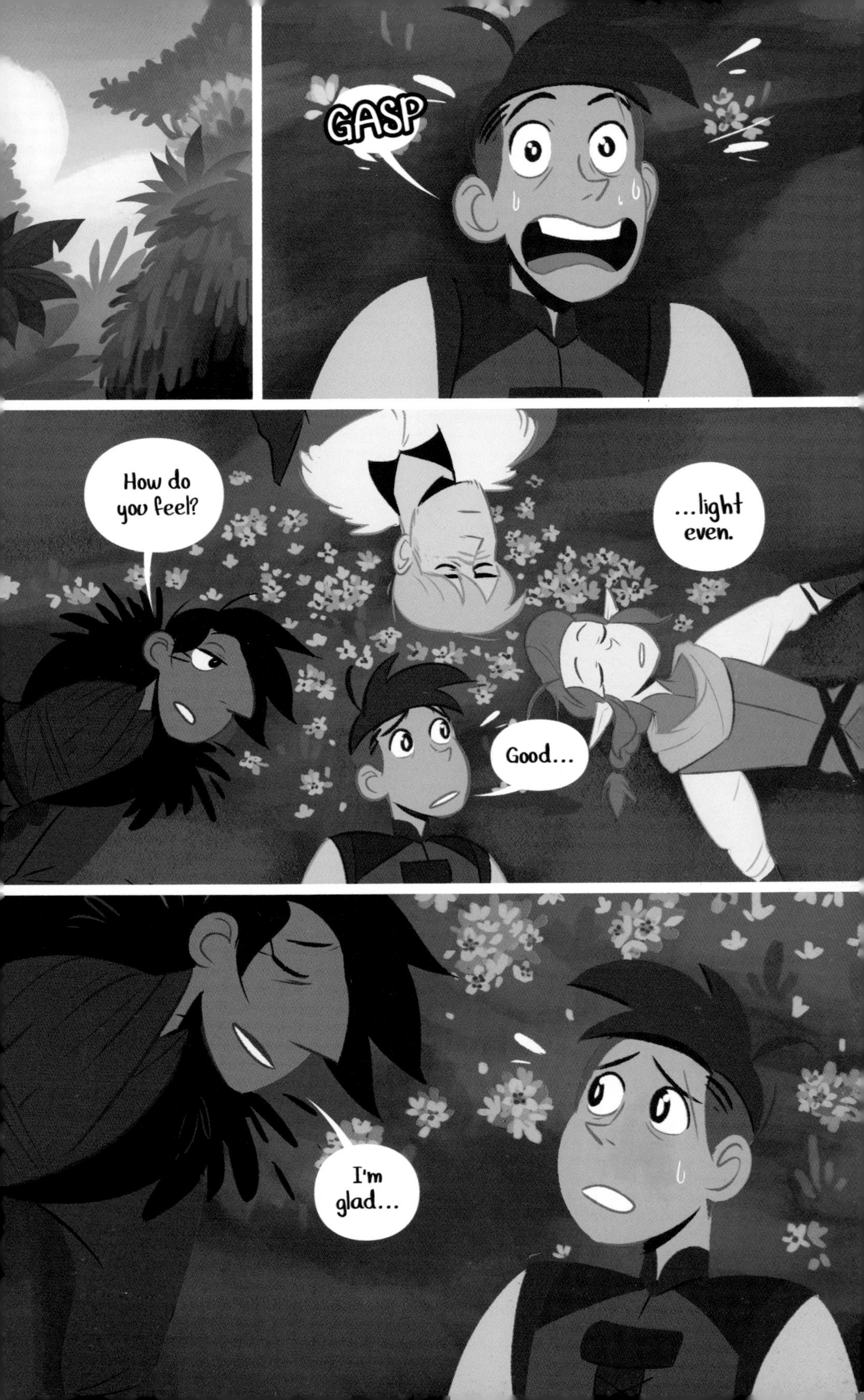
GASP
How do you feel?
...light even.
Good...
I'm glad...

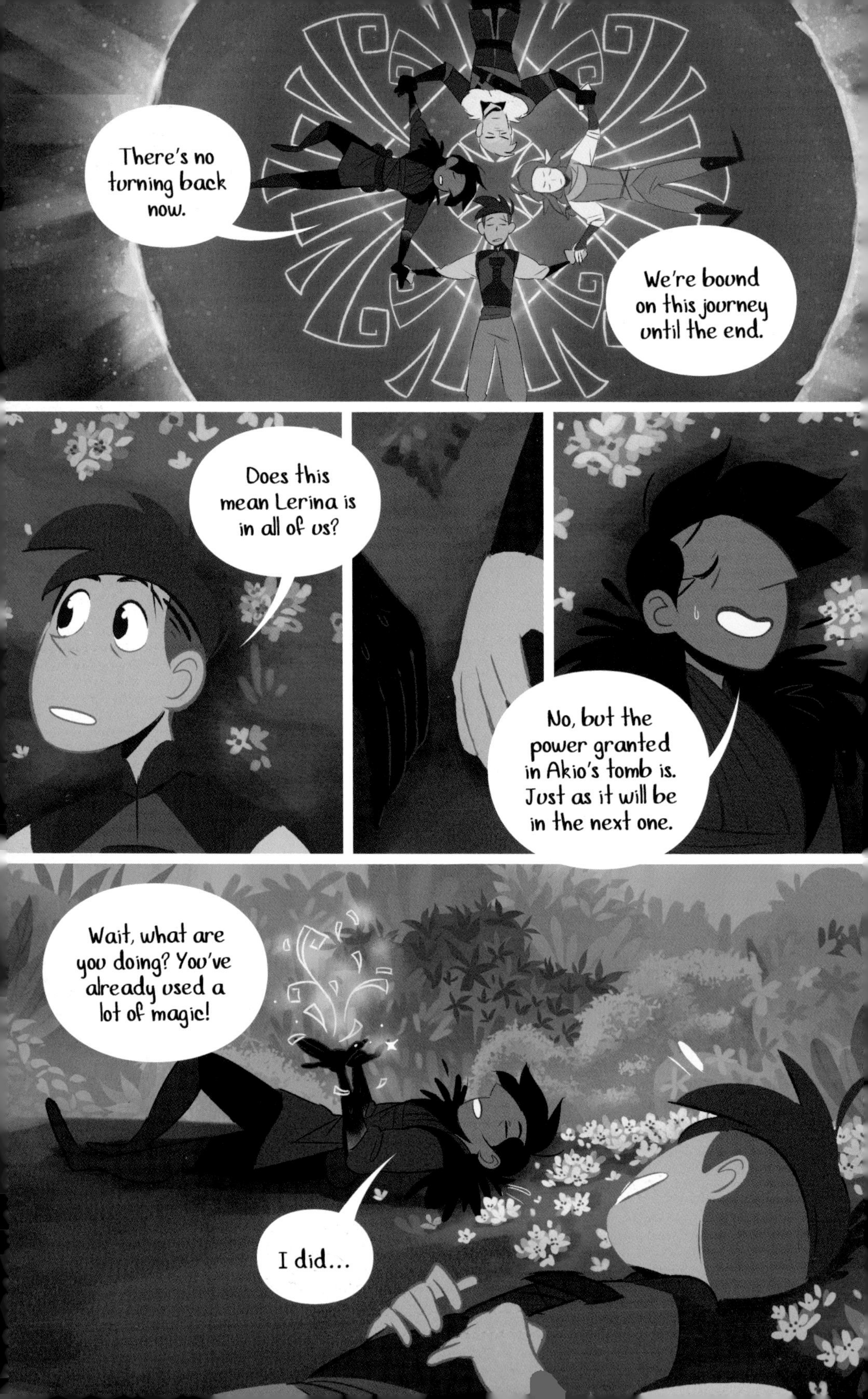
There's no turning back now.
We're bound on this journey until the end.
Does this mean Lerina is in all of us?
No, but the power granted in Akio's tomb is. Just as it will be in the next one.
Wait, what are you doing? You've already used a lot of magic!
I did...

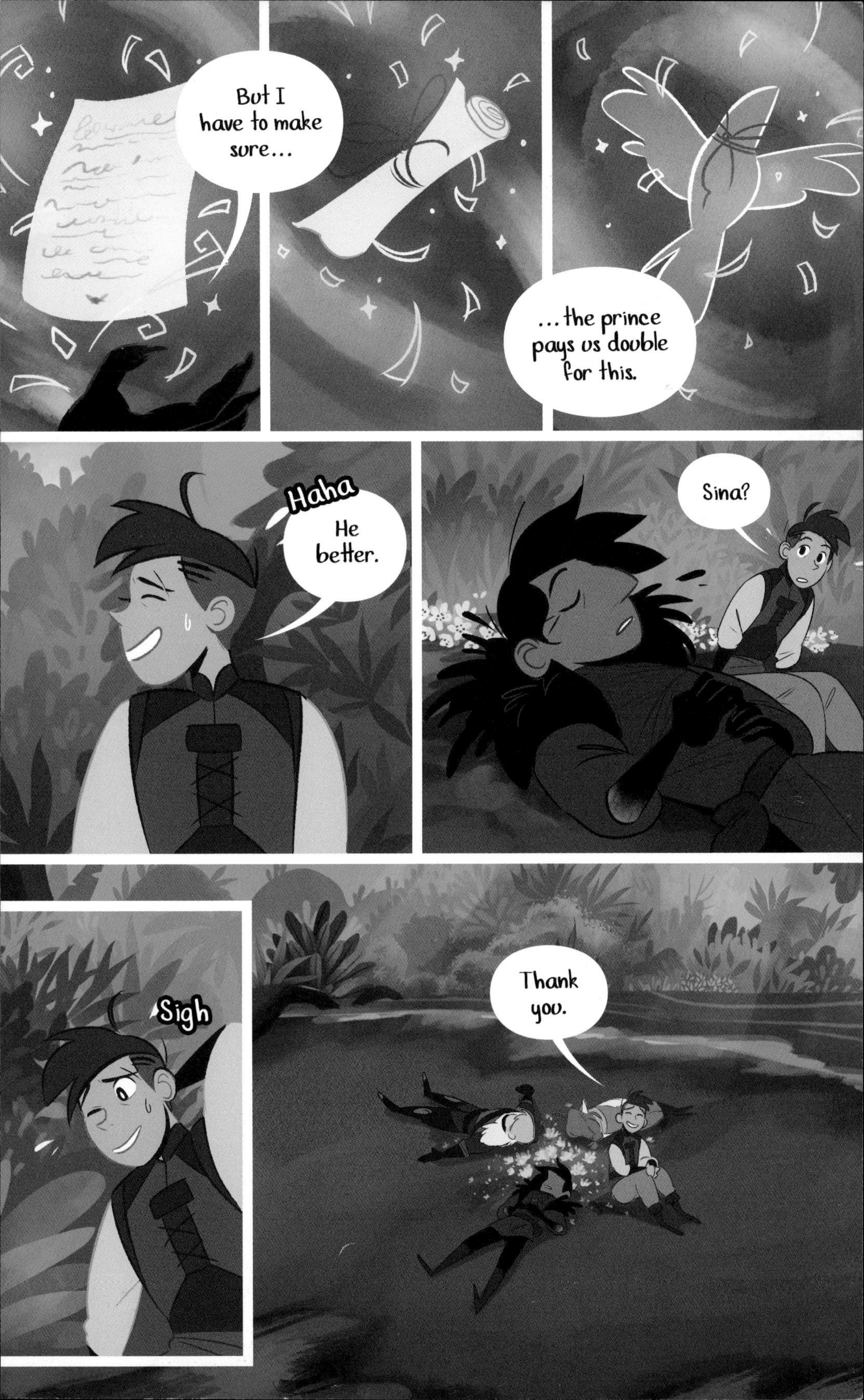
But I have to make sure...
...the prince pays us double for this.
Haha
He better.
Sina?
Sigh
Thank you.

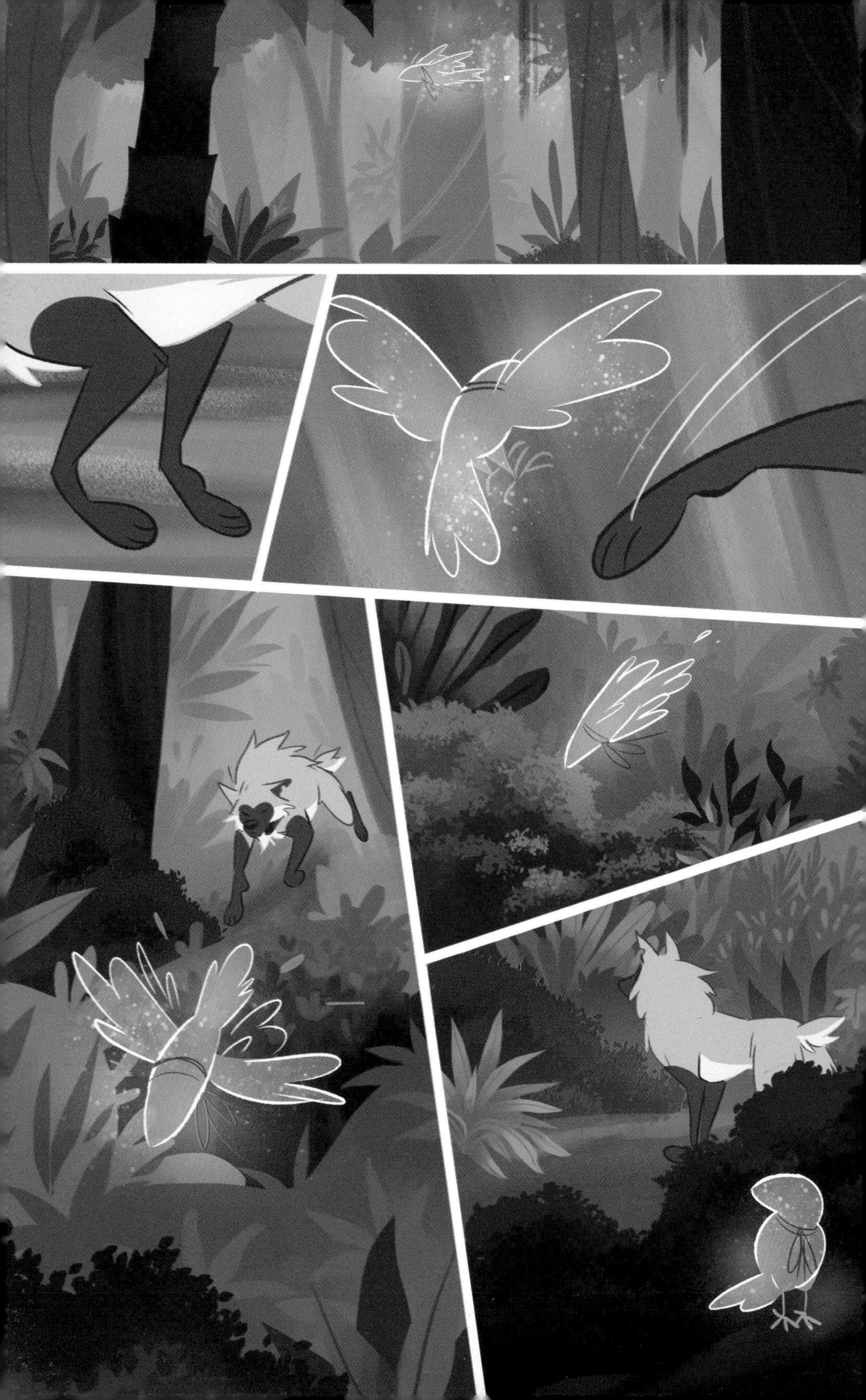

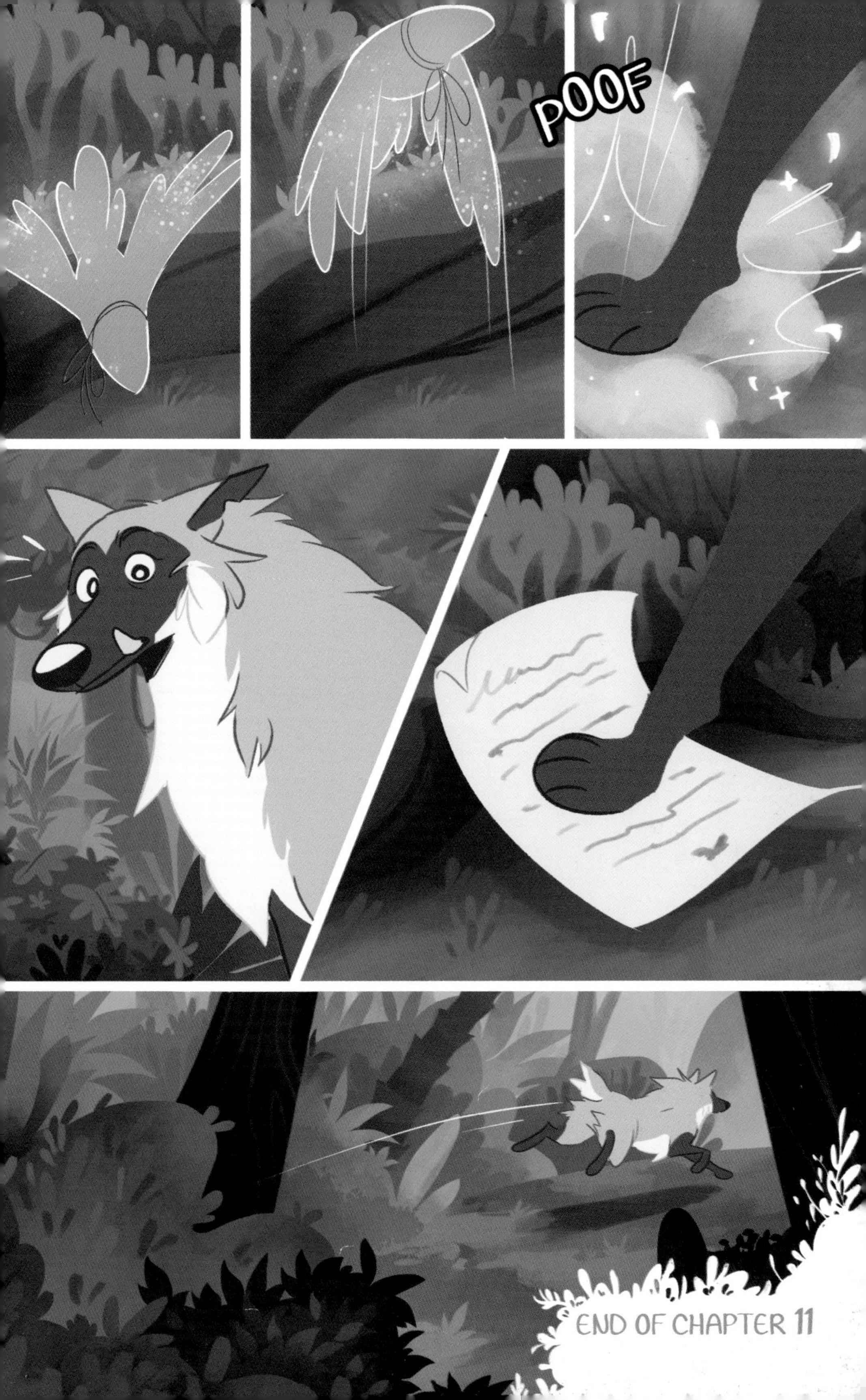
POOF
END OF CHAPTER 11

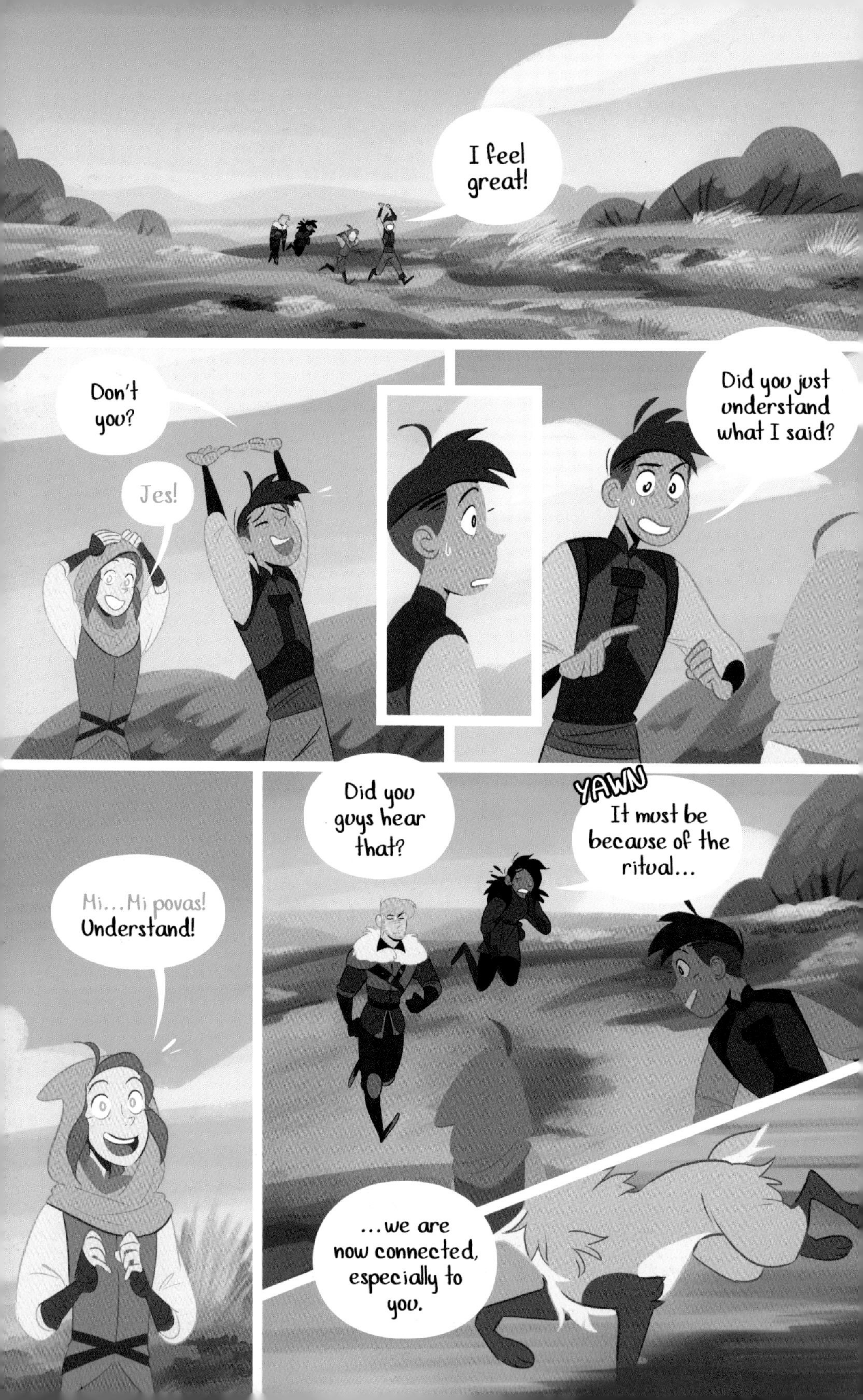
I feel great!
Don't you?
Jes!
Did you just understand what I said?
Mi...Mi povas! Understand!
Did you guys hear that?
YAWN
It must be because of the ritual...
...we are now connected, especially to you.

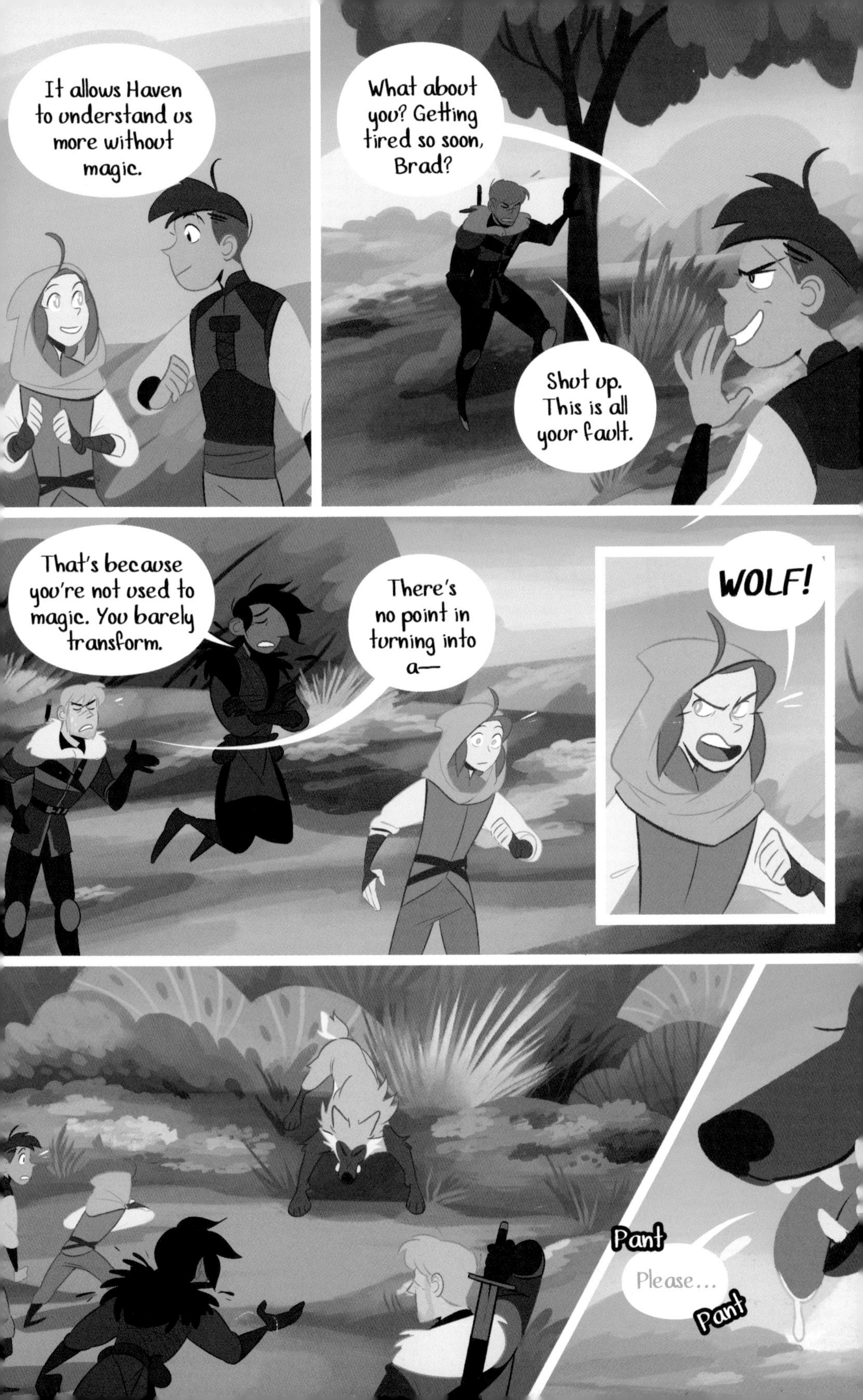
It allows Haven to understand us more without magic.
What about you? Getting tired so soon, Brad?
Shut up. This is all your fault.
That's because you're not used to magic. You barely transform.
There's no point in turning into a—
WOLF!
Pant
Please...
Pant

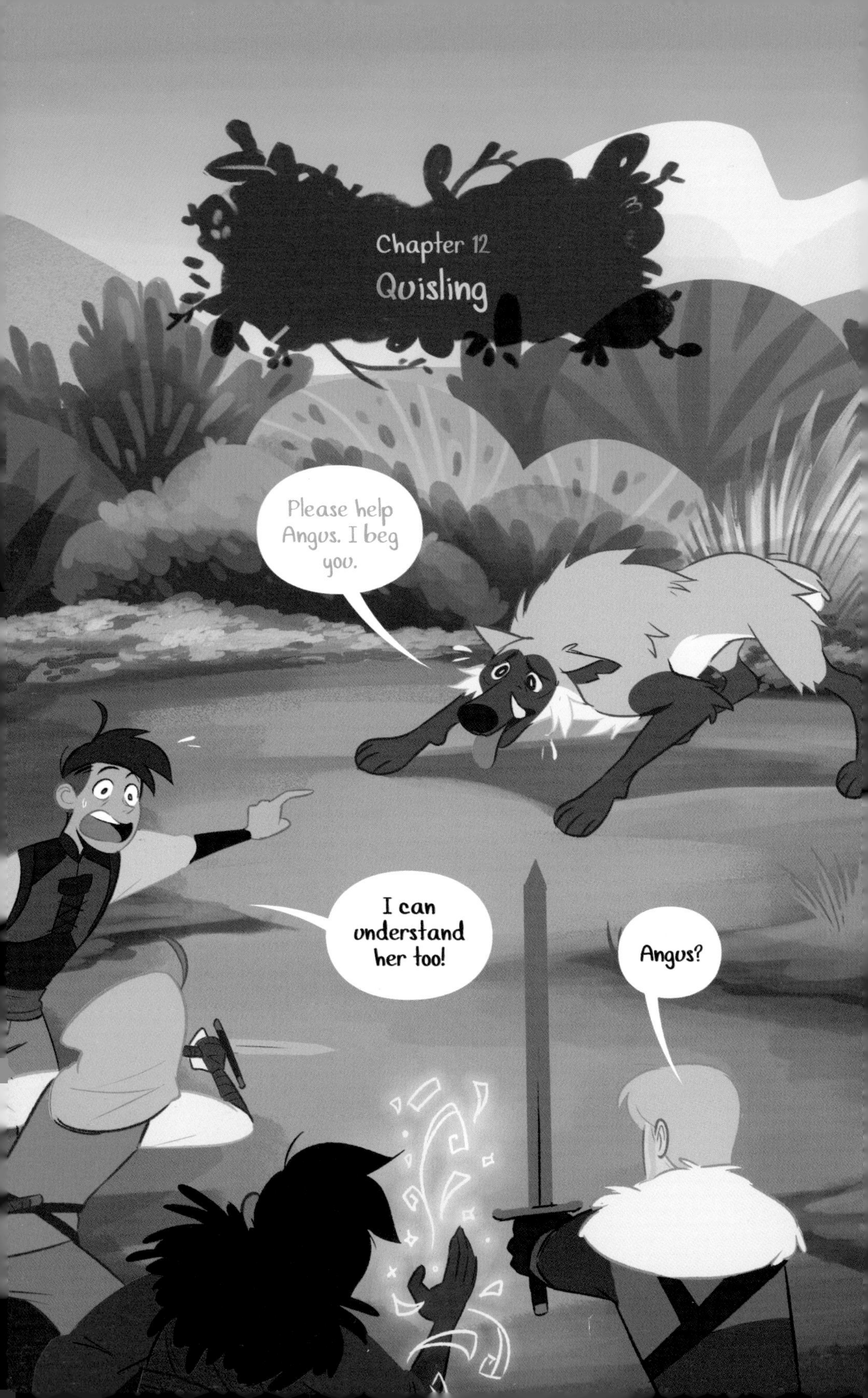
Chapter 12
Quisling
Please help Angus. I beg you.
I can understand her too!
Angus?

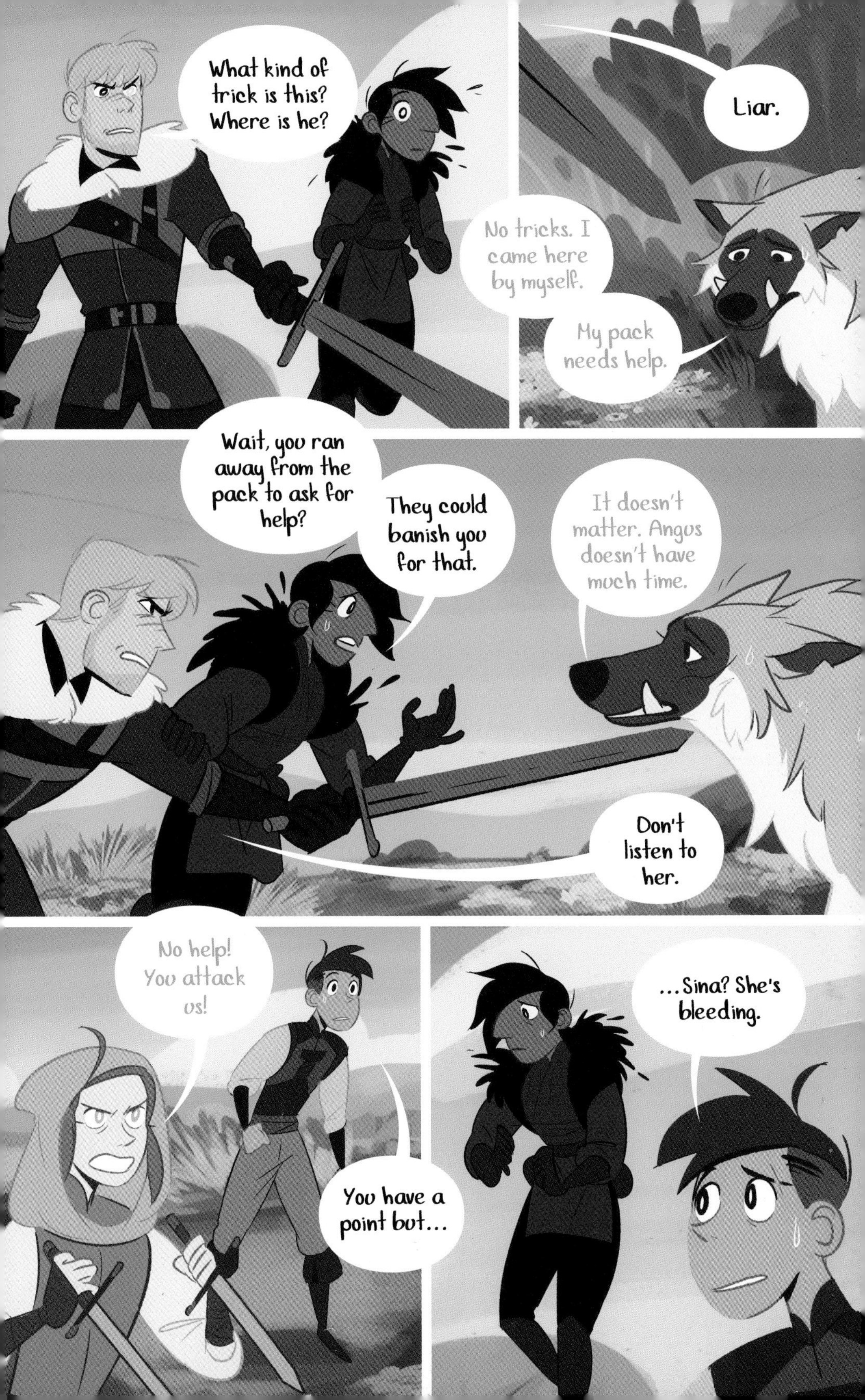
What kind of trick is this? Where is he?
Liar.
No tricks. I came here by myself.
My pack needs help.
Wait, you ran away from the pack to ask for help?
They could banish you for that.
It doesn't matter. Angus doesn't have much time.
Don't listen to her.
No help! You attack us!
You have a point but...
...Sina? She's bleeding.

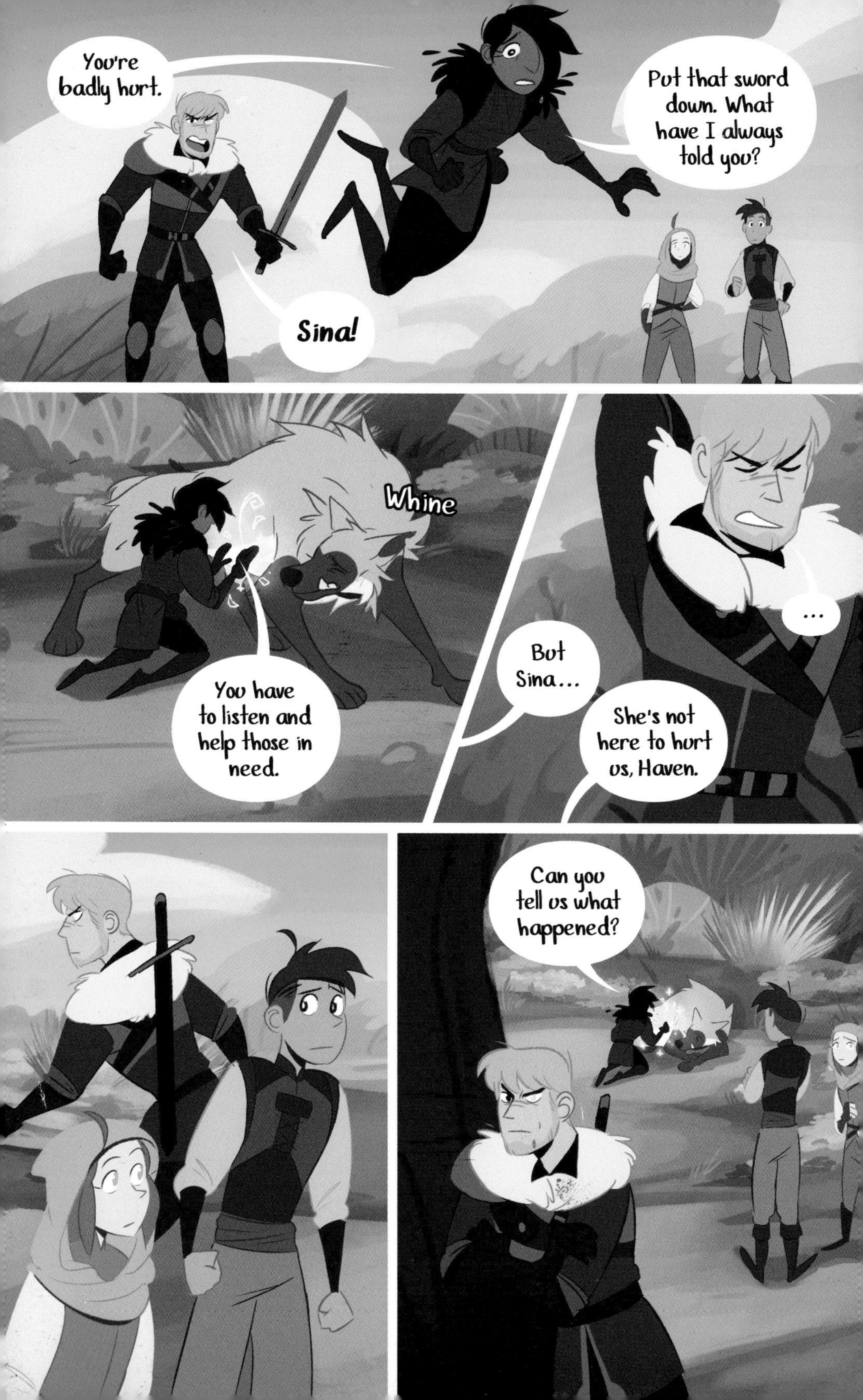

You're badly hurt.
Put that sword down. What have I always told you?
Sina!
Whine
You have to listen and help those in need.
...
But Sina...
She's not here to hurt us, Haven.
Can you tell us what happened?

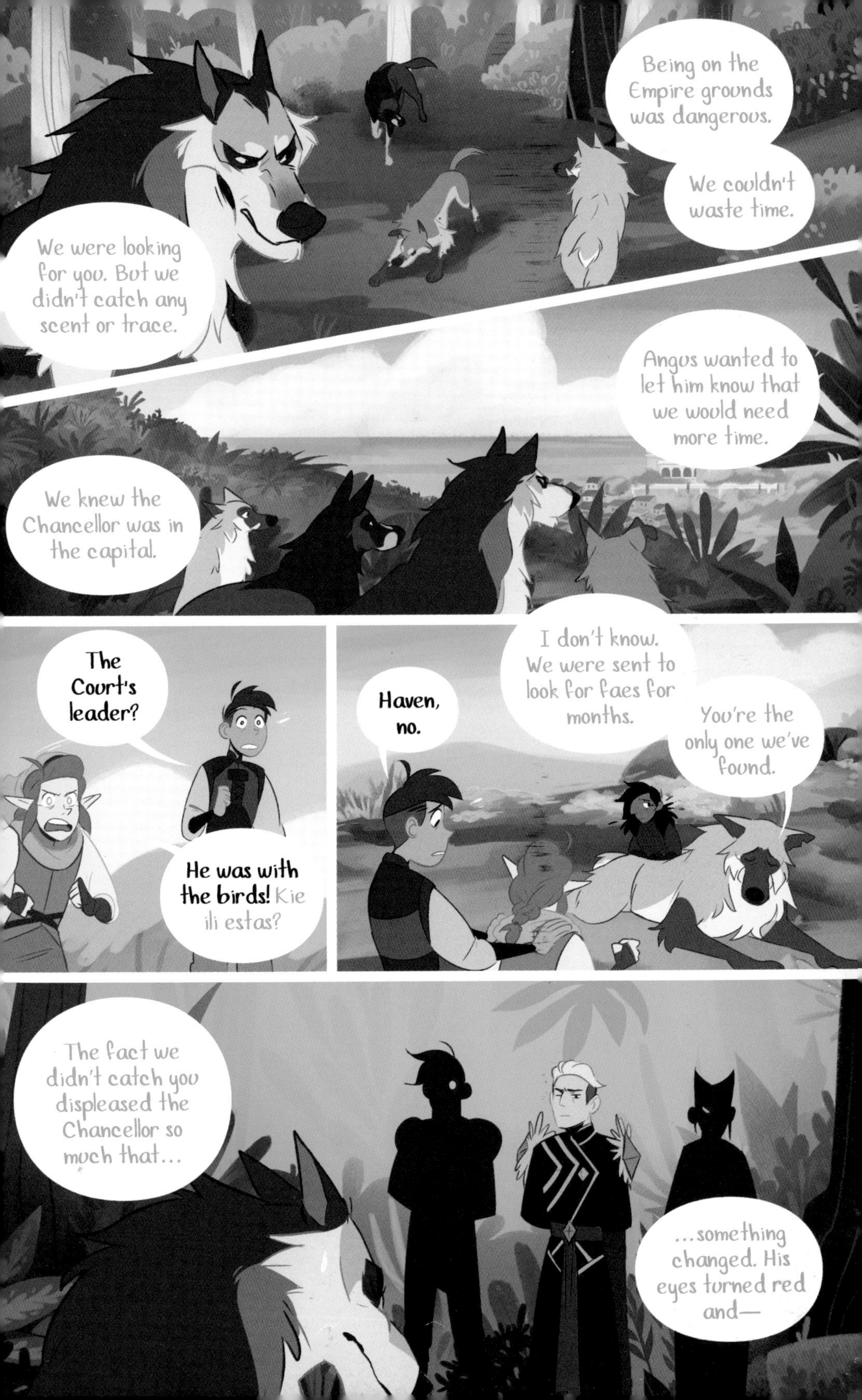

We were looking for you. But we didn't catch any scent or trace.
Being on the Empire grounds was dangerous.
We couldn't waste time.
We knew the Chancellor was in the capital.
Angus wanted to let him know that we would need more time.
The Court's leader?
He was with the birds! Kie ili estas?
Haven, no.
I don't know. We were sent to look for faes for months.
You're the only one we've found.
The fact we didn't catch you displeased the Chancellor so much that...
...something changed. His eyes turned red and—

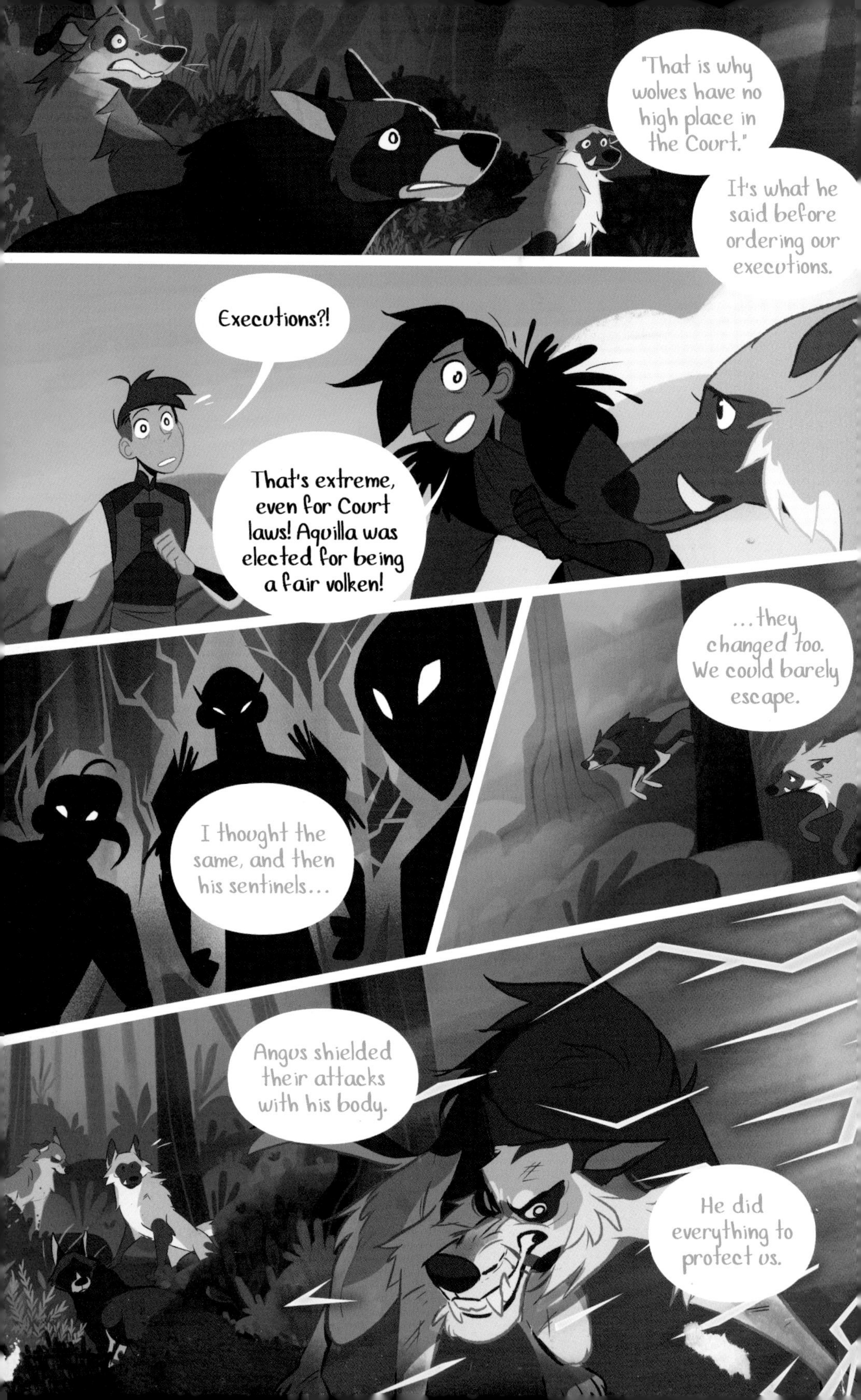
"That is why wolves have no high place in the Court."
It's what he said before ordering our executions.
Executions?!
That's extreme, even for Court laws! Aquilla was elected for being a fair volken!
I thought the same, and then his sentinels...
...they changed too. We could barely escape.
Angus shielded their attacks with his body.
He did everything to protect us.

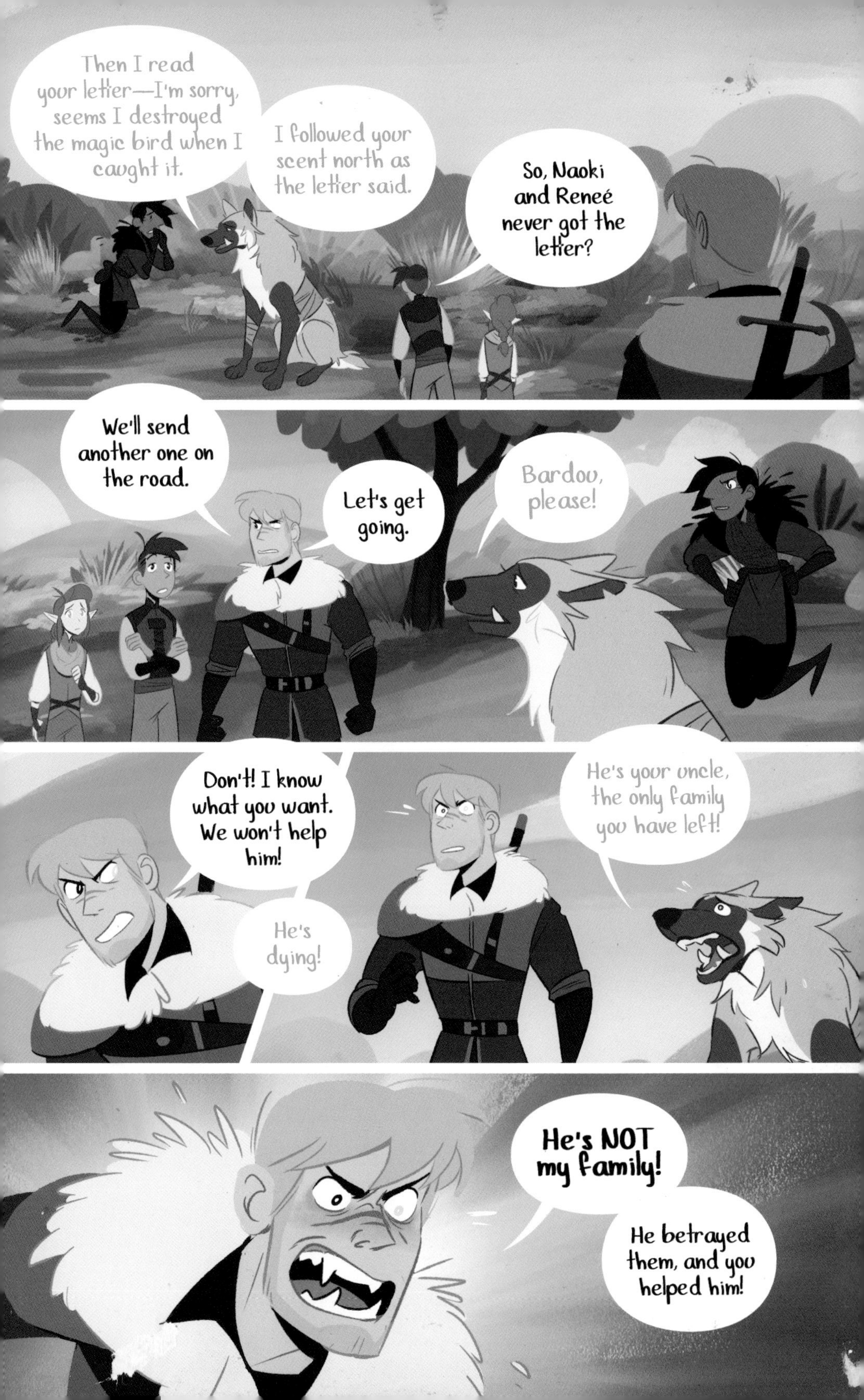

Then I read your letter—I'm sorry, seems I destroyed the magic bird when I caught it.
I followed your scent north as the letter said.
So, Naoki and Reneé never got the letter?
We'll send another one on the road.
Let's get going.
Bardou, please!
Don't! I know what you want. We won't help him!
He's dying!
He's your uncle, the only family you have left!
He's NOT my family!
He betrayed them, and you helped him!

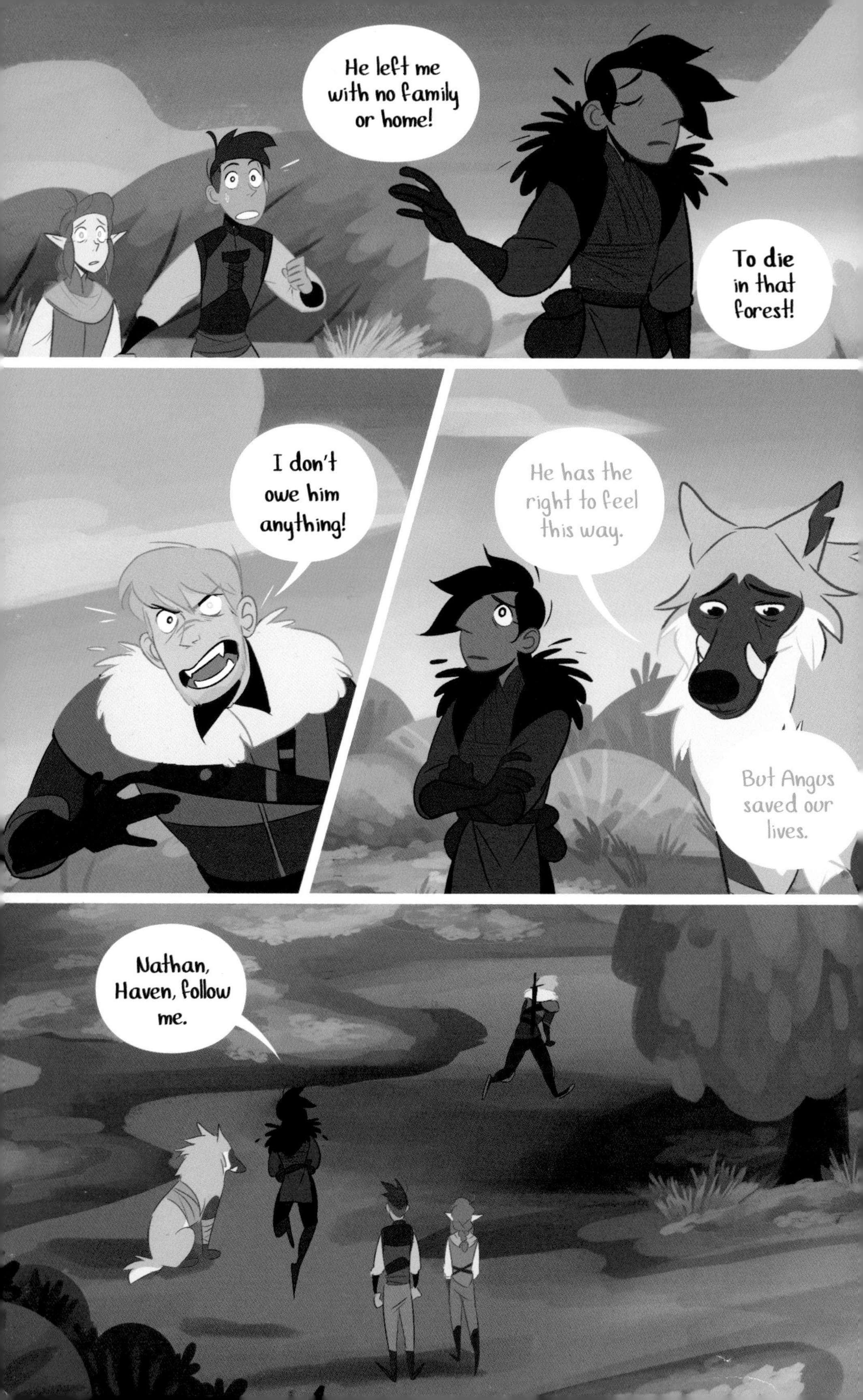
He left me with no family or home!
To die in that forest!
I don't owe him anything!
He has the right to feel this way.
But Angus saved our lives.
Nathan, Haven, follow me.

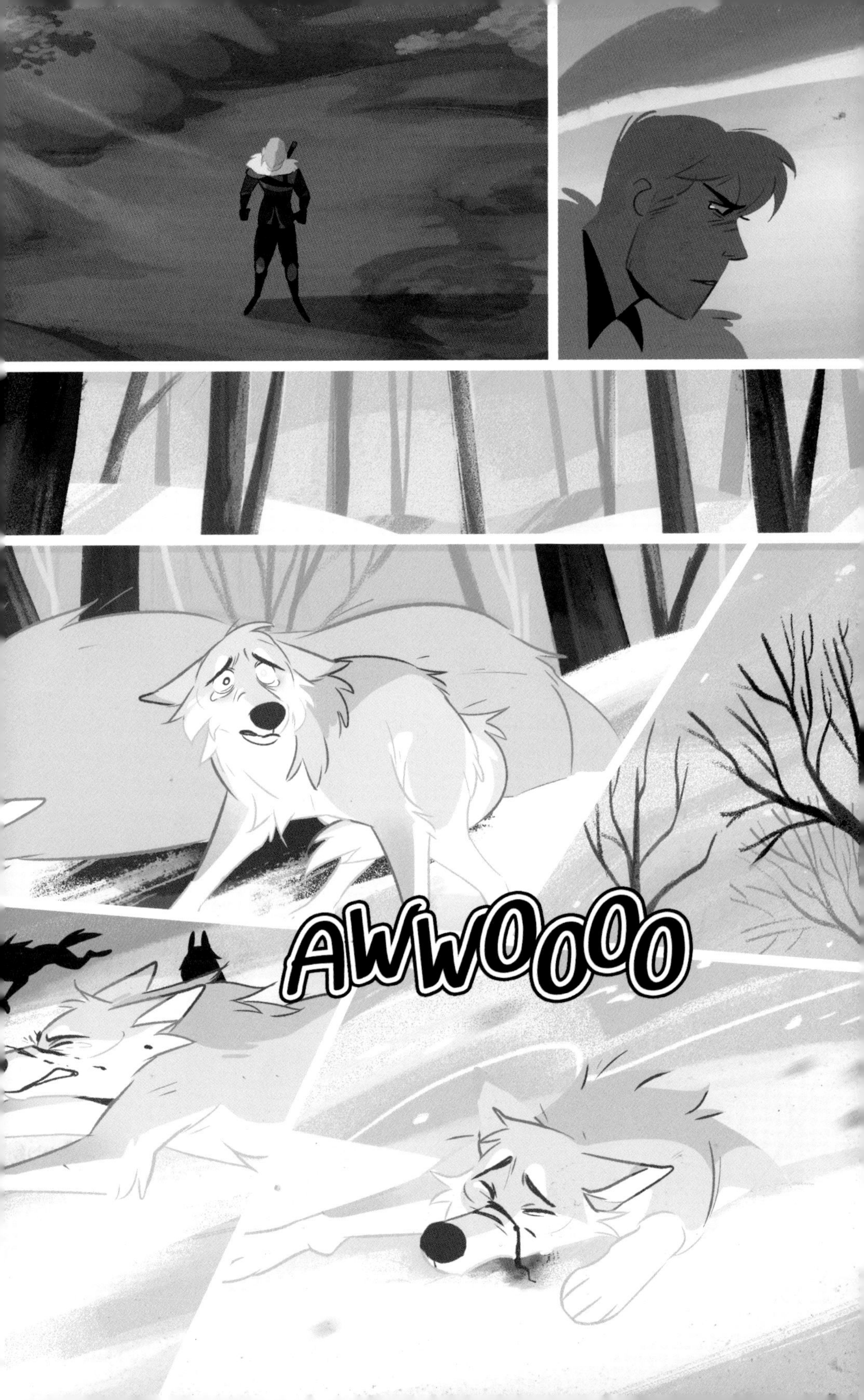
AWWOOOO

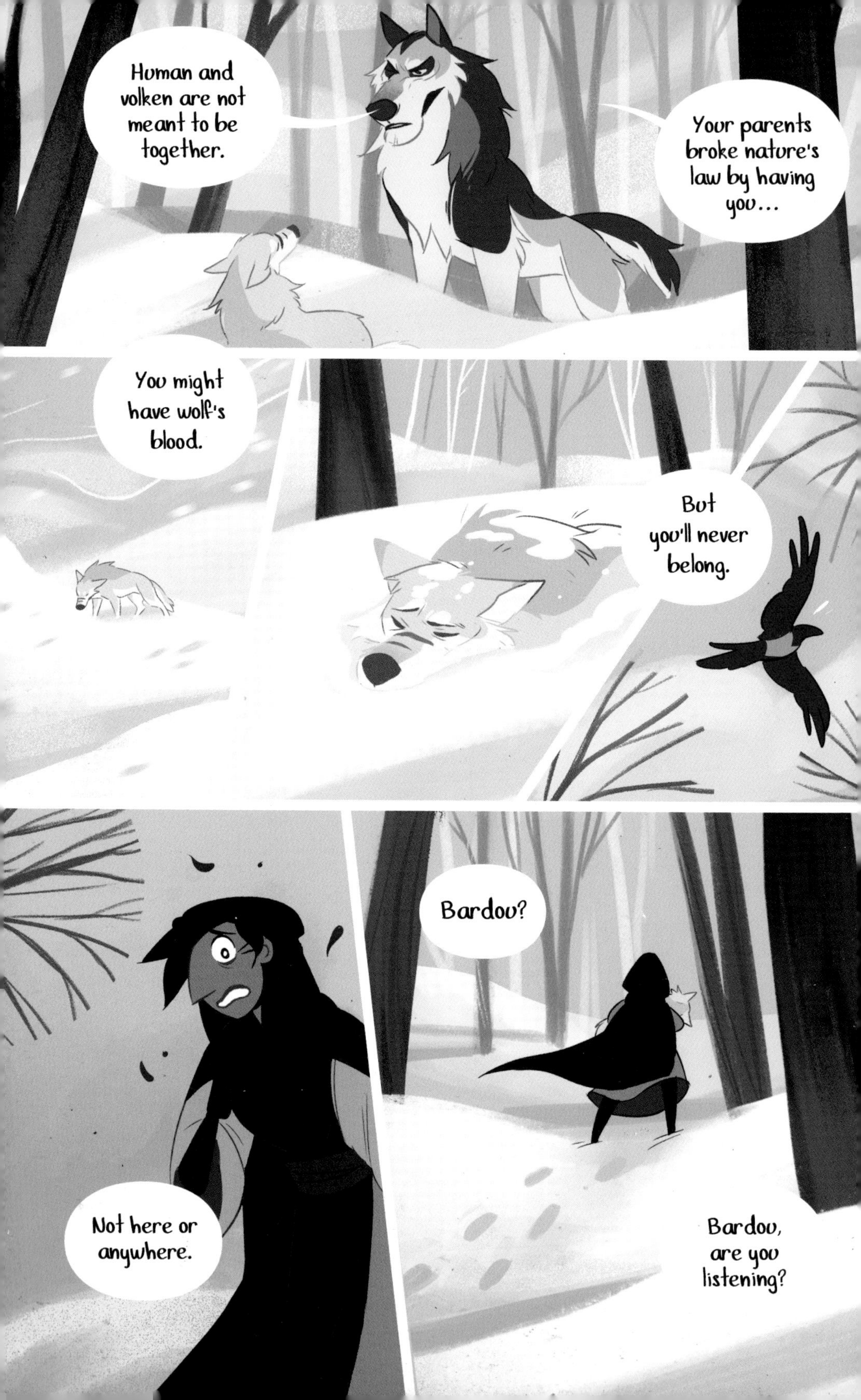
Human and volken are not meant to be together.
Your parents broke nature's law by having you...
You might have wolf's blood.
But you'll never belong.
Not here or anywhere.
Bardou?
Bardou, are you listening?

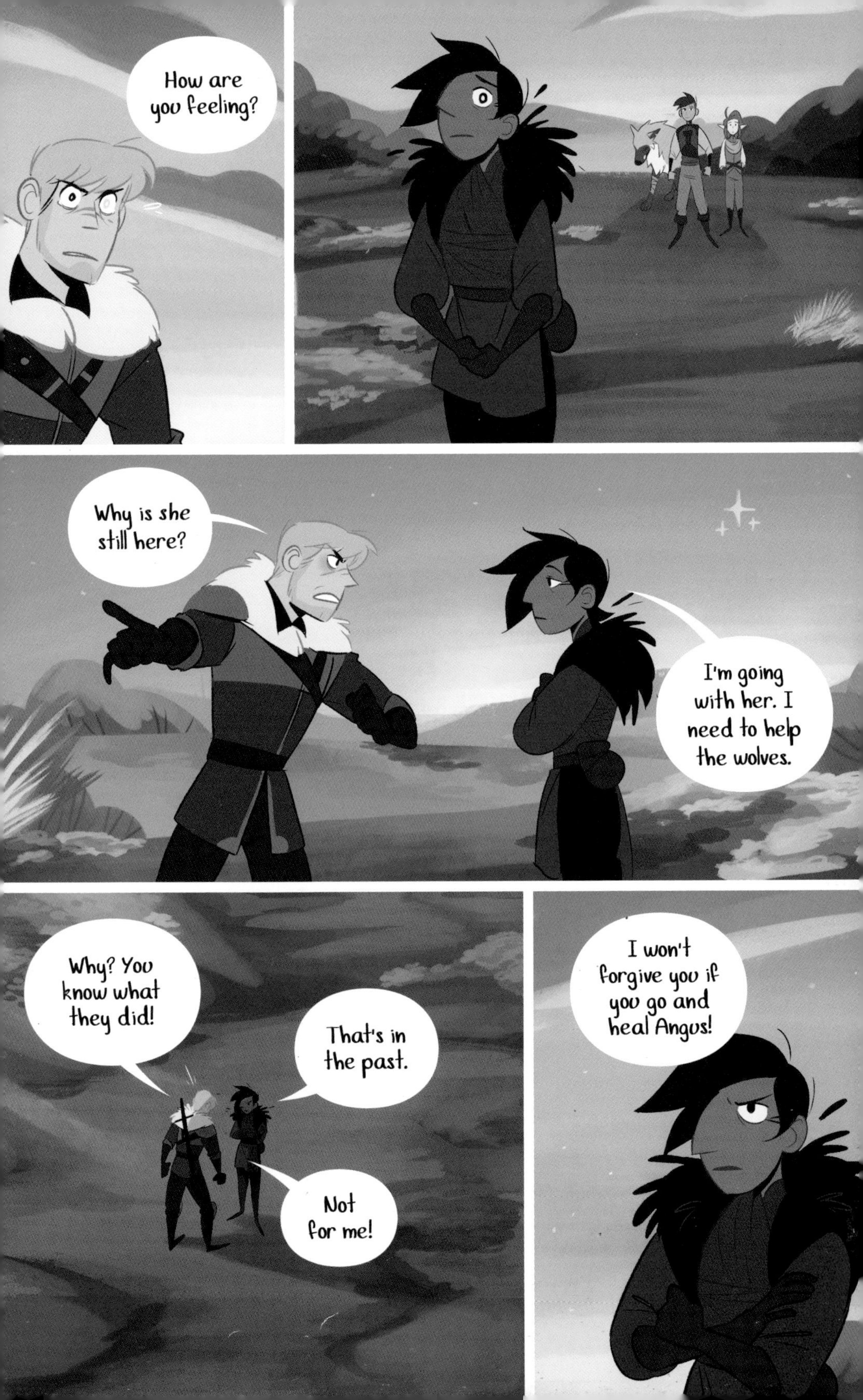
How are you feeling?
Why is she still here?
I'm going with her. I need to help the wolves.
Why? You know what they did!
That's in the past.
Not for me!
I won't forgive you if you go and heal Angus!

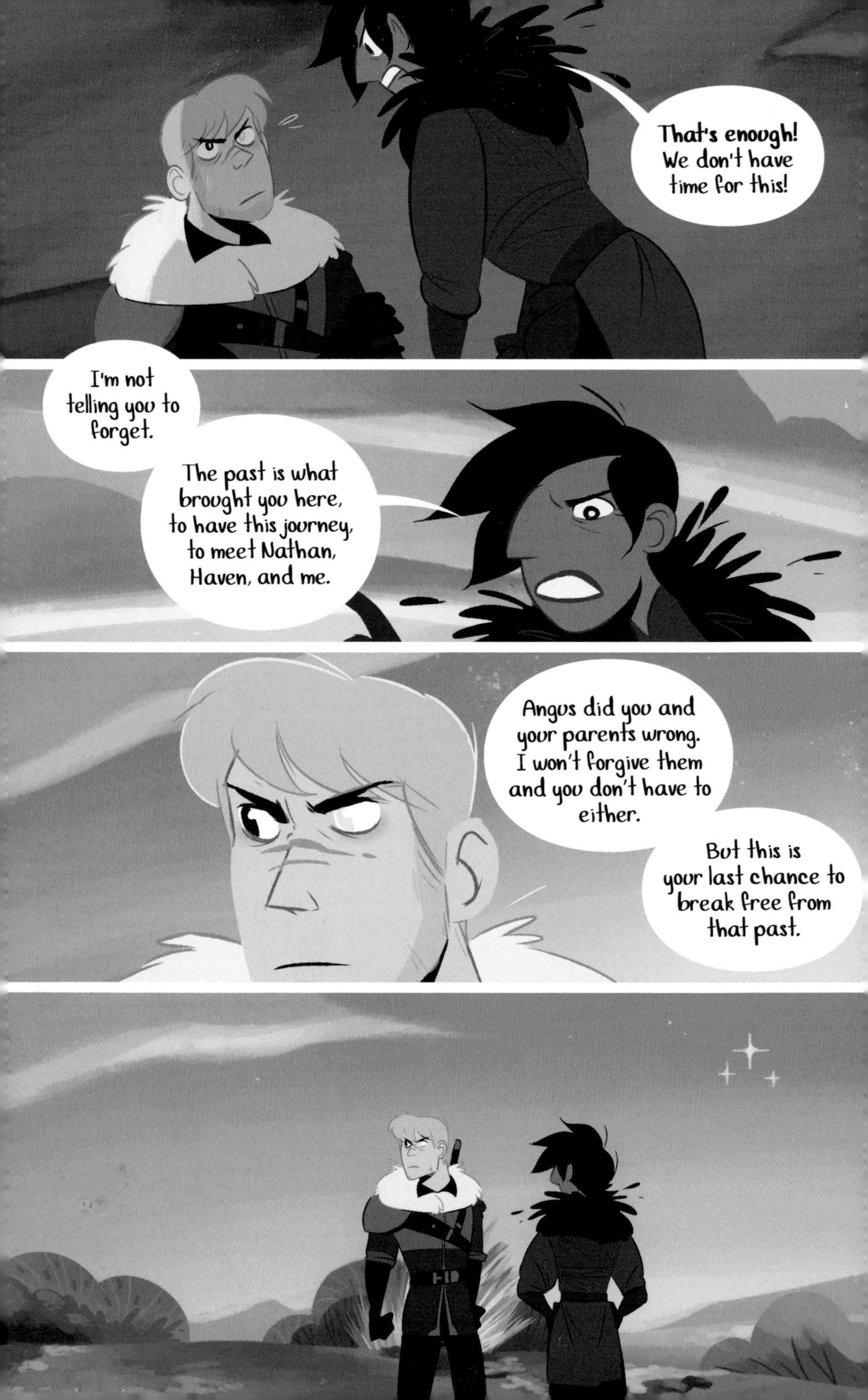
That's enough! We don't have time for this!
I'm not telling you to forget.
The past is what brought you here, to have this journey, to meet Nathan, Haven, and me.
Angus did you and your parents wrong. I won't forgive them and you don't have to either.
But this is your last chance to break free from that past.

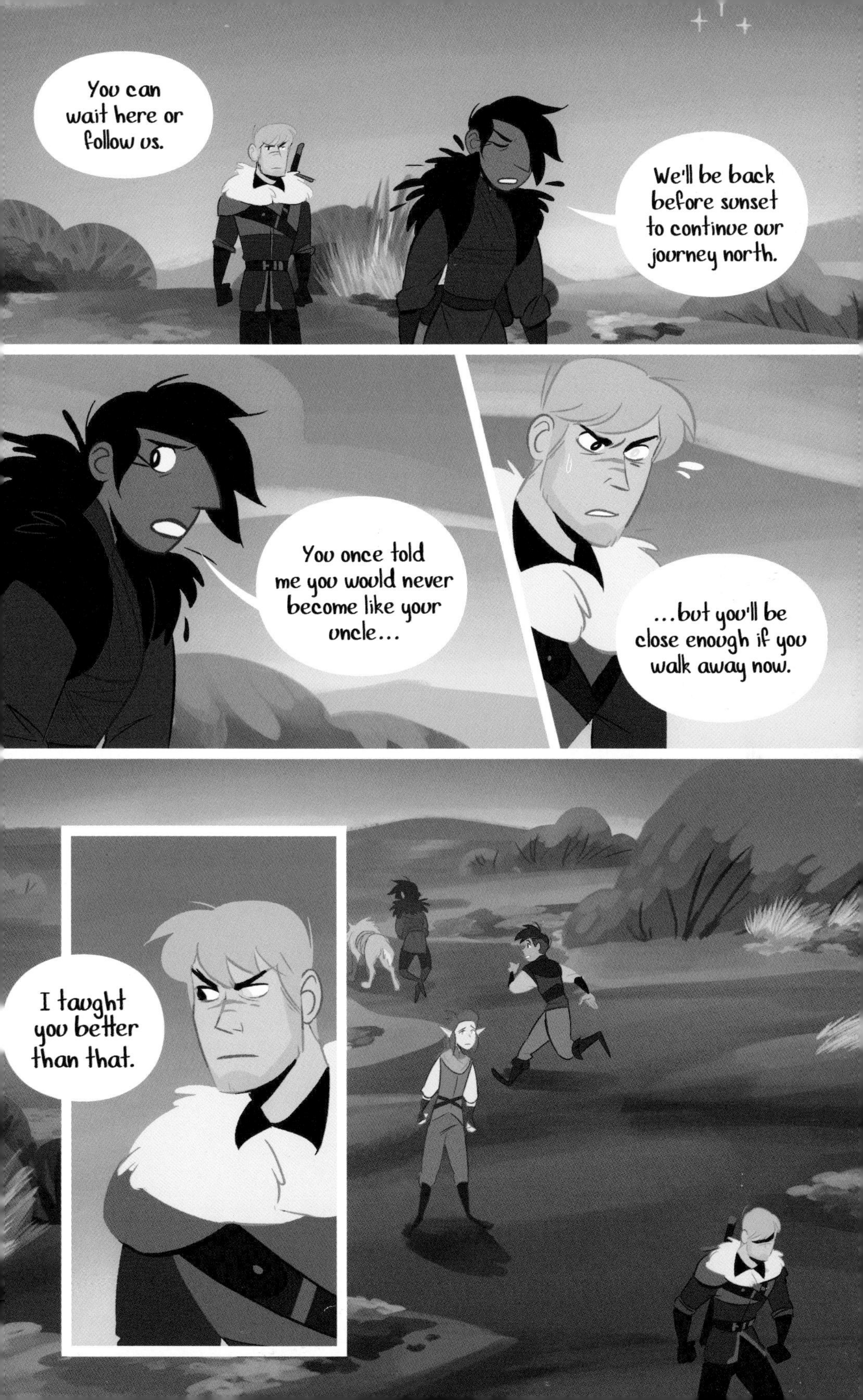
You can wait here or follow us.
We'll be back before sunset to continue our journey north.
You once told me you would never become like your uncle...
...but you'll be close enough if you walk away now.
I taught you better than that.

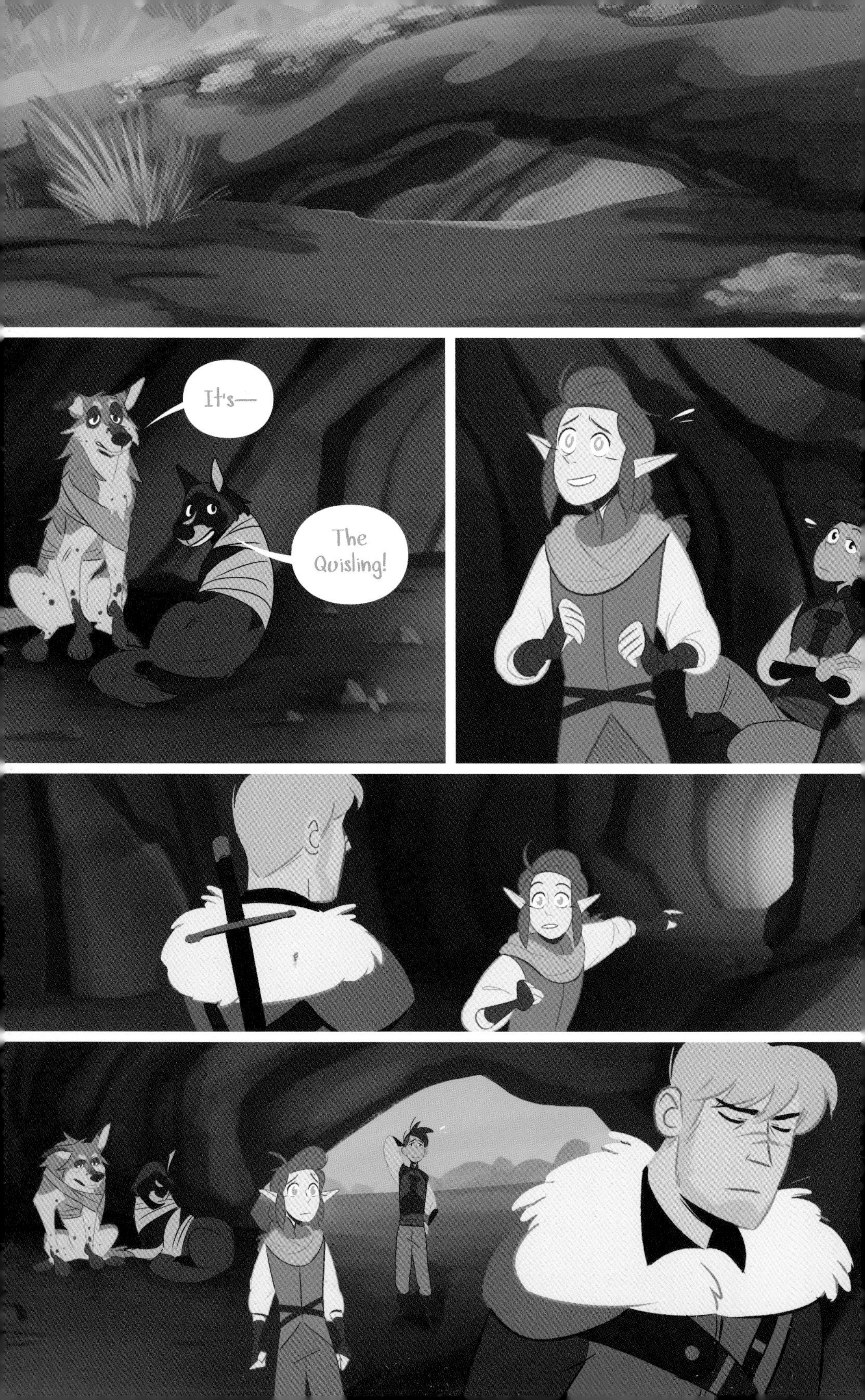
It's—
The Quisling!

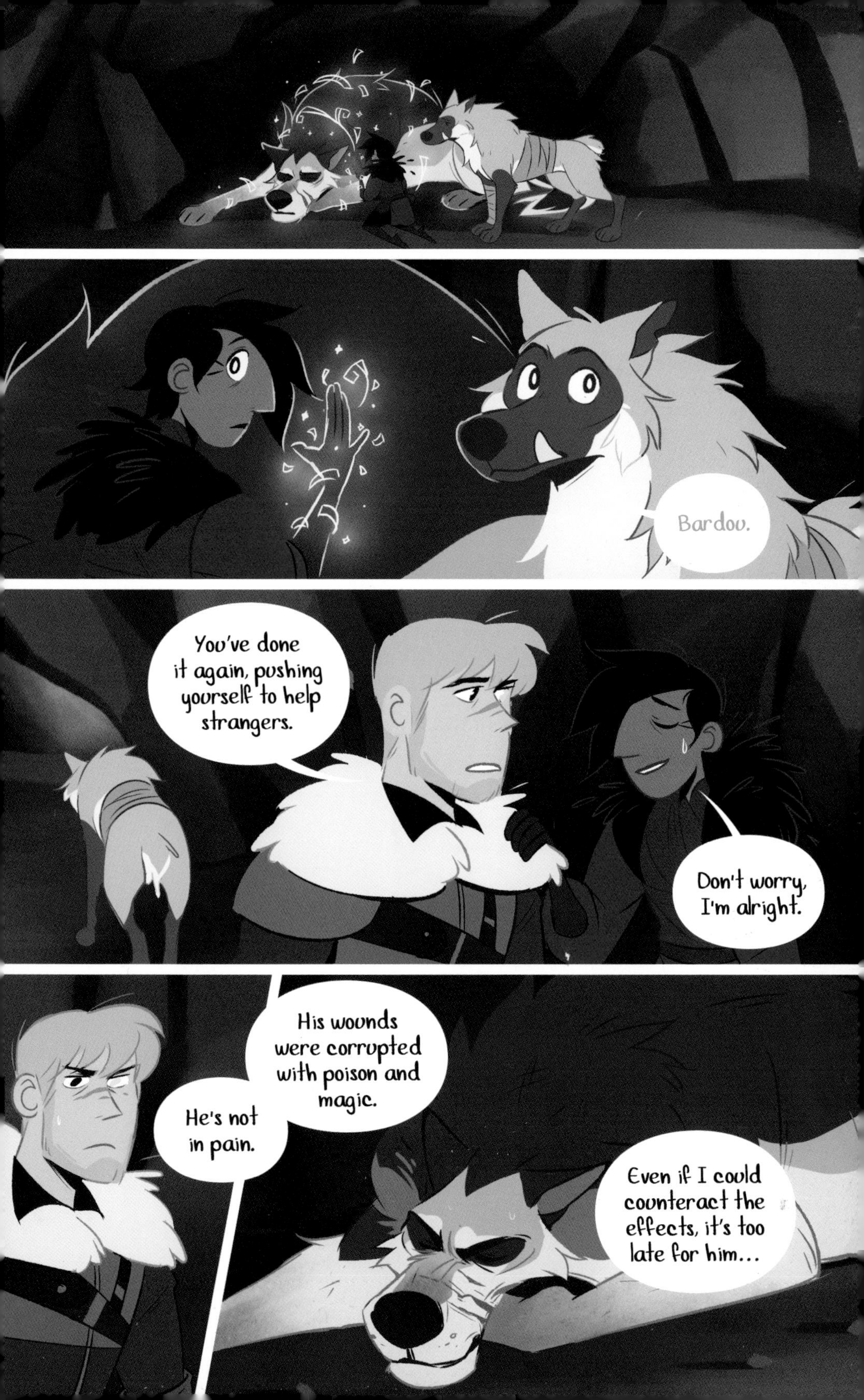
Bardou.
You've done it again, pushing yourself to help strangers.
Don't worry, I'm alright.
His wounds were corrupted with poison and magic.
He's not in pain.
Even if I could counteract the effects, it's too late for him...

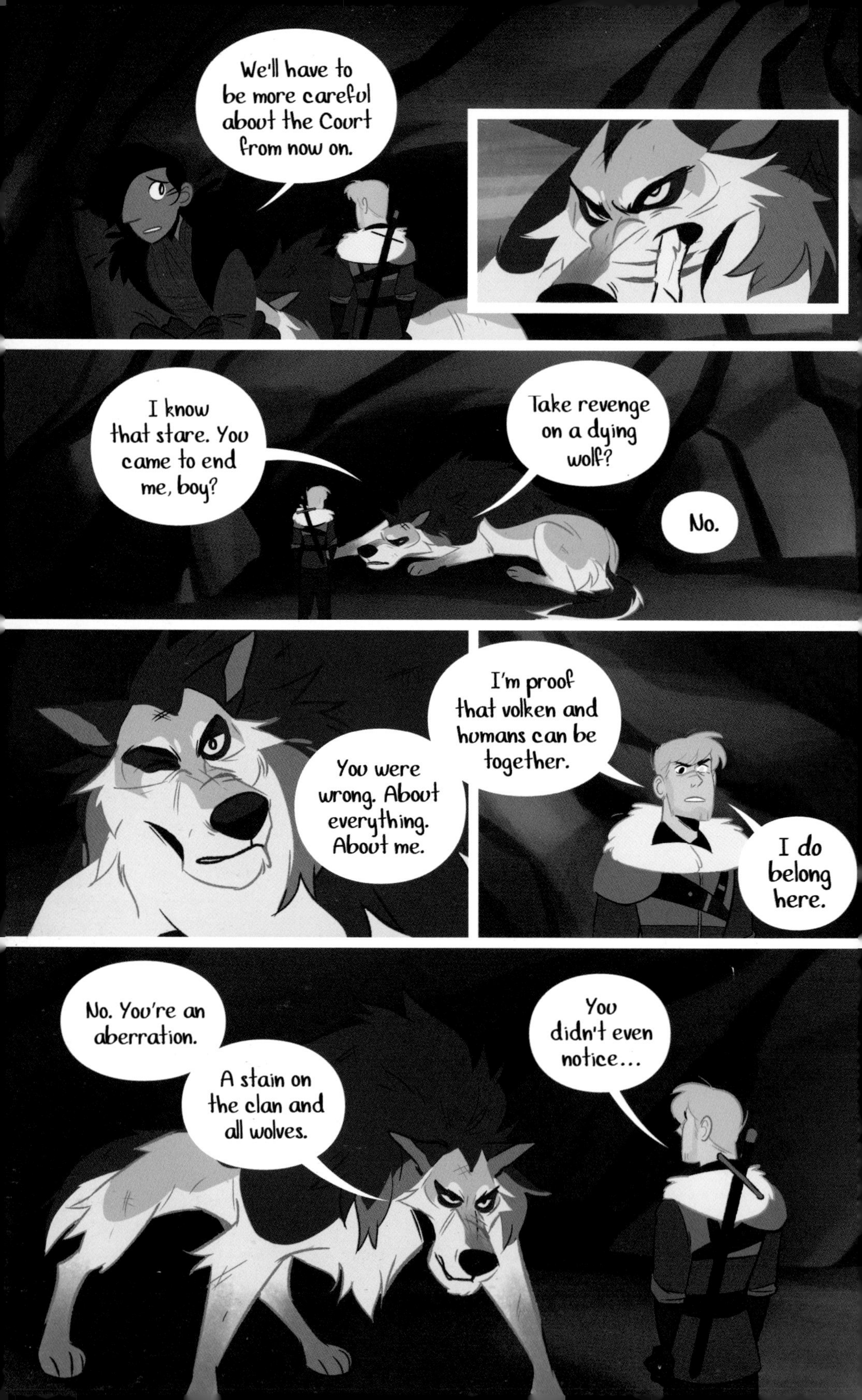
We'll have to be more careful about the Court from now on.
I know that stare. You came to end me, boy?
Take revenge on a dying wolf?
No.
You were wrong. About everything. About me.
I'm proof that volken and humans can be together.
I do belong here.
No. You're an aberration.
A stain on the clan and all wolves.
You didn't even notice...

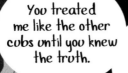

You treated me like the other cubs until you knew the truth.

Doesn't that tell you something? I am as much volken as you.

You're nothing like me!

If my mother never told you who my father was, it was out of love.

For both of us.

Your mother was a traitor!

Boss!

Don't push yourself!

Your mother didn't care about anything but herself! Not the clan or me!
I don't regret telling everyone what she did.
Meddling with that human, having you, raising you among us!
If anyone at the Court knew...
...they would've murdered us all! The clan knew that!
I saved them! I was meant to lead them! Not you!
Boss!
I know, Uncle ...I know.

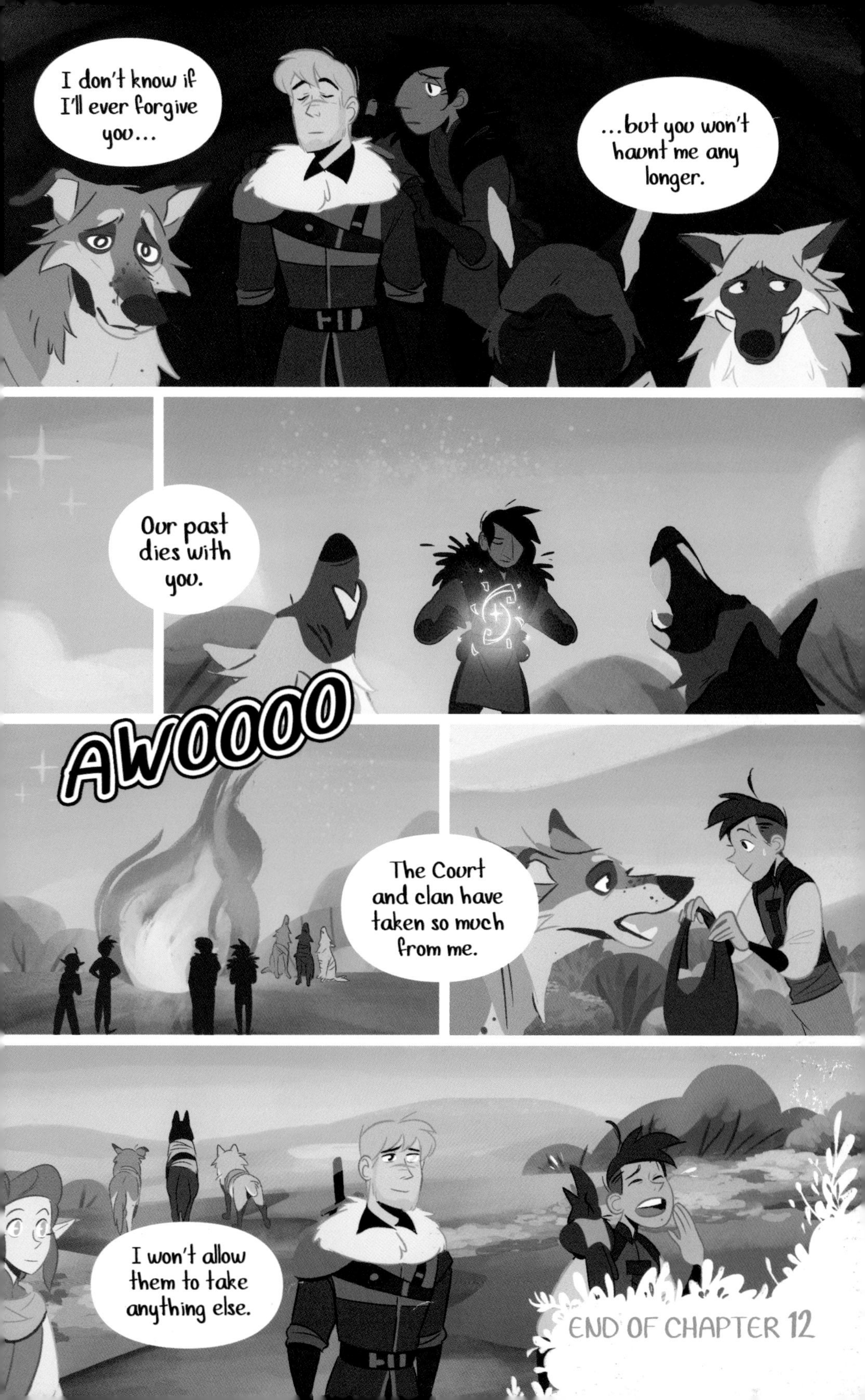
I don't know if I'll ever forgive you...
...but you won't haunt me any longer.
Our past dies with you.
AWOOOO
The Court and clan have taken so much from me.
I won't allow them to take anything else.
END OF CHAPTER 12

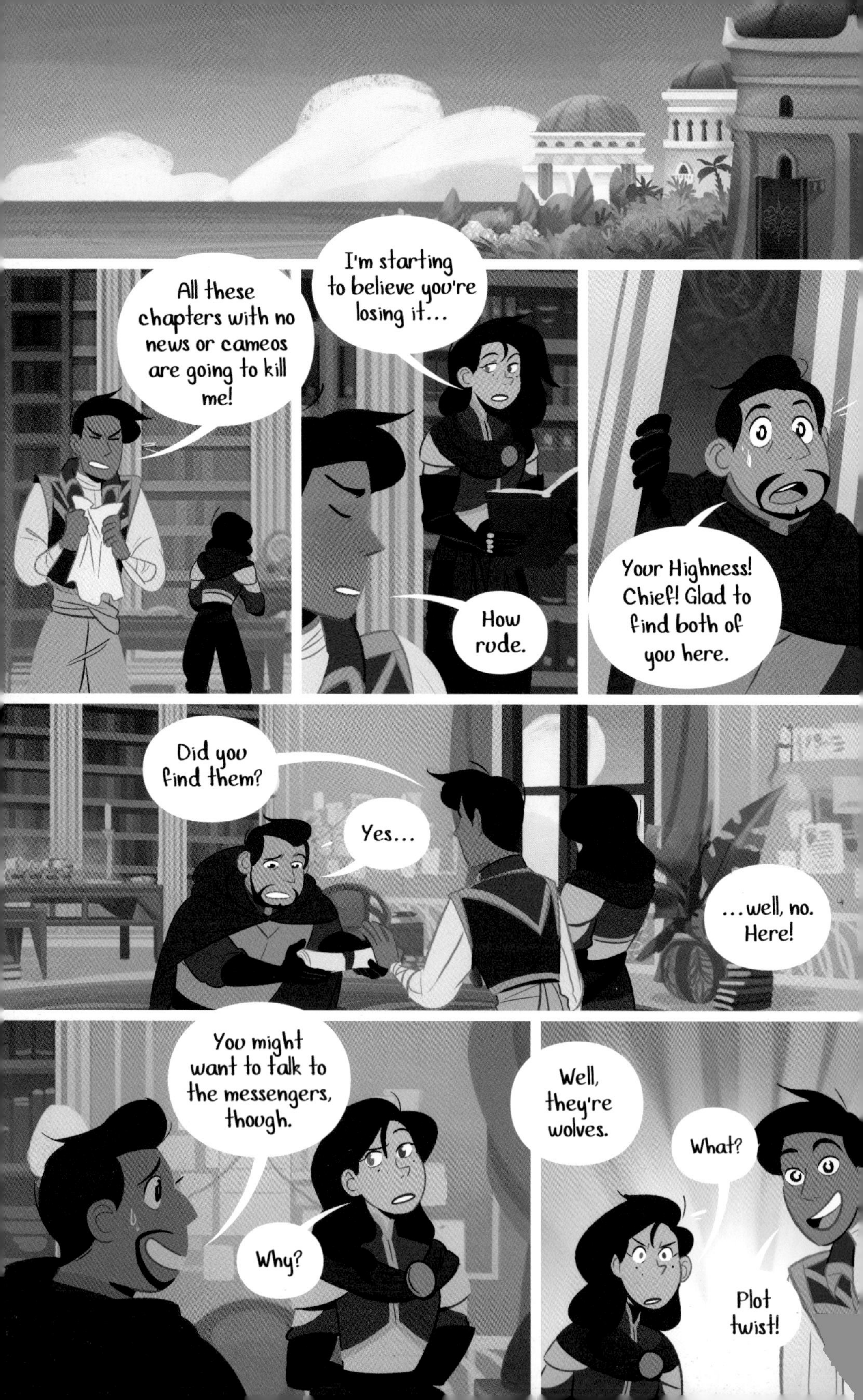
All these chapters with no news or cameos are going to kill me!
I'm starting to believe you're losing it...
How rude.
Your Highness! Chief! Glad to find both of you here.
Did you find them?
Yes...
...well, no. Here!
You might want to talk to the messengers, though.
Why?
Well, they're wolves.
What?
Plot twist!

"Hi, Ren! Sina asked me to write this letter. She's busy healing a wolf (I'll explain that later)."
"How are you? I almost died of a magic overdose but I'm okay now!"
"Anyway, your boyfriend prince was kind of right."
Hey! He said I was right!
Haha, take that, Dad!
Nathan, I'm going to kill you.
"We're headed north to find the second temple. Also, you better watch out; it seems Aquilla is sending the volken."
"The wolves can explain it to you. They also need a new job. Sina and Bardou said they might be useful to you. Write you later!
—Nathan"
Okay, we'll see what we can do with you.

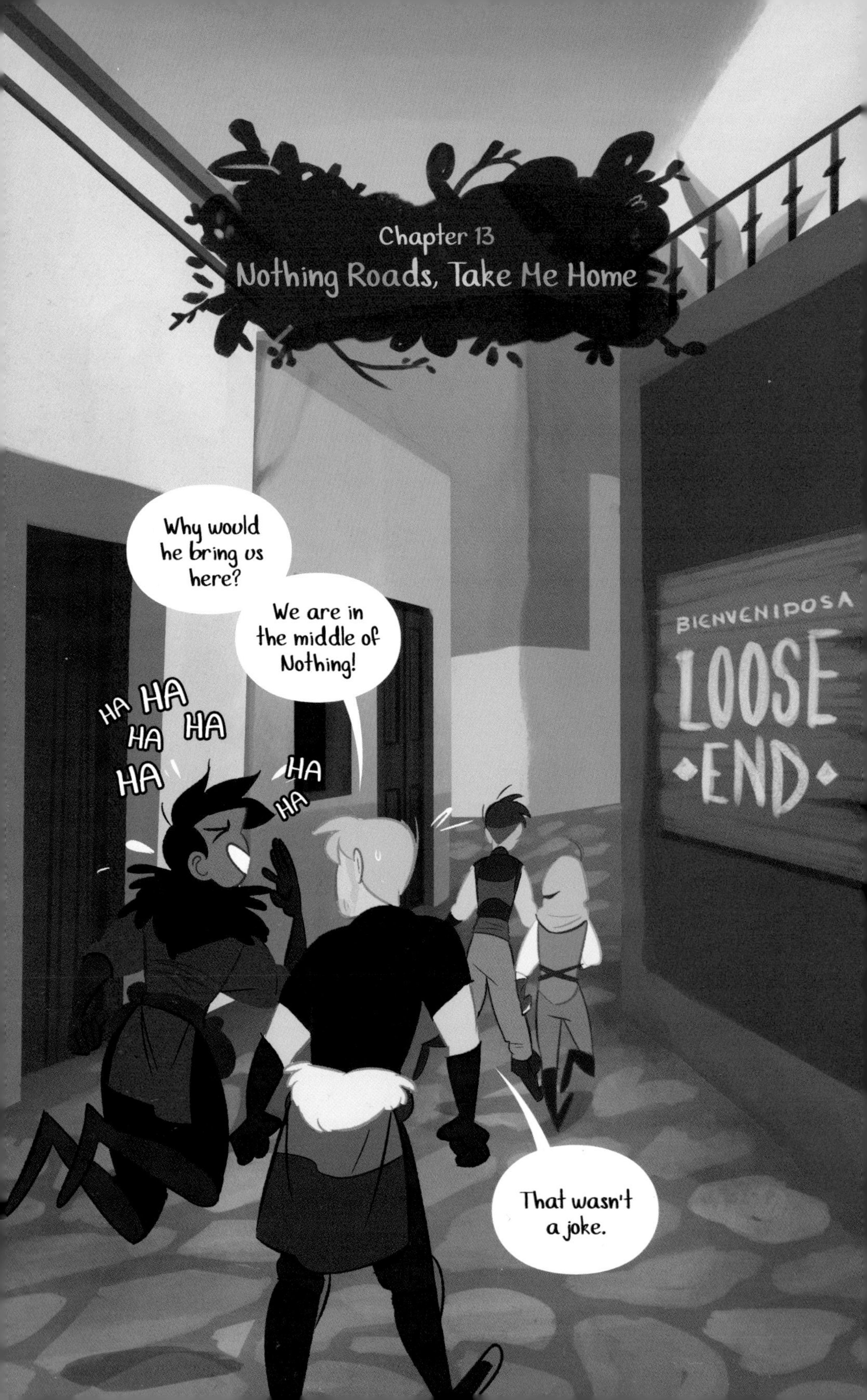
Chapter 13
Nothing Roads, Take Me Home
Why would he bring us here?
We are in the middle of Nothing!
HA HA HA HA HA
HA HA
BIENVENIDOS A
LOOSE END
That wasn't a joke.

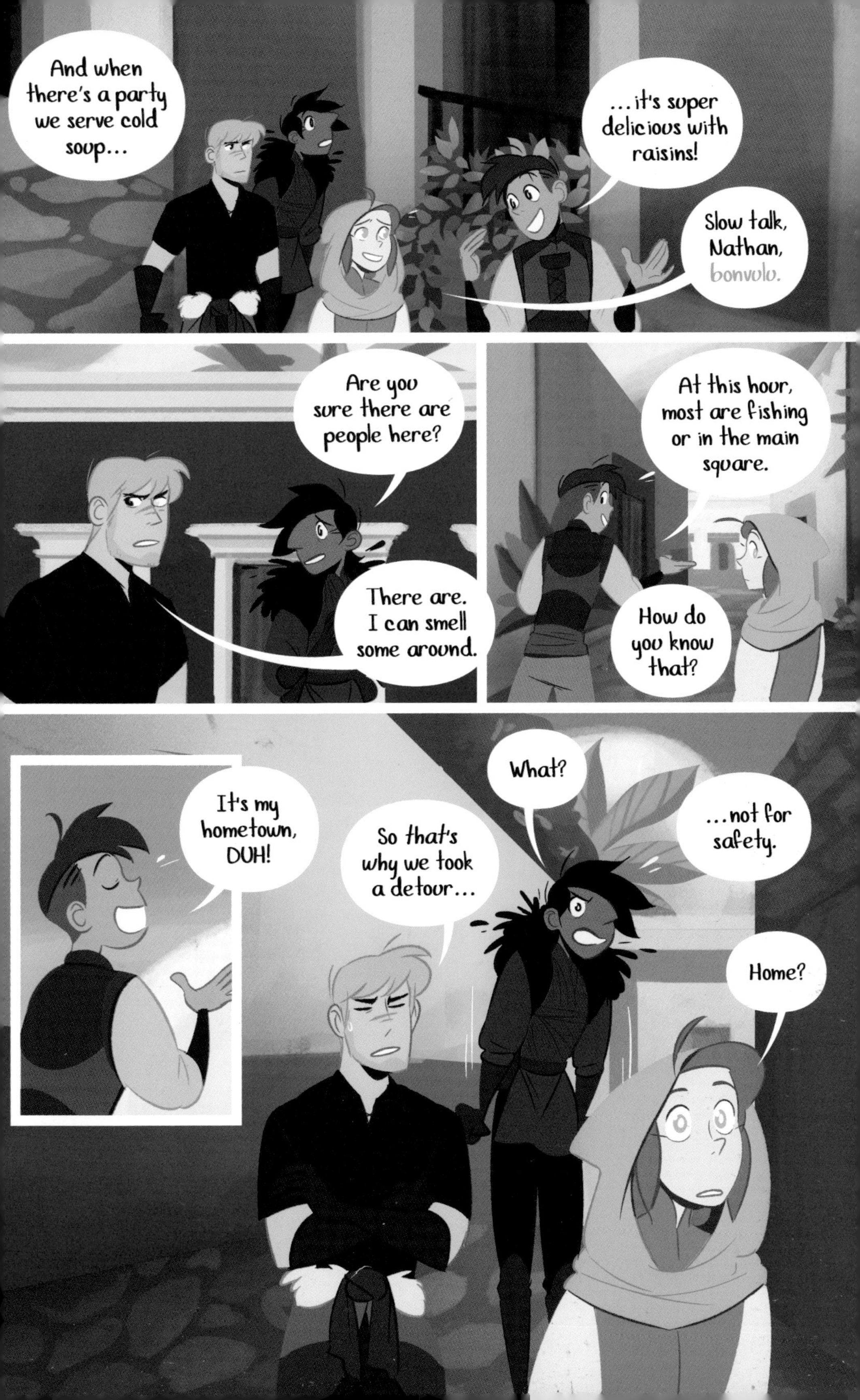

And when there's a party we serve cold soup...
...it's super delicious with raisins!
Slow talk, Nathan, bonvolo.
Are you sure there are people here?
There are. I can smell some around.
At this hour, most are fishing or in the main square.
How do you know that?
It's my hometown, DUH!
So that's why we took a detour...
What?
...not for safety.
Home?

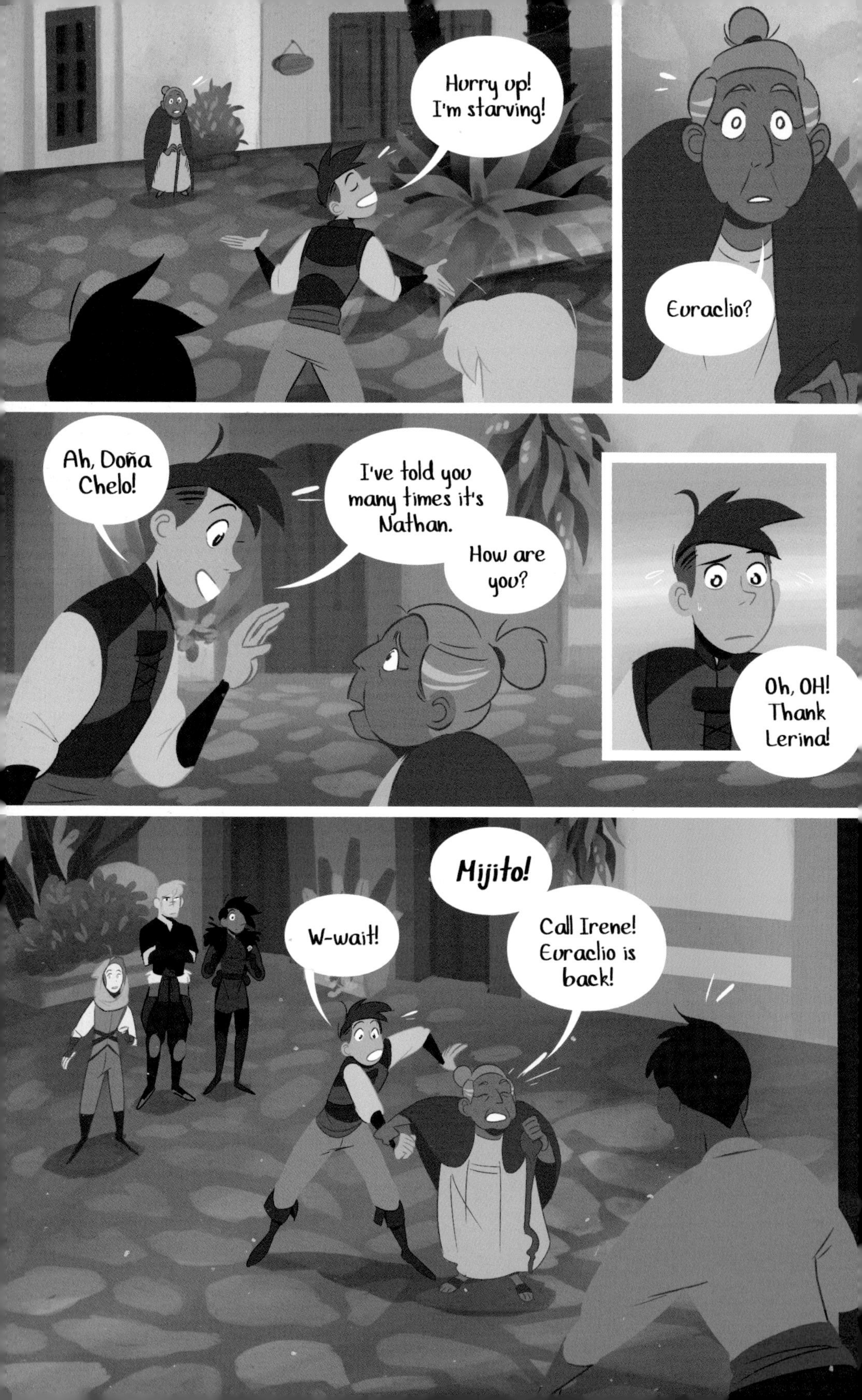

Hurry up!
I'm starving!
Euraclio?
Ah, Doña Chelo!
I've told you many times it's Nathan.
How are you?
Oh, OH! Thank Lerina!
Mijito!
W-wait!
Call Irene! Euraclio is back!

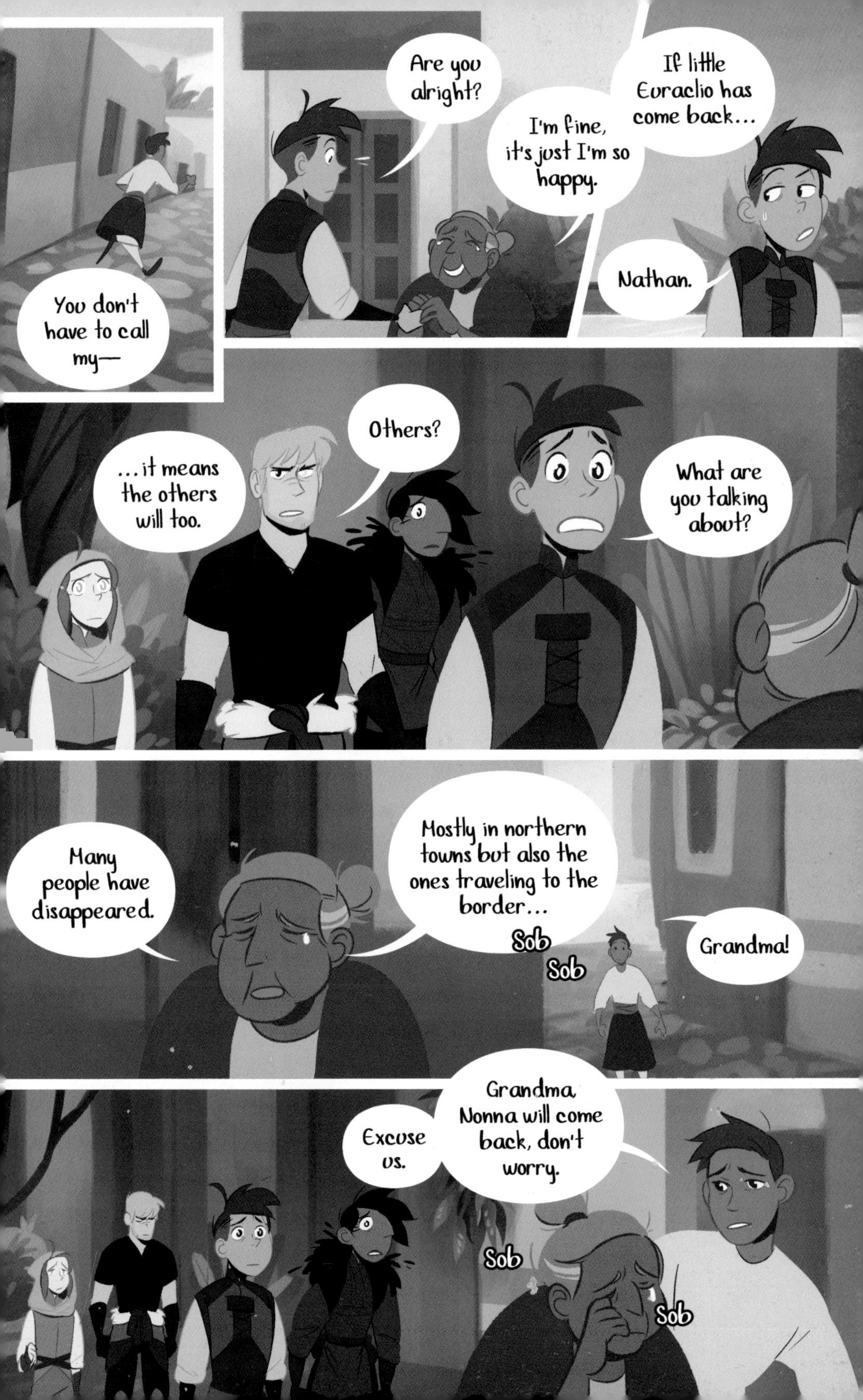
You don't have to call my—
Are you alright?
I'm fine, it's just I'm so happy.
If little Euraclio has come back...
Nathan.
...it means the others will too.
Others?
What are you talking about?
Many people have disappeared.
Mostly in northern towns but also the ones traveling to the border...
Sob
Sob
Grandma!
Excuse us.
Grandma Nonna will come back, don't worry.
Sob
Sob

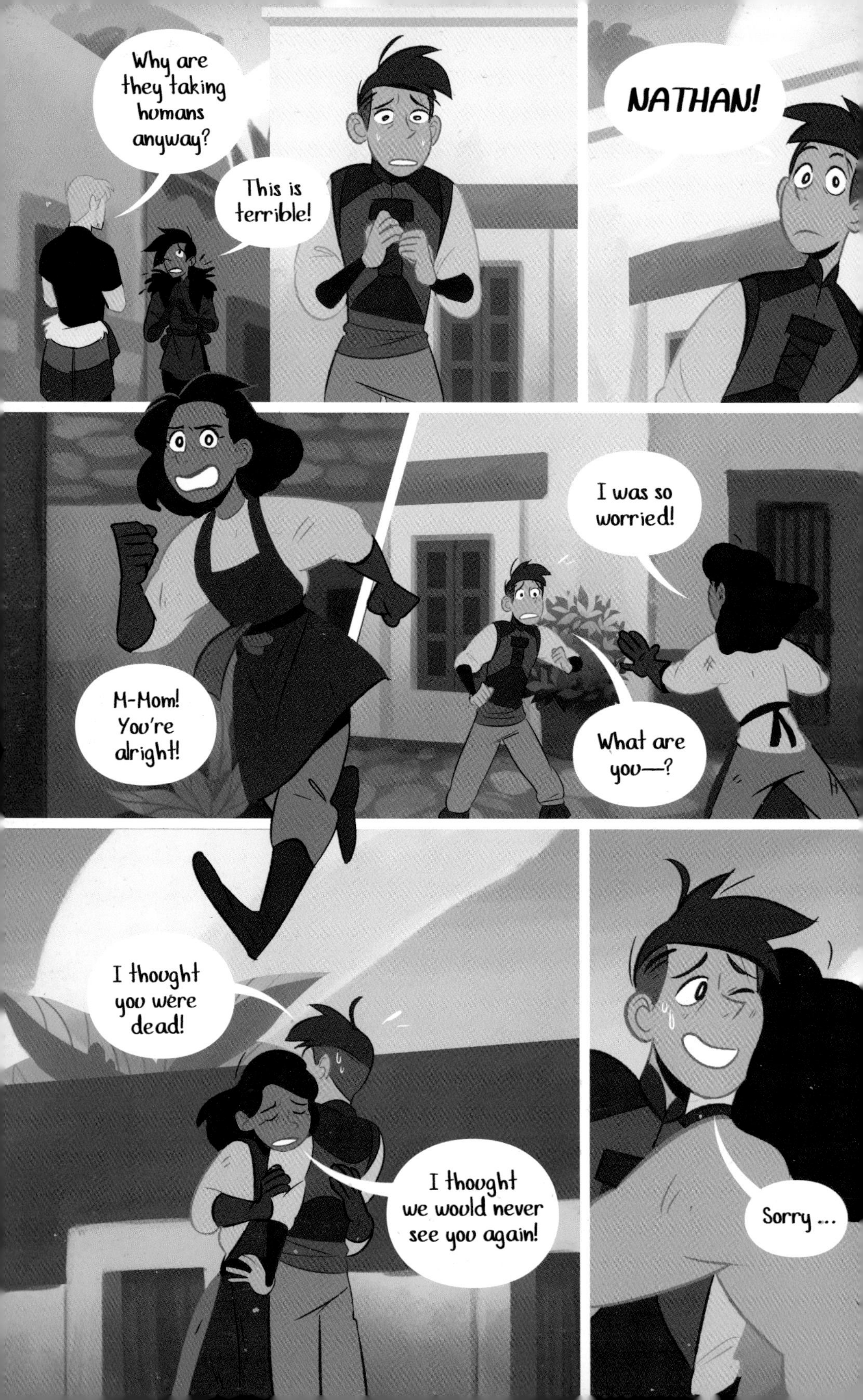
Why are they taking humans anyway?
This is terrible!
NATHAN!
M-Mom! You're alright!
I was so worried!
What are you—?
I thought you were dead!
I thought we would never see you again!
Sorry ...

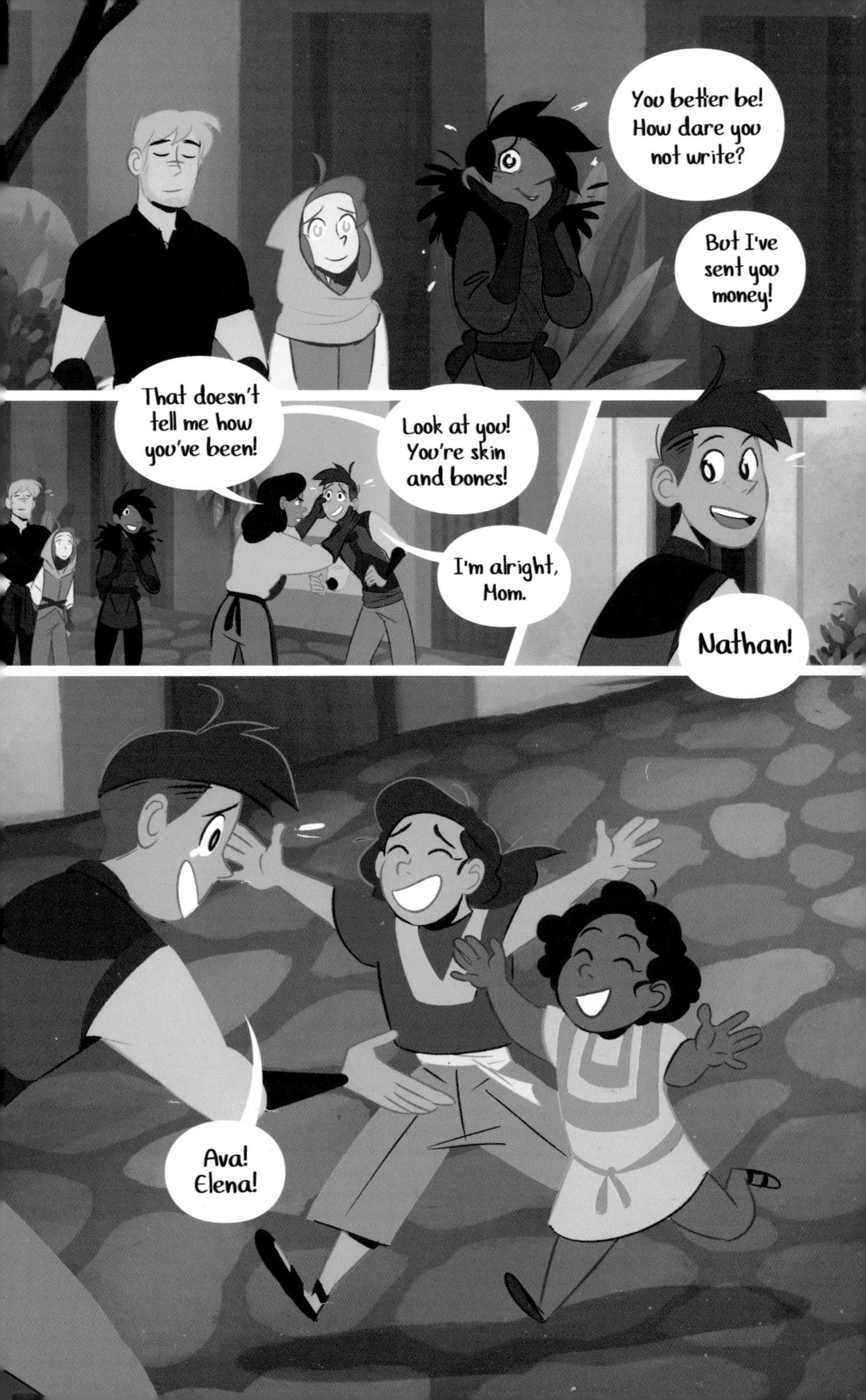
You better be! How dare you not write?
But I've sent you money!
That doesn't tell me how you've been!
Look at you! You're skin and bones!
I'm alright, Mom.
Nathan!
Ava! Elena!

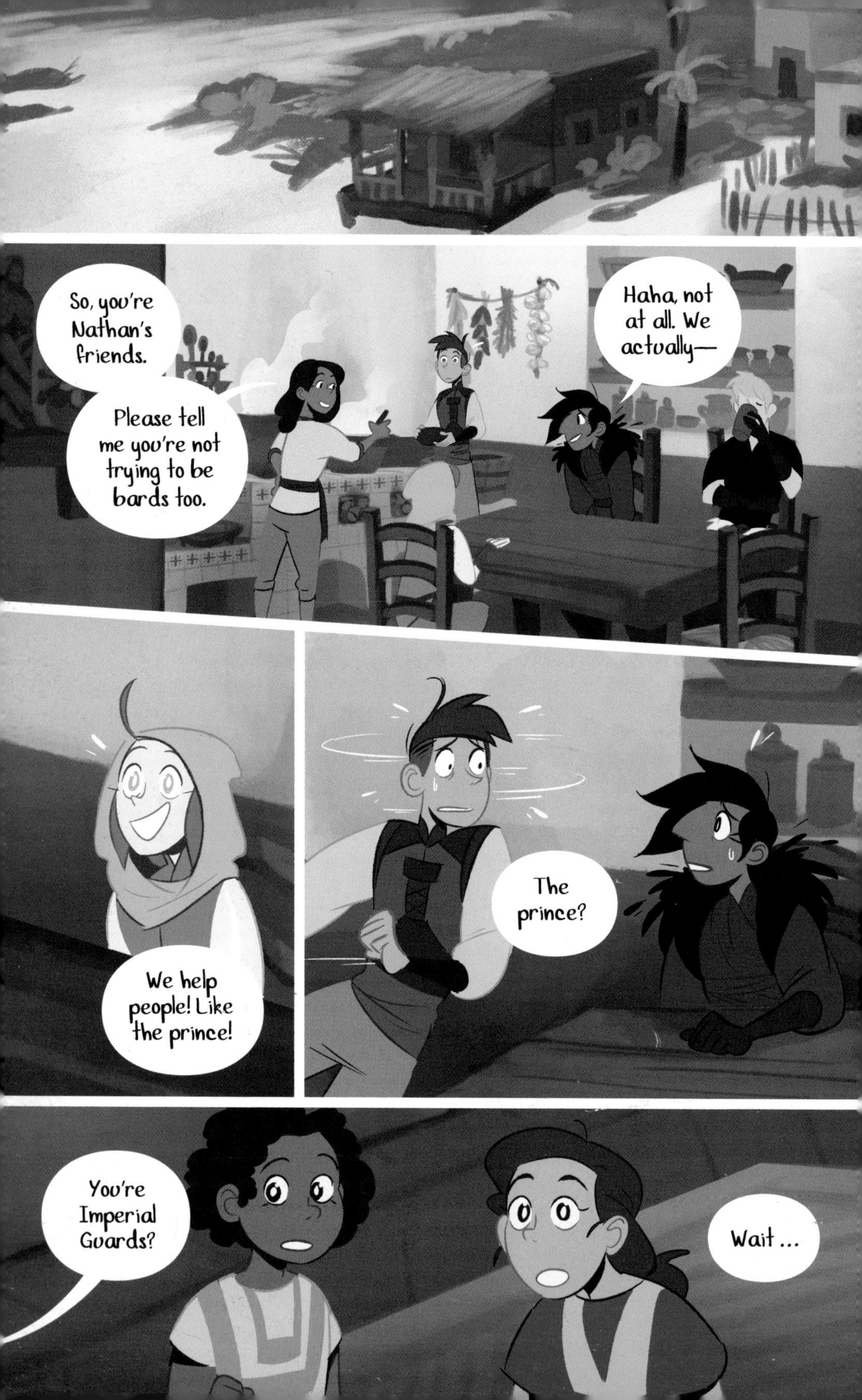
So, you're Nathan's friends.
Please tell me you're not trying to be bards too.
Haha, not at all. We actually—
We help people! Like the prince!
The prince?
You're Imperial Guards?
Wait ...

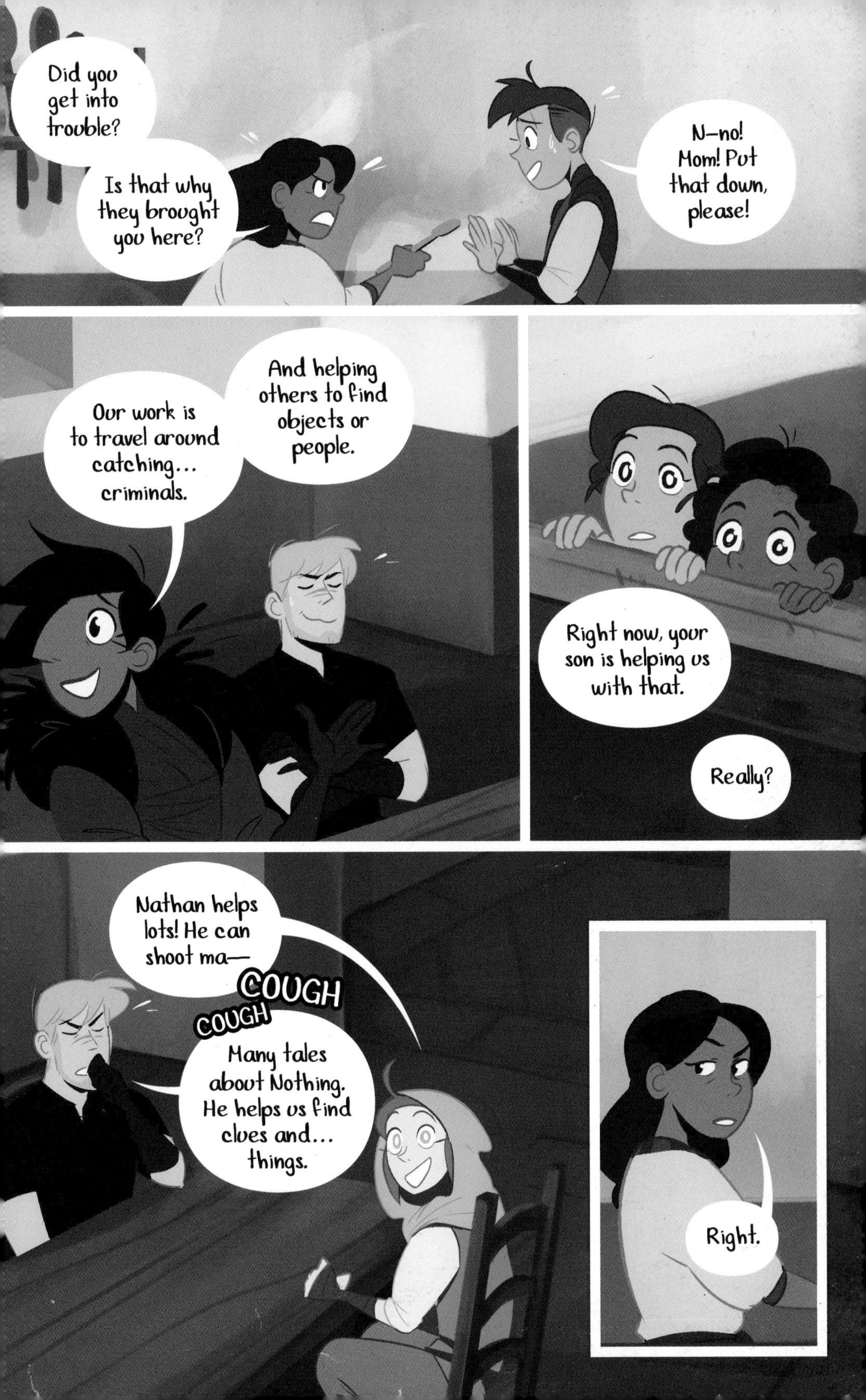
Did you get into trouble?
Is that why they brought you here?
N—no! Mom! Put that down, please!
Our work is to travel around catching... criminals.
And helping others to find objects or people.
Right now, your son is helping us with that.
Really?
Nathan helps lots! He can shoot ma—
COUGH
COUGH
Many tales about Nothing. He helps us find clues and... things.
Right.

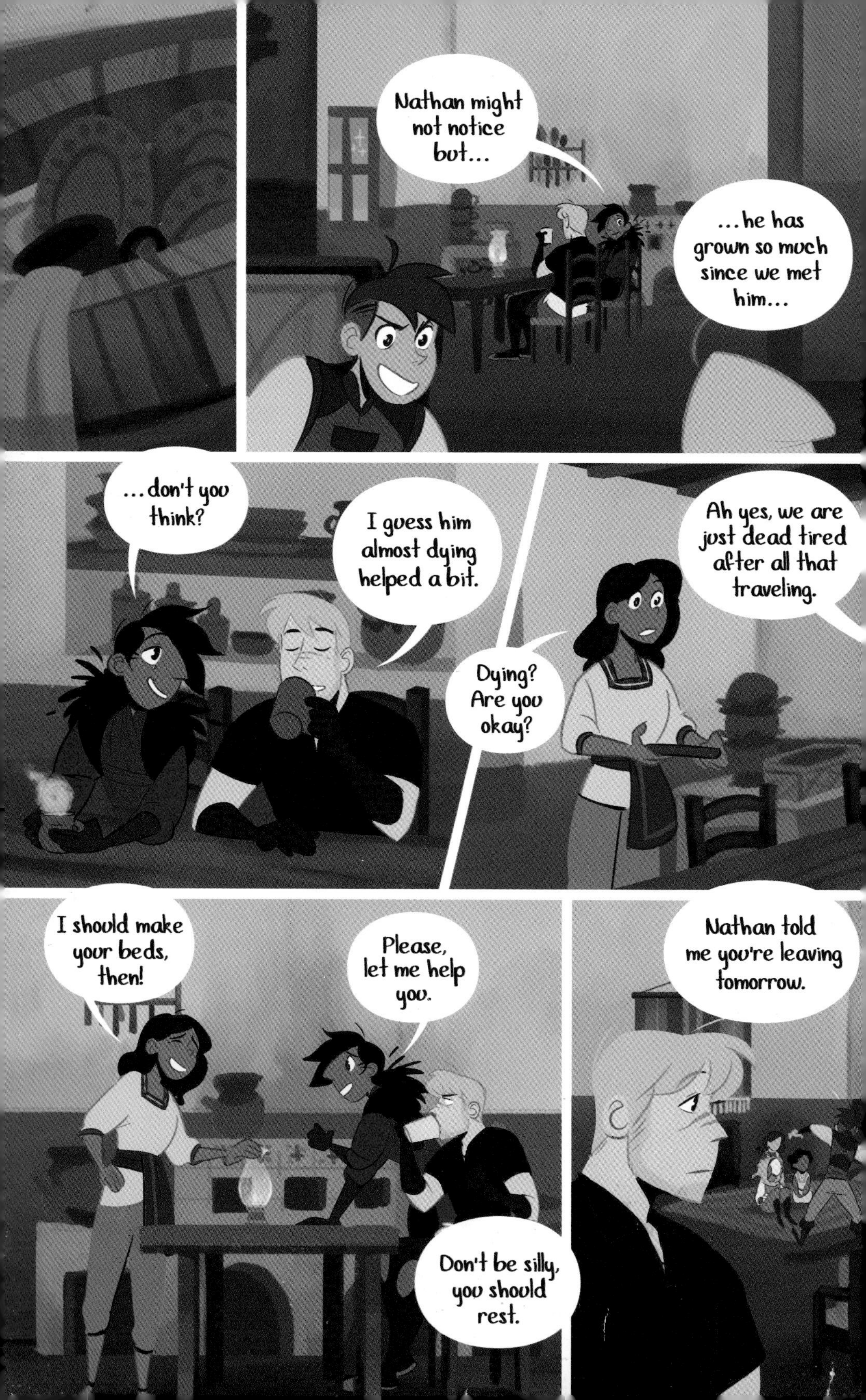
Nathan might not notice but...
...he has grown so much since we met him...
...don't you think?
I guess him almost dying helped a bit.
Ah yes, we are just dead tired after all that traveling.
Dying? Are you okay?
I should make your beds, then!
Please, let me help you.
Don't be silly, you should rest.
Nathan told me you're leaving tomorrow.

When all seemed lost, the Shadow Knight arrived!
With his deadly daggers, he fought the evil volken general.
And his soldiers that were attacking the village.
"You have no power here!" the knight shouted, striking a final blow to the general.
Making the volken soldiers shriek in fear, fleeing.
Everyone was safe, so the Knight rode to the horizon, leaving with the sun.
For it's said that he wanted people to thank...
...Lerina and the stars for their rescue. The end.

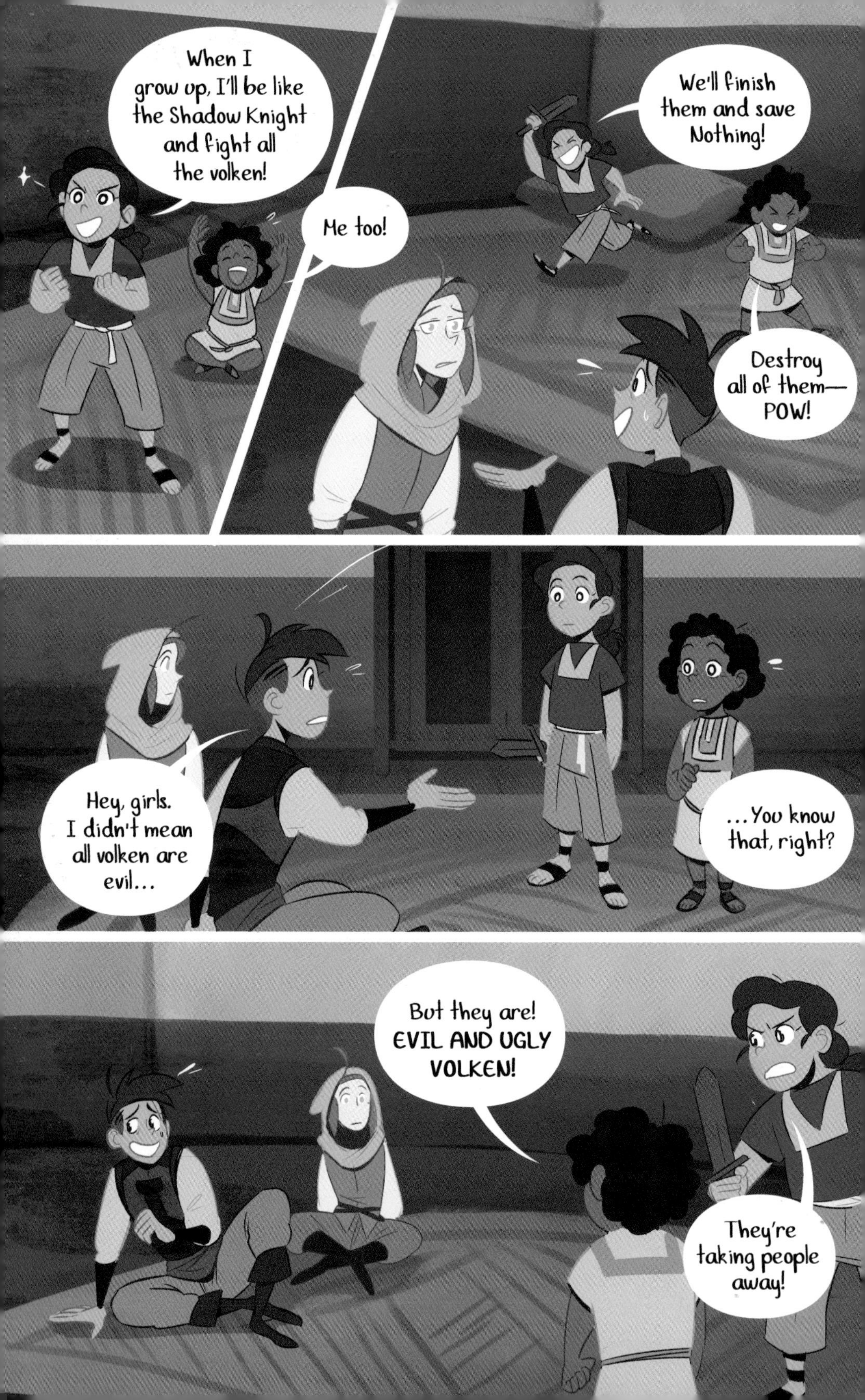
When I grow up, I'll be like the Shadow Knight and fight all the volken!
Me too!
We'll finish them and save Nothing!
Destroy all of them—POW!
Hey, girls. I didn't mean all volken are evil...
...You know that, right?
But they are! EVIL AND UGLY VOLKEN!
They're taking people away!

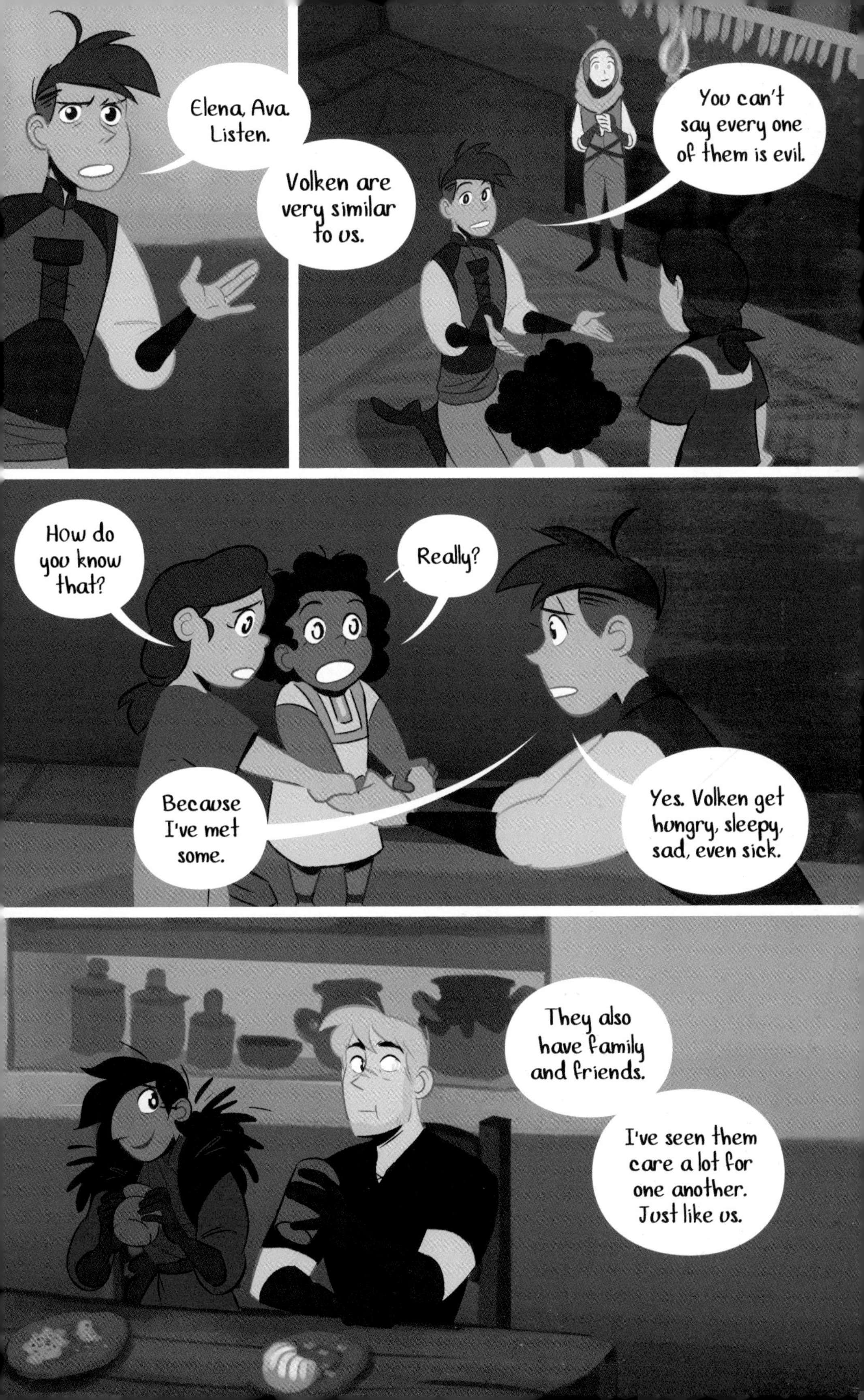

Elena, Ava. Listen.
Volken are very similar to us.
You can't say every one of them is evil.
How do you know that?
Really?
Because I've met some.
Yes. Volken get hungry, sleepy, sad, even sick.
They also have family and friends.
I've seen them care a lot for one another. Just like us.

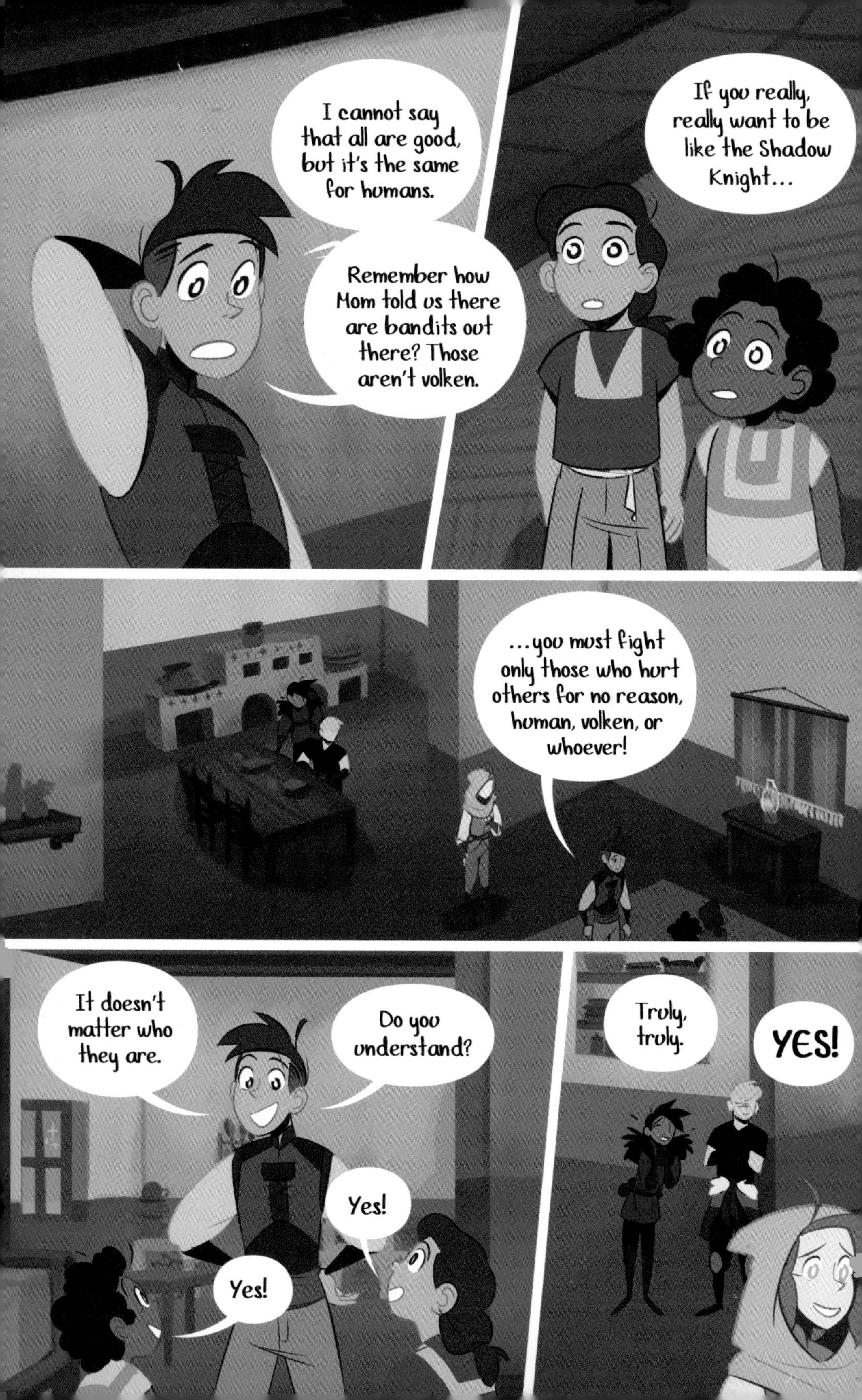
I cannot say that all are good, but it's the same for humans.
Remember how Mom told us there are bandits out there? Those aren't volken.
If you really, really want to be like the Shadow Knight...
...you must fight only those who hurt others for no reason, human, volken, or whoever!
It doesn't matter who they are.
Do you understand?
Yes!
Yes!
Truly, truly.
YES!

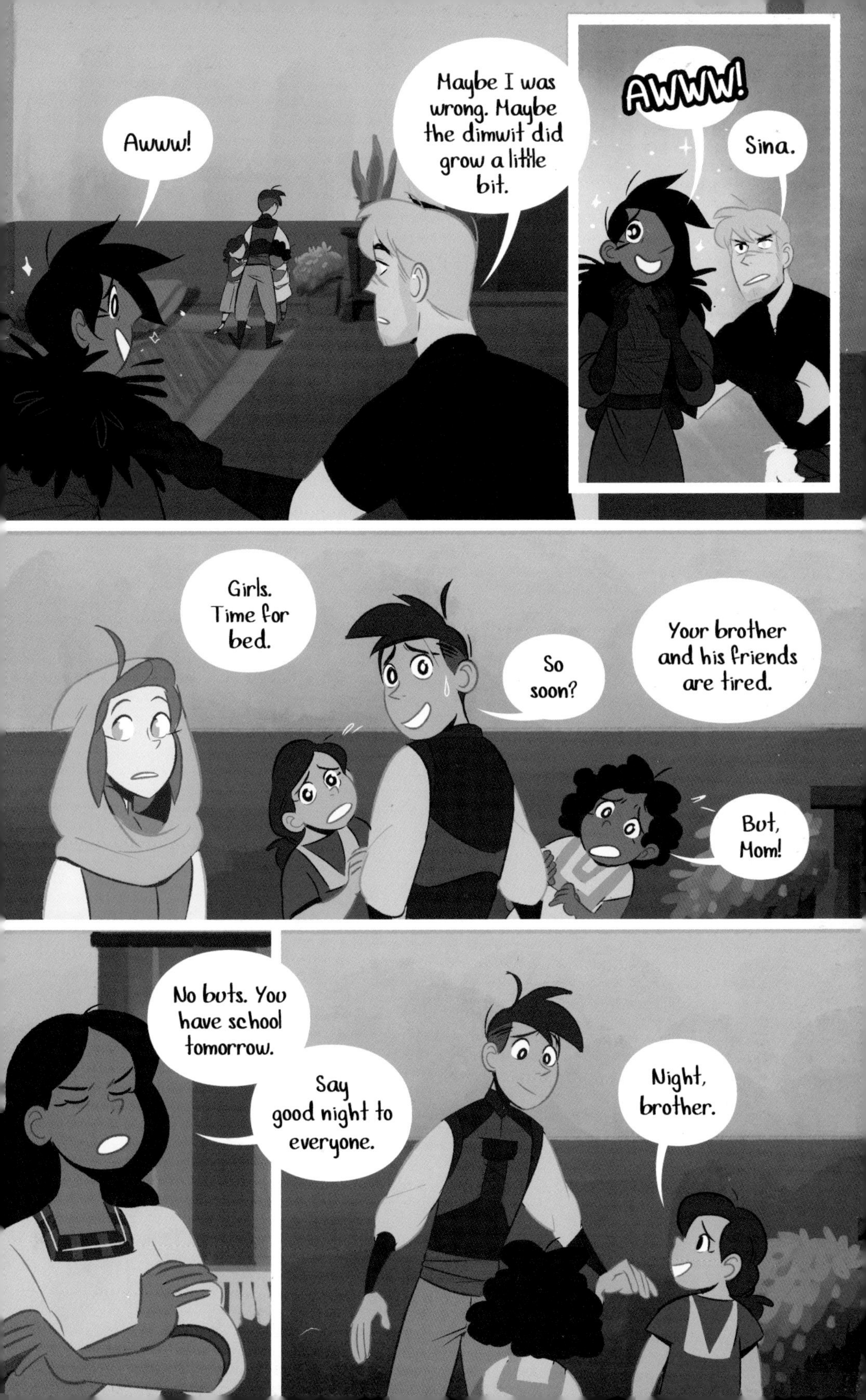
Awww!
Maybe I was wrong. Maybe the dimwit did grow a little bit.
AWWW!
Sina.
Girls. Time for bed.
So soon?
Your brother and his friends are tired.
But, Mom!
No buts. You have school tomorrow.
Say good night to everyone.
Night, brother.

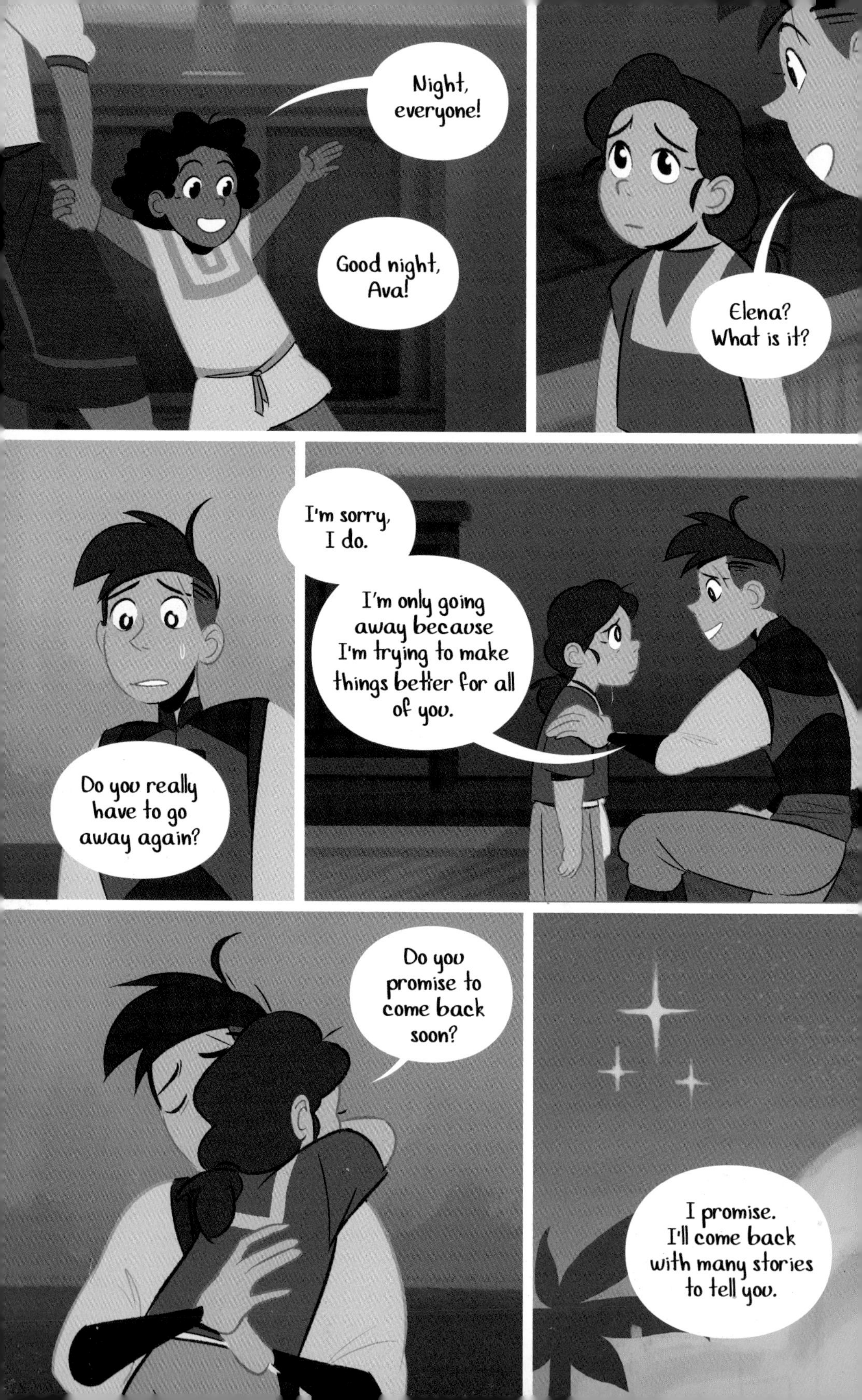
Night, everyone!
Good night, Ava!
Elena? What is it?
Do you really have to go away again?
I'm sorry, I do.
I'm only going away because I'm trying to make things better for all of you.
Do you promise to come back soon?
I promise. I'll come back with many stories to tell you.

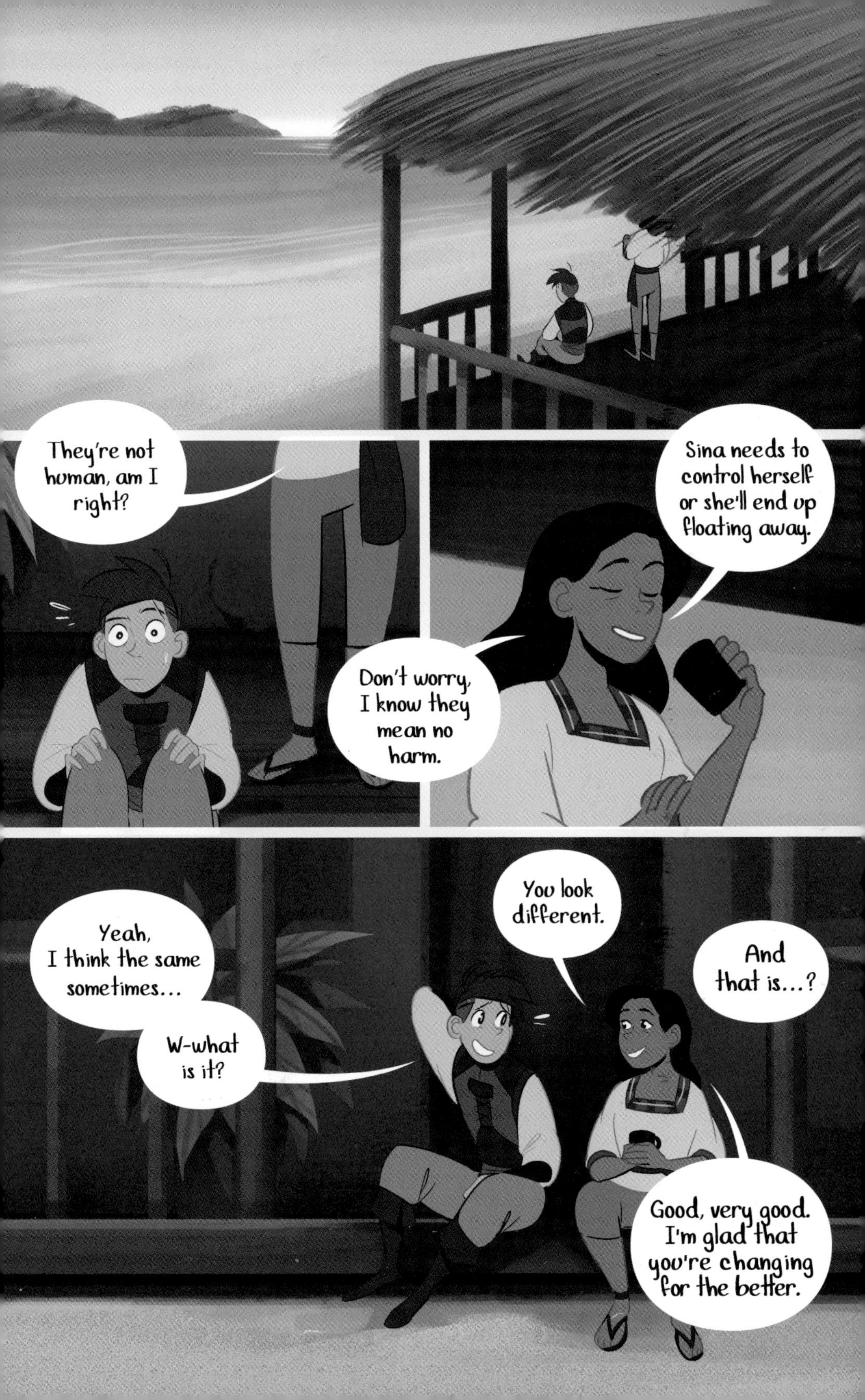
They're not human, am I right?
Sina needs to control herself or she'll end up floating away.
Don't worry, I know they mean no harm.
Yeah, I think the same sometimes...
You look different.
W-what is it?
And that is...?
Good, very good. I'm glad that you're changing for the better.

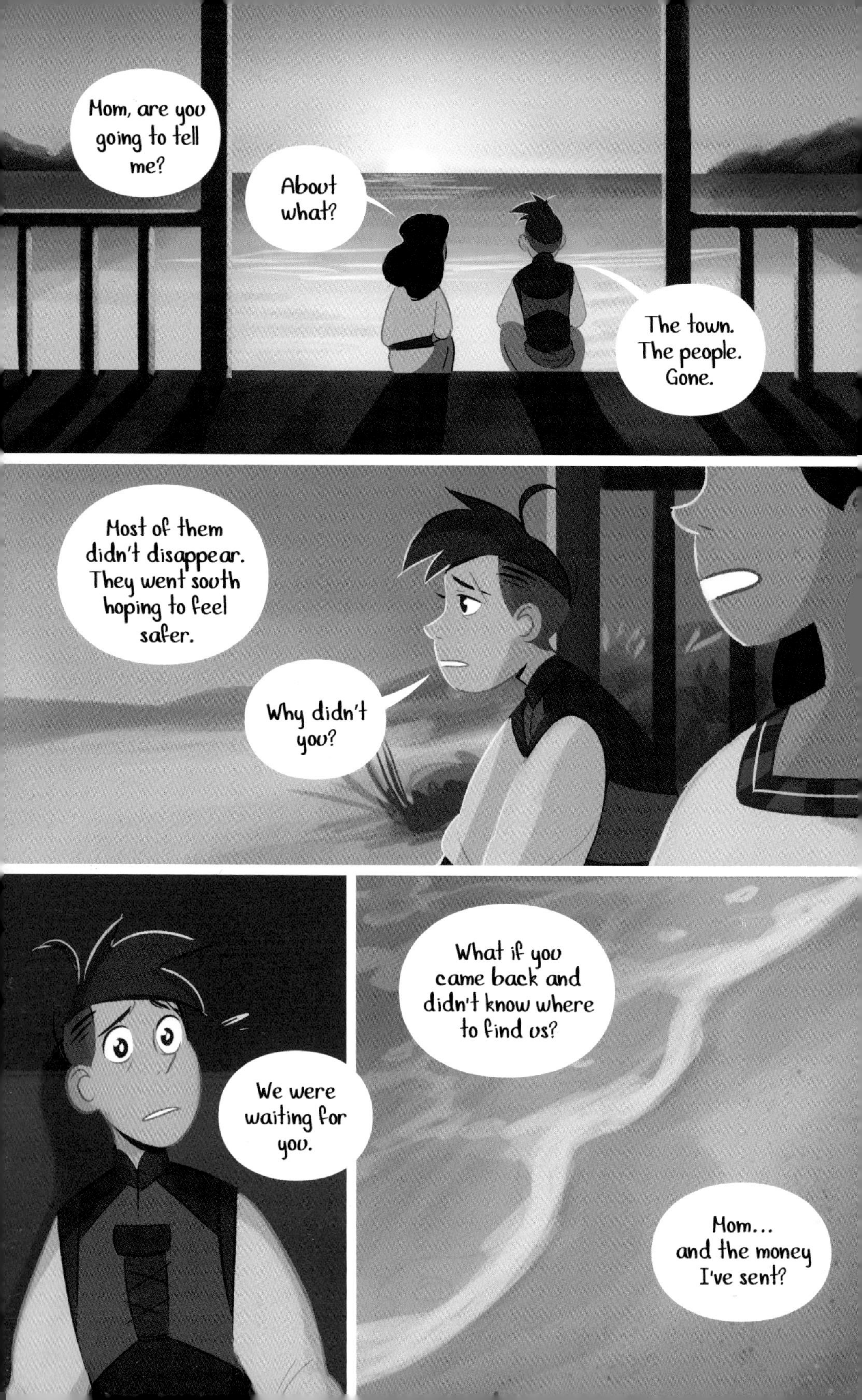
Mom, are you going to tell me?
About what?
The town. The people. Gone.
Most of them didn't disappear. They went south hoping to feel safer.
Why didn't you?
We were waiting for you.
What if you came back and didn't know where to find us?
Mom... and the money I've sent?

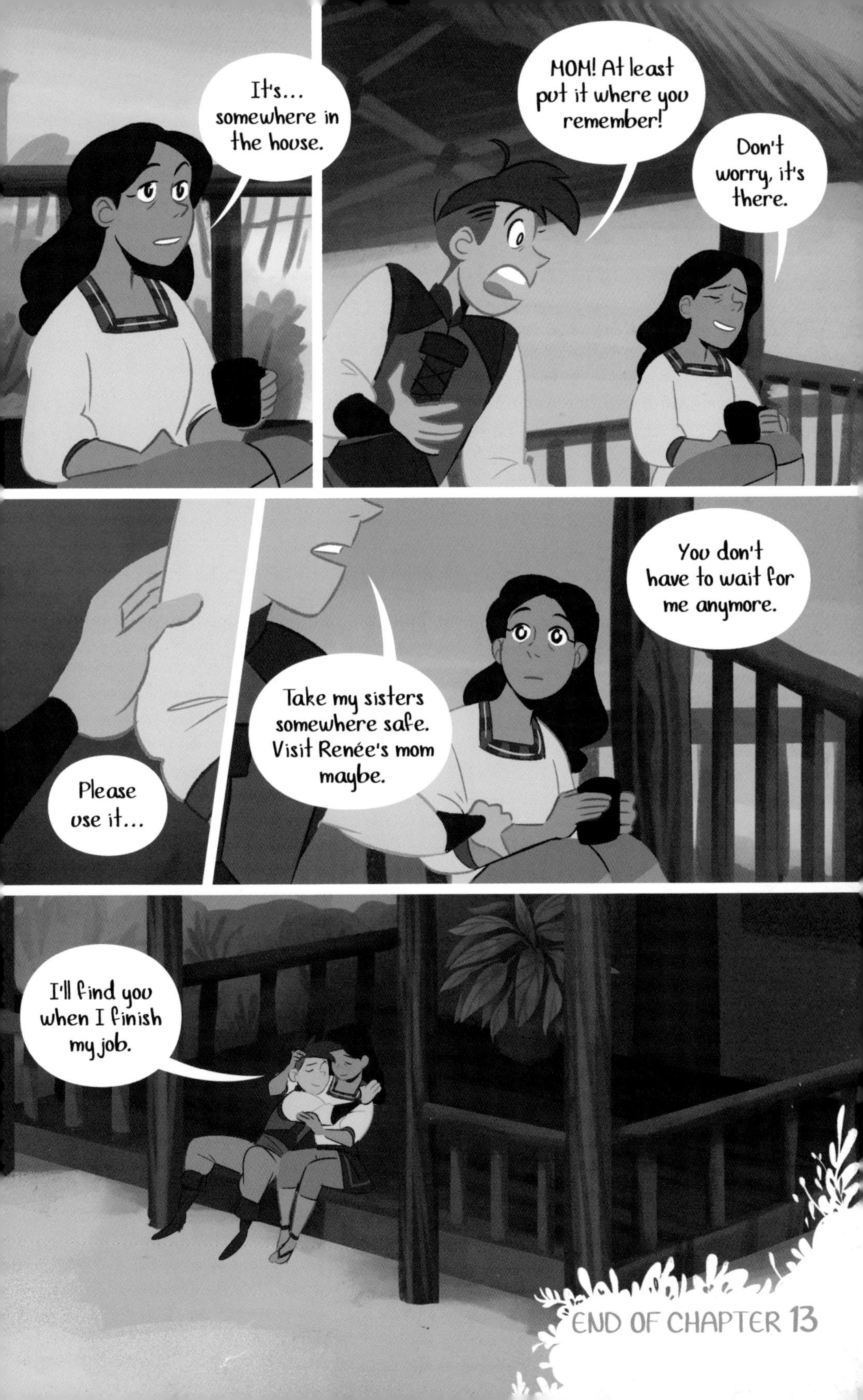
It's... somewhere in the house.
MOM! At least put it where you remember!
Don't worry, it's there.
You don't have to wait for me anymore.
Take my sisters somewhere safe. Visit Renée's mom maybe.
Please use it...
I'll find you when I finish my job.
END OF CHAPTER 13

Nathan? Your family will be okay?
They'll be fine. Mom is quite strong and scary.
Didn't I tell you? Mom's a blacksmith, fiercest of them all!
Scary?
Not only does she make weapons, she knows how to use them too!
In my "fierce scale" Mom is number one, then there's Ren in second place, and Sina in third.
Hey! How come I am third?
You're too soft.
I'm not! Well, maybe a little.
So, what's the plan, chosen one?
Haha, very funny, Ben. But I'm glad that you asked...

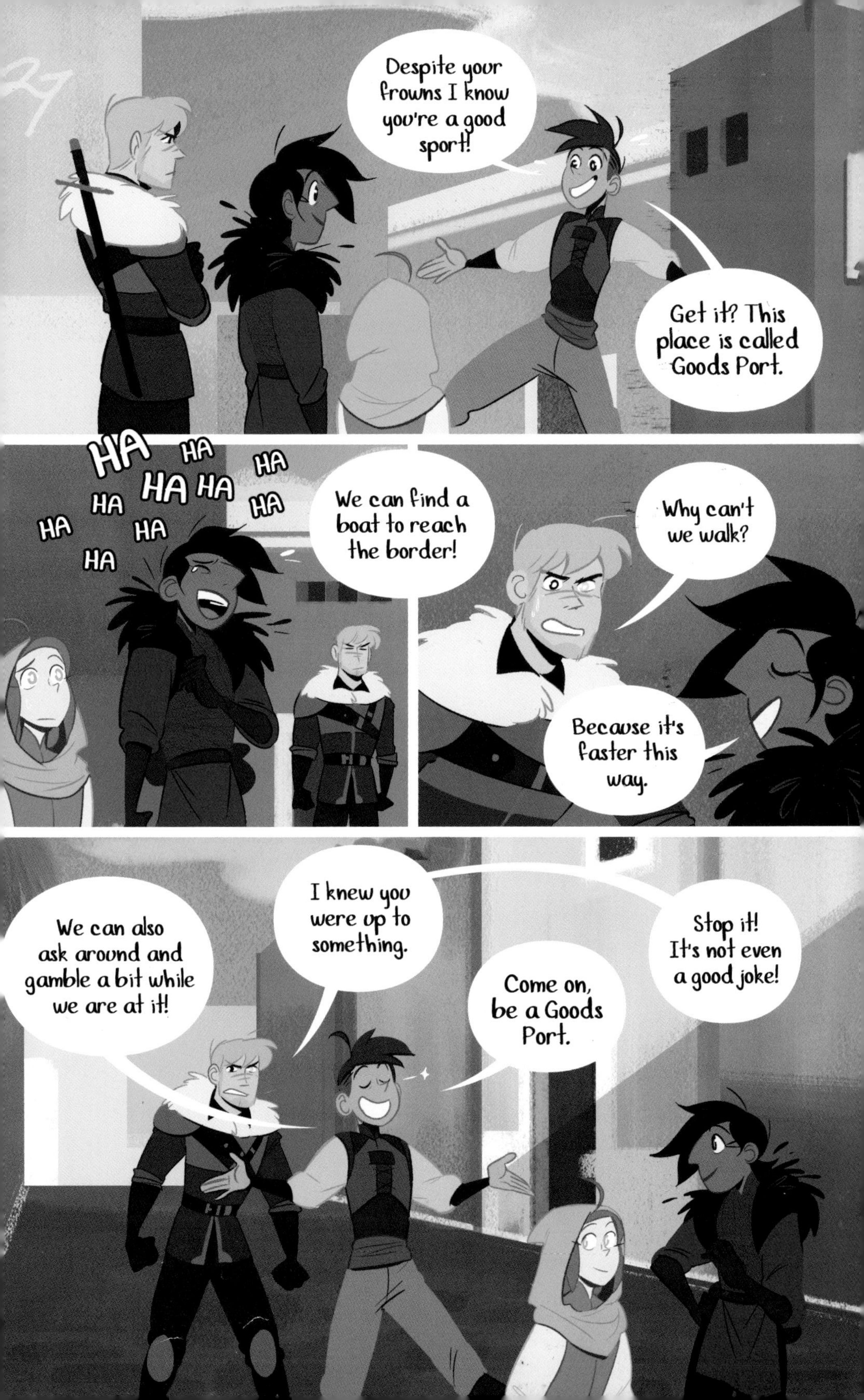
Despite your frowns I know you're a good sport!
Get it? This place is called Goods Port.
HA HA HA HA HA HA HA HA HA HA
We can find a boat to reach the border!
Why can't we walk?
Because it's faster this way.
We can also ask around and gamble a bit while we are at it!
I knew you were up to something.
Stop it! It's not even a good joke!
Come on, be a Goods Port.

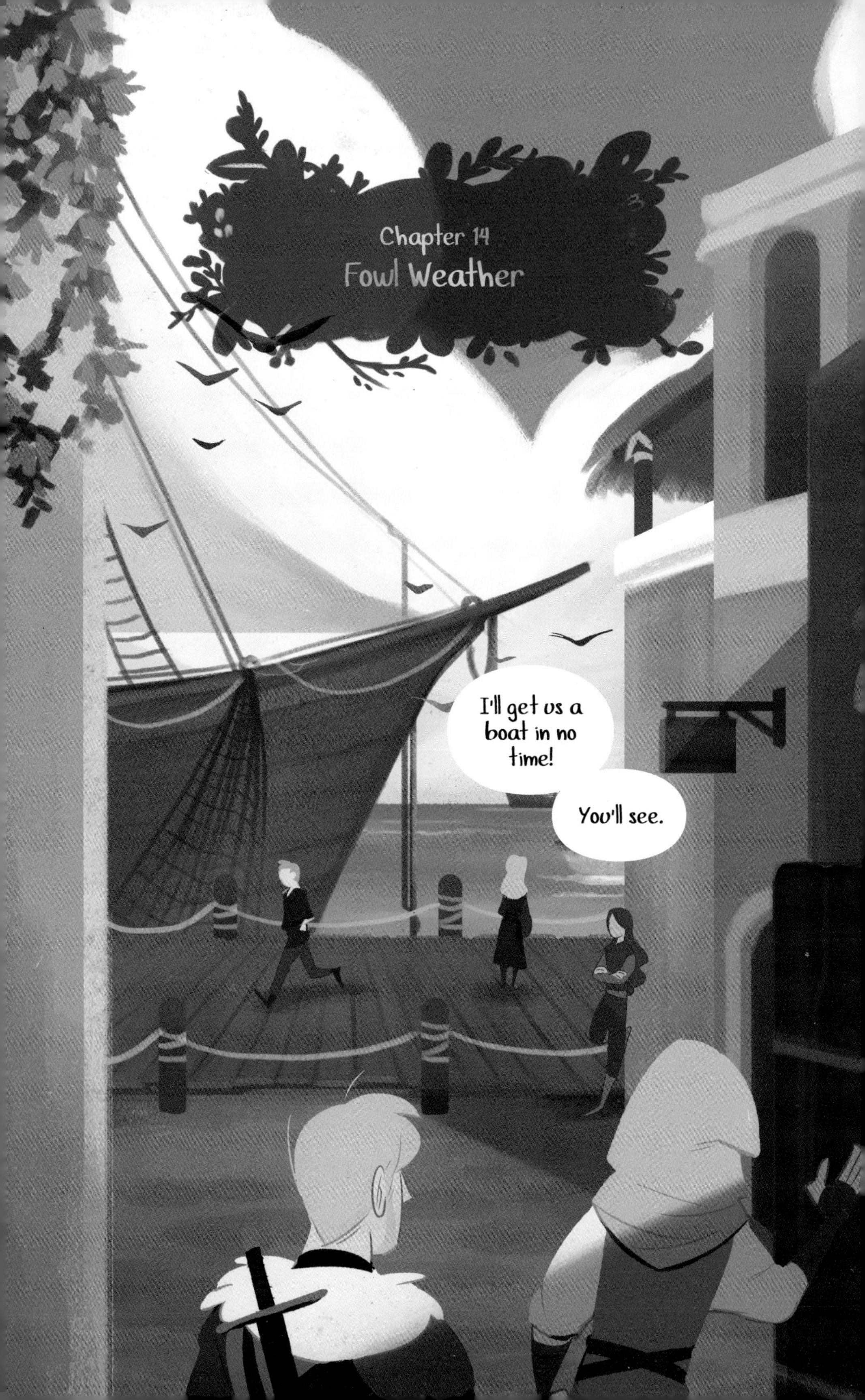
Chapter 14
Fowl Weather
I'll get us a boat in no time!
You'll see.

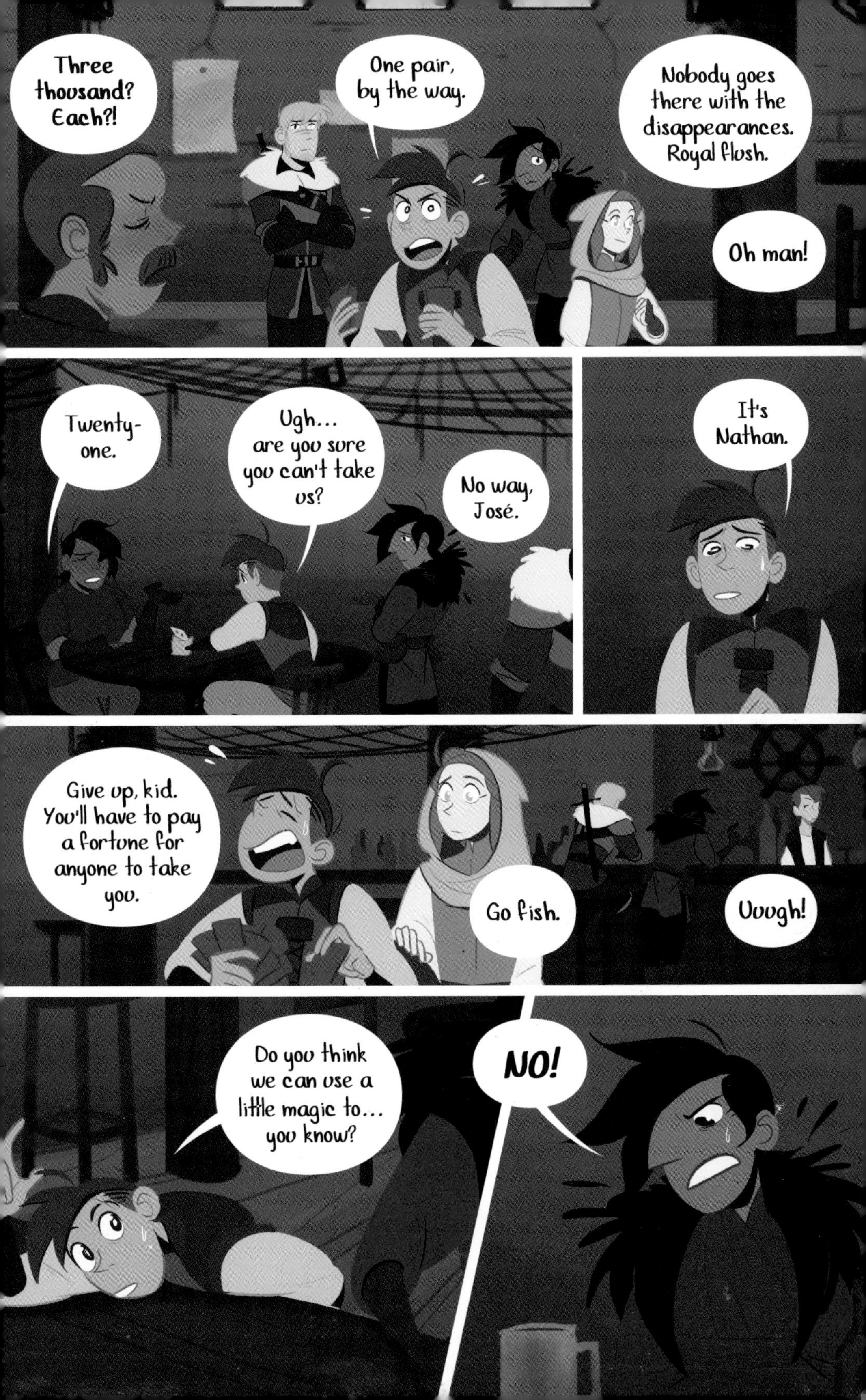
Three thousand? Each?!
One pair, by the way.
Nobody goes there with the disappearances. Royal flush.
Oh man!
Twenty-one.
Ugh... are you sure you can't take us?
No way, José.
It's Nathan.
Give up, kid. You'll have to pay a fortune for anyone to take you.
Go fish.
Uuugh!
Do you think we can use a little magic to... you know?
NO!

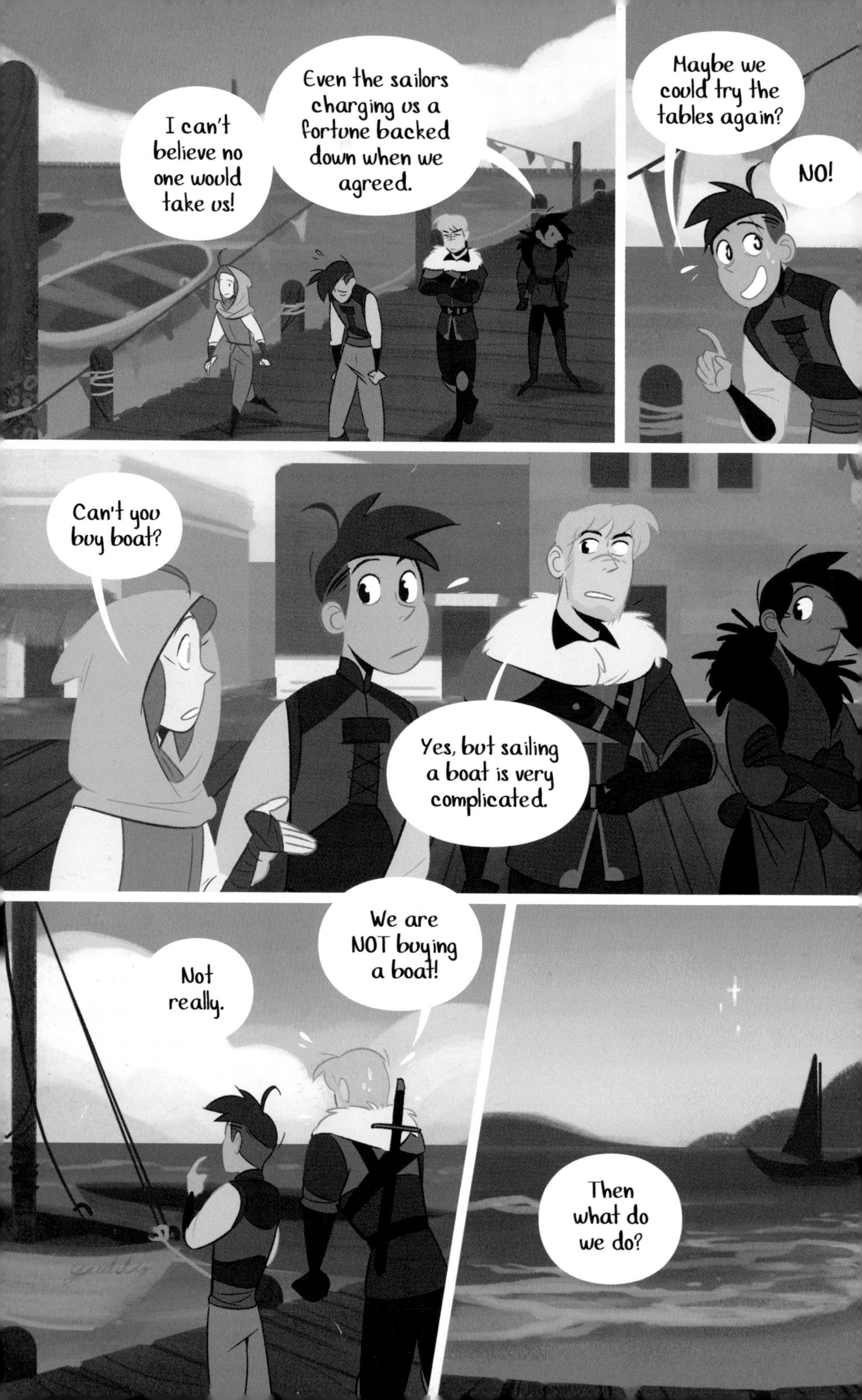
I can't believe no one would take us!
Even the sailors charging us a fortune backed down when we agreed.
Maybe we could try the tables again?
NO!
Can't you buy boat?
Yes, but sailing a boat is very complicated.
Not really.
We are NOT buying a boat!
Then what do we do?

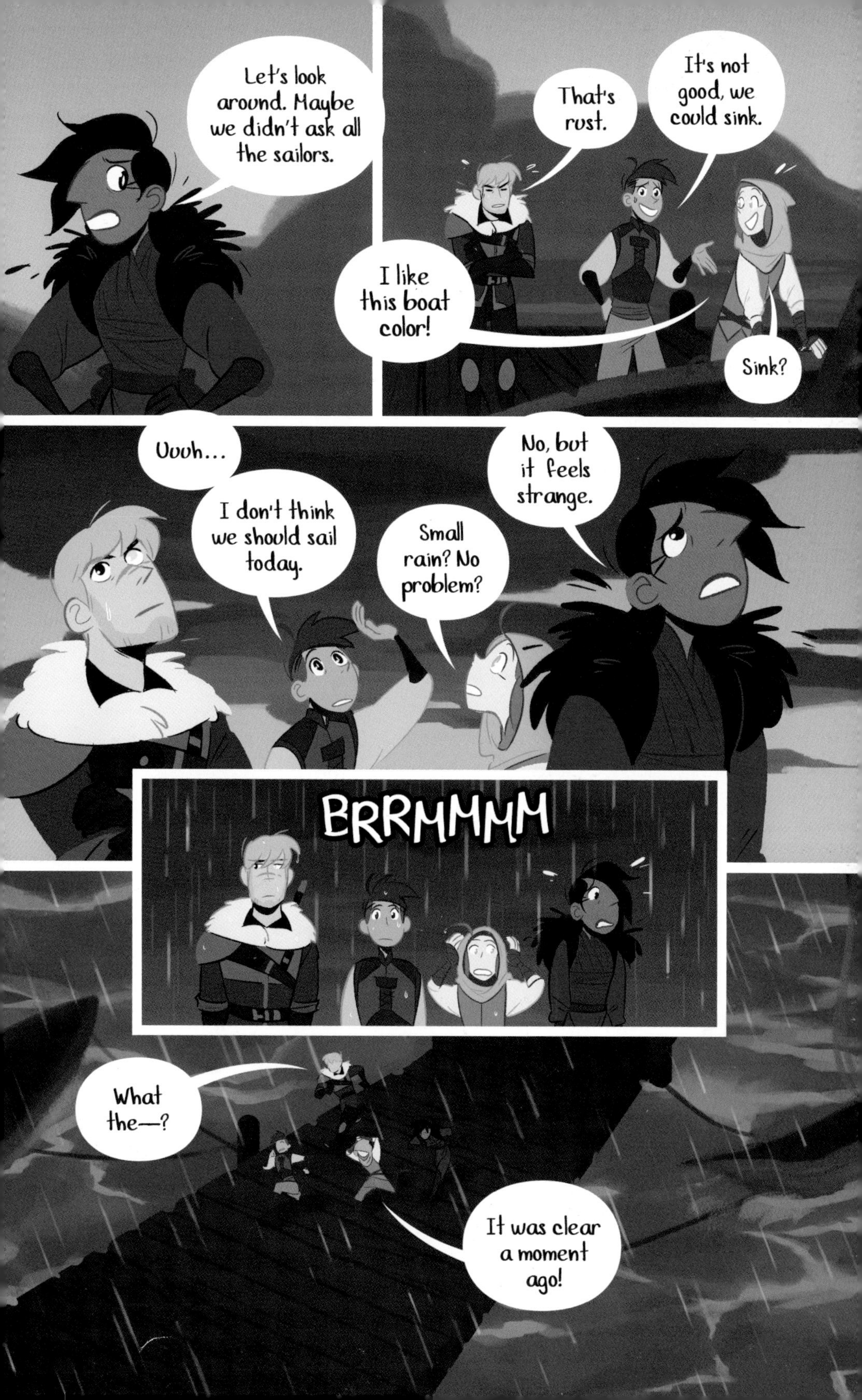
Let's look around. Maybe we didn't ask all the sailors.
That's rust.
It's not good, we could sink.
I like this boat color!
Sink?
Uooh...
I don't think we should sail today.
Small rain? No problem?
No, but it feels strange.
BRRMMMM
What the—?
It was clear a moment ago!

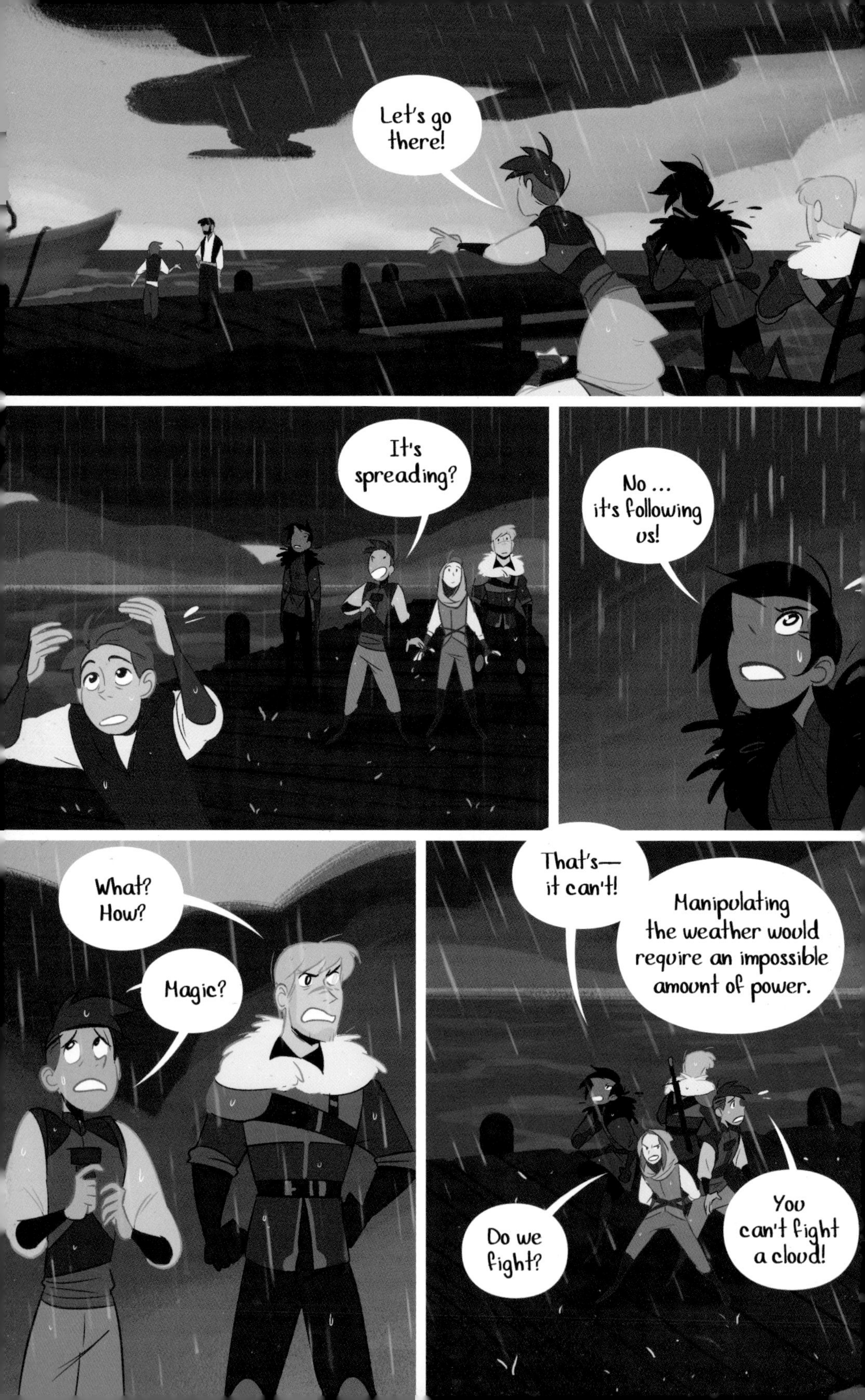

Let's go there!
It's spreading?
No ... it's following us!
What? How?
Magic?
That's— it can't!
Manipulating the weather would require an impossible amount of power.
Do we fight?
You can't fight a cloud!

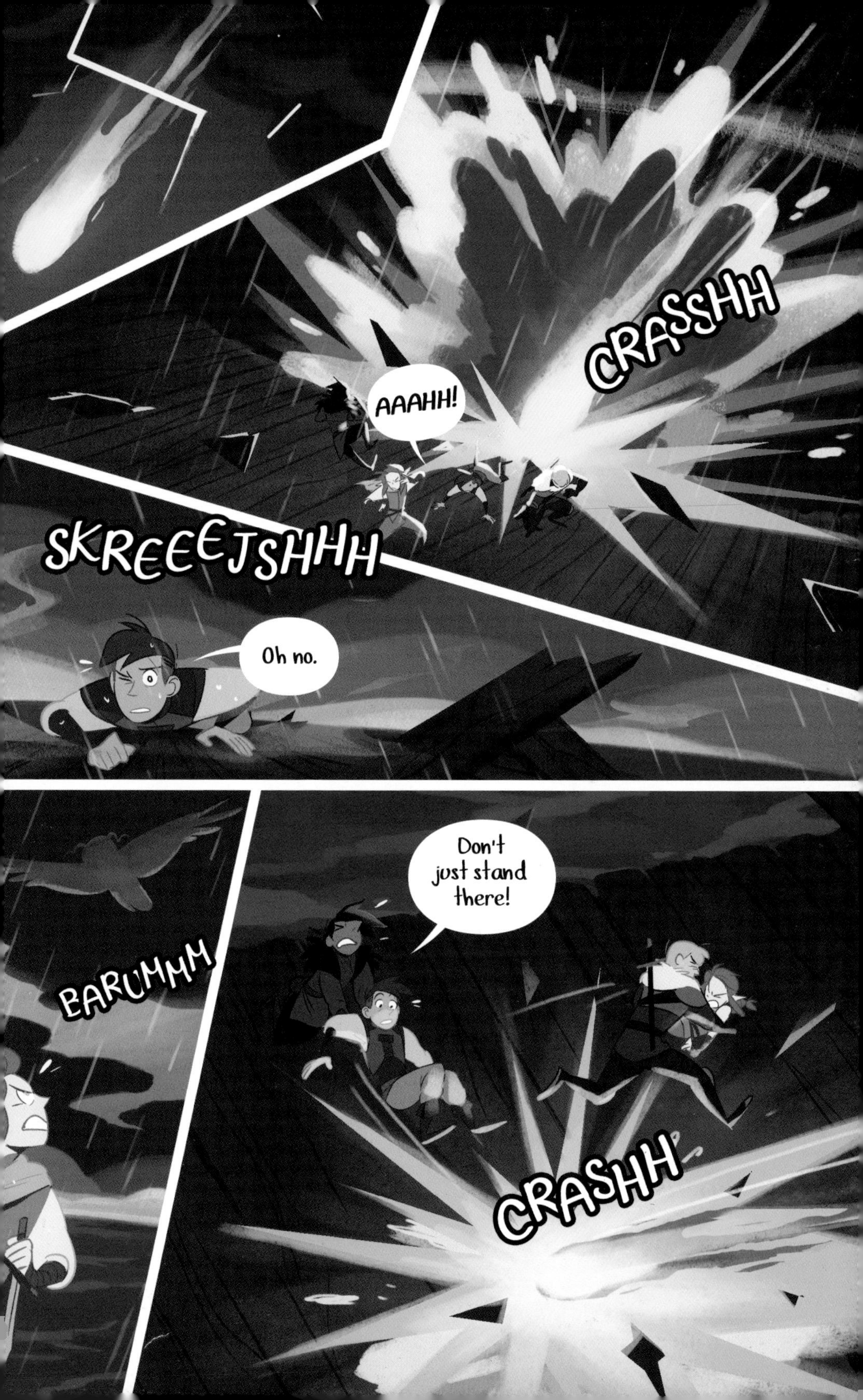
CRASSHH
AAAHH!
SKREEEJSHHH
Oh no.
Don't just stand there!
BARUMMM
CRASHH

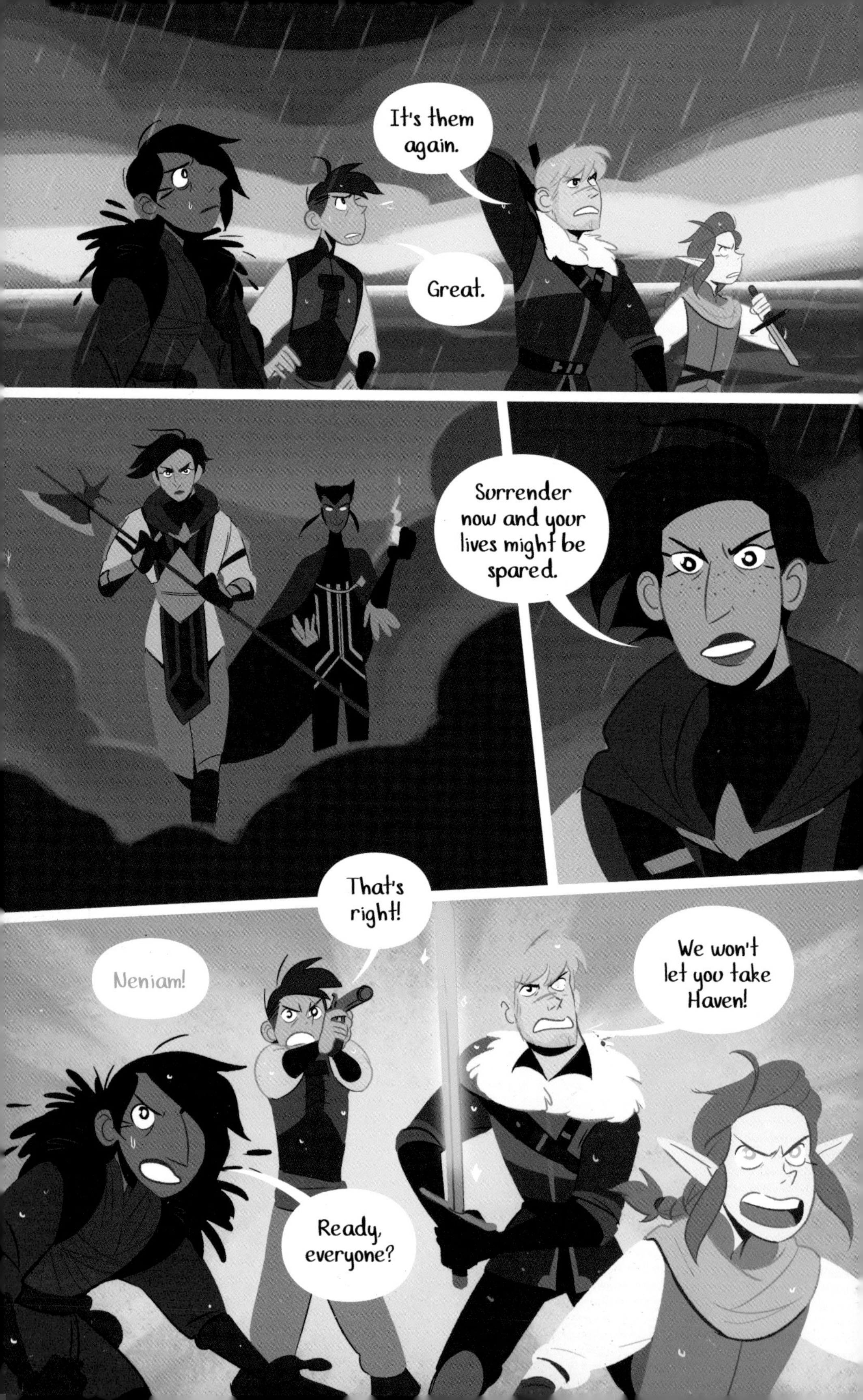
It's them again.
Great.
Surrender now and your lives might be spared.
That's right!
Neniam!
We won't let you take Haven!
Ready, everyone?

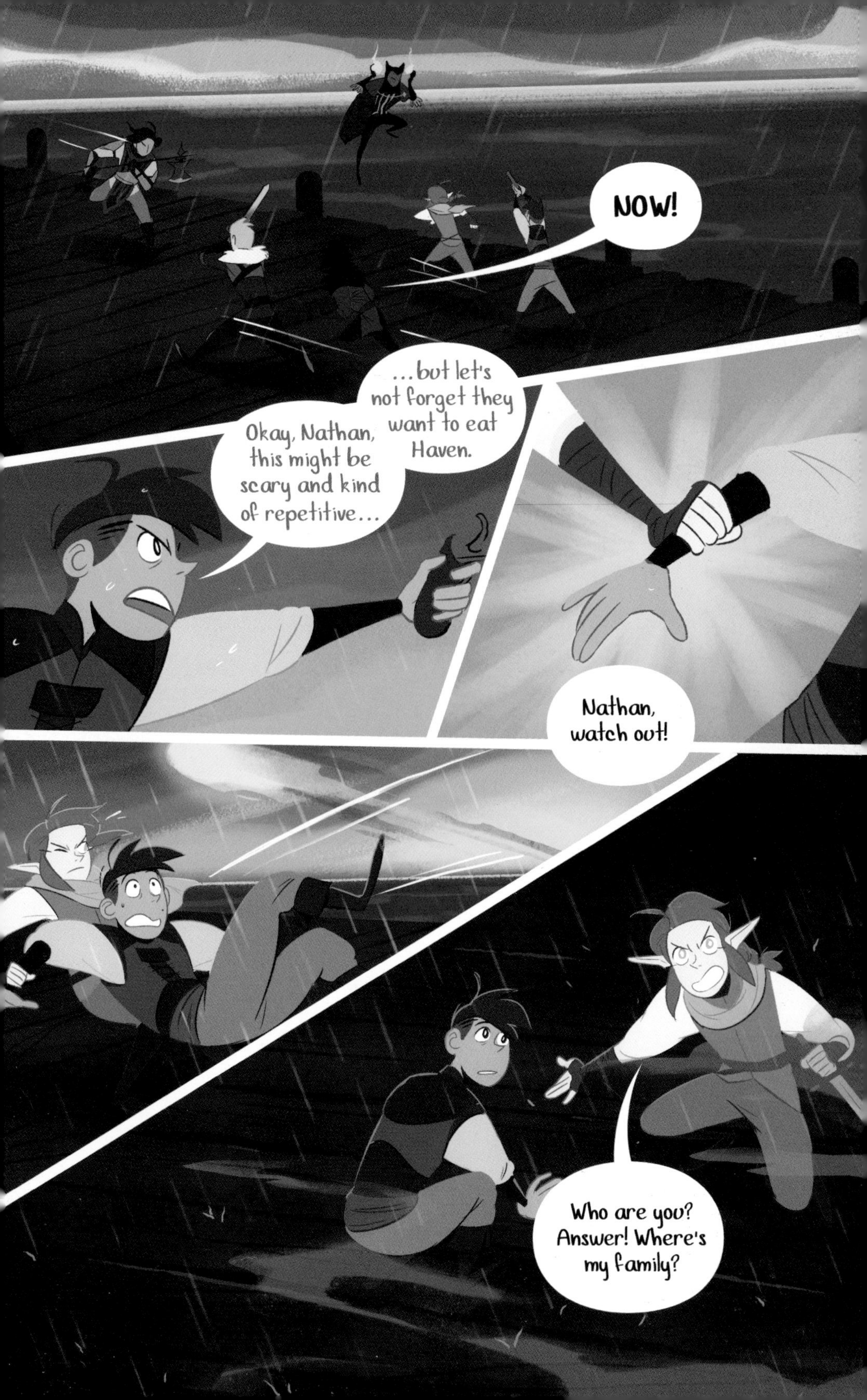
NOW!
Okay, Nathan, this might be scary and kind of repetitive...
...but let's not forget they want to eat Haven.
Nathan, watch out!
Who are you? Answer! Where's my family?

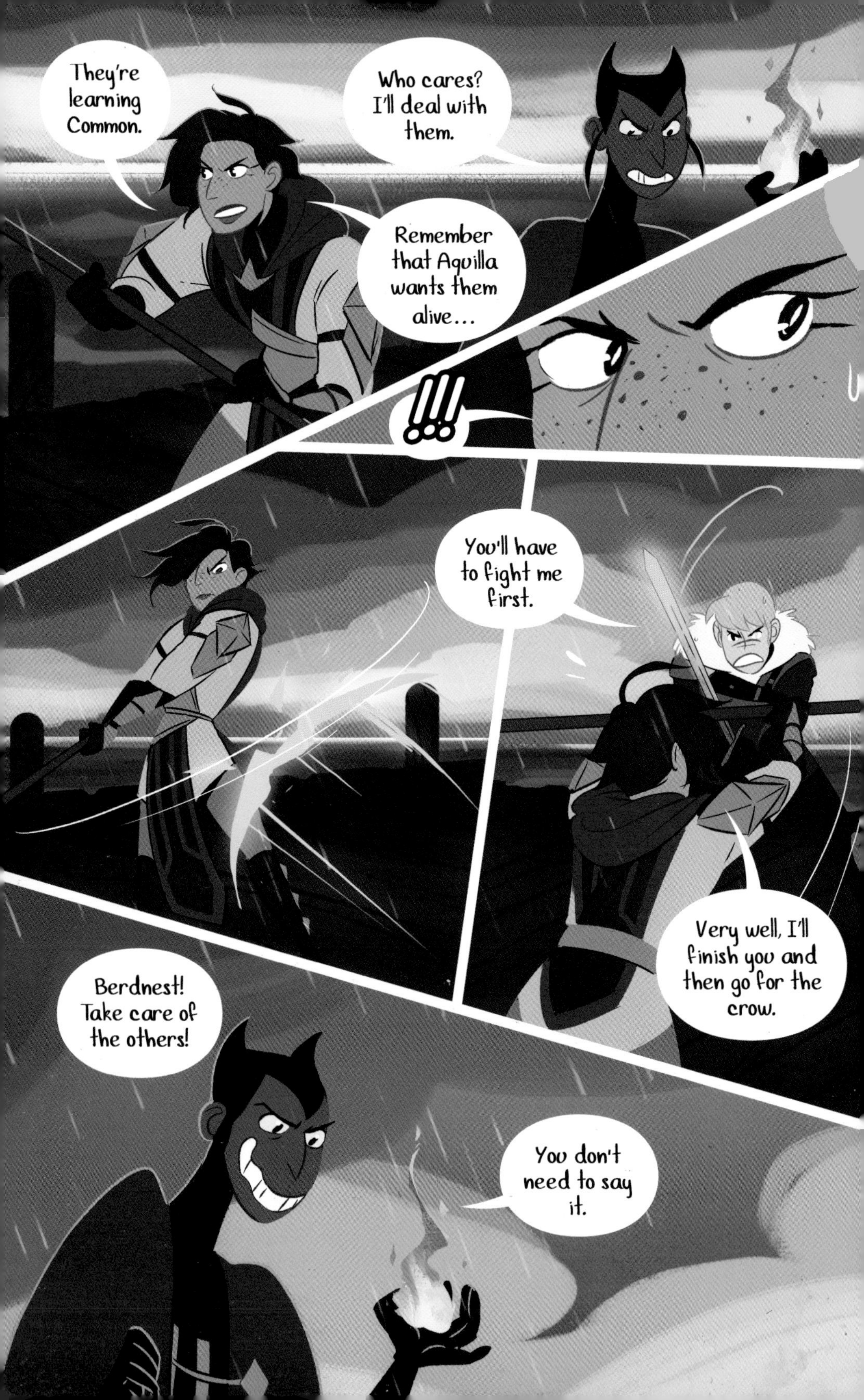
They're learning Common.
Who cares? I'll deal with them.
Remember that Aquilla wants them alive...
!!!
You'll have to fight me first.
Very well, I'll finish you and then go for the crow.
Berdnest! Take care of the others!
You don't need to say it.

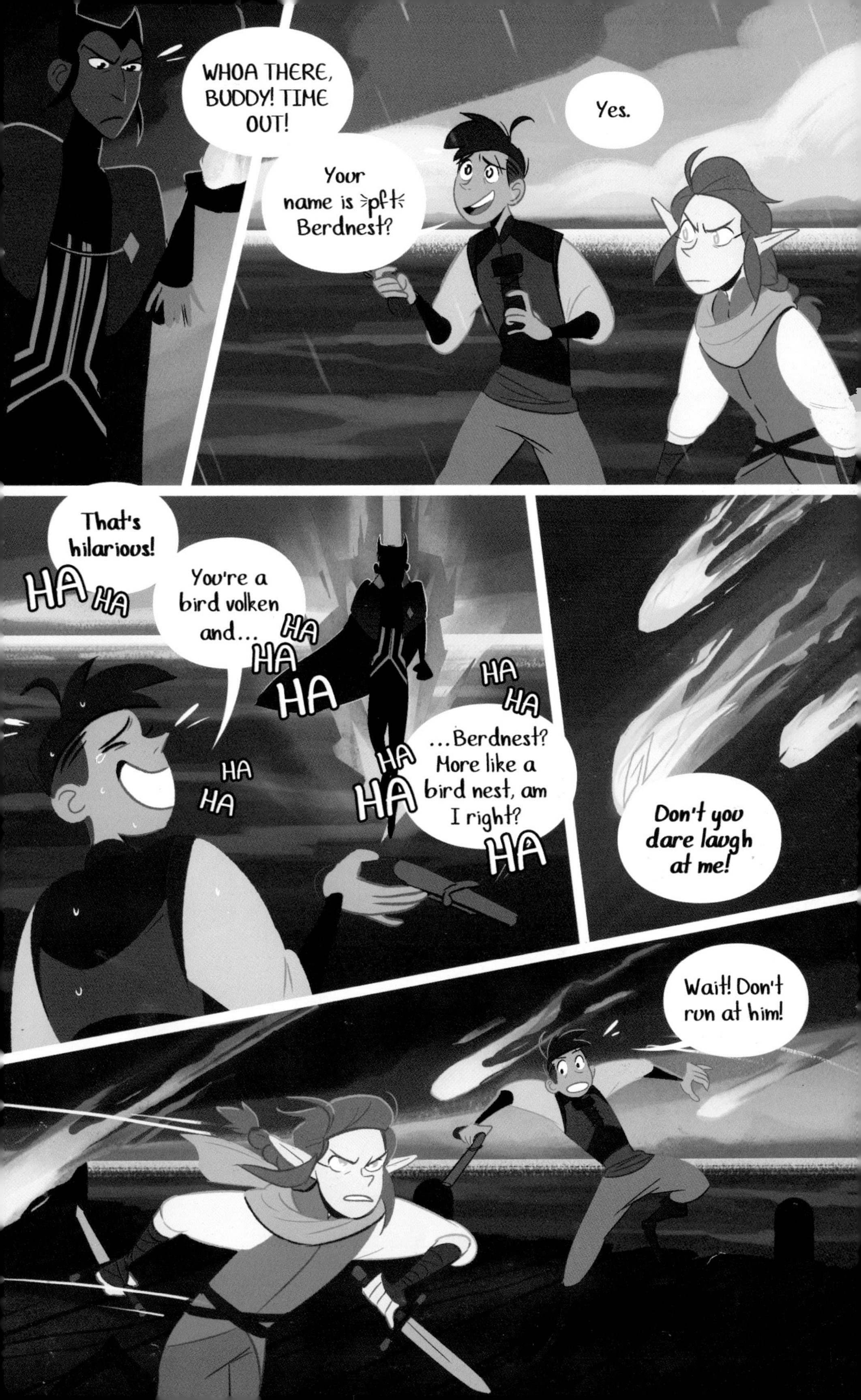
WHOA THERE, BUDDY! TIME OUT!
Your name is >pft< Berdnest?
Yes.
That's hilarious!
HA HA
You're a bird volken and...
HA HA HA
HA HA
HA HA
HA HA
...Berdnest? More like a bird nest, am I right?
HA
Don't you dare laugh at me!
Wait! Don't run at him!

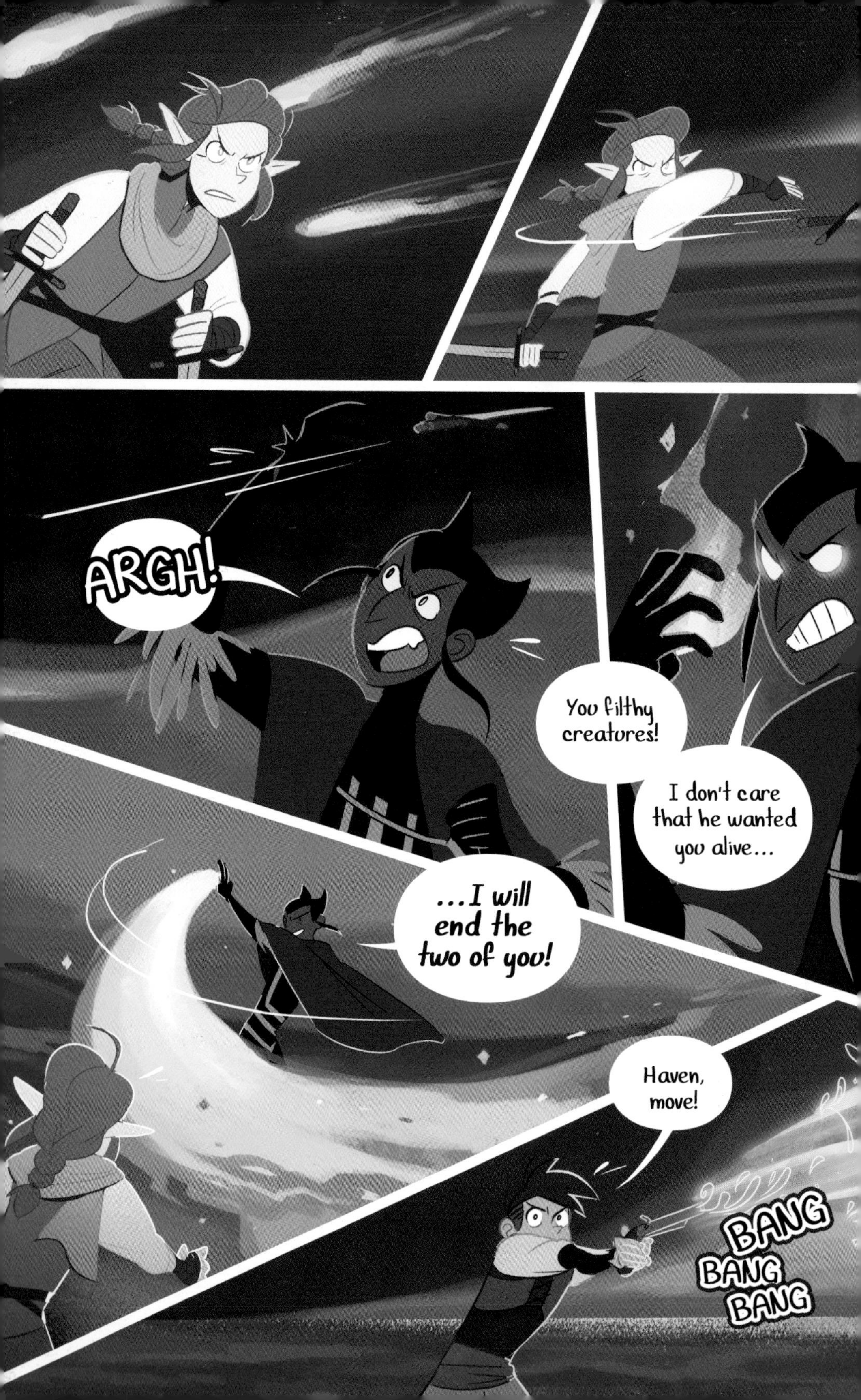
ARGH!
You filthy creatures!
I don't care that he wanted you alive...
...I will end the two of you!
Haven, move!
BANG
BANG
BANG

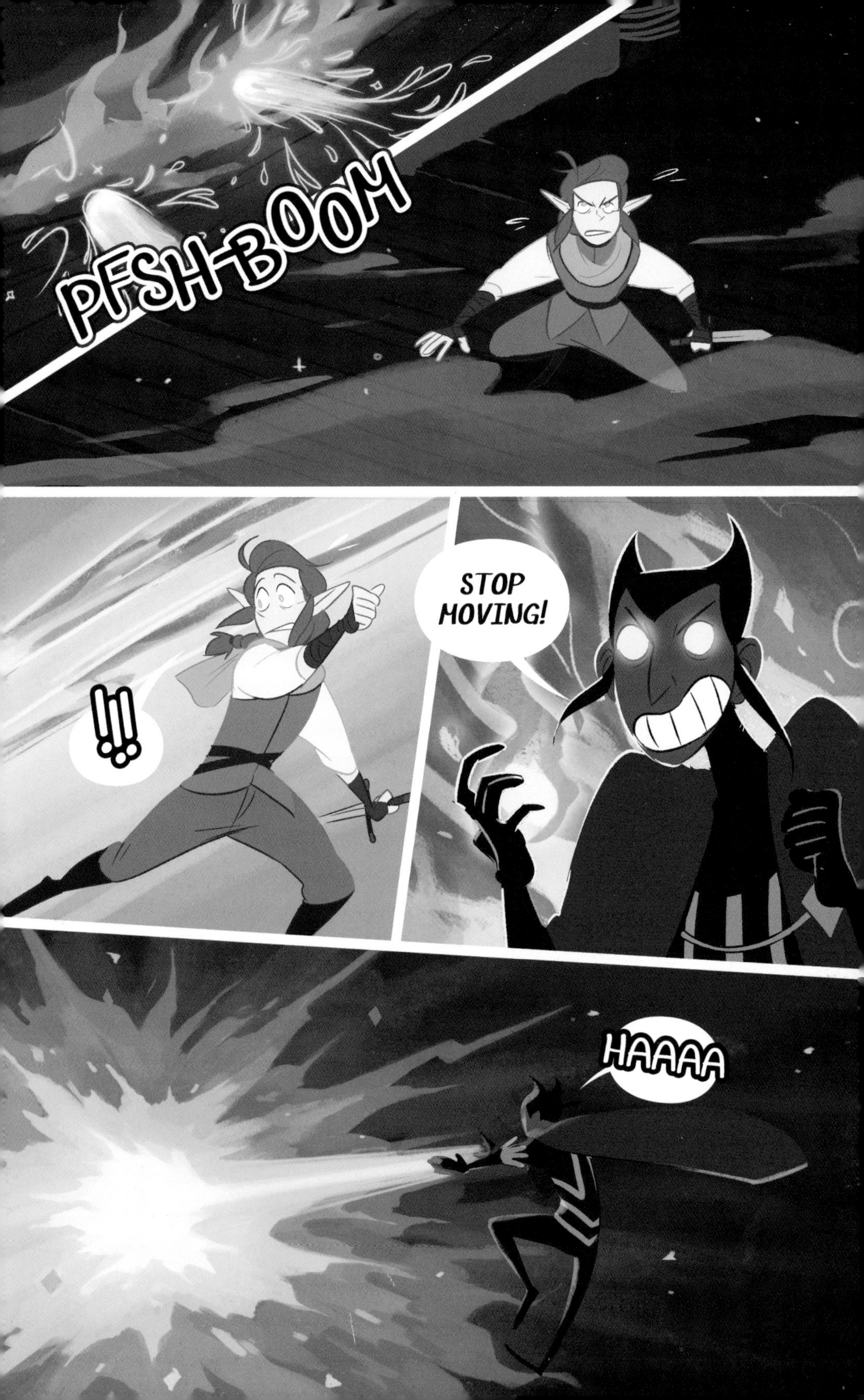
PFSH-BOOM
!!!
STOP MOVING!
HAAAA

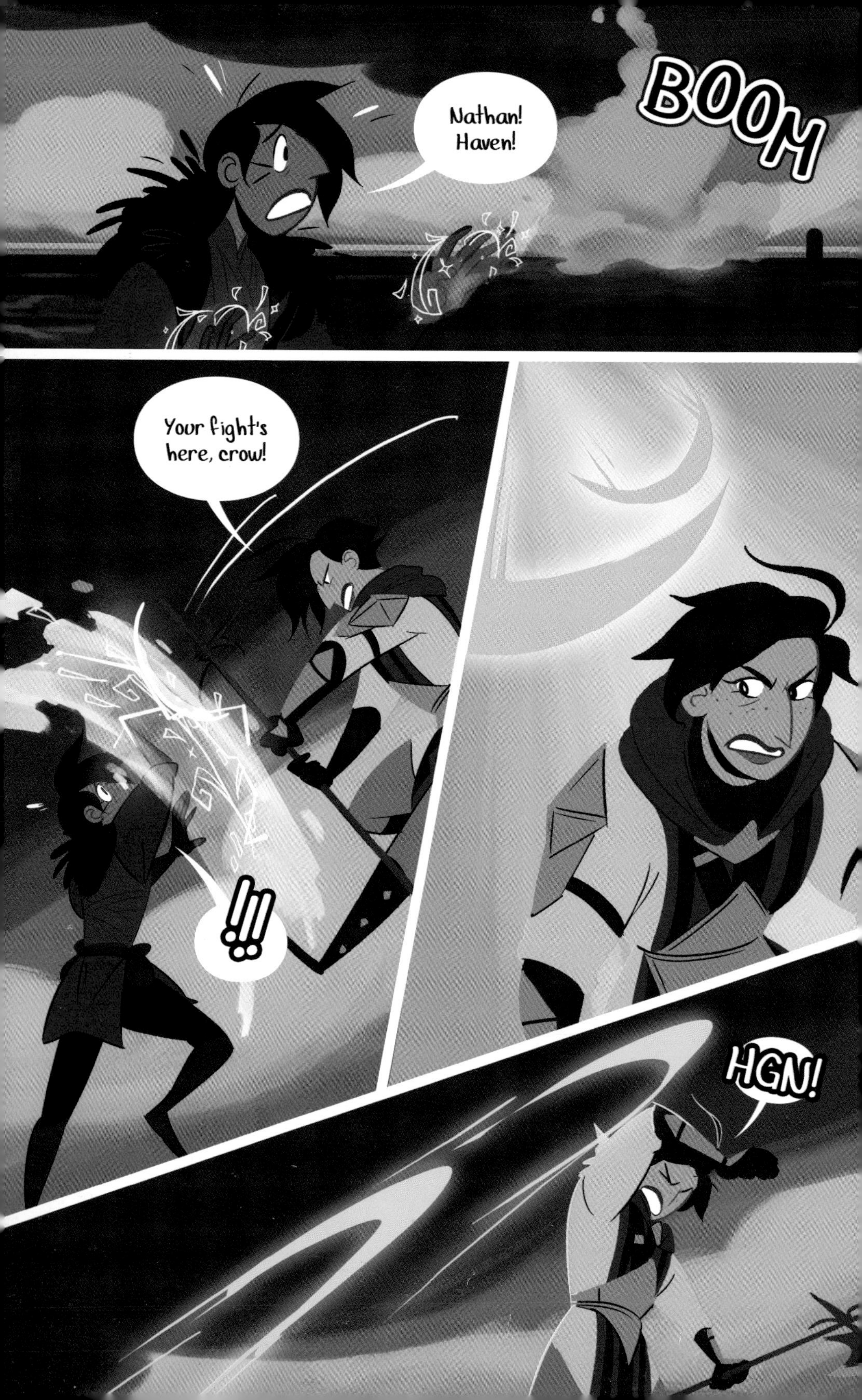
Nathan! Haven!
BOOM
Your fight's here, crow!
!!!
HGN!

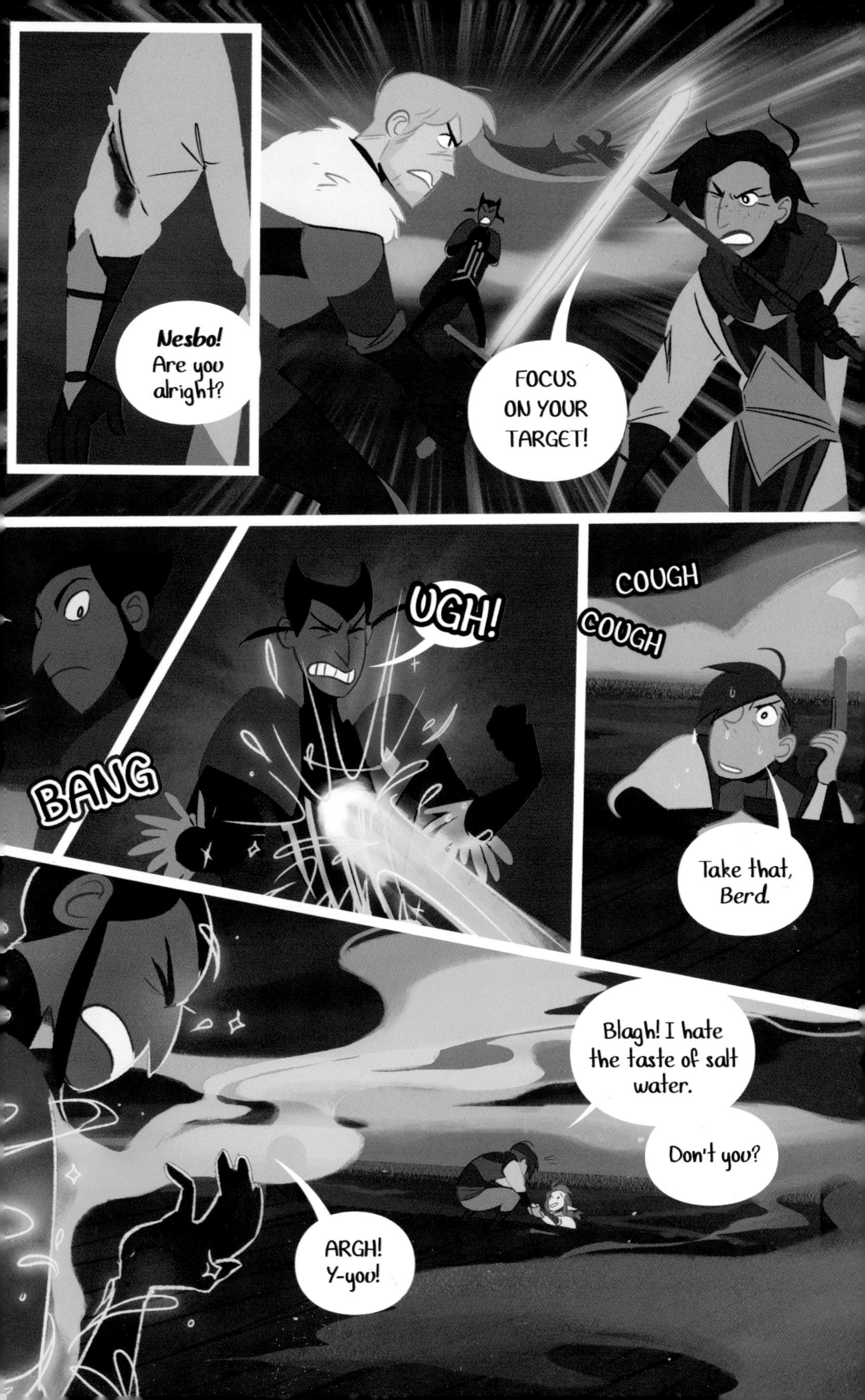
Nesbo! Are you alright?
FOCUS ON YOUR TARGET!
UGH!
BANG
COUGH
COUGH
Take that, Berd.
Blagh! I hate the taste of salt water.
Don't you?
ARGH! Y-you!

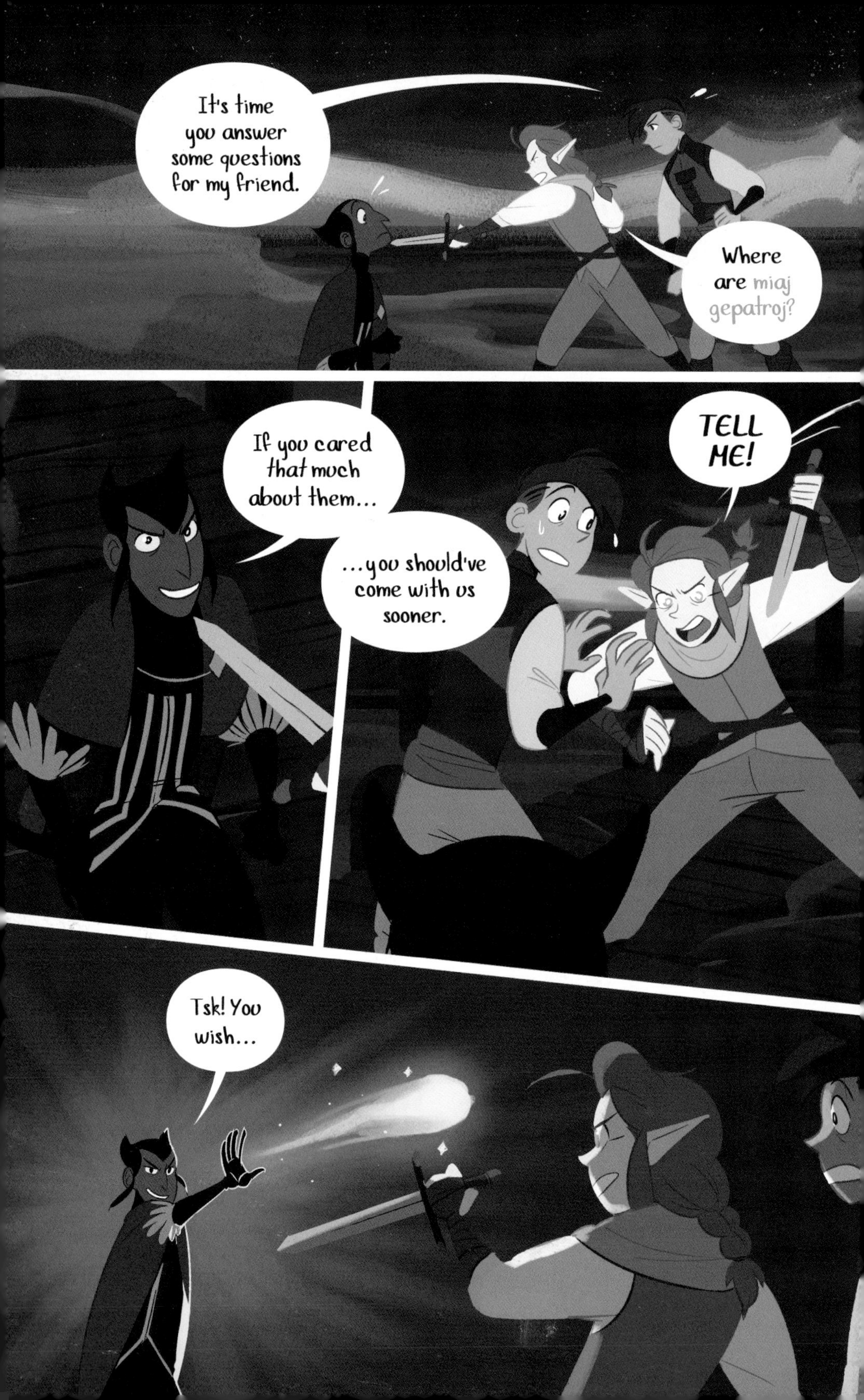
It's time you answer some questions for my friend.
Where are miaj gepatroj?
If you cared that much about them...
...you should've come with us sooner.
TELL ME!
Tsk! You wish...

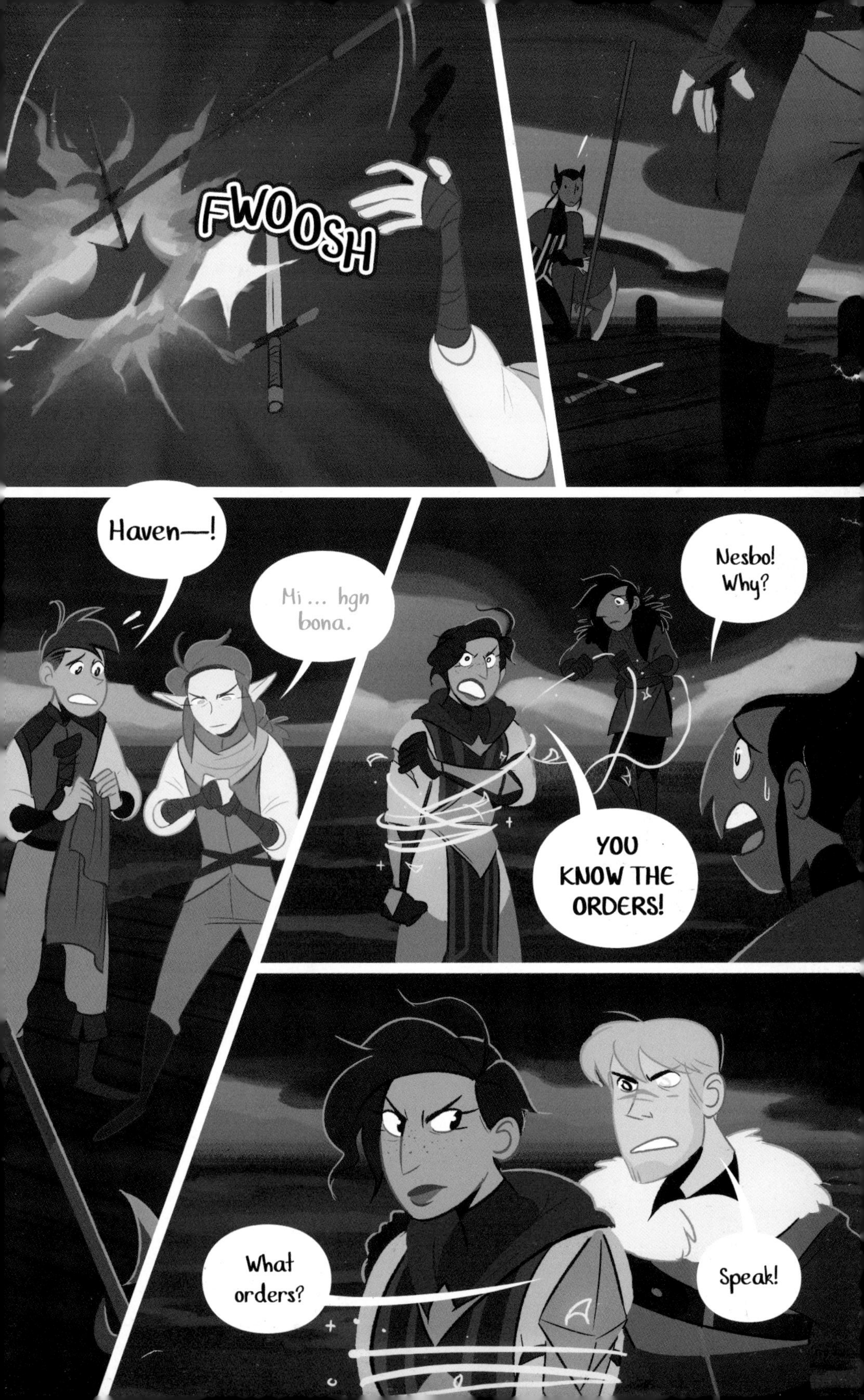
FWOOSH
Haven—!
Mi ... hgn bona.
Nesbo! Why?
YOU KNOW THE ORDERS!
What orders?
Speak!

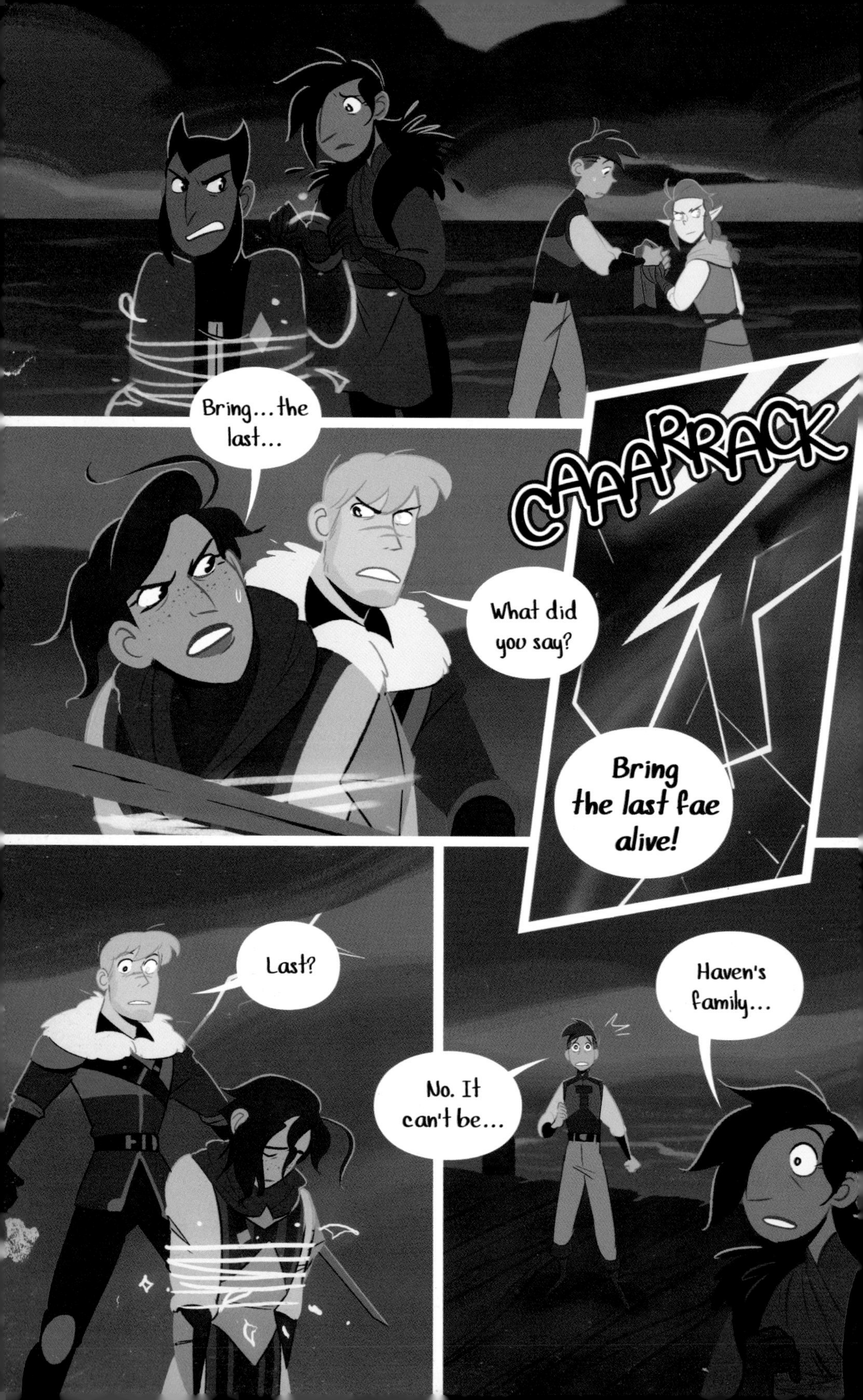
Bring... the last...
CAAARRACK
What did you say?
Bring the last fae alive!
Last?
Haven's family...
No. It can't be...

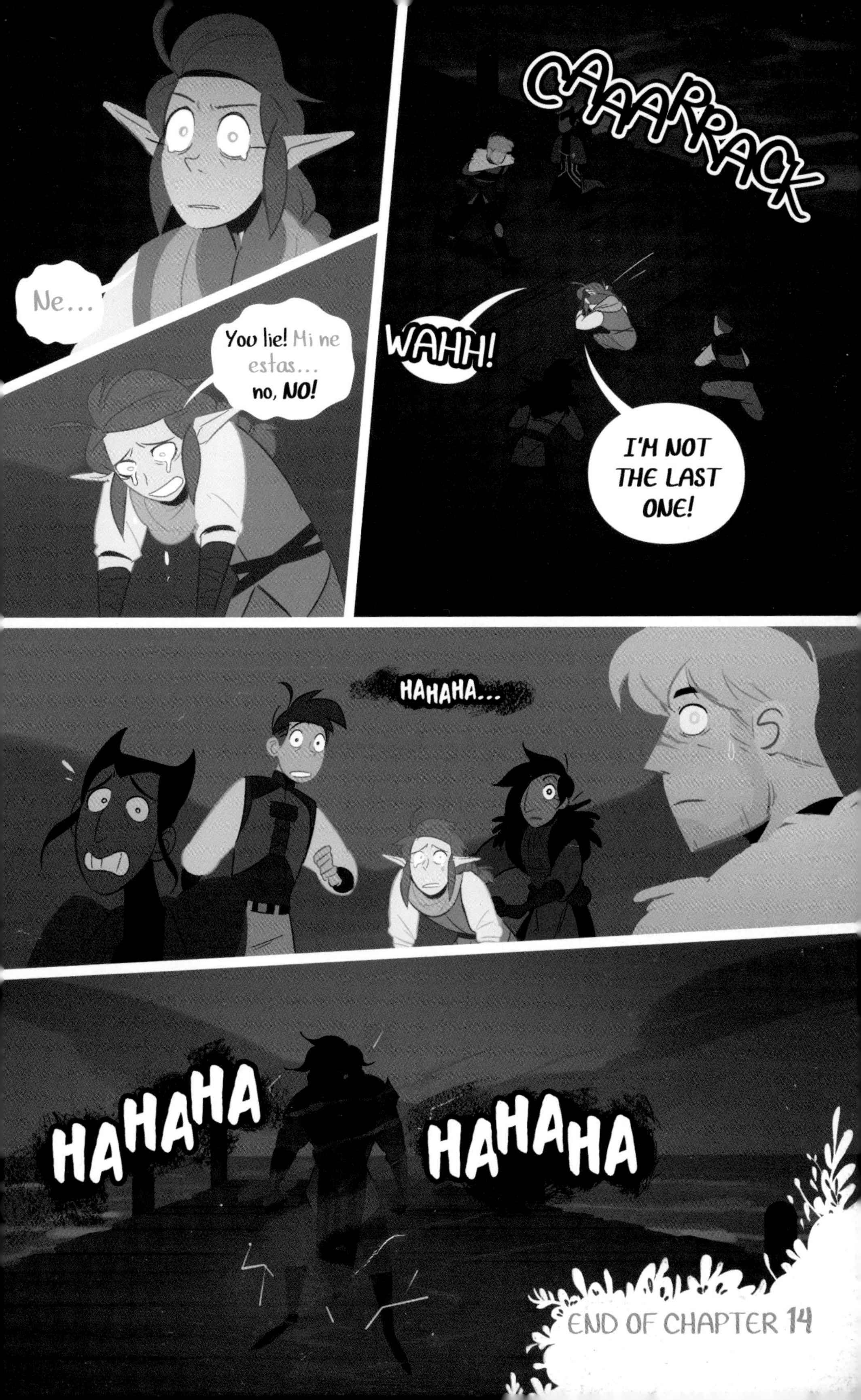

Ne...
You lie! Mi ne estas... no, NO!
CAAARRACK
WAHH!
I'M NOT THE LAST ONE!
HAHAHA...
HAHAHA
HAHAHA
END OF CHAPTER 14

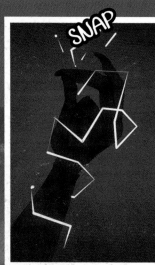

SNAP

I'm sorry! I didn't mean to harm the fae! I—

N-Nes...

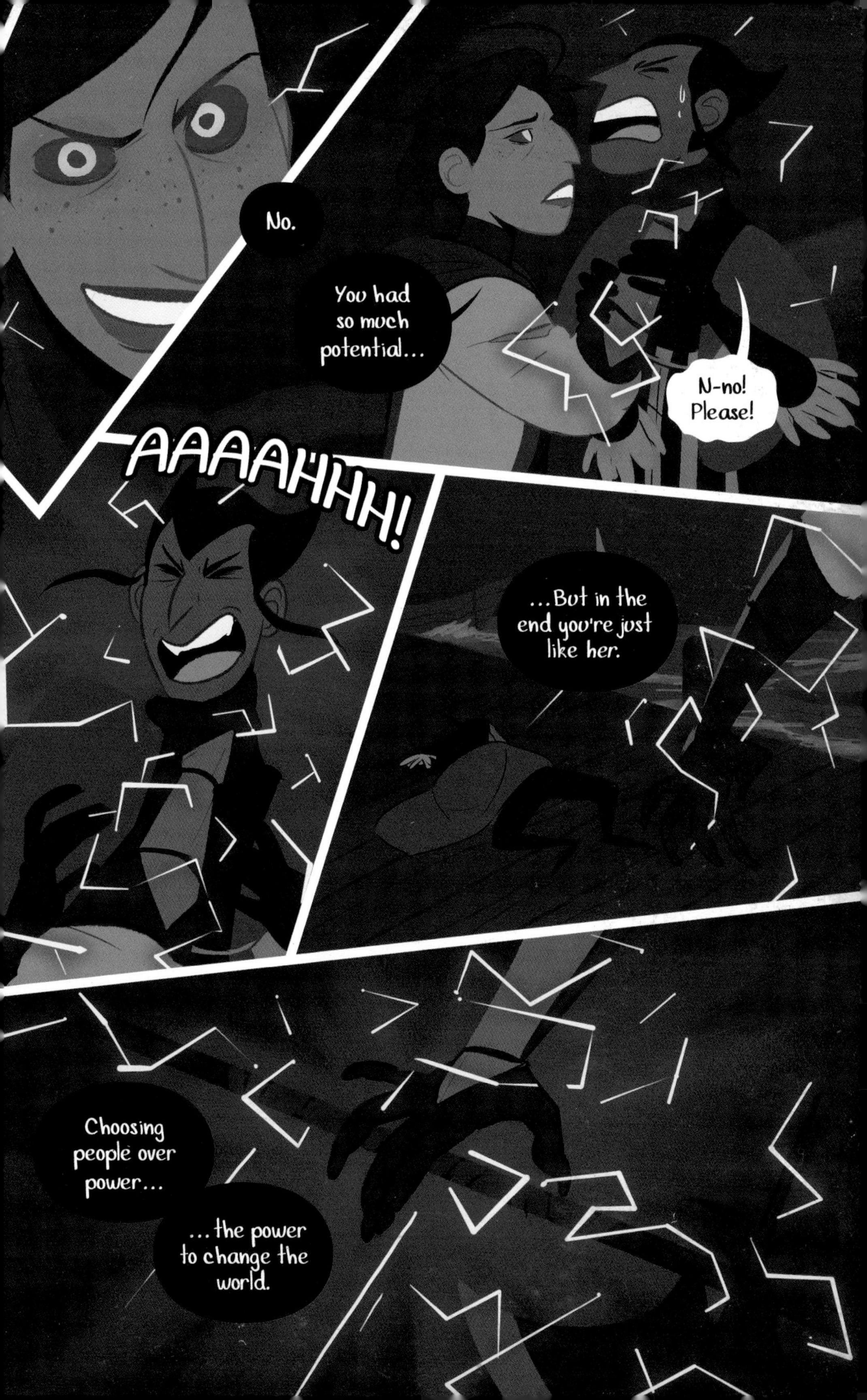
No.
You had so much potential...
N-no! Please!
AAAAHHH!
...But in the end you're just like her.
Choosing people over power...
...the power to change the world.

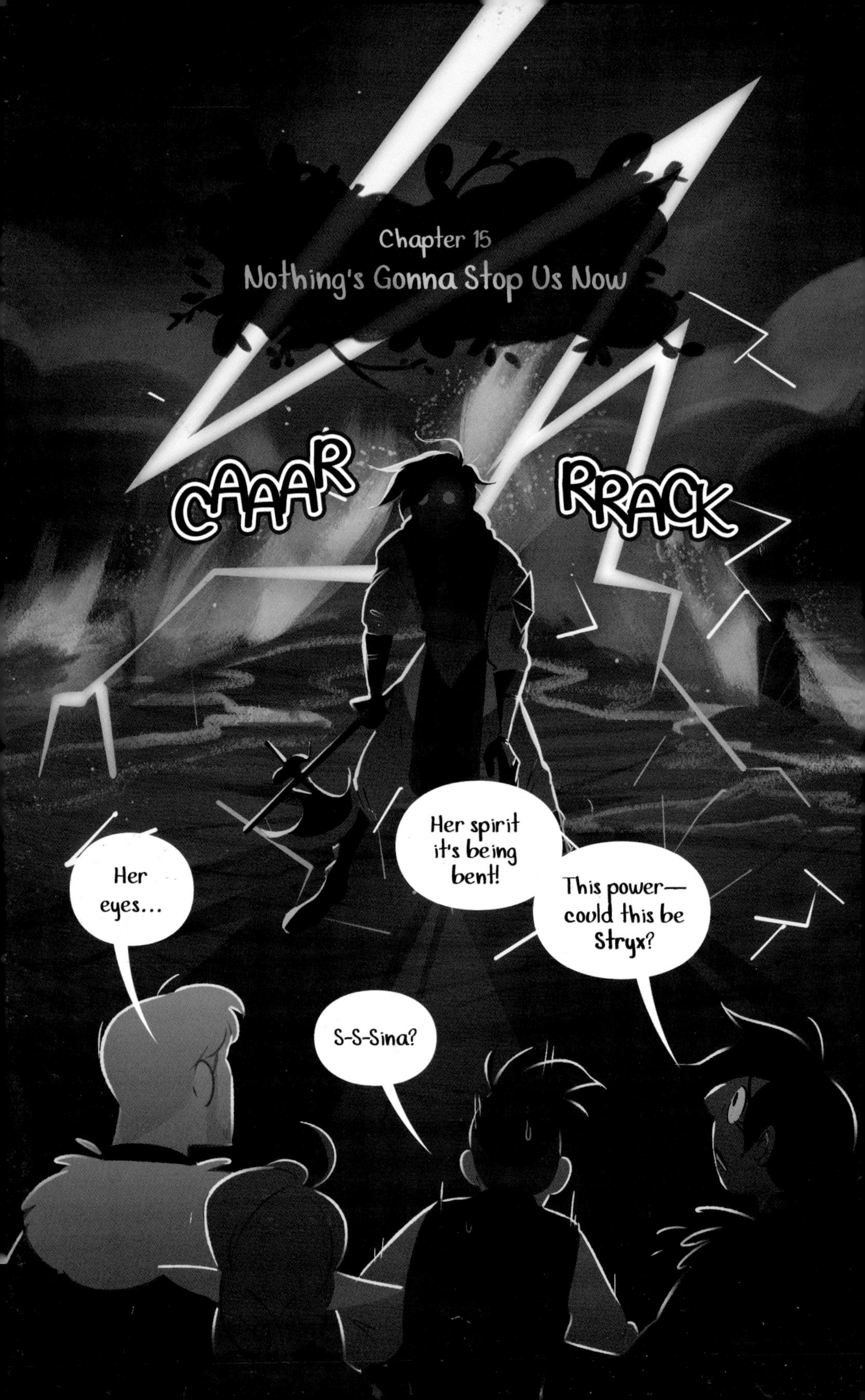
Chapter 15
Nothing's Gonna Stop Us Now
CAAAR
RRACK
Her eyes...
Her spirit it's being bent!
This power—could this be Stryx?
S-S-Sina?

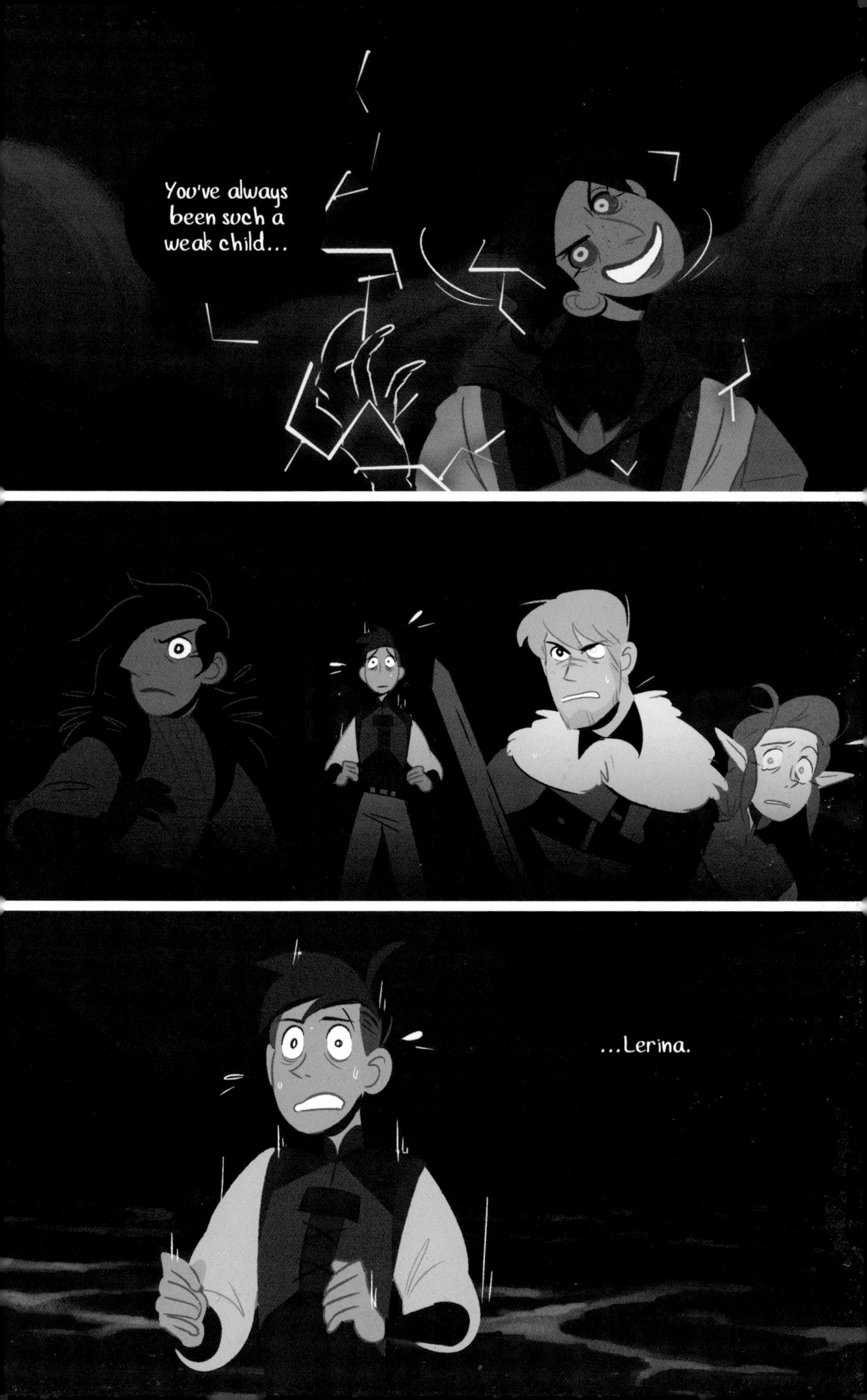
You've always been such a weak child...
...Lerina.

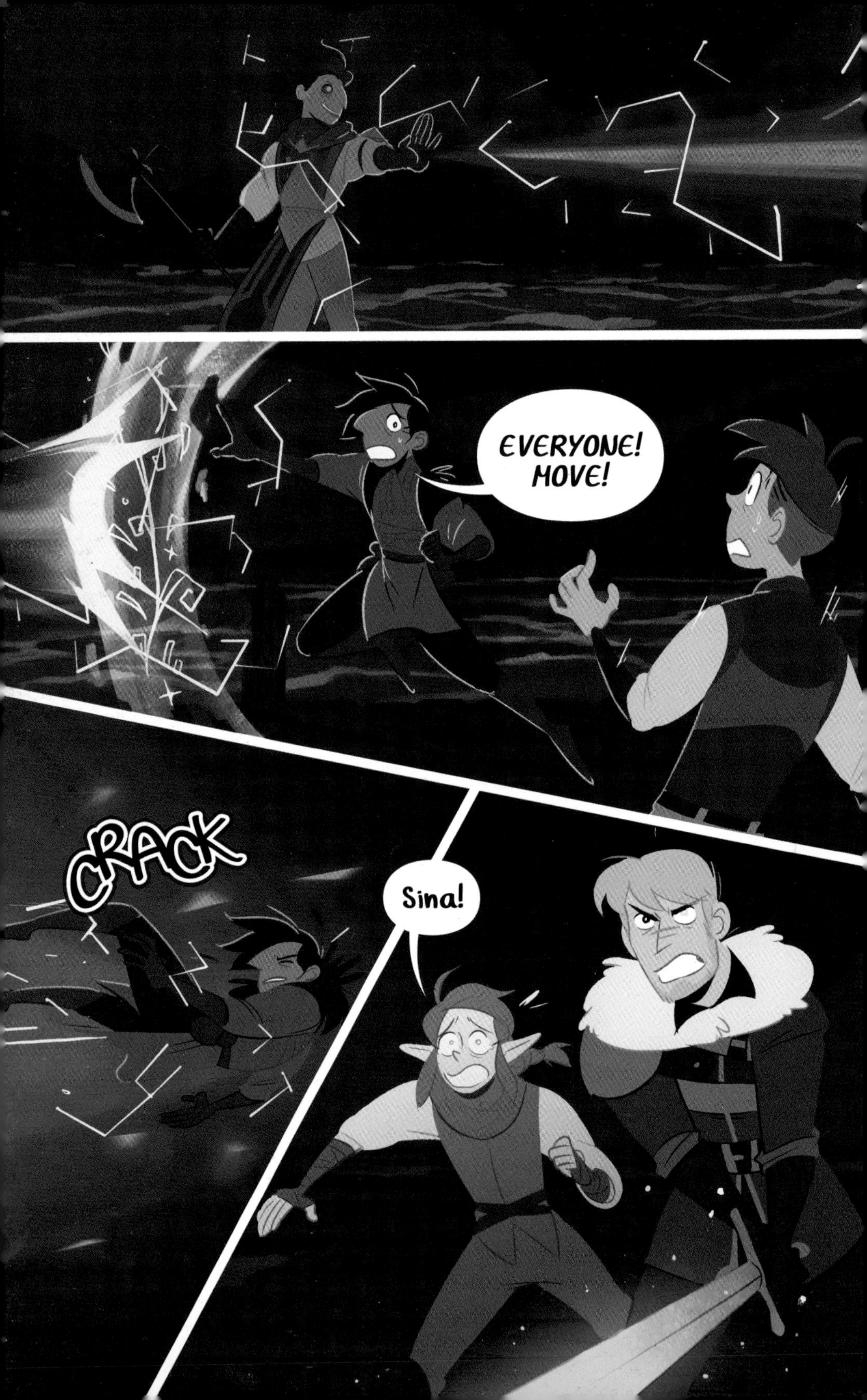
EVERYONE! MOVE!
CRACK
Sina!

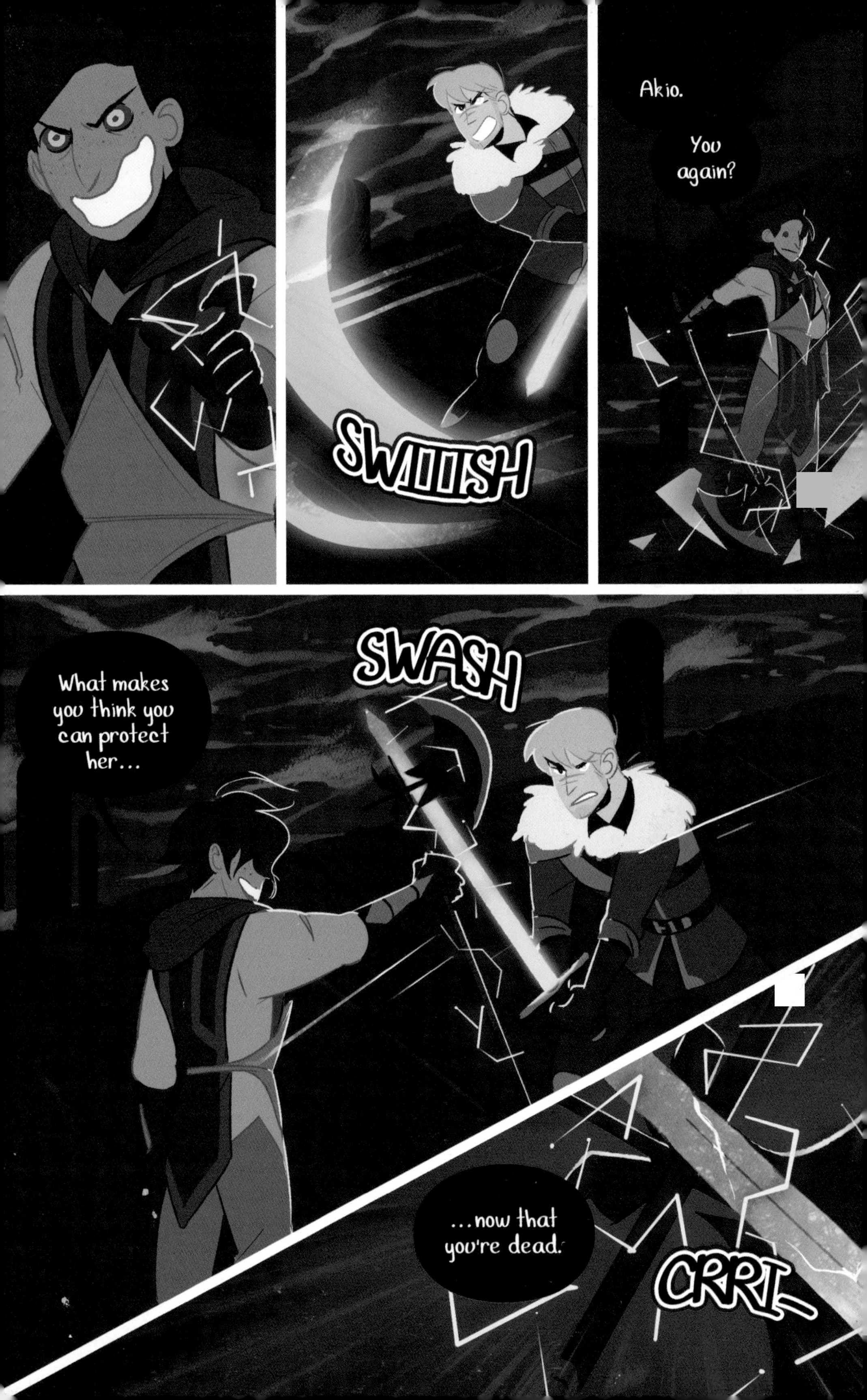
SWIIISH
Akio.
You again?
SWASH
What makes you think you can protect her...
...now that you're dead.
CRRI_

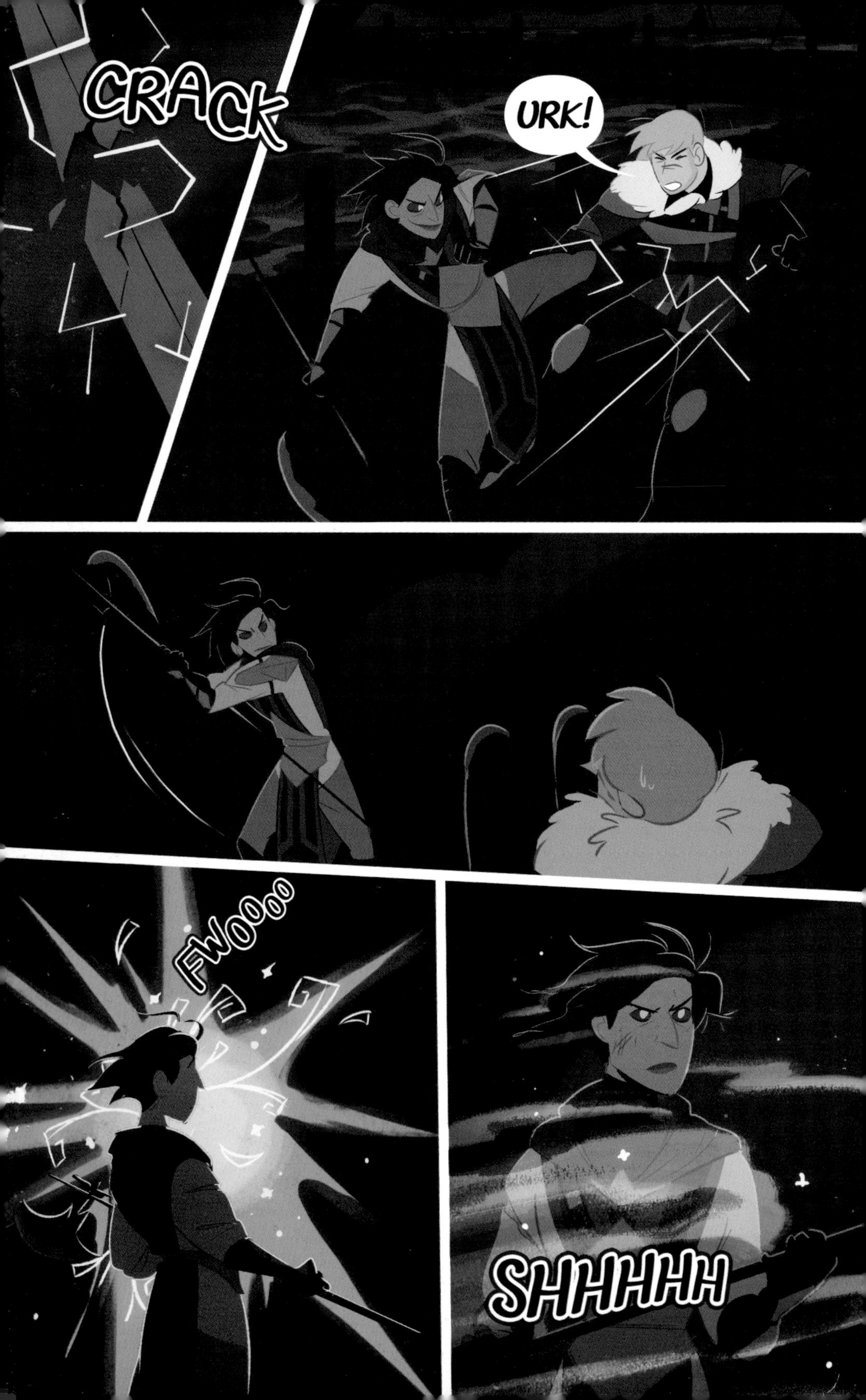
CRACK
URK!
FWOOoo
SHHHHH

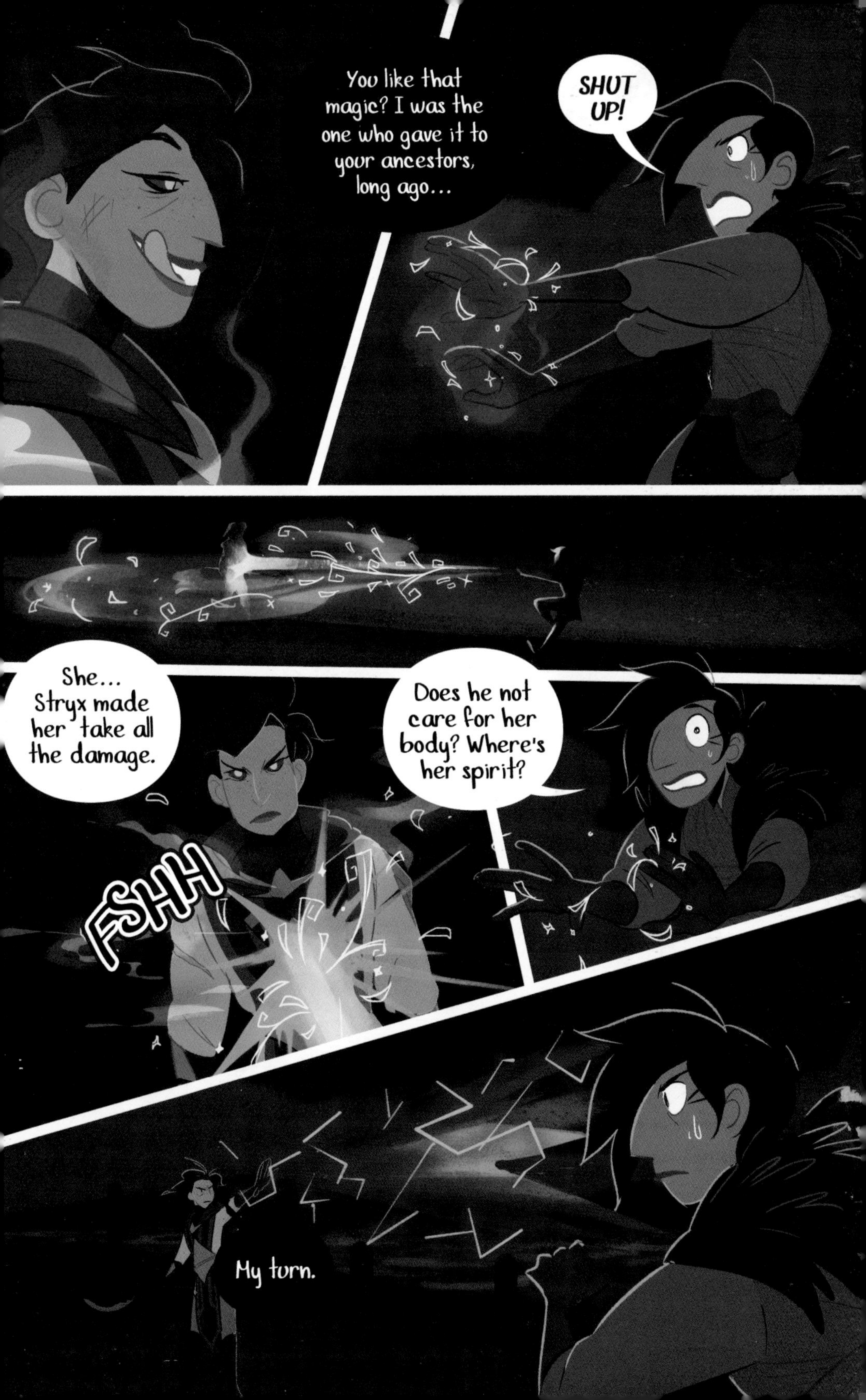
You like that magic? I was the one who gave it to your ancestors, long ago...
SHUT UP!
She... Stryx made her take all the damage.
Does he not care for her body? Where's her spirit?
FSHH
My turn.

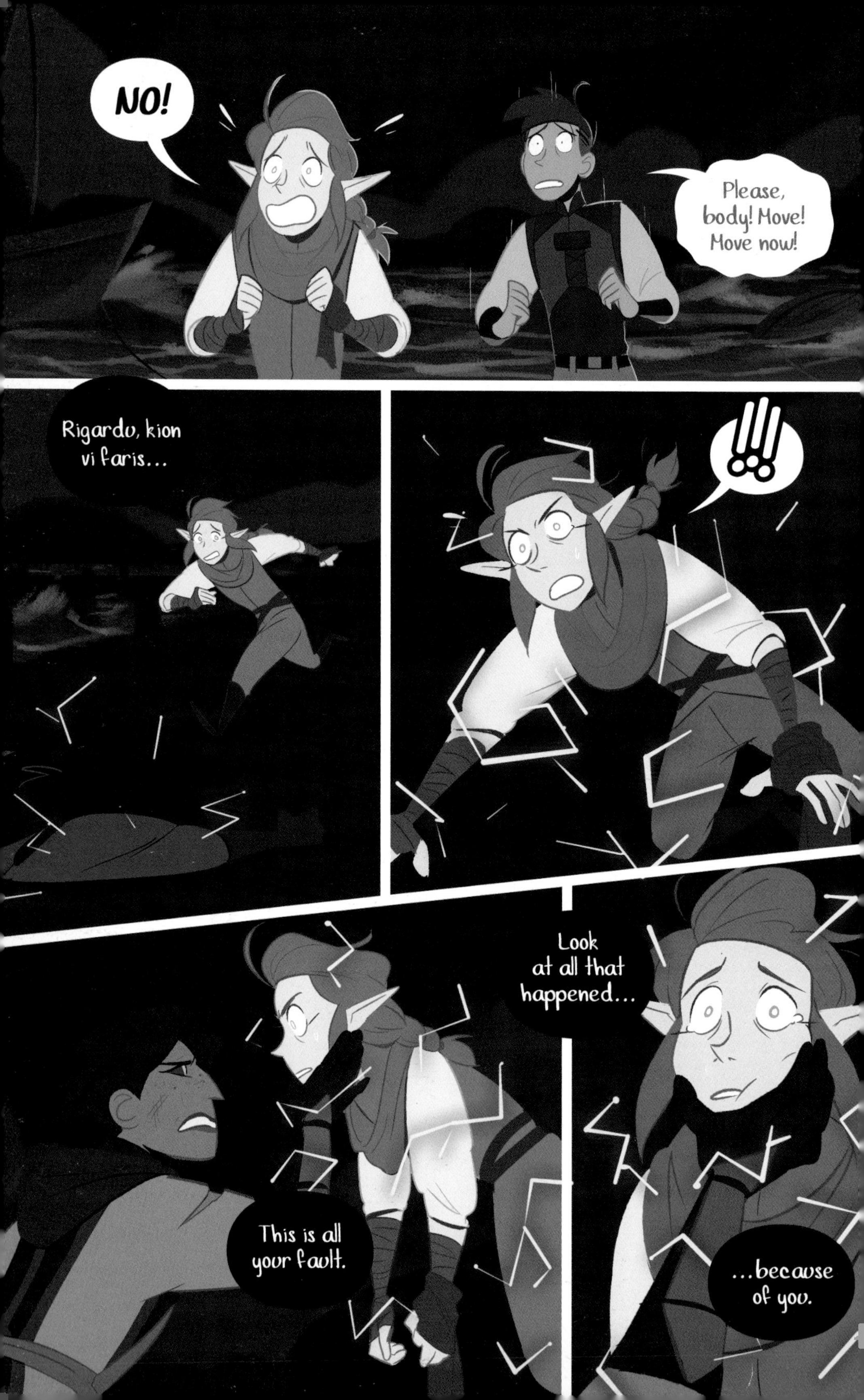
NO!
Please, body! Move! Move now!
Rigardu, kion vi faris...
!!!
Look at all that happened...
This is all your fault.
...because of you.

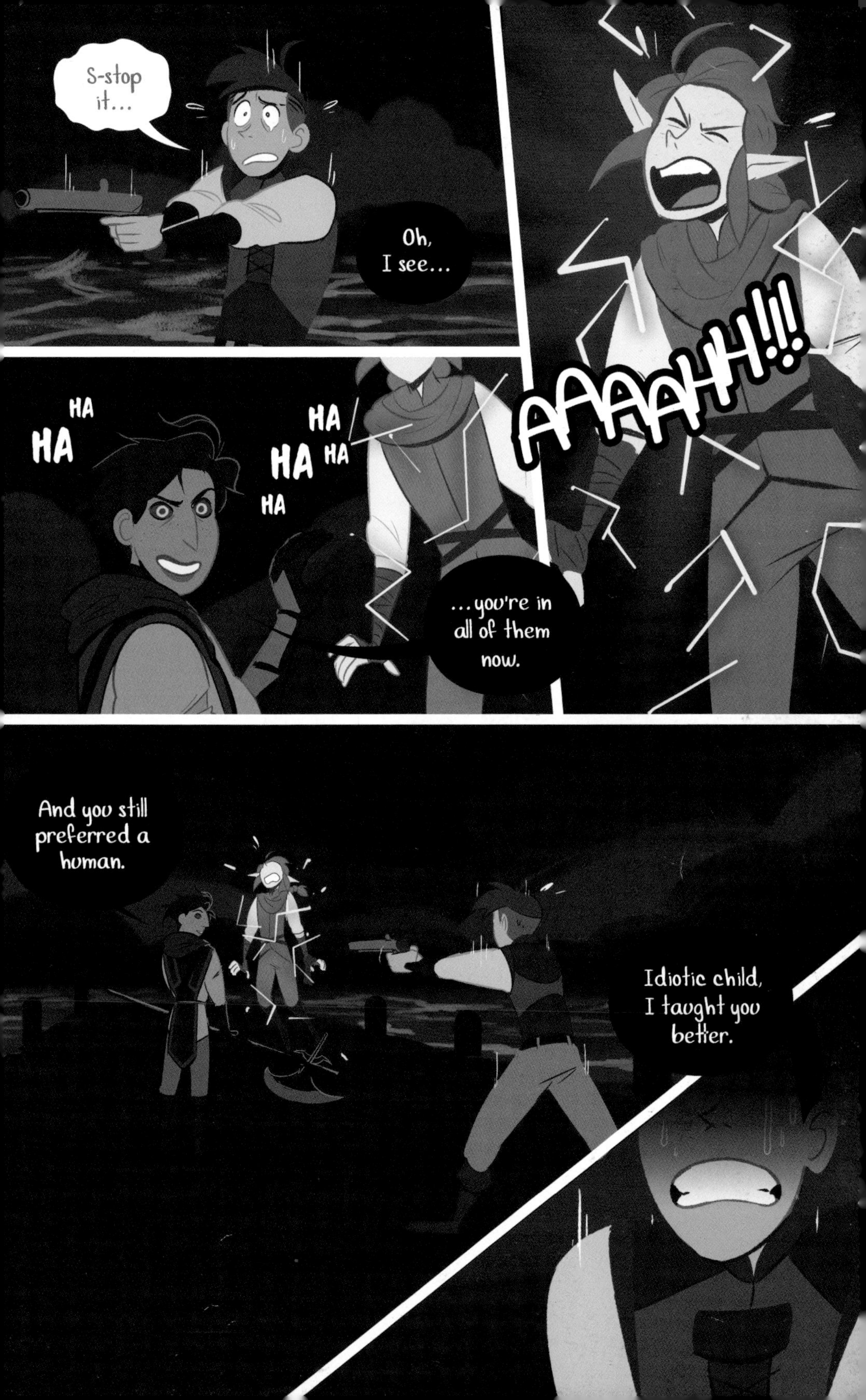
S-stop it...
Oh, I see...
AAAAHH!!!
HA HA
HA HA HA HA
...you're in all of them now.
And you still preferred a human.
Idiotic child, I taught you better.

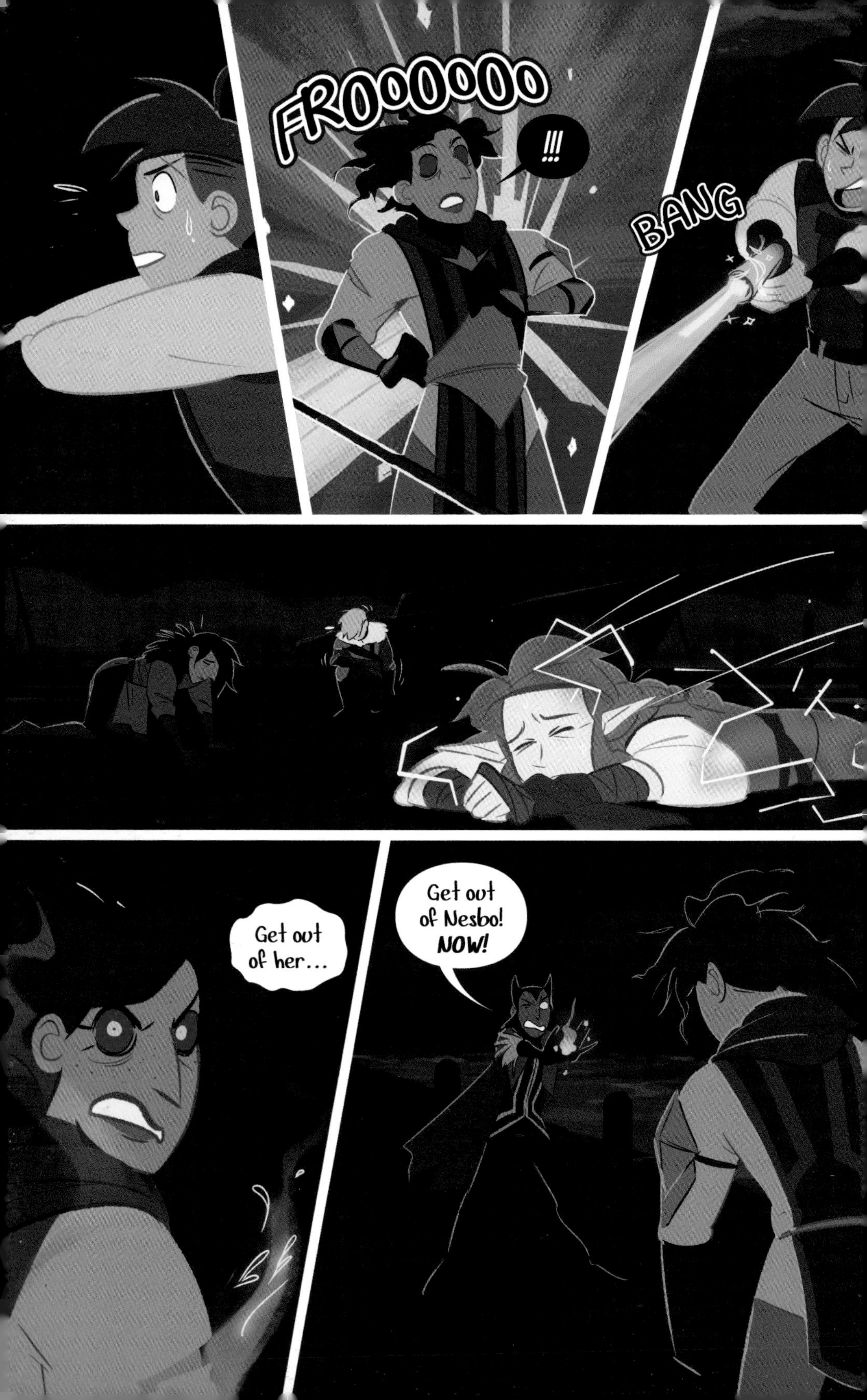
FROOOOOO
!!!
BANG
Get out
of her...
Get out
of Nesbo!
NOW!

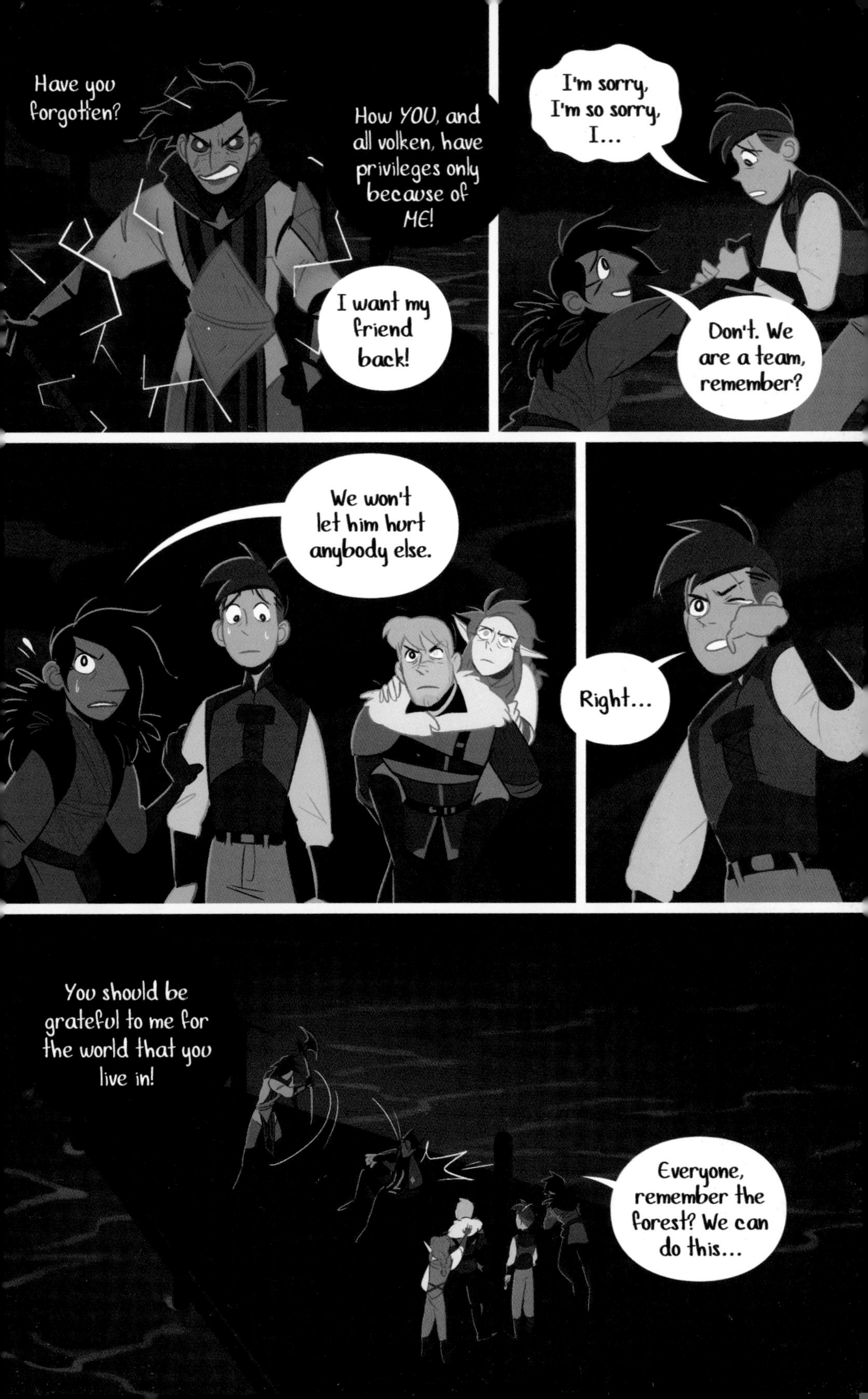
Have you forgotten?
How YOU, and all volken, have privileges only because of ME!
I want my friend back!
I'm sorry, I'm so sorry, I...
Don't. We are a team, remember?
We won't let him hurt anybody else.
Right...
You should be grateful to me for the world that you live in!
Everyone, remember the forest? We can do this...

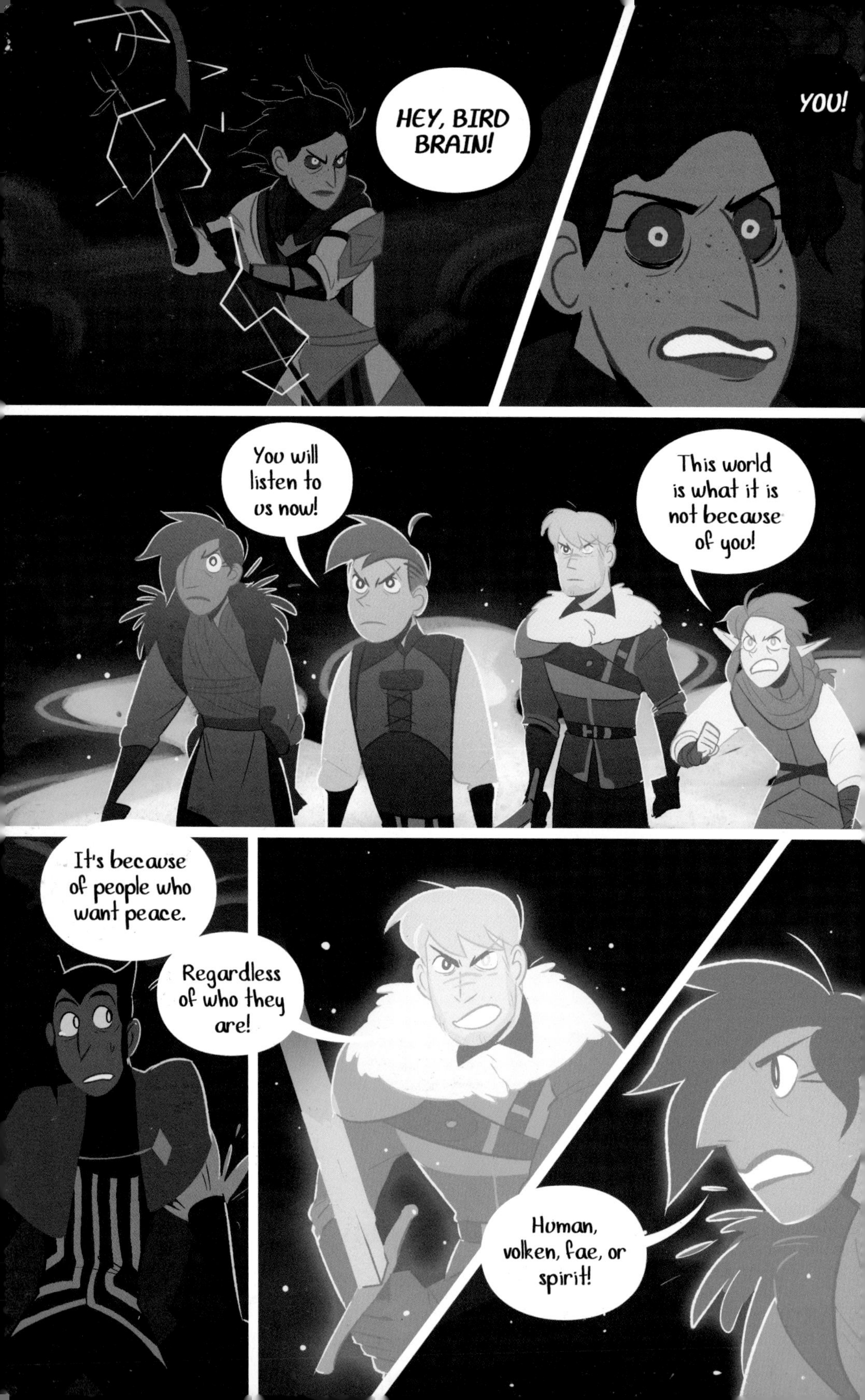
HEY, BIRD BRAIN!
YOU!
You will listen to us now!
This world is what it is not because of you!
It's because of people who want peace.
Regardless of who they are!
Human, volken, fae, or spirit!

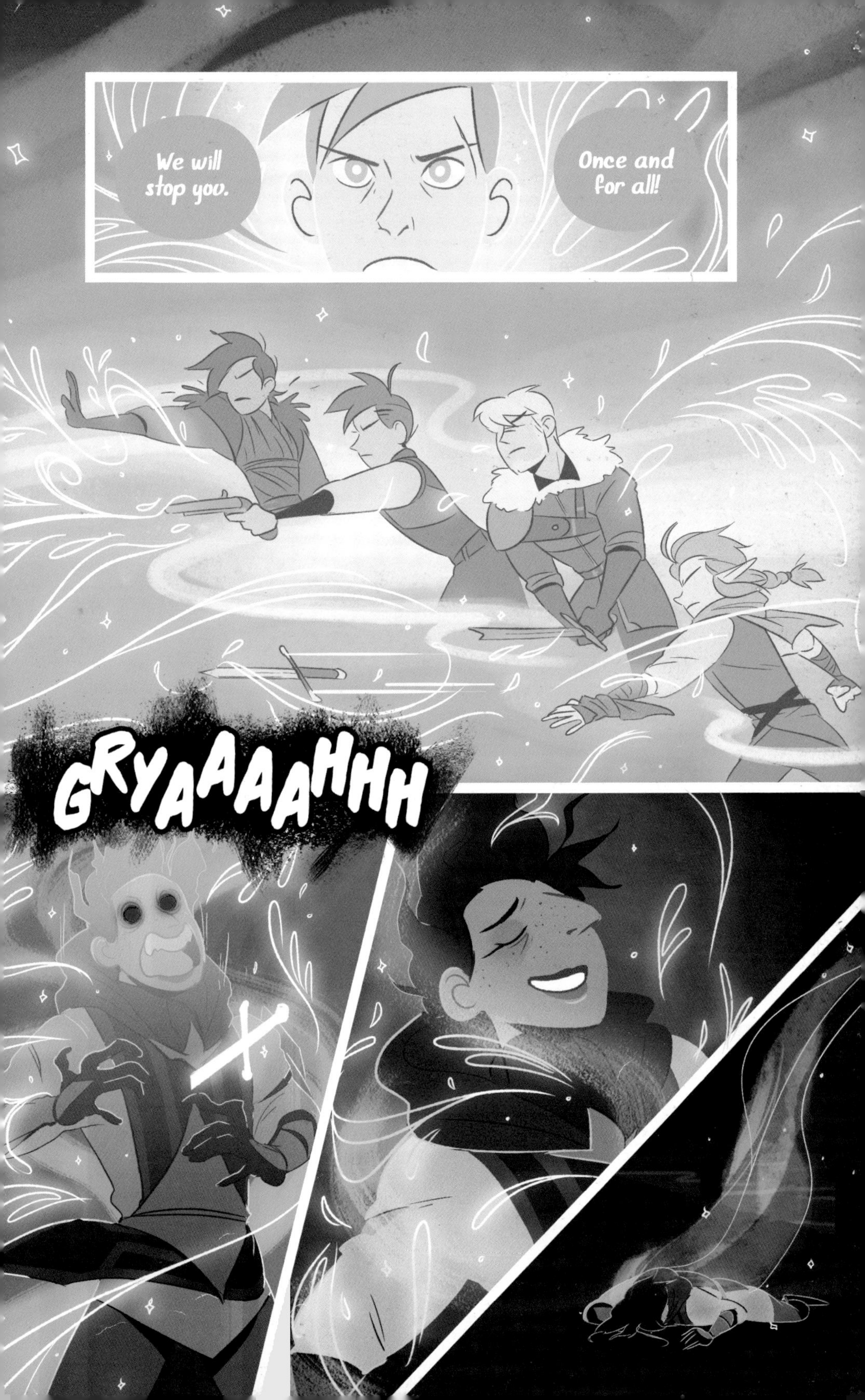
We will stop you.
Once and for all!
GRYAAAAHHH

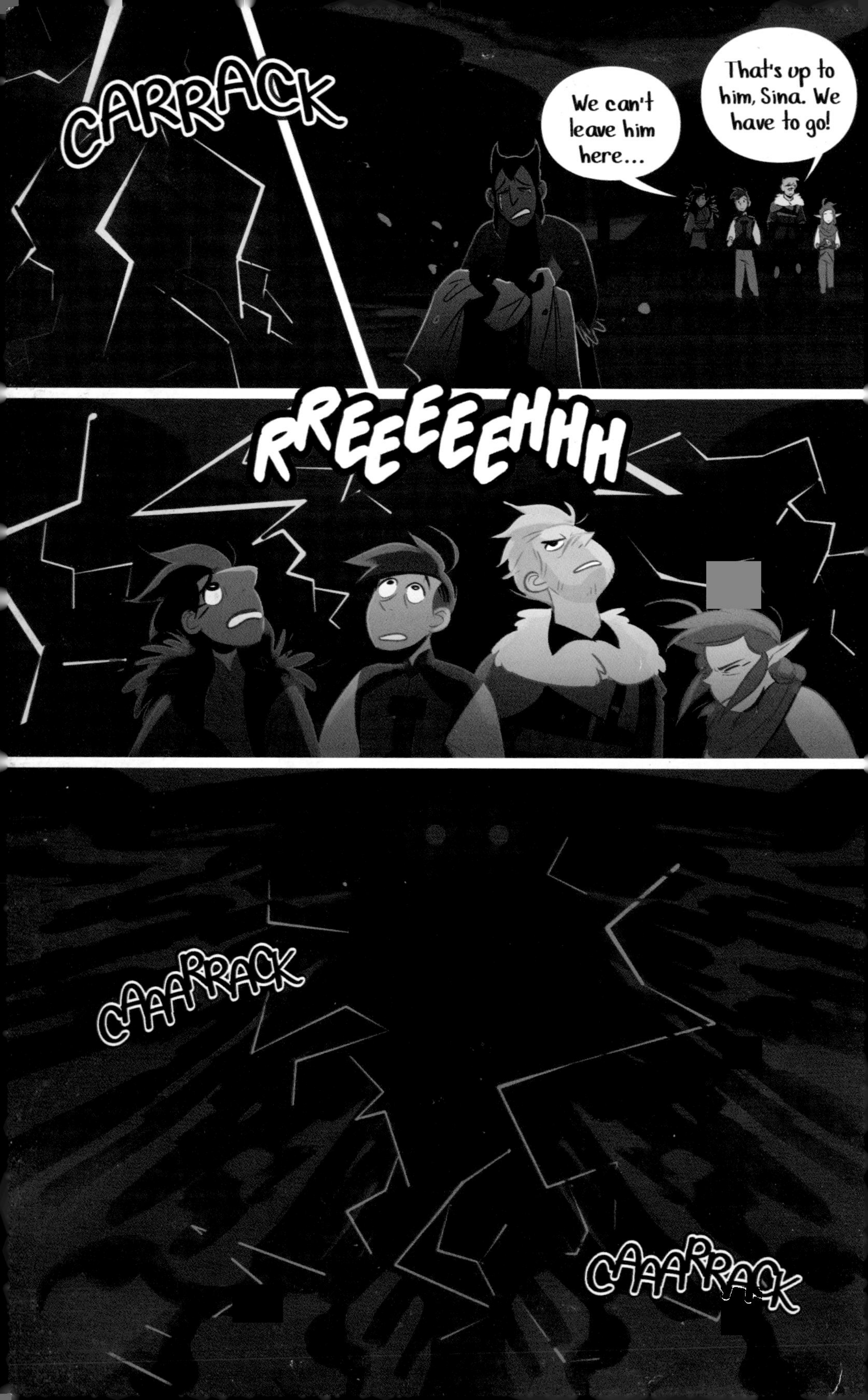
CARRACK
We can't leave him here...
That's up to him, Sina. We have to go!
RREEEEEEHHH
CAAARRACK
CAAARRACK

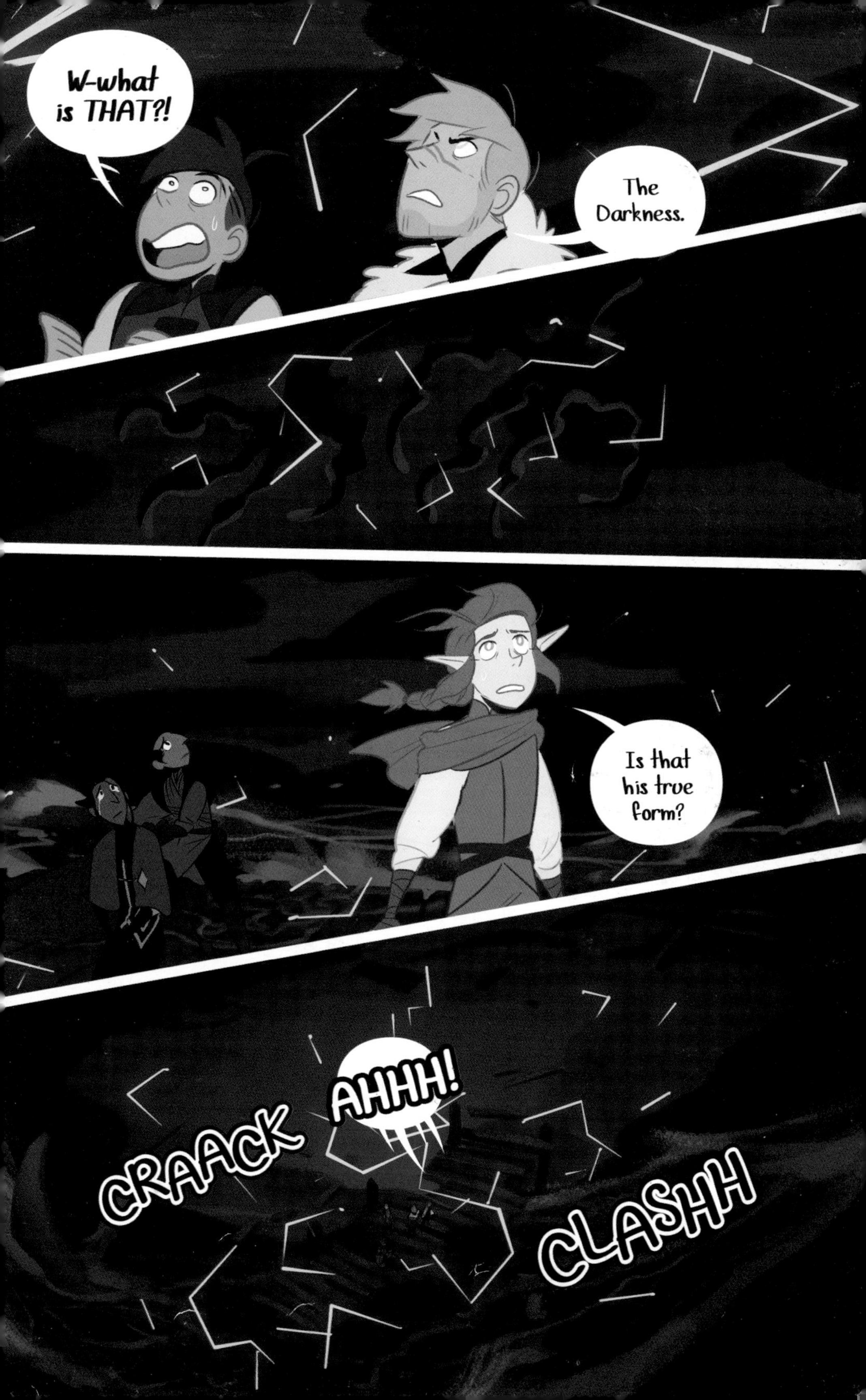
W-what is THAT?!
The Darkness.
Is that his true form?
CRAACK
AHHH!
CLASHH

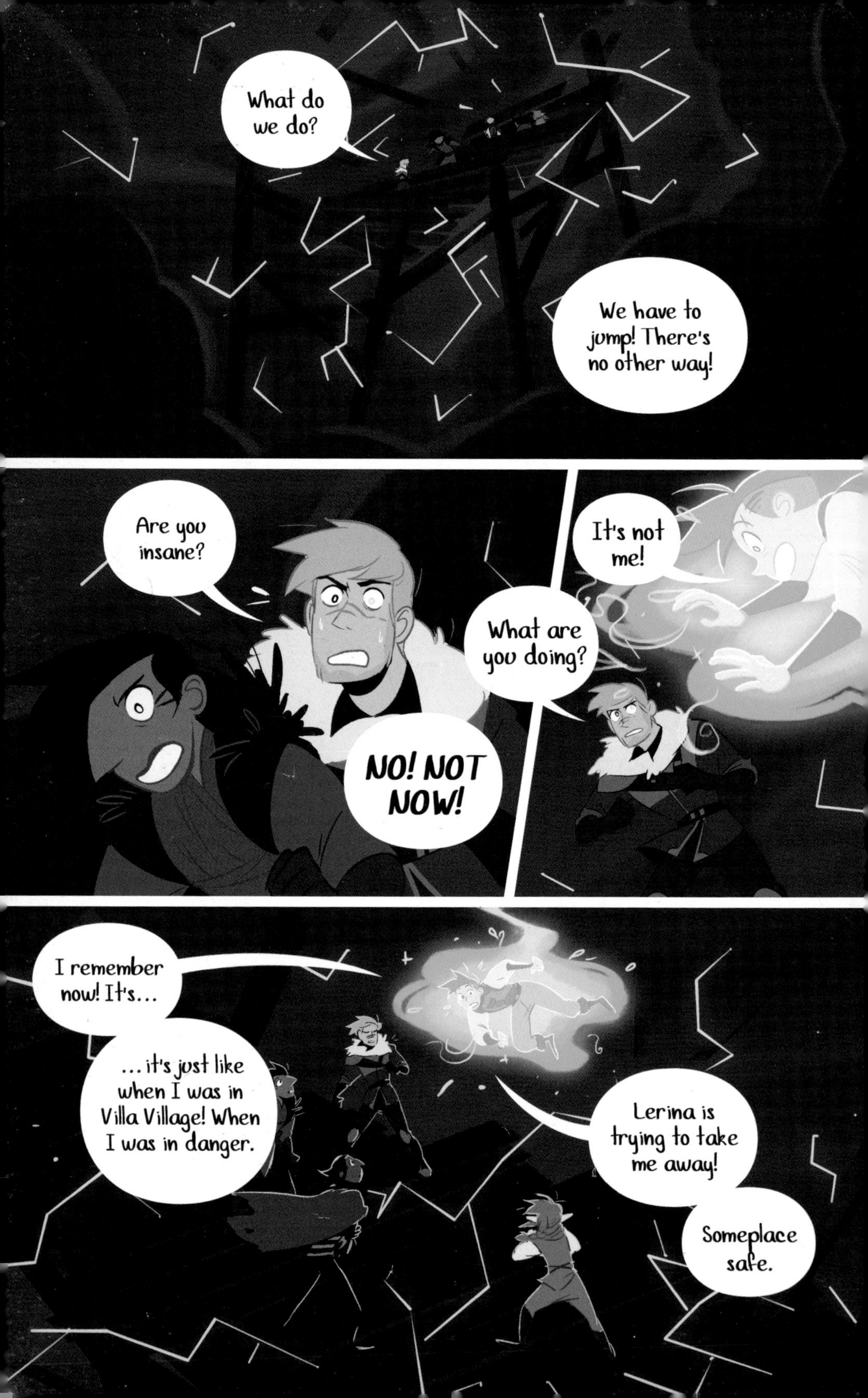
What do we do?
We have to jump! There's no other way!
Are you insane?
NO! NOT NOW!
It's not me!
What are you doing?
I remember now! It's...
... it's just like when I was in Villa Village! When I was in danger.
Lerina is trying to take me away!
Someplace safe.

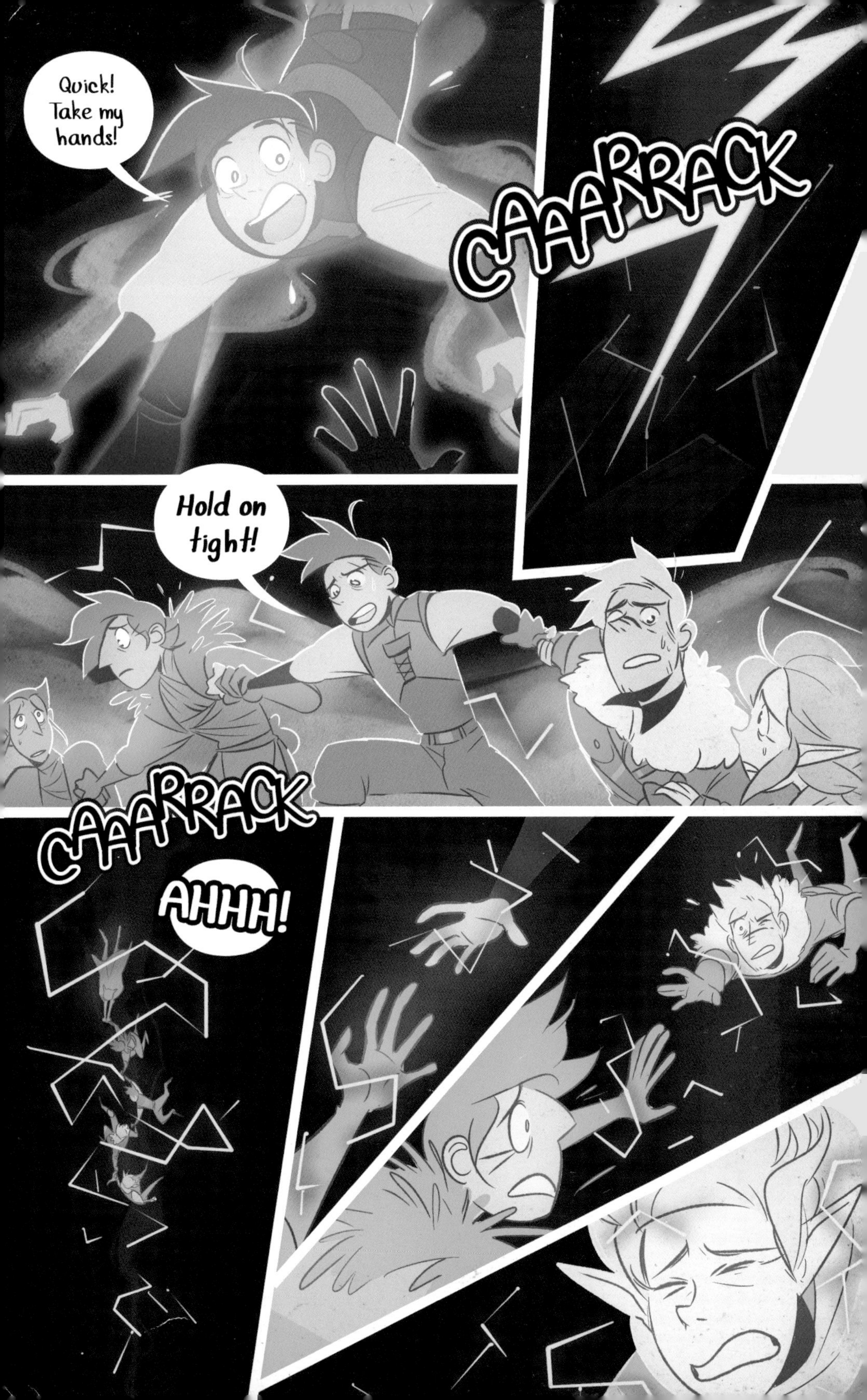
Quick! Take my hands!
CAAARRACK
Hold on tight!
CAAARRACK
AHHH!

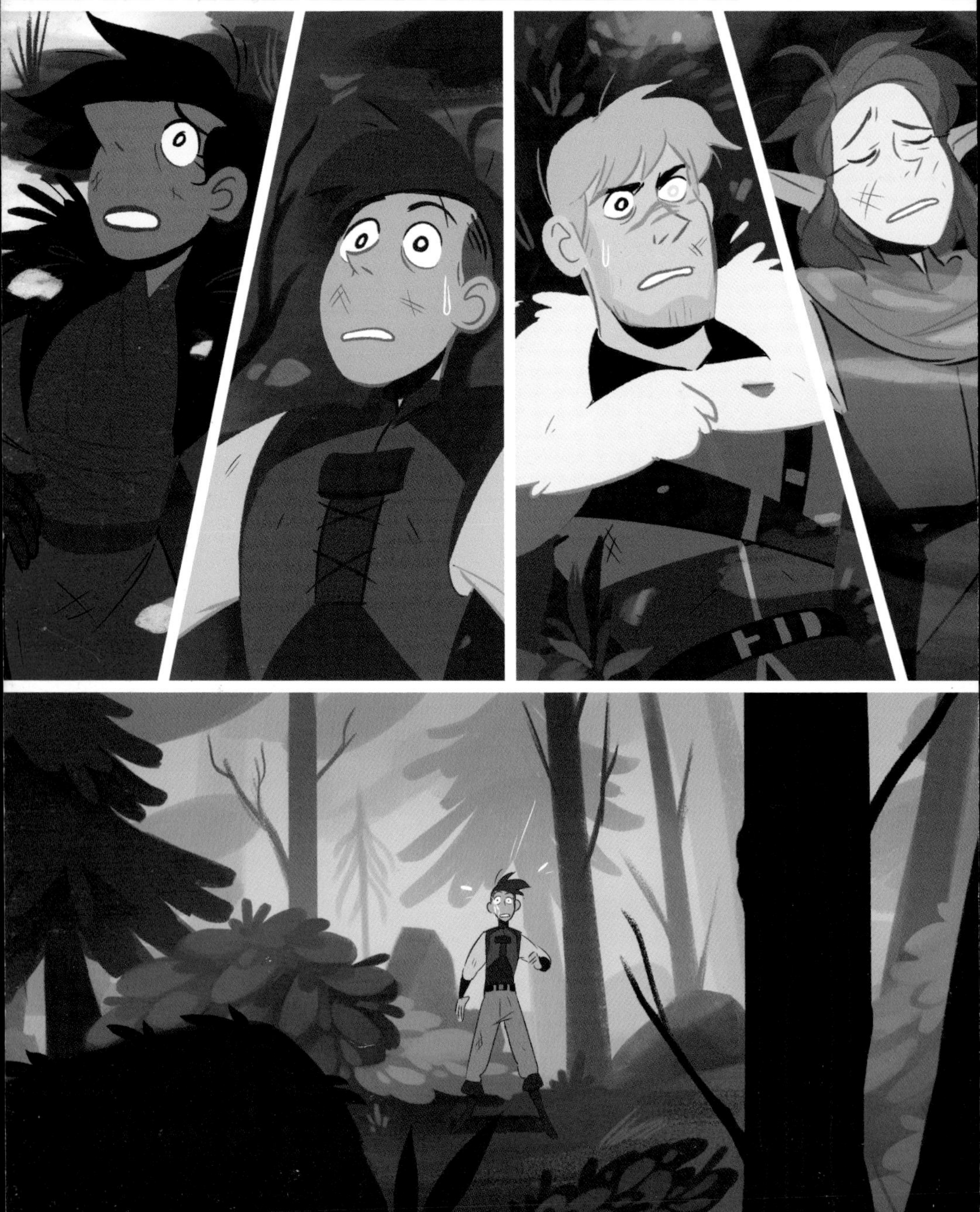

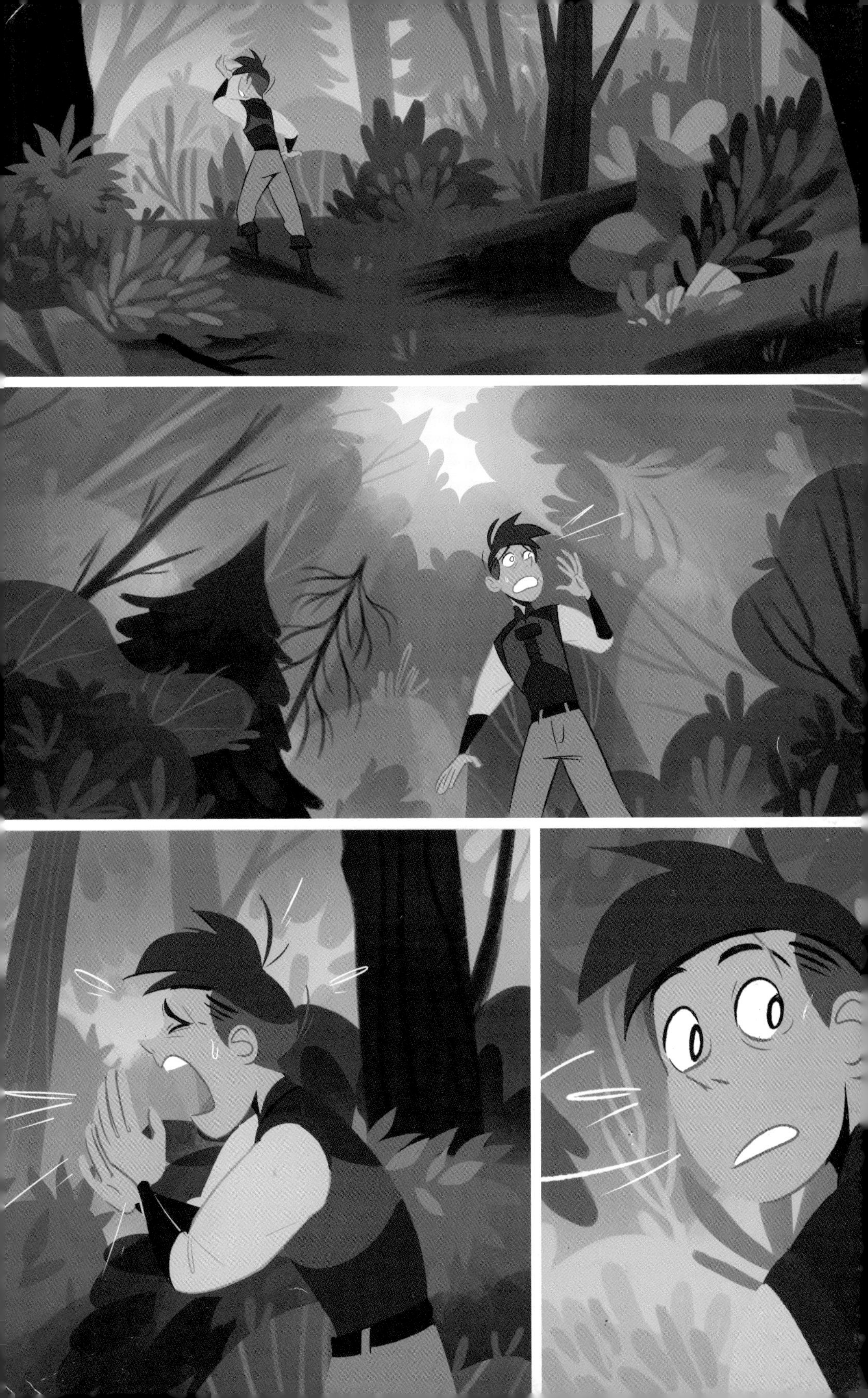

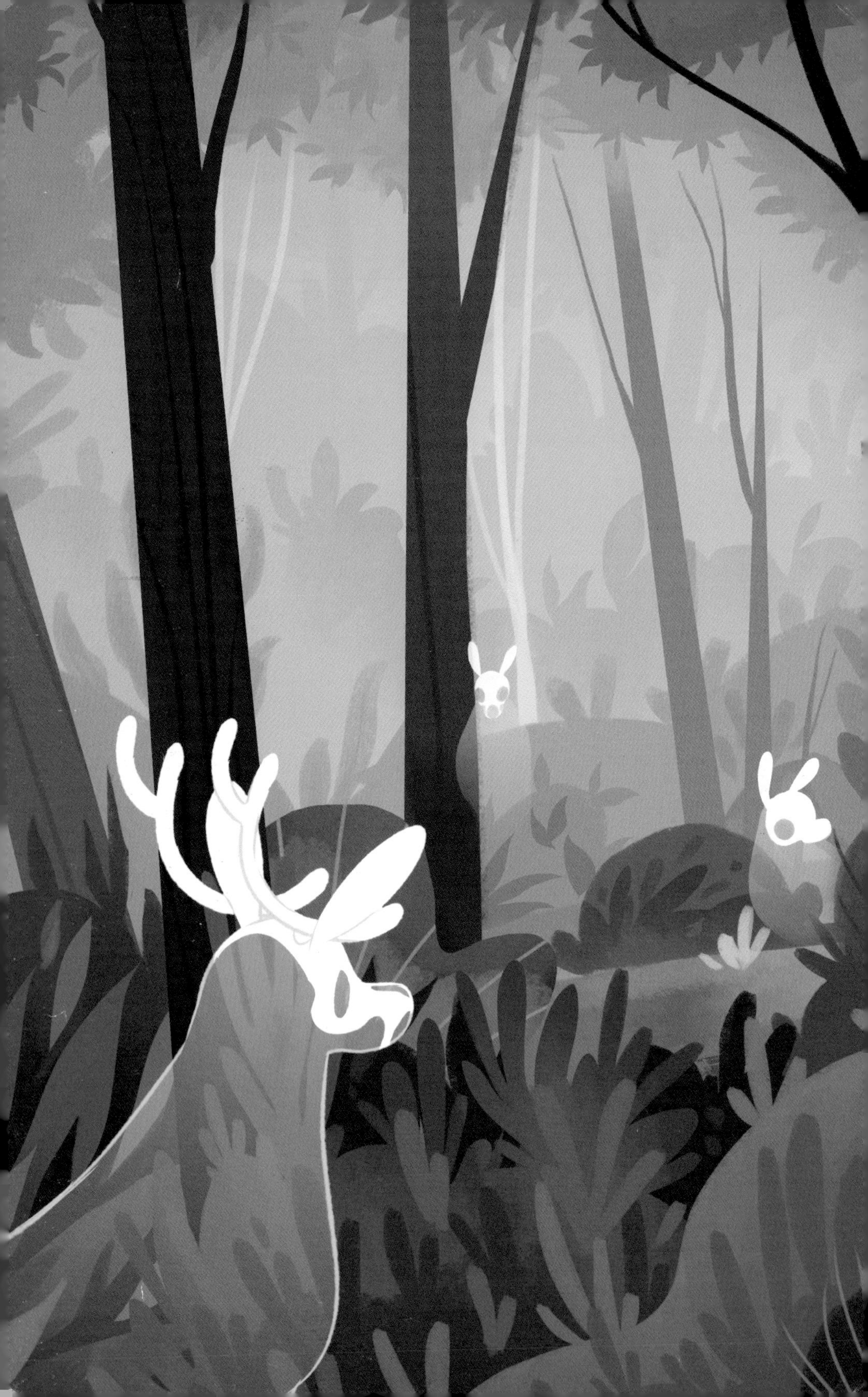

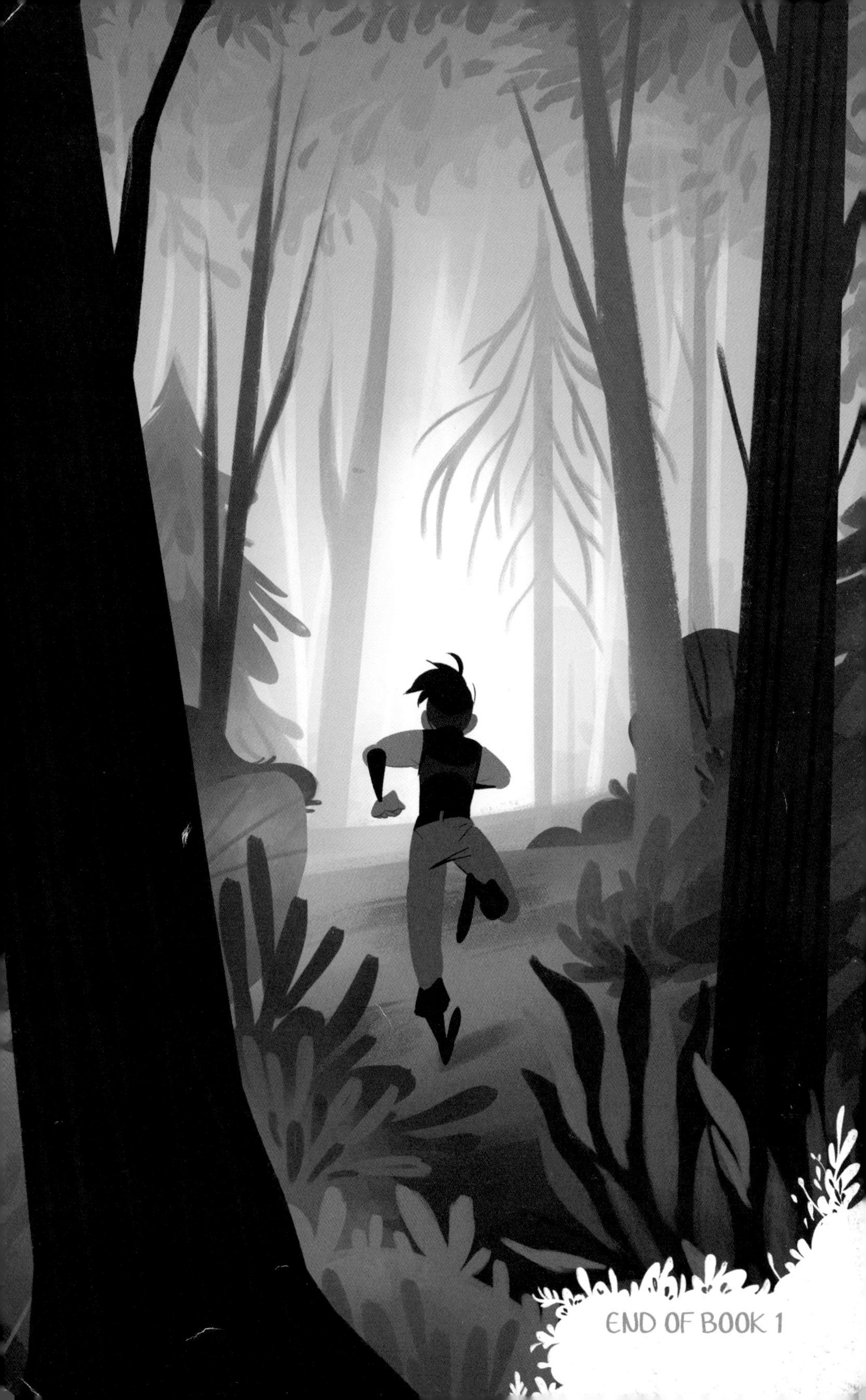
END OF BOOK 1

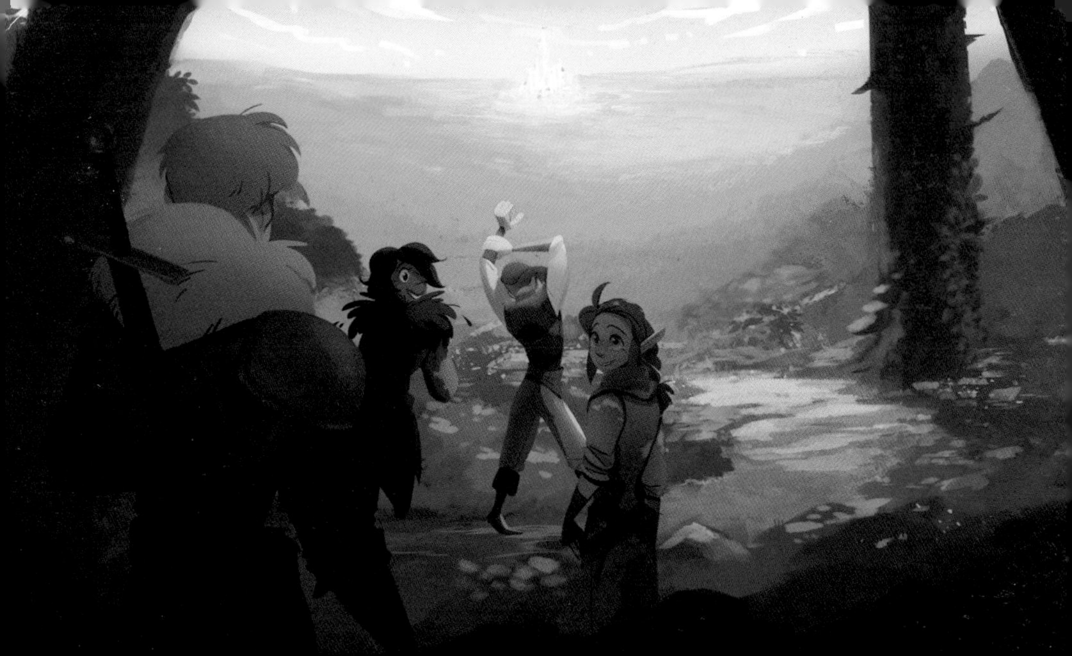

Acknowledgments

To all the people who were with us these past few years: thank you. Even if you believe you did nothing, those little nothings helped us get here.

Our beloved partners, Sergio and Luis, for your company, love, and understanding.

Our parents, siblings, nephew, and nieces, who maybe at first didn't understand the gist of it all but would still root for us.

Mark, for the comment we believed was spam, then made us believe that our project could be more.

Ben, Tanu, Molly, Amy and the team at Katherine Tegen for your patience and guidance.

To all the readers when this started as a little webcomic on the vast internet, and to our patrons that supported us through this entire process.

To you, reading this. Thank you.

—Ale and Fanny

STARTING NOTHING

This story, back in 2016, with only Nathan and Haven in our heads, was something for us to do for fun while drawing and writting stuff.

Many things changed since then, but some remained the same: Nothing was called "Granda," and Haven was a rebellious heir to the throne; Nathan has always been Nathan, a magnet for trouble.

In 2017, we decided to turn our silly little story into a webcomic, thinking it would be a great way to make a portfolio. We never expected things to happen the way they did.

Alejandra Green & Fanny Rodriguez
Fantastic
tales of
Nothing

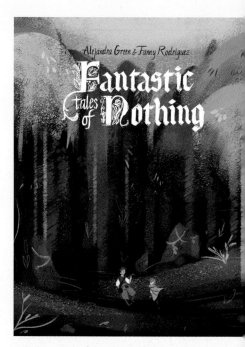

Early concept for creating a webcomic.

he
he
he

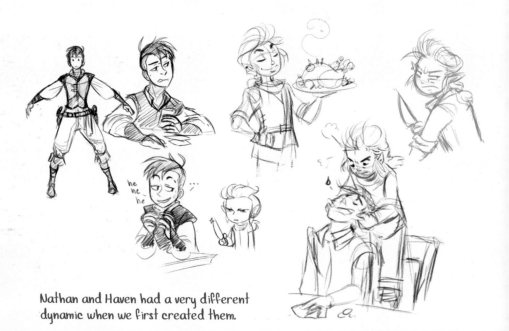

Nathan and Haven had a very different dynamic when we first created them.

HOW EVERYTHING WAS DONE

Each page is a labor of love, madness, and teamwork. Here's a quick view of how each page was done after the script was approved.

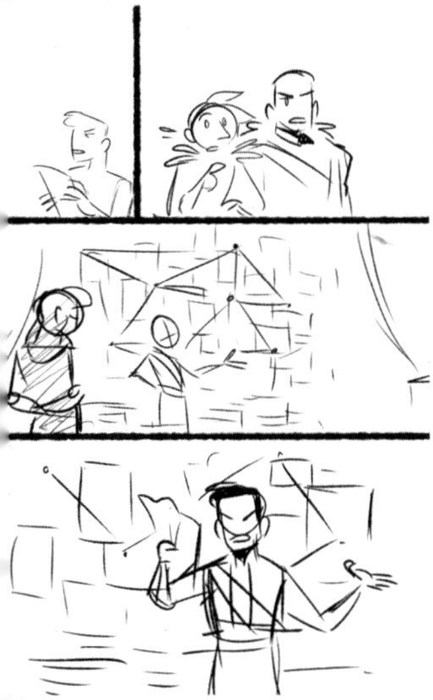

ugh thumbnail from script

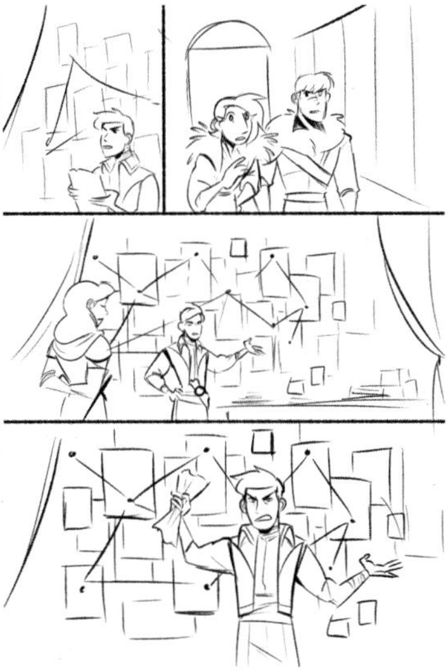

Cleaner sketch for review

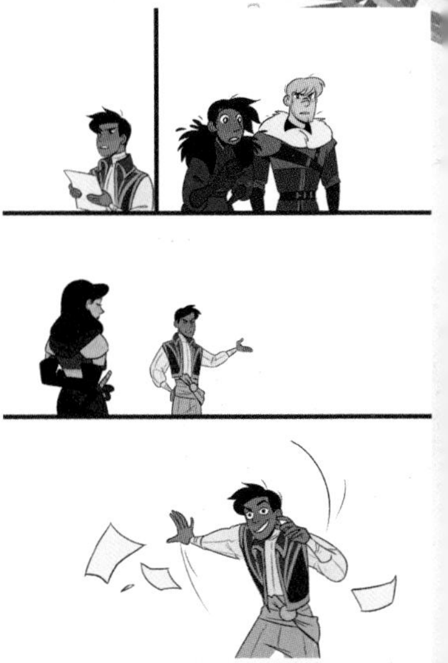

Line art and flats

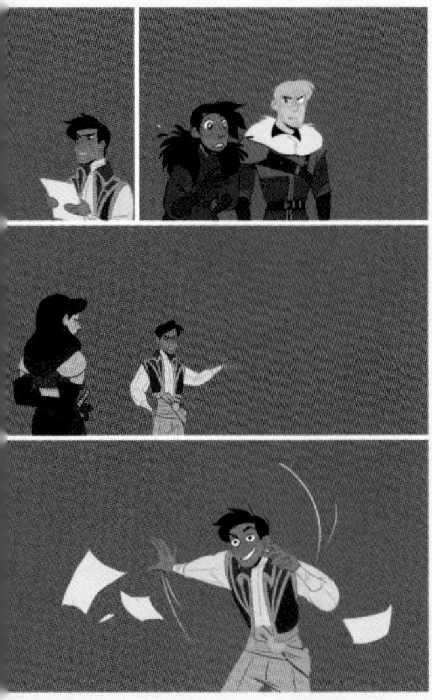

lored line art and details

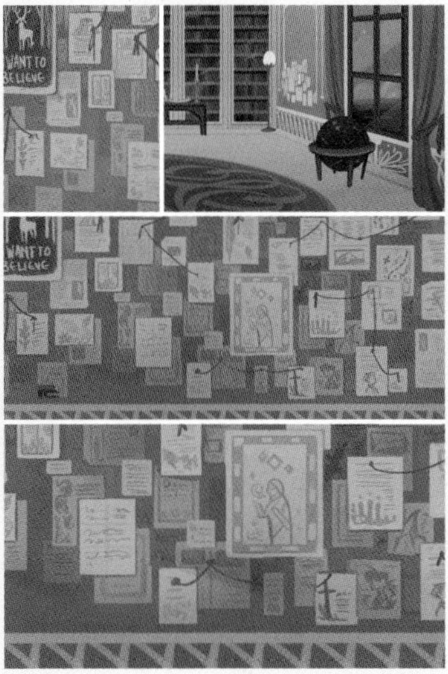

Background painting

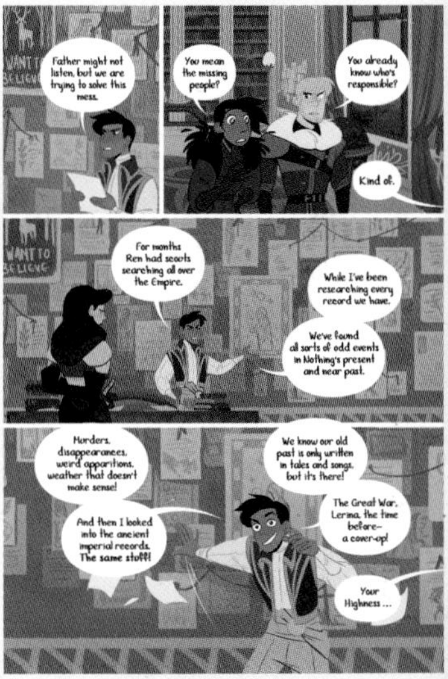
Father might not listen, but we are trying to solve this mess.
You mean the missing people?
You already know who's responsible?
Kind of.
For months Ren had scouts searching all over the Empire.
While I've been researching every record we have.
We've found all sorts of odd events in Nothing's present and near past.
Murders, disappearances, weird apparitions, weather that doesn't make sense!
And then I looked into the ancient imperial records. The same stuff!
We know our old past is only written in tales and songs, but it's there!
The Great War, Lerina, the time before— a cover-up!
Your Highness ...

Final composition and lettering

Early concepts of Nathan and Haven

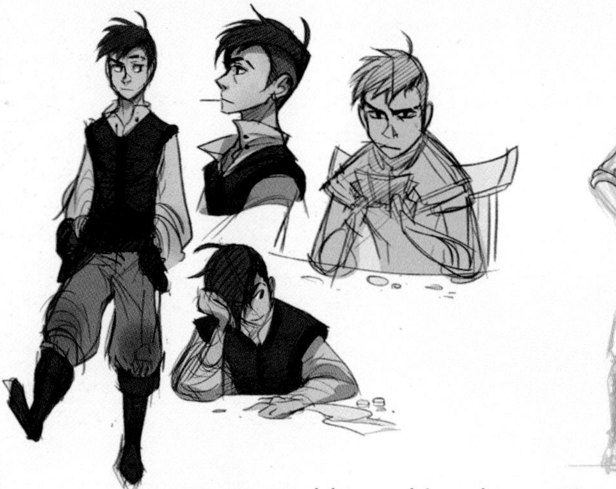

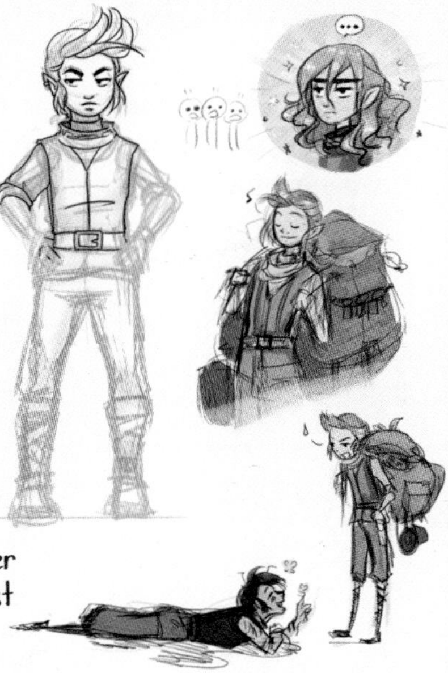

Haven changed the most from their earlier concept. Also, Ale says they're the hardest character for her to draw.

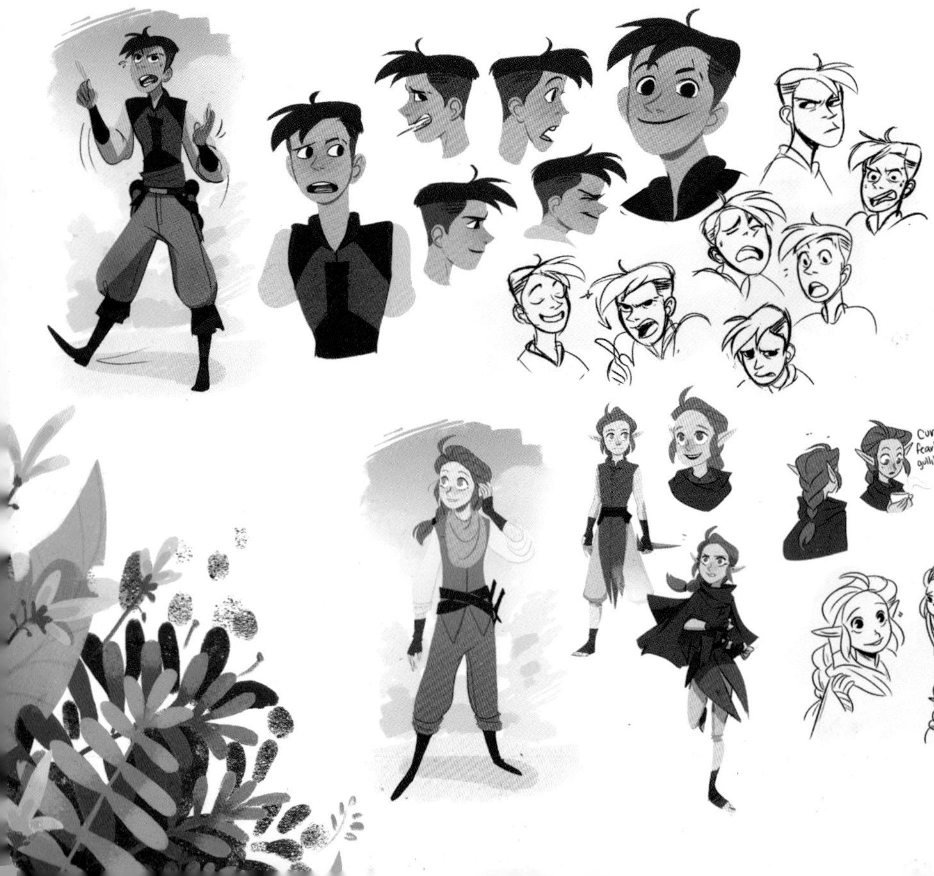
Curio
fearl

Early concepts of Sina and Bardou

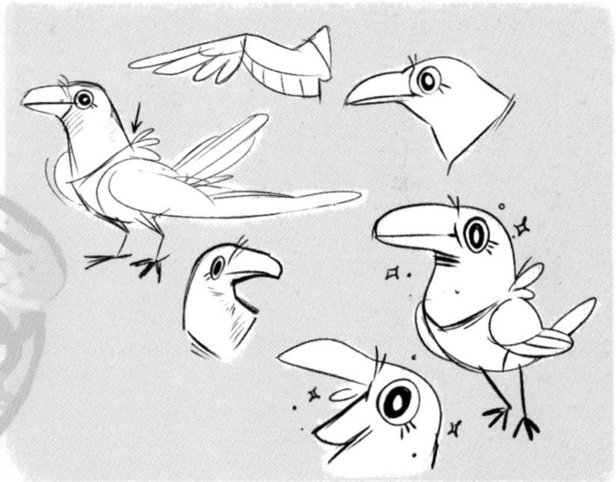

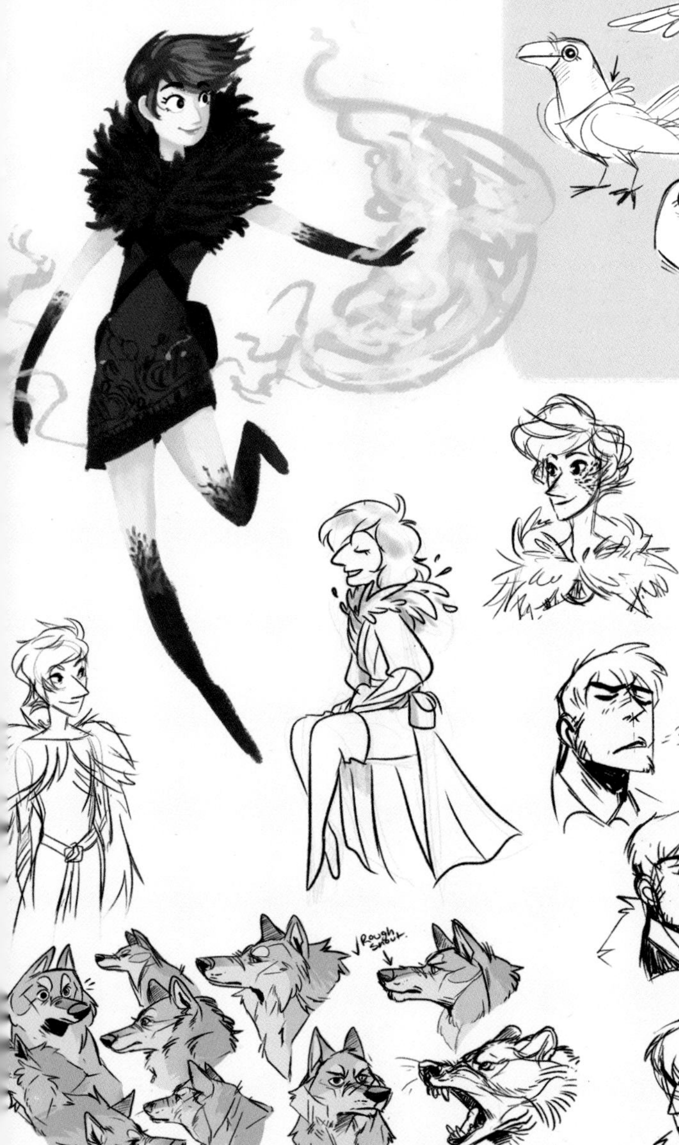

"Many of Sina's early sketches turned into nothing" —Fanny

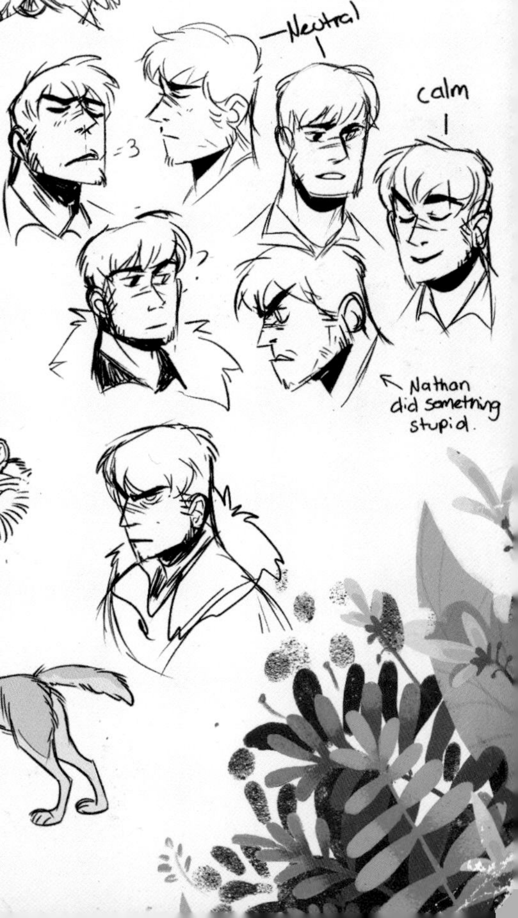

Neutral
calm
=3
Nathan did something stupid.

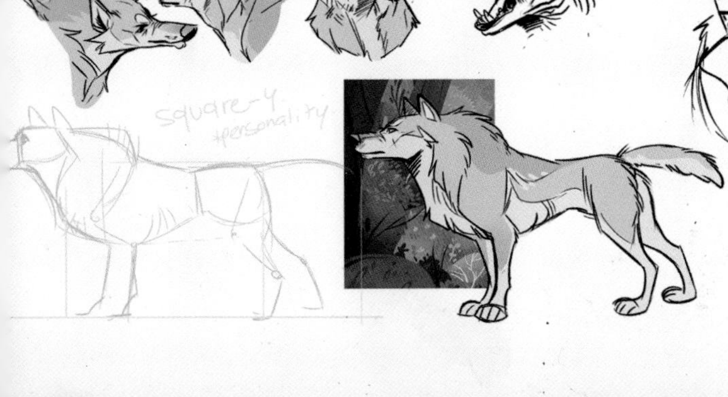

Rough Snout.
square-y
+personality

We love Renée and Naoki; they're fun to draw and write. We might simply have a bias and root for them secretly.

Fun fact: Naoki knows this is a book.

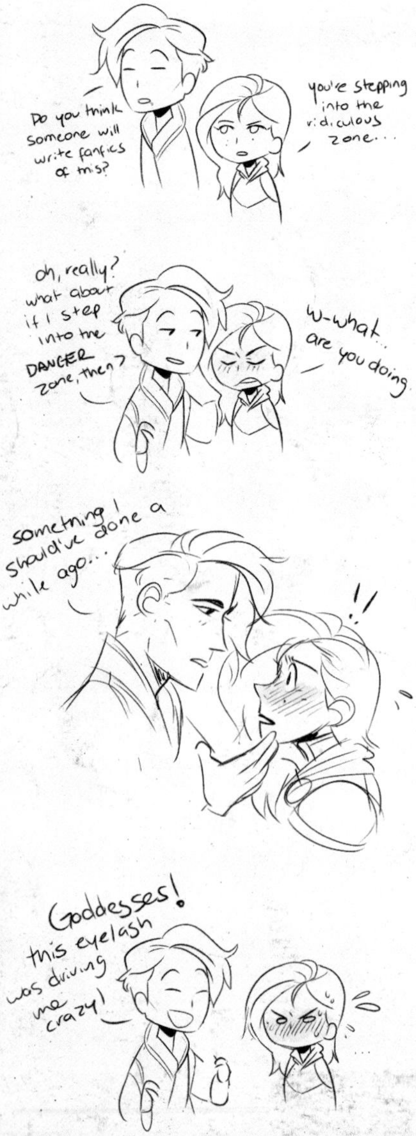
Do you think someone will write fanfics of this?
you're stepping into the ridiculous zone...
oh, really? what about if I step into the DANGER zone, then?
w-what... are you doing?
something I should've done a while ago...
!!
Goddesses! this eyelash was driving me crazy!

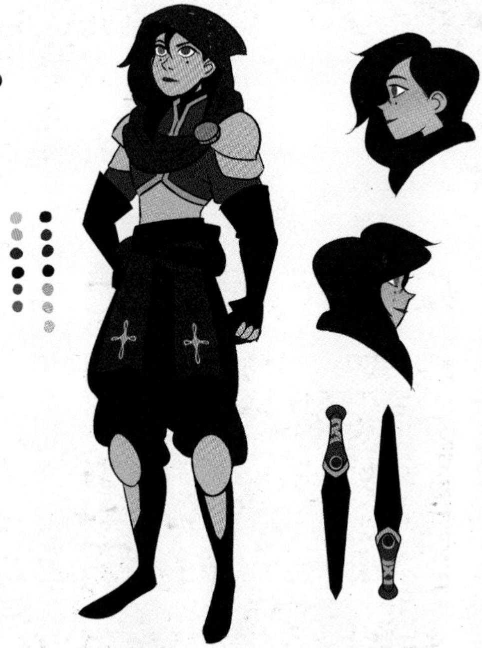

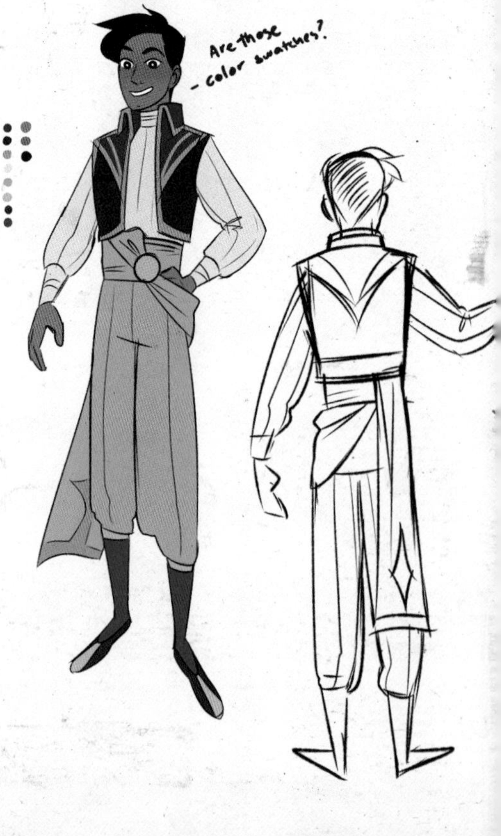
Are those color swatches?

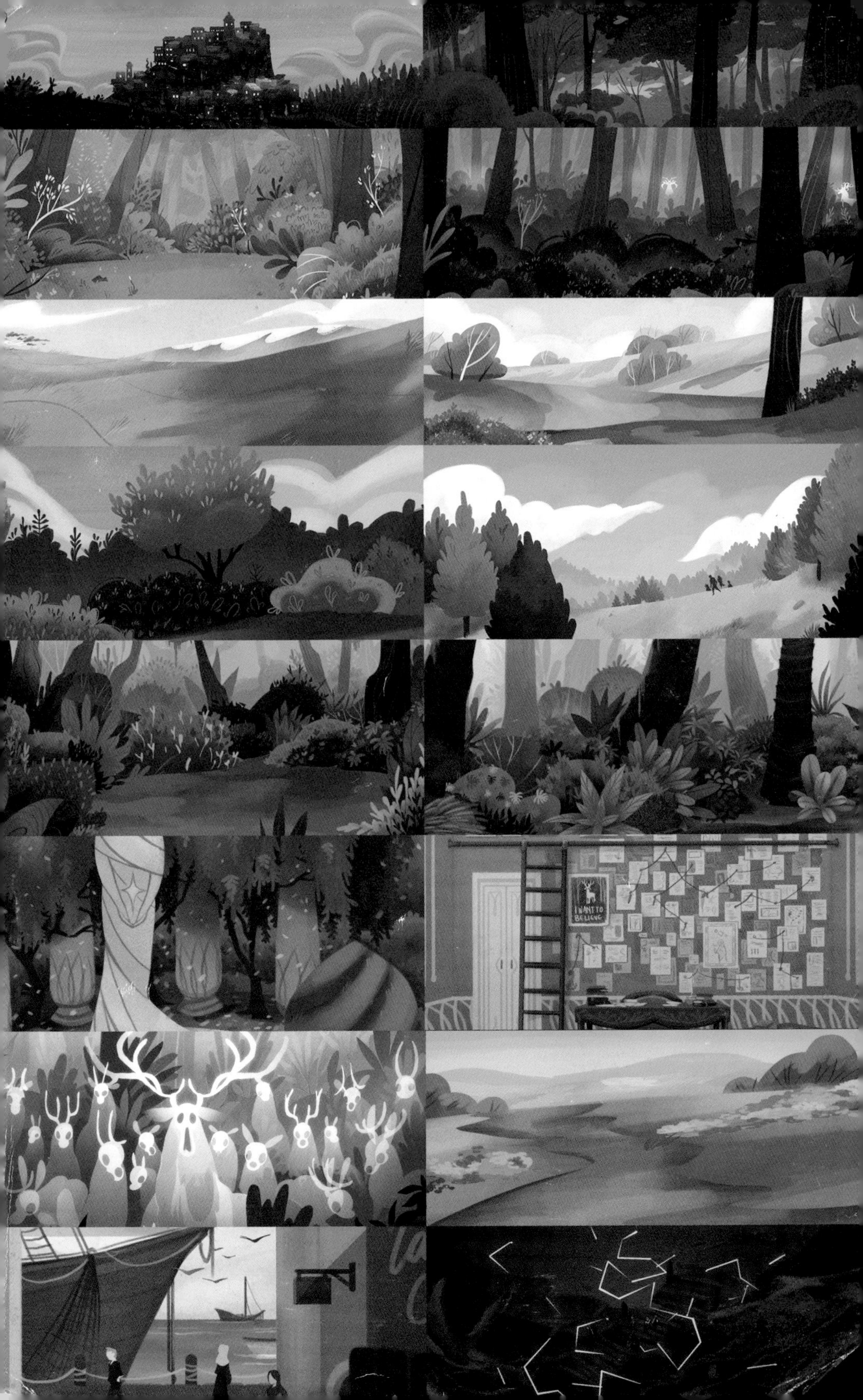
I WANT TO BELIEVE

A not so long time ago, two friends went on an adventure.
One that would change their lives...and ours too.

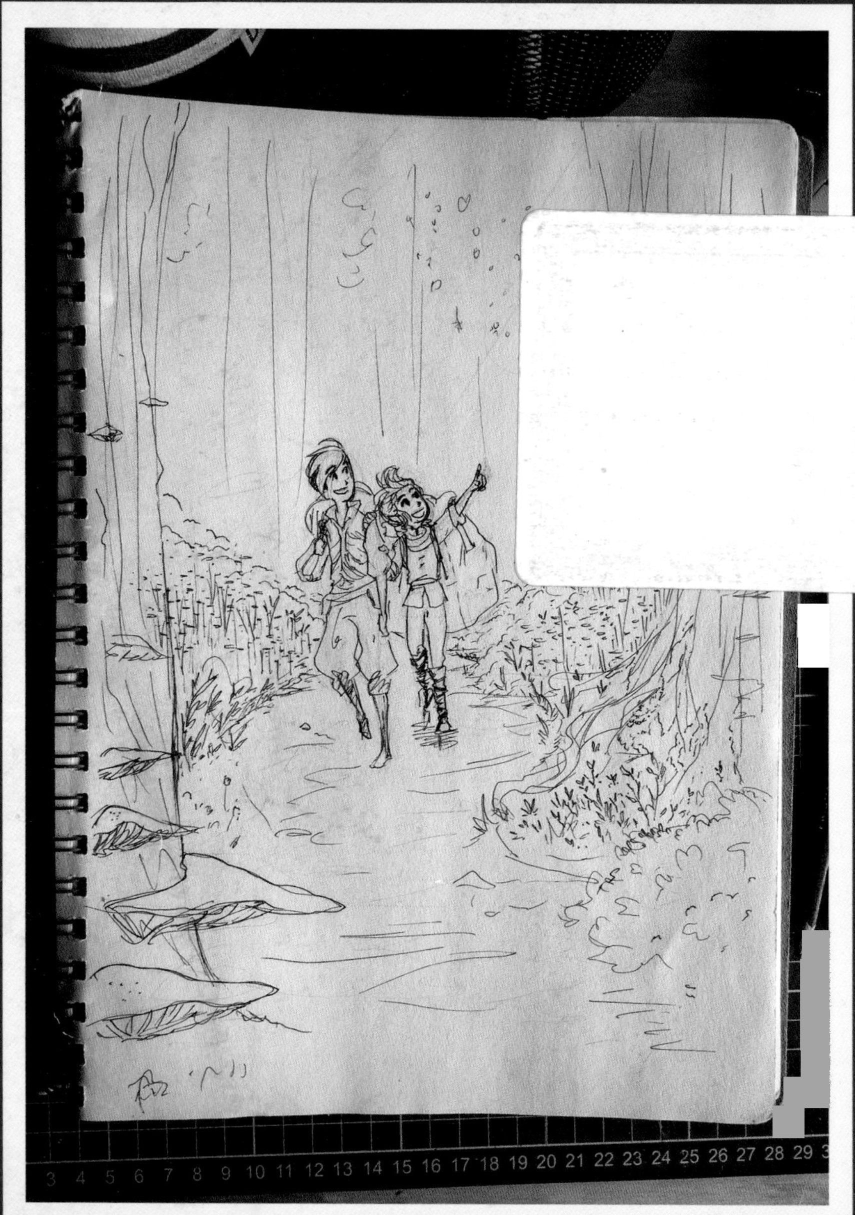

The very first doodle of *Fantastic Tales of Nothing*, back when Ale and I sat across from each other at our old job.